PENGUIN BOOKS

THE BONE PEOPLE

KERI HULME, a Maori, grew up in Christchurch and Moeraki, New Zealand, and has written many poems and short stories.

PEPA HELLER has been a professional tattoo artist since 1996. The owner of Bohemian Tattoo Arts in Tauranga, New Zealand, he draws inspiration from Maori and Pacific styles.

THE PEGASUS PRIZE FOR LITERATURE

THE BONE PEOPLE

The Booker Prize–winning novel *The Bone People* begins in a tower on the New Zealand sea. The woman who lives there is Kerewin Holmes. Part Maori, part European, she is an artist estranged from her art, a woman in exile from her family. One night she is disrupted by a speechless, mercurial boy named Simon who tries to steal from her and then repays her with his most precious possession. As Kerewin succumbs to Simon's feral charm, she also falls under the spell of his Maori foster father, Joe. Out of this unorthodox trinity Keri Hulme has created what is at once a mystery, a love story, and an ambitious exploration of the zone where Maori and European New Zealand meet.

"This book is just amazingly, wondrously great."
—Alice Walker

THE PENGUIN INK SERIES

For seventy-five years, Penguin has paired the best in literature with the best in graphic design. In celebration of our anniversary, a selection of Penguin's most distinctive contemporary books now features covers specially designed by the world's top illustrative artists.

KERI HULME

THE BONE PEOPLE

PENGUIN BOOKS

PENGUIN BOOKS

Published by the Penguin Group
Penguin Group (USA) Inc., 375 Hudson Street, New York, New York 10014, U.S.A.
Penguin Group (Canada), 90 Eglinton Avenue East, Suite 700, Toronto, Ontario, Canada M4P 2Y3
(a division of Pearson Penguin Canada Inc.)
Penguin Books Ltd, 80 Strand, London WC2R 0RL, England
Penguin Ireland, 25 St Stephen's Green, Dublin 2, Ireland (a division of Penguin Books Ltd)
Penguin Group (Australia), 250 Camberwell Road, Camberwell, Victoria 3124, Australia
(a division of Pearson Australia Group Pty Ltd)
Penguin Books India Pvt Ltd, 11 Community Centre, Panchsheel Park, New Delhi – 110 017, India
Penguin Group (NZ), 67 Apollo Drive, Rosedale, North Shore 0632, New Zealand
(a division of Pearson New Zealand Ltd)
Penguin Books (South Africa) (Pty) Ltd, 24 Sturdee Avenue, Rosebank, Johannesburg 2196, South Africa

Penguin Books Ltd, Registered Offices:
80 Strand, London WC2R 0RL, England

First published in New Zealand by Spiral/Hodder & Stoughton 1984
First published in the United States of America by Louisiana State University Press 1985
Published in Penguin Books 1986
This edition published 2010

5   7   9   10   8   6

Publication of this book has been supported by a grant from the National Endowment for the Arts in
Washington, D.C., a federal agency.

PUBLISHER'S NOTE
This is a work of fiction. Names, characters, places, and incidents are either the product of the author's
imagination or are used fictitiously, and any resemblance to actual persons, living or dead, business
establishments, events, or locales is entirely coincidental.

The Bone People was originally produced and published in February, 1984, in New Zealand (reprinted
May 1984) by a Spiral collective—Irihapeti Ramaden, Marian Evans, and Miriama Evans—assisted by
Anna Keir, Basia Smolnicki, and Lynne Ciochetto; and supported by Amster Reedy; Bill MacKay;
Huirangi Waikerepuru; Joy Cowley, whose generous help was given "in gratitude for over twenty
years of support from women writers"; Juliet Krautschun; Kathleen Johnson; Keri Kaa and the Maori
students at Wellington Teachers' College; Maori Writers Read participants and the series organizers,
Janet Potiki and Patricia Grace; Pauline Neale; Commission for Evangelisation, Justice and Development
(Wellington Diocese); Government Printer (Publishing Division); Kidsaurus 2; Maori Education Foundation;
New Zealand Literary Fund; Willi Fels Trust.

LIBRARY OF CONGRESS CATALOGING IN PUBLICATION DATA
Hulme, Keri.
The bone people.
1. Maoris—Fiction.   I. Title.
[PR9639.3.H75B6   1986]   823   86-5026
ISBN 978-0-14-311645-5

Printed in the United States of America
Set in Kennerly

Publisher's Note

The Pegasus Prize for Literature has been established by Mobil Corporation to introduce American readers to distinguished works from countries whose literature too rarely receives international recognition. In the case of New Zealand, the literature of the Maori people was singled out for this recognition. The Prize for Maori Literature was awarded to *The Bone People*, by Keri Hulme, in July, 1984, after a committee of distinguished scholars selected it from among the best Maori novels, stories, and autobiographies written in the past decade. The novel, first published earlier in the year by Spiral Collective, has also won the 1984 New Zealand Book Award. Hulme is the author of a book of poetry and prose, and a forthcoming collection of short stories. *The Bone People* is her first novel.

Chairman of the Pegasus Prize selection committee was Sidney Mead, professor of Maori, Victoria University. Other members of the jury were Arapera Blank, Glenfield College, Auckland; Elizabeth Murchie, Waiariki Community College, Rotorua; Wiremu Parker, Maori Studies Department, Victoria University; Ann Salmond, Anthropology Department, Auckland University; and Terry Sturm, English Department, Auckland University. In its selection of Keri Hulme's novel, the jury cited "a new kind of insight into writing and . . . a very polished technician, who knew the word, knew how to handle it, and knew how to make it work for her."

For American readers, *The Bone People* may evoke the works of

Carson McCullers, for Hulme's characters—like McCullers'—are outcasts who find moments of solace away from their inner turbulence and isolation in their contact with one another. While Hulme's canvas is vaster and more ambitious in its scope than McCullers', it is populated by only three main characters: the reclusive artist Kerewin, the mute boy Simon, and his violent, loving stepfather Joe.

The book's first publication in New Zealand is in itself a story of the dedication of three Wellington women who formed Spiral Collective to bring out the book after it had been rejected by some of the country's major publishers. It has since won two major awards and been republished in New Zealand by Spiral and Hodder and Stoughton.

On behalf of the author, we wish to express our appreciation to Mobil Corporation, which established the Pegasus Prize and introduced it in New Zealand.

The Bone People
Motueka 1966—Moeraki & Okarito, 1978

Ki a taku whanau—
Mary, Bill, Raynee, Diane, John, Mary, Andrew, Kathryn, Bob,
Robyn, Wesley, John, Barry, Patrick, Maryann, John Peters:

ki a nga whanauka mate—
ki a aku morehu tupu—
tenei pukapuka, he maimai aroha.

I thank these people and groups of people, without whom *The Bone People* would never have been completed, never been published:

my family
The New Zealand Literary Fund Advisory Committees
The committee awarding the Robert Burns Term Fellowship
    (Otago University 1977)
The Maori Trust Fund
    (for the prize for writing in English 1978)
The ICI Company
    (for the generous contribution to the 1982 ICI Bursary
    which enabled the final final rewrites)
Arnold Wall
Judith Maloney and Bill Minehan (remember the wake?!)
Rowley Habib
and particularly,
the Spiral Collectives, for friendship and faith.

KERI HULME

Preface to the First Edition

STANDARDS IN A
NON-STANDARD BOOK

The Bone People began life as a short story called "Simon Peter's Shell." I typed it out on my first typewriter, nights after working in the Motueka tobacco fields. The typewriter was a present for my 18th birthday from my mother, but that's another story.

"Simon Peter's Shell" began to warp into a novel. The characters wouldn't go away. They took 12 years to reach this shape. To me, it's a finished shape, so finished that I don't want to have anything to do with any alteration of it. Which is why I was going to embalm the whole thing in a block of perspex when the first three publishers turned it down on the grounds, among others, that it was too large, too unwieldy, too *different* when compared with the normal shape of a novel.

Enter, to sound of trumpets and cowrieshell rattles, the Spiral Collective.

The exigencies of collective publishing demand that individuals work in an individual way. Communication with me was difficult—I live five hundred miles away, don't have a telephone, and receive only intermittent mail delivery—so consensus on small points of punctuation never was reached. I like the diversity.

The editor should have ensured a uniformity? Well, I was lucky with my editors, who respected how I feel about . . . oddities. For instance, I think the *shape* of words brings a response from the reader—a tiny, subconscious, unacknowledged but definite response. "OK" studs a sentence. "Okay" is a more mellow flowing word when read silently. "Bluegreen" is a meld, conveying a colour neither blue nor green but both: "blue-green" is a two-colour mix. Maybe the editors were too gentle with my experiments and eccentricities. Great! The voice of the writer won through.

To those used to one standard, this book may offer a taste passing strange, like the original mouthful of kina roe. Persist. Kina can become a favourite food.

An explanatory dream: I am in an openwindowed railway carriage, going slowly round some mountains. I say to an unknown friend, "Hey! These must be the Rimatakas," and sure enough, across the pasty mountains rolls the inscription RIMUTAKAS 10,000 FEET HIGH, liquorice black on almond icing, and the carriage turns into a Club Room. The lady in charge has a smile hedged with teeth. "O yes, you can become a member. It'll cost $10." I offer a plastic card very bloody conscious I don't have a dollar, let alone ten. I say, guiltily, whakama, "This jersey I'm wearing, the moth holes only came up now. It was really white before." She smiles, and goes away into the dark. It really surprises me when she returns with a jug of beer and another smile for me and my friend. We all sit there, dozens of us, train rocking sadly, mountains cold, moth-holes, but not a squashcourt in sight.

Make of it what you will.

Kia ora koutou katoa.

Keri Hulme 1984

Contents

THE BONE PEOPLE

Prologue

The End at the Beginning

He walks down the street. The asphalt reels by him.
It is all silence.
The silence is music.
He is the singer.
The people passing smile and shake their heads.
He holds a hand out to them.
They open their hands like flowers, shyly.
He smiles with them.
The light is blinding: he loves the light.
They are the light.

. . .

He walks down the street. The asphalt is hot and soft with sun.
The people passing smile, and call out greetings.
He smiles and calls back.
His mind is full of change and curve and hope, and he knows it is being lightly tapped. He laughs.
Maybe there is the dance, as she says. Creation and change, destruction and change.
New marae from the old marae, a beginning from the end.
His mind weaves it into a spiral fretted with stars.
He holds out his hand, and it is gently taken.

. . .

She walks down the street. The asphalt sinks beneath her mus-cled feet.

She whistles softly as she walks. Sometimes she smiles.

The people passing smile too, but duck their heads in a deferen-tial way as though her smile is too sharp.

She grins more at their lowered heads. She can dig out each thought, each reaction, out from the grey brains, out through the bones. She knows how. She knows a lot.

She is eager to know more.

But for now there is the sun at her back, and home here, and the free wind all round.

And them, shuffling ahead in the strange-paced dance. She quickens her steps until she has reached them.

And she sings as she takes their hands.

. . .

They were nothing more than people, by themselves. Even paired, any pairing, they would have been nothing more than peo-ple by themselves. But all together, they have become the heart and muscles and mind of something perilous and new, something strange and growing and great.

Together, all together, they are the instruments of change.

In the beginning, it was darkness, and more fear, and a howling wind across the sea.

"Why not leave him?"

They can't whisper any more.

"No guarantee he'll stay on the bottom. Besides, we'll have to come back for the boat."

The voice. The nightmare voice. The vivid haunting terrible voice, that seemed to murmur endearments all the while the hands skilfully and cruelly hurt him.

"We'll have to move soon."

It is happening again, and like the time before, there is nothing he can do to stop it. It will take away the new people, it will break him, it will start all over again. He cannot change it. And worst of all, he knows in an inchoate way that the greatest terror is yet to come.

There is a sudden pause in the crashing of the waves, and a drawn prescient hissing.

"Jump now! Take the jacket, I'll swim. I can take care of him. . . ."

Even now, the barb of laughter in his voice.

Take care? Aiie!

In the memory in the black at the back of his eyes, there are words, different words. Help, but not help. Words. There were words.

But then the overwhelming wrenching groan of the boat as she struck the rocks.

In the beginning, it was a tension, an element of strain that grew and crept like a thin worm through the harmony of their embrace.

"What *is* it you want?"

"Ahh nothing . . . you're all the man I need."

Chuckles in the warm dark.

Sitting up then and saying to him urgently:

"You *must* have a son. You *must* have people."

It gnaws at him. She knew, somehow, that she wasn't going to be the person who gave him a son, who gave him people. And she never told him.

Then, he had only chuckled again and said, "Well, we got him on the way, ne?"

But the undefinable careworm was still there.

After the storm-night, they talked about the tide-washed child.

"I think he likes us," he had said.

"He needs you . . . look at him hold on though he's not himself yet."

"Shall we keep him then?" half-joking.

She had answered "Yes!" without hesitation.

"Before our baby? Before our son?"

"Before them all, man," and she had turned out of his arms and danced, in lumbering triumphant glee.

Then the worm of care had gone. They were whole and sound together until the night they took her away.

It gnaws at him: the last words she gave him as they wheeled her under the flaring lights. Harsh and whispered, "O Ngakau, mind our child."

Timote was already dead.

She meant the other one, the one who sat on his lap unmoved it seemed, while he was shaken and robbed of breath by sobbing.

"Hana is dead, dead, dead . . ." the pale child held his hand, and looked into his face with alien sea-coloured eyes, unclouded by tears. Marama said how bitterly, how hysterically upset he had been. But he never showed it to me.

It gnaws at him: he has this one thing left of her, this second-hand, barely-touched half-formed relic of her presence.

And he no longer really wants it.

And he knows the rock of desolation, and the deep of despair.

She had debated, in the frivolity of the beginning, whether to build a hole or a tower; a hole, because she was fond of hobbits, or a tower—well, a tower for many reasons, but chiefly because she liked spiral stairways.

As time went on, and she thought over the pros and cons of each, the idea of a tower became increasingly exciting; a star-gazing platform on top; a quiet library, book-lined, with a ring of swords on the nether wall; a bedroom, mediaeval style, with massive roofbeams and a plain hewn bed; there'd be a living room with a huge fireplace, and rows of spicejars on one wall, and underneath, on the ground level, an entrance hall hung with tapestries, and the beginnings of the spiral stairway, handrails dolphin-headed, saluting the air.

There'd be a cellar, naturally, well stocked with wines, home-brewed and imported vintage; lined with Chinese ginger jars, and wooden boxes of dates. Barrels round the walls, and shadowed chests in corners.

All through the summer sun she laboured, alone with the paid, bemused, professional help. The dust obscured and flayed, thirst parched, and tempers frayed, but the Tower grew. A concrete skeleton, wooden ribs and girdle, skin of stone, grey and slateblue and heavy honey-coloured. Until late one February it stood, gaunt and strange and embattled, built on an almost island in the shallows of an inlet, tall in Taiaroa.

It was the hermitage, her glimmering retreat. No people invited, for what could they know of the secrets that crept and chilled and chuckled in the marrow of her bones? No need of people, because she was self-fulfilling, delighted with the pre-eminence of her art, and the future of her knowing hands.

But the pinnacle became an abyss, and the driving joy ended. At last there was a prison.

I am encompassed by a wall, high and hard and stone, with only my brainy nails to tear it down.

And I cannot do it.

I

Season of the Day Moon

1

Portrait of a Sandal

I

" . . . **L**ike our bullock, Jack. Bugger'll be on the old age pension before *he's* killed."

"Yeah, but look who's laughing meantime?"

There was a rattle of laughter round the bar.

Kerewin, sitting apart, rang a coin on the counter and beckoned the barman.

"Same again?"

"Yes please."

> *This ship that sets its sails forever*
> *rigid on my coin*
> *is named Endeavour.*
> *She buys a drink to bar the dreams*
> *of the long nights lying.*
> *The world is never what it seems*
> and the sun is dying . . .

She shrugs.

Wonder what would happen if I started singing out loud?

The beer moves in a whirlpool to the lip of the glass: the hose withdraws.

"Had a nice night?" asks the barman politely.

It's the first thing anybody has said to her.
"Yeah."
He hands her back the change.
"Fishing been any good?"

> How long did it take to get round town that I had
> bought a boat?

"O fair enough," she says, "fair enough."
"Well, that's good. . . ." he mops the bartop cursorily and drifts away down to the other end of the bar, to the talk and the ever-curious people.

> It's late, Holmes, way after eleven. There's no point in
> staying.

There had been no point in coming to the pub either, other than to waste some more time, and drink some more beer.
Guffaws.
Somebody's in the middle of a rambling drunken anecdote. A Maori, thickset, a working bloke with steel-toed boots, and black hair down to his shoulders. He's got his fingers stuck in his belt, and the heavy brass buckle of it glints and twinkles as he teeters back and forwards.
". . . And then fuckin hell would you believe he takes the candle. . . ."

> I'd believe the poor effing fella's short of words. Or
> thought. Or maybe just intellectual energy.

The word is used monotonously, a sad counterbalance for every phrase.
"And no good for even fuckin Himi eh? Shit, no use, I said. . . ."

> Why this speech filled with bitterness and contempt?
> You hate English, man? I can understand that but why
> not do your conversing in Maori and spare us this con-
> tamination? No swear words in that tongue . . . there he
> goes again. Ah hell, the fucking word has its place, but
> all the time? . . . aue.

Kerewin shakes her head. No use thinking about it. She drains her glass, slips off the stool, and heads for the door.

The group at the end of the bar turns round to stare. The man stops his yarn and smiles blurrily at her. She didn't smile back.

"Goodnight," calls the barman.

"Goodnight."

. . .

The crayfish moved in silence through clear azure water. Bright scarlet armour, waving antennae, red legs stalking onward. Azure and scarlet. Beautiful.

It was about then she realised she was in the middle of a dream, because living crayfish were purple-maroon and orange: only when cooked, do they turn scarlet. A living boiled cray? A crayfish cooking as it walked calmly through a hot pool?

She shuddered. The crayfish moved more quickly through the blue crystal sea and the fog of dreaming increased. . . .

. . .

It is still dark but she can't sleep any more.

She dresses and goes down to the beach, and sits on the top of a sandhill until the sky pales.

Another day, herr Gott, and I am tired, tired.

She stands, and grimaces, and spits. The spittle lies on the sand a moment, a part of her a moment ago, and then it vanishes, sucked in, a part of the beach now.

Fine way to greet the day, my soul . . . go down to the pools, Te Kaihau, and watch away the last night sourness.

And here I am, balanced on the saltstained rim, watching minute navyblue fringes, gill-fingers of tubeworms, fan the water . . . put the shadow of a finger near them, and they flick outasight. Eyes in your lungs . . . neat. The three-fin blenny swirls by . . . tena koe, fish. A small bunch of scarlet and gold anemones furl and unfurl their arms, graceful petals, slow and lethal . . . tickle tickle, and they turn into uninteresting lumps of brownish jelly . . . haven't made sea-anemone soup for a while, whaddabout it? Not today, Josephine . . . at the bottom, in a bank of brown bulbous weed, a hermit crab is rustling a shell. Poking at it, sure it's empty? Ditheringly unsure . . . but now, nervously hunched over his soft slug of belly, he extricates himself from his old hutch and speeds deftly into the new . . . at least, that's where you *thought* you were going, e mate? . . . hoowee, there really is no place like home, even when it's grown a couple of sizes too small. . . .

There is a great bank of Neptune's necklaces fringing the next pool.

"The sole midlittoral fuccoid," she intones solemnly, and squashes a bead of it under the butt of her stick. "Ahh me father he was orange and me mother she was green," slithers off the rocks, and wanders further away down the beach, humming. Nothing like a tidepool for taking your mind off things, except maybe a quiet spot of killing. . . .

Walking the innocent stick alongside, matching its step to hers, she climbs back up the sandhills. Down the other side in a rush, where it is dark and damp still, crashing through loose clusters of lupins. Dew sits in the centre of each lupin-leaf, hands holding jewels to catch the sunfire until she brushes past and sends the jewels sliding, drop by drop weeping off.

The lupins grow less; the marram grass diminishes into a kind of reedy weed; the sand changes by degrees into mud. It's an estuary, where someone built a jetty, a long long time ago. The planking has rotted, and the uneven teeth of the pilings jut into nowhere now.

> It's an odd macabre kind of existence. While the nights away in drinking, and fill the days with petty killing. Occasionally, drink out a day and then go and hunt all night, just for the change.

She shakes her head.

> Who cares? That's the way things are now. (I care.)

She climbs a piling, and using the stick as a balancing pole, jumps across the gaps from one pile to the next out to the last. There she sits down, dangling her legs, stick against her shoulder, and lights a cigarillo to smoke away more time.

Intermittent wheeping flutes from oystercatchers.

The sound of the sea.

A gull keening.

When the smoke is finished, she unscrews the top of the stick and draws out seven inches of barbed steel. It fits neatly into slots in the stick top.

"Now, flounders are easy to spear, providing one minds the toes."

Whose, hers or the fishes', she has never bothered finding out. She rolls her jeans legs up as far as they'll go, and slips down into the cold water. She steps ankle deep, then knee deep, and stands, feeling for the moving of the tide. Then slowly, keeping the early morning sun in front of her, she begins to stalk, mind in her hands and eyes looking only for the puff of mud and swift silted skid of a disturbed flounder.

> All this attention for sneaking up on a fish? And they
> say we humans are intelligent? Sheeit . . .

and with a darting levering jab, stabbed, and a flounder flaps bloodyholed at the end of the stick.

Kerewin looks at it with slow smiled satisfaction.

> Goodbye soulwringing night. Good morning sinshine,
> and a fat happy day.

The steeled stick quivers.

She pulls a rolledup sack from her belt and drops the fish, still weakly flopping, in it. She hangs the lot up by sticking her knife through the sackneck into a piling side.

The water round the jetty is at thigh-level when she brings the third fish back, but there has been no hurry. She guts the fish by the rising tide's edge, and lops off their heads for the mud crabs to pick. Then she lies down in a great thicket of dun grass, and using one arm as a headrest and the other as a sunshade, falls quietly asleep.

It is the cold that wakes her, and clouds passing over the face of the sun. There is an ache in the back of her neck, and her pillowing arm is numb. She stands up stiffly, and stretches: she smells rain coming. A cloud of midge-like flies blunders into her face and hair. On the ground round the sack hovers another swarm, buzzing thinly through what would seem to be for them a fog of fish. The wind is coming from the sea. She picks up the sack, and sets off for home through the bush. Raupo and fern grow into a tangle of gorse: a track appears and leads through the gorse to a stand of windwarped trees. They are ngaio. One tree stands out from its fellows, a giant of the kind, nearly ten yards tall.

Some of its roots are exposed and form a bowl-like seat. Kerewin sits down for a smoke, as she nearly always does when she comes this way, keeping a weather eye open for rain.

In the dust at her feet is a sandal.

For a moment she is perfectly still with the unexpectedness of it.

Then she leans forward and picks it up.

It can't have been here for long because it isn't damp. It's rather smaller than her hand, old and scuffed, with the position of each toe palely upraised in the leather. The stitching of the lower strap was coming undone, and the buckle hung askew.

"Young to be running loose round here."

She frowns. She doesn't like children, doesn't like people, and has discouraged anyone from coming on her land.

"If I get hold of you, you'll regret it, whoever you are. . . ."

She squats down and peers up the track. There are footprints, one set of them. Of a sandalled foot and half an unshod foot.

Limping? Something in its foot so that's why the sandal is taken off and left behind?

She rubs a finger inside the sandal. The inner sole was shiny and polished from long wearing and she could feel the indentation of the foot. Well-worn indeed . . . in the heel though there is a sharpedged protrusion of leather, like a tiny crater rim. She turns it over. There is a corresponding indriven hole in the rubber.

"So we jumped on something that bit, did we?"

She slings the sandal into the sack of flounders, and marches away belligerently, hoping to confront its owner.

But a short distance before her garden is reached, the one and a half footprints trail off the track, heading towards the beach.

Beaches aren't private, she thinks, and dismisses the intruder from her mind.

The wind is blowing more strongly when she pushes open the heavy door, and the sky is thick with dark cloud.

"Storm's coming," as she shuts the door, "but I am safe inside. . . ."

The entrance hall, the second level of the six-floored Tower, is low and stark and shadowed. There is a large brass and wood crucifix on the far wall and green seagrass matting over the floor. The handrail of the spiral staircase ends in the carved curved flukes of a dolphin; otherwise, the room is bare of furniture and ornament. She runs up the stairs, and the sack drips as it swings.

"One two three aleary hello my sweet mere hell these get steeper daily, days of sun and wine and jooyyy,"

the top, and stop, breathless.

"Holmes you are thick and unfit and getting fatter day by day. But what the hell. . . ."

She puts the flounders on bent wire hooks and hangs them in the coolsafe. She lights the fire, and stokes up the range, and goes upstairs to the library for a book on flatfish cooking. There is just about everything in her library.

A sliver of sudden light as she comes from the spiral into the booklined room, and a moment later, the distant roll of thunder.

"Very soon, my beauty, all hell will break loose . . ." and her words hang in the stillness.

She stands over by the window, hands fistplanted on her hips, and watches the gathering boil of the surf below. She has a curious feeling as she stands there, as though something is out of place, a wrongness somewhere, an uneasiness, an overwatching. She stares morosely at her feet (longer second toes still longer, you think they might one day grow less, you bloody werewolf you?) and the joy-ous relief that the morning's hunting gave, ebbs away.

"Bleak grey mood to match the bleak grey weather," and she hunches over to the nearest bookshelf. "Stow the book on cooking fish. Gimme something escapist, Narnia or Gormenghast or Middle Earth, or,"

it wasn't a movement that made her look up.

There is a gap between two tiers of bookshelves. Her chest of pounamu rests in between them, and above it, there is a slit window.

In the window, standing stiff and straight like some weird saint in a stained gold window, is a child. A thin shockheaded person, haloed in hair, shrouded in the dying sunlight.

The eyes are invisible. It is silent, immobile.

Kerewin stares, shocked and gawping and speechless.

The thunder sounds again, louder, and a cloud covers the last of the sunlight. The room goes very dark.

If it moves suddenly, it's going to go through that glass.
Hit rockbottom forty feet below and end up looking
like an imploded plum. . . .

She barks,
"Get the bloody hell *down* from there!"

Her breathing has quickened and her heart thuds as though she
were the intruder.

The head shifts. Then the child turns slowly and carefully round
in the niche, and wriggles over the side in an awkward progression,
feet ankles shins hips, half-skidding half-slithering down to the
chest, splayed like a lizard on a wall. It turns round, and gingerly
steps onto the floor.

"Explain."

There isn't much above a yard of it standing there, a foot out of
range of her furthermost reach. Small and thin, with an extraordinary face, highboned and hollowcheeked, cleft and pointed chin,
and a sharp sharp nose. Nothing else is visible under an obscuration
of silverblond hair except the mouth, and it's set in an uncommonly
stubborn line.

Nasty. Gnomish, thinks Kerewin. The shock of surprise is going
and cold cutting anger comes sweeping in to take its place.

"What are you doing here? Aside from climbing walls?"

There is something distinctly unnatural about it. It stands there
unmoving, sullen and silent.

"Well?"

In the ensuing silence, the rain comes rattling against the windows, driving down in a hard steady rhythm.

"We'll bloody soon find out," saying it viciously, and reaching
for a shoulder.

Shove it downstairs and call authority.

Unexpectedly, a handful of thin fingers reaches for her wrist, arrives and fastens with the wistful strength of the small.

Kerewin looks at the fingers, looks sharply up and meets the
child's eyes for the first time. They are seabluegreen, a startling
colour, like opals.

It looks scared and diffident, yet curiously intense.

"Let go my wrist," but the grip tightens.

Not restraining violence, pressing meaning.

Even as she thinks that, the child draws a deep breath and lets it out in a strange sound, a groaning sigh. Then the fingers round her wrist slide off, sketch urgently in the air, retreat.

Aue. She sits down, back on her heels, way back on her heels. Looking at the brat guardedly; taking out cigarillos and matches; taking a deep breath herself and expelling it in smoke.

The child stays unmoving, hand back behind it; only the odd sea-eyes flicker, from her face to her hands and back round again.

She doesn't like looking at the child. One of the maimed, the contaminating. . . .

She looks at the smoke curling upward in a thin blue stream instead.

"Ah, you can't talk, is that it?"

A rustle of movement, a subdued rattle, and there, pitched into the open on the birdboned chest, is a pendant hanging like a label on a chain.

She leans forward and picks it up, taking intense care not to touch the person underneath.

It was a label.

1 PACIFIC STREET
   WHANGAROA
PHONE 633Z COLLECT

She turns it over.

SIMON P. GILLAYLEY
   CANNOT SPEAK

"Fascinating," drawls Kerewin, and gets to her feet fast, away to the window. Over the sound of the rain, she can hear a fly dying somewhere close, buzzing frenetically. No other noise.

Reluctantly she turns to face the child. "Well, we'll do nothing more. You found your way here, you can find it back." Something came into focus. "O there's a sandal you can collect before you go." The eyes which had followed each of her movements, settling on and judging each one like a fly expecting swatting, drop to stare at his bare foot.

She points to the spiral stairs.

"Out."

He moves slowly, awkwardly, one arm stretched to touch the wall all the way down, and she is forced to stop on each step behind him, and every time she stops, she can see him tense, shoulders jerking.

Lichen bole; glow-worms' hole; bonsai grove; hell, it
seems like 15 miles rather than 15 steps. . . .

She edges round him at the livingroom door, and collects his
sandal from the hearth. It is coated with silvery flounder slime.
"Yours?"

There is a barely perceptible nod. He stares at her unblinking.

"Well, put it on, and go."

The rain's still beating down. She shrugs mentally. Serve him
right.

He looks at the sandal in her hand, glances quickly at her face,
and then, heart thumping visibly in his throat, sits down on the bottom step.

O you smart little bastard.

But she decides it is easiest to put the sandal on. Then push him
out, bodily if need be.

"Give us your foot."

With the same fearful stareguarded care he has affected throughout, he lifts his foot five inches off the ground. Kerewin stares at
him coldly, but bends down and catches his foot, and is halted by
a hiss. It, sssing through his closed teeth, bubbles of saliva spilling
to his lips.

She remembers the strained walk, and looks more closely, and
in his heel, rammed deep, is something; and the little crater in the
sandal comes back to mind. She shuts her eyes and, all feeling in her
fingertips, grazes her hand light as air over the protrusion. It was
wooden, old wood, freshbroken, hard in the soft child-callous. Already the flesh round it is hot.

"We jumped on something that bit," her voice mild as milk, and
opens her eyes. The brat is squinting at her, his mouth sloped in a
shallow upturned U.

"I suppose I can't expect you to walk away on that," talking to
herself, "but what to do about it?"

Incongruously, he grins. It is a pleasant enough grin, but before
it fades back into the considering U, reveals a gap bare of teeth on
the left side of his jaw. The gap looks odd, and despite herself, she
grins back.

"I can take it out before you go, if you want."

He sucks in his breath, then nods.

"It'll probably hurt."

He shrugs.

"Okay then," hoping she has taken the tenor of the shrug rightly.

She gets bandage from the coffee-cupboard, a pair of needlenosed pliers from the knife-drawer, disinfectant from the grog cupboard.

"You better ahh tell your parents to get you a tetanus shot when you get home," picking up his foot again, conscious of the eyes, very conscious of paleknuckled fingers gripping her step.

She sets the pliers flush with the end of the splinter, carefully so as not to pinch skin. There's an eighth inch gap between the jaws when they're closed on the wood. She holds it a moment, setting aside every sensation beyond splinter, pliers, her grip, and then presses hard and pulls down in one smooth movement. An inch of angular wood slides out.

The child jerks but might be pulling against a fetter for all the effect it has. She scrutinises the hole before it closes and fills in bloodily. No dark slivers, clean puncture, should heal well; and becomes aware of the hissing and twisting and sets the foot free. The marks of her grip are white on his ankle.

"Sorry about that. I forgot you were still on the end of it. The foot I mean." With the careless suppleness of the young, he has his foot nearly on his chest. He broods over it, thumb on the splinter hole.

"Give it here again."

She swabs the heel with antiseptic, bandages some protective padding over it.

> Sop for your conscience, Holmes me love. He can limp
> away easy into the rain.

She stands, gesturing towards the door.

"On your way now, Simon P. Gillayley."

He sits quite still, clasping his foot. Then he sighs audibly. He puts the sandal on, wincing, and stands awkwardly. He brushes away the long fringe of hair that's fallen over his eyes, looks at her and holds out his hand.

"I don't understand sign language," says Kerewin coolly.

A rare kind of expression comes over the boy's face, impatience compounded with o-don't-give-me-that-kind-of-shit. He takes hold of his other hand, shakes it, waves tata in the air, and then spreads both hands palms up before her. Shaking hands, you get what I mean? I'm saying goodbye, okay?

Then he holds out his hand to her again.

Ratbag child.

She's grinning as she takes his hand, and shakes it gently. And the child smiles broadly back.

"You come here by yourself?"

He nods, still holding onto her hand.

"Why?"

He marches the fingers of his free hand aimlessly round in the air. His eyes don't leave her face.

"Meaning you were just wandering round?"

He doesn't nod, but makes a downward gesture with his hand.

"What does that mean?"

He nods, repeating the gesture on a level with his head.

"Shorthand for Yes?" unable to repress a smile.

Yes, say the fingers.

"Fair enough. Why did you come inside?"

She takes her hand away from his grasp. He has finely sinewed, oddly dry hands. He points to his eyes.

Seeing, looking, I suppose.

She feels strange.

I'm used to talking to myself, but talking for someone else?

"Well, in case no-one ever told you before, people's houses are private and sacrosanct. Even peculiar places like my tower. That means you don't come inside unless you get invited."

He's looking steadily at her.

"Okay?"

The gaze drops. He takes out a small pad and pencil from his jeans pocket and writes.

He offers the page to her.

In neat and competent capitals . . . how old are you, urchin? I KNOW I GET TOLD SP

"And you keep on doing it? You're a bit of a bloody hard case, boy."

He is staring straight ahead now, eyes on the level of her belt buckle.

> He gets told, meaning he must do it frequently . . .
> unholy, he's a bit young to be a burglar, maybe he's just
> compulsively curious?

"Well, there's a couple of cliches that fit in neatly here. One, curiosity killed the cat. Two, it takes all sorts to make a world. You want some lunch before you go? It might stop raining in the meantime. . . ."

He looks up abruptly, and she is startled to see his eyes fill with tears.

> What in the name of hell have I said that would make
> it cry?

. . .

He cripples over to the sheepskin rugs near the fire at her invitation. He sits down carefully, cradling his foot. She has a suspicion he is exaggerating his hurt.

"You like raw fry?"

Uhh? What?

> Is his face really that easy to read, or am I just looking
> harder because he can't talk? Probably years of practice
> at non-verbal communication.

She wonders how many years. He looks as though he might be, ummm? She has no idea how old the brat looks. She hasn't ever had anything to do with children.

"Raw fry is vegetables and stuff, like bacon or eggs or fish, all cooked together. It tastes okay."

There's no obvious answer.

"Well," she says after a moment, aware now there is an appraisal of herself taking place, "that's all that's going. Like it or lump it."

> I wonder if I still look peeculeear?
> Heavy shouldered, heavy-hammed, heavy-haired.
> No evidence of a brain behind those short brows.
> Yellowed eyes, and eczema scarred skin.

Large hands and large feet, crooked only if you look
closely.

Everything beautified by me knuckleduster collection.
Today, greenstone water middlefinger; kingfisher glitter
of opal ringfinger; winedark garnet one little finger, turquoise stud the other; and that barred charredlooking
silver hulking hunk of thumbring.

Encased in jeans, leather jerkin, silk shirt, denim jacket,
knife at side, bare footed. (Which reminds me, they're
cold.)

A right piratical-looking eschewball I suppose I look,
but what the hell.

Out with chopping board and cooking paraphernalia. She guts
green peppers, slices hapless onions into tears. She is immune to
the eyesting of onionjuice.

The click and squich of the knife cutting food.

Her breathing.

The steady downbeat of the rain.

The fire crackle.

It is unnaturally silent.

The guttersnipe still watches her, twisted and still like a small
evil buddha.

"Um, you expected back soon?"

He shakes his hair.

"Your people know where you are, even?"

All the answer is a well-screened stare that sinks slowly down
to his foot level. Mentally she balls fist and projects thumb.

Figs to you, boyo.

. . .

There isn't a proper table in this level. The room is for eating in,
sure, but also for listening to music, playing guitars, or quietly dreaming by the fire. Seawatching. Meditating. So, all the table is a dropleaf
bench, attached to the wall. Sometimes she uses it for eating off:
more often, she puts her plate on the floor by the fire. Now, she sets
a knife and fork and plate of steaming hash at either end of the
bench, and two mugs of coffee like a line of truce in the middle.

"If you want something to eat, it's here."

He arrives at the table with a stilted gait, eyes the food, eyes her, eyes the stool, and elects to kneel on the latter, head on one hand, eating from a fork in the other, ignoring his knife and herself. He eats neatly, with unchildlike precision and more quickly than she can. When he has finished, he pushes his plate to the middle of the bench, folds his arms, rests his head on them, and stares at her. A pair of seagreen eyes watching one from table-level is disconcerting, to say the least.

Kerewin sets her knife and fork down with a click! and ceremoniously lowers her head to table-level, and stares back.

The child's eyes widen.

She keeps on peering beadily across the table at him.

And the boy starts to giggle. A breathy spurt of chuckling that bubbles eerily out of him. He sits up straight, and pats the table, shaking his head.

"Good. I take it you've got the hint."

She calmly continues eating.

> So he can giggle . . . I wonder what stops him from talking?

. . .

One of her family used to say,
"And the rain was fairly pissing down."
It conveyed exactly how the weather was,
"And ther rain" (shaking head slightly)
"was fair-lee *piss*" (grimace and smash fist through the air)
"sing down" (eyes wide with surprise at the violence of the rain).

The gusto, the singsong level and fall of the speaker's voice made it real.

Anyway, she thinks, regretting again the gulf between her and her family, it *is* pissing down now. I better get some lamps out. The room is all shadows. She looks at the chance-guest, sprawled in front of the fire.

> Made yourself thoroughly at home, haven't you, guttersnipe? Well, you're about to get the boot.

"Give us a look at that, that pendant you wear please? I want to check the phone number."

He sits up. Six fingers, three fingers, three fingers again, and a large airy Z.

He waits, hands at the ready in case she hasn't understood.

"Thanks."

She's already at the radiophone.

It's her concession to the outside world, the radiophone. No one can ring her up unless they go through a toll-operator, kept by the Post Office especially for subscribers like herself, but she can ring anyone she likes. An expensive arrangement, but Kerewin has more money than she needs and likes privacy. Besides, while the toll-operators are busybodies, they can supply local information, especially one whom she's cultivated, and she values that.

"Hullo Miz Holmes."

"Morning," she says gravely. "A Whangaroa number please, 633Z. I assume it's a party line."

"It is," says the operator. After a minute he adds, "Dear me."

Click buzz whirp, and then a long series of monotonous burrs.

"Were they expecting you to ring?"

"Nope."

"O. Shall I keep the call in?"

"Just a minute." She winds the mike sound right down and asks the child, "That phone number is for your home?"

He nods, smiling a smug sage smile.

She brings the mike sound up again. "Keep it in please, and when someone answers, ask them to come out to Paeroa to collect something of theirs."

The operator laughs.

"Good luck," he says strangely, and hangs up.

Kerewin stares at the mike. All the world is a little queer except. . . .

"You going to have your coffee?" She asks without turning round.

A click.

"O you icthyphagal numbskull," she leans against the stone wall, and looks at him.

"I forgot," she says, weary rather than apologetic. "I take it that's for attention?"

He shakes his head. His hair falls over his face, and he sweeps it off automatically. He inches off the sheepskins, and suddenly smiles.

An amerindian opening parley. . . .

She hunkers down under the transceiver shelf and watches him.

He shakes his head quickly, and snaps his fingers once. It is a sharp crisp sound. She remembers that until she was ten, the only fingersnap she could make sounded like a boneless phup! no snap near it.

The child nods and snaps his fingers twice.

Not a parley, a language lesson,

and she's tempted to snap her fingers three times and say Maybe.

"I get that. Out of sight communication with you is one for no and two for yes, am I right?"

and snaps her fingers twice for emphasis.

He claps his hands together twice, deliberately, sarcastically.

Smartass, says Kerewin inside herself, grinning in an unfriendly way at him.

"Well, the coffee on the table will be cold by now. That's why I wanted to know whether you still wanted to drink it."

Snap.

"Okay. You want something else to drink? I have," counting off the list on her fingers, "wine and mead and sundry ales, beer and liqueurs and spirits, none of which you're getting. Water and milk and applejuice; limejuice, lemon and orange; cider of my own brew- ing, and teas, Japanese, Chinese, Indian, and herbal of many kinds. So which?"

Coffee, he mouths, with exaggerated lip movements, Coff-feee, and the teeth-bare gap is there again.

Contrary little sod.

"You just said you didn't want any?"

He makes a series of corkscrew spirals near his ear.

"You're nuts or you change your mind? Don't answer, I agree with both interpretations . . . anyway, you've missed your only chance to try Holmes' famous herbal tea, a soporific manuka brew, foolish child. Actually," she says, getting up, "it tastes disgusting, but it's very useful if you're an insomniac."

His face shows, What the hell are you talking about?

"If you're projecting what I think you're projecting, boy, the answer is, obfuscation is my trade. I didn't get to be thirty odd and horridly rich by being intelligible, hokay?"

She's grinding a handful of coffee beans by now. The mill had belonged to a great great grandmother, who brought it all the way from the Hebrides a hundred years ago. When she parted, in violence and tears, from her family, she had made a special expedition

Call it by its right name, o my soul

to gain the coffee-mill.

By thievery and stealth in the dead of the night, I ac-quired thee. . . .

She ran her hand lightly over the little machine, and talked loud nonsense to cover her pain.

The child sits, his eyes hooded, and doesn't make any response.

. . .

The rain hasn't eased.

The radiophone hasn't buzzed.

For a cat, when in doubt, wash: for a Holmes, ruffle a guitar.

She takes her oldest guitar down from the wall, and picks a se-ries of delicate harmonics to check the tuning. Then, the body of the guitar cuddled into her, she plays wandering chords and long pure notes and abrupt plucked melodies. The music melds into the steady background white noise of the rain.

At the end of it, she sighs, and props the guitar against herself.

"Do you like guitar music, ahh, boy?"

His eyes are shut and his mouth is open, and she is unsure whether he is ecstatic or gone to sleep.

He blinks rapidly and nods, Yes.

"Mmmm." She lays the guitar down. "What do they call you in-cidentally? Surely not Simon P. Gillayley all the time?"

He shakes his head, and presents his forefingers straight out, about two inches apart.

She rubs her eyes ostentatiously.

"Yeah?"

The boy looks at her with disgust. His lips are pinched as though he's tasted something bad, and his nostrils are flared, eyes narrowed—and suddenly all expression is wiped. His face is a blank, a mask showing nothing, and his eyes are cold. I'm not talk-ing to you. I don't like being played with. He turns his back on her.

Ratbag, smartass, and sulky with it.

Kerewin shrugs, and picks up the guitar again.

Shall we be nasty and throw it out right now? Nah, our
sense of hospitality won't stand for that . . . yet.

Once the guest has eaten and drunk at your table, the guest be-comes kin . . . beggar or enemy, friend or chief, if they knock on your door, it will open; if they seek your shelter, it will be given, and if they ask for hospitality, give them your bread and wine . . . for who knows when you may need the help of a fellow human? In-sure against the chance, and at least endure every miserable sulky dumb brat that you happen to find in your windows . . . thrum, golpe, golpe, rasguedo, and she launches into an ersatz flamenco rhythm.

The rain responds by pissing down harder than ever.

. . .

She hangs the old guitar back on the wall, stroking its amber belly and wondering what to do next, and the radiophone buzzes.

"Hello?"

"About that number in Whangaroa you want . . ."

"Yes, yes?"

"Have you got Simon Gillayley there?"

A long pause while she reassembles her proposed conversation, Sir/Madam, your son is loitering in my tower and will you kindly remove the same. . . .

"How the berloody *hell* did you know?"

He laughs drily.

"It happens often enough."

She throws a glance at the sullen little boy, still crouched back to her on the hearthskins.

"Ohhh."

"His father is out, y'know."

"I don't," says Kerewin shortly. "I never saw the brat until a couple of hours ago."

The operator giggles.

"You've missed a lot . . . anyway, I thought I'd better let you know in case there's trouble."

Pregnant pause.

And what bastard news comes forth?

"His father, Joe Gillayley, nice bloke incidentally, well, he won't be home till late. Guarantee it. If he gets home, that is."

She swallows. "I see."

"If I were you," the operator sounds happy he's not, "I'd ring Wherahiko Tainui and see if he or Piri'll come and pick up the boy."

"And what's this Wherahiko's number?"

"O, I've already tried it for you, and they're out at the moment too. Shall I give you a call when I raise them?"

Kerewin draws in her breath, "I. . . ."

"Or would you like me to get them to ring you?"

"That would do, but. . . ."

"Of course, it might be an idea to ring the police now. They know what to do. . . ."

"I beg your pardon?"

"Nooo, on second thoughts . . ." the man taps his mouth piece. "Tell you what, whether I can get hold of the Tainuis or not I'll ring you before I go off at seven thirty. How'll that be?"

"Fine," says Kerewin, "but. . . ."

"Rightio." Click.

What the hell do I do now?

She walks slowly to the window, frowning.

Round all the arc of glass, trickling rivulets of rain. Outside, greyness, deep enough for twilight. At the horizon it is hard to see where the sea leaves off and the sky begins.

The police will know what to do? What am I sheltering? A criminal, some kind of juvenile delinquent? Hell, hardly . . . it doesn't look more than, than about, o five years old?

It must be more than that, though. I'm ahem (polishing mental nails) exceedingly bright, and I didn't write coherently until I was seven—coherently enough for the adults to always understand what I mean, that is. But then again, I could talk. Vociferously.

A sudden gust slashes against the windows.

I can hardly send him out in *that*.

Outside, the wind would be howling and hard. There is a stand of alien pines half a mile along the beach, and she can see them bending from here.

Something touches her thigh.

She spins round, viciously quick, her palms rigid and ready as knives.

The urchin has sprouted by her side, asking questions with all its fingers.

"Sweet apricocks and vilest excreta . . . boy, don't do that again."

It was like watching a snail, she thinks coldly. One moment, all its horns are out and it's positively sailing along its silken slime path, and the next moment . . . ooops, retreat into the shell.

The urchin has snatched its hands behind its back and is standing fearful and still.

"Ahh hell," says Kerewin, her actor's voice full of friendship, "it is just that I get easily surprised by unexpected contacts eh. Besides, I couldn't follow what you were saying . . . if you make everything nice and simple and slow, even snailbrains like myself might gather what you mean. See?"

It may have been the genuine amusement in her voice that fooled it, for the horns come out again. Only this time he looks at her carefully while he gestures. Seven fingers spread briefly, and then one hand describes fluid circles.

"Umm, meaning?"

The child sighs. His hands writhe together a moment, then he shakes his shoulders, and reluctantly takes out his pad and pencil again.

We don't seem to like doing this.

He writes quickly, pad on foot-propped-up thigh: he stands remarkably steady on his uninjured foot.

In the darkened room, his eyes have lost their opal brilliance. They scan Kerewin's unmoving face as she reads.

TAINUIS HOME AT SEVEN I AM MEANT TO BE THERE CAN I STAY HERE SP (<u>SIMON</u>)

She grins at the underlining. She says, quite kindly,

"Thanks for the explanation. I've got a message out for your father to come and get you, so I dare say he'll be here shortly. And no, you can't stay. I'm not keen on anyone staying here, particularly children."

The boy sits down, right where he'd stood.

She gathers the dishes and stacks them in the sink. She goes and sits down under the portrait that dominates the room. She lights a cigarillo, and starts talking to herself.

"Once I had to work at horrible jobs to earn enough money to buy food to eat in order to live to work at horrible jobs to earn enough . . . I hated that life, I hated it to my bones. So I quit. I did what my heart told me to do, and painted for my living. I didn't earn enough to live on, but I wasn't too unhappy, because I was loved at home and I loved what I was doing. Money was the only problem . . . then it all changed. I won a lottery. I invested it. I earned a fortune by fast talking. And while I was busy blessing the god of munificence, the lightning came. It blasted my family, and it blasted my painting talent. I went straight out of one bind into a worse one. Very strange. I never could understand why. . . ."

She leans back against the wall, and knocks the edge of the portrait.

"That is an enlargement of a painting by Fujiware Takanobu. He was a genius, who could capture a soul in limning and pigment, and do this in such an ascetically elegant way that the heart stands still to see it . . . one time, I could do something like that. Not any more, o child, not any more. . . ."

She doesn't look at the boy.

"I am in limbo, and in limbo there are no races, no prizes, no changes, no chances. There are merely degrees of endurance, and endurance never was my strong point." She adds a moment later, casually conversational, "I'm just gonna stick on some socks and shoes before my toes drop off. Then I think I'll light some lamps. You think it's getting too dark?"

O god if there is one, running up the spiral to the bedroom, careless of the cold and the hard knock of the stone steps against her feet, get rid of that child. I need my peace. I need to get drunk.

She longs for the Gillayley father to arrive and carry off his offspring, right now. A loud and boisterous Viking type she'd bet, from the child's colouring. Yer rowdy Aryan barbarian, face like a broken crag, tall as a door, and thick all the way through.

She slips on thin leather kaibabs over woollen socks, and when the numbness of her feet has warmed to prick and needle sensations, walks silently back down the stairs.

The child is now sitting in front of the portrait of Minamoto-no-Yoritomo, and he's looking at it fixedly. He doesn't shift as she softfoots it into the room.

Ah to hell, I'll start drinking anyway.

"Crystal goblets, earthen cups," meandering over to the grog cupboard as she chants, "juice of grape, or squshed hop?"

She settles on stout, opening a couple of bottles with her knife, flicking the tops into the sink. Bugger the dishes, they'll be there tomorrow. She pours a schooner full, and settles back on the sheepskins

> (Momentarily, she sees the chain at the freezing works where fresh-killed sheep carmine-throated, are grotesquely hooded by their own skins. The skins slip along the floor as the white carcasses jerk and sway above them on the moving hooks . . . what deaths to occasion your comforts?)

and takes a deep swallow of stout.

It goes down, bitter as bile.

"Have to stoke the fire soon." It has settled into a red bed of embers.

"Light the lamps soon too."

There's a scratching noise, lighter than a mouse-scrabble but still heard over the rain. The boy is writing again.

She turns round a bit, nonchalantly, so she can see the child if she wants to.

"Becomes a ritual, eh? Build wood and coal into a fire. Care for the wick in the lamp and grow a light from kerosene."

The urchin has sidled crabwise closer. He's waiting to see whether she is going to notice him.

Kerewin turns round a bit more.

"You brought me a message?"

TIL TONIGHT PERHAPS. TIL JOE COMES PERHAPS. CAN I HAVE A DRINK PERHAPS. SP

Wonder what the latest word we've learned is?

She grins inwardly but says, "Of stout?" astonished and puritan and also dodging the issue.

The boy nods, looking surprised at her tone of voice.

"Well, okay then I suppose."

She finishes her glassful with a hurried swallow and pours him a drink.

A twelve ounce schooner should stop you, my lad, and again the inward grin, this time mean with anticipation.

Over he comes, hitching along the floor, crawling actually like he's half his age, with a smile in place that lacks even a vestige of embarrassment. The bandage shows startlingly white under the frayed jeans cuff. Good as your remaining teeth boyo. Thin-fingered hands round the glass—so you still need two for drinking a full one, eh? Split chin upwards, and the dark grog practically seen outside your skinny throat . . . what's the mark? Pink and satin-shiney, like a scar.

She fingers the two scar-like lines that run in parallel across her own throat, while staring in awe as the child keeps on swallowing and swallowing, downing the drink without needing a breath it seems.

He lowers the glass at last and grins hugely.

"Something tells me," says Kerewin, fascinated, "that that is not your first drink. I think I better get another glass for me, and you can keep that for your own." She fetches a mug and another two bottles from the cupboard.

"Well," raising the mug in a loose salute, "kia ora koe, and we might as well have a session."

Glass to glass, chink.

The boy chokes a little.

Kerewin staring at air rising in the black depth of her drink:

"Why do you want to stay tonight? Aside from the fact it's raining?"

Gillayley:

shrug.

"Write it down dammit, if you can't think of any other way to say it. A shrug tells me nothing."

He looks slyly sideways, away from her eyes.

"Well?"

Gillayley:

sigh. Followed by a hiccough.

He hears the sound with an expression of pained surprise.

She collars the last of the bottles of stout, and watches him from under her lids.

> I'll be hellishing popular if I send it home drunk.

"I'll put it another way then . . . why don't you want to stay with the Tainuis, whoever they are, for the night?"

SHE PETS ME AND CRY FOR JOE SP

"You needn't sign these damn things. I can see who they come from . . . pets you? Who?

MARAMA. SHE KISS ME AND

she's leaning, watching over his shoulder now,

"I know, cry for Joe . . . ah sheeit, archetypical small boy distaste! I love it, I love! Ah beautiful!"

> Hey easy, a couple of bottles of stout shouldn't cause that
> much mirth . . . but look at his face, delicious! Careful,
> now he's looking at you like you were kind of nutty. . . .

She sobers. She says straightfaced,

"I'm sorry, but that just seemed funny . . . now I understand, and sympathise a little. I don't like people kissing and fussing over me either. Can you tell me when Joe—uh, he's your father?"

Groggy nods.

"When Joe is likely to be home?"

Obligingly, the urchin writes a clear answer.

NO. SP

The initialling is obviously a reflex.

"Well, unless your father arrives first, you can stay here until the Tainuis ring. Okay?"

His hand comes out, pauses, and then as if reaching over a barrier, takes her hand. How touching, says Kerewin's innermost being, the Snark, squirming through a gamut of connotations, that *and* the guileless Gillayley smile. Too much.

"Agreed then. Sooo, it's about lamplighting time, not to mention fire-resuscitation. You want to help? You can uh, hold things," removing her hand but gently.

As she collects kerosene and lamps, putting much into the child's ready arms, she considers two things.

Is it better the devil you don't know?

Or simply, variety is the spice of life?

And she wants to know more and more, the halloween pumpkin grin renewing the query every minute, how the brat comes to lack teeth on one whole side of his jaw.

The lamps are hung, hissing quietly: she gets busy on the fire, piling logs and heaping coal on top. The coal dust flares and crackles, and all the shadows in the room retreat to the corners.

For the first time she can see the child clearly. Slender and prominently boned, his smallness making him seem frail. A tallowness about his face, a waxen depth that accentuates the bruise marks of tiredness under his eyes, and the narrowness of his face.

> Hey where you been?
> Watch you been doin?

For, as he stands there waiting on her next move or gesture so he may make his reciprocal offering, all the vivacity has gone out of him.

> My god, he really is desperately tired.
> Well, the long walk—if he walked here.
> The tension of being caught, and wondering what I would do.
> The drink of course.
> And maybe all this is like a fine drawn duel to him, words against his miming.

"You're tired, Simon?"

He examines the question, screwing his head into his shoulders, and nodding once.

Yes, more than tired.

"Well, why not go to bed until someone calls?"

He even starts to droop wearily, but he frowns. Yes, again, but it's given reluctantly.

"My bedroom's upstairs. You can use it for a while. This way," and she vanishes up the dark spiral.

She don't like me around much.
I'm staying though.

He stands still a minute, gathering his strength for the long walk up the stairs.

. . .

A spiral staircase can be surprising, because you can't see more than a step and a half in front. Kerewin, coming rapidly back down to find out anything that may have happened, nearly knocks the child all his slow progress back.

"Whoops and hie," grasping the handrail to halt herself. "I wondered where you'd got to."

He looks to his foot, and up again, apologetically.

"Well, keep going, the trek'll soon be over." She edges carefully past him. "It's colder up here than I thought. I'm going down to get you a hottie."

This godzone babytalk. Hottie lolly cardie nappy, crappy the lot of it, she snarls to herself. But what to say that the kid'd recognise? I'm gonna get you a bedheating hotwater bottle?

She's back with it as the boy arrives at the doorway.

"Go in, then. It's not as bad as it looks."

Actually, she is proud of this room. The bed and roofbeams are hand-adzed totara, and the floor is covered with palecream sheepskins. There is a double-windowed oriel, and the glass is a shallow summer sea, aquamarine and pale beryl green. A lot of leaded panes like jewels. One could sit on the broad sill and absorb sun and sea alone.

"Charmed magic casements, opening on the foam of perilous seas," she quotes blandly, seeing his stare fixed on the window. "I'd open them and show you a forlorn fairy or something except you'd probably die of pneumonia soon after."

Silence. "Well," she says, "here's the hotwater bottle, there's the bed. Get under the eiderdown on top, you should be okay. The toilet is through that door," pointing, "you want anything else?"

The child shakes his head numbly.

It hasn't taken long for the rot to set in. Suggest I know he's tired, and he's ready on the instant to flake.

"Right. If you do, come downstairs and ask; otherwise, I'll come up and wake you round seven. Sweet dreams meantime," and she walks slowly out the door but speeds down the stairs.

"Ahhh," stretching long and hard, "peace and tranquillity."

Freedom from overseeing eyes.

. . .

II

It is now early evening, dark sky outside studded with rain-washed stars. The rain has eased to a thin drizzle.

She drinks another bottle of stout, but her hands become restless. She gets down her golden guitar, and plays low languorous chords, watching the night grow deeper all the while.

But she keeps on listening with one ear for any sound from upstairs.

Blast the brat, he's beginning to haunt me.

An enemy inside my broch . . . a burglar ensconced here.

and it suddenly occurs to her that the child may really have been stealing and has been playing for time ever since.

God o Hell, my jade.

Ahh, come on!

He's not old enough to know greenstone from greywacke.

But what say someone else has heard about it, some local brand of Fagin, and. . . .

She lays down the guitar and pads swiftly upstairs.

Past her bedroom. Listen. Not a sound.

Into the library.

There's a drawing light on the desk. She takes it to the full extent of its cord, and shines the light onto the chest. She opens the lid, her heart thudding. On trays in the pale pool of light, a hundred smooth and curvilinear shapes.

> Two meres, patu pounamu, both old and named, still deadly.
> Many stylised hook pendants, hei matau.
> Kuru, and kapeu, and kurupapa, straight and curved neck pendants.
> An amulet, a marakihau; and a spiral pendant, the koropepe.
> A dozen chisels. Four fine adzes.
> Several hei tiki, one especial—so old that the flax cord of previous owners had worn through the hard stone, and the suspension hole had had to be rebored in times before the Pakeha ships came.
> A very strange pendant she had picked up long ago on Moerangi beach. As always her hand goes to it, stroking it, I am here, I am here.
> Jade of my heart, your names a litany of praise; kahurangi; kawakawa; raukaraka; tangiwai; auhunga, inanga, kahotea; totoweka and ahuahunga. . . .

It's all there.

She derides herself, You idiot, did you really think that, that *scarecrow* would pinch your precious hoard? Ea, you ought to give the berloody lot away. . . .

She says softly,

"It's becoming too precious. Too important. To care for anything deeply is to invite disaster."

She picks up the curious pendant one last time, to fondle and admire before she goes downstairs.

At seven precisely the radiophone buzzes. The operator answers her "Gidday, and Hooray" with "Miz Holmes, there's been some kind of holdup."

"O," a sinking premonitory feeling in her stomach.

"Yeah, I been doing some quiet checking up. The Tainuis left for over the hill early this morning by all accounts, and Simon Gillayley was supposed to be with them."

"Bloody hell," says Kerewin, "but his father? His mother? Anyone?"

"Lessee, Hana died two, maybe three years ago. If Joe's not around, the Tainuis usually are."

"And Joe isn't around?"

A long pause.

"No," he says, and she can hear him chewing his lips. "Ah, has there been any trouble?"

"No. I fed him, he sat round, and then went off to bed at my suggestion. He seemed helluva tired. I assume he's still there."

A current of surprise wafts to her.

"I take it he takes off fairly frequently?"

"O periodically," the operator's tones are restrained, "like about twice a week."

"So I got the impression you are surprised by something?"

"Yeah, when you said there's been no trouble. There always is. The kid's got a touchpaper temper. Also, he specialises in sneak-thievery and petty vandalism."

A little break of silence while she absorbs that lot.

"And," adds the operator, "it's well known he's not all there. Emotionally disturbed or something."

"Well, he's been no trouble so far." She feels somehow defensive of the child.

"Lucky you," and there's another pause. He says, "As I see it, you've got alternatives. You can ring the cops and have him picked up. That makes life hard for Joe, and as I said, he's a good bloke. It can't be easy bringing up a kid on your own, even the ordinary kind . . . I don't think the police have come into it since Simon tramped all Mrs Hardy's lettuces to death. Or you can keep him there until morning, say late morning, because I guarantee Joe'll be up and about by then. And choice number three, throw him out on his ear right now."

"It's still wet," she says briefly. Then, intrigued, "Why on earth did he stamp on Mrs Whatsit's lettuces?"

"I don't know. Can't have liked their faces or something. As I said, the kid's batty. Deficient."

"So I don't really have alternatives?"

"If he's no trouble, your words, and you're too humanitarian to kick him out or get the police in, no, you haven't got much choice."

"Not humanitarian, worried about my lettuces . . . actually the slugs got all the last lot so it doesn't upset me one way or the other."

"Well, in that case I'll leave a note for the graveyard shift to get hold of Joe, and if you sleep in late, you shouldn't have anything to worry about."

"Thanks"

"And listen, Joe'll make everything right by you. He's good like that."

"Yeah. Thanks again."

"S'all right," says the operator, cheerful and kindly, "Let's know what happened sometime eh?"

"I will. Goodnight."

"Goodnight . . . O. . . ."

"What?"

"Check your silver," click.

Ha bloody ha. I'll just turn the brat upside down and shake him thoroughly before he leaves.

And speaking of leaving, the stout is due to exit.

Running up the dark stairway, surefooted, lightheaded, giddy in the spiral between the walls. . . .

> Her original plan had included a garderobe, but there'd been problems. A convenient stream was one, the stench another. Let Genet sniff his farts like flowers, she preferred other incense. So a modern watercloset flush in the medieval stone. . . .

She sneaks to her bedroom doorway: there is a curled shape dimly visible on the bed.

No movement. No sound. She cannot hear any breathing.

A sudden absurd fear, that the unwelcome guest has somehow changed into an even more unwelcome corpse, grips her. Stupid! she says furiously, Stupid! She stalks down the stairs, shoulders high, still listening intently.

> Frae ghosties an ghoulies
> an longlegged beasties
> an things that gae bump!
> in the night,
> guid God deliver us. . . .

"Stupid," she tells herself out loud, when safely in the light and warm of the livingroom circle.

> But what would you have done if he really had died?
> Forget him. He'll go away with the morning.

She has no appetite for food now. She hunts out the sleeping bag she had last used during Tower-building, and gets ready to go to sleep.

But she sits a long time, staring at the fire.

"Of all the daft days . . . fit for the logbook, I think."

She takes it from the bottom shelf of the grog cupboard, and dreams what to put in it.

The pages are mainly blank, because there are 1000 pages. There are no headings, dates, day names. She has filled in some pages at random with doodles and sequences of hatching. Small precise drawings and linked haiku. Some days were a solitary word. "Hinatore" says one, "Nautilids!" another.

She notices the child's battered sandal by the andirons and draws it with careful realism on a page she marks "Today."

Then she lies back in the sleeping bag, hands behind her head, and listens a long time to the rain. . . .

. . .

III

Between waking and being awake there is a moment full of doubt and dream, when you struggle to remember what the place and when the time and whether you really are.

A peevish moment of wonderment as to where the real world lies.

And there is nothing so damned and godforsaken, thinks Kerewin, as to wake up looking at a pile of dead ashes.

Not only looking at: practically in. With some atavistic instinct her body had moved closer and closer to the only source of heat as the room grew colder during the night.

> Interesting if the whole lot had caught fire, eh. Immolated Holme in more ways than one . . . what would burn

though? me; the matting probably; shelves and grog and
the records and stereo; cupboards; o precious guitars—
and then the stone walls would stop it going further.
But a fine contained inferno. A private introductory
malbowge.

She shudders and crawls out into the cold.

What a mental inventory to make—the worldly goods
to accompany the cremation to Valhalla—and at the
hellish time of

and she suddenly remembers, standing naked and shivering and
glowering at the world, the guest. The vandal, the vagabond, the
wayward urchin, the scarecrow child—
six thirty three ay em.

It is dark outside still. The moon glows palely, slewed away in
the west. And through the thickness of the Tower walls, she can
feel frost.

Aue and ach y fi, the cold and my chilblains. And that
bloody little bugger upstairs. All miseries hemming me
in together.

"Sheeit and apricocks," says Kerewin to the immune walls, and
gathers her clothes on, hustles them on, and sneezes and shivers
her way to the shower room.

Somewhat warmer, cleaner, and altogether more self-possessed—
that is herself some twenty minutes later. Now venturing into her
bedroom with the same lightstepping care she would use on looking into a taniwha cave.

"Brushing the embers out of my hair and whistling merrily," she
announces, "it's me."

She can hear breathing, but the boy's idea of a comfortable bed
was to pile the quilt in a heap and crawl somewhere inside the centre. She can't see any part of him.

"To unearth anything, we begin by digging," but she isn't very
keen on the idea.

"Hey! You there?"

No answer. No movement.

So she untangles the end of the eiderdown and pulls it away.

He sleeps, pale and quiet, his mouth open. The small
angular face no longer looks tight and strained. He
sleeps in a strange twisted fashion, head turned to one
side, body warped round. He also sleeps with his
clothes on, sandal and all.

His eyes slide under their lids side to side, and open. His arm
comes over abruptly, shielding his chest, and the other wraps across
his face in an instant.

Then, out of his unsure second, he lowers his arms, looking surprised and sheepish all in the one face.

"Well, good morning, and where did you learn that luverly
block?"

The boy raises his eyebrows for an answer, disclaiming knowledge. The bruiselike shadows under his eyes have deepened to
mauve.

"Did you have a good sleep? Or are nightmares catching?"

He smiles.

"Mmm. Well anyway, in case you're wondering, it's tomorrow,
the Tainuis are safely over the hill, your father is picking you up
sometime this morning, and what do you want for breakfast?"

From hearsay, children wallow in milk. She considers her normal breakfast, black coffee and yoghurt, while watching something
like guilt slide across his face and vanish, and composes a list of
alternatives.

"You like, say, porridge? Coffee? Milk? Fruit? Blackpudding-
eggsanonions?"

He nods to the lot, sitting up now and holding his hands with
the fingers spread out.

God knows what it's trying to say, but she answers,

"Hokay, so you'll be eating for a month of Sundays."

He leans back on his elbows and yawns a yawn that is partly
sighed.

"I'll leave you to get up then. You know where the bathroom is.
I'll be down on the next floor, doing exciting things like lighting the
fire and burning the breakfast."

He looks at her uneasily. As she goes out the door, he clicks his
fingers.

"A yes? Or what?"

He pantomimes while she ponders aloud, "Sleep? Definitely sleep . . . okay, did I sleep? Nope? Where did I sleep? Nope? O, did I have a good sleep?"

Impatient fingers, Yes, Yes, Yes.

"I did, o politeness-impersonated. Aside from the penitential part," and leaves him to consider that.

The only time she regretted having a range was now, early on a cold morning facing a grate full of ash. So much easier to flick switches . . . she loathes all the cold iron frame of it until the fire is lit and it begins to live again.

Upstairs, Simon is thinking. What does she talk like that for? To fool me? and shakes his head in exasperation. Kerewin's multi-syllables were, for the main part, going straight in one ear and out the other, leaving behind an increasing residue of strange sounds and bewilderment.

> What does that mean, penitential?
> "That's the penitentiary, you. So watch it."
> Joe to Luce: "Tell him you mean jail. And it's not for you, tama."

But he couldn't place or connect that either. He kneels for some minutes on the end of the bed, trying to dredge up more past conversation that contained the word, but that's the only bit that sounds similar. So he gives up, and limps down the stairs, more mindful of his heel than when he had first slid out of bed and kept going straight on down with the shock of impact.

. . .

She made a thick oatmeal porridge that bubbled and klopped like a waking mudpool; fried half a loop of black pudding and two onions and several eggs in butter; made coffee and toast with quick and careless efficiency: then loaded the lot in assorted hot plates and bowls and mugs onto the dropleaf bench.

"Eat."

She is a slow and methodical eater, not from convictions regarding health but because she enjoys food of all kinds immensely. Save for offal: umble pie ain't for her eating. Brain, tripe, liver and guts—nuts to 'em. But o for the black blood pudding and the merry kidney stew!

The boy finishes before she does again, ducks his head and eyes her over his arms again, but this time he grins as he does it.

And maybe it is because it is a new day with the sun just coming up, but the annoying nature of his presence has faded. Despite herself, she becomes involved in a conspiracy of smiles.

> Which is bloody stupid. But then again, a smile doesn't
> cost that much, and he's not a *bad* looking goblin.

She starts washing dishes, slinging him a teatowel. "Here, payment for board," fervently hoping his minor speciality won't manifest itself. But he does dishes very well, spending long careful moments doing clusters of soap bubbles to death, and not dropping a single cup.

. . .

Kerewin sits smoking, crosslegged by the fire, watching her smokerings dissolve over the still spread form of the boy,

> who is thinking, not half so much asleep as he seems,
> It looks like someone tried to cut her throat.

What the hell have you done to your hair? Kerewin thinks. Nothing, I'll bet. Snarled, entangled, a ravelment. Slept in, obviously.

Almost telepathically, he lifts a hand, becomes absorbed in combing a knot out with his fingers.

"You want to wear it like sailors used to," says Kerewin suddenly. "In a queue, tied at the back of your neck." Tightly.

He grins in the crook of his arm.

"I'm going to have a wander round my garden. See how the weeds are doing."

The room is warm, and lightening all the time, but once out of it, the chill comes seeping into her. Downstairs, the very air feels frozen. She pushes open the door, and looks out on a whitened world.

A bird hops on the hardened grass, and the hopping is audible. She can hear the grass blades snap. It is perfectly still everywhere.

There is a raw smell, like smoke, in the air. Every inhalation catches in the throat, and stings the soft lining in her nostrils.

A soft shuffling creep, and Simon stands in the doorway beside her, cloaked in her jerkin. His left sandal is on, but unbuckled, and slops with every step.

"You'd be better back by the fire."

He sniffs.

She shrugs, and walks to the nearest piece of garden, stands, thumbs in belt, kicking the rockhard earth.

"About ten degrees," she estimates.

The ground looks less frosted by the manuka hedge. Everything appears as though it will survive. She culled out two days ago, leaving only what she thought were plants accorded to the season. Not sacrificially, either.

She catches the glint of his hair out of the corner of her eye; Simon, hopping in the frost, laying tracks in the glitter, dark dead grass steps for tomorrow.

"Be careful! Go . . ."

as he inevitably skids

"easy," she says belatedly, watching him pick himself up.

Not a sound. Not a whoop of dismay or pain. Just her breathing, and his.

Not a prepossessing sight, this silent child: hair a bunch of tangles, fingers chilled orange and blue, and his nose running with the cold. Swaying somewhat drunkenly as he attempts to put his sandal on, shivering so his teeth chatter.

She retrieves her jerkin and drapes it over his shoulders.

"Come on. I think we'd better go inside again. There's nothing much to look at this time of the year anyway."

From the jarred look on his face, she gathers the fall hurt his dignity more than anything else.

"O, and a handkerchief," amused and revolted by him at the same time.

He wipes his nose cursorily with her handkerchief and pockets it.

From the bright chill outside to the chill gloom inside, and up the dank stairway.

The boy goes up each step cautiously, bringing both feet to a standstill before he ventures to the next step.

> Bloody hell, brat, life might be a deathmarch, but do you have to make it so obvious?

The clock on the wall shows just after eight. Late morning, the operator said, so there's hours to go yet. . . .

"What'd you like to do? Play draughts or something?"

He frowns. He blows what looks like a silent raspberry.

Her turn to frown, "Ah, wait a minute, I have it. No, it's a game, not a wind . . . if you don't know it, we won't play it. I thought you might, and it's the only childish thing I have a board for. What do you know in the way of games then?"

He shakes his head forlornly.

"Hell, you must know one or two. I mean, I've come a couple of decades since childhood and I still remember dozens. You're still mired in the state, damn it."

He stares. Not rudely; apologetically.

"Well, would you like to learn chess? That's a game I like, and I think you will too."

After all, the Russians teach their babies to play. . . .

The green in his eyes seems to be ebbing out of them, leaving them dark blue holes.

He raises both hands in the air, a strange gesture of surrender, and lets them fall.

Although close to the fire, he's shivering.

What in the names of all gods and little fishes is the matter?

She shakes chess from her mind and looks down at him.

A pair of dilapidated sandals, brown, left foot holed and losing its buckle strap; jeans, denim, once green, now worn to a dun no-colour in most places. Frayed at the cuffs, and torn on the left inner leg;

elastic belt, dark green, missing buckle decoration. Ineptly put on leaving out two belt loops;

a t-shirt, originally cream or white presumably, although they might make them that off shade of grey (and the rest of you could do with a wash too, boyo);

and then there's this flannel shirt, grey and thinnish, with no cuff buttons.

That outfit can't be overly warm, even with some ounces of hair to help.

He stares her scrutiny out, bleakly.

She picks up her jerkin, laid on the table by the child when they re-entered the room, and throws it at him.

"Put that on for a while, eh? And would you like a coffee before I start to teach you chess? It was a bit cold out there, huh?"

> She saw I am cold
> She saw I am cold

He is exultant with the attention. The defensive tautness of his face eases, and his smile is soft and incredibly young.

Brilliant, touchingly grateful, and toothless, she thinks, grinning back to him, but blinking at the age the smile seems to reveal him as.

> I am in her jacket to warm,

he croons inside himself,

> She saw I am cold
> and I am in her jacket to warm.

It runs through his mind like a refrain. Warmness begins to seep back into him, easing the terrible ache, relaxing him like a drug.

"Hey!" calls Kerewin, and whistles, a piercing sound like a shepherd calling his dog.

The boy sits up suddenly, shaking his head.

"Oath, I do believe you were nearly asleep," and Simon grins sheepishly, clutching the mug of coffee to him.

. . .

She sets out the chessmen, naming them as she does, and demonstrating the move of each piece. She is patient and gentle, intent on sharing the pleasure the game gives her. Over the chessboard she is completely relaxed: the barriers of unequal intellect, and the child's dumbness, have ceased to exist. He is a person to whom she is teaching chess, and the thing that matters is that he enjoys his initiation.

He picks up the moves of bishop and rook, king and queen, in what seems to her like a surprisingly short time. But the way a pawn captures, and the eccentricity of the moving knight befuddle him.

"No, one ahead, and *one* to the side," showing the move for the fifth time. There is a scraping sound behind her. She swings round to it, and freezes.

The man standing in the doorway smiles benignly.

"Sorry to creep up on you like that, eh. I banged on your door the last five minutes till it swung open, but nobody came. So I just came up, hearing the voice."

He is a thin little man, with large brown eyes. He stands at ease, watching over her shoulder as the boy gets to his feet.

"James Piripi Tainui," he says, not looking quite at her. "Piri, they call me." He lifts his hands. "Come here you. You're for the high jump, I think."

Kerewin says slowly, not at all friendly,

"I was expecting his father. I was told the Tainuis were all over in Christchurch. And it's one helluva early."

The man smiles, a pink gummed grin, gentle and considering.

"Haimona, do some explaining eh."

The boy folds his arms and spits on the floor.

Piri Tainui groans.

"Here we go again," he says, "Look Himi, Joe's in bed and I just come home last night. There's this bloke on the phone at some horrible hour saying you're round at that queer place, excuse me, on the Paeora beach, and someone's to pick you up. Well, Joe's out cold, it's got to be me. Don't make things difficult, Himi."

Kerewin frowns, Himi? O probably transliteration for Sim but where've I heard it?

Piri turns to her, hands beseeching aid.

"Lady, I don't know who you are, but thank you for keeping him the night. Joe'll be round later to make things right, eh, but he can't come now. I thought I had better get here first thing in case there was any trouble. Sorry it's so early."

"There's been no trouble." Her frown vanishes. She stands up, holding out her hand.

"My name's Kerewin Holmes, Kerewin or Kere is what I get called. I'm glad you've come, early or not," and Piri shakes her hand murmuring Howd'y'do? and still not looking right at her.

She turns to the child.

"Well, it looks like someone else is going to have to finish teaching you that game. You left anything behind?"

The small face turns masklike. He shakes his head briefly, and shoves his hands deep into the pockets of his jeans, strolling across the floor to Piri Tainui with only the suggestion of a limp.

Faker.

But she shrugs.

"Been nice knowing you, Simon Gillayley," and belatedly offers Piri a coffee. He shakes his head, still smiling, still avoiding her eyes. He says to Simon,

"Say thank you to the lady eh," and the boy flashes her a brash smirk.

"That's all?" asks the man, and the child turns fast and angrily on him, digging two fingers veed in an obscene gesture at his face.

Piri doesn't move. "E, it's not that bad," he says, very quiet, very gentle, then picks him up.

"Well thank you," he says, stroking the boy. Simon's face is unreadable, still as stone, as though it is frozen.

"That's okay. Sorry you haven't got time for a coffee," leading the way downstairs.

Across her bridge she can see a car.

"You got here all right, no bogging down?" making polite conversation as they walk over the frozen lawn. "I keep on meaning to get that track graded, but you know how it is."

"O yeah. It was a good trip though. No trouble at all."

"Okay, well we'll see you again some time, Mr Tainui. Thanks for coming." The man grins elfinly.

"Goodbye Simon."

The boy gets woodenly into the car, making no gesture of farewell.

Berloody stuff yourself then, thinks Kerewin as the car drives off. Good riddance, you sullen little creep.

It's when she's putting the chesspieces away that she notices the boy has left his sandal behind.

And taken the black queen.

2

Feelers

I

On the floor at her feet was an engraved double-spiral, one of the kind that wound your eyes round and round into the centre where surprise you found the beginning of another spiral that led your eyes out again to the nothingness of the outside. Or the somethingness: she had never quite made her mind up as to what a nothingness was. Whatever way you defined it, it seemed to be something.

The spiral made a useful thought-focus, a mandala, anyway.

She brought her eyes back to it, and reread a letter in her mind. Written on pale pink paper, unfranked envelope and no stamp, the whole therefore delivered by hand. Envelope and paper the same genteel pink: the best matched stuff for refusing invitations and writing duty letters.

The writing was firm and flowing. Nicely sloped, easy to read, looked curiously delicate. Small letters and the pink paper maybe made for that impression. A prim hand.

Dear Ms Homes,
(a fair enough phonetic rendering of her name, presumably extracted from the urchin)

> Thank you very much for looking after my son this
> weekend.

His impromptu 'visits' seldom have such a happy result.

He enjoyed himself so much that he has indicated he'd like to return!

Heh heh. Heh.

But I would naturally obtain your opinion and permission first.

And you'll get the opinion all right.

I'm deeply obliged to you, and I would welcome any opportunity to help you in any way. I should like to convey my thanks in person. Would it be convenient for me to come and see you this evening? If not, would you please ring Whangaroa 633Z? Otherwise, I look forward to meeting you.

Joseph N. Gillayley.

No flourishes in the signature. Joseph N. Gillayley, what sort of person, he?

Joseph Nothing Gillayley.

Literate. Tidyminded. Widower, said the operator. With a kooky child. A right stubborn illnatured mess of a child.

Only,

"You're for the high jump," the little man had said. And,

"Joe is out cold," or words to that effect.

Put "tidyminded" with "drink" and you get the rigid dignity-on-a-high-horse that intensely dislikes anything or anyone getting out of the way. The dedicated drinker of this sort never gets messily drunk. Nastily, but not messily.

Focus the picture again. Not a roaring Viking. A pale cold-eyed man who expects too much of his offspring so the offspring goes defensively wild.

The long hair didn't fit, though. Nor did the scarecrow appearance. Nor the maternal sympathy, ease-up child, the little man showed. Or the boy's readiness to get near a stranger.

A small dry hand, with fine sinews, long fingers, she remembered.

He liked it here? Hah! Though the man could hardly write, "My son loathed your cooking and was contemptuous of your resent-

fully given hospitality so can I come and tell you so?" even supposing the boy could indicate that.

To ring or not to ring?

Envision the breeder from the bred, and find if the reality cor-
responded with the vision?

Hmmm.

She stared at the spiral.

It was reckoned that the old people found inspiration for the
double spirals they carved so skilfully, in uncurling fernfronds: perhaps. But it was an old symbol of rebirth, and the outward-inward
nature of things. . . .

Half an hour of your time, my sweet soul. That would be all. You
might even learn something new.

She doodled a finger in the centre of the spiral.

> You might, says the snarky inner voice, find out where
> guttersnipe Gillayley lost half his teeth. And get your
> queen back into the bargain.

"True," says Kerewin, "I might at that."

. . .

"This evening" by Gillayley time, was half past six.

She hears the crunch of gravel through one slit window. It has
been a dreary and tiring afternoon, pinching clay, punching clay,
trying to make a worthwhile shape. Nothing grows under her anx-
ious hands. She feels empty and sour.

To hell, why didn't I ring and say No? Perhaps I could hide and
they'll go away?

But she goes down a level, and washes her hands; down another
level, and stirs the fire along.

She squints out the livingroom window. Hard to see in the dark,
but she can make out two figures, one half the size of the other.
The urchin back as well . . . let's hope there's not going to be a
scene of any kind. Now why should I think there's going to be
a scene?

. . .

As she opens the door, Simon stumbles in.

He has apparently been leaning against it, knocking on the wood.

Remembering Piri Tainui's remarks, she had listened for knocking, but it hadn't been audible until she was nearly into her entrance hall.

Hoowee, remind me to install a bell, an alarm, a photoelectric eye. . . .

she steps to one side to avoid the child's entrance, but not fast enough. He is mysteriously happy to see her, taking her free hand and kissing it, grinning widely, his eyes sparking green in the lantern-light.

"Uh yeah, and how are you?" embarrassed by this wholehearted greeting, lowering her eyes.

His foot is still bandaged, still lacking a sandal. She raises her gaze, and Simon's gesture leads it on to the other person, waiting quietly on the threshold.

"Urhh," says Simon—it is a sound: his fingers snatch at the air and swing abruptly to his throat. The person reaches down and takes hold of his shoulder gently.

"I'm Joseph Gillayley. I'm glad to meet you."

A deep voice. She is looking at the hand, and wondering at the way it has suddenly linked them all.

A dark hand, broad and strong-looking, with neat blunt nails.

Her eyes travel rapidly up the arm and flick to the man's face.

"Hello . . . o," she gestures with the lantern, and Simon swallows audibly, and draws her hand to his shoulder.

"Kerewin Holmes," she says as their hands touch.

A hard warm hand, and her eyes go back to his face.

He smiles, an amiable grin.

Hell unholy! It's that joker from the pub. . . .

and the pink paper plus the stream of fucks becomes a roaring ribald laugh in her mind. She grins hurriedly back. You and your berloody doorway Vikings Holmes, and uptight dignities . . . though it's a nice grin, merry as his fosterling's, it *must* be fostered, and her smile grows, rounding her cheeks and squinching her eyes narrow.

"And I'm very glad to meet you," she says, the laughter in her mind sneaking into her voice. "Both," she adds to the boy, and he chuckles, strange little sound in the shadows.

Joseph Gillayley laughs quietly, bassing behind it.

"Well come!" says Kerewin. "Come on up. There's coffee at the top, and it'll be a helluva lot warmer."

. . .

Simon drops by the fire, spreadeagling himself.

Joseph stands in the doorway, his black eyebrows quirking.

"Well, I like it," she says defensively.

"O?" he asks. His big hands spread. "O, the room? It's magnificent . . . that window. . . ."

He stands still a moment, then shakes himself. "No, I was watching my son. Sorry," again the odd shaking. "I can't get over the way he's made himself at home."

"O. O yeah," she shrugs and pours a cup of coffee. "You drink coffee, Mr Gillayley? I know your son does."

He turns from contemplating the boy's relaxed sprawl, biting his lower lip.

"Yes, I do, thank you." He looks down at the grass matting. "Um, would you mind calling me Joe? This," pointing at his son, "refers to you as Kerewin." He glances up, checking for approval, disapproval.

"Good. It'd please me if you called me that too." She pours coffee into another mug. "I don't like getting mizzed or mistered either."

Joe smiles. His lips are full, and beautifully outlined.

"Joe," he says, pointing to himself. "Kerewin," he bows gracefully, "and Simon pake."

He straightens swiftly. "Did it surprise you, the contrast?"

His smile has deepened, not with derision or hurt or contempt, but as though it is a good joke.

"You bet!" She leans back against the bench. "You know what? I was expecting something big and blond, and for some unaccountable reason, dumb and boisterous to boot. And aside from the blond part, I couldn't reasonably justify . . . O God! I didn't mean dumb that way, I meant stupid. . . ."

Joe says quickly,

"It doesn't worry either of us. Truly."

He looks back to his child.

"Simon, get up from there, and come and give," he hesitates, "give Kerewin a hand. And can I help you too?" he asks.

"Yeah, grab your cup. Do you have sugar? Because the only stuff I've got is brown. I've got a few kinds of honey though."

"Brown sugar'll do nicely." He spoons two measures into his cup and Simon's.

"Listen you," he calls. "Come over here. At once."

The child rolls to his back and shakes his hands in the air. He gets to his feet in a hurry though.

"That bit of byplay meant Okay," says Joe, staring at the boy. He switches his gaze back to Kerewin, mellows it with a smile, "or shall we say, I'm coming or doing, so you needn't yell."

"I know this bit," and she snaps her fingers for Yes and No.

"Most of it is shortcuts." He blows on his coffee. "One time we tried proper sign language. It got him good at spelling, but it was too slow. He likes to say things as fast as possible, preferably without having to write them down. All you need to know about his hand-language is that it's mainly derivation. You know, from an object, or a way of doing things that is ordinary, or from ordinary things, or things . . . O b, bother," and the bother sounds so forced after the fluent stream of obscenity a few nights back that Kerewin laughs out loud.

"A right mess-up," says Joe, his face darker by a flush. "Was it the bother?" She nods.

"Well, I'll admit that it's not what I'd ordinarily say, but I was getting mixed up. I was lecturing, or trying to." He is looking down at the floor again. "Umm, Kerewin?"

"Yeah?"

"I'd like to talk to you a bit if you've got the time to spare. Otherwise, I'll just say thank you properly, and we'll go?"

"By all means, talk."

They went to the fire and sat down round it.

. . .

"Well, it was this chessman, the queen. Borrowed," he says with a grin, handing it back. He lets his hand drift down to settle on his son's shoulder then. "I was going to give him a hiding, because that seems to be the only way to get across the message that he's not to go roaming off to other people's houses and burgle them or whatever . . . and he produces the chessman. Sort of like a truce-flag?" Joe's hands go up, imitating Simon's gesture. Simon is still, holding his cup.

"Up till then, all I knew was that he had gone to your place and broken in, and that you'd looked after him until Piri picked him up. Piri said you seemed a nice sort of person. A lady, he said you were. Sim wasn't sure whether you were man or woman until Piri said that," the man's grinning again.

Kerewin smiles into the fire.

"So Haimona brings out this chesspiece, not to save himself the beating so much as to say something about you, you know?"

"I can imagine."

"Well, it started me thinking. He said how you started to teach him chess, and how you were patient with him when he tried to talk with you."

She remembers her sneers, and jibes, and coolness, and decides Simon/Sim/Haimona is a diplomatic little liar.

"And that you didn't exactly like him, but you were still kind and patient. That was impressive, because generally he's either treated as an idiot, or deaf as well as mute—you've no idea how many people raise their voices to him! Or they talk over him, as though he'll vanish and not be an embarrassment any more. It works too. He generally vanishes from that kind of person very fast." He broods a moment, hand back on his small son's shoulder. "So there it was. We spent an hour wondering why you were different, decent. And—how can I put it?" speaking to Simon now. "Good for you? Good for him," says Joe, looking straight at her.

Kerewin looks back, eyebrows raised.

The man eases down to lie supported by his elbows.

"I mean, it can be bad at school. He comes in for a lot of, o, a lot of petty bullying and shitslinging there. Not just because he's different being dumb, but because he's a bit of an outlaw." The child and his father swap grins. "Like this Monday, well Monday last week. He missed two schooldays before the weekend, and when he went to school on Monday, someone started having a go at him. 'Cops get you again, Gillayley,' style of thing."

Joe draws a deep breath.

"If you push him hard enough, he'll fight you to make you understand. It's his last resort, spitting and kicking . . . he'll do his damndest to punch into you what he wants to say. That's bad, I know, you know," wagging a finger at the boy, "but he's still trying to talk to you," lifting his eyes to Kerewin, "you know?"

"I can imagine," she says again.

"If you won't listen after that, or you fight him back, he'll despair, and literally throw himself on the ground. And stay there, and shake. It looks like a fit. It isn't. Say the medics. It is sheer frustration and despair that you won't listen, you won't converse, when he's got something to say that's important to him."

Kerewin nods.

"So last week, the little bastards do this push-and-tease-the-oddie business until Simon stupid obliges them by giving up and getting sick. And then you won't go to school for the rest of the week, will you?"

Simon is squinting at the gold grass floor.

"So. Today, I came here and left the note and then I took the morning off work, and went along with him to school to find out what started everything off this time. And all those sweet smiling little kids said, "Your Simon started it, Mr Gillayley, he's bad isn't he?" And they all believe it, or know it's a very safe bet, on his past record, that I'm going to believe it ... but I don't know. . . ."

Kerewin asks,

"What did the teachers say?"

"Nothing much. They didn't see it happen. Anyway, they've more or less given up on him now. Because he can be unapproachable—you've never been coldshouldered till Sim's done it to you, believe you me! Even I've been on the receiving end. . . . Some of the teachers tried to help. In his first year there, last year, one lady tried very hard, but it was too soon after. The death of my wife. And he was upset about that. So this year, they shoved him in the special class to begin with, all the slow learners and near nuts and that. Patently ridiculous, because he can read and write as competently as kids twice his age. Well, nearly. So then they put him in Standard One, and he's not fitting in there either. They recommend an institution of some kind or the other. For handicapped kids, you know the kind."

He leans over and ruffles the boy's hair.

"And they'll put you in that kind of place over my dead body," he says grimly.

"Look," he says, after a minute, "he's bright. He can understand anything you put to him, Kerewin. He doesn't need special care and attention. He just needs people to accept him."

She thinks.

There is something peculiar about all this pleading. As though I'm being set up, or primed. . . .

She says carefully,

"You mentioned he was considered to be a bit of an outlaw. My radiophone operator said, quote, he's a wellknown local oddity, specialising in sneakthievery and petty vandalism, unquote. Is it just because he doesn't get on with people at school, or is there some other reason?"

Joe flushes.

"I should imagine his muteness, and the fact that my wife died, and he doesn't get a woman's care. I should think those reasons make him a bit unsettled."

He is watching the floor again, away from her, away from his son.

"There is a wildness in him sometimes," he says. "It comes maybe from those reasons. Like the running away . . . the child psych said he was trying to find his own mother, his other parents, even if he doesn't think that knowingly. That he won't face up, can't face up, to them being gone. Not here," still looking downward, still with the dark flush suffusing his face.

There's something bloody peculiar about this whole conversation. It doesn't feel right. Has he got some strange hope I'm going to be the kid's substitute mother? Bloody oath . . . and all you can do, Simon obstinate, is stare unconcernedly into the fire.

Almost as though he caught her thought, the boy turns round and smiles broadly to her. She smiles back, wondering again what happened to his teeth.

"How old are you, Sim?"

She says to Joe, while watching for the child's answer, "I guessed anywhere between five and ten, going by size and behaviour. I still would, but after what you've said, I'd bring the upper limit down."

The boy is looking at her in a considering way, mouth down at the corners.

Joe says softly, "He doesn't know. I don't know. Nobody does." He picks up a chip of coal and flicks it into the fire.

"Well, you can see I'm not his blood father," he says into the silence. "Do you remember a Labour weekend three years or so back, when there were terrific storms? Out of season storms?"

"O, vaguely."

"Well, a gale caught a boat here then. A stranger cruiser. It sank off the end of Ennetts Reef. Everybody aboard came ashore. One way or the other."

The man has been talking quickly, almost convulsively, his eyes on the boy who is uncaring, not hearing, it seems.

"Well, meet some jetsam," he says, and his eyes glint, belying the callousness of the flippancy. The deep lines round his mouth are charmed into emphasis for his smile.

> I bethought you grim and forty, but now I doubt you're
> much older than me. Maybe not as old as me.

The lines on his face seem drawn by an inward corroding bitterness, not age. A carelessness of life, an abandonment, death of wife and death of him, she thinks, as her answering smile begins.

"I see. Wreckage washed ashore as opposed to goods found floating. Thanks for answering. I shouldn't have been inquisitive, but it intrigued me. I don't have experience of children of any age group, but his years seem to vary a hell of a lot. One minute he looks about five, and the next he acts as though he's ten times as old."

"Excuse all this," she adds to the boy, who had sat up at the last exchange of smiles, proffering his father the black queen Kerewin had left on the floor.

"That's the way it seems to me every so often too," says Joe agreeably. "Ahh yes Haimona, the chess. . . ."

The grin slides in again, above the strong spade-shaped chin.

"No," he says, "it's maybe seven, possibly eight, but probably six. Maybe even younger, but not likely. God knows. Nobody was at all sure how old you were originally," talking now to Simon P, "and you weren't much bloody help," says Joe.

Simon smiles a bland smile that somehow makes his face seem empty.

Joe turns the queen round in his fingers, examining it from all sides.

"Kerewin, politeness aside, was he good?" His voice deepens further, sounds less strained. The scarring lines that run down his cheeks and embitter his eyes and the corners of his mouth, lighten a moment. "You see, you. . . ."

She says hurriedly,

"O, he was an excellent guest. He slept most of Saturday, and Piri Tainui arrived before lunch yesterday. At breakfast practically. He was no trouble, I assure you."

"Lucky for you," says Joe to Simon. "Good for you," he amends, and shuffles the child's fringe back off his face. "Hell, I feel as awkward as a cow in a bog . . . I was going to say that you strike me as someone who'd accept a nuisance, and not make a fuss about it, Kerewin. So, for a beginning I thought, if he'd made a pest of himself, I'd fix that up before we went any further."

> Fix it up how? And where are we going? And me not
> make a fuss? Sheeeit,

but she smiles nastily, while saying,

"I had every intention of shunting him outa here within minutes of his discovery. But then there was his foot. And it started raining. So we had lunch. And *then* there was the question of who to send him to. All in all, he stayed. If he had made a nuisance of himself or pinched something, or something," now she can feel herself starting to blush, "I would just have dropped him quietly from the top of my Tower."

Joe laughs.

So does Simon, but stops his laughing short.

"Save a lot of future trouble too, eh," says the man. "Look, would it offend you if I offered payment, say for his board?"

"Yes."

"Back in the bog," he says and laughs again, humourlessly. "Well . . ." dark head downbent, long brown fingers still fiddling with the chesspiece, "that's some of the background. It happens often enough, eh, but generally me or one of my Tainui relations pick him up and bring him home before he really gets anywhere. Or the police," he says, staring at the boy again.

Simon is tracing the intricacies of the tatami mat with his forefinger, absorbed in doing so.

"O."

"You know, this is the first time he's ever ended up really staying with someone." Joe is still frowning at his son. "I was very curious to find out what was the attraction," glancing at her. Again that charming unlining smile.

"Surprise, surprise, nothing sentient. It was the Tower itself, I expect. I've had other people come and gawk at it, but never anyone inside before. Now, that's a thing," she looks at the child. "Is he good at climbing?"

Joe shrugs. "Not particularly. Why's that?"

"Because he managed to get up into a window that has only a chest below it, and the distance between the chest and the sill is rather more than he is, and it's all smooth stone wall. If you follow?"

"O?" says Joe, but enquiringly to his son, who sits up and gestures something too fast for her to follow.

> You need eyes like an archerfish, able to see what happens on two planes at once. One set for watching the hands, and the other for watching whatever it is he mouths.

Joe interprets, after looking at her puzzled face,

"He stood on the upraised lid of the chest and hoisted himself up. But the lid fell down and he wasn't game to jump to the floor."

"Of course . . . simple and obvious when you know how." She grins, more to herself than either of them. "The only way I could see him doing it was like some kind of caterpillar with suckerfeet, humping up the wall."

The man guffaws unrestrainedly, "Hear that, e tama?" and the boy smiles, politely, a mere facial twitch that lasts physically for two seconds but somehow lingers.

"Anyone like more coffee?" asks Kerewin hastily. She gets up before they answer, and brings the pot across. The trip is mainly to hide her face. There is something rather hardboiled about that brat, who can smile as he's bid and wind up looking like he's wondering how you'd taste.

As she tops up the cups, the boy stands and limps over to the shelf with the chessboard. From the corner of her eye, she watches the limp. Much reduced, indicative of a mild twinge in the heel. Bloody little fraud, she thinks, but nods to him when he turns round, questioning with his eyes for permission to take the set down.

"You were being taught to play . . . here, show us what you can do, eh." Joe slides forward to lie at the boy's side, picking up chess-men and placing them in the formal doubledrawn ranks.

It's the evident familiarity, she tells herself, fingered communion with knight and king and queen. She has a sudden longing to talk with someone and play live chess, rather than the mummified games set and dried in books.

Simon, after watching what Joe is doing, sets up his end of the board. He kneels up, shifting a shoulder hesitantly, and points to her.

"Ah sheesh," says Kerewin. "I caught three flounders a day or so back, and I've been keeping them fresh in a water-safe. I'm going to stuff 'em with celery and crushed pineapple. I'll serve them with a salad and baked potatoes." She stands, and the little errant verte-brae in her neck and back snick into place. She is looking at the floor now. Or rather, at her boots.

> Kaibabs of cut gold suede, creased and scuffed to barefeet
> fineness by long wearing. How well shoon you are. . . .

"Actually, this is an invitation to tea if you haven't already had it, and I can thereby bribe you to have some games of chess with me. It won't take long . . . unless of course you have something else to do, in which case I apologise for being importunate."

The red tide pours into her face and she shrieks at herself, inside herself, You never meant to say that! You meant to get them out of the way. . . .

The child is begging Can we stay? with his hands.

> Careful. I might end up by liking you, brat, if I'm not
> careful.

Joe stands, and places his hands over the child's hands.

"It doesn't need you to plead it, boy . . . what can I say, Kerewin? I'd stay here all night and play chess with you if that's what you want, and it doesn't need an offer of tea, either. Because you looked after Himi, and I'd like to do that."

> Heap coals of fire upon my head.

"We didn't have tea," he says. "We came straight here after I got home from work. I didn't even have a shower, or get this one dressed up . . . which reminds me," shaking Simon gently, "I thought

I told you to have a bath, and get Piri or Marama to see to your foot?"

Simon raises his eyebrows, Did you?

"Arggh," and shakes him harder. To Kerewin, "That's settled then. Can I give you a hand with the spuds or anything?"

For seconds she has stood in a state of self-blankness, observant of what's happening but out of contact with her body: then the hands shift off the child's shoulders, and in a flood of sensation she is aware of the rustle of the man's felted wool coat, the breadth of his shoulders contrasted with the child's bone-thinness; the black-ness of his long straight hair; the half-wonderment, half-weariness of his face.

And the fact that he is exactly as tall as herself. Deep brown eyes on the same level as her stonegreyblue gaze.

"O yes," she says. "Not so much give me a hand, but if you want to go and have that shower, or wash Simon, you might as well do that now eh? There's plenty of hot water."

"That would be all right? It'd be no trouble?"

"Tchaa! What trouble? Your son can show you where the shower is. The first door inside the bathroom is a linen cupboard. Help yourself to towels and whatnot. There's first aid gear down here. Somewhere," she says, gesturing vaguely around.

Urchin Gillayley, catching her eye, points to knife-drawer and grog cupboard.

"Okay, so your memory's good," she mockbows to him.

His father laughs. "Only when it suits him . . . my thanks. I'll have that shower, and wash him too, then come down and give you a hand with tea. Then we'll play a chess marathon, and you can have the pleasure of wiping me out piecemeal and tidy every game."

He grins. "I'm not a very good player."

Kerewin grins back. "I am," she says.

. . .

We came on the bike, he'd said. Him in front, because then I can be sure he's not going to fall off. He's good at falling off things. . . .

The bike was parked on the other side of her bridge. He had a what he called 'Morning after emergency kit' there. . . . "You know how it can get, you wake up feeling like yech, so I carry the basics with me. Washing gear and a spare shirt, and gear for Himi in case it's needed."

He went into the night to get it, carrying his son.

She was taking the skeletons out of the flounders, wielding knife and scissors with practised skill, when the man arrived back in the kitchen level, child leaning against one shoulder, a dufflebag over the other.

"Nice walk," he says gaily. "It's still drizzling though."

"Yeah, I can see it on the window there eh."

They look on with interest.

"You a cook or something?"

"Or something."

She is filling the flounders with neat little mounds of pale green celery and yellowish pineapple. "Really I'm just a brilliant amateur. In everything," she adds sourly.

"It looks very nice. Though I never seen that done to a flounder before," watching her sprinkle parsley on top of the fish.

"O, it's past caring what happens to it now."

She slides the flounders into an oven dish and the butter sizzles round them.

"Twenty minutes or so, and they'll be done."

"A hint, tama. Come and show us where this shower is. I never had a Tower shower before," giggling as they go out.

> Overpowered, he cowered, glowering amidst the flowers,

and she sits by the fire spinning-ower compositions for the sheer hell of it.

That's an odd child. And an odd man.

> The coal sinks down in its red bed, and the little violet flames run flickering over it.

She wanders across the room and lifts her golden guitar down from the wall. It is easy, leaning over the ambered belly, to put thought through a filter of slow-picked arpeggios.

An odd child, with its silence, and canny receptiveness.

> Orange-red sparks climbing in skewed lines to die out in the glimmer dark pile of the soot.

An odd man, looking so bitter until he smiles.
A harmonic bells out under her fingers.

> Why the wariness and drawn-eyed look of the child?
> Why the bitterness corrupting the man's face?
> And why, above all, the peculiar frisson of wrongness
> I keep getting from some of the conversation?
> O it's riddles, and no thing of mine,

and she quickens her chording to a heavy downbeat strumming.

. . .

In the bathroom, Joe can hear the guitar, the rhythm of it rather than the chords: the walls are too thick for more.

"She can play . . . dry yourself," to the boy, as he begins putting on his own clothes.

His body is squat and heavily muscled, except for his legs, thin-calved and spindly.

A long pale scar runs over the brown skin, from his right shoulder blade down in a curve across his ribs.

"You've been lucky as hell this time," watching the boy dress, grimacing at the child's thin body. "Behave yourself, Haimona. Don't let's spoil it, eh."

He says meditatively, "It would be nice to have a friend again, somebody we could talk with who wasn't a relation."

The boy raises his eyebrows.

"Out, and be careful of your heel."

When the boy has gone, he looks round the bathroom. He gathers the used towels—she's dead keen on this dark green colour, everything's it—and as he picks them up, something falls ringing to the floor.

A broad gold circle with an inset stud of greenstone.

"O shit, o sweet Christ."

Simon had stood there, dressed himself there, and *that* had fallen from Simon's pocket.

"O you bloody little sod."

He thinks a minute, rubbing the back of his neck, We done already? Because bloody Himi can't keep his hands off anyone else's gear? and then he leaves the ring on the sill, next to the basin.

. . .

The boy slid in through the doorway, and went over to the fire.

Kerewin, armed with knife and spatula, was manoeuvring whole flounders on to plates. Joe came in, holding out the towels.

"Chuck 'em on the floor there, I'll see to them later," and she gets the last fish out without breaking off so much as a sidefin bone.

"That smells like good food. We timed it nicely, eh?"

"Perfectly."

"Would you mind if I put something on his foot first? I've got something to say to him too, but it'll only take a minute."

"Fine, go ahead," and handed him the first aid box.

He went to the boy and spoke in a low voice, so low it was almost covered by the rattle of the crockery and cutlery she was laying out.

But it was still loud enough to hear:

"E noho ki raro. Hupeke tou waewae," and the boy sat quickly, looking at his father wide-eyed. "E whakama ana au ki a koe."

Kerewin was wide-eyed too by now, shuffling the plates discreetly louder.

> Really? You're ashamed of him? And more pertinent, why? And I don't think I'll disclose meantime that I can speak Maori.

"Kei whea te rini?"

She stole a surreptitious glance.

The boy flushed violently, reached for his back pocket, and then the colour drained out of his face.

Joe bandaged his foot, and didn't say anything more until he finished and the child stood. Then he hit him hard across the calf of his leg. The sound cracked around the room and Kerewin looked up sharply.

"Kaua e tahae ano," as the boy staggers straight, and then Joe turned to her saying,

"That was just. . . ."

She says evenly,

"The ring was borrowed more likely. I have so many I wouldn't miss one or two. Still, thanks for caring. This dinner's getting cold while the beer gets warm."

He stands open-mouthed.

Well, you've certainly got all *your* teeth.

"E korero Maori ana koe?"

"He iti iti noa iho taku mohio," she answers blandly.

"I don't know whether to be delighted or horrified," his heavy shoulders fall. "I don't know whether he was going to bring it back or not, but it fell out of his pocket when he was getting dressed, I think. I'm very sorry, but I left it upstairs and I hoped you would. . . ."

"Don't be. Hell, you want to see what I used to pinch as a child. It's not stealing properly. It's just something takes your passing fancy, so you take *it* to amuse yourself with for a while."

"He will learn not to steal," says Joe, his mouth tightening.

"Yes." She turns round, hearing the slipping step come up behind her, and looks into eyes that are now intensely green. "Help your-self to fish or fandangles here, I don't give a damn. But tell your father first. Saves trouble, eh?"

It wasn't the stealing that bothered him, or the blow she'd bet. It was being found out.

But the grin he was offering was pure bedevilling merriment.

"So okay," Kerewin shrugs, "and how about tea?"

. . .

Simon poured the beer: the head took half the glass.

"Spoiler," said Joe.

It settles down, a hundred thousand bubbles snapping out, cream diminishing to clear brown liquid.

"I'll pour my own, thanks" she said, and did, ignoring the child's pained expression.

She settled comfortably back, hand curled round her glass, and watched the chequered board.

Joe was the sort of player he said he was, not very good.

"A while since you played?"

He smiled ruefully. "I used to play at college. Then I played my wife a few games, after I quit there. I haven't played since she, for a while."

The hesitancy, the catch in his phrasing. He doesn't like mentioning her death.

She considered her next move for two seconds before making it.

"O hell." Joe screwed his eyes shut. "I should have seen that two moves back." He opened his eyes and sighed. "Sim, get my smokes from your bag, eh." He looked at Kerewin,

"I resign?"

"Well, you can play it out if you really want to, but you're doomed." She sounds smug, she knows. But she likes winning.

The child brings back a packet of cigarettes. He takes out two, and lights them.

She says hastily,

"I don't smoke those cigarettes, thanks all the same," and Joe replies,

"The other one is probably for him. If he had proper manners," reaching up and catching Simon round the waist, and sitting him down on his lap abruptly, "which he hasn't, and can't seem to learn, he would have handed you the packet first."

The boy's already got one cigarette in his mouth, giving the other one to Joe.

"Ka pai, e tama . . . but see you remember others first next time." Simon gestures to Kerewin in a quick pointed traverse that sweeps to her face round to her side pocket and back to himself. Then he lies back in the strong circle of his father's arms, and blows a smoke-plume at her with calm expertise.

"Even so, you still offer . . . he says you smoke something you keep in your pocket, but if you want a smoke you can have his?"

"Ah, no thanks . . ." she took out the silver container lined with cedar wood that held her cigarillos. "He's right, I normally smoke these. A pipe or cigars on occasion, but rarely cigarettes." She lit a cigarillo. "Ahhh," hunting for words that didn't sound too critical or meddlesome, when Joe says,

"Him smoking eh? Well, he's allowed to when I'm around. He doesn't inhale much, just plays at it. Makes him feel grownup or something," and he leans over and kisses Simon's upturned face. "No harm done anyway."

"None of my business, I know, but it's a little unusual to find the matter treated rationally. Most parents I've had the misfortune to meet don't think about it at all. They instantly assume if their young kid smokes, it's wrong. Doesn't matter if they smoke themselves—watch out, kid! A good example of how parents in our society tend easily to tyranny—I shall make or mould my child as I see fit, without too much reference to the developing personality or needs of the child." She grins suddenly. "And here's me talking who classes children as something more remote from humanity than your average snail!"

Joe smiles. "You're a dispassionate observer, or at least uninvolved . . . it's awkward to treat this one as my personal property. He's apt to remind me he's a developing personality about two dozen times of an evening. In a particularly stressful way, at that."

"Heigh ho for children's lib," as she puts down her beer, and begins to set up the chessboard again.

. . .

Smoke clouds grow and dwindle. The game continues, a leisurely vying of mental strength. And a reaching out from either side, a growing pleasure as the knowledge comes. This is someone I shall be able to call friend.

. . .

Simon comes over, and looks, and cuts his throat crossways airily.

"Go get lost," says Joe, "I can see I'm not winning without your cheerful interpretation." Kerewin coughs.

"Simon? There's another bottle of beer in the cooler. Would you open it for us, please?"

And,

"You can pour my glass if you want, yes."

"Don't get sarcastic, that's all," says Joe.

Barely a head on it, professionally poured.

"See?" says Joe, spreading his hand, "told you, eh? Smart arse," he mutters to himself. Pushes his king over.

. . .

And the third game.

"Moonmaker, sunraker, o wild song for my ruby guitar," sang Kerewin, very quietly, "ah hah," sneaking up on a bishop.

And Simon, ceased from wandering round the room, lay peacefully stealing fallen chessmen from Joe's side of the board and adding them to Kerewin's hoard.

It was a much longer game.

He can feel mind muscles long-unused, stretching and beginning to feel their way to action again. He played with concentration and was aware that the woman was directing only half her attention to the game, and that the half was enough.

"You are too good," he burst out, "too good. I feel as though every move I make is manoeuvred, that I'm doing exactly what you want me to do."

"On the contrary," she said mildly. "I play opportunist chess, and it's largely dependent on what you do. Or don't," grinning wolfishly.

He looked at her. Looked at his doomed bishop and castle-bound king. Looked at small Simon smiling his gap-toothed happy-idiot smile up at his marvellous newfound friend.

(SHE GOT RINGS. SHE PLAY THE GUITAR FOR ME.
"She liked you?"
NO.)

"Aue," said Joe, but wasn't miserable at all. In this strange round room, warm and full of a golden feeling of companionship, Himi good and sweet beside me, how could I be? "E hoa, I think you just won again."

. . .

Dark man lying full length by the fire, pale child huddled at his side.

The firelight dances, ruddying them and the chessboard, all men now neatly packed away. Wars of small kingdoms in forgotten lands, what do chessmen dream of in the dark? She was brewing cocoa, a final drink before the Gillayleys left.

For herself and Joe at least: the boy had drifted off to sleep towards the end of the last game, and his father was reluctant to wake him.

"He doesn't sleep well," he said. "If he falls asleep, I leave him sleeping. Else I have to feed him dope, so he'll go down at night."

Evocative phrase, 'go down at night'—down to Sheol or some other gibbering dark, or ride the restless tumbril of dreams. . . .

"Dope?" she had asked.

"O, some stuff from the medic. Red and syrupy. Doesn't taste too bad."

Stirring sugar and cocoa and a little warm water together, until the whole achieved the consistency and fragrance of melted chocolate:

"Joe, why doesn't he sleep well?"

The man's smile is crooked.

"Bad dreams. He doesn't like going to sleep because he'll dream bad dreams." He twisted round and looked in open wonderment at the still child. "Spooked, would you believe?"

"Spooked, I'd believe."

He wasn't quite joking, nor was he truly serious. There was a strained gaiety in his voice.

"Scared of ghosts and things in dreams . . . if I was proper Maori I'd. . . ."

Into the following silence,

"You'd what?"

"Hah, I don't know." He laughed quietly. "Maybe take him to people who'd know what to do, to keep off ghosts in dreams." Laughing again, a dry unfunny sound like a cough, "See? Bloody superstitious Nga Bush? Get the Maori a bad name, eh?"

Kerewin, carefully looking into the cup,

"When I worked at Motueka in the tobacco a few years ago, I knew two girls who were really spooked. One was Pakeha, the other, city Maori. They heard things breathing on them at night, and there was no-one there. Damp patches appeared on the ceiling and the floor of their bach, and no-one spilt anything. And books and jugs would fall over when there was no wind, and no-one to touch them, eh. And then the footsteps started, and they couldn't sleep any more . . . the whole thing was quite stupid, but it had gathered a menacing quality from somewhere. Or something."

Joe was staring, unmoving.

"So the Maori wrote to her mother, who went into a trance, and found out an aunt of the girl didn't like her going round with another woman. She had spooked them. Makutu, nei? The mother said to go to a Catholic priest and get some holy water, and bless themselves and the bach. She was one of the people who know what to do."

"It worked?" There was tension tight in his voice.

"It worked. No more odd things happening. No more scared girls." She brought over the mugs of coffee. "Probably one pissed-off aunt though," she said, sitting down.

Joe grinned.

"Ah hell, I should've kept inside the faith. Might have helped me after all." He said it lightly. Then, slowly, "You speak Maori, and know a bit about, about things. Are you Maori by any chance?"

Kerewin, blue-eyed, brown-haired, and mushroom pale, looked back at him. "If I was in America, I'd be an octoroon." Paused. "It's very strange, but whereas by blood, flesh and inheritance, I am but an eighth Maori, by heart, spirit, and inclination, I feel all Maori. Or," she looked down into the drink, "I used to. Now it feels like the best part of me has got lost in the way I live."

Joe was very still; so softly, that it was almost on a level with his breathing,

"That's the way I feel most of the time." More loudly, "My father's father was English so I'm not yer 100% pure. But I'm Maori. And that's the way I feel too, the way you said, that the Maoritanga has got lost in the way I live."

He shook his head and sighed.

"God, that's funny. I never said that to anyone before, not to Piri or Marama or Wherahiko, or Ben. Not even to my wife."

"She was Maori too?"

"Tuhoe."

"Yeah."

He drank the rest of his cocoa at one swallow.

"Ho well." He slides his hands under Simon and gently lifts him, and stands in a graceful exact movement straight to his feet. The child doesn't stir.

"Kerewin. . . ."

"Yes?"

"I don't know how to say thank you except this way." He says very formally, "Ka whakapai au ki a koe mo tau atawhai."

Kerewin smiles. "Ka pai, e hoa."

Joe gives her a brilliant smile back. "We see you again?"

She considers, for all of a second,

"I'll give you a ring, eh?"

"Yes. Well," moving to the doorway, "anything you want or

need, and think I can help, just give me a yell. You got friends," he smiles to her again, "one crazy kid and a mixed-up Maori. Should take you far. . . ."

"How about this non-painting painter who's not sure whether she's coming or going? You'll get a long way with me, too. . . ." She's aware that this is the first time she's said "Pax, friends," to anyone for a decade.

"Do you need a hand to carry that bag?"

He shakes his head. "Would you give us the parka out of it though? I'll bet it's still drizzling outside."

"It is."

Holding the sleeping boy with one arm, Joe adjusts the parka over his own head with the other, so the jacket forms a tent-like covering, sheltering the child as well as himself.

"You'll be OK on the bike?"

"We're used to it. I'll just park him in front and he'll probably go back to sleep before we're out of your road."

Kerewin chuckles.

"I'll believe it, unlikely and all as it sounds."

. . .

Rich night. A promise of times to come . . . maybe.

She sat a long time by the fire after the echo of the bike's engine had died.

No sound now but winds and trees and the omnipresent sea.

. . .

II

Going! Going! The clock's just gone eleven.

She stretched and groaned and yawned herself awake.

"Gorecrows, gorecrows," moaning it for no good reason except it fitted the sound she wanted to make and her bloody turn of mind.

It was raining. Heavy grey clouds rimmed the horizon of the livingroom circle. A small patch of blue sky scarred with white said the day was trying to come fine.

There was a template of a drawing in her mind, spidery and shadowed, a remnant of dreams. She doodled with a fine-tip on a block of heavily textured paper, making tangles of lines, but the spidershadow was still obscure. She felt it to be worth digging out.

"You *are there!*" digging the tip hard into the paper, grooving it and spoiling the woven abstract patterns. "Ah to hell, come *out.*"

Ripping the page off the block and hurling it against the wall didn't achieve anything. Hitting her closed fist on the table didn't do much either. She jammed her hands into jean pockets, breathing hard.

"Get your fishing gear, Holmes."

Funny how words echoed now, where before they sounded right, her voice for her ears.

"Calm down, o soul. Be reasonable, a serene and rational being."

Her heart belies the words, therdunk, therdunk, beating harder and harder.

I am exceedingly angry for no good reason.

"Ah shit and apricots, why'd it have to be this way?" calling loudly, anguish in her voice. "I have everything I need, but I have lost the main part."

"Damn. Damned. Damned." Thumping the handrail so it quivers, all the way downstairs. At the bottom, the flukes are shaking.

She soothes them with a finger, and then leans her head upon them.

"If the weather stays fine, I'll take a trip out past the heads. Set a pot or two, and then be with dolphins for hours. I'll use the ber-loody boat for a change instead of having it barnacle up at the mooring."

She pulls the door open: the blue piece of sky is shrinking. The lowering bulbous rim has edged forward.

"Ahh, bugger it all," but she has lost her anger. She's filled with a soft woolly despair. "It'd figure," resigned, "go upstairs and sit in your big chair and twirl merrily round. Contemplate your easels. Pretend you're an artist again. Pah!" spitting.

The spit landed on a dandelion.

It was an even bet it would have. For, regardless of winter frosts, dandelions grow here all year round. They know where they're welcome. She cultivates them, doping the ground with things dandelions like, and helpfully spreading seed by blowing the clocks.

> Wine. Ersatz coffee. Salad greens. A diuretic, if I need such a thing. Pickles from the roots. Dry the leaves for a green stock for soup. And tea can be made from the leaves as well . . . not to mention the superb aureoles glowing, a feast for the most miserly eyes. What more could you ask from a simple plant?

She apologises to the spat flower, and turns to go inside.

When round the edge of the wall, something. Steps light and limping on the grass.

"God in hell, it can't be."

God in hell, it is.

There stands the guttersnipe on top of her flowers, a grin wide and welcoming on his face.

"Haunted," she says to him, without a hello. "Trailed by ghosts."

The grin becomes a ghost of itself.

"What on earth are you doing here? It's Tuesday and a schoolday."

It's exorcised entirely.

He holds a note out to her, and stands frowning, rubbing a groove in the damp grass with the toe of his sandal.

"O boy, here was I wondering what to do now I can't go and play with my especial snouted friends, and guess what turns up?"

She stuffs the note into a back pocket, and holds out her hand.

"C'mon urchin, you're just in time for lunch," and laughs at the double meaning.

He takes the hand but doesn't move, looking up at this lady of the fire, outlined by the retreating sun and full of a strange gaiety that seems close to despair. He holds her hand more tightly, sweeps his eyes from her wild flurry of hair down to her bare feet, what is wrong? Where is it wrong? Can I help? up to the odd pendant that hangs, like his label, in the middle of her chest. Only her pendant is made of a blue stone, carved like a complex opened knot.

"That," she says, after tracing his gaze, "is a sort of Sufic symbol. Worked quite cunningly in turquoise. The circle is silver."

She takes her hand away to hold it closer for him to see, poised between her forefingers.

She doesn't like holding hands.

He is amused.

"Okay," mistaking the small shark grin, "so I gloat too much on things I like. Inside, Gillayley, before I change my mind and send you away.

"Not really," she says, inside the hall. "I suppose it's a compliment that you want to stay, eh. But only God knows why," and she sighs.

She stands at the bottom of the spiral and chants,

"There is both amber and lodestone.

Whether thou art iron or straw,

thou wilt come to the hook."

She stops, frowning at the silent crucifix.

"Why should that come to mind?" Over her shoulder to the silent child, "From the Masnawi by a poet called Rumi."

Jalal-uddin the Sufi.

Ah hah, back to the Sufic knot. Not to mention fishing. Quid est.

In the living room, he looks round and sighs. Then he turns to her and hunches his shoulders. He stands there, staring.

The silence, o my soul, is getting awkward again.

She hums to herself, while stoking up the range.

He whistles and she looks round. He sits down, and takes off the dufflebag he carries.

Takes out two parcels, one large and wrapped in very greasy brown paper, the other small and neatly folded in a black silk wrapping. He beckons.

"Gillayleys bearing gifts?"

She crosses to him and sits down too.

Four mutton birds, plump and pale. "E hoa, I've sent lunch. . . ."

"Succulent. Do you like 'em, boy?"

He nods, and pushes the silkwrapped bundle to her.

"Joy, another whatisit."

It is more difficult to open this one. The wrapper is a scarf, and the ends have been knotted together again and again.

"This is to keep something in? Or me out?"

There's no answer.

> We're not in a very communicative mood today, are
> we? Sullen urchin.

She resorts to using her teeth on the knots.

"Ah, got it."

A small battered case of black morocco. She sniffs the leather. Under the smell of the hide is a subtle musk, which grows stronger as she holds the case in her warm hand. "Fascination. Now, how do we get in?"

There is no obvious fastening.

The boy takes it, and presses the two front corners. The top lifts slowly as he hands it back.

"Thank you,"

> and all expectant we lift the lid to find,

and what she sees is entirely unexpected.

It is a rosary of semi-precious stones. A Christian rosary presumably, because the beads tell decades, lots of them, each decade separated from the next by large beads carved from turquoise. The decades are alternatively of coral, the red Italian kind, and amber, and each begins and ends with a bloodstone.

There is no crucifix. The beads trail off from a small gold plaque, and the chain that joins them ends in a solitary link. There is a ring on the rosary. The chain of beads has been broken and rejoined through it.

She looks at it closely. A signet ring made of very soft gold. 22 carat. There is a curious coat of arms engraved on the ring. A long-necked bird like a heron, with wings outstretched, is nesting in flames.

"A phoenix, bejabbers."

The bird was engraved over a saltire. There is fine lettering round it, but incredibly, it looks as though someone has filed that down so it can't be read.

"This is magnificent," holding it up. "Is it yours?"

He shakes his head, pointing at her.

"Mine? Do you mean as a gift? Like hell!"

The boy takes out his pencil and pad.

YOURS

"My dear child, you do mean it as a gift for me?" He nods. "But you—or Joe—can't give me something like this. It's beautiful, but also valuable."

She loops the decades round her hand: the beads are cool and smooth. "Superb," she whispers to herself. "Flame and water, earth and air . . . amber and coral, turquoise and bloodstone."

She hands it, almost reluctantly, back to Simon.

"It's like, o like something you are offered but which really belongs to a family. Do you know about Te Rangi Hiroa and the cloaks? No? I'll tell you sometime, but for the meantime, I have touched your gift, appreciated its richness and your intention, and that is enough for me."

The rosary hangs in her outstretched hand, swaying.

IT IS MINE I GIVED IT TO YOU.

"Gave," she says, her head bent. "You can't, boy. I know it's yours to give, all right," but she's remembering the ring last night, and wondering where this might have come from, "but it is too rich a thing to give to a chancemet friend. I thank you for your thought, truly, but it remains your rosary."

Rosary. He mouths the word, closing his lips on it as though tasting the sound.

"Rosary . . . you didn't know the name of it? Do you know what it is?"

His face is troubled.

IT'S MINE, thumb jabbed back at himself several times.

"Yeah," she says gently, "it's yours. It's also something you use when you pray. Joe hasn't told you?"

No.

She draws the loops through her fingers, counting off the de-cades. "Unusual. There's the full fifteen here. Most rosaries today are really chaplets, and have enough decades for only one set of mysteries." Ah, look at him Holmes, you're spouting garbage and gobbledygook as far as he can make out. . . . "Generally, only those used by religious have fifteen decades. I've got one myself, a pleas-ant ebony and steel-linked one, complete with brass medallion and silver Corpus, obtained long ago from a Cistercian."

This one, gold and gems, seems too worldly for a religious to handle. Her fingers arrive at the plaque again. Squinting, she can make out a monogram, much worn as though someone has fingered it for years. The letters flow into one another, but look like gothic M.C. de V.

She can't think of a Latin tag that fits the letters. Mater Compassionem de Virgo? Not only bastard Latin, but it doesn't sound orthodox.

She turns the plaque over. There's a surprisingly clear intaglio of the icon, Our Lady of Perpetual Succour.

"Well, well."

She adds after a minute, "The beads keep track of the prayers you say, tell you what kind of prayer to say next. You ever want to know them, I can teach you."

He makes no move to take the rosary.

She hands it to him again, so close that he can't avoid taking it. He frowns, and writes on his pad. Then he kneels up and puts the rosary over her head, passes her his note, face tight, mouth tight, all of him condensed and taut as though ready to spring or explode.

IT IS YOURS I GIVE IT TO YOU

> Ah hell, what do we do now? Give it back and precipitate a scene?

because there is a rising flush on the Gillayley face and his tension is becoming almost unbearable.

Instead, she makes the circle of beads into three loops, and settles them round her neck.

"Okay, I thank you very much for your gift."

> I can always sneak it back to Joe.

Oddly, the rosary feels comfortable and familiar, clinking against the Sufic maze. And more oddly, the small boy is delighted with himself for succeeding in giving it away. Relaxed as water now, positively hugging himself for joy of it all.

Nutty child.

"Umm, d'you mind telling me what this is for?"

He shuts his eyes and shakes his head.

"You don't mind me asking? Or you're not telling?"

The pad and pencil are slipped deliberately back into his pocket.

Which reminds me. No more initialling each note. I musta
got into the familiar category, or some damn thing.

"Then what's it for?"

The boy goes on shaking his head, so his hair falls screening his
face.

The way it flows out with each turn of his head reminds her of
the skirts of dancing dervishes as they spin to ecstasy.

Exceedingly nutty child.

"Hei. Well, we'll leave the matter there then." Gets to her feet,
and puts the muttonbirds into the range oven, in an unlidded
baking-dish.

"Come on," she says to the entranced child, "downstairs and
help us collect some puha to go with them."

. . .

The muttonbirds turned golden in their own rich fat: the puha
steamed quickly in water. Kerewin cut slices of brown wheaten
bread and left them unbuttered. Then they feasted. Muttonbirds
have a lot of bones, some dark, some pale as bones should be. They
licked each one clean of flesh and fat, and wiped their fingers and
faces on bread before eating it. Picked up puha in their fingers: its
slightly bitter taste was astringently refreshing. A mouthful of bird,
and one of bread, and a fingerful of puha, and then back to the
bones.

He had muttonbird fat on his face, in his hair, all over his hands.
And breadcrumbs . . . gone was the neat precise eating of the weekend. This was hog in and enjoy.

And I probably look as bad, feel as good.

At last she said, leaning back against her chair,

"Do you know what was in that note from Joe?"

Simon sighed happily.

He wiped his mouth on his hands, and his hands on his jeans.
Grinned at her while he did.

Then took out his notebook and wrote, JOE PICKS ME UP
TONIGHT.

"You know." He has left delicate fingerprints of grease on the paper. "Well, I'm sort of pleased that you like being here, but what precisely do you think you're going to do?"

The little boy shrugged.

"Because I'm going upstairs to do some drawing in a minute."

Simon licked his fingers, then held up the pencil and pointed to himself.

Nice economical way to say, I'll draw too, assuming that's what he means.

She stood, looking at him.

The fey swirling mood had ended.

But, a tendency to steal and damage . . . not all there, said the radiophone voice.

Joe had written:

Many thanks for the best night I've had in years. I'll buy a book on chess today and see if I can't beat you some day at your own game. There's a bloke plays at work— I'll ask him for a few tips.

Muttonbirds for lunch, and

You know, you got a fan. He thinks you're marvellous (so do I). Want a kid? Going cheap . . . if he's any trouble, pack him home. That'll be a better inducement to good behaviour than any hiding I threaten. Bit of cheek, eh, this letting him go back to you without so much as a word of permit from you. (But it's just before 7, and I don't think you'll welcome a call this early.) Let us know if you're doing something and don't want him round—Piri'll pick him up. Otherwise I will, tonight. Na tou hoa, Joe G. XXX

Very different note from the formal thankyou of yesterday.

But where's the brat been since 7 this morning? And what's all this about? It doesn't feel right. Yet nobody's stomped on my heart except family, so why am I so mistrustful of people?

A meal, and a chessgame or two, and he signs the letter with kisses like a lifetime friend. And this one, grinning like a gargoyle from his chair where he's kneeling, brings a ring for a ring untaken, and the making of a garden of prayers. I don't understand it. . . .

She wasn't smiling back at the child.

> Was it being a listening ear for the man?
> Someone to tell troubles to? Suspicions? . . .
> And what is the attraction for a disturbed and zany child here?
> Me? Nah, he knows I don't much like him.

"What about school though?" undecided what to do.

He frowns briefly. Picks the notebook off the table, and weighs it in his hand, then takes a slip of paper from an unsealed envelope in the back of it.

It is another note from Joe, this time excusing his son's absence from school on the grounds of sickness for the week to come.

Simon is writing while she reads it.

I AM SICK SOMETIMES

"Conveniently, like now?" She returns his excuse. "How often do you actually turn up at school? Monthly? Or just a couple of times a year?"

He's writing again. JOE SAYS I GO, I GO

"I'll bet." She thinks, Hell, imagine if they both think I'm going to put up with him all the times he misses. No way.

He is looking at her narrowly.

I KNOW WHAT THEY DO. He stops, searching for a word, his teeth clenching in exasperation.

She sits down at the table again.

"You know what who does?"

He grinds his teeth.

"Is it about school, and your absence therefrom?"

No.

Then he nods.

Shakes his head.

He is actually shaking all over with the effort of trying to find a way to show what he wants to say.

"Is it a word you need? Or a whole sentence?"

He hits the table with the pencil and it breaks. Point smashed.

He puts his face in his hands.

She picks up the pencil, takes out her knife and sharpens it care-fully, whittling away little resinous curls of wood. There is a faint fresh smell of cedar: it must have been an old pencil. As she makes a new point on the lead, she says slowly,

"If you like, we could start again at the beginning of this conver-sation, and feel our way to the words you want."

He puts his hands down on the table and avoids her eyes. He's been snivelling but quietly.

"So. Here we are at the beginning. How often do you go to school?"

MOST DAYS

He looks at that, shakes his head, and with one hand guarding his eyes, amends,

SOME DAYS

"And that's of each week?" Yes, he nods. "For some days of each week, the days Joe says you're to go to school, you go to school. Right?"

He is grinning again. Weirdly, through the tears and the bread-crumbs and the muttonbird grease. MOST TIMES, writes Simon recalcitrant.

"Occasions Joe don't know about, you play hooky? Stay away from school?"

"Goodoh," to his nod, privately thinking Ratbag.

The child hugs himself, and his face goes tight again. He points to her face.

"I show an expression of disapproval or something?"

He looks puzzled momentarily, and then shakes his hand, No. He screws up his mouth at the notebook and pencil, and writes reluctantly,

I WONT STAY HERE ALL THE TIME. I KNOW WHAT THEY DO.

"I'm beat. If you mean you're not staying here all the times you're absent from school, you're dead right. I'll be doing other things often, and won't want you underfoot. But as to this other—you know what who does? To whom?"

Simon looks at the table.

"Hey listen, some things are easier if you're not concentrating on them. Come and do some drawing with me, and forget the lost words for the moment eh? If it's important, you'll find a way to tell me, and I'll find a way to understand."

He slides off the chair and comes round the board table. He stares at her for long moments, his face unreadable. No expression in the intent stare. Then he holds his hand out, reaching for hers.

She gets up quickly, forestalling the contact.

"You'd better have a wash, eh. I mean, I'm going to. Before drawing. Grease and chalk and charcoal don't go well together."

Babbling again, Holmes. He's not contagious.

> But hands are sacred things. Touch is personal, fingers
> of love, feelers of blind eyes, tongues of those who can-
> not talk . . . oops.

Simon still has his hand out, and his smile there, turned smirk, as though he knows perfectly well her reluctance to touch any-body's hands and is amused by it.

"What's this for now?" but gives her hand.

Thanks, mouths Simon, kissing her hand, the grin widening after.

> O those bloody nonexistent teeth . . . draw out where
> they went, anything, but the staying barbs of this gentle
> courtesy.

Kerewin appalled.

. . .

She works with charcoal, every shade of black bearing across the white paper.

Trying again to catch the spider shadow of the morning's dream-ing, but netting at random this time.

Smudge. Then a razorfine line, so keenly black it aches. Illusion of looking into a knife-thin ominous chasm.

She makes several more of them, slewed at intervals, and in the midst of them, quite suddenly, near the oily-looking smudge, she has captured something.

. . .

He can't help glancing up at the slit window.

He had heard the door bang shut, and the sound of singing, and he had climbed up into that window. But the sounds came closer, and he thought of what the owner of the house might do to him . . . the ground was far below, the floor inside in shadow at his feet. If he jumped . . . the pain in his heel had him part-crippled already, and if he hit it on the floor . . . so he had stayed, stiff and horribly scared.

> Two times ago, he had been trapped. And the young man, very young man smooth and bearded, the young man who held his shoulder had pushed him hard against the upright of the fence and

He felt sick to the pit of his stomach, and his mind blackened. This time! said the voice urgently.

The sun on his back in the window, and how the figure below had turned and looked straight at him, though he hadn't moved at all.

. . .

She stands back from the board and looks at it for a long time. Her gut sense says that any alteration will rip the network and allow the lively shadow to escape. Yet it feels unfinished . . . she closes her eyes hard, and in the dullred at the back of her lids, sees what she needs.

Redbrown, redbrown as red chalk, earthcoloured reminder.

"Stammel and murrey," she murmurs happily, "ruddle and madder and o solferino," hunting with gusto through the chest of chalks.

. . .

It had looked with fear and surprise at him, but had made no move to harm him. Sharp flames flickered round it, like small fiery knives. But it listened, listened sometimes with care. And when it found out he was hurt, even that small hurt, it had helped.

The elation built up in him. He battered it down, but it kept coming back. Not again, he told himself, I don't believe it. Not again.

The name was Kerewin Holmes, and he had said it inside himself, melding it to his name, all the times it prowled round the room, or made the meal, or took him up the narrow haunted stairs that twisted upon themselves, like the inside of a corkscrew.

And there were things hanging on the walls, and dark secret places where small trees grew, and gardens of brightly coloured toadstools, and it had passed these as though all houses had such things in their walls.

Even with his hurt and tiredness, the elation kept growing.

Big and strong, strong as Joe, stronger than Joe it came with sure suddenness, Kerewin Holmes covered with flames like knives. And a fierce hidden flame inside it, that sometimes dimmed taking all the over-lights with it, sometimes sank so far down that he was afraid it would never emerge again, and he would be left to face a husk that babbled. It is a beginning again he hugs it close in his inside self, a beginning again, afraid and excited at the same time.

A beginning, and I never thought there would be another beginning. Just the end.

The end is still there, he told himself that while it talked at him.

The words, the words, that chattered and bubbled round his ears . . . words that had been spoken across his head before, but never to him . . . many parts to them, to be stored and untangled at leisure. Like 'penitential'. . . .

He can store any sound he wants to, and duplicate it inwardly.

"Aside from the penitential part," says Kerewin again, and her voice seems to float to him across the strange round room.

. . .

A border. A deep thick border, encrusting that left side. Make it totally opaque, with nary a vestige of underlying paper showing. Then, skim it out, thin it gradually to a mere shade of itself, finest earth-tinted mist seeping to but not onto the edge of the dark web.

Then one could never be sure that the red was not an evil devouring fog, creeping up to the netted shadow's last stronghold, last retreat.

She grinds the chalk heavily across the paper, layering it, pressing its essence out, until chalk and paper seem to blend. The red becomes an encroaching fungus that spreads gradually but with terrible sureness to the thing that whines and wriggles and can't get out from between the prisoning chasms that bite down to it like knives.

. . .

A fly droned through the air.

He stretched himself quietly on the floor, arms away from his sides, flat on his face, so he went nearly cross-eyed looking at the interwoven grass matting when his eyes were opened.

The elation was still at home in him. It had come to climax last night when her hand and Joe's had touched, with him aching and unsteady and overwhelmed with joy in the centre.

The horror was still at home in him.

It was almost always there.

The only defence he could raise against the dark and the horror and the laughing terrible voice were his golden singers, the sounds and patterns of words from the past that he had fitted to his own web of music. They often broke apart, but he could always make them new. So he lay prone on the floor, and listened to them, and made Kerewin part of them, part of his heart.

. . .

The hours sing by.

She begins a pattern of scrolls, but their coils become tangled and hectic so she screws them to oblivion. She starts on another group of curves. Over on the stand, the creeping fungus with its screaming centre is drying under a coat of clear sprayed varnish. Every time she looks at it, she feels a shiver of pride and satisfaction.

> Another real thing! I am not dead yet! I can still call
> forth a piece of soul and set it down in colour, fixed
> forever. . . .

The curve-group isn't working out.

"Sss," says Kerewin and swings round at last. "Hey you!"

She has forgotten about him till now: his self-effacement is perfect.

She looks down, worried that he lies so still, guilty because she had forgotten completely he was in the room.

Then Simon turns his head, and his eyes are open and unblinking. For a moment, they look at each other.

> Hell, his eyes go funny colours,

but she says gruffly,

"Up. Come and look at this."

He doesn't like it, his face whitening, and his eyes going darker still. He cups one finger in his other hand, tightens the hand as the finger tries to get away.

Kerewin grins with triumph and delight.

"That is it!" hands on hips. "That is exactly what I wanted to show. And even you see it!"

"What have you done?" and picks up the pad before he can take it. "Nothing?"

Nothing.

. . .

Joe comes hurrying up the stairs, Simon a step behind him.

"Ready for tea?" he calls. He still has his helmet on, plastic-guarded face, green swelling head, a warrior fresh returned from the mundane war.

She thinks, Berloody cheeky, mate. First send the kid here, and then expect tea again—there's limits to tribal affinities, and is going to say something sharp and icy when the man takes off his helmet and holds it out to her.

"He did tell you?"

"Tell me what?"

"Uh uh."

Simon takes the helmet and holds it to her instead.

"About tea," says Joe, eyeing his disorderly son, who has spent the last two minutes dancing round him. He had come down as soon as he heard the bike, and Joe had wondered at his pallor.

He says, "You forgot to say, didn't you?"

Me?

"Yes, you . . . o crikey, I thought one simple message would be safe enough unwritten. Kerewin, e hoa, I had a brainwave when I sent this one here. Since you gave us tea yesterday, I'd get tea tonight. Did you like your lunch?"

"Yeah, superb. I haven't had muttonbirds for months, and I didn't think the season began for a while."

Joe grins. "Secret source. Well, those were for him staying here, whether he stayed this time or not. I know he stayed, I checked with Tainuis on my way home. So then I rushed and got tea ready. It's special. Wild pork and corn. I even bought a bottle of wine to go with it, and that's something for this beer drinker to do. Why didn't you?" swinging round on his son, "why not?"

He is annoyed that all his effort and anticipated joy may be wasted. "Why not, eh?"

Simon, unfazed, writes SURPRISE on his hand.

"I'll say it's a surprise, but a bloody nice one too," says Kerewin. "I was just thinking about lighting that cursed range and getting some sort of hash for tea, and here I am offered a feast. Wait two seconds while I change my rings to some suitable for dining out in," and she cackles, derisive of herself. "Are you really serious? You actually want me to come and have tea with you?"

"Hell, yes. It's not a joke or anything. Listen, bloody brat, do as you're told, not keep things for surprises. That sort of practice backfires."

The boy nods, about one affirmative for each word.

"Distinctly sarcastic," Kerewin watches him with glee. "Well, it's nice to get a surprise like this, so faulty memory or delibera-tion, it turns out well. How're we going?"

"O, I got the bike." He takes the helmet from the boy and hands it to her for the second time.

"Not berloody likely!" jumping back like it was a head offered her on a plate. "I mean, where does Simon go?"

"You don't like travelling on bikes?" asks Joe anxiously. "I'm careful, I'll go slow."

Kerewin pulls at her hair. "I keep thinking, the only times I've been on bikes, about what happens to this precious brainpan of mine should we come off."

"That's the helmet's worry . . . look, truly, I'll go slow. There's not likely to be any traffic till we get to town. And we stick Sim in front as usual. I get caught," shrug, "I get caught."

"Okay," she says dubiously, and slides the helmet gingerly over her head. She puts on her denim jacket as they go through the en-trance hall. Sounds are distant and muted through the fibreglass. Joe is talking to Simon, and she can see Simon answer, but she can't follow what's being said. She gets smiles from both of them, when-ever she looks their way.

Even behind the man's broad shoulders the wind struck into her face. Swept across her eyes, stinging them to tears, and whipped round those curls stranded outside the helmet. And it was cold. The blow of air against her face bit through her lips and chilled her teeth. The lack of balance she felt, no control over speed or direction, made her feel unaccustomedly small and powerless.

She shut her eyes until the bike stopped, because seeing only the dark was better than the blur that rushed past previously. Not fast, the man had said: then what was speeding like?

"Sheeit," says Kerewin, standing unsteadily. "Remind me to buy a car." She takes the helmet off: her mass of hair is crushed and subdued.

"You know what?" she asks the grinning Gillayleys. "My teeth are numb. What the hell does pork taste like when eaten with numb teeth?"

Unanswerable. . . .

• • •

So here we go, walking creepfooted into the Gillayleys' den, following the hand-in-hand two of them.

A neat lawn bordered by concrete paths. No flowers. No shrubs. The places where a garden had been were filled with pink gravel.

The hallway was dim, an unshaded bulb dangling from the ceiling, no carpet. There was not a suspicion of dust anywhere, nor any sign of flowers.

Joe sprouted from a doorway.

"Kitchen," he says. "Come in."

The kitchen is gas-heated, square and bare, almost institutional in its unadorned plainness. Table and four straightbacked wooden chairs. Battered fridge with chipped enamel; stainless steel sink and bench; a scarred clean cooker. There's a decrepit Coronation teacaddy on a shelf over the bench, with a saucer holding soap and sinkplug beside it, and at the end of the bench, there is a canvas-covered birdcage on a stand. She is surprised by that, although she can't say for why.

Joe invites,

"Sit down, make yourself at home," and goes on busying himself with the pots on the cooker.

Simon slides round the door. He has a way of edging into a room very close to the doorpost furthest from anyone. He goes to the birdcage, slips off the cover, and snaps his fingers. Joe looks round automatically, and the boy gestures to the cover. "I forgot, and it's your job anyway. Feed him while you're at it."

The bird is a budgie of inquisitive green: it has no sense of occasion or time, cracking its beak and twittering as though the day has just begun.

She looks at it politely while Simon deftly slips in seeds and shows where it runs up and down a ladder, and looks at itself in a mirror. She dislikes birds in cages.

"Get a bottle out of the fridge Haimona, and give it to Kerewin to open, eh."

A semidry white wine: the top snaps off and a very small cloud of whitish vapour oozes out.

Simon makes a noise like Frrrsh, flinging a hand way in the air.

"You'll go frrsh in a minute if you don't give us a hand," says Joe, coming over with a pile of plates and cutlery.

"Sorry. Forgetting my manners," says Kerewin. "Can I give *you* a hand with the spuds or something?" and Joe smiles, remembering his own offer.

"Nope. Just nourish up your appetite."

"Rightio."

"Haimona!"

So the boy brings the salt cellar and the pepper grinder. A butterdish. Mustard already mixed in a pipkin. A dark sort of sauce, smelling of plums. Pulped apple spread on a wooden plate. A bowl of salad greens that sends fingers of scent stealing all round the room. Garlic, a mild vinegar, lettuce, and is that chicory?

"This appetite is in danger of becoming uncontrollable."

"Zoom," says Joe, and whips across the room with a haunch of basted brown pork on a platter. He waves it back and forth directly under her nose. "Kapai?"

"Ahhh," mock swooning off her chair to be an untidy heap sprawling on the floor, and he nearly drops the lot, giggling.

She must enjoy this. And if bloody Haimona doesn't wreck things, maybe she'll want to come back again.

He scurries back to the stove, an incongruous movement for his wide-shouldered figure, and begins ladling out the corncobs.

Simon is already kneeling on his chair, sharpening his knife and fork together.

"Quit 'at," growls Joe when the boy does it in earnest, making a sharp metallic squealing that sets all their teeth on edge. Simon stares back insolently, but stops the racket.

We'll fix you, tama, you keep behaving like this.

But he fills the three glasses smiling, and goes to his seat, and still standing, gives the toast.

"Kia ora koe," to Kerewin.

"Kia ora korua," she says in reply.

While the wine goes down, she thinks

> What's strange? No pictures, no flowers, no knicknacks I can see? Maybe, but not all homes have that sort of thing. Is it the barren cleanliness, the look of almost poverty? Contrast that with the brandnew 750 c.c. bike he's got and this wine . . . liebfraumilch doesn't come cheap.

The pork is meltingly well-cooked, full of the sweet slightly gamey flavour of a beast fed in the backbush all its short life. The salad is excellent, and the corn good enough for frozen stuff.

"You're no amateur when it comes to cooking, eh?"

He is strangely bashful. He mumbles under his breath, and Simon mouths SPEAK UP SPEAK UP so obviously that Kerewin sputters and chokes on her wine.

"Shuddup," he pushes his child's hair all over his face. "No more wine for you, smartass."

The boy's been drinking with them glass for glass, although his glass is considerably smaller. Still, his face is flushed and his eyes too brilliant.

"I like cooking," says Joe, "so what do we have for tea? Mainly fishnchips . . . I'm generally feeling too tired and it's a helluva lot quicker and easier. No dishes either. But every so often, I like to do something special, like this. I learnt how, off Hana. Man, could she cook. . . ." his voice trails away, and he stares over Kerewin's head, his eyes glazing. Shakes his head sharply after a minute and says roughly,

"You touch any more wine and I'll belt you, guest or no guest."

Simon had sneaked himself another glassful, grinning conspira-torially at Kerewin.

Now he subsides to the back of his chair and scowls sulkily at his father.

O dear. It'd spoil the meal if they fight. . . .

She belches quietly, and says, peacemaking,

"That is the best meal I've had since lunchtime, bar none. Seri-ously, Joe, it was splendid."

Joe brightens, stops scowling back at his child.

"You liked it truly?"

"Man alive, it was, he, kapai. . . ."

He squares his shoulders, and the sour expression vanishes.

"I'm glad. It is a small thing to offer you, but I hoped you'd like it."

"So much I'll even offer to do the dishes, and *that*, friend, is un-heard of from a Holmes. At my place, I leave 'em for a month or so until I run out of plates."

"Uh uh. That's my job, and his," jabbing a finger at Simon.

He stands, slightly unsteady, they've drunk three bottles of good German wine between them.

"Well, you've got a relief for tonight." She heads for the sink.

"E!" he calls out. "We'll leave them for the morning. Let's go to the sittingroom. I've built a fire. The room'll warm in no time."

. . .

He shows her over the house first, the child beside her, holding her hand again, and making surreptitious comments with his fin-gers. All of them are lost on Kerewin who is using most of her at-tention to stay straight and look sober.

The house has six rooms, the pattern typical older State house, found in thousands all over the country.

A bedroom with a double bed in it, antiseptically clean, with heavy curtained windows.

"My room," says Joe, flicking the light on and switching it off again.

"His room," gesturing into a small lighted sunporch. "Sweet Jesus, tama, must you chuck all your clothes on the floor? Pick 'em up."

She gets a good look while the child gathers the clothes and dumps them on his bed. The room is on the righthand side of the hall, going in, right at the back of the house. Sparsely furnished like every room she's seen so far; a wooden dresser against the wall, a three-quarter bed. On the bed though, is a bright coverlet made of squares of crocheted wool; all colours, orange and violet, scarlet and shocking pink and vermilion, cornflower blue and sunflower yellow and limeleaf green. It is the only burst of colour she's seen in the house, excepting the budgie.

> That's one thing—everything is so drear. Small wonder
> the brat escapes twice weekly. . . .

"Nice counterpane," she says, and Joe answers, "O, Marama made him that. She's Piri's mum, and considers herself your nana, right?"

The boy, having rearranged the disorder in his room, nods. He looks resentful at having had to do it.

"Out," says Joe, and waits till the child has gone into the hall before switching the light off.

Next place on the guided tour?

"O, that's the bathroom."

Spruce, clean tiled floor—hellishing cold on these winter mornings because there's not a bathmat in sight.

Simon disappears into the toilet.

"Go get undressed when you've finished," Joe says to him. "You can stay up a while yet."

He whispers to her, "With any luck he'll flake."

For the first time she wonders whether the man has anything else in mind other than conversation. In which case, he has struck out.

"That's the spareroom. Only junk in there."

But she realises she misjudged the words. In the sittingroom he says,

"I don't want to give him his dope on top of the drink he had. I didn't realise he was getting himself quite so much, or I would have pulled him up short before. But anyway with luck it'll send him to sleep naturally."

The fire brightens this room, but there is nothing in it otherwise that is cheering. A faded sofa beneath the window that looks out into the street. Three chairs with pale spots and rings from slopped glasses on the arms. And a glass-doored china cabinet with nothing in it.

He has been following her guarded survey, and when he sees her glance linger on the empty cabinet, he chuckles.

"Ask Himi where the stuff inside went," he says cryptically.

"O?" but the man just grins.

He sits on the hearthrug, poking at the fire, whistling softly to himself. He makes no attempt to start small talk, and she appreciates the silence.

Simon comes in, his feet bare. The bandage she had put on, is gone.

Joe says, "All right?" and at the child's nod, "Come here, then." He scrutinises the child's heel and comments.

"So far the splinter has grown to be about as big as he is. Wonder where it'll stop?"

"It was about an inch actually. Big enough if you stepped on it suddenly, I suppose." Joe's eyebrows rise.

"I thought about half an inch, and then I was being generous. Tough luck, tama. Where did you go to step on it anyway? Probably deserved it, eh."

Simon kneels beside him, but disdains to answer. Instead, he reaches up to Kerewin, inside the denim folds of jacket, to where the rosary is lying.

"O," says Joe, surprise and something akin to awe in his voice. "You're giving them away?"

The boy looks at him, still wine-flushed, but now his eyes are dark.

Kerewin says slowly,

"They were his gift to me this morning, and I appreciate them very much. But maybe an heirloom isn't to be alienated?"

Joe shakes his head. "They're his, to do what he wants with them. More later, eh." Back to his son, "Miracles never cease. Do you remember, hey no. Let's forget that a moment. Kere wants to ask you a question."

"I do?"

He weaves a hand at the china cabinet.

"O yeah. What about the cabinet, Sim? Why's it empty?"

Simon's stare at his father is both reproachful and vindictive.

Joe laughs, at him.

"It was a sore subject. Once upon a time it was full of trinkets and junky glass stuff, the sort people give you but you never really need."

"Mathoms."

"Really? Well, anyway, the cabinet was stuffed with them. One time, Simon got wild at me, I even forget what for now, and cleared the whole lot out. By the very simple expedient of throwing them at the walls. There was one hell of a heap of glass splinters. With weird little bits sprinkled through it—some of those uh mathoms are held together with very strange things. Little springs and sprigs of plastic and odd rubber bands."

"Goodbye the debris of years," she says, not knowing what else to.

"Yeah, that's what I thought too, after I calmed down. Most of the junk had been souvenirs or birthday presents or wedding gifts. A lot of sentimental memories attached to it, but not much other value." He looks down blandly at his child. "There is a moral to that, Kerewin. Haimona is rough on possessions, his own or others'. I was surprised to see his beads as a gift to you, but it's entirely in keeping with this iconoclast." He ruffles the child's hair back into place. "Hana, my wife, hung some pictures in his room, quite colourful and pleasant. I thought he liked them. They went west a year back, didn't they?"

"You just throw whatever's handy when you get wild?"

"Uh huh," Joe answers for the boy. "From your tea to a half gallon of beer a certain Saturday morning. That little effort nearly brained Piri's two year old we had visiting. Lost skin over that, didn't you?"

The boy has the non-expression on his face again. Utter disinterest.

"Okay, I think we'd better change the subject," says Kerewin, "shatteringly interesting and all as it is."

Joe laughs.

. . .

An hour later, the conversation has meandered round to fishing: seafishing, which is Kerewin's favourite and speciality, versus river and lake, at which Joe modestly admits being expert.

"Not really," he says ruefully. "I just know where the fish are to be found. It's getting them out in an orthodox manner that both-ers me."

"Ministry of Works minnows," chuckles Kerewin, but he affects shock.

Simon is nearly asleep, but he stirs every time one of them moves to stoke the fire, or pass across smokes.

"Excuse me a minute," says Joe at last, and goes into the kitchen, returning with a round bottle a minute later.

"Come on, tama. Bed time."

Two teaspoonsful of what looks like raspberry syrup.

She looks at the label.

"Trichloral!" the word makes her voice resound in a squawk. "Hell, he's a bit young for that kind of draught, isn't he?"

"I said last night about the sleeping bit," says Joe softly. "At least this way we both get a good night's sleep. Otherwise, it's nightmares at two in the morning, and three hours spent getting him calmed back to normality. And that's no joke night after night after night."

"I shouldn't imagine so."

He's holding Simon as though he were a baby. It renews her sense of the boy's slightness.

"E moe koe," says the man tenderly, kissing the child, dark hair overlapping fair.

"See if you can't do something unusual tomorrow," setting him on his feet, "like be good for a change."

Simon grins, nearly out on his feet. He staggers to Kerewin, holding out his arms, and Kerewin ducks.

"E, he just wants to say goodnight," says Joe.

When was the last time I kissed anybody?

as the child kisses goodnight, and winds his arms round her neck. And stays there. "I'll take him if you like," Joe stands quickly and opens his arms, aware of her increasing embarrassment even if Simon isn't. "I'm not used to children," she says, standing too, and holding Simon awkwardly from her. "Ummm. . . ."

How to pass across one nearly comatose brat who is quite securely entwined round my vertebral column?

His arms are anyway, scores the snark snidely. A child
as a muffler? Come now. . . . There was a young lady,
from Munich I think, who anxiously said, with embarrassment pink, I can see that you're staring, at the scarf
I am wearing. Well, it's kidstuff arranged in a rink.

Ooouuhh.
She stares into the fire as Joe takes the child to bed.

The last time I kissed was with my elder brother, before
the big breakup. His kiss tasted of rum. That one's kiss
tasted of raspberries, from the drug to keep away dreams.
What sort of dreams does he have that are so terrible?

Jetsam, she ponders. The old meaning was goods thrown overboard to lighten a ship . . . dreams of being left, bereaved, dreams of
drowning while your people sink in the hungry waves?

"Joe," as he comes back and closes the door, "do you mind me
asking about what you said last night?"

"Not at all. What was it?"

"When you said, apropos of Simon's age, meet some jetsam?"

"O that. Well, it was strictly true for one thing. It'd take a while
to explain . . . are you really interested? I haven't had anyone aside
from people in pubs to talk about my odd child for months and
months and months."

"I like listening. I've got time. And I'm curious to know what
makes him dream nightmares at his age."

"Don't ask him," he says seriously. "He can't explain it to himself, let alone me, and he hasn't enough words to tell other people
about it."

He stretches.

"Ooooweee . . . e, would you like some more wine while I talk?
There's a bottle left still, and I meant it all to go with dinner." He
stands waiting. "O, and just in case you think I have bad designs,
I don't think you do, but just in case and with apologies for raising
the subject, I'm not intending to take advantage of you in any way.
You know," he has darkened with embarrassment, and fumbles for
more words.

"I didn't even think it."

You lie in your teeth.

"You said tea, Joe. It was delicious. My mind ends at my stomach anyway, but I certainly didn't think you were playing some under-hand game with it. Like the oldfashioned *Drink is the downfall of many a nice girl*," she throws back her head and laughs. "Besides, I think I could drink you under the table where wine is concerned. I've had lots of practice."

"So have I," says Joe sadly, "but you'd like the wine?"

"A very good idea."

. . .

He lay on his back on the floor, his arms crossed over his face, and talked. Or rather, recited, as though he had memorised what he wanted to say a long time ago. "Three years back, in early spring, we had a storm of unusual intensity. That's what the radio called it. We called it a bastard. Quote: 'The town of Whangaroa in the South Island was lashed by a storm of unusual intensity today. Sev-eral houses lost their roofs, and a garage near the centre of the town was totally demolished by fierce gusts. Two people are be-lieved to have drowned when a launch was driven onto the south-ern tip of Ennetts Reef about two miles north of the township. The police are seeking information on the survivor of the wreck . . .' That's getting ahead of things, so I'll unquote." Joe smiled over his arm. "But they also mentioned that one of Ben Tainui's prize heifers was a casualty. They raise Charolais, y'know."

"Yeah really?"

"Yeah, really. Anyway, about four that afternoon, one of the families round the Head phoned the police to say a launch was in difficulties off the reef. The sea was rough but the coppers asked a friend of mine, Tass Dansy, if he'd take the boat he used on the Chathams run, and go and have a look. See if he could get a line to her. There were no other craft here anywhere near as good as Dan-sy's for heavy seas, eh. They tried, Tass and his mate, and two cop-pers, for over two hours. Tried to get close enough to send a line over for a tow, and by that time the wind had reached sixty knots and was still rising. Eventually, the launch banged into the end of the reef. The coppers and the mate saw three people go overboard, a man holding a child, and a woman. But Tass swears to this day that he saw another man slip over the bow, and he thought there might have been someone else as well. He was in the wheelhouse and had the best view, so he's probably right. But we only found three. They put out a call for volunteers to search the beaches after the launch went down. I went. Hana was seven months gone at the time, but she was okay, and I didn't worry about leaving her alone in the storm. This old place'll stand up to more than that sort of wind."

He sighs.

"Here I am, walking the beaches in a bloody howling gale with seven other mugs, and wondering what on earth possessed me to do so. We were strung out in a long file along the shore. Trover, he was a constable here then, shouted out after about half an hour. I never heard him above the wind, but I saw his arms wave us in and came running. He had found the man, and a very obvious body he made, too. His head had split open on a rock when he came tumbling through the surf. The cap of his skull was sliced off and his brains washed out. It was like a cup, his open head, with the face still there on one side"

"Grisly." She begins to see why the child might have nightmares.

"O Himi wasn't with him," Joe somehow catches the tenor of her thought. "Anyway, this bloke. His face was nice, pleasant, open. Relaxed somehow, as though he didn't care about dying. He was tall and beautifully muscled, a body like an athlete's. He was naked, his clothes probably torn off during his passage in, but none of them were ever found. I never saw his eyes open. Trover radioed the copshop to say we'd found one, and the station 'phoned for an ambulance to come from 'Wera, and we kept on looking. You know my cousin, Piri Tainui?"

"I've met Piri for five minutes, when he picked up Simon on the weekend."

"Yeah. Well, he found the woman. She had drowned apparently. The other constable, some foreign name like Kosinski or something, but he was a nice bloke, tried artificial respiration. It didn't work. Because the lady had a broken neck aside from anything else, the pathologist said. She was partly clothed in a loose blouse thing, with a thonged sandal somehow still on her right foot. Her toenails were painted black. She was well-shaped, but flabby. I remember thinking, God help me, that she looked a right tart, lying there spread among the weed. Her hair was hennaed. It might have been blond at some stage. The bloke had black hair, by the way, but crewcut. The woman had blue eyes and they were wide open, staring as though she couldn't believe she was dead. She had a watch on her right wrist, which is a bit unusual. The glass was smashed, and it proved useless for identification purposes. Her clothes weren't any help in that line either."

He sits up, and lights a cigarette.

"About half after seven, I was sent back along the beaches, while the others went to scour the far east of the headland. It was dark, very dark, and the wind hadn't dropped any. I had to fight to keep on going, to stop myself from being blown backwards. I hadn't gone that far when I saw something at the water's edge. I thought, ahh Ngakau, it's a weedtangle again, get going. The shore was littered with them, and it wasn't the first time I'd mistaken one for a body, eh. You started seeing bodies everywhere, you know?"

He looks down at the stream of smoke flowing out of his cigarette, shaking his head. "Then I saw his hair . . . long then, even longer than it is now. He was thrown mainly clear of the water, but a high wave from the receding tide would drag at him. He was front down, his face twisted towards me as I ran skidding over the sand and weed. There was sand half over him, in his mouth, in his ears, in his nose. I thought, I was quite sure he was dead. But I cleaned out his mouth and nose, and pressed water from his lungs, and breathed for him."

He is silent for a minute.

"He has got that of me, I suppose. My breath . . . I was surprised when he started coughing. I hadn't any hope in my heart at all. He was so small, and limp. We didn't think he was much more than two or three, thin and fair with arms and legs like sticks. Sweet Lord, was he skinny! You think he's bad now," grinning at her, "you ought to have seen him then. . . ."

Silence again.

"His eyes were black, all pupil, and he didn't see me at all. I thought he was a girl at first, you know because of the hair, but when I picked him up I saw his penis. He had on the top half of a pair of pyjamas—still around here somewhere as a matter of fact. Common kind, you can buy them at any Woolworth's. And a life jacket. One of those orange things that are two pockets of kapok and a collar for joining them. They go over your head?"

She nods. "I know them."

"He was almost literally black and blue all over from cold and bruising. I didn't know it till after, but his left hand was smashed, his left arm broken in two places, three ribs on that side were fractured, and both his collarbones were cracked. Like he had hit something very hard, arm first. I just picked him up, and wrapped him in my coat, and ran back, was blown back, shouting like a lunatic with the wind cutting into my kidneys like a knife. And after that, everything is a bit blurred. The ambulance ride into Taiwhenuawera with two corpses for company. Long waiting, or it seemed like it, in hospital rooms with huge bright lights. Examinations, and him screaming his head off. He seemed to come back to life very quickly. Scared as hell, but even when he was half-conscious, he was clinging like a leech to my hand all the time he could and they'd let him. Shock, exposure, pneumonia, he should be dead, said the hospital, and enumerated the breaks. I stayed the night with him, because he was upset whenever I stopped holding his hand, and Hana came up and stayed with me." He adds, "Did you know Hana was a nurse?"

He leans forward and stubs out his smoke, avoiding her eyes.
"No."

"Two other things," he says, after a while. "He had obviously been in hospital before, and it was clear early on, from the way he reacted, that the other time had been bad. X-rays showed he had had widespread injuries to his pelvis and hips, and they would have kept him in hospital for quite a while, the medics reckoned. The other thing is, he never talked. Screamed, my God could he scream! He was, and is, a fluent screamer. But he never said anything, or acted like he was used to talking. The ENT bloke who examined him said there was no physical reason to prevent him from speaking. He's got all the gear needed, eh. But if he vocalises, he throws up, and violently."

"Words?"

"No, just sounds."

"Hmmm."

"Well, there was a coroner's court, to get back to the story. I testified. Piri testified. Tass Dansy testified. Half of Whangaroa testified, one way or the other, and enjoyed it very much. The pathologist said the woman was in her late thirties, the man in his early thirties, and both had been in good health. No distinguishing marks or scars—most unusual, said the pathologist, and left it at that.

"The police never got a report of any people of their description missing, and they made enquiries as far afield as Britain. The bodies and the survivor were, and are, unidentifiable. The one object that might have helped is in two hundred fathoms of current ridden water, and nobody wants to have a go at getting to it. You know, I often wonder about the others on board, because I think there were others. Aside from Tass seeing maybe a couple extra, Himi used to be scared of meeting people, like he expected to see some-one from the wreck he didn't want to see."

"How much does he remember?"

"Nothing that he's telling, if he remembers anything at all. Sweet Jesus, he was too young to know how old he was. He didn't even know his name, or if he did, he couldn't ever tell us. Hana called him Simon Peter because he initially reacted to that name most of all. We tried lists of them, hundreds . . . actually, he reacted to quite a few, some of them odd as hell. We thought they might have been people he had known or places he'd been to or something like that. I'm pretty sure that O'Connor was the name of the people he was with, for instance."

"People he was with? Not his parents?"

"Not according to blood groups, definitely not his parents."

"A real live mystery . . . what other names?"

"Well, one morning he heard something on the radio and got re-ally agitated. Tried to drag Hana to listen to it. What he wanted to hear was over by the time she got there, so she rang the station and they kindly sent her the news broadcast, because that's what it was. And the item Himi went almost berserk over was about a shark attack on a Dunedin beach."

"O, I remember that."

"Well, where did it get us? Nowhere, because he shut up tight and wouldn't say any more. Another thing used to be Citroen cars. He had a bee in his bonnet about them for some reason. And fires . . . he doesn't mind them now, but at one time he was even afraid of matches."

"A strange collection . . . how do his beads fit in? Are they your, were they your wife's?"

Joe shakes his head.

"The case was my wife's, that's all. Those beads were his lucky talisman for over a year. He wasn't separated from them ever. Not in bed, not in the bath, not anywhere. Nobody got to have a good look at them for quite a while. They were in the pocket of the woman's blouse. They were shown to him to see if he knew them. He knew them all right. He grabbed them, kissed the ring on them, and thereafter wouldn't let them go. For over a year, as I said. If you wanted to see them, you had to fight him for them, literally. One time, when the police were still trying to find out who he was, a senior detective type came from Wellington to photograph them, and try and question Himi. He would have been about four at this time, I suppose."

Again shaking his head before a vivid memory.

"And my oath! the racket! We told him we were only going to look at his precious beads, but it didn't make an iota of difference. In the end, I grabbed his arms and pinioned his legs, and carried him out of the room, after Hana had removed the beads. We were regarded as poison for a month after."

"He holds grudges, eh?"

"No," says Joe, very slowly, "no, he doesn't hold grudges. He was just too frightened of us to trust us for a while; and that's after we had looked after him for over a year. By the way, he's only sort of adopted. Because no-one can find out who he is, it couldn't ever be finalised. And besides, my personal status had altered the last time they asked about him. Hana, and my other son, had died by then."

"I am sorry." They are always inadequate, words . . . if I knew you better, or I was a warmer person, I would hongi, but. . . .

"Yeah." He sits, looking into the flames. "Timote was ten months old, and Hana was thirty, and they died of flu. Which has always struck me as stupid and unfair. Imagine, flu!"

He spits. There are tears filling his eyes.

She doesn't say anything.

"O drink up, Kerewin. I'm boring you." He puts the bottle down. "Excuse me please, I'm going to check on Himi." He strides out of the room, banging the door shut.

O hell, she thinks, a fine end to the night. He's a right emotional boil, and so's the kid, and I suppose no wonder the both of them.

She looked at the wine settling flat in her glass, and drank it, morosely.

. . .

Kerewin, beneath the distant luminous dust of stars: so that's what there is to know of Gillayleys in their queer strait antiseptic haven. She stretched her arms, wide as a cross, and something small and bony snapped in her chest.

She swore and closed her arms in a hurry.

> Snapped a wishbone without a wish . . . what would I wish for anyway? A return of the spirit of joy? It won't come back by wishing. . . . Maybe, considering this rintin shambles of a night, I should wish something for them . . . for Simon, what? A real name? No, something better. A shield to raise against his dreams, and for the other, a relief of that need he shows so plainly, for dead wife and dead child. But there's only one way to do that, send him to them. . . .
>
> Anyway to hell, I forgot to wish.

She walked on, her bare feet sinking in the sand. There was a crust on it from the past night's rain. No-one walked on this beach much.

> O chief of my children, primate of woes, come sink in the fleece of your old mother, Earth . . . but seriously Holmes, there is something wrong with the brat, be-yond what Joe says. For that matter, there's something wrong with the fella as well.

Chanting into the night,
"O all the world is a little queer, except thee and me, and some-times, I wonder about thee."

> I know about me. I am the moon's sister, a tidal child stranded on land. The sea always in my ear, a surf of eternal discontent in my blood.
>
> You're talking bullshit as usual.
>
> Only what to do about the urchin's bitter dreams? Or the

man's evil shadows—the ghosts riding on his shoulders?

The miasma of gloom that shrouded his lightning smile?

He'd come back into the room, the tears barely dried on his cheeks, cups of coffee in his hands.

"Do you know what? He's smiling in his sleep."

She got the impression that that didn't happen too often.

The coffee was strong and sobering.

"I've got to go to work tomorrow eh."

"That's today now."

"Yeah, that's the hell of it."

"I used to hate that," she said. "Having to get up at some ungodly hour to go to work. Feeling out of kilter with my body time. That's the thing I value most now, that I can get up at five, before the sun's awake if I wish, or stay in bed till tomorrow."

He sighed. "I'd love that. But I work in a factory, work in a factory, work in a factory...."

"I know. I've worked in factories too."

"You know what I think's worst? It's not getting up."

"The monotony? Noise? The twits around you? Bosses?"

"No, being a puppet in someone else's play. Not having any say." He spread his hands and looked through the fan of fingers. "It has its compensations, I suppose. I've paid off the house, and I've got some money in the bank. We're clothed and we eat. All the good old pakeha standbys and justifications. Though it's hard hours. I start at seven and I never get home before five. Sometimes six. Even seven. Too long to be away from Haimona, eh?"

"Sounds it, a bit . . . what does he normally do during the day then?"

"School," said Joe laconically. "He's meant to go to my cousin's afterwards. And when he goes to school, he mainly does too."

She asked hesitantly,

"If you don't have to work, all the time, why don't you take a break?"

"I'd dearly love to take a decent holiday. I've got several weeks coming to me . . . but I don't know. I've tried it all ways. Stayed at home, and we got in each other's hair. Sent him to Tainuis while I took off, and he fought Piri's kids, antagonised all the adults, even Marama. And *she* thinks he's an angel incarnate. So then I tried one of those bus-tours, last Christmas. We went north. I thought he might like seeing all the places I grew up in. Something a bit different from here."

He leaned back and lit himself another cigarette.

"Sweet Jesus, was that ever a disaster. I wound up locking him into the hotel bedroom wherever we stayed for the night, and going down to the bar and drinking myself blind. Right way to win friends and influence people, eh. You can imagine what we were like during the day . . . I won't do that again."

He bent his head.

"I forget how much I paid out for damage to hotel bedrooms, but it wasn't altogether his fault I suppose."

The fire crackled.

Kerewin said,

"You like fishing, don't you?"

"Yeah."

"Well, I could find out whether any of my ex-family are using the baches at Moerangi. That could be an idea for a holiday you might like to consider. Not much to do except fish, but it's nice there. Quiet. Healing."

Joe nodded, looking at her quizzically.

"Ex-family?"

"O, we rowed irreparably . . ."

We wounded each other too deep for the rifts to be healed.

She sat down on the damp sand, stretching her legs in front of her and leaning back on her hands.

Strange.

Webs of events that grew together to become a net in life. Life was a thing that grew wild. She supposed there was an overall pattern, a design to it.

She'd never found one.

She thought of the tools she had gathered together, and painstakingly learned to use. Futureprobes, Tarot and I Ching and the wide wispfingers from the stars . . . all these to scry and ferret and vex the smokethick future. A broad general knowledge, encompassing bits of history, psychology, ethology, religious theory and practices of many kinds. Her charts of self-knowledge. Her library.

The inner thirst for information about everything that had lived or lives on Earth that she'd kept alive long after childhood had ended.

None of them helped make sense of living.

She watched the sealight grow.

> What the hell did I offer my sanctuary to him and the brat for? Though I've left myself an out . . . I can always say They are there. Maybe I should just sneak away to the baches myself . . . they used to say,
> Find the kaik' road
> take the kaika road,
> the glimmering road of the past
> into Te Ao Hou.

The moon came out of a cloudbank.

> Ah my shining sister, bright core of my heart, maybe this year in Moerangi I'll find a meaning to the dream?

A mist was obscuring the depth of stars. The night grew towards dawn.

She got up unsteadily and stretched, groaning against the stiffness.

> Sitting on wet sand, what'd you expect numbskull? Numb bum, rather . . . anyway, twenty minutes' walk to bed, and a long lying in . . . thank God for wine, and so easy sleep. Moerangi can rest holy and ghostly in my dreams tonight.

And as for those teeth?

She grinned.

Undoubtedly, somewhere beneath not too distant waves, deceitfully mirroring a babyhood of milk and honey, small ivories. . . .

. . .

> She stares at the screaming painting.
> The candlelight wavers.
> The painting screams silently on.
> She hates it.
> It is intensely bitter.

O unjoy, is that all I can do? Show forth my misery?

All the fire has gone.
She is back in the haggard ashdead world.
She picks up the painting and slides it away behind her desk.
There are a lot of drawings, paintings there.
The new one can scream in company.
And what's the use of keeping them?
A pile for keening over?
"You are nothing," says Kerewin coldly. "You are nobody, and will never be anything, anyone."

And her inner voice, the snark, which comes into its own during depressions like this, says,

> And you have never been anything at anytime, re-member?
> And the next line is. . . .

"Shut up," says Kerewin aloud to herself. "I know I am very stu-pid." But not so stupid as to take this.

> I am worn, down to the raw nub of my soul.
> Now is the time, o bitter beer, soothe my spirit;
> smooth mouth of whisky, tell me lies of truth;
> but better still, sweet wine, be harbinger of deep and
> dreamless sleep. . . .

"Wordplayer," she says sourly. "Mere quoter," feeling her way down the dark spiral to the livingroom circle.

And until the time Joe wakes, groaning at the shrill snarl of the alarmclock, groaning at the thought of another dull and aching day; until the time Simon wakes, and listens, and dresses very quickly, and exits via the window for his new retreat;
until then, Kerewin drinks her way into a kind of cold and uncaring sobriety.

It's as though nothing has changed.

3

Leaps in the Dark

I

WHAT DO YOU SEE AT NIGHT?
    "In dreams?"
He shudders and shakes his head emphatically.
"In the dark you mean? What do I see in the dark?"
No. He waves the paper, WHAT DO YOU SEE AT NIGHT?
"Okay, what do I see at night? Stars?"
No.
"The night itself, like darkness?"
No, no.
"Ah you mean something that can't be seen, like ghosts?"
No, a lot, frowning.
"Hell Simon, I see the same things I see during the day except they are, they seem so dark as to be deprived of colour. I don't see anything different."
He tries again.
ON PEOPLE? scratching his head with the pencil, frown still in place, writing again finally, ON PEOPLE.
"I don't see anything on people. Do you?"
He nods wearily. Then he keeps his head bent, apparently unwilling to look at her.
Kerewin's turn to frown.
What the hell would you see on people in the dark. Shadows in the daytime, yeah, but at night?

It's the word shadows that gives her the answer.

"Wait a moment . . . Sim, do you see lights on people?"

Head up fast, and his bright smile flowering. O Yes.

. . .

In the library, the books spread round them,

"Well, that's what they are. Soul-shadows. Coronas. Auras. Very few people can see them without using screens or Kirlian photography. Only other person I've met before who could see them unaided, could see them all the time, night and day. That's where you had me puzzled, fella."

He touches by her eyes.

"No, I can't see them. I'll bet Joe can't either."

Right, says the boy, grinning wolfishly. He writes quickly, SCARED SAID NOT TO SAY.

"Yeah, I can understand why. It's a bit scary when someone can see things about you that you can't see for yourself . . . if he said not to say, why'd you ask me?"

YOU KNOW. YOU ANSWER.

. . .

I know, I answer eh?

She settles herself more comfortably in the bed, crosses her hands behind her neck and stares into the dark.

Well, I do know a lot. Encyclopaedias of peculiar facts and wayward pieces of knowledge. Myths and legends by the hundred . . . but not generally the kind of things a child wants to learn.

These odd conversations we hold. Glance and gesture, intuition and guess, brief note and long wordy enquiries and explanations . . . and Sim drinks up answers so avidly. All kinds of answers. Why? is the boy's motto, why does, why is, why not? Food, weather, time, fires, sea and season, clothes and cars and people; it's all grist to the mill of why.

I know a lot and I answer, but increasingly I have my own why.

Why isn't Joe doing the answering?

. . .

When I go to the pub these days, the locals talk to me. I have, for example, been fed incredible tales of Simon's wildness by one Shilling Price. Just as well Joe keeps him toeing the line, he says, or we'd all be bowled over eh?

Bill the barkeep says discreetly that old Shillin's apt to exagger-ate y'know? Take it all with a grain of salt, he suggests, and then proceeds to regale me with the time Simon set off all the town's lamppost fire-alarms. He's a bit of a devil, that boy, finishes Bill.

Hmmm. I get the feeling that the child's exploits are only toler-ated because Joe is well-liked.

. . .

He's certainly a mystery.

The more he comes round, the more I'm intrigued.

His background is old hat to the town, to Joe—but it fascinates me. So why not try and find out who he is? I could kill a bird or two thereby: give Sim an understanding of his dark past, that shield against the dread unknown in nightmares he needs. And Joe, who worries about what he's taken on—I suppose you would worry about fostering a moody little nobody, it might turn out cuckoo in more ways than one—Joe could reconcile himself with a known quantity.

I think it's because Joe's afraid of what might be in his child's past that he keeps Simon on so short a lead. Like tonight, all amica-bility:

"E Kere! *Good* to see you again!" mmmm, hongi (it's been all of a day). Picks up Sim, kisses him, "You been good, e tama? Had a good day?"

"Weelll," I'm grinning as I say it, because what happened did look funny. This pintsize hero taking on an adult. Not to worry, I assure Joe, it was just that the mail bloke got a bit huffy when Simon P badfingered him. "That replacement fella, who's taken over Grogan's run for his holiday, you know him?"

Joe knows, nods coldly, his eyes on his son. Simon's shrinking back against the wall. I don't get to finish the story because the boy gets hit, twice, hard. "I told you before, don't you ever. . . ."

Apparently, digitus impudicus is out, no matter what the circum-stances (the new postie was inept: leaning out of the cab of the van, he missed my mailbox altogether and the letters dropped in the mud. I'm swearing Oshit and Sim goes round, picks it all up, salutes the bloke rudely, bloke glowers, goes to cuff him, child ducks, bloke smacks hand against my box, swears. Sim ups him again, bloke practically froths at the mouth. He stamps on the accelerator, and stalls van. I get sore cheek muscles from laughing so much.)

I had already learned that any kind of thieving is totally forbidden. So is anything resembling lying it seems, and woe betide the brat if he doesn't do whatever he's told to, more or less on the instant. The matter is settled right then, thump, that's it. It always looks so ridiculous, Joe hefty and twice his child's size—but that's the way we do it in good old Godzone. Besides, the man is tolerant to a fault in other ways, and he's always lavish with praise, with cuddling and kisses . . . anyway, the hell with it, what business of mine is it how he chooses to bring up his son?

So. We take up an old cold trail—what clues do we have, Sherlock? (Hey, that's good! why haven't I thought of it before?)

A rosary and a ring. A dead boat in deep water, and two dead people. An inarticulate child, a tongue-locked mind.

So, again. Jewellers, libraries, police, hospital records, natter to Dansy, check out boat registration lists. . . .

She thinks about the possibilities for a long time before dropping off to sleep.

. . .

The boy turns up every other day now, regular as clockwork with the morning mailvan (Grogan's back).

"Hello," he says, as Simon scrambles out with her letters. "Nearly hit a cow this morning down near Tainuis' bridge. You know it?"

"Bridge or cow?"

The driver guffaws. "Bloody good," he says. "Other than that, no news. O, except they've got a new barman at the Duke. Just hired today. Not a local." To Simon, "You have a nice day, and thanks for the help."

Boy earns his ride, says Grogan. "Helps me no end, putting the stuff into all those bloody boxes miles off the bloody verge. Inconsiderate bastards." He winks at Simon. "Won't charge you this week, Sim."

One morning, Grogan leans conspiratorially out of the cab and asks in a loud whisper.

"Do you *like* having him around?"

"Um, yeah." (Simon relaxes.)

"The old lady and me think it's a bloody good job too. About time somebody did something bloody useful instead of just bloody talk." Slaps Kerewin on the shoulder. "*Good* on yer, girl."

Hot shit and apricots thinks Kerewin, bristling.

"Hooray," says the postie cheerfully.

"Hooray to you too."

Simon gives him the fingers as the van skids in a half-circle away.

"Watch it you." She shrugs. "Ah, hell, a year of being the eccentric avoidable, and all of a sudden I'm *in* with the locals."

Me image hath gone down the drain.

. . .

Writing,

Hello.

It is six and a half years since I last wrote. Well, six years and five months, and an uncertain number of days, 21 or 22, because I lost track of time then, for a weekend or so. . . .

A lot has happened. I have a home, befitting the eccentricity of a Holmes. I am still myself, iron lady cool and virgin. Maybe not lady. But what to call that sport, the neuter human?

There has been little in the way of true joy.

I don't paint much any longer.

I can't, I can't, I can't.

I have taken to wandering a lot, gyrovague, te kaihau. There is a long desert beach here, my bush, and whispering stands of alien trees. An estuary. The sea all around, waves at night, and my retreat. Unsullied sky (except when I care to build a fire . . .) I am beginning to wonder why I started this parade of excised feelings again.

O yes.

Dear paper ghost, I know a little more about Simon P. P for pestiferous, prestidigitous, (and as his father has it) pake.

Simon P?

Simon the shadowed. Oddbod, spiderchild. A very unlikely but strangely likable brat. Me new toy is to discover whence Simon the Gillayley came from. Why there is a suggestion of the numinous in his shadow. Who else do I know who listens to the silence of God on lonely beaches? (Ah hah! That would be telling. . . .)

Anyhow, I know more.

And I don't know what's worse: knowing as much nothing as I did before, or being cognisant with this futile misleading much I have now.

The saga:

Armed with the ring and the rosary, I went to the library. In Debretts, after hunting through a thousand dusty pages, found a saltaire with phoenix on flame-nest superimposed. Arms of a doddering Irish earl in his eighties. He had two sons. One died in World War II, and the other popped off in 1956. Remarried, with no issue, was the Irish earl. Fat lot of help.

I looked around the pile of peerages and lesser landed gentry, junk from the old dead world. Five hours of scurrying through those pages, and this is all we've got?

The librarian smiled.

Librarians' smiles look like bookends.

And there wasn't a Latin tag, Mater Compassionem de Virgo, or any such mixture.

. . .

Next, the jewellers.

My tame silversmith said the trinket was nice work, maybe fifty years old. Haven't seen any of that coral around for a while. Cabochon turquoises, v. similar to your ring. Very nice amber. Bloodstones—hmm, not really possible to say where these particular bloodstones originated. Can tell you one thing though. The turquoise isn't American, and the gold is very pure. Nowd'youwannasell?

Fat lot of help.

. . .

The fuzz really tried to be helpful.

I have a sneaking suspicion they have a sneaking fondness for the bandit child. They let me read all the reports on the dead boatcrew, and the follow-up after. All more or less as Joe told it.

"How's young Gillayley getting on these days?" asked a young constable, brown dewy eyes and a fresh fluff of moustache. "No more escapades?"

"Not recently," said another, "been very quiet out there these days."

They all grinned at one another like it was a conspiracy.
Fat lot of help.

. . .

So then, after the jeweller, the police, the library, the hospital records, even the local, it was a dead end.

Think sideways.

I had a child who was so old.

Many tales of infamy.

One tale (I incline to the suspicion) of emotionally biased fact.

A ring that led nowhere (you ever meet a ring that went somewhere?).

A rosary that served as an endowment and nothing much else.

An unreachable boat, no registration number known.

Corpses in a graveyard, decently interred after neat indecent dissec-tions.

A strange wayward shut-and-bolted mind.

So what the hell, I wrote to the Irish earl.

Winter grew on—half a month more and it'll be the midyear school holidays, and the urchin won't need lies any more to cover the track of his days. He's grown a quarter of an inch, sideways. He looks that much less like a famine victim. The cheekbones don't sear through the skin so sharply. And he's not nearly as restless.

Behold, Holmes! Anchor and salvation of an erstwhile happy family. I hope. Joe is beamish—when he's not glowering. Joe? Don't let's digress any more, g. reader. But I better record this deathless bit:

Last month SP was an imp incarnate. We were shown a hectic quick-silver series of mood-reversals. For instance, one moment kneeling (it never sits) enjoying dinner, and the next, for some unknown reason, it slams the plate on the floor (the plate broke). No reason given: just a silent snarl as it tromped round my livingcircle, kicking at the windowbase. Stop that Sim. Kick. You'll break the berloody window and I'm sour enough about the plate. Another boot. Stop it you little bastard, or I'll stop you. And what does Simon the self-possessed do? Breaks down snivelling. Not cries of desolation. An abject self-pitying whimpering. Which continued, despite threats and blasphemy until Joe arrived to take him home (about 40 min-utes' worth). What are you crying for? asks the Kati Kahukunu (he's prob-ably my 23rd cousin but we haven't swapped whakapapa yet). Nothing, whines our Simon shaking his hair, nothing. Right, says Joe, belting him smartly across the arse, there's something to cry for. Now stop it.

I can see I do not possess the family touch.

Anyway, back to the reason I dragged you out of the cobweb pile, self-odyssey.

Today I got a letter.

It's an airmail letter.

A sheet of onionskin paper, with a heavily embossed coat of arms. Ah so, phoenix on flamebed and NON OMNIS MORIAR in gothic type underneath. I shall not all die?

> *Mr (sic) K. Holmes,*
> *The Tower, Taiaroa PB,*
> *Whangaroa, Wetland (Sic),*
> *New Zealand.*

Sir,

> *I am directed by His Lordship, the Earl of Conderry, to ac-*
> *knowledge the receipt by him of your letter dated April 30th. I*
> *am to inform you that, if the ring is genuine, and not a copy,*
> *then it belonged to His Lordship's younger grandson. This per-*
> *son, about whom His Lordship has no wish to know anything*
> *more whatsoever (underline, underline) was disinherited for*
> *disgraceful propensities four years ago. He is known to have*
> *resided in your country during his worldly peregrinations. His*
> *Lordship wishes you to understand clearly that he has nothing*
> *further to say on this subject, and asks that you refrain from*
> *entering into further correspondence with him on this, or any*
> *other matter. He will not reply to any such correspondence.*

> > *I am,*
> > > *Sir,*
> > > > *Yours faithfully,*
> > > > *scrawl.*

Apparently one Gabriel Semnet, Secretary to His Lordship the Earl of Conderry. Isn't that luverly? Can't you hear aristocratic nerves jangling all the way round the world? Sucks to his ancient overbearingness . . . though I do like that bit about disgraceful propensities. Wonder what they were? However, assuming this isn't a wild goose chase, I think I have a peer's re- mittance man to track down in his haunts of vice in this lowly colony of NZ.

I have a purpose in life again!

But I've also discovered I'm a snob. For my first thought on discovering there was a possible though improbable connection between Simon P and decayed Irish nobility, (bastardy? greatgrandsonship? the tenuous link of gifts?) was:

Ah hell, urchin, it doesn't matter, you can't help who your forbears were, and I realised as I thunk it, that I was revelling in the knowledge of my whakapapa and solid Lancashire and Hebridean ancestry. Stout commoners on the left side, and real rangatira on the right distaff side. A New Zealander through and through. Moanawhenua bones and heart and blood and brain. None of your (retch) import Poms or whateffers.

This is getting boring, ghost, I'm gonna immure you again. See you in another six years.

snapping the book shut.

. . .

"Did you know your son might have Irish connections?"

Joe sputters.

"The IRA? Yeah, I'd believe . . ."

"No, you silly bastard. Look at this."

He reads the letter, frowning.

"Where on earth did you come by this? I didn't know anything about it. . . ."

"I did the obvious thing. Went to the library and checked through the reference books until I found a coat of arms that matched that ring. You know, on his rosary. Then I wrote to the bod concerned and asked whether he had any antipodean relations who might be sporting such a thing, and that's the answer. I wish I could get a photograph of the old bugger. There might be family resemblances or something. To wit, Sim's split chin. Or the eyes. Or something. D'you reckon he looks Irish?"

Joe's still reading.

"Jesus," he says in a worried way, "what does he mean by disgraceful propensities?"

"Weelll, I should imagine in that ingrown aristocracy it could mean anything from an improper preference for Scotch whisky, to a practised predilection for raping the cat."

He chokes on his coffee.

. . .

There's a full moon up, and the growing night is cold, silver, serene.

Kerewin sits patiently, chin cupped in her hands, watching the suneater flicker, miss a beat, die.

It's run for quite a while after the sun went down. 18.55.25 she notes, stopping the watch, and entering the time. She adds another dot to the graph—yep, the gradual decline, an inverse phi curve. Strange that the suneater's curve keeps pace with some of her own.

She had begun a book of biorhythmic cycles for herself a long time ago, and when she first began to explore the little machines, she had been curious to find out whether they might reflect cycles too. The suneater's chart has been going for sixteen months: her set, for five years, six years o God this December. And I thought a year would be enough to discover the rhythms of my body and mind . . . I'll finish it this year. The thing's become an obsession.

For what does five years of accumulating snippets of wisdom add up to? Knowledge that I'm a changeable sort of person. . . .

O well.

She flicks the crystal casing of the suneater. Pretty toy. Pastime. As useful as all my other toys and time-passers. As useful and pointed as myself.

. . .

Joe, coming through the library circle doorway next night.

"Himi said you were up this . . . holy God, what is *that*?"

A blob of shining light, making butterfly oscillations.

It came from a mirror focused on a crystal to which was attached many fine copper wires. The crystal was set between two magnets, and it was turning blurringly fast.

"O that? One of my little um concoctions? Conundrums, anyway."

He came across and peered at it.

"It's a motor?"

"It might be if I could rig the thing up in some fashion to a driveshaft or belt. But the damn thing just goes phhfft! if you start hooking other bits to it. So I keep it like that, purring nicely along eating sunlight."

Eating sunlight . . . he winces.

"How did you make such a *thing*?"

Horror in his voice and eyes.

"You really wanna know?" She exudes fake eagerness to tell. "Well, I have a grasshopper and haphazard mind y'know, a brain that listens to all sorts of things as well as itself." Patter, patter. "Annnd, one day this idea plopped into my mind that mirrors and sunlight and crystals and magnets and whatnots *should* . . . anyway, my gut tingled the right way. So I made it." She flipped a hand at it. "Kerewin's little toy, mark 18."

"But how?"

"I dunno. I've made a lot of the little beasties. One works off steam produced by strong sunlight. Very sporadic. Not satisfactory. Another one that I *really* like works off goodtempered humans. At least, it only goes if you touch it, and only if you're happy. You sulk, it sulks . . . o, they're fascinating wee things but not useful, if you get what I mean?"

Joe shudders slightly.

"I haven't the faintest idea why they work. Or even how," she adds.

"You give me the cold bloody horrors sometimes, Kerewin."

She smiles, her smile full of fangs.

He thinks,

> Sometimes she seems ordinary. She is lonely. She drinks like I do, to keep away the ghosts. She's an outsider, like me. And then sometimes, she seems inhuman . . . like this Tower is inhuman. Comfortable to be in, pleasant, if you ignore the toadstools in the walls, and the little trees and glowworms in holes by the stairs, and the fact that nobody else in New Zealand lives in a Tower . . . maybe I've got it all wrong. . . .

He had thought, from Kerewin's guarded talk over the past month that she had broken up with her family over a relationship they didn't approve of. She didn't approve of? That her loneliness, being apart from her family, had driven her to this part of the country where none of them lived. He could understand that.

He shakes his head.

Don't worry your heart, Ngakau. Just *like* her.

He says to Kerewin's grin,

"If I had that thing in my house, I wouldn't sleep until I knew what made it work."

She picks it up.

"Here you are then."

It burrs on, quivering with light, whining with energy, unholy, in her hand.

"Shit no!" ducking even touching it. "I only meant that it's not normal . . . I've never even heard of anything like it, and if I'd made it, I'd want to find out o I dunno . . ."

"My poor innocent suneater . . ."

She's put it down, and is refocusing the mirror.

"It doesn't worry me. I figure if I'm meant to find out more about it, I will."

He shakes his head dubiously.

"You know what that reminds me of? Things Himi makes. Things he reckons make music."

"O yes. The music hutches . . ."

> . . . that had been a week ago, when she'd gone for a walk along the beach. The boy had tagged after. He sat down a little way apart when she stopped for a smoke. He started picking up debris off the beach, and randomly at first, and then with a steady and abnormal concentration, he had built a spiralling construction of marramgrass and shells and driftchips and seaweed.
> "What are you doing?"
> He whistled and pointed to it.
> It whistles?
> He lay down on the sand with his ear by it, and she went to him, puzzled. Simon got up quickly. Listen too, he said, touching his ear and pointing to her. So she did, and heard nothing. Listened very intently, and was suddenly aware that the pulse of her blood and the surge of the surf and the thin rustle of wind round the beaches were combining to make something like music.

She adds, "They only make music when someone's listening. They're focusing points more than anything, and I'd love to know where he got the idea for them."

Joe says sourly,

"O God knows where. He started making the bloody things about a year ago. Now he's obsessed by them."

He scowls.

(The child, when first discovered building them, had written for him THEY MAKE MUSIC. He was feeling wild and joyous from the vigour of the seawind and the roar of the sea, and had hugged him tightly, and called him a nutcase. But he was worried by the look in his eyes. Secretly, when Simon was sleeping his drugged uneasy sleep, he had stolen back down to the beach, and examined by torchlight the structure his strange little son had built.

Feeling foolish, he had lain down beside the husk and listened, absorbed, for nearly quarter of an hour. Then he became scared, squashed it flat, and strode home with the wind whining round his heels. Because he heard, thought he heard, a faint but growing music from Simon's creation . . . nothing he could really hear, a sound of darkness that seemed to sing . . . he had never told Simon about it, and he never listened to the music hutches again. And he stopped the child making them whenever he caught him at it.)

He says now,

"He's, he's disturbed enough without doing anything that adds to it."

"Is he adding to it? He might be lessening any disturbance by listening like that."

The scowl deepens.

"E Joe, I know about these things . . . I used to know a rock that talked, and look at me!"

He still frowns.

"Ah hell man, it took me years to realise I was projecting all my troubles through that rock. . . ."

She pats the desk by the suneater.

"Stop frowning. This fella won't stop for an hour or so yet. Come and get tea before the dark takes over."

. . .

They had begun competing as to who could produce the most unusual or tasty tea. It had become a kind of ritual, one night at the Tower, one night in town.

The day after Kerewin had gone to Pacific Street for the first time, Joe had rung and asked,

"Is ummm. . . ."

"Yeah, strangely enough."

They giggled at each other.

"Come and have tea here when you pick him up," said Kerewin. "We spent most of today catching an eel."

"Ka pai, but you let me get tea on say, Friday though?"

A cousin of his in Kaikoura providentially sent over kinas on the bus that day.

So Kerewin's next meal featured a salad with fourteen different greens in it, all plucked within a one-mile radius of the Tower. Sorrel, wild turnip, lambsquarters, dandelions, pikopiko curls, puha, cress, young yarrow . . . "In summer, I can make you an even better one," she said.

"I don't know," said Joe, between large mouthfuls, "this tastes good, but isn't that chickweed?"

"Yeah, and you know what else?"

"No. Please."

She told him anyway.

Joe's next entertainment was a fish-chowder.

"It's different," he assured her. "It's got fourteen kinds of eyeballs in it."

He had gone to especial trouble to get the fourteen different fish. "Even unfroze a whitebait," he told her. "Enjoying it?"

"Yeah," said Kerewin, deftly avoiding another eyeball. She noticed Joe wasn't too keen on swallowing them either.

He admitted when she finished, "There was really only cods' eyes there . . . unless you count the scallop's . . . but there truly was fourteen different kai moana. I thought you'd like the macabre touch?"

She looked at him consideringly.

"Mmmm. But you wait and see what's going to be lurking in my next offering."

. . .

Despite the hammer she gave him,
("Ah hah, worrying isn't it? Do you eat it, or does it eat you?")
tea this night turned out to be rock oysters.

"The only patch of rock oysters on this coast," says Kerewin tri-umphantly. "I couldn't believe it when I saw them first. I don't think anybody else knows about them. They're a freak colony. I've taken care of them since I found them, but I figured now they should be harvested for their own good."

They knocked them off the rocks in dozens—

"Kerewin, isn't this illegal?"

"Yep. Isn't it enjoyable?"—

and carried half a sackful stealthily away.

. . .

Back in the livingroom circle, Joe asks,

"Do you remember asking us if we wanted to come and have a holiday at a place of yours?"

"Yes." She looks at the dirty white shell, shining white and brown inside with purple shadows where the muscles had hung on.

"Well, I can take holidays soon, and Himi's got the May holi-days coming up. Can we?"

"Yes."

He wipes his hands on the seat of his jeans.

"You coming too?" very casually.

She bites the last oyster in half.

"Umm, I don't know."

. . .

It is very peaceful. Leaning back, eyes closed, she can hear the firecrackle, a rattle from something the boy is playing with, the rustle of Joe's paper.

"Hey, did you read this?"

"Nope. What?"

"Some tripe from these back-to-the-landers. You won't believe it, but here goes. . . .

"The breeding of guinea pigs requires a minimum of land, little time, and practically no outlay. They feed on scraps, grass-clippings et cetera, and their flesh is nourishing and tasty. They return a rea-sonable amount of meat per beast . . . shit, they give *recipes* even! I ask you, can't you just see Mrs Average slaughtering little Mary's pet guinea pig for the Sunday roast?"

She grins, eyes still shut.

"Nope, not yet. But if food ever got really short, I can see the knives come out all over suburbia . . . they've got a point, these fanatical fellas. The more self-sufficient you are the better."

"I had noticed . . . don't you bloody dare!"

The sudden yell jerks her eyes wide open.

The boy stands quickly as Joe orders, "Give them here. At once."

A box of matches, tossed to the man.

"Sailing bloody close to the wind, Haimona."

Simon stares back, unmoving, his body taut, his face hard.

Joe throws the box in the air, again and again.

"Just what in the name of all gods and little fishes is going on?" she asks plaintively.

Joe sighs. He catches the box a final time, then holds it up.

"He thinks it's funny to flick matches. You know how?"

He faces the fire, takes out a match, holds it against the striking strip with his thumb, and flicks it. The match flares explosively into flame and arcs into the fire.

"Dunno who taught him to do it," he says wearily. "Maybe he taught himself. But he had one all lined up ready for a go. At you."

She looks at the child, and then down at the floor. There's the match, lying right where the brat dropped it at Joe's yell.

You poisonous little creep.

"You," to Simon. He doesn't move.

"Turn round," Joe has a snap in his voice she hasn't heard before.

The boy turns slowly, insolently slow. He doesn't look at her, staring off to one side.

"I don't think that's funny, throwing fire at people. Why do you?"

The angular face is blank as a mask.

"Ah to hell with you then." Kerewin swivels her chair around, turning her back on him.

"What were you saying, Joe?"

He's still eyeing his son, his own face set and hard.

"Well," eyes unmoving, "Well, I was going to say that I had noticed this place is pretty self-sufficient."

She settles back in the chair again, and makes her voice low and easy.

"I'm a secret back-to-the-lander." She laughs. "Not really, but you know originally this place was going to be a dome or a yurt or an icosa. I was going to build it out of recycled goodies. Run goats and fowls, and a guinea-pig or two, and have a vegetable garden about six acres square. Then one night, while I was still in the planning stages, I sat down on the beach and thought, Holmes, what do *you* want? Because all these were other people's ideas . . . nothing wrong with them, but they didn't really fit me."

She lights her pipe, the flame glowing orange in the dim room. She can see Joe relaxing, his gaze now turned to her.

"I decided I didn't want livestock, because they demanded care and involvement . . . and anyway I'd never wanted *them*, just eggs and milk and meat. I could get that elsewhere. I'm a fisher, a forager, a hunter-gatherer, not a farmer. I don't grow much, though I like my herbs. . . ."

"And dandelions!" The man is smiling again.

"Wow, you've noticed . . . I'm probably the only person in the country who nurtures the dear golden souls."

Simon is still standing, left in the dark, rigid and lonely.

She does something she hasn't done before, turns and reaches to him, sitting him down on her knee. For a moment he stiffens, looks at her quickly, his eyes shuttered.

"You're making the place look untidy, wickedness," says Kerewin easily, but she won't smile at him. Something flickers in Simon's eyes, then he smiles tentatively, folding his lids over the light come back.

Don't look in. Nobody look in.

"Mind you," continuing as though she hadn't moved, "I also look after a stand of mushrooms hereabouts, and my patches of puha and my karengo beds are very carefully tended."

"Aue," Joe shakes his head. "E hoa, ka pai."

"What for?"

He stands up, and stretches, and doesn't say why. Just, "My turn to make coffee?"

Kerewin shrugs. "Okay. Good idea."

As he goes past them towards the bench, he reaches out and taps Simon's face. The boy flinches, but the tap can't hurt him.

"Lucky," says Joe, and continues on his way. For a moment, the boy is tense, then he smiles weakly at Kerewin—a lameduck grin, I'm wrong and I know it—and twists sideways, and leans against her.

"You going to sleep?"

He glances up, then puts his thumb in his mouth and starts sucking it.

"Yerk," says Kerewin, grimacing, but makes no other comment.

She says to Joe,

"This place is almost self-sufficient. The range can live off driftwood. There's a coal seam on the property I could mine, and extract kerosene for the lamps if I needed to. I've got four solar panels providing hot water, and two that charge the nicad batteries . . . only the stereo and the drawing light need the electricity anyway."

"Why the emphasis on self-sufficiency? Do you believe in the millenium or something?"

"Nope. I just like to be able to do most things for myself."

"I've noticed that too," says Joe.

. . .

Later that night he said, "You're very tactful."

"Peaceloving is the word. There seemed to be a fair sort of row brewing there."

He sucked in his breath. "It was a bad thing he was going to do."

The child is back in his arms, and sound asleep.

"There is a vicious streak in him, Kere, and I'm frightened it might be bred into him." Face full of gentle sadness, "I don't know what to do sometimes."

"Buggered if I would either. Probably pick up the nearest hunk of four-by-two and wallop him with it if he ever does flick a match at me. Warn him." She chuckled.

"Mmm . . . it's okay for adults, we can hit back, but he'll take on kids, and kids smaller than he is too. Like he fights a lot, when he's at school."

"Candidly, there can't be too many there who're smaller than he is."

"Maybe not . . . but he starts the fights I'm told. And he fights dirty."

"He likes fighting?"

"I don't think so . . . well, I don't know. Every time there's trouble, and I go along to find out what started *this* lot, I get about fourteen conflicting stories. But fairly often, Himi's started it. It's not always the others picking on him."

She puffed quietly on her pipe.

"You, uh, put a slightly different emphasis on a similar statement when you first came here."

He quirked his eyebrows and grinned, impishly. He looks so like Simon for a second that it's funny.

"I couldn't tell you all the bad bits at once."

She laughed.

"All things considered, I don't think he's too bad a kid."

"O true," said Joe quickly, "I mean, it's so bloody awkward for him not being able to talk out loud. He gets to screaming pitch very quickly with anyone who doesn't bother to try and understand him. Hardly anyone bothers. You're the rarity, eh."

"Yeah, rara avis all right," she kept her face straight.

"He, well, as for the others . . . they start off with good intentions, I think, but then they get embarrassed, or say he's cute, or put words into his mouth. . . ."

"Hassles," said Kerewin equably.

But she thought about it.

. . .

Just for an experiment, she went into Taiwhenuawera, where she hadn't been before, and spent the day as a mute.

She smiled at questions in pubs, and wrote down answers. She went into shops and bought things by listing them or pointing. She had quite a time getting a bus ticket back to Whangaroa.

It was infuriating. Everyone she met talked more loudly than normal, as though the volume would penetrate the barrier of her silence. Many people stared and whispered to each other behind their hands. And some, kind in manner, simplified their speech and repeated key words, as though she were dumb as well as mute.

. . .

II

On the Friday night of bad memory, she had gone into her cellar, cultivated spiderwebs and all, and selected a bottle of dandelion wine, first of the vintage she laid down a year before.

She is just sitting down to admire the bottle, 1979 says the label, Estate bottled, when the radiophone goes.

It's Joe.

"Tena koe," he says.

His voice sounds odd, hesitant, timid.

"Tena koe."

Pause.

"Uh, Haimona there?"

"No, haven't seen him today. I thought he was going to school?"

"He was, but I've just met Bill Drew and he says Himi didn't turn up."

His voice has returned to normal.

She can hear the background clamour now.

Joe adds, "There was a bit of fuss this morning. He wanted to go and see you, and I insisted he went to school."

"Fair enough. He hasn't been all week."

"He didn't think so. I had to play heavy father." Pause. "Looks like he skipped it, anyway."

She hears a door bang, and the noise of voices and laughter becomes louder.

"Just a minute, Kere. . . ." Muffled sounds. He's covered the speaking end. "You still there?" he asks a moment later.

"Of course."

"That was Polly Acker, eh." He laughs. "You know, the lady with Pi Kopunui?"

"No, I don't . . . wait a mo, is she the one they call the half-n-halfer?"

"Yeah! Half-and-halfer!" He sputters. Now he sounds drunk. "Anyway she just said she saw Haimona at Tainuis' this afternoon. By the gate. So that settles that, eh?"

"Mmm."

"Probably didn't want to go to you because he thought you'd tell on him eh."

She is obscurely hurt by that.

"Bloody hell, Joe, I'm not your son's keeper. I don't give a damn what he does and where he goes, as long as he doesn't annoy me. I'd no more *tell* on him than. . . ."

"Easy, e hoa, easy. I was just joking sort of . . . uhh, what's the time?"

"Close to six." It's getting dark, outside.

"You doing anything important? Because it's my turn for tea, ne?"

"Well, nooo . . ."

The fire's bright. Bream is playing Recuerdos d'Alhambra in the background. Half a dozen potatoes, still in their jackets, are baking in the oven. She's made garlic butter, and has two ham steaks ready to fry. The dusty bottle waits, wine glinting golden inside.

The first bottle . . . to drink and eat in peace, in music. She's had little enough of her own company these past few weeks, and she is beginning to hunger for solitude.

"Look, what say you come here? I'll send a taxi, you have a night out, meet some of my friends? I'll arrange for a meal."

"What about Sim?"

"O him, he'll be okay at Tainuis'. Marama and Wherahiko think the sun shines outa his arse excuse me. He's the whitehaired boy round there, literally. You'll come? Please?"

Goodbye potatoes in their jackets, ham, and Bream, and dandelion wine . . . because who's the only live and caring chessplaying friend you got round here?

"Okay man. I'll see you say, in half an hour?"

Joe says O hell good, that's good.

"You at the Duke?"

"Course!" The background racket blares up again. "God, here's
Pi. Looking for his missus." Giggle. "See you Kerewin." Clunk.

She stands looking at the radiophone.

> Dammit. I don't want to go out. I don't feel like it at all.
> On the other hand, for a friend he don't ask much . . . he's
> given more than he's got, even taking childminding—if I
> can in all conscience call my casual overseeing 'minding'—
> into account.

She puts on her denim jacket, scraping a fishscale off one sleeve,
then asks the radiophone operator to get her a taxi.

It's the talkative one. Old Eyes-and-Ears. Not to mention tongue.

"Hear you and Simon Gillayley have hit it off?"

"He's a much maligned child."

"And Joe too, they say."

"They say what?"

"O, just that you've been to his place, and he's been to your
place." He adds hastily,

"They say it nicely."

"They couldn't say otherwise, considering."

"Your taxi's on its way. Uh, considering what?"

"Innocence, built-in chaperone, and the laws of slander," says
Kerewin curtly.

The operator choked.

"Of course," he says in a neutral tone. "Of, course."

"Would you put in a call to Wherahiko Tainui please?"

"Well, they're still over the hill at the moment. . . ."

"No they're not. Simon's round there now."

Silence.

"He might be with Piri Tainui, would you mean Piri Tainui?"

He's speaking very cautiously. "I'm sure the old people aren't
back yet."

She frowns at the mike, "You're positive?"

"I've had a telegram to ring through to them as soon as they
got back. I've been trying their number every quarter of an
hour."

"That's very odd. Would you try Piri then, please?"

The operator breathes heavily.

"I'd like to, but I saw him down at the New Railway just before

I came on shift, and I don't think anyone could raise him at the moment."

"But you said. . . ."

"I meant the boy could be at his house. And that hasn't got the phone on. It's the sleepout on Tainuis' farm. Lynn and co used to live there with Piri, and Simon used to go there a lot. Before."

She ignores the invitation to gossip.

"Well, that is berloody odd. I wonder where he's got to then?"

"Uh o," says the operator. "We've been expecting this. You like me to ring Sergeant Trover?"

"No. I'll check with Joe first. Thanks all the same." You incredible busybody you.

"That's all right," says the operator happily. "Have a nice time." Click.

. . .

The taxidriver was taciturn. He said Good evening. Yes to her directions, and nothing thereafter.

She walked up the driveway of the Tainui farm, shivering.

Another frost. . . .

Two dogs in a wire run began to yelp and snarl as she came near the house. There weren't any lights on. She could see the dark bulk of the sleepout: no lights there either. She knocked on the door of the house. No answer. Walked to the sleepout and yelled,

"E Himi! You there?"

The dogs barked louder.

Nothing else stirred.

"Ahh to hell," and walked back to the taxi.

"Pacific Street now."

The taxidriver grunted.

It was darker and colder by the time they arrived at Pacific Street.

There was milk in the box at the front gate. She collected it, checked the letterbox for mail, and tramped up to the front door.

It stood slightly ajar,

"Simon?"

She stands in the hallway, listening.

No sound.

She walks into the kitchen and switches the light on. There's a plate on the bench by the sink, and another in pieces on the floor.

"You just throw whatever's handy when you get wild?"

"Uh huh. From your tea to a certain half gallon of beer on a Saturday morning."

Breakfast too, by the look of things . . . she puts the milk in the fridge, and then examines the floor. The plate had been partly filled with porridge: there were splatters of the stuff all over the place. She picks up the broken pieces of plate and puts them on the bench, and cleans up the rest of the mess. She notices that while Joe has left it, he has rinsed his own plate.

The budgie hasn't been covered, the milk hasn't been taken in . . . looks like nobody has been here since this morning . . . so much for hunches, thinks Kerewin. Anyway, if Joe is happy about him roaming all round the show, why should I worry?

As she walks out to the gate, the smell of the sea comes strongly.

Of course, she thinks, it's only a couple of hundred yards to the wharves.

. . .

The smell of the sea was the smell of blood.

He didn't know why the two should smell the same, because they were very different, but they seemed to be inextricably mingled. Where one was, there was the other.

From where he knelt, it was easy to watch the Tower door.

Kerewin had left. Joe hadn't arrived.

He unwrapped the sack from round himself, and stood unsteadily, shivering.

It's all quiet.

Stupid Clare, he says inside himself, as he limps towards the Tower.

He has called himself that, Clare, Claro, ever since he can remember. He doesn't know if that's his name, and he's never told it to anyone. He has a feeling if he does, he'll die.

Stupid Clare, again and again, with each halt step.

If he hadn't thrown the plate, he wouldn't have got the kicks.

On the other hand, if he hadn't thrown the plate, it might have got worse.

As it is, his face is hot and numb at the same time, and he is light-headed.

I hope it is warm. O Clare, I hope it is warm.

. . .

Joe stands beaming at the door.

"Tena koe!" he cries. "Haere mai, nau mai, haere mai!"

Two or three of the regulars look up from their beer.

Shillin' Price says, "Gidday Kerewin." The barman nods to her.

Joe yells,

"Meet Pi! Missus! And Polly!"

There's a group of people in this corner. Shrouded in smoke, the brown faces stare at her with bright unfriendly eyes.

"Tena koutou, tena koutou," she says, "tena koutou katoa." As always, she wants to whip out a certified copy of her whakapapa, preferably with illustrative photographs (most of her brothers, uncles, aunts and cousins on her mother's side, are much more Maori looking than she is). "Look! I am really one of you," she could say. "Well, at least some of me is. . . ."

"Tena koutou katoa," she says again, lamely.

The old lady Joe had called Missus looks at her keenly, grunts, then says "Heh heh heh."

Polly Ackers spares a glance from her cardplaying to grin at Kerewin, glower at Joe.

"Your turn, fuckwit," she says to Pi.

Pi Kopunui (Joe enlarges, "Pi, he's a cousin on my mother's side eh." High pitched giggling. "Most of them are Tainuis of one kind or another") picks up a card, lays a card down.

"Game," he says briefly to Polly Ackers, then turns to Kerewin.

He comes across and hongis. He is warm and big and smells strongly of beer. "Tena koe, kei te pehea koe?" he says, hugging her. "Joe's said a lot about you these past weeks."

He whispers, "He's got a skinful."

A skinful?

O, he's drunk. . . .

Very.

He's very glad she came, Joe tells her and the whole pub, six or seven times.

Kerewin begins to think of many reasons why she should suddenly go back home.

But after another jug, the man quietens, pales, excuses himself. He comes back looking rather more sober.

The old lady grins.

"He puku mate, nei?" Heh heh heh.

She has a husky kind of chuckle, like a mummified laugh.

Joe grins back at her, weakly. "Ae."

A moment later he says, "Kerewin? Like to come have a meal now?" His voice lowers,

"Sorry about all that."

"That's okay." To hell, everyone gets drunk once in a while.

"I was uh worried that you might not want to come out with me."

"I see."

"I've got a meal arranged. . . ."

"Well, we might as well have it then."

He looks round the pub.

"Piri was coming along too, but I don't see him. He must have flaked."

"At the New Railway as a matter of fact."

"O?"

"The phone operator mentioned it. When I asked him to ring round and find out where Simon had got to."

Joe grips the back of the chair.

"O, Himi's okay. He'll be with the Tainuis."

"He won't. They're over the hill. Still. And he isn't at your place either. I checked."

Anger is welling up in her. Joe doesn't give a damn where the child has gone. And he must have known the Tainuis weren't home when he rang her.

O yes, he knew all right.

His head is downbent, and his knuckles have gone pale on the top of the chair.

Pi is looking at him, and shaking his head slightly. The old lady has stopped puffing her pipe. She holds it inches in front of her, poised and still. Polly is frowning, her eyes fixed on the cards.

Joe sighs, relaxes his grip on the chairback, shrugs.

"E hoa, I'm *used* to him going off, remember. He knows how to look after himself. That's why I'm not worrying much. Everyone knows him, eh . . . hell, I expect Morrison or Trover any moment."

There's a forced cheerfulness in his voice.

The other three are all looking at him now.

"Don't you worry, he'll be okay." He reaches for her shoulder, laying his hand there. "But thanks very much for taking a look for him."

She hasn't watched his face fully. She has been looking at Pi and Polly and the old woman. They have all looked at each other and then down at the table, and avoided looking at Joe again.

She has a strange feeling that a chance has passed, but she could not describe the nature of the chance, or even why she feels there was one.

. . .

For the first time since they met, she feels alienated from Joe.

All the while she ate and drank and talked smoothly, inconsequentially, the feeling that there was something very wrong between them grew and grew, until there was a wall up.

A glass wall: she talked, watched him respond to the words, watched his words come at her, made a suitable reply. Nothing communicated.

She was glad when Joe said with embarrassment that it ah was rather late, and uh, he would have to get up very early to check on his son's whereabouts, and ah. . . .

His face looks slack and debauched and aged.

"Right," she said cordially, not looking again at his ruined face, "thanks for the evening. I'll see myself home, and if the boy turns up, I'll let you know."

. . .

The door is shut.

She had left it pulled to, with the handle on halfcock.

She knows he will be inside.

"Sim? You there?"

Her voice echoes.

No whistle. No fingersnap. No sound.

She shucks off her jacket, and goes silently up the stairs.

No sound yet.

The fire has died down. The coals are coated with ash and little light escapes, but there is still enough for her to see the shape of the child kneeling on the sheepskin mat, head on his arms, arms resting on the hearthbox.

"Haimona? Simon?"

He doesn't stir. His breathing is even, but somehow thick.

Stupid kid, out all day and caught himself a cold I'll bet. And that's a damned uncomfortable position to sleep in. But then he's got a knack of going to sleep at peculiar angles.

She lights the lamp, stirs up the fire, moving quietly.

The child doesn't move.

At last she says, "Hey Haimona," taking him by the shoulders.

Bed for you, boyo, and berloody oath, that means I get the sleeping bag and the floor again, and

Shit and hell.

The child looks up at her, and there's the ghost of a grin on his battered face.

O hell, you haven't been asleep. . . .

Then he turns away, his hand holding hers, and his hand is shaking.

"O shit and hell," she says aloud, but this time she moves, crouching down beside him.

"O hell, boy, what've you been doing to yourself?"

As gently as she can, she turns his head back, hand under his chin. He doesn't resist but he keeps his eyes closed.

His eyelids are swollen, buddhalike, and purple. His lower lip is split, and blood has dried blackly in the corners of his mouth. Bruises across the highboned cheeks, and already they're dark.

He has been struck hard and repeatedly across his face.

She looks at the hands still holding hers. Unmarked.

"Joe hit you?" her voice as neutral as she can make it.

He opens his eyes. No, he says silently, No.

"Who then?" anger running in a hot flood through her. "Bloody who?"

He stares through the slits of his swollen lids.

"Who, Sim?"

He moves his head reluctantly, side to side.

"Someone at school?"

The fingers say, No No No. . . .

"Damn it, someone you know? I know?"

The child is still.

"Ah sheeit, kid. . . ."

She stands, balling her fists, raises them in the air, lets them fall.

"You don't want to talk about it, okay. I'll just get you a doctor, ring Joe, and they can take it from there."

He gropes for his pad, not shifting his head. As Kerewin moves to the radiophone he holds a hand up, and she stops, still looking at him in that cold angry way.

NO DOCTOR JOE OK IM OK

"I'll bet," she says.

He holds his clasped hands up.

"You begging?" asks Kerewin sourly.

The hands come undone as he makes an affirmative.

"Well, don't. What's wrong with getting a doctor? You need one. You scared of them or something?"

A limp fingerfall.

She realises Yes isn't really an answer.

She looks down at him, shaking her head grimly.

> Supposing nothing's broken inside, his skull okay and none of his facebones cracked, then it's only cuts and bruises. It won't scar him. He'll heal well and quick enough. And it's late to call a medic out.
>
> But what if he's got . . . fractures, concussion, deeper damage?

"Joe can decide," and the child actually smiles.

Not very much, but enough for her to decide it's a smile rather than a grimace.

"I don't know, boy, I really don't. . . ."

The operator is surprised.

"Well, I never," he says chirpily, "at home all the time eh?"

"Not quite home, and not quite all the time . . . leave that in till Joe answers, will you?"

The burr-burr goes on for minutes.

"Anyhow, how'd you know he was here just from me ringing Joe?"

The operator giggles.

"Feedback. One of the good things about this job, y'know. Tass Dansy, you know him?"

"Yeah, by repute."

"Well, he saw Simon staggering along the road near your turnoff, and when he made a toll-call a coupla hours ago, I asked him, he told me, you know how it is?"

> With you, I can imagine.

"Mmmm, what do you mean, staggering?"

"Tass's word, not mine. Is the boy all right, or is something the matter?"

"He's okay. Just a minute, please. . . ."

She turns the sound down, and tells Simon, "Come over here." No please about it. The anger still burns.

He has folded himself back over the hearthbox. He stands awkwardly, and she can hear him hissing with the effort.

Staggering isn't quite the word, but he's limping badly . . . sweet hell, if I can get hold of the person who's knocked him round, I'll make them rue the day they were. . . .

"Hello?" says a voice in her ear.

"Hello Joe?"

"Uh, Kerewin? Uhh," she hears him rubbing his face, and the discreet clit! as the operator gets off the line.

"Sorry to wake you up man, but you can guess who's turned up?"

"Uh . . . . . . good."

> Even allowing he's tired, stupid with sleep, and still heavy with drink, that is one hell of a pause.

He asks hurriedly into her silence, "Everything's all right?"

"No."

Another silence. She hears the sound of his fingers massaging his face again.

"Has he done something wrong or something?"

"Or something. Joe, you didn't by any chance mean, when you said earlier that you'd had to play heavy father, that you'd bashed him?"

More silence.

"O no way," but the denial sounds wavery. "Sure, I hit him a couple of times, but—"

"Where?"

"Where you normally hit kids."

His breathing has quickened, and the slur from sleep and drink in his voice has gone.

"Not across his face?"

"Hell no . . . is he hurt there?"

The deep voice has sharpened with concern; the denial is positive. Now it sounds like Joe as she knows him.

"Well thank God for that."

"E?"

"Ah sorry, e hoa. For a horrid moment I thought, well, someone's been playing amateur gestapo, and I thought, I mean. . . ."

"O God . . . is Himi right there? Can I speak to him? Now?"

The child is weeping. He takes the mike, and taps it three times.

"E Himi, what's the matter? You all right?"

The small click of the child's nail tapping the receiver once, wait for it, twice.

"I'm glad," says Joe simply. Then he scolds, "Why didn't you come home? Why did you bother Kerewin? Why'd you. . . ."

It seems the tinny distant voice berates the child for minutes.

Kerewin, still wild at an unknown assailant, tires of the scolding quickly.

> Why bawl the brat out, when maybe it's not his fault,
> when maybe it happened near here, when he's hurt,
> and especially, when he can't answer?

She leans over and plucks the mike out of the boy's unresisting hand.

"You're being boring, Joe."

He stops, shocked. "O Kere, I didn't realise that—"

"Shit, man, he's hurt and all you can do is fill his ears with a diatribe? Be a bit realistic . . . do you want me to get a doctor?"

He says quickly,

"He's very scared of them. I don't think that'd be a good idea. Unless he's hurt badly?"

"Weelll, he's bruised. Bruised a lot. I don't think anything's really damaged though. You want to risk waiting for the morning?"

"That'd be best," says Joe promptly. "I'll pick him up before I go to work tomorrow, and we'll go see Lachlan then. For some reason, she's less of an ogre than the others."

"Okay. It's your kid . . . you want to tell him goodnight? He's not looking particularly happy."

In fact, he's still crying, leaning against the wall in a sagging hopeless fashion.

"Ae. E pai ana, e Kere, e pai ana."

"That's okay," but the thanks in Maori don't, this time, draw the normal emotional response. He could be saying The moon, the moon, going by what she feels.

"Here's Simon," she says.

"I'm sorry," says the man, "I'm truly sorry. I didn't mean to upset you, when you've been in trouble, to hurt you. I'm really sorry."

The little boy nods, apparently unconscious of the radiophone.

"Take care of yourself, e Himi, and we'll see you tomorrow morning, early. E moe koe, e tama, and kiss Kerewin goodnight for us. E moe koe."

The child holds the mike, staring into it through the blur of tears for quite a time after Joe has hung up.

. . .

She washed the boy's face with witch-hazel and warm water, and gave him a mug of hot milk that had honey and some of her manuka brew in it. Then she carried him up the spiral and deposited him on her bed.

It was after she'd collected her sleepingbag that she remembered the limp.

"What's the matter with your legs?"

OK, say his fingers, they're okay.

"Why're you limping then?"

He grimaces. He kicks at the air, a short distance only. But they're OK, the fingers assure her.

"Who kicked you?"

No response.

She shakes her head doubtfully.

"Your legs, boyo . . . you want some help for them?"

No. He looks at the floor, and then up at her, suddenly smiling. OK, he gestures again, firmly.

But it looked as though he had needed that moment to gather his strength to smile.

"Okay, Simon pake . . ." and Joe's word for him is right. The brat is as stubborn as they come, when he wants to be.

"You know how to turn that lamp off?"

Yes.

He's leaning against the bed now.

She asks again from the doorway, "Who did it, Sim?"

His face twists, but he says nothing.

She exhales noisily.

"So be it. Sleep well, sweet dreams."

But her impatience shows through her voice and gives the words a sardonic ring.

. . .

Joe arrived before seven the next morning, creeping up the stairs in the near dark and whistling her awake.

He clucked over his child's bruised face, over the obvious pain he showed walking, and—strangely to Kerewin's eyes—held Simon's hands a long moment, and said something very softly and very quickly, so she couldn't catch the words.

He refused coffee or breakfast for either of them.

"I've got an appointment, out of surgery, so I'll go along now," he said. "We'll see you soon."

She didn't see either of them for over a week.

. . .

"What else was there?"

She stands on the footpath, tapping the stick thoughtfully, carefully, against her teeth.

> Of course, tobacco. What you came to town originally
> for. Sweet hell, who else could blunder through life like
> this but me?

A car slams on its brakes, stopping with a squeal a couple of
yards before her. The driver curses and leans on his horn. Up you,
thinks Kerewin, and keeps on strolling across the road.

In the sweet tobacco-scented gloom of the little shop, she says
to Emmersen behind the counter,

"You ever noticed how the only time traffic moves in this
one-horse town is when you go to cross the street? I think they sit
there, waiting for hapless pedestrians."

Emmersen grins obligingly. He'd seen the near-accident from the
window. He doesn't say what he thinks. Kerewin is too good a customer.

"I managed to get you some more of that Dutch aromatic," he
says.

"Goodoh. I'll have it. Any Sobranies?"

His eyes flick to the side, "Gidday!" he says, and then he smiles
back at her, "I got some, yes."

A pair of thin hands wind themselves round the middle of the
stick at her side.

"Well, I never, look who's here. . . ."

Simon P, with a smile all over his face and his eyes green blue as
a hot summer sea.

Me! he mouths, and grins more broadly still.

"Yeah, who else?" she laughs and reaches a hand to him.

"Well, possibly me?"

Joe is standing in the shop doorway, with a grin as broad as his
son's.

"Berloody oath! I thought you two had gone walkabout or
something. . . ."

> Ah dammit, slow down heart . . . ridiculous, ridiculous,
> you who love your own company, you should be feel-
> ing dour not spasming with delight.

"Tena koe," he adds, and comes to her, and places his hands on
her shoulders, and hongis quickly. "If we'd known you were going
to be glad to see us, we would have come much sooner. . . ."

She shakes Simon's hand, "It's good to see you both again," peering hard at the boy, "and you're looking remarkably good."

"In all senses of the word," says Joe cheerfully. "Has it ever been a quiet week . . . better get him squashed like that more often eh?" He laughs and scuffles his hand through the boy's hair.

She feels her stomach muscles tense, and the joy leaves her.

"I think not," she says coolly.

But the child is swapping bright smiles with his da: they clearly think the idea funny.

Well, my soul, it takes all sorts to make a world. . . .

She shrugs lightly, and takes her hand from Simon's hold.

"The Sobranies?" she suggests to Emmersen. He is standing smirking at them.

"O yeah, right away . . . I got a couple of cartons of the black ones, OK?"

"Uh huh. Cigarillos?"

"Something new and special you may care to try . . . I'll just get 'em from the back."

He nods to Joe, smiles at Simon, and vanishes.

"Ahh," sighs Joe, positioning himself, back to the counter and resting on his elbows.

"Dunno how much you missed us, but we missed you a lot, truly," his dark eyes are serious. "And it was really because we thought you might like a rest from us that we didn't bother you."

"Considerate . . . I did wonder where you'd got to, briefly."

The boy is climbing his fingers up the whorls carved in the stick: his face is nearly clear of bruising. Only yellowing contusions round his eyes, and at the corners of his mouth. And he's moving easily—one way, she thinks, children have it all over adults. Fast clean healing.

She asks, "Did you find out who was responsible?"

Joe touches a finger to his lips, as Emmersen comes in. "Muri iho, e hoa."

"Have to learn to speak that, one of these days," Emmersen says. "Maybe I'm a bit old to learn though . . . how about these?"

"Never seen them before. Were they recommended or something?"

Emmersen opens a box.

"Try one," he offers. "The sales bloke reckoned they were strictly for connoisseurs, and I figured you were a connoisseur."

Joe giggles. "Knows how to sell, eh?"

"At connoisseur prices too, I'll bet." She sniffs the slim cigar and rolls it gently between her fingers. Tightly rolled leaf, not too dry. She lights it.

Everyone's looking at her, brown eyes, seagreen, pale-blue: all expectant, waiting for her decision. She keeps them waiting for three draws.

Then she says, "Weelll . . ." and passes it to Joe.

"O thanks . . ." He breathes out a fine plume of smoke. "Hmmm . . ." He hands it back.

Emmersen is twitching with ill-concealed suspense. He smiles anxiously, and she smiles blandly back.

"Haimona?"

She passes him down the cigarillo and the boy chuckles.

He leans against her, holding the smoke in front of him. He makes a performance of inhaling a mouthful, tasting it, and expelling the smoke in a thin jet.

Joe puts his hand over his mouth.

Emmersen's eyes are bulging, and he's gone a strange raspberry colour.

Kerewin asks the child, "You'd buy it, or you wouldn't?"

Emmersen chokes.

Simon hands it back to her. He scratches his head, holds his chin, darts a green glance at Emmersen, obviously wonders whether or no, and finally shakes his head.

Emmersen has gone redder still.

"O bad luck," says Kerewin. "Joe?"

"I like it actually. Bouquet a bit tart, and it hasn't got the bold maturity of your Cuban '65, and and . . ." he's starting to break up. "For goodness' sake, put the joker out of his misery, Kere."

Emmersen swallows. "I thought . . ." he begins, the flush fading from his face, leaving it normally sallow. He swallows again. "I thought," and there is a note of real misery in his voice.

Kerewin interrupts.

"I was in two minds about this purchase. I thought if I could have got a majority consensus . . . anyway, he's too young to know a decent smoke from your average dockleaf. I'll have what you've got. They are good."

Emmersen's sigh is loud with relief.

"Just for a moment there," shaking his head, "you had me worried . . ." he's smiling his nervous smile, "though I did think you were having me on, but . . . but. . . ."

Kerewin smiles too, her lips lean and her eyes narrow.

"But you never can tell for sure," she leers. "On the other hand, the day I take Simon's advice as to what to smoke, is the day I enter my dotage. Hell, *he* smokes his father's cigarettes."

Joe says, "Hey! What d'you mean . . . ?" and Simon giggles, and Emmersen, busily wrapping up the tobacco and Sobranies and cigarillos before she can change her mind, laughs uproariously.

. . .

Joe says with embarrassment they'd been looking for her, because uh he wondered if Himi could stay a couple of nights? He explains in a rush. Wherahiko Tainui's got a bad heart, he's been going over the hill for specialist treatment, now he's been told not to drive anymore, and Marama can't drive, Ben is busy, and Piri's tied up with his job, and the other son is outa town and,

"Berloody oath," Kerewin bangs the stick down hard on the road, "of course Simon can stay. I wondered where he had got the bad habit of begging from. I can hear, loud and clear."

Joe grins shyly. "Well you know, I don't want you to think I'm just using you, as a babysitter. Just visiting when convenient, even if it looks like that. Truly it isn't."

Kerewin says drily that if she had thought that, they'd've both got the message, weeks ago.

. . .

She asked, when Simon was in bed, why he wasn't staying with his Tainui relations. Joe looked away from her. "The less he stays there the better," he said bitterly. He never said despite his "Later," who had hit his son in the face, and Kerewin, sensing a family quarrel, didn't bring it up again either.

. . .

On the second day, Kerewin said,

"We'll make use of the fine weather. Both the tide and my stomach are right for pipi-hunting. So put your jacket on, eh."

She sighed luxuriously.

"And just think, muttonbirds next month, and the whitebait season soon after. Who could ask for more?"

Simon raised his eyebrows, and then put on a smile so she wouldn't notice the dark seeping into his eyes.

I could, he thought.

. . .

The truck stopped beside them, halfway to the beach.

"Kia ora korua," said Piri, climbing down out of the cab. He leant over to greet Simon, then stopped, as though the child had struck him. He tipped the boy's face towards him and studied it a moment.

"Run into another door?" said Piri lightly, and then he turned to Kerewin, his eyes hard. She shook her head, and he looked back again to the boy.

"You didn't run into a door," and Simon stared at him, his face unmoved. "Did you?" as he released the child.

Simon kept on staring at him, without moving his eyes. Piri bit his lip. He started to say something, stopped, then shrugged.

"O well," he said at last. "O well." He smiled quickly at Kerewin, his eyes still hard. "Nutty child, eh."

"Unlucky, but not, I think, witless."

Piri's real grin bloomed.

"Right. Tell Joe I need to see him about a dog when he gets back, eh." He kept on smiling. "He'll understand."

Simon has her hand, and is shaking it unobtrusively. Once, pause, once again. No. Don't. What? She glances at him, but he is staring at his feet.

"Okay, when I see him."

"Right you are," Piri climbs back into the cab. He slams the door. "You going to town or anywhere I can take you?"

"Just for a walk."

"Good day for it. We'll see you later then. E noho ra, Himi, Kerewin."

"Haere ra, e Piri."

Simon didn't let go her hand, nor did he wave goodbye.

The truck vanishes.

"Yeehai, boy, what was that all about? Don't you like Piri?"

He shrugs.

"Well, what was the handtugging in aid of?"

Nothing says the boy, a thumb and forefinger making O.

"I take it all back. You are nuts."

He shrugs again, looking at her with the bland say-nothing expression.

"Beach and pipis then."

. . .

"Here," she says, standing right on the edge of the low tide mark. She spades out sand with the butt of the harpoon stick, but water rises in the hole faster than she can throw it out. She resorts to shovelling with her hands. She jars her finger and whoops with delight.

A small triangular shell, like a chip of dirty china. She scooped it out and dug her knife into the back of it, severing the connector muscles. The shellfish went limp and oozed water. She tore off the top shell and cut the fish from the bottom one, and ate it.

He watches, his mouth agape in horror. She digs again, this time in the middle of a group of siphon holes, and uncovers a colony.

"Want one?" He closes his mouth with a snap, and shakes his head vehemently.

She chuckles, and prises another shrinking pipi from its shell.

He flutters his hand with distress.

"It moves, it's alive? Yeah, I know. So is an oyster when you eat it. And that was what you were enjoying a couple of weeks ago. Very nice, weren't they?"

His mouth draws down.

"I can assure you," speaking thickly, her mouth full of soft sweet and salt flesh, "that an organism like this doesn't feel pain as we do. It doesn't realise its impending death. It's just cut and gulp, and that's it for the pipi." I bloody hope so, anyway.

"You understand Sim?" Schloop, carve, swallow, as she downs another pipi.

The little boy quivers.

"Look, it would be wrong, very wrong, to eat a fowl or a frog alive supposing we had the stomach to do it. But not these."

She hopes he won't ask why, because she isn't sure herself. She suspects it's because even a lowly frog, not to mention a fowl, could make one hell of a racket as you gnawed 'em. All the helpless pipi could do, was spurt a feeble squirt of water and die between your teeth. Dammit kid, you've started to make me feel guilty.

The boy sighs.

He goes away by himself, and stands on all the tell-tale siphon holes.

She follows, and wherever his footprints become many, digs down, and brings up another horde of pipis, thanking the child in a loud voice as she does so, until Simon P is stamping any old where in despair.

"Hey!" she calls at last. "I've got enough. E tenderheart, it's all over, the massacre. You can stop protecting them now."

She giggles over the full kete, and he comes back dumb with rage and glowering, and hits at the bag.

"Go easy, fella. You'll damage yourself, doing that."

He shakes his head fiercely, and begins crying.

"Whatsamatter? You crying for them? Believe you me, this is what their mothers brought them up for. . . ."

Tears dribbling down, channeled toward his pointed chin, Kerewin, you piss me off. She grins at him, standing there hunched and miserable in the winter sun.

"Hell, I wasn't trying to upset you. Much, that is."

He doesn't smile.

"Berloody oath . . . look boy, to the best of my knowledge, and that's considerable, it doesn't hurt shellfish to be eaten straight from the shell. Not as it would hurt us to be gobbled up whole. I believe the scientific expression is, the shellfish receives a terminal negative stimulus, okay?"

> And I hope the multisyllables intrigue you enough to
> stop your weeping because I'm beginning to get some
> kind of guilty indigestion.

He sniffs, sighs resignedly, crouches down by her, and pats her shoulders. Then he holds out his hand.

"O?"

Points to his mouth, and the kete.

"You wanta pipi? After all that bloody fuss?"

She gives him two, ready shelled. He eats them slowly, screwing his face up and weeping all the while. He begs for more when he's finished.

"I do not understand kids," says Kerewin to the world at large, and gets up, to hunt for more pipi.

. . .

She lay back on her elbows and watched him wander along the beach. He fossicks, picking up tide debris, bringing it back to her.

She assumes he wants to know what they are, so identifies each object.

"Gull's feather. Wouldn't hazard a guess as to the species."

"That's a segment of sea biscuit. Not for eating, you silly little bugger. It's an echinoderm."

"Um, lamanaria of some kind . . . lessee, this is the Coast, and it's a roughish beach and the weed's got no side-spikes. Yep. Lessonia variegata for your information, boy, and get it to hell away from here. Sandflies love it for a breeding ground."

"Fishbone. Haven't the faintest idea as to what kind of fish, but the bone's a vertebra."

"*That* is part of an electric light bulb. Probably chucked overboard by a marauding squid boat. I wouldn't bother keeping it, unless you want to go in for some kind of revengeful voodoo. Then I'll help you."

"O those. Co-eye, kor-fie, alla same tree."

He wrinkles his nose, Yeah?

"That's part of a poem, believe it or not. These are seeds of a tree, golden seeds for golden flowers, seaborne to make more sea-trees. Well, it's a coast-dweller, anyway."

He's still puzzled.

"The kowhai is a tall thin tree, with greybrown bark. It blooms in the earliest part of spring, with flowers that the tui and korimako love. It likes coastal areas, and lets its seeds fall into rivers and the sea. And they are carried to other beaches so the kowhai blooms through the land. A sea-tree emblem for a sea-people, only the people haven't woken up to the fact they *are* a sea-people yet . . . anyway, co-eye English pronunciation, kor-fie Maori pronunciation, alla same tree, getit?"

He reaches over and pats her on the shoulder again. It is a curiously adult gesture from a small boy. He smiles as he does it. Don't get upset, Kerewin, I believe you.

Romance on.

Kerewin lifts her eyebrows until they disappear into the brown bush of her hair.

"And the same to you, urchin ... collect as many as you can, and I'll show you how to make a necklace from them. Made so you can plant the seeds at a later date, if you want."

He comes back with a handful and puts them carefully in her pocket. Wanders off down the strand again.

The wayward brat ... she squints at the winter sun, and closes her eyes. She keeps seeing scarlet patterns that jiggle and flash.

A touch on her hand.

She stiffens, then relaxes.

"What's up?" closing her eyes again.

He blows in her ear gently, and she shudders at the unexpected breath.

"Meaning?"

He sits back on his heels, and smiles with half-closed eyes, shaking his head all the while.

> He'd thought,
> knowing names is nice, but it don't mean much. Knowing this is a whatever she said is neat, but it don't change it. Names aren't much. The things are.

Laughing secretly at himself. Because you can't say names, Clare. But he'd come back anyway, and blown into her ear.

> A whole stream of names that is. Do you like them? Segment-lamanaria-vertebrae-lessonia-variegata-marauding-voodoo-korfie and ALL.

Her eyes flicked open quick again, and were as sharp and threatening as glass splinters.

It was just air, see? he'd thought hurriedly, my hand was more real, see? But Kerewin didn't ever get really wild. She just sat there, frowning at him.

> She'll get to know it, one of these days

He'd sat, smiling his knowall smile into the sun, until, tired of making explanations for words, he lay down and went to sleep.

The first thing he saw, right by his eyes when he wakened, was the sea biscuit shard. He took his time about waking, doing it slowly (because it is Kerewin sitting there, still squinting at the sun, still dreaming) until he was clearheaded and calm. Then he picked up the shard: still lying sprawled, he started building. The sea biscuit in the centre, a network of dry marramgrass stalks on top, the feather, a sliver of driftwood, a seaweed bladder, a pipi shell . . . putting them together neatly, quickly, and it seemed to Kerewin's bemused eyes, inevitably . . . it finally stands about six inches high, sturdy yet delicate, an odd little temple, a pivot for sounds to swing round. . . .

He moved a few inches to lie down beside it, ear nearly touching the thing.

Slowly his eyes closed, and his mouth loosened, opened. His expression was one of rapture.

. . .

Is it being trusted?

She tamps the tobacco into the bowl more firmly.

It's almost a feeling of protection I have . . . because he's leaving himself so wide open? I could sneer, or scold, or stomp on it, or him . . . but he seems to have decided I'll do none of these things. So that's him trusting me, and this, this *peculiar* sensation that tightens my chest and throat is the spinoff.

The snark says, Maybe he's discovered how to use a new kind of soundwaves. You know what happens with subsonics. . . .
Ah shuddup. . . .
The child is motionless. If she listens very carefully, she can hear his breathing. It is abnormally slow.

Simon P. Gillayley, no wonder you're considered an oddball. Emotionally disturbed, not all there, says the grapevine . . . do you do it often, lie before what's essentially a rubbishpile and fall into a trance? What with

that, and fighting, and stealing, and absconding from
school not to mention home . . . and anything else I
haven't heard about yet? . . . the hat fits. The reputation's deserved. And yet . . .

Unbidden the thought drifts in, Why does he trust me?

Why should he trust me? I don't trust anyone, I've
never trusted anyone. Not even as a child, when everyone is supposed to be innocent enough to trust the
world. Maybe I became too early aware of myself, aware
of the shivered base that we all have to build on.

"You're too clever for your own good," they'd said, her parents
and relations, friends and enemies. She poohpoohed it every time.
"Nobody can be too clever," she retorted, missing the point. She'd
decided before she was twenty, that they were right after all. She
knew too much. The smarter you are, the more you know, the less
reason you have to trust or love or confide.

So this one is very stupid?

Simon touches her hand. His eyes are wide open and sparkling,
and he's grinning fit to split his face.

. . .

III

"E hine!"
She comes to the car.
"Joe'll be here in a minute."
"I know. How are you? Well in every respect?"
"Yes. I'm fine."
"That's good." He sits back into the shadows a little, his hands
folded in his lap.
His face is tired but his eyes are stern, aloof. He is not a friendly
looking man.
His wife, smiling and nodding with every phrase he says but
not so far venturing a word herself, is small and plump and full of
friendship. She had waved out before the car stopped, snared

Simon and cuddled him, crooning over him while the old man sat stiff and straight and unsmiling in the back.

Wherahiko Tainui asks, "Was it a good two days?"

"Fair enough. The weather was good."

"And what do you think of him?"

"Who?"

"Joe's boy, Haimona."

"O, Sim." She rubs her forehead thinking, This is an inquisition and so far they haven't even bothered to introduce themselves. Well, Joe said over his shoulder, This is Kerewin, before catching his child up, but neither of them had acknowledged it. She says coolly, "He strikes me as being older than his supposed years, and sort of wild."

"Wild?" Wherahiko pounced on it as though it was an insult, "wild?"

She shrugs.

"As though he is growing up wild. Fey."

Marama says comfortably, "I think I know what Kerewin means, love," beaming at her. "He seems older because he doesn't act like most kids, and he seems wild because he does unexpected things."

"That's more or less it. Wild in the uncontrolled sense."

Wherahiko grunts. Marama says,

"We've heard so much about you, dear. Why haven't you called in?"

"Well. . . ."

"You were probably waiting for an invitation," says Wherahiko, and all of a sudden he smiles, and the wrinkles and creases cause his face to lose all its fierceness. "Now you've got it," he adds, and Marama says, "Anytime you'll be welcome, any time at all."

"Well, thanks. I will call in." Within the next decade, she thinks, still cool at being treated in what she considers to be a rude and casual manner.

"Tomorrow," says Wherahiko.

"What?" She is startled.

He stabs a finger toward Joe and Simon coming over the lawn. "We want to talk to you, or at least, I want to talk to you . . . Marama can have you after," he grins again. Then his face falls back into its ordinary severity. He whispers, "I need to talk to you about them both."

And she turns bewildered, to watch Joe and Simon laughing and sparring in the sunshine. Two days apart, and they make it seem a year of bitter separation by the way they carry on reunited.

"Tomorrow then dear?" Marama is saying. "Any time you like, Kerewin love," and the two old people flash her smiles.

. . .

"I'm invited to the Tainuis' tomorrow," she says to Joe, "and I'm buggered if I know why."

"O, they been wanting to meet you for a while now." He shrugs one shoulder. "I thought they'd never get round to asking you though. They're both very shy."

"That's one thing they didn't strike me as being . . . I'm a shrinking flower in my own fashion, so what're you doing tomorrow?"

"Avoiding Marama or Wherahiko, I hope," and he says, after her startled "What?" "O there's been trouble between us that goes back to Hana's death. We had a proper go coming back over the hill." He shrugs that uneasy one shoulder lift again, as though he is hunching to take a blow on his body instead of his face. "It started when I wouldn't let them have Himi to look after when Hana died. They never forgave me. They still think I'm making a pissawful job of bringing him up. Whatever I do with him is wrong . . . they'll probably tell you some awful lies about him and me."

Kerewin laughs.

"As though I'd believe them . . . I've seen enough to know you're doing a great job. You've got patience and time and love, and that's what he needs."

He looks at her quickly,

"Yeah, that's what he needs . . . would you mind if I didn't come with you then?"

"Okay. I might see if I can invent an excuse for not going anyway."

He looks unhappy, but he smiles gently at her.

. . .

Jesus, thought Joe, this whole thing is going to explode and come crashing down round my ears, but what can I do? What in the name of heaven can I do?

It's not wrong, he tells himself. Well, not bad wrong. What else is there to do?

He won't listen, he won't behave, he won't do as I say, what else is there?

He hugs himself, deriding the movement of self-sympathy as he makes it (Ngakau, you're as bad as he is).

The feeling of roosting in a false calm, knowing that the mother of all hurricanes was about to break loose and destroy the world, was getting stronger daily.

You should explain it, he says to himself forlornly. She'll probably understand . . . if they just tell her pointblank . . . he shudders. I can't tell her yet, it's not the right time. She doesn't know us well enough, know me well enough. Anyway hell, it's not *wrong.*

He dreads tomorrow.

. . .

She remembers the afternoon as a golden easy haze, wound through with talk and laughter. A sweet three hours with the only jarring note her own conscience.

And you were going to turn them down cold.

Drinking the wine Marama bought especially for her visit ("We don't drink," says the old lady, and Wherahiko adds, "The doctor told her and me if we boozed, we'd keel straight over. I don't believe him," he chuckles richly, "but I'm not dead keen to prove him right, eh"): eating the food that had been especially prepared for her ("Ben killed the pig last night when we got home, eh. Nothing like really fresh pork for a roast, though I'd choose to hang him for a while if I wanted him for a pickle.").

And you were going to say you had to see a man about a dog or some such. . . .

She recalls suddenly, while Wherahiko is showing her the family photo album (there is a wedding picture of Joe and Hana, and a family shot of the Gillayleys in their heyday, Joe beaming, Hana a serene non-smiler, Timote a toothless grin, and Simon looking wild and smaller and unhappy, his fingers wrapped in Hana's skirt—"He used to hate having his photo taken," says Marama fondly, as she looks over her husband's shoulder), that Piri had said he wanted to see Joe about a dog.

Piri is still at work. The only other brother here is the eldest son Ben, a short nuggety blackbrowed man who seldom smiles. When he does, it is slow and beautiful like a rare flower unfolding.

Wherahiko asks a lot of questions, about herself, about her work, about the Tower, about her view of the world.

Marama asks a lot of questions, too: what does she think of Joe? what does she think of Himi? What does she think of solo parents? What does she think of Whangaroa? It is always Himi she comes back to. The child is ever Haimona/Himi here, never Simon or Sim. She tells anecdote after story after joke about him and his father. But it is gentle humour, as the inquisition of herself is gentle, and they offer a lot of information about themselves while they question.

They show her over the farm. They hold one another often, two old people sick in body and sound in mind, still eager for life, still eager to share it. When she leaves, they hongi, then hug her in farewell.

"Come back soon!" calls Marama, waving goodbye behind the gate.

"I will too!" she calls back, "very soon!"

She means it. It's been a delightful time.

It's only in the dark of the Tower that she realises they never told her anything about Joe and Simon she didn't really already know.

. . .

On Wednesday, Joe rang at midday.

"Hello, guess who's got the afternoon off?"

"You, by the sound of it."

"Right! The stupid machine I push levers on has broken itself, thank God. While they fix it, they said to clear off and enjoy myself on the company's time. I didn't need to be told twice."

"Understandable . . . what do you want to do? Go fishing or something?"

"Well I thought, since Haimona's at school for once, if you're maybe free?"

"I am." Mooning over old and beautiful sketches she had done two years ago was only being involved in sour reminiscence.

"E ka pai . . . well, I thought you might like a drink at the pub. Not like last time," he says hastily, "hell, was I ever sorry about that . . . I was almost glad Himi was hurt, because it meant I didn't have to stay round too long."

"I'm an ogre?" she asks incredulously.

"O no," he sounds shocked. "What I meant was that I had behaved badly, and you knew it, and I knew it, and I knew you knew it."

"Well, to say something very original, that morning I knew you knew I knew you knew, you know. So to speak."

He giggles.

"You do have a knack of saying things *so* unequivocally."

"Shuddup. I'll see you down at the Duke in about an hour?"

"Beaudy."

. . .

And this afternoon is flowing along nicely on small talk and beer. Two in a row, great! she thinks. Then Piri comes over.

"Gidday," she says, grinning happily.

"Gidday," he replies, with a grin for her: it flits over his face and is gone by the time he looks at Joe.

"Get up. I want to talk to you."

Joe puts his schooner down slowly. "Why? I'm drinking with Kerewin. What's so important that you think you can interrupt us?"

"You know bloody well what. Excuse us. Kere."

"Okay," she says with surprise.

> There's a side to that little man I would never have expected.
> All steel and anger . . . he's walking away as edgy as a cat to a fight.

And Joe walks meekly after him.

Piri says at the other side of the room,

"Have you told Kerewin?"

"Sweet Jesus, no."

"That's the only reason Pa held off. You tell her first, and make it bloody soon. If you don't, we will. He says you deserve that chance. I don't think so."

"Piri, I need a little more time, just a bit," his face twists as Piri turns away, pursing his lips in disgust. "Look, I'm begging you. Just some more time . . . I don't want to ruin things."

Piri looks at him with unveiled contempt.

"Ruin what? You've already done the ruining."

"Ah hell, I'm under pressure all the time. You don't know what it is to be lonely," he stops quickly, recalling Piri's runaway wife. "I mean, I can't help it if I blow sometimes. And you know it's not just bloody one-sided. He's—"

"Shut up." Piri leans his head back, his eyes half-closed, as though the full sight of his cousin was more than he could stand. "You've turned sour, Joe. You're bent. You've got all the resources of family in the world, and you won't let us help. We've stood enough of it. You're spoiling something special and bright and you fucking know it. I think you enjoy it."

"Don't talk stupid, I don't enjoy—"

"Shut up. That was the last time. You do it again, and it's not just Kerewin we'll clue up. And not just Kerewin's company you'll lose."

He swung on his heel and went out.

Joe looks down, his eyes filling with tears. "You degenerate bastard," he says, but he doesn't mean it for Piri. "There's your word to go ahead," he tells himself. He shrugs hard, as though to dislodge something clutching his shoulders, and goes back to Kerewin.

"Everything okay?"

Now's the time.

But he freezes at the thought of telling. Not yet, he thinks, smiling desperately, I *can't* tell her yet . . .

"Yeah, just another snarl-up with damn Tainuis, eh," pushing his hand out as though pushing the quarrel away. "Okay me and Himi go on that holiday sometime next week? When school breaks up?"

"Surely."

Why the tears, man? Why the tears glittering at the sides of your eyes?

. . .

A little while later, a lot of beer later, small talk under the bridge and the deep talk now beginning to flow, there's another interruption.

A slender man glides up and stands by Joe. He has a permanent smile fixed to his face.

"Well, well . . . do introduce us, my dear?"

"Jesus! What're you doing here?"

The man smiles a little harder. "*Always* a case of mistaken identity . . . I don't know how I do it." The smile razors coldly over Kerewin. "*This* is a change . . . aren't you going to introduce us?"

Joe grimaces. "E hoa, this is another Tainui, Luce Mihi by name. Luce, Kerewin Holmes, an artist."

The man raises his eyebrows.

"Really?" His handshake is cool, his hand limp.

Affected twit, she thinks, smiling as artificially back while saying, "Glad to meet you, the place seems littered with Tainuis."

"O, *littered*'s the word, m'dear. Too apt."

He turns his smile deliberately back to Joe.

"Well, shall I sit down, my kissing coz?"

"Why?" asks Joe harshly.

"Thanks, sweeting. What news in the dear old burgh, Hohepa?"

"Nothing much."

The thin eyebrows swoop up again.

"Hohepa! I've only been here two days, and already I've heard the most *fascinating* things . . . Sharon told me a little tale yesterday, for instance. The dear saw sweet Simon over at you know who's . . . following in his father's, well maybe *not* footsteps but you'll gather my meaning hmm?"

"Who is you know who?" Joe is not smiling.

"Why, Binny Daniels," and the permanent smile widens a fraction to reveal startlingly white teeth underneath.

Joe looks at his cousin, his eyes snapping.

"I'll see Simon about that."

His voice is too tight, too controlled.

"Deary, Hohepa," each word spaced by exaggerated last vowel sounds, "that's being a little heavy." He slid out of his seat, cool as a snake. "I was just sharing the *news,* sweeting. There's no need to get all rough."

He flips his hand. "I dare say the child could stand a little gentle *hand*ling. You really should thank Binny. If he was cleaner, and touchable, *I* would. Even though his taste is generally execrable."

Joe grits his teeth.

"Bye for now, my coz."

Luce fed himself back into the five o'clock crowd.

"That bastard is poison." He is squeezing his schooner viciously as though it was his cousin's neck. "He's bloody poison. A bloody poisonous *liar*."

Kerewin, who has heard about Binny Daniels, is having difficulty swallowing her beer.

"If you say so," she says at last, pacifically. O hell, I hope so. "If you say so." The easy drinking has clearly come to an end.

· · ·

He knocked on the door.

Shuffle, shuffle.

Pause.

"Hoose there."

"Joseph Gillayley."

Sucking sound and whistle of breath.

"Geezus Mr Gillayley . . . gee-zus." The voice trails down to a frightened whisper. "Geesuss, what yer want?"

"Has my son been round here?"

He's been round here all right.

Luce wasn't just making it up.

"He just, he just, was over the fence one day an I said LookIwonhurtyerboy, don't jump like that. He was scared."

"Open the door."

"No." Almost a whimper. More sucking sounds.

Joe studies the flaking paint on the door. Pale dirty green, blistered and sunstained.

One minute more, and I'll kick it down.

"Lissen Mister Gillayley, he didn' do nuthin. Nuthin wrong. I didn' do nuthin wrong.

"He was scared about some money stole in school. So I give him a dollar. He's a nice little boy. That's all."

He'd know the little bastard steals . . . Christ, when's *that* going to surface?

But it sounds plausible . . . except not money for nothing. Not charity from this stinking old faggot.

"You expect me to believe that shit?"

"No."

The chain clinks again, and suddenly the door scrapes open.

"No," says Binn again, "I got me reputation. But that's the honest bloody truth, so Jesus help me."

He is trembling at the knees, his chin is wobbling. There are stains all over his cardigan and shiny trousers. He stinks of urine and stale sicked-up sherry. There is a shine of dribble down one side of his bristling chin.

He holds his chin high though, so the scrawny neck stretches.

"No, I got me reputation," he says again, and lowers his head in defeat.

Waiting for Joe to knee him one, or belt him.

"Did he ask for the money?"

"He sez he was scared about it. I think that's what he sez any-way." The old eyes are rheumy and opaque. "I wouldn't touch your pore little boy, not the way you think. He was scared, he wanted some money. I had some, so I give him a dollar. Christ, there's nuthin wrong wiv that?"

Joe looks at him long and hard, and the old man's eyes flinch, and come back to him, and flinch again, and still return.

"No, there's nothing wrong with that for you," says Joe at last.

. . .

He went home, and prowled through the rooms until he found the boy in his bedroom.

"Where have you been since school finished?"

The boy gets off the bed, looks at his father sideways, moves sideways, gesturing as he goes, moving faster, faster, panicking now, Out, Out, Out. Joe puts his leg across the doorway, blocking it off just before the child reaches it.

"Where's out?"

A blank stare. Not blank. Scared as hell.

Joe reaches out and slaps him across the face.

"You go to Tainuis' when you're told. Or to Kerewin's. Don't have me chasing all round the countryside after you. You get into trouble too easily. And stop the tears. Marama's not here."

YOU PROM, the boy is writing, finger against his hand.

"Shut up." He puts his hands on his hips. "Luce said you were over at that creep Binn's place. Did he handle you?"

The child shudders, shaking his head No No No, so the tear-tracks skid off at right angles. He writes again, finger on hand, BINN OK.

"What'd you go there for?"

Simon swallows.

"Come on, save some skin."

MONEY fingers Simon.

"Wise. I heard about that too." He unbuckles his belt. "Shirt off, boy."

The boy looks once to the door, once at his father's face.

As he takes his shirt off, Joe thinks, What the hell, he'll do as he's told for two days and then go his own way again. I might as well not bother. But he's my child, my responsibility. I've got to do it, wrapping the end of the belt round his fist.

Through the beer fog, he was saying, You promised. Not to hit me on the face again.

That's the only thing he'd mean by You prom.

It irks him.

> Why should I feel guilty? Why does he always find some sneaky way to make me feel bad? He's the bad one.
> And you don't learn, Himi, that's why you get the hits. You won't learn. You shiver already, but as soon as it's over, you'll be out doing some other stupid thing and earn yourself another lot.

He shrugs his heavy shoulders.

> What else can I do, Hana? What else is there to do?

He hits the boy until he grovels on the floor, gone beyond begging for it to stop.

"*Don't* go to Daniels' place again, hear? He's not a good man. Bloody old pederast," he mumbles as he buckles on his belt.
His own hands are shaking now.

He pulls the boy up from the floor, and then because he is suddenly sorry for him as he stands there swaying, white and sick with pain, he says,

"Look tama, that was for your own good. I'm not much drunk am I? I aren't just mad, am I? It's because you mustn't go there, Himi. I'm sorry to have to hit you so hard, but you've got to learn to do as I say."

Like a voice in his head, You didn't tell him not to go there.

Joe shakes his head.

"Otherwise, otherwise," he looks blearily into the child's darkened tearclouded eyes, "you could get really badly hurt. And I don't want you hurt, tama."

Sweet Christ, don't look at me like that.

. . .

"Pedderass?" she scans the note again, wrinkling her nose. "Would you mean pederast?"

Simon lifts his open hands to her, I don't know.

Where the hell does he get these words from?

And abruptly, with painful clarity, heard the languid Luce Tainui say, "Why, Binny Daniels." Two days ago in the Duke, and still the hooks in that conversation stick in her throat like a half-swallowed bidibid. She says, swallowing,

"A pederast is a person who makes love, has sex that is, with children. Particularly young boys. Why?"

Anger is starting to drive her heart harder.

Simon gives her another note. The purple shadows ringing his eyes make them curiously luminous and birdlike.

IS BINN?

Sheeit. Binny Daniels is the proverbial dirty old man. A solitary gaffer in a long khaki coat, caught several times and finally put away for a year for feeling up schoolboys. Now he drinks in solitary at the Duke, where the regulars rubbish him savagely and aren't above sly punches, and the barman doesn't serve him very often. He buys half a gallon of sherry and trundles off home to bed with it, early each night.

"Yes, Binn Daniels is. Did he bother you?"

The boy shakes his head, already busy on the next note. He is writing more than gesturing at the moment.

HE GIVE ME A KISS AND SAY I CAN HAVE MONEY ANYTIME. HE STINKS

"Ulp," heart beating hard as haka-stamping, and as war-ready. "That was all?"

It had better be, but the child shifts uncomfortably. He has been moving and walking as though he was a wooden doll ever since he arrived this morning. She half expects to hear his joints click; Simon the graceful burdened with twitches. An experimental act, she'd thought, a phase, a put-on, but now buggery comes to mind. I'll gut and deball the old bastard if he's touched you.

The bruised-eyed child shakes his head, but he means nothing, nothing happened.

NOTHING, he writes, BINN OK.

Nothing, he emphasizes, shaking her hand once, ready to touch as ever but flinching before the cold anger in her eyes.

> So I'd better believe you rather than make a fuss. But where'd you get that bruise Sim? And why're you look-ing so strained? I think I'd better do some asking round. About all sorts of things . . .

"Good." She says it lightly, and grins down at him. "That stink isn't the only thing sour about that old man. He could do you con-siderable damage . . . sunchild, do me a favour?"

Simon, weak at the knees with relief that the flickery swords of flame have been sheathed, and that Kerewin is still Kerewin and not wild at all with him, would do anything in the world for her. His smile is full of promises.

"If you want money, come here for it. I've got more than enough. If you want kisses, there's all your Tainui relations ready and will-ing, not to mention Joe. But don't go round to Binny Daniels' place again, eh. Not for any reason whatever. The bloke has a nasty rep-utation, and he earned it."

He crosses his heart and cuts his throat, I promise, I promise, and he asks for two dollars, and thanks her profusely, and he smiles all the time.

. . .

"You been back to Binn Daniels?"

He is startled out of his retreat. No No he says, lifting his head from his arms.

"Where'd you get this from then? You pinch it?"

The boy shivers. No, barely moving his head. His eyes are fixed on Joe.

Kere, he mouths, and his shoulders slide up to hunch by his ears.

Possible, thinks Joe, but is it begged or stolen? and at that moment, Simon offers a note. He is shaking now, a hopeless seemingly
uncontrollable shudder.

Joe goes over to pick it up from him. GAVE SHE GAVE IT, but
the child won't look at him, and the knuckles of his clenched fists
show through as though the skin is transparent.

Ahh, what can you do Ngakau?

> Once on Monday night, because the suspense of wait-
> ing over Kerewin's visit to the Tainuis' farm got too
> great, and the boy woke up at the wrong time, and
> blundered into the kitchen at the wrong time.
> No school Tuesday.
> Once on Wednesday: Binn Daniels.
> School all right, sent home with a headache at lunch-
> time, God knows he'd have an ache everywhere else,
> why not his head?
> Thursday.
> Sneaked off to Kerewin's Friday morning, but she sent
> him home in the afternoon claiming she wanted to draw
> in peace. He doesn't remember why he thrashed him
> last night. It had been a forgotten, better forgotten
> night. Only when he'd wakened the child for breakfast
> this morning—"Himi, it's nearly nine o'clock, where
> the hell are you?" thinking, I'll bet he's drifted off to
> Kerewin again—he'd been curled up in a foetal ball on
> top of the bedclothes, arms wrapped round his chest,
> knees drawn to his chin, and his face still wet from
> weeping. He couldn't stand properly. Hunched over
> and moaning, he clung to Joe.
> "Whatsmatter?" His head was throbbing horribly.
> "Sweet Jesus, did I do that?"
> Which was silly of him to ask, even considering the
> nature of the morning. Who else would?

Don't hit him any more, man. You'll break him again.

He's been kneeling here all of the morning. Keeping out of the
way.

The shower wasn't much help. Nor were the aspros.

Ahh god, Ngakau, you and your bloody temper. He eases himself down beside the boy, and lights himself a smoke.

He passes it across to his child,

"You feeling any better?" his voice very gentle.

The boy coughs and hacks on the smoke like he's an old man of eighty, and the tears spin down his cheeks, while his fingers shake on the cigarette, but you can always win him by declaring peace. After a while, he even smiles.

"It's been a bad week, e tama."

The boy leans against him, sideways, gingerly. Joe slides an arm round him, touching and no more. "I think we'll go on that holiday very soon," and Simon grimaces.

He don't want to go? Don't ask for the moment. . . .

"You know if Kerewin's coming?"

She don't say, says the child.

"O don't she?" Joe smiles at him, "o don't she?" he breathes out. He ruffles Simon's hair, smoothes it again. "Tama, you've never told Kerewin, have you?" in the same quiet-as-breathing voice.

His son shakes his head.

"Why?"

There's a long silence.

Because she'll know I'm bad, the boy mouths, and starts crying. Because she'll know I'm bad, he says it again and again, gulping miserably through the silent words, She'll know I'm bad.

"O Christ," says Joe, and cries with him.

• • •

He rings Kerewin at two, and gets her out of bed, it seems . . . she snarls into the mike, "Who the hell is it?" and takes a lot of sweet talking before she's at all conversational.

"Two in the afternoon," he joshes at last, "you'd better admit it's late in the morning for waking e hoa!"

"I had a very late night," she says briefly.

"Drawing?" he asks, and after her "Yes", "Have you finished?"

"Why?"

"Well, Himi really wants to come round, but not if you're busy like yesterday."

"He won't bother me today. I stomped most of yesterday's work to death anyway."

He's sympathetic. Then he adds, The boy is a bit under the weather with flu, does she mind? he truly wants to come?

"If you don't think he's going to keel over or anything."

"No way," Joe assures her, "he's just a bit achy with it." He doesn't think it's a catching kind, well, *he* hasn't got it, and he has had every opportunity to . . . he won't send him for an hour or two yet, but expect a taxi before I go to the pub, eh. "I still got the washing to finish," mourns Joe. "You wouldn't, by any chance, want to try your hand at some interesting washing?"

"No bloody way, man. Okay, I'll expect Simon soon, and you when you arrive, doubtless." "Right," says Joe, crossing his fingers, it might be okay yet, I've patched up all the fights, tama's coming better, it'll be all right, "And thanks from the bottom of my heart, Kere. Ka pai, e hoa."

. . .

She breakfasts on coffee and the first of a new batch of yoghurt. After that, a desultory picking at things to do. She makes the bed for the first time that week, picks up her golden guitar, but puts it down without playing anything. She goes upstairs and touches the shelved rows of charcoals and inks, chalks and felt-tips, tubes of oils and watercolours and acrylics; touches them all, no more.

> It's the bad mood I woke up in. It makes for an oppressive quality to the day.

She wonders briefly if anything is wrong with any member of her family.

> We used to have links . . . but now?

She opens another bottle of dandelion wine, but only drinks a glassful.

> Not even in the mood for drinking? Hell my soul, you must be in a bad way. . . .

Looking down at the sunlit sea through the great sweeping curve of window, Fishing? Nope?

By the sill, in a heap and scatter of shining stones, is the rosary Simon gave her.

> Been playing with it, brat? Or you're an indian giver?
> Where'd I leave it? Ah yes, up a floor in the box with
> my rings . . . you been secreting away a few of those
> too, fella? I better check, later. . . .

She picks the beads up, runs them through her fingers. Amber and gold, turquoise and gold, bloodstone and coral and still more gold. Redolent with luxury: not the sort of thing she could envis-age swaying next to a sackcloth habit.

> Who owned you?
> Prayed with you?
> Played with you?
> What prayers said, in what moods?
> Joy, or grief?
> Love, or anger,
> Or tears?

The beads slide by her fingers.

It's a long time since I prayed this way, she thinks. Why not today? Give deity some prayer-flowers. Say hello to the most gra-cious lady of them all, sister to tuakana sister, blessed among women, Hello Mary.

She folds the beads in a triple coil round her neck, and walks downstairs, and outside, and away along the beach.

. . .

The door is open.

He sidles inside.

He whistles as shrilly as he can.

No answer. No-one home?

The entrance hall is cool and quiet, full of shadowy green light.

The crucifix on the rounded back wall is in a pool of light, like it stood under shallow water.

He looks at the brittle metal man, stripped to his pants and nailed to the wood. His face is turned to one side. Right, he wouldn't want anyone to see what was in his eyes.

There is a hole in the brass chest, on top of the swelling ribs. But the metal man's fingers aren't curled tight against the pain.

They stretch out, open and loose, still as prongs.

He shivers.

Why does she keep a dead man nailed on the wall?

Ask her Claro. But keep the smile on, Claro.

He keeps straight, and he walks well, and he smiles in case she comes round any of the stony bends.

But there's no-one upstairs.

The fire is out.

Ah hell, no-one cares.

He stalks over to the dropleaf table.

There's this bottle on it, full of shivering gold drink. Pale gold, sunlight shot with silver.

The smell comes lazily out, sweet and compelling.

He listens carefully.

No footsteps. No noise.

Besides, she doesn't mind if he has a drink, she's given him plenty of glasses.

So, into the cupboard, squinting over the cups . . . that's the small brown mug with the blue sigs? . . . um, listening carefully to his head, sigillations whatever the hell *they* are.

He's had it before. It's the right size, tika size, fitting his hand. 'll do.

Methodically, he pours a cup, drinks it down steady in one long heady breath, and pours another. And five cups after, he's feeling fine, thank you, easy in the stomach and pleasantly relaxed in the shoulders and back. Only trouble is, the bottle's about shot.

A marine, says Kerewin, throw that marine away.

He wanders to the cupboard, and looks the full bottles over.

That squat and bulbous one, full of green . . . stuff. Grass juice, maybe?

He screws the cork out of it. The sides of the cork are sugary and they grit as it turns.

And if that's grass juice, spit spit urrkk, it's not the clean healing smell of grass.

It's a rank bitterness, something decayed then pickled.

I'll try anything once, but that's had its chance . . . how could she possibly drink that? Maybe someone swapped the real drink for rat poison. Cat's milk, piss, like Piri says . . . something horrible, anyway.

He moves on to the next bottle, and swigs a sample.

Too sour. His tongue is numb under it. He purses his lips and spits the mouthful back into the bottle.

This?

Another gold drink, a darker gold, the yellow of dry gorse flowers nearly. It smells as musky as gorse. He rather likes gorse.

> I sat in the middle of that bush one whole afternoon,
> and nobody could see one damn thing of me. . . .

("Simon! You don't come here censored immediately. I'll I'll I'll. . . .")

They couldn't get in. They would have got scratched to pieces getting through that hole, *I* did.

Haven't gone there for a while, Clare.

Too wet.

It's a place strictly for summer.

So he pours a cupful of the gorse drink, tastes it . . . slightly sour, but it only tingles on the lips and tongue . . . and it goes down smmmoooooth . . . could stand more of that, Clare.

So?

You got that berloody cup, boyo hokay?

Why does she always hokay okay?

It's sokay hokay okay ay? he sings in his head. And tokay . . . that was another one, tokay.

> A drink fit for kings, she says. The Sun King especially.
> And no, you can't have any. Youth needs juice neither
> for longevity nor aphrodisiac. Sun king maybe, sunchild
> no way . . .

I'm the sunchild, because of my hair . . . he shuffles his free hand through the length of it.

> Struth mate, that mop needs cutting. Six inches more
> and you'll be treading on it, hah!

. . . and there'll be another fight.

He shudders.

I can't help it, it's too much . . . there can't be a fight. I won't. This time, I won't. I'll ask her to say she cut it.

He went to turn round and bumped into the cupboard door. Sat down involuntarily on the floor. It doesn't hit him as bad as he thought it would.

Claro?

Echo.

I think you're getting drunk . . . the voice that says it recedes through his head back out into . . . he tries following the voice with his eyes, looking backwards and up into his head until it hurts. Caint be that drunk, stuhupid Clare . . . he croons, an audible out-side singsong to the inside talk.

> When you're really full, you don't hurt anymore, and you don't care anymore, says Joe. That's why, tama. Even though you gotta come back for tomorrow, for the night you're safe and sound.

Sound?

Listening carefully, There's no sound.

C'mon, she comes home, you'll get a thick ear or something.

So what's new?

He splashes more of the gorse drink into the cup. Most of it's pouring on the floor, but he keeps going, wobbly as hell, until enough gets into the cup to fill it.

That all tastes rather good. Especially good. Bloody good. He smiles happily and blearily for quite a while, and then frowns.

Why am I happy?

Joe don't get no happy.

Joe gets bloody mean.

Shitty's the word, he thinks sourly. He gets sooo berloody shitty . . . stop crying, you. I can hear it.

It's me. I always do the wrong thing. I don't, I don't try to, it don't matter what I do, it's always wrong.

He sniffs through a maudlin stage to a realisation that the bottle he's cuddling is empty.

He goes to stand, and slips in the puddle of gorse juice.

That's strange . . . I'm floating. . . .

It seems to go on for minutes, and then Thunk. Hard on his hip on the floor.

Godbloodyshitandhell.

It hurt. It hurt him a lot.

He picks up the fallen bottle and snarls, I'll show you, throwing it away with all his strength.

A fierce crack! somewhere, and then an odd muted splintering sound, like ice ringing on stone.

Jesus oath, says Simon to his heart, what was that?

Frightened to look, but looking anyway, twisting his head off the floor until his neck creaks.

But there's one hell of a blur hereabouts . . . caint see no thing Claro.

Shrug, shrug, kneeling up, and shuffling on his knees to the cup-board, hip aching like it's fresh hit.

That's beer. I don't want any damn beer.

Sniffs in the next bottle he pulls a top off.

????

Again.

Delicious.

He nurses this bottle carefully to the cup's rim, and pours a bit in.

Chocolate. Thick and syrupy and sweet.

So clink! knocking the bottle, cheerful again, here's to you Kere and to you Joe he says kindly, silently, sprawled against the cup-board held by his arm, clink, and that's for me eh Clare, and he drinks to them all.

. . .

Kerewin stares.

You wouldn't believe it. You couldn't.

You come in, feeling clean and straightened out and high on ho-liness, and what awaits?

One drunken kid, lying hunched and untidy all over the floor. Snoring like a bluebottle.

Two bottles overturned, and alcohol rife through the air.

O hell, look at the window!

She shakes her head in disbelief.

Two hours and he does this much damage?

Man alive, a six year old debauchee. . . .

Her heart mourns the window (but I can buy another one).

She walks across to the cupboard, avoiding the puddles (O tatami, you weren't got for this . . . to be good and golden for bare feet not to be . . . I *hope* that's drink . . . still, if the worst comes to the worst, I can always turn it over . . .) and digs him in the ribs with the toe of her foot.

No response. Not so much as a blink or an offkey snore. He dreams on oblivious, sound in his stupor.

It would be kind to let him sleep it off. I'm not kind.

So she picks him up, her heart kicking with a kind of misgiving at his lightness, and climbs the spiral to the shower, and turns the water on at needlespray and coldest. For a minute he lies under the blast, limp as a skin in her hold.

Then he jerks, and screams.

Highly startled, she drops him. She has never heard him scream before.

"He screamed, my God could he scream. He's a fluent screamer. . . ."

It's a fierce high agonising to the ears sound.

The child goes on screaming. He starts to fight the cubicle walls, the floor, the water, in a blind panic to get anywhere out.

She watches, pulled back clear of his flailing arms.

He's not seeing where he is. He's terrified.

Then, understanding part of his terror, she reaches in and turns the spray off.

The boy crouches in the inch of water, shuddering and retching and sobbing. He is sickly white, and he hasn't opened his eyes yet.

"Simon."

It stills him a little. More shivering and gasping, but the screaming panic is done. So she repeats his name again and again, kneeling down by the shower stall.

Conversationally she says,

"Did you think that was the sea or something? The same water where you almost drowned? I'm sorry, it was a foolish thing for me to do . . . I didn't think deeply, you see. I just said to myself, the urchin's riddled out of his mind. So many sheets in the wind there's none left to steer the ship with. So get him sober fast. And how to do that? O easy . . . like in the song, you know it?"

Singing softly,

> "What shall we do with a drunken sailor,
> ear-lie in the morning?
> Put him the scuppers with a hosepipe on him. . . ."

"Only, there's just a shower here. No scuppers, no hosepipe . . . but it wasn't the wisest thing in the world to do, I admit that now."

He is nearly quiet, only the occasional whimper, though his breathing rushes yet.

She sighs,

"Actually it was a bloody stupid thing to do, eh?"

> Godgodgodgodgod, thinks Simon.
> It is a beat in his head in time with the drips. With the steady splat of water running on to the cold steel floor under his hands.
> In time with the aching pulses in his thighs and back and chest and legs.
> But listen: snap. Cigarillo case. It *is* Kerewin.
> Scrape of match, and a flare of flame.
> The water is nearly all out of his ears.
> There's a rattle as she puts the matchbox away.

"So hokay? You know where you are now? Third floor the Tower, all over the shower . . . or are you still a bit under the weather?"

He puts out his hand, groping blindly, and Kerewin takes it, holds it gently.

"Sorry about that, Haimona. I sure as hell didn't mean to frighten you . . . wake you up in a rough fashion, yes. I was nasty, I meant to do that. But not to scare you, really."

He shakes her hand, goes to shift upright, and his other hand slips under him and he skids forward on the shining steel floor nearly chinning himself before Kerewin's grip pulls him up short.

"Sweet hell, boy, easy."

She leans in and lifts him to his feet, steadying him out the door.

Rat-tail hair and soaked clothes, a sodden sorry sight.

"Struth fella, talk about a joygerm . . . but I don't suppose you feel like smiling."

She has conned that the tears are still running off his face mixed with water. He can feel it, the way she's looking.

"I think you'd better have a proper shower," says Kerewin gentlevoice. "Then you'd better go to bed for a while . . . I forgot about that bloody flu you're smote with. Help us undone with your clothes, e Sim."

It is because I am tired, he weeps helplessly. I can't stop. I can't say. I *can't.*

We've had it, he thinks. It's finished and it's all my fault.

He is shaking again.

He can't remember when he last felt this sick.

He makes no protest, gives no resistance. He even helps undo buttons and slide off clothes.

And Kerewin didn't say a word.

Except when he was naked, she took one of his hands, and turned him round carefully, supporting him so as not to make his head spin more, and then she tipped his face up towards her, and stared into his drowned eyes, as though she were seeking a meaning to it there.

"Why didn't you say *anything?*" There was pain in her voice, "Why did you keep quiet?" but he shook his head.

And that was all she said.

. . .

DAY INTO NIGHTMARE.

What the *hell* do I do *now?*

O, I know what I'm supposed to do. Ring up Child Welfare and report the bloody mess he's in.

"Excuse me, I know a small child who's getting bashed . . . it looks like he's been thrashed with a whip (but I hope to God not)."

I can just hear it.

"You've known him *how* many weeks and you never suspected he was getting so badly treated?"
"Uh, well, he's very good at hiding his pain."

I can just hear it.
She is furious with herself, not only because she must have hurt him.

Joe, you good kind patient sweet natured gentlefingered everloving BASTARD.
But I knew all along, herr Gott. Something always felt wrong.

No, I didn't.

I had suspicions when he was here with his face battered.

But he never said it was Joe, and Joe didn't admit it was him.

I've seen him slapped.

Hell, everyone slaps kids.

I really didn't know. I really didn't. Just the nagging feeling that something was wrong between them, right from the first.
Christ, no wonder he always sleeps in that twisted fashion.

Joe.

(No more chess.)
(No more gay and grogging nights.)
(No more joking ritual of meals.)
(No more sweet and drifting conversation.)
(No more heart-sharing.)
(The end of the dream of friend.)

Joe Bitterheart Gillayley, what on earth possessed you to beat up Simon?

I mean, *Simon.*

That's Haimona, cherished and cuddled and kissed.

That's Haimona, quickwitted laughingeyed and bright all ways.

That's Haimona, all three feet nothing and too few pounds of him.

So okay, he can be a fair little shit at times, but you know why he is.

God in hell, even *I* know why he is.

It's the sick twisted secrecy of it.

I'll bet he threatened the child with murder if he revealed his wounding.

And the urchin flinched the first morning I knew him.

(And where did you learn that luverly block? Conditioned reflex, ma'am.)

And by the look of the scars on him, it's all been going on for a long long time. Man, I wouldn't bash a dog in the fashion you've hurt your son.

I'd shoot it, if the beast was incorrigible or a killer, but never lacerate it like *that.*

Aue, Joe.

From the nape of his neck to his thighs, and all over the calves of his legs, he is cut and wealed. There are places on his shoulder blades where the . . . whatever you used, you shit . . . has bitten through to the underlying bone. There are sort of blood blisters that reach round his ribs on to his chest.

And an area nearly the size of my hand, that's a large part of the child's back damn it, that's infected. It's raw and swollen and leaking infected lymph.

That was the first sign I had that something was wrong. Despite his soaked clothes, his T-shirt stuck to his skin.

He didn't make a sound. All his crying was over.

And he wouldn't meet my eyes.

Somehow Joe, e hoa, dear friend, you've managed to make *him* ashamed of what *you*'ve done.

Neat job.

. . .

She wiped up the puddles from the matting—the tatami is tightly woven and more or less waterproof—and scrubbed away the stain the creme de cacao had made.

She gathered the shards of bottle, and tapped her nail against the cracked window.

She went and rang a Christchurch number and ordered a new pane of glass. They yelped with surprised joy, Yes Miz Holmes, consider your pane on the way. . . .

. . . Pane? A massive bowl-like curve, specially made, specially transported, and specially installed. Costly, rather. But the crack was unsightly, a blow to the eyes, although the pane would still keep out wind and rain.

She sat down with a cup of coffee at the ready, and made a fire for company.

Simon is upstairs, sleeping I hope.

(Washed and dried with extreme care: ointment, anointment, much good may they do him. Covered with padding and gauze, all the places where the cuts are open or bonedeep. A dessertspoonful of milk of magnesia to stop his retching.

"Happens when you drink that much," she lied to him cheerfully, while praying in a cold way that he hadn't been hit too hard in the stomach. The child had managed a sickly grin.

And a cup of warm milk to help remove the taste of the spoonfuls of painkiller and sleeping potion he had obediently swallowed.)

Dammit, I could have led him ground glass and he'd have passively opened his mouth and sucked it in . . . may the painkiller work. I can't stand the way he kept on shaking, then wincing.

She sipped the coffee thoughtfully.

Joe will be at the Duke. God knows when he'll get away from there, but he'll probably turn up here soon after. Heaven keep me from kicking the bugger to death

when he finally arrives. So, gentle soul, you still have a
few hours to decide what to do next.
And what can I do?

I can do nothing.

Make Simon keep quiet about this discovery. How?
Say nothing to Joe—at the moment, I'd have to bite my
tongue through.
Tell nobody—let it continue, let the child endure it by
himself.

No way.
I could tell Joe, but not tell anyone else.

Who else to tell anyway? The fuzz? The welfare? That
means the experts get to wade in, but how does the sec-
tion in the Crimes Act go? Something about assault on
a child, carries a sentence maximum five years, child removed from environment detrimental to physical or
mental health and wellbeing . . . sheeit and apricocks,
that's no answer.

But just telling Joe wouldn't do anygood . . . I'd have to look out
for the child, and that means getting heavy. Getting involved.
She shivered.
It always happened.
You find a home and you lose it. Find a friend, grow a friendship,
and something intervenes to twist it, kill it.
So what the hell can I do?

. . .

She takes down a long narrow black-silk wrapped bundle from
the niche by the guitars. Lights incense, arranges the table, and ma-
nipulates the yarrowsticks. Forty-nine stalks worn to the smooth-
ness and oily shine of muchfingered bone, and somehow they assist
a contact with an ancient, compassionate wisdom.
The hexagram given is Kuai, Advancing Again. 'One who is determined to proceed must first demonstrate the offender's guilt in
the high court,' it says. 'At the same time, one must be aware of the
peril such action will place a person in. As well, one's followers

must be made to understand how reluctantly one takes up arms. If
this is so proceed, and good fortune comes. . . .'

Peril and guilt and reluctance. . . .

And the mysterious lines of the Duke of Chou, hideously apt,
but dismaying:

> One walks slowly and with hardship because of flaying.
> If only one could act as though one were a sheep, and
> let the decisions be made by a companion, one could
> still accomplish something of the plan. But advice is not
> listened to, and alone one can do nothing. . . .

The pine scent of the incense is cool, acrid, remote.

Alone, one can do nothing. . . .

She rocks to and fro.

The amplifying hexagram, made from the moving lines, is Hsu,
Biding Time.

. . .

> Simon stamping along the beach and grizzling audibly.
> He's tired and it's cold, and his arms ache from carrying
> two pieces of driftwood. (She is carrying what feels like
> half a ton deadweight of rata, and Joe is bowed under a
> mighty pile.)
> "We'll soon be home, tama."
> "Not long to go now, Haimona."
> "Just a little way now, eh."
> The snivelling goes on.

> Suddenly Joe swings round and down. He crouches in
> front of the boy, reaches out and touches him briefly on
> the lips. Hush up . . . in Simon's language. The boy gives
> him a brilliant smile. Attention, attention, he loves it.
> "Okay, come on up, sweetheart," Joe lifts the child,
> one-armed, sets him on his hip, and staggers on down
> the beach.

She gets down the golden guitar for the second time this nightmare day, but this time picks out the ragged beginnings of a tune.
Then it swoops, it flies, it glides . . . it sounds thin, only the guitar's

voice singing the overture to La Gaza Ladra. It needs an orchestra, a synthesiser to do it justice. Or even that music box.

> She opens the lid to the gaudy little box, and the melody jangles out.
> "Well well, me favourite piece among others ... overture to The Thieving Magpie and where'd you get it?"
> Joe grins. "It's not mine. Himi picked it for himself." He touches the fluorescent pink lid. "Okay taste in music but eecch colour sense eh ... I was buying smokes last month and he was with me. Started playing with Emmersen's display of these boxes while I was talking tips. And Emmersen said suddenly, Hey look at your kid, he's dancing, and there's Himi showing—"
> "Sim *dancing?* That I've got to see."
> "He does it a lot ... play the tune, and you'll see soon enough. Anyway, he fell in love with this thing, and I like to see him happy. I said leave it alone, but gave Emmy the wink and he picked it up without Himi seeing and stuck it in with the rest of the gear."
> He beams at her. "You should've seen tama's face when I unloaded it. He still plays it about twenty times a day. When he's home."

. . .

She thinks, I'll wait. I'll do nothing except watch out for the brat. Say nothing to Joe but wait for a good time to tell him my mind on the whole bloody thing. Preferably with my fists.

And I feel eyes on me.

She turns to the door.

"Hullo."

What else to say? Somehow, knowing about the crosshatch of open weals and scars that disfigure the child has made him back into a stranger.

He's wan and unsteady and there's a look on his face as though he's just chewed bile. Very sour, very surly brat. He stands there scowling, wrapped in one of her silk shirts.

"Quick sleep?"

He hasn't reacted to her words, standing there, shaking steadily, but his eyebrows still superiorly high.

It is a surprisingly arrogant look, nose in the air, highchinned, proud-headed. The aloofness of his bearing, wobble and quiver and all—the fact that he still manages to look aloof despite the shakes—is offensive.

> And what the hell have I done to deserve this cold-shoulder carry-on?
> You do this too often, and I can understand why Joe would have a go at you . . . ah come on, Holmes! Bash him like he has been because he's indulging in some kind of kiddy snubbing? And how often does he do it? Never before to you.

But she is staring as coldly, as arrogantly back.

And then the child slumps, slithers down to a heap on the floor, a very surprised look coming over his face as though he didn't intend doing *this* at all.

And all Kerewin can think of, in her guilty astonishment, is to say,

"Are you okay?"

. . .

"That flu you mentioned?" says Kerewin.

"Uh huh."

"I think it's caught up with him."

"Uh huh. He okay?"

"He's better in bed than out of it, I think. I gave him a drink and some dope, and a hottie and one of my shirts for pyjamas, and sent him off to bed."

"Great."

The man's practically asleep, sprawled lithe and careless as his son can be on the sheepskin mat in front of the fire.

He greeted Kerewin fondly and drunkenly an hour ago, gave her the parcel of chicken pieces he'd won in a pub raffle, raved on about a game he'd seen played in the afternoon, sipped a coffee, and then curled up by the fire.

He hasn't noticed anything untoward. Her manner may be reserved, her voice tight and controlled, but he's got warmth and com-

panionship enough for a dozen, and he's determined to give some
away. And after the talk, he's determined to go to sleep.

Why bring Himi up now, thinks Joe dreamily. It's good he's gone
to bed because it's late, and if he's caught a flu—did I say he caught
the flu?—well, he'll get over it all right. He's rarely that kind of ill.

"But as soon as he's better, it might be an idea we head south for
that holiday, eh."

That penetrates.

Joe raises his head.

"We?" he asks joyfully. "All of us? You coming too?"

"Yes," she says. "I think it might be a damn good idea if I come
along in case you," she stutters over the next few words,

> Bite or slight or might happen? thinks Joe sleepily, I
> dunno. . . .

as she finishes, "and anyhow, I can use a change of scenery too."

Joe grins slowly and secretly, hiding the smile in the crook of
his arm.

> Ahh tama, she likes us eh. She wants to be where we
> are, after all. It'll all work out fine, Himi, all work fine,

and he gives up the struggle to keep listening to whatever Kerewin
might say, and falls very peacefully asleep.

II

The Sea Round

4

A Place to Sleep By Day

"Tea time," says Kerewin, and turns the car off the main road.
"Bloody pines," snarling to herself.

"Huh?"

"Look at it."

Cutover bush going past in a blur. Where it isn't cutover, it's pines. They start a chain back from the verge and march on and on in gloomy parade.

"This place used to have one of the finest stands of kahikatea in the country."

"And they cut it down to make room for those?"

"They did," she says sourly. "Pines grow faster. When they grow. The poor old kahikatea takes two or three hundred years to get to its best, and that's not fast enough for the moneyminded."

She pulls up hard. "I hate pines," she says unnecessarily.

Joe grins. "I gathered. They've got their uses though."

"O there's room in the land for them, I grant you, but why do they have to cut down good bush just to plant sickening pinus? Look at that lot, dripping with needle blight dammit . . . this land isn't suitable for immigrants from Monterey or bloody wherever. Bring the kete, eh."

She slams the door when she's out.

He looks at his son.

"What's she in a bad mood over?"

Simon winces. Joe lowers his voice. "You hurting?"

The boy says No. He's spent the last three days in bed, all taken care of by his father who's suitably sympathetic to, and thankful for, flu, this time.

Might've been a lie when I said it, but thank you for making it come true. He strokes the child's hair. "Sure?" he whispers.

Sure, he nods.

"Well, it must be the pines that have upset her." He leans over the seat and picks up the kete, full of sandwiches and teamaking gear. "You feeling hungry, e tama?"

He winces again.

"Ah hah, that's the problem is it?" Joe grins cheerfully, "Don't worry. We'll eat your share, and you can have a double helping at tea or whenever we get to this place."

He picks his son up, and joins Kerewin.

It's a good place where she's standing, despite the alien trees. There is a stone-bottomed creek twenty yards away, and the ground slopes towards it. The sun is high, and the air is warm and windless.

Kerewin has taken her jacket off, and is booting pinecones.

"Now that's a good way to show your opinion of them." He plonks the kete on the ground, and sets Simon beside it.

She lays her boot into another cone, and it cracks against a tree trunk fifty feet away.

Joe whistles. "Mighty! I'll bet you didn't intend to hit it though. . . ."

For answer, she kicks again, and a second cone shatters on the same tree. She rubs her nails on her shirt collar, and breathes on them carefully.

"Right," says Joe, challenged, and zooms in on a grand-daddy cone, thick and hard and bristling with club-ended spines. It explodes on impact.

He shakes his head in mock surprise.

"Gee, poor tree . . ."

"Poor bloody cone, more like. Anyway that was a fluke," Kerewin dismisses it. "We'll try for best out of three. You've got to hit under that bole, and pinecones that break up before arrival don't count."

"Done. Haimona, be scorekeeper."

The boy, looking less unhappy now he's out of the car, kneels up to watch.

"Turn and turn about," says Kerewin, "And you can go first."

His cone gets there, offcentre and under the bole. It skids off at an angle on impact, still intact.

Simon coughs, and hides his eyes.

"Any rude remarks from you Himi, and you can pick up all the pieces after."

"Fine performance," she says, and Joe smirks, "Yeah, it wasn't too...."

"I meant the fingerwagging," she says, and launches herself at a hapless cone.

It speeds in, dead on target, and splits neatly in two, halves lying defeated at the base of the tree.

"Haiieee," sighs Kerewin, "who is like me?"

The boy whistles, and holds up two fingers.

"An extra point for prowess? Accepted with thanks, but really unnecessary."

"Cheating. We didn't agree on that."

"So? He's the official scorer. You appointed him yourself."

Joe mutters to himself, sights, and sends the pinecone flying with a short vicious swipe.

"Equalled mine, shall we say?" she says thoughtfully.

The cone bursts right on the bole in a shower of chips.

She boots another one away. It doesn't break, but is accounted better than Joe's first effort by the official scorekeeper.

"Help yourself to the liquorice allsorts, fella me lad," she turns to Joe, smiling smugly. "Loser stands me a drink, eh?"

"Bribery and corruption," he growls, and kicks hard.

It is spectacular, soaring away in a magnificent parabola and whistling down to hit directly under the bole. He rubs his hands, and smiles nastily. "A jug for me, nice and cold."

Kerewin frowns at a pinecone. It is a fat little brown one, its knobs still closed, not too heavy but weighty enough. She swings her leg and hits the cone with calculated force.

"Beuteefull, beuteefull," she intones solemnly, listening to pine chips raining down. Perfectly on target, and this spectacular disintegration at the end of it.

She turns to Joe, who has flung himself down on the ground.

"Two perfect and an excellent against two perfects and a fair, right Simon sunshine?"

Joe whimpers.

"You can't tell me he's an unbiased judge."

Facedown, he can't see the coldness that comes into Kerewin's eyes.

"O, he does all right. That's a glass of pure iced orange juice you owe me, and endeavour to see there's three shots of tequila in it."

He lifts his head and brushes some of the pineneedles out of his hair. "Done," he says in a normal voice, and then drops his head again and says sobbingly, "Beaten, beaten by a mere female. I can't stand it," pounding the ground with his fist.

"I think you better bring your da a drink of something quick. The sunshine's addled him. Or maybe it's the pinescent. It does peculiar things to people. . . ."

The boy comes over, radiating concern, mouth full of liquorice, hand full of a cup of soft drink. He dribbles the drink carefully into his father's hair and the man shrieks in surprise.

"Oath tama!" scrambling to his feet and grabbing for his son.

She stiffens. You hit him and I'll drop you like a log.

But Joe is smiling, and Simon ducks behind Kerewin giggling wildly, and whichever way Joe swings to catch him, dives the other way.

"When you two jokers have finished using me as a maypole in your catch-as-can, we might get some tea and tucker," says Kerewin plaintively.

. . .

They went on into the McKenzie country.

"Over there, there's Simon's Pass," says Kerewin.

"O? Simon's Pass?"

Joe looks at Simon. Simon says nothing.

"Who was this Simon anyway?"

"I don't know. All I've ever found out was, he was a Maori boy who rode a white horse called Dover."

"Evocative."

"Yeah . . . whenever we came this way as kids, my mother would say, There's Simon's Pass, we're nearly there, and when we asked who Simon was, that's what she'd say."

"Are we nearly there, then?"

"Not berloody likely. That was just to shut us up."

. . .

The sun's come out again.

When they came out of the high country, they'd been enclosed in mist and greyness.

The cold seeped into the car, the dampness into their spirits, and they'd driven in silence.

But here, back by the sea again, it's light and warm.

"Let's stop," suggests Joe. "Boil a tea, maybe look around a few minutes?"

Kerewin glances at him.

"You're not in any hurry to get there?"

"You are?" he counters. "I mean, we got three weeks."

She grins.

"Okay . . ." the car is already slowing, ". . . what's the matter with Sim? Flu still getting at him?"

I think I know, but we say nothing. Yet.

"Carsick," says Joe, and the boy stirs. He is white and quiet. He looks at her and nods.

"Hell's bells, why didn't you say so before?"

"O, he'll be all right. He's always like it. Some fresh air and some fresh tea'll put life back into him. That's why I suggested the stop."

She shakes her head wonderingly. "I must say I like the lack of fuss. Every other kid I've known, and that includes self, is yelping I-wanna-cat as soon as they feel remotely queasy. It's the fun of having the car stop, or seeing your parents turn green. Very civilised, boy, very stoical, but if you had yelled we could have fixed the queasiness hours ago."

She pulls off the road near a solitary pine. "More blight," morosely, but brightens, "We can use the bugger for firing, though."

She has set up a waterheater and loaded it with pineneedles and bark by the time the man and his child are out of the car.

"Only thing wrong with yer average pine . . . soot. It fouls up the smokestack of this thing remarkably," popping a small twig down with great cheerfulness.

Her waterheater is shaped into two parts, cylinder on top of cone. Fill the cylinder with water, feed anything flammable down the narrow top of the cone and away she goes. The fire is protected: the water heats fast.

The black smoke disappears: pale flames dance at the mouth of the firehole.

"Ready in a minute . . . e boy, go look in that blue canvas satchel on the back seat, and you'll find a small bottle . . . wait a moment, you'll find a lot of small bottles. Better bring the whole bag to me." In an aside to Joe, "I been waiting to try this goop out for years," leering fiendishly as she says it.

He smiles. "Sometimes you're very nice," he says enigmatically, and she has time to think about that before the child comes back with her bag.

The bottles are all gillsized or smaller, and contain oils or powders or pale liquids.

She pours a spoonful of liquid from one into a cup of cold water.

"Drink it slowly," and the child swallows it, obediently slow.

Sometimes Sim, you're too damn trusting.

"What is it?" Joe has knelt down, with his arms round the boy.
"Aha." She's watching Simon closely. "It's a patented Holmes mixture. Herb extracts and things. Incidentally, I have tried it on myself, and it doesn't taste too bad."

"I'd say it even works," he says a minute later. The colour is coming back into the boy's face. "What herbs? We could make a million, eh."

"Distillations of mint, koromiko tips, manuka inner bark, and a little of the wicked weed . . . I don't think so. It takes too much time to gather and brew if you were doing it commercially. OK just for yourself, though. It's effective for period pains and flu-type nausea, so I figured it might work on carsickness too."

He uses one hand to sort through the little bottles, still holding onto the boy with the other.

"Bit mysterious, your labels . . . what's Morph, and Wit Haz? Or Unhappy Sun Bum's Oil for goodness' sake?"

"Aw come on, they're all obvious. Work 'em out."

But she hustles the bottle back into the satchel quickly.

"You okay now?" and Simon gives her a thumbs up sign. "Right. We'll have some tea, and then get on the road again. You want to drive this last stretch, Joe?"

"Not unless you're tired. I'll hold him, and we'll contemplate the scenery. He's less likely to feel sick again that way."

"I'll believe you. I've never been travel sick, car, ship, train or plane. Though I haven't tried elephants or camels yet. Or flying saucers or carpets, come to that."

"There's always a first time, scoffer. I thought I was immune until I took a canoe trip one Waitangi Day regatta. O sweet Lord was I glad when the canoe tipped, and I could decently and secretly puke in the water."

"Urk for the other swimmers . . . or did they all drown?"

"Waikato's a fast river . . . besides there were quite a few of us feeling offcolour. I think it was the mussels beforehand, they might've been bad . . . could've been the couple of half g's I had though, or that hunk of pork. Or the kinas, or the. . . ."

"You hungry, man? Well, endure. It's only another forty miles to home sweet home and tea."

. . .

There was a wide bay, so wide that the hills to the north were purple and hazy in the late afternoon sun. There was a small town, a straggle of houses and cribs, with a fishing fleet and store as reasons to unite them.

They passed it by.

There were rounded greenish hills that grew flax and scrawny windbeaten bushes in their gullies. There were beaches covered in grey sand and beaches clothed in ochre golden gravel.

And there was the sea.

. . .

She let the car drift round the corner, revving so it corrected the slide into a turn after a judicious wheel twist.

"Sheeit! They've made a road out of it."

Joe bit his lip.

It doesn't look much like a road. A double rut of loose shingle, and thistles growing up the middle hump. Ramshackle wire fences drooped on either side, almost overpowered by weeds.

"Kerewin says we're nearly there, sleepyhead," and the child yawns, and sits up in his lap.

There is a clump of macrocarpa shadowing the next bend in the ruts. A small neat house stands to the left, and two old dog kennels under the shade of the trees, with a cattlebeast skull between them.

"Ned Pita's place," says Kerewin. "Now, there always used to be," and she brakes hard. Two steers loom in front of them, out from the shadow of the trees. "Bloody normal, nothing's changed," and to Joe, she sounds relieved, as though she expects everything to be different.

One beast breaks into a sharp trot, heading down the hill, and the other turns and baws mournfully, head up. She edges the car at the steer, and it backs off, swinging its head side to side, favouring first one foreleg then the other in an uneasy retreat. There's a lot of cattle around. They stand in blank-eyed clusters, except for the beast trotting away in front. She accelerates, and the animal speeds to a rocking gallop, flinging its tail high.

"Stuhupid beast," snarling at it as though it caused her personal offence. It finally swerves to the side, its barrel heaving after the effort.

"Fences down, I take it?"

"Fences mainly non-existent. It's poor hard land to farm."

They're cruising down the last stretch of track. It winds to the beach. A cluster of baches in the hill-hollow to the left, and three against the right. In front, there is another line of cribs right on the beach, and beyond them, the grey Pacific.

"This is it. This is home."

She stops the car by an ochre-coloured bach at the end of the beachline, by the shelter of a massive thicket of African thorn. She gets out, and stretches her arms high about her head, weaving her body back and forth under her stiff shoulders. She drops her arms suddenly, throws back her head and screams,

"YAAAHEEEAAAA!"

and runs on to the beach.

Joe looks at Simon.

"Sea air," he says mildly to the child, who is staring at the run-ning woman in disbelief.

. . .

She's standing on the orangegold shingle, arms akimbo, drinking the beach in, absorbing sea and spindrift, breathing it into her dusty memory. It's all here, alive and salt and roaring and real. The vast cold ocean and the surf breaking five yards away and the warm knowledge of home just up the shore.

"Ahh," she sings wordlessly, hugging herself, oblivious of the two behind her. She stamps her feet in the shingle, bends down and throws off her boots, and stamps again, bare feet tensing against the damp cold stones.

"I am back!" she calls in a high wild voice, "I am here!"

The wind blows more strongly it seems, and a larger breaker than the ones before comes crashing down in front of the woman and sends long white fingers speeding towards her. The foam curls round her ankles and Kerewin cries aloud with joy.

"O Thou art beyond all good but truly this land and sea is your dwelling place. . . ."

She spins round, dancing herself round, spreading her arms wide in a welcome, her eyes alight.

Tendrils of her joy and possession steal to them, and the man runs across the gap calling, "Tihe mauriora!" and Kerewin laughs and holds him and hongis. And the child runs into them both, liter-ally, blind in his need to be with them.

She picks him up, and holds him one-handed on her hip.

"Tihe mauriora to you too, urchin."

One arm still round Joe's shoulders: they are knit together by her arms. She can feel their heart beats echo and shake through her.

She says softly, but clearly above the thunder and swash of the sea,

"Welcome to my real home. For now it is your home too."

Nobody says anything for minutes.

Aue, if only we could stay like this, thinks Joe, and at the other side Simon stares down at the nearby waves with no fear at all.

Then Kerewin shakes her head and says, "O berloody oath, can you see my boots round here anywhere?"

"That big sea," she adds thoughtfully, and puts Simon down on his feet, and unlinks her arm from Joe. She grins to the child, "Tuppence a sock boy, and a shilling a boot, shall I translate?"

He grins back, shaking his head. Nothing for nothing, his hands making noughts and circles in the air.

They find one sock, sodden and sandcovered.

"Well, the sea'll give the rest back," she says resignedly. "Or it won't, as the case may be. I prefer going barefooted anyway."

"May you what?" asks Joe, watching Simon. The boy crouches, and unbuckles a sandal, and looks at his father again.

"O sure, if you want to. It's your feet."

> He-ell, watching the child take off his sandals and socks, now there is a thing about childhood I had forgot. Imagine having to ask whether you can go barefoot or not. . . .

But she remembers similar requests and prohibitions now, from twenty years and more back. "The childhood years are the best years of your life. . . ." Whoever coined that was an unmitigated fuckwit, a bullshit artist supreme. Life gets better the older you grow, until you grow too old of course.

Simon stands, walks round, grimaces.

> Cold and hard, the gravel under your tender unaccustomed feet?

"Yeah," aloud, Kerewin the unsympathetic, grinning like a hyena, "bit hard on the soles until you're used to it eh . . . o, and a warning for you. See that thorn bush?"

The thicket rears behind them, a livid green impenetrable mass, studded with wicked-looking pale spikes.

"Walk wary of it. There's bits and pieces of it strewn all over the beach. You stand on a hunk, and you'll think the splinter you got a while back, nothing, nothing at all. Okay? Watch where you're going, especially near the bushes."

Joe says, "Somehow I find the idea of shoes extremely appealing. It's winter, remember you fellas? Kerewin, look at your feet. They're turning blue for goodness' sake." Her toes have gone a dull bruised-looking pink.

"It is a bit chill," admitting it with reluctance. "I suppose we better get a fire going . . . c'mon, I'll unlock a bach or two, and we can settle in."

. . .

She tells them, "We own five of these baches, all of us owning them, not anyone separately."

"What if some of your people turn up and want a bach?"

"Well, we'll only be using two. Besides," she shrugs, "I sent a telegram saying I would be here until the middle of June. That'll keep them away."

The two baches she opens squat next to one another, an iron boatshed between them. They are roughcast buildings, one supplied with electricity, the other heated by an old coal range. Small, neat as the inside of ships, with that compact air of a cabin, the baches contain a minimum of furniture.

"That one is known as the New Bach," she says, pointing to the ochre crib next to the thorn bush, "because we acquired it last of all. This one," over the small footbridge past the boatshed, "is called the Old Bach because we got it first. We're fairly pedestrian with names here."

The stream that flows onto the beach between the two baches is no good for drinking water, she says. "If you saw the cattle staling in the pond you'd know why, eh. So all the water we got is rainwater. The tanks are full, but it pays to go easy on it." Joe, walking behind her over the footbridge to the old bach, "These fences are pretty heavy . . . what comes lolloping up that you've got to keep it out?"

"The sea. See up there?" gesturing to the south end of the beach. "Those concrete foundations?"

"Yeah."

"There used to be baches on top of them. The sea ate 'em. Our black bach right at the end—we call it the Black Bach, incidentally," her grin flashes at him, "that one only survived because of the way it's dug into the cliff. The sea bashed into it but the pullback action never could get into effect . . . I think," her voice has grown suddenly dreamy, "I'll go along there and see how the old place is. The boat we'll be using is stored there. After I've said hello to that, I'll walk along the tideline for a way and a while. See you later."

. . .

Joe looks round the old crib.

The firelight from the range is flickering on the ceiling, but the kero lamps glow bright and steady.

The beds are made up on the bottom two bunks, and he's unrolled the sleeping bag for the child on the bunk above him. On the other top bunk, he's put their suitcases and the two guitars. He has arranged the food they brought in the cupboards. Bread and butter and bacon in the safe in the boatshed; milk in the fridge in the New bach; fruit and vegetables tucked away tidily in boxes and bowls; Marama's cake and biscuits in tins. . . . "Watch out for the furry gentlemen," Kerewin had warned. "Meece love here."

There are traces of them in all the cupboards . . . or there were. He's been working on that with disinfectant and hot water. It looks like nobody has stayed in these baches for a while.

And to top it off, he's got a pot of soup near the boil on the range, and a kettle singing briskly beside it.

"Haimona?"

The boy looks down from his bunk.

"You busy?"

He smiles and shakes his head.

"Like to go and find Kerewin while I make the toast?"

He nods and kneels up, holding out his hands.

"Okay . . ." lifting him down. "Going to take you a while to get used to going to bed upstairs eh?

"Lazybones," he adds, shuffling the boy's hair out of his eyes. Simon peaks his brows . . . If you say so.

Joe laughs. It's funny how much he says, makes you think he says, with so little . . . how green your eyes are tonight, tama . . . I'm happy to see you happy. He leans over and kisses the boy.

"Put your shoes on before you go out. It's getting dark, and you won't be able to see where to put your feet."

. . .

The wind has dropped.
It is growing very dark.
The shag line has gone back to Maukiekie, bird after bird beating forward in the wavering skein.

The waves suck at the rocks and leave them reluctantly.
We will comeback sssssoooo . . . they hiss from the dark.
Maukiekie lies there in the evening,
that rock of an island,
not much more than an acre and bare
except for a mean scrub of bushes and brown guano-
eaten grass,
where the shag colony spreads its wings in the sunlight
and haggles over footspace at night;
Maukiekie at nightfall,
all black rock crusted with salt and birdlime
and sleeping life, and
nearest to land
the stone hawk, blind sentinel
watching the cliffs.

Aiieeee, pain and longing and relief . . . too long I've been away
from here. Too long that's been just a memory.

Tears come to my eyes whenever I hear a gull keen, or watch a
shag pass on whistling wings.

O land, you're too deep in my heart and mind.

O sea, you're the blood of me.

The night darkens.

It is too easy, sitting here in the rock seat, to put words to the
seasounds. Words round the waves breaking on shore, smacking
the rocks. Especially now, when it's quiet, and there's only yourself
listening in the dark.

(Well, there's them . . . and I think it was a mistake I brought
them . . . but how can I send them away now?)

But my family is gone.

I am alone.

Why did I lose my temper that night and wound everybody
with words and memories?

("It's the bloody horrible way you've remembered everything bad about everybody, and kept it and festered
it all your life . . .")

They started it.
I finished it.

They are gone beyond recalling.

I am gone too.

Nothing matters anymore.

She stares into the dark. Maukiekie is just a shadow on the sea, wound round with crying birds.

> Twenty-five years. That's a long time. A quarter of a century.
>
> A generation. They were the only people who knew me, knew anything of me, and they kept on loving me until I broke it . . . do they love me now?
>
> Six years is a long time to be alone. To be unknown, uncared for. Cut off from the roots, sick and adrift.
>
> They must have wiped me out of their hearts and minds . . . why can't I do that?
>
> Why do I keep on . . . careful, you're wallowing, back in the slough of selfpity and greasy despair . . . but why do I keep on grieving? When all meaningful links are broken? Forever.

(Because hope remains. Get rid of your hope, Holmes me gangrenous soul. Do you really think you could apologise? Say you were wrong? Ask for forgiveness that might not be given? Never!)

She shudders.

Aie, quit it. Listen to the sea, not to words in your head. . . .

There is an alien sound, a slight scrunching sound like someone . . . ahh, yes.

She watches him trudging past in the dark.

> You really are a very stupid child. For all you know, there might be something terrible lurking in the shad-owed cliff at your side, just waiting to sink its fangs in your flesh . . . (a mad sheep, woman? Don't be barmy!)

But she warms to the thought.

> And who knows what might rise out of the sea and come groping and flabby and inevitable and smother you forever? Doom! doom! the taniwha hath come! You have no imagination whatsoever, you unintelligent little

creep, or you would never have come this far down an
unknown beach at night. For all you know, I could be
waiting to push you into the sea . . . look at the stupid
brat, will you? He'll be halfway to the lighthouse before
he decides I'm not along that way after all. . . .

She wondered what would happen if she shadowed him and
leapt out and grabbed him. Probably kill him with a heart attack.

Lay off, Holmes. He can't call out, he can't see you, he's
doubtless doing his feeble best, and he's a nice child,
most of the time.

The nice child is now standing still, shivering, looking down the
long dark noisy stretch of beach.

O Kerewin, where are you?
I wish I could

he swallows hard.

You cry Clare, and I'll kick you.
I think I better go and get Joe.
No, you said you'd look.
But. . . .

"E Sim!" calls Kerewin from behind him, "over here, boy."
He hopes she can't see his tears, because there's nothing to cry
for. It's dark, he reassures himself, it's very dark.
Kerewin is whistling for him to follow the sound. He arrives at
a black wall of rock. The whistling is coming from above his head,
but he can't see the woman anywhere.
"Can you get up?" says her voice.
He stands numbly, shaking his head.
"Reach up your hands," and as he does so, surprise, warm strong
hands out of nowhere hold his wrists.
"Easy does it," she says, and lifts him upwards. "God, Sim, how
much do you weigh? I have more trouble with fish. . . ."
He doesn't know. He's not even interested. He's more inclined
to wonder where he is, where they are, but how to ask?
Kerewin is still tching to herself over his frailty. Beneath her
arms he feels slight and breakable, ribs a brittle cage for his heart,

neck a thin stalk for the hair to depend on. Yet you're a tough little bastard for all that, or you'd never have got to be this old.

"Hard to talk in the dark, eh?"

Yeah.

"Joe got tea ready? You sent for me?"

He taps her hand twice.

"Well, I suppose we'd better get going then . . . I'll show you this place in the morning. It's a good place if you like to sit and think. Or dream."

She stands up, the boy still in her arms.

"Can you see in the dark? Aside from seeing soul-shadows?"

He twists round to see her face, to see if she is joking. He can't see much aside from the white flicker of her eyes and teeth, and the life that sheets her. He shakes his head.

"Rightio . . . there's one thing I can do . . . like an owl, a rabbit, a possum, I can see the land at night. Don't move much or you'll have us off balance."

She walks down the slope from the rockseat and then moves faster, faster, until she's running over the line of rocks, a series of jumps and fast steps from one spur of rock to the next, no step on the same level, until she comes to the strip of sand at the end of the line.

"Wow!" she's breathing heavily. "It's been a good while since I last did that."

The boy stumbles on the beach as she puts him down.

"Tired or scared?" she asks lightly. He had stayed rigidly still while she ran.

Simon turns round and lifts his arms to her for an answer. Scared or tired, he's still a trusting idiot.

She laughs.

"Ahh, it's not far to walk . . . there's another game I'll teach you some time here. It's played with waves, and we used to call it the tide way. It's probably a helluva lot more fun than running over rocks at night especially if you can't see where you're going . . . but we'll save that for a tomorrow, sunchild."

I wasn't scared, you knew where to go, but I want to ask you, I need to ask you, he wraps his arms round himself, trying to recapture the warmth and strength she had held him with, and follows her.

Outside the bach door, where there's light enough for him to see her face, for her to see his hands and face, he points to himself and her eyes.

"I see you? . . . o, you mean before, when you were looking for me?" There's a muscle ticking in her eyelid.

"Yeah, all the way," says Kerewin, and laughs again.

. . .

She wakes startled, her heart thudding. The air is full of alien sound and movement. Joe is up: she can hear water being sloshed on the floor. There is an acrid smell about.

"What's the matter?"

She sits up shivering.

"Anything wrong?"

Joe pads over, torch in one hand. She can just see the boy lying against him, cradled in his other arm.

"It's all right," he whispers. "Sim's been sick, that's all."

"O." She settles quickly back down under the eiderdowns. "Can I help?"

"No, I'm just cleaning up." There's amusement in his voice. "For a small boy, he can surely throw up plenty."

Yech.

"Yeah, I'll bet." She's glad to have never wiped up anyone's vomit.

"It was probably the car, the travelling. After-effects. You know."

"Yeah," says Kerewin. "Mmmm," sleepily.

Joe grins to himself.

"You know what?" he asks Simon, very softly, his mouth close to the child's ear.

Simon taps his neck, No?

"I think she's glad I didn't ask for help . . . she's gone back to sleep a bit too quick, eh?"

The boy giggles.

"Hush up."

He kneels again, and mops up more of the mess on the floor.

"She sounded like she might have thrown up too, if I'd said Yes, I need help. That'd be a bit hard on me, eh."

Finger brushing his neck, light as a moth touch, No.

"Cheeky brat," Joe whispers.

She can hear the rustle of his voice, and the boy's quick
hushed laughter, but the sea is loud, louder. . . .

It's good lying against Joe like this, thinks Simon. All the muscles
are soft, the strength in abeyance. He has let his own body go completely limp, relaxed into the curve of arm, the curve of his father's
chest.

Joe finishes the floor, and shines the torch round to check—yep,
sick over my bed too—he's only just made it over the side of his
own bunk.

"Talk about making a thorough job of it, Himi . . . that must have
accounted for everything in your gut from last week on."

After he's done rubbing and wiping, he creeps over and puts a
pot on the still-hot range, and heats milk.

"Think you'll go to sleep all right, without any more dope?"

Simon nods, smiling at him in the firelight. He gestures to Joe.

"With me?" the man murmurs. "It's a bit cramped in those bunks,
fella."

He pours the milk into two mugs.

"Might be an idea though . . . you really finished being sick?"

The child giggles softly again as he tells him No. He has found
the whole episode hilarious apparently.

Joe hefts him higher against his shoulder, and sits on the floor
with the boy in his lap.

"You truly all right now?"

He nods, and then leans his head back to look up at Joe. One
of his hands rests on the man's wrist, loose and quiet. With the
other he touches his forehead, and then his scarred back, and gestures to the bunk where Kerewin sleeps.

He can feel his father's heart start to beat urgently hard. He
stretches up and touches Joe's lips.

"She's keeping quiet? Or I'm to?"

The whisper is high and strained.

Both, say the upraised fingers. It's okay, he mouths, it's okay, and
suddenly the word is turned into question and entreaty, Okay?
Okay?

"Aue, aue . . . okay, tamaiti, okay . . ." he strokes Simon's hair
away from his eyes, and kisses him. "Taku aroha ki a koe, e tama."

All still, all silent, except for the sea.

They can't even hear Kerewin's breathing.

Joe sighs.

"Eh, I don't know why I hit you," he says in a low voice, talking more to himself than his child. "I'm drunk or I'm angry, I'm not myself . . . even when it's necessary to beat you o I don't know, it's not like I'm hitting you, my son . . ." Simon moves, and Joe looks down to see what he's saying.

It feels like it is, says Simon wrily.

He closes his hands over the child's small hands.

"Thank you for not holding grudges," his voice lower still, husky and shaking a little. "God knows I deserve your hate . . . but you don't hate," he says wonderingly, "you don't hate."

The boy looks at him, eyes glinting in the firelight, saying nothing. Then he smiles, and leans over, and bites Joe's hand, hard as he can.

"Shit!" the man gasps, hissing with pain, and pulls his hand to his mouth. "Bloody brat, what's that for?"

Aroha, mouths the child, grinning, aroha, and his smile is wickedly broad.

Joe sucks his hand until the ache dies, then holds it out in the firelight.

"Look at that, you. . . ."

Neat set of teethmarks, halfmoon on one side, quarter circle on the other.

"Aroha my arse, utu more like," says Joe ruefully. "Drink up your milk, and we'll go to bed."

. . .

Lying awake in the night when no-one else is, warmed by the boy at his side. (Simon is asleep, face down on the man's arm. Kerewin hasn't stirred from her close inviolate solitude.)

My hand hoods, holds your head against my palm.

Shifting his arm a little,

You are still too thin, but you've always been slight . . . and it's been better since Kerewin arrived. Well, not so much arrived as you discovered her . . . I wonder what she really thinks of us?

Me?

She never shows anything much.

She's still wary of you. I can't imagine her cleaning up after you . . . what'd she say if I mentioned you wet the bed every so often. Probably be very cool and polite about it. "O really? Well, lack of control over micturition in children Simon's age isn't uncommon, particularly in moments of stress." Taha, Ngakau, you're putting words into her mouth. You don't know what she'd think.

He lets his hand fall, away from the child's head.

Himi, what are we going to do? It's all very well for you to tell me to hush up, but what am I going to say tomorrow? How am I going to look her in the eyes now? Same way you been doing it before, you great pretender.

He reminds himself, It's been okay today. Been all right this week . . . when did she find out? And how? He wouldn't tell, because of what he said, it makes him look as though he's been wicked.

He is, sometimes.

Flicking matches, and stealing.

And when he loses his temper, he can get vicious . . . what had Piri's kid done to him? I was the one doing the teasing, and who nearly got his brains bashed out? Timote, the bystander . . . yeah, but who treats Himi viciously when they lose their temper?

He shifts uneasily in the sea-hushed dark.

There's trouble at school . . . I don't know what it is, but there's trouble going on . . . Jesus, why does he have to go to school? He's smart enough to do without it. If Kerewin would only have him for a while . . . or I could stay home . . . it's too much of a struggle to get him along there every day, even though everyone seems sympathetic now. Even most of his classmates.

O but he learned early on that his handicap made him peculiar, and having only one parent wasn't normal, and not knowing his original parentage or background or even his proper name, was downright wrong.

And how've I helped with all that? mourned Joe. Not going to school triggered off the first time of all.

> The air is sweet, but his lungs hurt as he takes in great gulps of air. There is no other sound than the persistent ringing chorus of treefrogs.
> No lights.
> No questions.
> No more cries.
> O, what did you do that for?
> You must be sick, man. He says it aloud, experimenting with a statement of guilty excuse.
> I must be sick, but who can I tell?
> And abruptly his noisy breathing changes to sobbing.
> A grown man down on his knees beneath the cool moon, crying out the pain in his heart and the guilt in his hands, with no-one to hear him anymore.

("Except me now," whispers Joe. "Nearly two years later, I can hear me cry. . . .")

It left a gap. It made a wound, for all the child's reacceptance of him. He'd gone back inside and cared for the boy as best he could, all apologies and endearments and tender loving care . . . and curiously Simon hadn't reacted with his earlier extreme fear at being held or thwarted in anything. It was almost as though he had been expecting it for a long time, and was now dully relieved that the worst had happened. The odd marks, the man remembers, the marks which had puzzled the people at the hospital . . . maybe even before . . . but he looked at me without resentment or fear, just looking. Observed me without communicating, He seemed to understand that time, how close I was to breaking point . . . but now? He must think it's just me taking all my woes out on him. That's not what it is, but he gets punished so often he probably doesn't believe I'm belting him just for wrongdoing. Or does he think he's that wicked? Good for nothing else?

She'll know I'm bad.

And is he now waiting for Kerewin to assault him too?

Joe shudders.

At the moment he'd rather cut his throat than hurt his son, but he knows from broken past resolutions, that come the morning if the child is sulky or rude or baulks at doing what he's told, he'll welt him with a cold and righteous intent. You've been bad, tama, and you're sure as hell going to learn . . . do I hate him then? But how can you hate someone and not know it? I love him. I just get wild with him every so often. Like I told him, it doesn't even seem like him I'm hitting. His disobedience or something, I don't know. Ah, you're screwed up in the head, Ngakau . . . and elsewhere, but it all comes back to the head.

His penis is erect, proud under his hand. He begins to relieve himself, cautiously but mechanically. He can hear Kerewin's quiet breathing, a woman asleep a yard across the way. A mile away.

> God, what makes her tick? She must feel like this some times . . . but she never shows it. She's as distant as a stone. I've never seen her excited by anything except odd colours and archaic words . . . and she hates touching. She even avoids Haimona's hugs and kisses, and as for mine . . . hai! Yet Hana was as ready as me, strong for love any time, right to the night they took her away from me . . . someone, sometime, must have hurt Kerewin. Like I've been hurt and putoff. But hassles with Himi aren't because of lack of sex. I was celibate for that year before I met Hana and anyway, I can get it now when I like . . . not that enjoyable, just bodymeeting, but it shouldn't make me cruel. I was never cruel to anyone then.

He shudders slightly and then relaxes, eased.

The child hasn't stirred. Still as if he's fainted. Still as if he's dead.

> What happens if I damage him badly? Or kill him?

He clenches his teeth.

> Like when I fought that shit Luce over his sneer that Himi would get to prefer the boys too, under my influence.
> "The look in your eyes, Hohepa, when you talk and kiss, my god, it's hot enough to turn me on at twenty

paces distant, let alone the pretty child himself. There's something very appealing about the half wild and the half broken-in—and you know what I mean by *that,* sweetie. And the way he kisses back . . . did you teach him? From Taki? Not from Hana, I guarantee, that puha mouth couldn't kiss. . . ."

"Shut your mouth about Hana. And shut your mouth about Taki. That's dead past and not to be spoke. . . ."

"O, I told him, dear. And do you know? He giggled. Fondly. Dear old Daddy, he loved the idea. Positively deelighted in—"

Wham. Straight into Luce's fine high nose.

And afterwards, he had gone home and yelled Simon awake. He had begun by scolding the child, but angered by his sleepridden look of bewilderment—deliberate, he's hiding behind it, I know his slyness—had finished by belting him until he fainted. Staggering then into the kitchen, sick from the party, sick from the fight with Luce, sick with this. But the only way to be less sick is to drink more, so the best part of half a bottle of whisky, searing down his throat. Muttering "Fallen boy, fallen boy," and remembering the sad-sweet months with Taki. I knew it was wrong, I know it was unnatural, but he was gentle, he was kind, I loved him and it was good.

And why why why did he have to *laugh* at it?

His rage mounted. Laugh at me, will he? Laugh, eh?

(And remembers this with most shame next morning, because it was only Luce's words, and Luce was born to make trouble.)

The child had crawled part way back to his bedroom. The tired sick way he moves, the mess of him, his cringing, the highpitched panting he makes instead of any normal cry—e this thing is no child of mine, levering the boy to his feet and pinning him against the wall, and punching him in the face and body until he whitens horribly and faints a second time.

And he had picked up the unconscious child with no feeling except hate in his heart, and thrown him on the bed. He had fallen loose and broken, and lay unmoving, sprawled still as if dead for hours.

And while he was full of remorse for what he had done to

Haimona in the daylight, he couldn't bring himself to seek help.
Aiiiee, imagine what they'll say, they'll do . . . so it's lies in notes to
school, Simon P has the flu, excuse, and lies to Marama, O Himi has
a friend, neat eh, he likes going there, lies to all and sundry for two
weeks. Then Piri finds out, and now they all think I am sick, am
warped, am a monster of cruelty. No blame on him, he's a godgiven
angel to them . . . and what does Kerewin think now? Aue, don't
think about that.

The child heals, at least his body heals; but then, and each time
after, he becomes both more diffident and more unruly . . . and the
worst part is that he still loves me. And what else can I do but kiss
him back, hold him tight, and hope that the bad times will finish
soon.

I kiss him too much. I hold him too much. Don't think on it, play
each day as it comes . . . don't drink so much, don't do such things
again. Forget it.

He bites his hand hard, and screws his eyes shut against tears.

Aroha, the child said, while smiling that wicked chal-
lenging smile, aroha.

"Ka nui taku mate, ka nui taku mate," and stops his whispering
in horror as Simon touches his face.

"Aie tama, it's just a nightmare . . ." he can feel the child's eyes
on his face, ". . . just a bad dream."

. . .

II

. . . and Kerewin turns to him saying, "That's okay with you then
sunchild?" from the top of the building where she's standing. Joe is
nodding, pleased and proud in the background, and he can feel the
sun on his shoulderblades, and he can scarcely contain the bound-
ing joy he feels. He throws off the chains from his head and his feet
and he cries "I'm home!" and Kerewin yells, "Hey Clare says
Homai!" and Joe says proudly, "I hear! What joy!"

He opens his eyes.

It's grey outside, he can see through the gap in the curtains. He can hear the rain beating down. Underneath that sound, the sea hushes up and down the beach.

He sighs.

It's the first day here, but already time is running out.

He leans over the bunkside.

Joe's head is practically buried under the blankets. All you can see are long strands of black hair . . . hey, wait a minute, didn't I go to sleep down there? His father's hand is curled tightly above his head.

Must have put me back here again. . . .

He glances at Kerewin.

She is tucked up neatly, her head on her arm. She doesn't sleep with a pillow at all. She seems to do without a lot. She doesn't sleep with pyjamas on either. She'd gone out while he and Joe got ready for bed, and coming back, turned out the remaining lamp, and got undressed in the dark. There was enough light from the range to show him that she didn't bother getting dressed again for sleeping.

Now she lies curled and still, her hair thick and curling round her face.

He sighs again.

In that dream, she had cut her hair very short. He hopes she doesn't. He can't bear his own hair being cut.

I don't see why it *needs* cutting, he thinks resentfully.

But Joe says, When you're old enough to take care of your own hair, you can decide how to wear it. Till then, I decide. Right?

You didn't say No to that, not without a fight happening. From experience, you should learn not to say No. . . .

He stretches, leaning an arm out to touch the green wall beside him, and the other to touch the yellow wall at the back of his head.

I wish somebody would wake up.

He turns carefully over onto his back, wincing. Still . . . he looks at the roof. There's the lamp hooks, and hundreds of spider webs . . . all Kere's people must be like her and grow spiders in their houses . . . he wonders if Kerewin knows about the little brown man with blue lines across his face who seems to sleep in the floor. Not on it, the floor looks like it's not hard for him, he just lay down, and went halfway through it. Then he became aware that Simon was staring at him, and grinned at him, and said something in a soft indistinct guttural voice.

It was Maori, like Joe when he's in a good mood at home, or in a bad mood and wants to yell me out with other people around. But, thinks Simon frowning, it wasn't quite the same. Some of the words sounded funny. Besides I can't remember what he said. It was just before I got sick.

Ho hum.

There's a lot of shelves here. Some over the bunk across the way, and at the end of the room near the range, and above the sink, all of them piled with books, and more books, and candles and lamps and boxes and tins of food. You could tell this was a home of Kerewin's family . . . books and lights and food, all the same.

The cloth Joe used for wiping up the sick has dried crinkly on the string above the range. Above it, on the mantelpiece he sup-poses, are more lamps and candles and boxes . . . anana! that's a mouse! A live mouse. . . .

It sits on the mantelpiece, and apparently doesn't see him watch-ing. It cleans its paws, and sits back on its haunches, nose twitching, ears alert, eyes bright and beady and ready for any movement.

But Simon doesn't move. The delight is back. Hey, a live mouse! I never saw one before. . . .

He levers himself up with infinite care, slowly, slowly—but the mouse drops to all fours and flicks away out of sight behind a lamp.

Aue, he thinks, but not with much disappointment, It'll be liv-ing somewhere in the bach, and I'll see it again today maybe. Or tomorrow . . . I won't tell Kerewin or she'll set a trap.

She'd exclaimed with disappointment over the empty traps in the new bach.

He's sitting now, the over-blanket drawn up round his waist. Aiii, as he straightens. I wish for one day it didn't hurt. But it's not all that bad, shrugging tentatively, experimentally. You'll do Claro, you'll do.

He leans over the side again.

Still nobody's moved. They're breathing very quietly, no snores. If he listens intently he can hear Joe, but the gusting rain drowns Kerewin out.

I might as well get dressed.

He's shivering.

He burrows for his T-shirt, takes his pyjama top off, and pulls the shirt on. The bandages Kerewin had taped on are loose now. Some-time today, I'll tell her. Or maybe I do something else? He closes his eyes and waits for an idea, but it's too cold to concentrate for long.

Where the unprintable as Kere says did I put that berloody jersey? I remember, end of the bed. Crawls out of the warmth of sleepingbag for it, but it's not there. Looks over the edge. Yeah, I'd believe it. On their berloody apricock floor.

So he creeps down the ladder, pulls on his jeans and his jersey, and sits gingerly down to put on his socks.

Now what?

Will Kere get mad if I try lighting the fire? No, it'll make a noise.

I'm thirsty.

He sneaks over to the tap and draws himself a glass of water.

It is cold, cold, cold.

I'm hungry.

He stamps lightly on the floor. Harder, but no-one stirs even then.

O to hell with this lot. I better wake someone up.

He blows on his fingers. They're starting to freeze too.

He thinks grumpily, I could freeze to death for all they care.

Who'll I try?

Joe? No, he was dreaming bad, so he'll probably be in a shitty mood today.

Bad mood? Fight? Ahh maybe.

It feels right, he thinks, tiptoeing over to Kerewin, kneeling down by the bunkside.

I'll surprise her, grinning already at the way she always reacts to a kiss. Draws back and looks as though she's going to spit.

He leans in and kisses her on the mouth, but for a moment there's no reaction.

Then Kerewin frowns. She opens her eyes and stares at him.

E Kere, it's me, don't look as though I'm not here,

his mouth is open with distress, and she starts to smile.

"Hello you," she whispers. "Up and about already?"

She rubs her eyes, and yawns, turns away from him and stretches. "Ye Gods, child, it's cold . . . you dressed warmly?"

He presses himself close to her, and then sits across her legs.

"O thanks. How t'hell 'm I supposed to get up?" But she's still smiling, and still talking in whispers. He wriggles closer, and mouths, Coffee?

"You want one, or do I want one?"

He points, You and me.

"And guess who's supposed to get it?" She closes her eyes.

He snaps his fingers. Wake up, or I can't talk to you . . . he crawls up the bunk beside her and blows on her face and on her shut eyes and in her hair. Her arm snakes out and pinions him, and shifts him backwards. But she's gentle doing it, and Simon in gratitude kisses her arm.

"Ah hell," says Kerewin, mockgroaning, "kid, you're impossible. Go have a mimi or something while I get dressed."

But he's comfortable where he is, thanks, getting warm again. He smiles at her, and steals more eiderdown. Sheesh, she says, and pushes him down into the covers, plonking all the rest of the bedding on top of him. She swings her legs over the side and pulls down her clothes from the top bunk.

He stares at her.

He's never seen Kerewin naked before. And she's pale, cream, except for her arms and feet, and face and neck. They're brown and freckled. She has no scars, not even the pale kind Joe has curving up his left side, no marks at all except for the strange ones across her throat, but hair grows thickly and oddly under her arms and at her crotch. Her breasts are small and pointed, and hang on her chest. He's seen breasts before—Piri's Lynn fed Timote for over a year, but hers were fat and brown. Kerewin's are that cream colour, different at the ends.

He suddenly realises, for the first time in his life, that his skin is the same pale shade, except for the scarred places.

"Berloody oath, another freezing day," she shivers, and the things round her neck, long piece of greenstone and small silver cross and the medal that is covered by a clear blueish stone, clink and jingle together.

She pulls on her silk shirt and jersey, stands up, drawing on her pants and jeans very quickly, slides back onto the bunk muttering, "Where the hell are my socks? Move over chief, I left them down the bottom there somewhere."

He waves a hand airily, I'll get them.

He shuffles up with them, moored by blankets, crawls onto Kerewin's lap and holds onto one wrist so that she can't easily chuck him off.

"Which is being awkward, you."

She slips on her socks onehanded, and looks at him. "You want a cuddle? Or you just being a pest?"

You got the idea, he smiles.

> Why can't it always be like this, when they like me?
> Why can't it be good all mornings?

She cups her hands over the boy's shoulders.

"Better?" she asks in a whisper.

He raises his eyebrows and purses his lips.

"As read . . . I'll see if I can't think of something that works quickly. Get down, Sim."

She reaches up to the other bunk and gathers his sandals.

"Put 'em on," she's whispering still. "Or, as my Nana used to say, you'll get a cold in the kidneys."

She can clean out the grate, raking the live coals forward out of their dun coating of ash, and set a fire, very quickly, very quietly.

They're eating porridge twenty minutes later, and Joe still hasn't stirred.

. . .

He woke suddenly, when the boy dropped the plate he was drying, and he woke in a foul mood.

He sat up so quickly he banged his head against the bunk above, and that didn't improve his temper.

"What'd you do? Come here!"

"S'okay, Joe. He dropped a plate. Accidentally." You hear the last word?

Joe muttered something unintelligible, clasping his head in his hands.

"What's that?"

"I said, Jesus what a morning."

"Oh. In that case I won't ask you the traditional question always asked of newcomers to Moerangi."

"Unhh?"

"That's, Did you have a good sleep? The answer's invariably Yes."

"Unhh."

"You knock yourself hard then, Joe?"

"Yes," he says shortly.

Kerewin looks at Simon and rolls her eyes.

"Well, we're just going along to the other bach. Have a happy getting-up. That's if you're getting up . . . it's ten after ten now."

He grunts.

A place to sleep by day?

Ta hell.

Only because you couldn't get a decent sleep at night.

. . .

It's a sour day.

His mouth tastes sour.

His eyeballs feel gritty.

His joints ache, he's got cramp in one shoulder, and chilled kidneys it feels like.

Half the bedclothes are on the floor.

The air is bitterly cold, and it's blowing a gale outside.

"Inviting. Deelightful. Just the place for a holiday," he snarls to himself. "O this is gonna be a fun fun time."

He crawls awkwardly out of the bunk, bruising his thighs on the concealed board edges, and knocking his head again.

He puts on as many clothes as possible, jersey and cardigan and thick woollen shirt, his woollen jeans. Feet and hands are stiff with cold, and he squats in front of the range, trying to warm them up.

"Jesus, I need a pee."

He huddles under further layers of clothes, jacket and parka and socks and boots, and braves the wind. And rain, it turns out. The toilet's got a leak in it, situated right over the tin, which is okay for the toilet but inconvenient for anyone doing their business. Wind leaks through the door, round his ears, up the can, and by the time he's finished he knows he's never been this achingly cold in his life.

Back in the old bach, he finds the fire is just about out. The porridge Kerewin made has thickened and congealed greyly in the pot.

He looks at it and shudders. The shudder continues as he

washes. The water is lukewarm, and seems to freeze on his face and hands. He gives up. His eyeballs can stay gritty, his mouth continue unclean. He pulls all his clothes tighter about him, warring against the seemingly permanent shiver that has taken up residence in his gut, and stalks past the fence over the footbridge into the other bach.

Kerewin looks up from the floor. She's lying by the heater.

"Hell's bells, the original abominable clothesman!" she guffaws. "You cold, Joe?"

The words are singsong and mocking.

"You cold Joe?" he mimics. "What do you bloody think?"

Kerewin looks at him for half a minute, saying nothing.

He thinks uneasily, her eyes are changing colour.

They've gone chill light grey.

He steps round her.

She says after him, "I'm not cold. Sim's not cold. If you are, make yourself a coffee, or have a whisky, or some damn thing. But don't vent your ill-humour on me."

The room was very warm when he came in. It's now noticeably colder, as though the temperature dropped ten degrees merely with him opening the door.

He remembers what Simon said last night, and the shiver in his belly continues, even after he's swallowed two cups of coffee.

. . .

Play the clown, one part of his mind argues. Lighten things up.

No way, I'm tired of being fall guy. Guy of any kind. I'll ignore them.

He studies the hundred or so paperbacks on the shelf on the far wall for a long time. Westerns, light romances, thrillers, crime stories, and all of a sudden, a Chinese Materia Medica. A little further on, Parasitic Infection of Echinoderms, a Preliminary Study. Readers Digests, National Geographics, Woman's Weeklys, and then The Chambered Nautilus Newsletter, pub, Delaware Museum of Nat. Hist.

Eclectic, he thinks, fascinated. Anything and everything, and presumably this is just the holiday reading.

"Heliogabalus: A Historical Analysis," back to back with "Owning and Training Your Staffordshire Bull Terrier." Piles of Giles, two Leunigs, and an early Searle underneath sixteen True Confessions.

In the background, behind the sounds of his exploring and sorting, there is an eery conversation going on.

"Shuffle then."

Cricklecricklecrickle.

Silence.

"Nah, three cards beats two pair, Sim."

Followed quickly by, "Why the hell didn't you say they were two pairs of eights? You barsstard."

Clinks as a pile of cents is trundled away, presumably to Simon's side.

"No."

"Okay, yes then."

"Ask yourself, I'm not."

"Uh uh, my fine feathered little friend, *that* will most emphatically take those."

Crickle crickle slip slip slip.

"Heh heh heh," followed by soft giggling from the boy.

"What're *you* laughing for?"

Silence.

"O, *sheeit.*"

Then, among the card noises, four "No's" from Kerewin, each one more annoyed than the last.

This is going to be one hell of a holiday, he thinks. I've got a suspicion today is going to live up to its morning.

He avoids looking at either of them when he turns around and sits at the table engrossed in his selection. From the snatches of talk that filter to him he gathers that the poker finished early, that Simon doesn't want to do anything thank you, and that Kerewin'll be damned if she'll have him hanging round in her hair.

He grins to himself, I give this venture two days and then we'll go home, and sinks deeper into reading. He had no idea that the chambered nautilus was such a fascinating creature, or that a mind could be as gently and whimsically dirty as Leunig's.

If there was any kind of rift between the woman and the child, it hasn't lasted long. They sit on one side of the table, eating lunch and swapping small talk, leaving him stranded by himself on the other.

It isn't that they're excluding him deliberately from the conversation. He has cut himself off, and he isn't invited, by look or remark, to rejoin them.

He attempts to, once.

"My mouth tastes like it's full of sawdust."

"Meaning the food is yuk?"

"No, no," he says hastily. "I didn't take the time to wash properly this morning. The water was a bit cold eh, and I've still got this thin North Island blood."

"You could have put more coal on the range and heated the water. Which reminds me, boyo. Get the porridge pot when you've finished your dinner, and we'll do all the dishes at once."

So much for trying, he thinks, and goes back to his reading.

And when he's finished the heap he brought across, he stares out the window.

The tide is nearly full out. The wind still blows strongly. Waves sweep up the beach, rise and crest, and are flattened to seaward flying spray. But over by that island—what did she call it? Makihea or something—where the waves are sheltered from the offshore wind, they are breaking in great showers of white spume. Gulls are making light of the wind, sailing in beautiful easy spirals away to the south. Other birds are beating in an ungainly way against it, getting nowhere fast.

"Kawau pateketeke? Kawau paka? Kawau tuawhenua? Kawau tui?"

"You're nearly right," Kerewin is back on the floor, playing poker again. "Stewart Island shags, and I don't know the Maori for that . . . kawau rakiura, perhaps? At least, it's most likely to be them. They live and nest on the island."

"Stewart Island? This far north?"

"O, I've seen them further north than this. Don't ask me how or why they came here though."

"Poor fellas probably got blown here by the wind."

"Unusual wind. The prevailing bree-eze is a northerly of some variety or the other."

"Bree-eze being a Holmes-type understatement?"

"Well, the one flaw with this place, aside from the trippers, the Japanese fisheries offshore, and the general pollution, is the ahh, rather regular wind we get."

"O," says Joe, forlornly.

"But don't let it worry you, man" saying it more kindly than she's said anything today, "Why, I've stayed as little as a month here, and had two whole windless days."

An opening. An invitation.

And anyway, what the hell is dignity good for? Keeping your nose high and your backbone stiff?

"Well, that doesn't sound as bad as I thought . . . you got a nice little pile of calcium around somewhere?"

"I could get you some if you really want it." Kerewin, watching him get up, sounds cautious.

"I thought I'd grow a streamlined sort of shell, so I could bask in comfort on the sand."

"O *splendid* idea . . . though did you notice those things whirling past the window a moment ago?"

"Yeah, the leaves?"

"No, they were limpets. . . ."

What's funny, asks Simon, what're you laughing for?

Joe squats beside him, and ruffles his fringe.

"The demise of gloom, fella, that's what."

. . .

In the late afternoon, the wind drops. One moment, the bach is being buffeted and the iron on the roof is singing, and the next, everything is quite still. The sea sounds very loud.

Kerewin stands. "Anyone coming for a walk? I'm clogged to here," waistlevel apparently, "with smoke, and the last molecule of oxygen escaped, screaming for all its dead siblings, two seconds ago."

"Yeah, it is that bit stuffy . . . where we going?"

"Where'd you like? We can go that way, and see the north reef. Or we can go that way, and see the south reef. Or of course we could go inland, and see a resentful steer or two."

"North, make it north . . . I figure every step I take south brings me that much closer to Antarctica."

"North it is then. That way I won't be able to show you where you were last night, me sleight-fingered knave, but then at the moment I don't want to either."

The boy grimaces.

"Y'know," she puts on her windbreaker, "I thought I was doing your child a kindness. I gave him 20 cents in cent pieces, and more or less the rudiments of poker. So far, he's won nearly three dollars off me, *and* had the gall to repay the original loan. The luck of ould Ireland indeed."

Simon isn't amused. He scowls.

Inside he shivers. Here we go. . . .

Joe says, "Really?" but doesn't sound sympathetic. "What do you mean, you don't want to go?" he asks his son. "Go get your jacket on, and back here at the double." The boy goes stamping out, slamming the door behind him.

"Uh ah," says Joe, moving towards the door.

"Uh uh," she says, putting her hand against it. "Leave him be, eh." She removes her hand.

One more step man, and down you'll go.

"If he really doesn't want to go for a walk, why make him? A drag for you, not to mention me, and a drag for Simon P."

"Fair enough," he says after a moment, "fair enough."

They wait outside the bach for the boy. And they wait.

"Ah to hell, he's probably holed up under the bunks or something."

"Well, we'll leave him under them . . . does he really do that?"

"On occasion," says the man sourly. "Goes to earth rather than does what he's told."

"Leave him a note saying where we've gone, eh," after another minute has passed. "That wind won't stand still for hours."

"The fifth commandment," Joe spaces his words to match time with his writing, "with Haimona," the note seems studded with exclamation marks, "is, Honour thyself and thyself, and don't give a damn about longevity, the land, or the Lord. There, and much sweat may it give him."

"What's on it?"

He's folded it already, and slipped it into the doorcrack.

"No threats . . . e Himi! Haere mai!"

He sang it out again, as they were moving down the beach.

"Silence and nothing moved . . . let the little termite stay happy in his hole, Joe. Forget him for a while."

"Yeah." He shook his shoulders and breathed out hard. "I just worry, that's all."

"Too much," she says blithely, "and watch your footing here."
She began to run nimbly over the rocks.

. . .

Watch my footing, thinks Joe in the night. Watch my footing.
He murmurs it aloud, into his sleeping son's ear.

Aue, what a day.
But it's over now.
And with luck and no more troubles, we're out of the
woods, hai,

sighing.
He whispers Ouch, for himself.
Kerewin the quick, she of the very fast very hard foot, sleeps
soundlessly as always.
"Christ alive," he says in soft wonder, "Christ alive, she's a
strange lady. What did she say? The world's a fiery wayward place,
why has it eaten me?"
Crippled with bellyache, her knees dug deep in the sand,
Kerewin had gone whiter than anyone he had ever seen.
"I burn to be out of it, and'll burn out of it," she'd groaned in a
kind of snarl, and had refused their hands.
He stretches gingerly, easing his bruised body to a new angle
without waking the child at his side.

But she'll be okay, little peace-and-war maker, as you'll
be okay now. As I will. As we all will be together.

Sweet dreams, he tells himself, and is still smiling when he
sleeps.

. . .

Kerewin has dreams of teeth.
Beginning with a replay of the time, the last time she'd been at
Moerangi, when after a week of agony, she'd looked at the inside
of her mouth in the mirror.
Jaw abcess.
Swollen gums, with pus-extended ridges.
Ah God, make it go away.

There was a matter outlet, not yet breached, a gumboil where some of the infection had gathered.

It was the constancy of the ache that was unbearable.

The dream had dwelt on the moment when she had taken a razorblade and attempted, using the mirror as a guide, to play surgeon and open the outlet the abcess had made for itself in her jaw.

She wasn't successful.

The next moment she was still looking in the mirror, and her two front teeth had changed to soft bloodstreaked stumps. The enamel all ground off, the spongy nerve and bone centre exposed . . . how to bite? She had only to touch them and she would dissolve in anguish. And then the teeth resolved themselves closer.

Her six front teeth loomed astonishingly white. But small yellowish holes of decay sat like ulcers near her gums, and there were brown stains from coffee and nicotine. In nearly every tooth, the enamel was marred by the black and silver inlay of fillings . . . except for those unexpectedly bright upper front teeth.

Dissolve.

There is a brilliant flare like a volcano erupting, shooting up through the after-image of the white teeth.

Draw back through a darkened window.

"Hell, what was that?"

"Fire," said Number Two laconically.

"Spotwelding," someone else suggested.

Sitting up, struggling against the weight of clothes and was it bodies? "What? What?"

There is a sharp drawnout pain against her throat as though someone has fastened their lips against it, suctioning.

Still struggling. Arms come out, and they're too warm. They surround.

It *is* fire out there in the landscape of dark lunar shadows.

Again the sharp smart at her throat.

She says to the man with the sallow face and shadowy trace of moustache on his upper lip, "Are you kissing me?"

He replies lazily, wearily, and with a shade of alarm in his dry voice,

"I wouldn't exactly call it kissing."

The pain increases.

At the top of her voice, in terror, "He isn't kissing me?"

The shadow people rush in, tearing. Warm gush down her throat.

Weakening into black horror.

She wakes, shaking.

God, did I yell?

She listens hard. The child is breathing through his mouth. Usual. Behind the even, noisy breaths, she can hear the soft, regular snoring of the man. Still asleep. Mother of us all, thanks. For that small mercy anyway. She is still shaking.

Dream vampires . . . what in the name of all holiness did I do to deserve *them*?

She edges out of the eiderdowns, shivering, and slips on her jeans and jersey.

Sneaks out of the room, opening and closing the door with stealth. She collects a thick canvas-backed blanket from the side-room, and goes out into the night.

It is quiet and dark, and it's drizzling. Although she can't see much, she can feel that dawn isn't far away. The ghost hour.

"Aue," sighing. She makes the blanket into a tent, and shelters in it. She lights a cigarillo, and smokes it, calming her breathing, listening to the sea.

The horror of the nightmare fades.

After a while—the drizzle gets heavier, it's nearly day, the sand gets hard under her behind, the smoke is finished, and her head is clear—she goes back to bed. There is an insistent but minor ache in her gut. It's like a period cramp, or the aftermath to a blow in the stomach.

But she hadn't been hit there.

She hadn't got hurt at all.

. . .

The air is full of spray. The rocks are black and jagged and wet. Not bare rocks: covered with life of all kinds, grapeweed and kelp, coralline paint and slow green snails. But the impression they give is desolation: black broken rocks, streaming seawater.

I feel an intruder, he thinks. Unwelcome. As though this is ages past and people haven't lived yet.

She apparently finds it homely enough. She smiled as she started walking away.

> The further she went from me, the more alien she became.

She is standing now at the far seaward end of the reef, on a black tongue of rock. A strange person in blue denims, sometimes obscured by mist from the waves that explode like geysers in the blowhole. She looks tense and desperately unhappy. Like she's at war with herself. Like a sword wearing itself out on its sheath. She doesn't look like a woman at all. Hard and taut, someone of the past or future, an androgyne. She hasn't moved from the rocks there for ten minutes. Still as a rock herself.

The whoomph! and hiss of the blowhole sounds again; the spray drifts behind her, hiding her again.

She hadn't said much, walking with him to the reef.

She hadn't said anything at all when he said, "I'll sit here and have a smoke eh. I don't think my shoes'll go too well on those rocks."

She just looked, then walked away.

He sighs and shivers. The very air is wet. And cold. He bends down to stub out his cigarette, and when he looks up, Kerewin is running back over the rocks towards him. She moves fast over the seaweed and studs of snailshells and limpets, never skidding or stumbling.

Eyes in her feet, he thinks, wondering what has made her run. Something in the water?

The tide is coming in?

"And you saw the sea," he says to her, his eyebrows lifting.

"Yeah." Nothing else. She isn't even breathing hard.

"I saw something," waving a hand at the beach. "Look what's crawled out of the woodwork." The small figure trudging along the beach doesn't wave back.

. . .

Simon sidles up, glares at them both, and declares war.

That was by holding up Joe's note, and tearing it carefully into bits.

Joe shakes his head and draws in his breath, saying, "E tama, tama. . . ."

Kerewin stares. "So what *was* in it? An invitation to commit seppuku?"

The boy sneers.

Joe stands. "Nope. It went, word perfect as far as I can remember it, 'We're going now. We can't wait all day. Kere is surprised at you. No wonder! You're being very stupid! Don't worry, I'm not mad. If you want to hide, instead of having a good walk, okay. And when you're finished, come out and make us a drink. It's cold out here, and it must be cold under there!' That's all."

"Innocuous, kind even . . . so why're you uptight?"

The boy scowls.

"You don't have to come with us you know. You can head straight back for the baches if you're in a bad mood. Speaking for myself, I've seen enough to sour today without having obstreperous brats around."

He goes on scowling at her.

"Whee! Shitty liver!" Kerewin laughs. "Or does ould Ireland fear retribution at the poker table?" and the child suddenly bends and picks up the nearest thing to hand and hurls it at her.

It's a green snail, a pupu, and it just misses Kerewin's eye.

Her hand flicks to one side in a blur of movement.

"Careful," she says, and all the laughter is gone. "Don't do that again, urchin. I'm just badmannered enough to throw something heavier back."

Joe hasn't moved but his fingers are twitching.

"I dunno, there must be something in the air that's getting to you fellas. Come on, let's all go back. The tide's on the turn, and it'll soon be blowing a gale again."

She squints at the sky. "And I wouldn't put it past it to start raining within the next ten minutes or so."

"Okay," says Joe quietly. He turns his back on his son, and clambers over the rock line to the beach.

Simon stays put.

As Kerewin moves away, she says, "You'll get very wet, you stay there too much longer. On the other hand, if you want to get wet, that's your business."

On shore she asks Joe, "He got enough sense to move once he

sees the water rising, or do we have to carry him away like a sack of spuds?"

"He stays there too much longer and I'll kick him all the way home," he speaks through clenched teeth.

"Ah come on, fella. It's not worth the fuss. He wants to play silly buggers and get soaked, it's on his head. On the other hand, you might just warn him at some private and convenient time, that I don't take kindly to having things thrown at me. Even by the gentle Gillayley himself. If that pupu had hit me, I would have hit him back. Even considering I know how much he gets whacked and all."

The air is still, waiting on the wind.

"Pardon?" says Joe.

"You know, and I know, that's a very difficult child to bring up. The word from me is go easy. Very easy. With kid gloves so to speak, instead of thumbscrews or whatever it is that you've been using so merrily to date."

"What?" says Joe.

He hadn't expected it to come up like this, be dealt with like this, not in his wildest moments. A calm, almost jocular—not threat, not piece of advice. It is something of both.

Kerewin's eyes are fixed on him. Dark and cold as the rocks now.

"Ahh Jesus!" the exclamation burst out of him. "Look at him e hoa! Look at him . . . he's trying to start a fight, and he'll keep on stirring until he gets one. He's like that a lot. He'll cause trouble out of sheer perversity."

"And you'll oblige him? Dammit man, you're an adult. Ignore him."

They're standing face to face. Joe plants his fists on his hips.

"I don't need you to tell me what to do, Kerewin. I don't need you to tell me how to bring up my son," his voice rises. He thinks, hears the same words from a year back, I don't need you to tell me what to do Piri, I don't need you to tell me. . . ."

Kerewin blinks. She folds her arms.

"So I'm not telling you. I am merely offering you a suggestion on how to keep the peace round here. This is a pleasant peaceful kind of place and we—"

"To hell. It's miserable. I've been cold and miserable ever since I arrived."

"Well go away then," Kerewin's voice is dangerously low.

They're glaring at each other now, Kerewin listening to herself saying, Stupid! Stupid! Break it up! in her head, and watching Joe's lips quivering uncontrollably with incredulity.

Hell, he is near breaking point,

and Simon comes off the rocks on to the ochre sand.

"Come here you!" Joe calls, and every word shakes. The scar up his ribs is blazing and Piri's retorts still shriek in his head.

The boy stops, and looks, and spits at him. His eyes flicker to Kerewin, and away, and he walks on again.

Incredible, Kerewin shaking her head in awe, fantas-tic . . . look at it, will you? Battered matchstick person flirting with death. You'd think he'd never been hurt at all, didn't give a damn about the consequences. Strolling away casual and apparently carefree . . . picking a fight? O you're right, man . . . but I wonder why?

The spit didn't hit—Simon's ten feet away—but Joe flinched as though it did. He shouted inarticulately, and lunged for the child.

Blown his top!
Blown his cool!
Berloody fool!

She is screaming with delight inside herself, trembling with dark joy. Fight. Fight. Fight.

O me killer instinct, riding high on my shoulders, wide with teeth and smiling!

And more or less under control, a pity.

"HAI," and the man stops involuntarily for half a second.

Plenty of time, plenty of time, sings Kerewin to self, floating over the barrier of space between her and the child, who has also been halted, midway through a cringe.

Ninny, she thinks fondly to herself, as she drifts to a stop beside him, trying to solve it all yourself, were you? And with violence yet, tchh, tchh. She notices, seeing every hair on the child's head distinctly, that there is a hole in his left ear. Like a small circle of flesh has been punched from the lobe. An earring? A brand? The awl mark of a slave?

The sand sprays outward, and Joe keeps coming, hands clawing for the boy. The man's eyes are blank.

I've driven him over the edge?

her body smoothly assuming a stance of defence.

How did she move so fast? It feels like I'm swimming in glue.

Nope, he's okay. If that clout had connected with your shell-like ear me sweet chy-ild though, it woulda broken de temporal bone
and de mastoid process
and de styloid process, ho hum,

as her hand caught the edge of Joe's fist and sent it flying harmlessly downwards. Her right foot arced into his kneecap a split part of a second later.

He sees the blows coming as blurs and can't avoid them. He goes down hard on the sand, but shoves himself back to his feet with extraordinary strength and quickness.

All right, woman, you think you can fight a man?

and strikes for Kerewin's face.

She weaves, seemingly. Her hand flows in between his moving fist and her face somehow creating a vacuum that sucks his hand upwards, outward, over her shoulder. She twists away from his falling body.

As he goes, This is wrong that's not what she should have done, and again he lands boneshakingly hard on the sand. Kerewin kicks him in the side and dances round Simon, who is lying nearby, flat on his face. She calls out, "Easy meat! So easy!" She is grinning wildly, her teeth bared.

Even as he scrambles to his feet, awkward and gasping, he wonders why the taunt should make him so angry.

Careful, that's Kerewin, someone says in his head but he yells at them "Fuck her!" crouching as he yells and powering his fists in a flurry of blows into her. *This,* he thinks with satisfaction, bloody kick me would you?

But none of the blows connect. It's like beating on air. She slips past the flailing hands and hits him on the mouth with the side of her open hand. It feels like being hit with a board. He staggers, is spun round and kicked viciously in the back.

"Upsadaisy," calls Kerewin. She is high with amusement, wavering and bobbing on her feet and grinning like a gargoyle.

He gets up raging. Stop her mocking, get her, *stop* her, but he whimpers as she whacks his face again and then steps sideways and drives her knuckles across his midriff. His breath fails him. He feels his hands drop, clench over his belly, thinks No what did I did she? feels his knees buckle, and the hard knock of a fist beating the small of his back, his kidneys, his bare spine. As he falls, Kerewin boots him in the ribs again. "Huh . . ." gasping continually, halfconscious and groaning for air. It aches when he tries to draw breath, chest and stomach, and his back is still curling away from the pain at its centre. He can feel blood trickling from his welted mouth. And somewhere, in the background, Simon is crying.

> But I didn't hit you . . . o sweet God it would be so easy to die. . . .

His breath is coming more easily. He keeps his eyes shut.

> But I better get up or Haimona'll be scared.

Haimona is.

All morning the feeling had grown, start a fight and stop the illwill between his father and Kerewin. Get rid of the anger round the woman, stop the rift with blows, with pain, then pity, then repair, then good humour again. It works that way . . . it always did. There isn't much time left for anything to grow anymore. It must be in this place, or the break will come, and nothing will grow anymore.

So start a fight.

Easy.

It had been.

But he didn't know what would happen after Kerewin winning. He thought, They'll kiss and make up, or I'll get a hiding, or maybe both, but he had shied away from thinking much about it. He hadn't reckoned on this, Joe bloody and moaning and breathless, and

Kerewin gone white and screaming to her knees beside him, and neither of them capable of anything else.

Everything's gone wrong. The world's turned on its head. Simon weeps.

She had stood gloating a minute after Joe went down for the final time, Ahh little eater of people-hearts, relish this . . . aren't you glad you never let me loose in a more warring time? Or maybe you howl and gnash your pointy teeth for the mistiming? Speaking of howling, trust old heart-and-flowers to be crying his eyes out . . . where do your sympathies lie, child? Entirely away from yourself? Survival ain't that way, Sim . . . though I do feel vaguely sorry for the fella myself now . . . she is starting to feel queasy at Joe's hard hurt breathing, so she goes to help him. Press the two points: one either side of the nose, pinch the heel, and it'll all stop, man . . . kneeling down to do it, and then screaming convulsively. She falls the last few inches to the ground. She twists over to one side, hands pressed deep against her belly, a simulacrum of Joe's agony a minute back.

It isn't mockery. The only thing she can think about the searing pain in her gut is that someone has stuck a knife into her.

"It's not, it's not," moaning aloud, hands still kneading.

"What's matter?"

He has got himself to his hands and knees.

"Fire-er-er," word lengthened sobbingly by the stabbing anguish, "O no, it's not."

It is diminishing. She huddles over, keeping her hands tight, lest her intestines fall out. Seppuku I kidded, it kids me not . . . what slipped or tangled or pierced? Joe presses her shoulder gently.

"Get your hand off me," she is panting hoarsely and sweat runs in steady drops down her face.

He takes his hand away. He sits wearily back on his heels, and reaches an arm out for his child. Whispering is all he can do, "Aue, tamaiti . . ." and Simon scrambles to him as though the arm were the only shelter left in the world.

. . .

She was still pallid and sick and ill-tempered when they got back to the old bach.

She'd refused help in walking, Joe's or Simon's.

"Okay, you lend *me* your shoulder, Himi, I can use it," the man said ruefully, and leant enough weight on the boy to kid him he was helping.

She'd refused food and drink and all care offered, and ignored Joe's tentative apology. She climbed into bed with her clothes on, burrowed under the eiderdowns and fell asleep, immediately, deeply, unnaturally.

She didn't wake until it was dark.

. . .

Joe says, unintentionally louder than anything he's said for the past two hours, "Well, maybe they only go when she whistles at them or something, honey, but I can't get them to light."

She whistles, a sharp three notes like anyone calling in their dogs.

"Nope?" she questions into the silence. "Hell, we'll just have to use matches afterall."

They laugh. They laugh heartily and immoderately considering the feeble nature of the joke, but it is warm kindly laughter.

And with undertones of anxiety yet, thinks Kerewin, but she grins at them widely from round the side of her bunk, a supple grin, an easy grin, a white flag of a grin for their white flag of laughter.

It seems silly to keep a war going. She is so deep in peace her very bones feel soft with it. And they're waiting, their smiles still at the ready, Joe with his hands cupped over the child's shoulders, Simon hanging with both hands onto one of his father's.

Like he's trying to throw him, judo fashion, she thinks irreverently, but likes the forgiveness and acceptance implicit in their pose.

"All right, people," she says, and swings her legs over the bunkside. The movement doesn't bring even a twinge to her belly-muscles.

> Weird, me soul . . . snatched out of thickets and thatches
> of furze and turned around taverns where thorns drank
> us . . . a rip from a burning bush or a ghost-dagger in the
> gut, but not even a small bulge of hernia or tender swol-
> len muscle to show where. . . .

The boy has danced away from under the shelter of his father's hands, coming to her, by her before her feet hit the floor.

Eyes so wide and dark you can read the question like type coming up on a screen, Are you all right now?

"Right as rain, Sim," she says, still smiling, and he hugs her, blending his ready tears with his jackolantern grin. "E Joe, your disgusting child is kissing me knees," she lifts the boy quickly and stands with him. "I don't mean that nastily, sea imp, I truly don't. It's just an odd place to get salutations, that's all."

Joe says simply, "He was worried, now he's glad. I was worried as hell."

She walks to the range where Joe stands, arms folded against his chest now, his face so puffed with bruises his grin is crooked.

"Jesus," he says fervently, "I'm glad you're okay. . . ."

"Um yeah. What's for tea?"

> Some of that is put on, mate. Nobody could sound *that*
> happy I'm all right after the smacking round you got.

"We haven't got any ready. We were too worried," he says again. "When you flaked, I didn't know whether to get a doctor or not. I didn't know where to get a doctor anyway. Your breathing sort of relaxed and sounded ordinary after a while, so we crossed our fingers and hoped. We didn't know whether you'd give us the umm boot, or whether you'd wake up wild again, or what. So we commiserated with one another on our various hurts, and kept a weather eye on your bunk. And then we woke you . . . wasn't it?"

"Well, it was nice to hear your voice again, loud and all."

The brown eyes level with her own are so open she feels she could slide in and poke round in the chambers of his soul.

> He really does mean it, Holmes. No illwill at all.

"What was it? The uhh?" waving a hand round the region of his stomach.

"I haven't the faintest idea. It's never happened to me before, but it might be an ulcer. I drink enough to support one."

"I hope not."

"You and me both, man. How're you?" It's a clipped-on casual query.

Joe grins lopsidedly.

"Battered but not broken. I got aches and bruises but that's okay. In an odd way, it is penance you know?"

"I can believe it." She shrugs. "I been wild at you since last week. Since I found out how you've whacked him. Nobody should take the kind of hidings he's been getting, not for any reason at all. But let's forget it. Drop the subject. If you can believe I'm both sorry and glad to beat you up, you can also believe the matter is closed as far as I'm concerned. Provided you don't beat him like that again."

"First things first," he says slowly, and Kerewin thinks, Yeah, here it comes, you were lucky and all that crap, but he goes on, "I'll tell you all the why of the past whenever you want to hear it. Meantime I swear, on his head," hand motioning to but not touching the child's bright hair, "not to hit him again. If he deserves it, I'll tell you and you can decide . . . I mean that, that if, uhh God—"

"Assuming I am willing to assume some responsibility for him," she interrupts coolly.

The man gazes into the fire.

"Yes."

"I sort of hoped," he adds, and falls silent again.

And I do believe he's going to cry.

She says quickly,

"Say a smidgin of responsibility, a scantling, a scruple of responsibility I accept. After all, you're not that big, boy."

The child grins.

Joe sniffs and rubs his hands across his eyes. "Ahh Kerewin, I don't know . . . I need a dictionary to talk to you." He thinks, You bugger, you cold lady you. "Anyway," breathing out heavily, "that'll be good. We'd love you to help . . . and the other thing is, I don't hold any grudge against you, but that's the first time any one person has dropped me in a fight without a weapon of some kind. How'd you do it?"

"Ah hah," says Kerewin, "geddown you," and slides Simon down to the floor. "Say you get that bottle of Tattinger I've been saving for emergency celebrations in the new bach. Then we can chat over it. I'll even cook tea while we do. But to be frank, you didn't have a snowball's chance in hell against me."

Joe doesn't answer, except to ask gently, before going out for the champagne.

"The ulcer?"

"Will be made comfortable and sedate by good wine . . . if it's an

ulcer. It might have been because I was using muscles and techniques I haven't used for years . . . anyway, the champagne please,
so we can celebrate."

As she stokes the fire she says to Simon, broodingly.

"Though I'm not sure what we're celebrating. Not what's happened certainly. The future, maybe. . . ."

Simon leans against her, and stares into the flames. His face is
composed and his eyes are unreadable.

. . .

By the time Joe returns, she has scrubbed potatoes and put them
in the oven; made a tangy mayonnaise from yoghurt and honey and
wheatgerm oil; grated carrots and sliced an apple thinly. It's a large
green grannysmith, and she only peeled it partly.

The boy plays teeth with the peel before eating it.

"Provide you with some you're missing eh?" and he grins a green
ghastly grin. He turns it on Joe when he comes in.

"Yurk, and after the way you eat toothpaste, too." He gestures
to the bottle, "I open it?"

"Yeah please." She goes on chopping up vegetables; cabbage into
shreds; clove of garlic squashed; piece of green ginger skinned and
sliced into fragments . . . "Quick stir of that lot, slather in the mayonnaise, and there's your salad, complete. . . ."

Joe sniffs.

"Smells piny. Nice."

"Tastes piny too. Great, if you like turpentine . . . where'd I put
the pork chops?"

"They're in the safe. I'll get them if you like, and you can continue the struggle with this cork?"

"S'okay, you're doing fine. I'll get 'em."

The stars glitter and wink in the deep of night. The rain still falls
soft on her skin.

> It was just beginning when we came back up the
> beach . . . hell, I can't understand him. Either of them. It
> doesn't make sense to be without any reproach . . . or
> are they both masochists? They don't act like they are,
> but it's a bloody kind of love that has violence as a si-
> lent partner. And Sim hugs Joe as if he's never been

thrashed, and Joe just grins at me amidst his bruises.
Penance? Strangeness? Hei, I don't know. . . .

Joe asks when she comes back in,
"Any champagne glasses?"
"No. Recycled peanutbutter jars that do double duty, beer and water. Even champagne at a pinch."
"Sacrilege," he says in a stagy whisper. "Two or three?" in normal tones.
"There's three of us."
"Ka pai."
The pinpoint bubbles tremble and sniz at the surface. The wine is pale as the light on straw.
"Ahhh . . . here's to peace and solace all round."
"So say we . . . and may the rest of this holiday be ah, as stimulating as this first day but a little more easy and quiet."
"Hear, hear," says Kerewin in a deep hollow voice. She asks a minute later, mouthfuls later, "Are you disliking this, fella, or is that face-twisting because of the fizz?" Joe squints at his child. "He doesn't like it. And you don't want to say, eh."
"Right. Rescue what remains, and fill his glass with mead." She reaches down a bottle from the shelf behind her. "He does like this. At least, he drinks it."
The boy blushes.
"O?" asks Joe. "Words behind words?"
"If only you knew . . . that's what started this whole thing off, believe it or not, but Himi can tell you if he wants. Only if he wants."
He doesn't want. He most emphatically does not.
"Okay, past is past," says Kerewin, and refills their glasses.
The silence is profound. Joe eyes Simon, and the boy stares guardedly at the champagne bubbles in Kerewin's glass, and Kerewin looks from one to the other, shaking her head. "You ever notice," trying to change the subject, "how loud your swallow is when there's no other noise?"
"Mmmm. O well, to hell. How long's tea going to be?"
"About half an hour. You hungry?"
"Very, but I was wondering how you have a bath round here, and whether there was time for Himi to have one before tea."

"Well, he could go and have a shower—there's one rigged up at the back of the boatshed—but he'd probably freeze to death before he got clean. The alternative is, you heat water on the range, and fill the old tin bath. It's in the boatshed too, but can come in here. It'll take about ten minutes for the water to heat, so you could squeeze in a bath between now and tea."

"Right. We'll get that over with."

. . .

Joe removes the bandages Kerewin had put on without a word. For a minute, strangely like his son, he won't meet her eyes. When he does, his eyes are full of tears. It takes Simon's slow headshake, straight stare at his father, so full of disgust, so full of disbelief, so exaggerated Regrets now? Ah come *on,* to break the tension.

"Ah you," says Joe, half-laughing, half-crying.

"Yeah, ah you," Kerewin grins helplessly to the child's sly grin.

There is, after all, really nothing else to say.

. . .

That curious impersonal property sense parents display over their young children's bodies . . . check this, examine that, peer here, clean there, all as though it's an extension of their own body they're handling, not another person. . . .

She's amused by that.

Ostensibly, she's revolving her ersatz champagne glass (very odd tit Madame de Poitier would have had to make *this* one, sausage-shaped and nippleless . . .) and watching the bubbles extinguish themselves. But out of the corners of her eyes, she studies the man and his child.

Most of the time, Joe sits on his haunches and oversees. Simon is way old enough to bath himself, but he checks what the boy does, and when he needs help, helps gently, competently.

Hell, the brat is positively chewed looking. Thick with wales.

He'll carry his scars for life. Yet he doesn't seem concerned.

He flinches occasionally but not away from his father's ministrations, from the touch of water . . . and the weird thing is, it's Joe who sucks his breath in each time, as though it was him that was hurting.

Bloody mixed up pair, she thinks, fashed in the head and still making it in the heart.

And now I'm embroiled. She asks, covering her moroseness,

"That hole in his left earlobe . . . what from?"

"Huh?" and they both turn to look at her, startled.

"During the contretemps this afternoon, I noticed Sim has a small hole in his ear. Is it from an earring?"

"God help us," Joe sounds stunned, "you saw that while hitting me?"

"Yes, and I haven't forgotten I said I'd tell you where I learned to fight."

"I'm not sure I want to know now . . . probably a pact and personal teaching from some taipo," he says in a soft aside to the child that she is meant to overhear. "That hole, yeah, it's from an earring. He had a heavy gold thing in it, like a keeper, when he arrived. He wore it until early this year. He got teased too much about it at school, so I took it out for him. He still carts it round . . . in your dufflebag now, isn't it?" and Simon nods.

"O. No marks on it, I suppose?"

"No marks."

"Pity . . . and pity you had it taken out, ould Ireland, because gypsy or hippy, pirate or fisherman, it'd become you," and the child blinks. "I mean, it would look good, besides being ever-ready coin for Charon, which would have been handy before," she says drily. "You won't need it for that now we've come to an understanding, though . . . speaking of which, e hoa, here's why you got clobbered this afternoon," and she launches into the tale of her year in an aikido dojo in Japan.

She had been attracted to aikido because she had heard that it was some kind of super-karate, the ultimate kung fu. It wasn't anything of the kind, she said, but it took a while for her to learn that.

"To quote a master of it, 'Aikido walks the way of the universal, and has as its sole aim, the perfection of humankind.' The techniques are based on unifying mind and body and spirit, but they're immensely practical in any kind of fight. But you're failing if your only aim is to beat up your opponent. I couldn't understand that . . . I was the ultimate warring barbarian. Slam crash along comes Holmes . . . chuck out yer morals and spiritualese, show me how to gut 'em in half a second flat. Stomp strangle and maim hooray! I didn't stay that long, not long enough to become really expert, but I can handle six ordinary attackers at once quite comfortably."

"No wonder you waded over me then. . . ."

"Yeah, it wasn't that difficult . . . but I've seen an old woman in the Hombu dojo take on ten armed men, knives and sticks and bottles, or rather let them take her on, and she just massacred them. Or rather, let them massacre each other . . . quite a sight," she shakes her head slowly. "Massacre in the figurative sense," she adds, seriously.

"I hoped you meant it like that."

"Mmm, well . . . I left Japan after a year, screaming about getting up at five every day to practise, practise, practise. Screaming about spending two hours every day in misogi breathing. Screaming about the food, about not being able to test the techniques I'd learned in match situations, screaming about everything."

"No contests?"

"They're forbidden . . . look, I'll quote you some words, and the thing might become a bit clearer. Just a minute."

She lifts down her guitar case, and takes a small book out of it.

"When I came back to good old Aotearoa after the Japan fiasco—I didn't get kicked out, incidentally, I kicked myself out—I started thinking about all they tried to teach me, and ended up agreeing with them. I didn't do much about it, I had started building at Whangaroa for one thing, and I felt heartily ashamed, for another. But I wrote out a lot of sayings that had been given to me, and added a few bits of my own," waving the book in the air. "That's part of this."

She sits back by the range. "These potatoes smell about done . . . you nearly finished?"

"I'll just wash his hair."

"Okay. Here goes . . . Aiki is not a technique to fight with . . . it is the way to reconcile the world, and make human beings one family. Winning means winning over the mind of discord in yourself. It is to accomplish your bestowed mission. Holmes addendum: and to discover your bestowed mission. Love is the guardian deity of everything. Nothing can exist without it. Aikido is the realisation of love. The way," stopping reading, and explaining, "Do is Japanese for a way. Ai means love, harmony, and ki is the vital spirit. Aikido can mean, the way of martial spiritual harmony, okay?"

"Okay," says Joe.

". . . The way means to be one with the will of deity, and practise it. How can you straighten your warped mind, purify your heart, and be at harmony with the activities of all things in the universe? You should first make God's heart yours. There is no discord in love. There is no enemy in love."

Joe is frowning. He doesn't say anything except, "Keep your eyes covered, tama" when he pours water over the child's soapy hair.

"Even standing with my back to the opponent is enough. When he attacks, hitting, he will injure himself with his own intention to hit. I am one with the love of the universe, and I am nothing else. There is no time or space before Uyeshiba of Aikido—only the universe as it is."

She stands, and puts the small book back inside the guitar case. The guitar strings hum faintly as the lid goes down.

"That writer was Morihei Uyeshiba, founder and master of Aikido."

The silence continues.

Coming back to the range, she opens the oven door and pokes the nearest spud.

"Done to a turn, e hoa ma. . . ."

Simon stands in a flood and shower of drips. Joe wraps a towel round him, and bundles him out of the bath onto the stool.

Joe, towelling the child dry,

"So you picked up the techniques, but not the spirit of it?"

The question was unexpected. The silence had lasted so long that she thought she must have bored the man with the length of the quotations. She answers,

"Since the techniques really concern spiritual development, I didn't pick up anything except enough physical knowledge to make me extremely dangerous in any fight with anyone who isn't an aikido expert. I'm good enough to take the beginners . . . I started out with a cold temper, fast reactions, a killer instinct, as well as Maori ancestors . . . all of which makes me someone to avoid when I'm in a nasty mood. Don't worry," she says grinning, her teeth shining red in the light from the open firebox door, "the philosophy is over for the duration, and I promise never to fight you again. Not without serious provocation, that is. Like not eating this superbly cooked meal . . . oops, the chops seem a bit crisp. . . ."

"I like burnt chops," says Joe. "Get some clothes on, honey, and we'll dry your hair after tea. Where do we put the bathwater, Kerewin?"

"Chuck it out the door."

After he has done so, he asks without preliminary, "Did you wonder whether that pain might be a consequence of sort of misusing knowledge?"

"I did, but I discarded the idea. Deity tends to exact revenge in more subtle ways than that."

"Yeah?" He doesn't sound convinced.

. . .

When she woke for the second time, it was nearly midday. She stretched cautiously, but all the pain had gone. "Downright peculiar," she said, and got dressed.

The Gillayleys were gone from the bach. The bunks were made, the breakfast dishes washed and neatly stacked to drain and dry.

"Kia ora!" read the note, and Simon had written it. "We are making lunch. See you. Arohanui, H & H."

> Joe's dictation, I'll bet . . . only he would end it, Hohepa
> and Haimona.

It was still drizzling outside. No fishing for a while yet, she thought, staring at the sea, and sighed. Another day inside . . . smoke, and card games, and guarded talk, and everyone looking sideways at each other. . . .

Despite the overt friendliness and reconciliation of last night, she can't believe the former delight in each other's company will be there. Sooner we finish this stay, the better, she told herself, opening the door to the new bach.

Joe swings round and grins. Simon isn't here.

"Uh, good morning, where's . . ." and Joe grins more widely still.

"Good afternoon to you!" he says cheerfully. "Right behind you, he's just been out for a piss."

And you passed me *that* close while I was doing it, Simon's mime is both graphic and funny. Like his father, he's full of smiles, and she finds herself answering them.

It might be okay yet,

her heart lightening, but even then she is unprepared for the flood of affection she feels for them both when Joe says,

"Now you're back, Himi, we can show her." To Kerewin, "It's because you said it would look good . . . first thing this morning, I had to put it back," sweeping Simon's hair away from the side of his face.

In the pierced lobe of the child's ear, the gold circle. Bright as the smiles, seemingly as unbroken as their friendship.

5

Spring Tide, Neap Tide, Ebb Tide, Flood

TIDE IN

The day is warm and the wind is light, but the sea is still rough and whitecapped.

"Tomorrow," says Kerewin, "better wait for tomorrow eh?"

Joe shrugs. He's easy, he says. The fish'll wait. "I'll try for some paua. Where's the best place?"

"Try the second arm of the reef, out where I was standing a couple of days ago. That's the only place I could see any sign of them."

So Joe heads north, the fork over his shoulder, while Kerewin goes to the other end of the beach.

"I'm going to do some sketching." She takes a pad and felt-tips and charcoals.

But she isn't drawing, thinks Simon. Sleeping yeah. It can't be sunbathing. She's lying wrapped in a rug under an umbrella.

He turns his attention back to the cliff above the black bach.

There is a hole there, two feet in diameter. He can see in for nearly a yard, then it tunnels away in a curve and the shadows become too dark to see anything. He'd like to wriggle partly in, stretch his arms out, explore, but there might be something quiet, with teeth, waiting further up.

"It's a rabbithole," Kerewin said. "There's still a few of them round here. The country holds a drive every few months with guns and dogs and a helluva hullabaloo, but there's always a couple missed it seems. Rabbits, I mean, not holes. . . ."

They kill them then, he thinks. Maybe there's nothing down the hole now. Maybe they're all dead.

He finds a stick and inserts it cautiously. It goes into the shadowed part, but he can feel more space beyond its end, even with his arm stretched in up to the shoulder.

He goes along to Kerewin and takes her hand and shakes her awake, and begins explaining. How can I find out what's there? he asks with writing in the end. Kerewin says sleepily, "Dig it up . . . you want to?"

He nods vigorously.

"Well don't expect to find anything marvellous," but tells him where to find a shovel in the boatshed. He digs for most of the afternoon before he gets to the end of the hole.

There's a round hollow, not large. It is lined with soft hair, and on that, huddled together, are two mummified baby rabbits.

He looks at them for a long time, not touching them. Sweat dribbles into his eyes, stinging them, but he stands quite still and looks.

The fur is dulled, the eyes shut and sunken. Their ears are stiff leather pieces, laid back on their dead bony shoulders.

He puts the dirt back on top of them.

I'm sorry, he thinks, shovelling faster. I didn't mean to worry you. I wouldn't have dug you up if I'd known you were there.

He fills back in all the dirt he dug up, and sits down on the pile for a rest. His hands are sore and his shoulders ache, and he's still sweating, even though the work is finished.

Joe comes along a little later, wet to the waist and whistling loudly.

"Hey, we got paua for tea, Himi!" he calls, and comes to the base of the cliff.

"What you been doing? Been busy?"

Digging, says Simon, showing how. On another piece of ground.

"Find anything in that hole?" asks Kerewin over tea.

Simon shakes his head, No, not a thing.

. . .

It's a groggy kind of dream. He knows it to be a dream even as it happens.

You're kneeling back by that hole. It's hot in the sunshine. You feel like crying, but you know something better, and you want them alive. So you start feeding them music, underbreath singing, and little by little the withered leathery ears fill out: flick flick, a tentative twitch and shake. The dead dried fur begins to lift and shift and shine. Those sunken holes of eyes and nostrils pinken slowly, like a blush stealing over, the eyes to moisten, darken, the nostrils to quiver, and then they open their eyes on you and they glow.

The music rings and swirls now, picks up like a lift of a wave, and the light has turned from ordinary sunlight to a deepening blue-green, shot with gold . . . you're inside a moving wave of sound and light and quick joy, and it steadies, stays, before the motion of descent can begin, and sicken.

The rabbits shift and nudge one another, start to joust with soft brown forepaws in a glad scrabble to get free of the hole of darkness, and scatter away into the green waterlight shine.

"I want to tell you," he sings fondly to Kerewin and Joe, who're holding his shoulders now, and they turn and stare at one another with delight. But when they look back, their faces waver and change, and the wave begins to move, faster and faster, and the light is turning to night.

He can feel the wire round his wrists again. There isn't any room to move, and there isn't enough air to breathe, and the voice, rich warm powerful voice, is questioning, questions he can never answer, and laughing when he struggles. The voice grows and echoes, and the pain intensifies, and he tries to cry out against it, but no sound comes. A bitter sting in his arm, and then the fingers bite him, pushing into the places where it hurts worst, and sending him down into the blackness where he cannot breathe. The lid closes over against his silent screaming, and the blackness floods everything.

And as he wakes, gasping and weeping and struggling futilely, he can still hear the voice in his head, singing his name in the deep of the receding dark.

. . .

They're sitting in companionable silence, sipping whisky.

Joe asks, "What was he playing at this afternoon with that shovel?"

"Digging up a rabbithole. He wanted to find out what was at the end of it."

He laughs softly. "Trust Himi . . . tired himself out nicely any-way. No dope needed, for a change."

More silence, filled with the slow breathing of the sea.

"You know something?" He shakes his head. "That's the first time I've seen him do anything like play."

"Yeah, well . . ." Staring into his glass. "He doesn't play much, I dunno why. We tried, Hana and I, gave him all kinds of toys at first. Blocks and dolls and trucks, but Timote knew more than he did when it came to playing with them. He didn't exactly ignore them, but it was like he didn't know why he should bother with them. We used to play with the darn things more than he did, showing him how and that, and he used to look at us rather kindly, but with distinct superiority . . . and then all the gear started getting lost. He gave some of it away quite openly to Piri's kids."

"Kids? I understood he only had one?"

"No, he's got four. Lynn, his wife, took three with her, and he looks after Timote. It's a bit daft," he says, swirling the whisky round in his glass. "Timote's the one who could have most used his mother's care, and the oldest, Liz, dotes on Piri and wanted to stay with him . . . but you can't order other people's lives, eh?"

"You can't . . . so Piri and Mrs Piri are separated?"

"In the process of getting as far separated as possible, but Piri doesn't want it . . . anyway, him and his toy phobia, well not a toy phobia, a disinterest. You know about the music things?"

"Yes."

"There's two music boxes. A little pile of junk, mainly clock in-nards, and I think they all get fed into his crazy constructions. He used to have that black case with his beads in it . . . he played with those for a while, when he thought no-one was around to grab them. And that's about it."

"What about the stuff he ah, borrows?"

He frowns.

"That's not so much to play with as gloat over, I think. A mad magpie instinct, you know?"

"I can imagine ... does he keep all the gear at home? You fall across say, hordes of old chess queens and things from time to time?"

He grins despite himself.

"Nope. Some of the things he thieves stay in his pockets. I think he's got a hideaway round the house for other stuff though."

"I know this is a sore subject with you and all that, but um, since I'm going to be shouldering that soupçon of responsibility, does he shoplift? Or is all the loot whizzed away from friends and relations?"

"I wouldn't know, e hoa, I truly wouldn't know." He shifts uncomfortably, looking down at his whisky again. "He swipes gear from everyone, you included, at some stage or other, and he's been accused of thieving at school. But nobody proved that one," thinking momentarily of what Binny Daniels said. He shakes his head, trying to shake the old man's words away physically, He adds heavily, "No-one's caught him shoplifting. Yet." He swallows the whisky in a hurry. "Aie, I don't know, Kerewin ... he's been told and hit a lot for stealing, but he still does it."

"That only shows that hitting him isn't a particularly good way to teach Sim."

She fills his glass, pours another dram for herself. She starts filling her pipe, her face thoughtful.

"What else can I do though?"

"Talk to him maybe. Try and find out why he does it."

"Last year," says Joe, cupping his chin in his hands, "I took him to a children's psychologist after a lot of hints from Bill Drew at school. The fella asked a lot of questions, but ... he was a nice enough bloke, I suppose, but his voice never got raised above a confessional whisper and his breath smelt of, I think, garlic and peppermint, and he kept on saying, "Not to worry ah Mr ah Gillayley, we'll soon know a little more.""

Kerewin chuckles. "Sounds a cretinous git."

He looks at her, and the lines on his face lighten a little. "Yeah ... I'll guarantee he never got to know that little bit more anyway, because Himi sits there and stares the whole time. The bloke puts out all kinds of puzzles and asks questions every minute in this low tell-it-to-me voice, and Haimona doesn't make a move. Sits there with his mouth open, looking like an idiot. Not a twitch or a squeak out of him, nothing eh, nothing at all. The child psych says after about half an hour, 'Ah Mr ur Gillayley, is he always this um nonre-sponsive?' And that bloody Sim sort of slides me a look sideways, and I can see he's nearly killing himself keeping a straight face. And I have to say in all seriousness, 'Ah no, Doctor, he's normally um very lively. I think it's just the strange surrounding eh.' And that was that. The fella made another appointment for us to come back, but by mutual consent, we decided it wasn't worth the trip into Taiwhenuawera.

"I think your son's got a rather wicked sense of humour."

Joe sighs, back to being serious again. "He's got a different sense of humour. Different sense of everything."

"Mmmm." She lights her pipe, and watches the match twist and blacken and go out. "You ever go to anyone else in the psych field?"

"We'd have to go to Christchurch, eh."

"Mmmm." After a minute, "It doesn't make sense. Neglected and unhappy kids steal to get attention. Sim's not neglected, but he's probably been unhappy because of the way he's been treated, and,"

Joe winces,

"disregarding his background, his handicap, he's had reason to go round pinching stuff to show people, 'Hey, here I am, I want you to help me.' But that doesn't tie in with not playing, and not own-ing stuff. I don't think so, anyway."

She takes the pipe out of her mouth, and swallows the glassful of whisky. "Ahh . . . does he play with other kids at all?"

"No, not at school. Not according to the teachers. He generally stays on the fringes of anything going on, looking . . . and he's never brought anyone home to play or gone to play with anyone as far as I know. He sticks round adults most of the time, or goes away by himself. He did used to play with Whai and Liz and Maurie—that's Piri's lot, and they're all nice kids—but there was a hell of a lot of fights."

"What over?"

"O anything and nothing. One moment they're all happy hide and go seeking or whatever, and the next boomf! Sim's in, boots and all."

"But there must have been some kind of provocation or misun-derstanding each time?"

"It's pretty hard to find out what started things when you've got a yard full of kids all yowling and hammering one another." He adds, "Liz always used to take Himi's side. . . ."

"Good for her . . . you could have asked them after though, Joe."

He shrugs. "Well, what with one thing and another, we never did."

"O." She lights her pipe again, and puffs away in silence.

> He doesn't seem to have thought about the boy in any deep fashion. Why Sim does strange or wild or bad things . . . he either kicks or kisses the brat, and hopes things'll work out. Like if he hits him enough, Sim'll stop stealing, without finding out what started him stealing in the first place. Or maybe the spiderchild has always been lightfingered?

and she's just about to ask him that, when the door opens, and the boy stumbles inside.

Joe takes one look, "Ah Jesus, nightmares," and kneels down, gathering his son into his arms.

Another time, she thinks.

. . .

TIDE OUT

Very early morning, fine and mild.

("You reckon we ought to go? After last night?"

"Yeah, he's all right. Box of birds.")

The sea is mid-tide, on its way out, but flat and quiet. The water curls sleepily onto the beach, stays awhile in a flat silver sheet, and then seeps back into itself. There isn't a wave anywhere to speak of.

"Um, has he been out in a boat since being shipwrecked?"

"No." He whispers it, reluctant to break the silence of the dawning.

"Ye gods and little fishes. . . ."

> What will we get? Pandemonium? Or he'll just be scared shitless?

She picks up a lifejacket.

"Give him that, it's smallest . . . this can be yours. O, and tell him he better go to the toilet now, because it's okay for pissing out there, but anything else is bloody awkward."

Joe glances at her and his eyes twinkle. He says in an ordinary voice, "Don't worry, he's already been. So've I."

"Okay. . . ."

"Can I carry anything for you?"

"No. I'll take the rods and the bait, and you can bring him. Led, carried, or whatever."

He goes back to the bach, and Kerewin heads for the boat.

Her craft back at Whangaroa is a 36 foot converted fishing trawler, with a 100 h.p. inboard. It has a galley, bunks, and lockers, and is equipped with everything she thought useful or decorative. Radar, depth sounder, electronic compass, marine radio, chart library. She could live on board, for everything necessary is there, from the small fridge and cooker to the extraordinary shower and WC arrangement. To date, she's taken the vessel out on three fishing trips. The Aihe II is, as yet, a plaything among playthings in plenty.

The craft waiting for her at the water's edge is a 12 foot clinker-built dinghy, and it's powered by a temperamental 5 h.p. outboard. There is a splashboard at the bow, and three seats, and no gadgetry at all. As Kerewin's brothers were apt to say, there was precious little comfort either.

But the boat is as old as she is. She practically grew up in it, learned to swim from it, row in it, handle it in seas and weather of most kinds. She knows and loves every inch of the nameless little ship, from the screw gouges the motor has made on the sternboard, to the set of grooves at the bow where she's hauled up the anchor times out of mind.

You've been taken care of, she thinks. Someone has repainted the boat during the past six years—the blue is darker than the last coat she'd given her—and one of the curved pieces of wood holding the port rowlock shaft has been neatly replaced. There's new canvas covering the lattice in her bottom, and the anchor rope is nylon now, not sisal.

But if only I could have taken you when I pinched the coffee-grinder. . . .

She'd swap the Aihe for it, right now.

She stows the two rods under the seats, the thermos flasks in the bowlocker together with fruit and smokes and sandwiches and firstaid kit. She can hear the crunch of footsteps on sand behind her, and Joe talking steadily, quietly.

"All well?" as she clambers out of the boat.

"More or less. Do you want a hand to shove off?"

"Help us get her right afloat, and then you and Sim get aboard. I'll do the rest."

The dinghy is heavy and hard to shift on land, but in the sea it's a different story. She stands, sea near the top of her boots, holding the boat steady as Joe wades to the stern carrying his son, lifts him aboard.

"Sit in the middle," says Kerewin to the child, who has squatted in the bottom as soon as he could.

"I'll sit with him." Joe climbs awkwardly over the side. The dinghy rocks and sidles, and the boy hunches his shoulders as though he's been struck.

Hell, we should leave him behind,

but she keeps her face impassive.

She pushes out hard, and in the same movement, swings herself nimbly up on the sternboard, kneeling by the motor a second before stepping onto the seat.

"You've done that a few times . . ." Joe has settled himself on the middle seat, holding Simon.

"Yeah, but you should have seen some of the other performances. Distinctly inelegant, to say the least . . . I've brought her in broadside, and nearly turned her over. Gone out on a wrong wave and ended up bum in the air, boots waving goodness knows where. Lost oars, dented her bow, bent the propeller blade on a rock I somehow didn't see. One of the neatest though," she's winding the starter cord round the motor-head, "was a time when I was half-drunk. I should never have gone out, but I wanted to check some pots," she pulls the cord and the motor sputters, but doesn't keep going, "damn." She squeezes the bulb on the petrol feedline again. "Anyway, I do this act, get her launched, push her out—it's a sea like this, calm as a duckpond—and swing myself on board. I ended up under water. I remember thinking, 'Shoot, were'd the boat go?' as I sank." She pulls the cord again, and this time the motor spins into life. She keeps it in neutral a moment, the noise crackling round the bay as she revs it. Before she puts it in gear she adds, "They were killing themselves on shore. They could see it was all going to happen. I apparently hopped up on the stern all right, and then kind of forgot she was still moving. She cruised out from underneath me while I was still plotting where to put my feet next."

In gear, and the boat heads out past the reef for the open sea. Joe says something to Simon, and maybe to her, but she can't hear what it is above the outboard's racket, so she smiles and shrugs to him.

The dinghy is riding badly, and normally she handles well in any kind of sea. It's the weight of the Gillayleys, parked midcentre so the bow lifts high.

"Hey! Go forward!"

"What?"

Kerewin idles the motor. "The boat's out of trim. Too much weight this end. If you go forward, we'll ride that much easier eh?"

Joe glances down.

"Ah hell," she says, and switches off the motor.

She has been avoiding looking at Simon on the principle that if you ignore something unpleasant, it often goes away. If the brat's going to throw a wobbly, she doesn't want to know about it. It is awkward not to see someone a yard away, however, once your attention has been drawn to them.

The boy is huddled into himself, even though his father's arms surround him. His face is white, and his eyes are tightly closed. Presumably he thinks that if he stops looking at the sea, it might go away too.

Is he sick with the motion, with fear, or with memory?
At least he's not making a fuss.

Then again, says the snark, he's inclined not to.

Afterwards, she doesn't know why she says it. She uses bits of languages a lot, but why this snippet at this time, except to preserve her hardboiled image, she really doesn't know.

"Sheeit," says Kerewin, "we'll have to go back. You can't have the bloody pauvre petit en souffrant like that," and the child's eyes snap open. They're black and blank and his face has twisted in terror. He jolts out of his father's arms as though he's been banged

with a cattle prod and falls against the side of the boat. Next moment, he's spewing his heart out over the gunwales.

Joe moves almost as fast as his child. The dinghy rocks wildly as
the weight shifts dangerously to one side.

She sits back hard into the opposite side of the stern, singing out
oaths in a stream, for Joe to get back, for someone to tell her what
on earth or heaven or hell is going on.

And all the time her busy mind, Pidgin French, M C de V, I'll bet
it was Saint Clare beach, Citroen cars . . . I'll lay a thousand on it
there's a French connection somewhere. Worldly peregrinations,
was it? Why not France as well . . . Watching the boy hawk, then
lay his head wearily against the wood, the vomiting spasm over, she
thinks wrily, But I don't think I'll pursue that matter right now. . . .

"Sweet God," Joe is saying in a shaky voice, "are you all right
now? I thought you were going to jump overboard."

"Beach and bed in ten minutes flat," says Kerewin firmly, and
reaches for the starter cord.

But incredibly the boy lifts his head and mouths No, shaking his
head to emphasise it.

So she waits, swapping looks of bewilderment with Joe. A minute later, Simon spits a final time in the sea, and determinedly slides
himself away from the side of the boat. He's still a sick bonewhite
colour, and his teeth are clenched tightly, but he fingers OK to
them, tapping his chest, OK.

"Himi, you deserve a medal," says Joe, his eyes shining.

"Or an anti-seasick tablet . . . they're in the bow, Joe, if he wants
one. Mind you lad, that was a fine display of intestinal fortitude . . . ur,
one way or the other," and she draws a muttered, "You bastard,"
from Joe, and a watery kind of grin from the boy.

"Speaking of bow lockers and that, would you pass me a cheroot
Joe? And there's limejuice in one of the flasks—you want some,
Sim? Nope? Hokay, if the smoke won't bother you, we'll have a
quick one and then be on our way."

It's growing lighter all the time. She chatters, mainly to Simon,
pointing out a circling mollymawk, a line of shags winging away from
Maukiekie, a penguin that surfaces not far from the boat. The boy is
relaxing, little by little. He kneels to watch the penguin, and doesn't
appear to mind the gentle lift and sway of the dinghy under him. Joe
broods in the bow, staring down into the clear green-blue water.

Like looking into his eyes . . . only nothing is moving
down here at all. . . .

"Right," she says, flicking the butt of her cheroot into the sea,
"we all ready?"

"Ae." Joe leans forward. "You all right down there, Himi? You
want me to hold you?"

The boy shakes his head, and Kerewin says,

"I'll take it very easy, just putter along. We've got as long as we
like. Any wind won't be here till eleven."

She grins at the child, still crouched on the canvas, his back to
the bow.

"And with any luck at all, fella, you'll shortly be catching your
first fish here."

"First fish," Joe tells her, adding with a laugh that Simon has the
luck of a proverbial dunny rat. "God knows what he'll catch."

She keeps the motor chugging along at half-throttle for minutes, covertly watching the boy. The colour is coming back into his
face, and as the dinghy moves steadily on, he ventures to kneel up
again, leaning his elbows on the seat behind him. Goodoh, she
thinks, and discreetly winds the throttle to fullspeed.

It doesn't take long to reach her favourite patch. She lines the
marks up, lighthouse centred on Puketapu, Rima lined with the distant pale dots that are the cribs on shore, and feels tears stinging
her eyes as she does.

So long, o my heart, so very long. . . .

She cuts the motor and the boat drifts a little way in a suddenly
resounding silence.

"Theoretically, we are now over an enormous number of blue
cod who never seem to have appreciated over the years that safety
isn't in numbers."

"O?"

"This is the cod patch. Provided everyone else hasn't also discovered it, and fished it out, I guarantee you a blue cod within seconds of your line touching bottom."

She baits up the hooks on one rod.

"You want this, or I give it to Sim?"

"Well, he'll probably find it easier to haul things up with that than a line."

"Okay. Lines are made up ready in the basket there." She slings him a handful of chopped butterfish: she'd caught three off the reef yesterday evening. "Bait one for me too, eh."

She leans to Simon, "You going to do your fishing from there, or from the seat, o neopiscator?"

"Actually, he's been flyfishing with me before. He catches trees quite well."

"Make that neomarinepiscator then, oh" the boy's sat up on the seat and very swiftly flashed Up you at her. "Why you dear child," says Kerewin sweetly, passing him the rod wrongend on, "I hope you catch grand-daddy shark."

Joe blinks.

"Here," he says. "Hold it like this, that bit in that hand, and your right hand on the reel. Now push that knob down . . . you don't have to stick it up in the air like that, keep the tip down. Just let the sinker take the line down, you don't have to heave . . . hell's bloody bells, watch where you sling that lead!"

She is sitting well back, feet propped against the gunwales, humming to herself.

Her line is hitched round a rowlock, and the sinker of her rod is nearly on the bottom. The line twitches.

"What say I give you a race? My catch against both of yours?" She's grinning ear to ear as she tucks the butt of the rod under one thigh, and begins hauling up the handline.

"Ha bloody ha," growls Joe. "How did you manage to get *this* tangled round *here*?"

The boy says nothing.

"Two!"

Good-sized cod, glistening blue-green. They flop and struggle, but she unhooks them swiftly, stunning them with a small brass priest. She winds up the rod-line.

"Ahh, make that four . . . either of you down yet?"

"No," says Joe shortly, tugging at the snarl of nylon.

"Pity. They're biting well."

She stabs each fish through the backbone quickly, then slits the thin connecting flesh bellyside of the spine. The rose-coral gills spread one last time, convulsively. She puts all four, bloody and the bluegreen splendour dulling now, in the basket under a wetted sack.

"Ho hum," rebaiting her hooks, "How yer goin?"

Joe bares his teeth.

"Tell you what man, give us that mess over here, and you tend your line eh?"

"You asked for it."

"Oath, what a foul-up."

"Year-ess," much more cheerfully, as he drops his sinker over the bow.

Kerewin works on the snarl, muttering inaudibly. Simon stares at the sea, the sky, at the dead fish, everywhere but at her. And just as Joe yells "bite" she gets the hooks free of the filament.

"Carefully now," she says to the boy, and he swings it into the sea.

Joe is bringing up his handline, fist over fist, the cord sawing into the wood of the bow.

"Big one. Maybe a couple on each hook eh?"

The boy yelps, and hauls on the rod. It's a light fibreglass boatrod, and the tip has bent nearly to the water.

"Hey, grand-daddy shark . . ." The reel of his rod has locked, and he isn't making any effort to wind in. It's taking all his strength just to hold on. "Just a minute, and I'll help you," says Kerewin. "It shouldn't catch you for a little while yet."

Joe looks over the side. His face twists.

"Haimona," he says in a strangled voice, "You've caught my fish."

She bends over for a look. "My goodness, and it's a *big* doggie too," and laughs all by herself for some time.

By the time Joe has chopped and carved and otherwise parted the ensnared dogfish and the two lines, Kerewin has caught a dozen more cod, three terakihi, and several sea perch. She throws most of the latter back.

"The way I figure it," leaning back comfortably against the motor, "anything that garish and spiny and above all, bigmouthed, doesn't deserve hooking as well. I'm basically a charitable soul, y'see. Besides they're not very good eating."

Joe grunts.

Simon's skywatching again.

Five minutes later, the man rebaits his own hooks and sends his line down. With noticeable restraint, he checks the baits of the boy's line, takes the rod off him, watches the sinker slide through the green water, and waits till it touches bottom.

He gives the rod back.

"Just sit there and hold it," he says coolly. The boy looks sadly at him. With both hands full he can't say a thing properly, but he mouths to Joe.

"Fish? What do you mean fish? Kerewin's probably caught them all," smiling a bitter smile, "but if she hasn't, I intend catching at least one. If a fish gets on your line, get it up yourself. Without tangling up *any*thing *any*where."

Kerewin sniggers.

"Sim, don't worry. With that proverbial luck of yours, you'll probably snag an octopus. It'll climb up your line and fall in love with your father, nestle tenderly up to him arm by arm by arm by yek," she spits violently. It's a fairly messy bit of bait the man chucked. "Joe," she says in a hurt voice, "me baiting you is one thing, but I'm supposed to get bites, not get fed," and cackles like a harpy. She stops immediately. "Waste of good butterfish," she says primly, and starts hauling up yet another cod.

. . .

Joe caught two sea perch. He didn't throw them back.

Simon got a bite. He sat holding the jerking rod tightly, hoping the fish would get off.

It did.

Then quite suddenly, the fish stopped biting. Kerewin carved up a seaperch, but even the change of bait didn't appeal.

"Ah well, we'll have a teabreak. The fish seem to have. Then we can go visit the groper patch. So called, I might add, because you grope round in it hopefully, not because it's loaded with hapuku."

The boy refuses sandwiches and fruit. "You still feeling queasy?" asks Joe. Simon says No, but looks involuntarily at the basket of bloody fish.

"That's making you feel crook?" Kerewin picks it up, as the boy touches his nose. "Yeah, fishblood doesn't smell too rosy . . . it's probably that shark goo up your end too, Joe."

She balances the basket on the gunwales and sluices it down

with the bailer. "Oath that's cold. They'll keep better for it, though."
Joe's removing the blood and guts that landed in the boat during
the shark shambles. "Watch that lot bring the toothy gentlemen
round. Cannibalistic creeps."

"I'll have a go at them with the gaff even," says Joe. "How long
we been out?"

"Nearly two hours."

"I thought so. That means I've averaged a fish and half a shark
an hour."

"Never mind. I've caught enough for a feed, and a small smoke.
And who knows what we'll catch in the groper patch?"

. . .

Simon's thumb.

It all goes sweetly until that happens.

Kerewin slung the anchor out as soon as she stopped the motor.
It's a smaller patch than the other one, she says, and if they drift,
they'll drift off it.

A breeze is up now, just enough to ruffle the water.

For some time, nobody catches anything, but it's pleasant sitting
in the sun. The sea is jade green here, still as a pool when the breeze
has passed. A jellyfish drifts by, glassy discoid pulsing, long purple
tentacles dangling after it in a backwards slant. Something elon-
gated and silver flashes down in the deep, too fast to see what.

Two mollymawks skid across the water on their pale feet and
settle close by the boat.

"They're hopeful," says Joe, but Kerewin says it's a good sign.
"They expect us to catch something they can share eh," and shortly
afterwards the man hooks a large trevally. "Great!" she rejoices,
"haven't seen one of those for damn near decades, and they're beautiful eating." "I'll catch us a couple more then" he jokes, and to their
rowdy delight and astonishment, he does so. "Bloody wonderful,"
says Kerewin. "Forget the terakihi, those are the fellas we'll have
for dinner . . . come on now, Sim. Catch us something spectacular."
He grins. His fear and sickness are forgotten. He settles down on
the middle seat, rod at the ready.

The mollymawks honk, and swim hopefully closer, and the
boy begs for something to feed them. "Look at them, fat as pigs
already . . . but I suppose it's their due."

She cuts a seaperch into filleted chunks, and gives them to the boy.

The birds squawl and splash and gobble the fish. A third molly comes cruising past, and skates in to land in the middle of the feast.

"It's a bloody circus . . . hey, that one's different. Not toroa."

"A variety I guess," says Kerewin frowning, "but I haven't seen his sort around before." The newcomer is the same size as the other two, but where their heads are neat grey with dark brows, its head is shining white. Its bill is orange, flushed pink at the base, and the other mollys have black and yellow beaks, razor-keen. They all have the same appetite for fresh seaperch, however.

"Chuck that new bloke a bit, Himi. I think the others are ganging up on him."

The boy draws his arm back, aims, and at that moment the tip of his rod saws down. He grabs the butt and hangs on. The molly-mawk, eye on the hunk of fish, nearly comes aboard, grabbing it.

"Out you cheeky bastard," yells Kerewin, and, "Hang on, boy."

Joe swings over from the bow seat and sits behind his son. "Want a hand?"

Simon shakes his head frantically. The rod is jerking down, down, down, in hard insistent tugs. The tip is under water, but the child clearly wants to catch whatever it is by himself.

"Okay, this hand's just here in case." He straddles the seat and holds the upper grip of the rod loosely. "When you want a rest, I'll take the strain." Sim nods. He's doing all he can, bracing the rod back.

"Looks a weight." She takes a waddy from under the stern seat, and slides the gaff up from the centre of the boat. "Keep it on, Sim . . . it's probably just a largish shark, but it might be a groper. . . ."

The tugging stops and the rod straightens. Simon's face is misery incarnate. "Wind in," urges Joe. "Wind in quick, he might just be tired."

The boy winds in hopelessly, shoulders sagging. Three turns of the reel, four, and five, and wham! down goes the tip again.

They all yell.

This time the fish pulls for over five minutes before the line slackens once more.

Joe braces the rod with both hands, and Simon winds in until again the fish hauls down.

"Oath, I wish I had a camera," says Kerewin.

The boy is gritting his teeth, hands whiteknuckled round the butt of the rod. Just as well Joe has him caged in his arms, she thinks. If that thing pulls really hard I'll bet the urchin wouldn't let go even if he went in the drink . . . wonder how much longer he can hold out?

It's a grim death struggle: the fish might be tiring, only might, but the child definitely is. Sweat streams down his face, overflowing his cheekbones and dripping off his chin. All his effort is concentrated on holding, waiting for the next period of grace when the fish will cease struggling for deeper water.

> Just as well the reel's star-drag geared . . . you'd have
> lost a finger by now, or skin at least, the power dives
> this fish is making.

Twice more Simon gets to reel in line, the second time making tens of feet, and each time after, the enemy on the other end drags the rod tip down again.

"Sweet Lord, my wrists are getting sore," says Joe, and Simon groans in real anguish as the fish beats down again.

But it is near enough to the surface now for Kerewin to glimpse it.

"Not a shark, boy! Lean the other way, Joe." She balances against the gunwale, ready with gaff and club.

Simon is breathing raggedly, heavily, but he's winding up steadily now.

There's a brief flurry as the fish breaks water, but it's finished.

"Groper!" screams Kerewin, and slides the gaff in at the mouth edge of the gills.

"Keep on winding, fella. Ah you beauty!" whacking the fish hard, "You beauty!"

"Himi or the fish?"

"Both! O my oath, superb."

Simon is laughing, eyes closed, head back against Joe.

As she brings the stunned fish over the gunwales, the man sees its full size for the first time.

"Sweet Lord, it's about as big as he is. . . ."

"And weighs a bloody sight more," grunting with the effort of lifting the groper inboard. "Okay maestro, you can put your rod down now."

The boy opens his eyes, and stares, awed. Bluegrey, massive, huge mouth, that's all he can take in at the moment. He's shaking now the long struggle is over. He lays the rod down on the bow side of the seat: there is enough slack nylon for Kerewin to ma- noeuvre the fish.

"Is it really your first catch?" and when the boy nods, still looking dazed, "Well, that's the best first fish I've seen in my life. Big, and the best eating kind in the sea, for my money. Beats Joe's trevallies, even," she grins.

He smiles, tipping his head back to catch his father's reaction.

"Ka pai," says Joe and gives him a kiss.

The groper chooses that moment to thresh convulsively in a final bid for escape.

"Ye gods!" from Kerewin in a highpitched shriek as the gaff twists loose.

"Getit!" roars Joe and dives to grab the tail.

The groper's head is on the middle seat and the tail is flailing the deck: a few inches more and the fish will make the sea. Simon seizes the nylon, Kerewin seizes the waddy and belts the fish vi- ciously hard thunk thunk thunketty thunk, the beat shivering through the boat. The groper's eyes become rigid in their sockets and protrude. The gills rasp once, then clamp together. It falls back into the bottom of the boat.

"Wow," she says weakly, lost for once for words.

"I think you've pulverised its skull," Joe is staring at the fish with horrified fascination. Then he shakes himself. "Hoowee, if we'd lost that after all," turning smiling to his son, "I don't know how we'd ever . . .

"O God," he says in a sickened voice, several seconds later. "Look what he's done."

Put a 5/0 hook deep in his thumb.

. . .

The spine of the groper was severed. It was bled, wrapped in the remaining wetted sack, and stowed under the middle seat. She chopped the trace off, leaving the hook still in its mouth. She cut through the nylon above the hook in Simon's thumb with more care, holding it below her cut so the hook didn't move. She examined the thumb very quickly. "It's in too deep," she said, and put the firstaid kit back in the locker.

The boy sat and looked at his hooked thumb. His face was back to being a waxen mask.

Kerewin wound the starter cord round, and the motor started first go. She kept it in neutral.

"Ready?"

Joe picked up his son, saying, "All right, stupid," as he did. But he held him as though the child could break in his hands. "Ready," he answered.

She slipped the motor into gear, and swung the bow round for Moerangi beach.

. . .

Joe steps onto the sand, still holding his son.

"Take the car. The keys are on the old bach mantelpiece."

He frowns. "What for?"

"The nearest doctor is at Hamdon. That's too far to walk."

"The nearest doctor he won't fight is three hundred miles away. I'll take it out here."

"Ah, come on, that's minor surgery. He needs a doctor."

She turns round as a wave breaks near the stern of the boat.

Simon swallows. He whistles for her to look, but his throat is too dry.

"Ah, Kerewin. . . ."

She turns back. The boy shakes his head, deliberately, emphatically.

"And that means no doctors eh?"

They stare at her, same set faces, drawn mouths.

"Aue. Well you better go away and do it then." She shrugs and sighs. "I'll put the boat away and fix up the fish."

"You manage the boat by yourself?"

"There's a winch up there. I can do it, easy enough."

"Okay." He turns away.

"Uh Joe . . ." and he swings back quickly.

"There's a flask of brandy in the top cupboard. If you give him quite a bit, but slowly, it'll probably make things a whole lot easier. For you both."

"Yes." He turns for the baches again. "Thanks."

. . .

She removed the gills from the groper head, and put it in a separate bucket. Good for soup, and plenty of pickings in groper cheeks.

She gutted the fish itself and thought in the middle of doing so, "Damn, we should have a picture of it whole. Though if I stick the head back by it, it might give an idea of the size. . . ."

Gutted, and the head off, it weighed over forty pounds.

"Impressive, urchin, impressive."

The gulls that have gathered shift off at her voice.

The cod take longer to process. She fillets each one, and the gulls return, swooping and shrieking over long pink intestines and yellowish glands and skeletons and skins.

She saves a few filleted bodies for cray pots.

The trevally and the terakihi are simple to do: she removes the heads, and flicks out the entrails, and scrubs the bodies clean.

She packs all the fillets and bodies, except the groper, into three buckets, and trudges back to the baches.

Joe is playing his guitar in the new bach. She kicks on the door.

"Ju-hust a minute!" he sings out. "Hello!" he says gaily, opening the door wide, "that didn't take too long."

O star of the sea, who got the brandy?

"No," she says warily. "Would you put these in the fridge," poking at the terakihi and trevally, "and just leave the rest in the buckets? I'll be back in a bit. I've got to collect the groper yet."

She passes the buckets oveer. "Sim okay?"

"Fine, fine. Grogged up to the eyeballs, and an interesting slice out of his thumb, which, curiously, he seems quite proud of. He wants his fish, I'm not sure whether to take to bed or not." Joe smiles and smiles at her.

"I'm getting it."

"Good." He picks up the buckets and shuts the door.

"That was very bloody peculiar somehow," she says to herself, and stamps away back down the beach.

Inside the bach, Joe pours another glass of mixture, for himself.

Port and brandy, horridly sweet, but he swallows it straight down.

He's buzzing with anger inside, like a stirred-up wasp nest, but he's determined not to let it out.

> She could have thought. She could have offered. If there was two of us, one could have held him steady, and the other cut. Even Himi can't hold himself still while someone's hacking into his hand.

The boy had been passive and giggly with drink when he laid him on the sofa.

"Do what you like, yell or kick me, Himi, anything. I'll be quick as I can." He had held the boy's hand in front of himself, so Simon couldn't see what he was doing. Cut, and hold the cut wide, so the barb pulled out doesn't rip flesh further.

He had thought it all out carefully, coming back in the boat, everything: what knife, which antiseptic, what to staunch the blood with, even how to make butterfly stitches—because he couldn't see either of them using needle and thread to seal the cut.

Blessing the first aid course taken so long ago at Teachers' College, he had got it all in his mind, so they could get it done quickly and smoothly, with as little hurt as possible. But he hadn't thought of Kerewin choosing to ignore them. Or that the hook would be rammed into the soft bone. Two yanks to get the bastard thing out. It makes him sick to remember it, and he can't stop thinking about it.

"Another one for you, e tama?" his voice is controlled, his smile in place.

After four glasses of port and brandy, Simon's nearly out to it. He's feverishly flushed, and his eyes keep closing when he wants them open. He makes a very limp Yes with his right hand. At the moment, all he wants to be is asleep. His left hand aches abominably. He keeps starting to think about why Kerewin wouldn't help, about what she said in the boat—he shies away from the words again, but the voice is back, and the songs are starting to sing themselves in the dark that is growing around.

("You sweet effall useless Clare, you caint do no thing
right.")

Joe comes in slow motion, saying something gentle, and holds
the glass steady for him to drink from. He smiles hugely at him to
show that
every
    thing
       is
          all

. . .

She sneaked back to the old bach for her camera. At the boatshed of the black bach, she arranged the groper corpse so that it
looked intact if you didn't look too closely. She laid a yard rule
alongside it, and took shots from three different angles.

"Now you'll have something permanent to show for your ef-
forts, Simon P Gillayley."

As well as another scar, says the snark.

Ah shut up, Kerewin tells it. I don't want to think about that.

She struggles back along the beach, weighed down by the groper,
telling herself all the way to forget it, getting more upset and angry
with every step. Coward, coward, you can't stand anything else's
pain, hide it away, darken it, sweep it outa sight and mind.

Why did the stupid brat have to grab the nylon anyway? I was managing it okay . . . just when everything
is starting to flow nicely, that berloody kid turns it into
a disaster area again.

She sticks the groper in the freezer in the new bach boatshed.

He wants the damn thing, he can go get it for himself.

She pushes open the door belligerently, daring the boy to make
any fuss, the man to make any fuss, anyone to remind her of what
happened.

Joe looks up and smiles.

He lays his guitar down and stands.

"Have my seat and I'll make a tea," he offers kindly. "You've been
doing all the work."

"Thanks."

She glances at the sofa. The boy's a hump at one end, covered by a blanket.

"He asleep?"

"More like deep in an alcoholic stupor, eh," he says it easily, grinning all the while.

More like pain and shock have finally got him,

seeing Simon slip into unconsciousness again, in the middle of his smile,

and bewilderment as to why you wouldn't help.

"Brandy *and* port?"

"It made it sweet for him. He gagged on just brandy. Don't worry, I'll get another bottle of each." His smile is becoming fixed.

Kerewin frowns and picks up the guitar. "To hell with that . . . if he wanted my tokay, he could have had it and welcome." She runs her fingers over the strings, still frowning to herself. "I can't understand why you didn't put your foot down and just take him to the doctor. I mean, they're used to kids being scared of them. They can cope with that sort of thing."

He drops the smile.

"He would either have fought all the way, or got hysterical. If he fought, he would have got hurt. If he started a screaming fit, well, it doesn't just last for a few minutes. It takes hours for him to get over it. This way might have hurt him a bit more initially, but it was quick and he didn't mind. Believe you me Kerewin, he's not just slightly scared of medics. He is terrified of them."

"Why?"

"I don't know," and hopes she'll drop the subject.

"What's he terrified of then? The surroundings? The doctors themselves?"

He shrugs and doesn't answer.

Drop it, lady.

"You said a while ago that he'd been in hospital before you picked him off the beach, and the way he reacted indicated he'd had a tough time then. Did he react the same way when you first took him to a doctor?"

In her way, she is trying to help. Don't blow, Ngakau.

He breathes out deeply. "As soon as he realised Elizabeth Lachlan was a doctor, yes. He had met her before at home though—she was a good friend of Hana's—and he liked her. He still likes her, but he manages to be very scared of her at the same time. You ever watched somebody throw up because they're afraid?"

"Aside from this morning, no."

"He does that every time it's necessary for us to see Elizabeth. And as far as other medics are concerned, he baulks absolutely. There's a limit to how far you can fairly push him. I can hardly thrash him because he's frightened."

"What other medics?"

"O, Elizabeth's locum. The hospital doctors. A bloke in Hamilton, that was when we were on that holiday bus tour . . . he got rundown from being travel-sick, and, I suppose, all the fighting. I thought a doctor might be able to give him something better than Dramamine eh, but as soon as Haimona sees the bag, that's it. He screamed himself into hysteria and that isn't exactly fun to watch or try to handle. The poor bloody medic didn't know what he'd struck. He kept looking at me sideways as though, This his kid or has he pinched it? In the end, he shot him full of tranquilliser, and I thought the needle would break, Himi's arm was that rigid."

Kerewin stops playing, zang in the middle of a chord.

"Needles. A lot of people are pathologically scared of them."

"I don't think so." He switches the boiling jug off. "The first time we took him to Elizabeth's didn't involve injections . . ." he stops, screwing his face up in perturbation, "Wait a minute, it did though. I'd forgotten that . . . he had a hell of a chest cold, and Hana couldn't clear it up. So we see Liz and she prescribes some goop or other, and he was okay till then. She suggested she give him a tetanus booster, because he'd had a course of that in the hospital . . . yeah, that's right." He snaps his fingers. "All of a sudden things happened. Sim went wild but not till then. Not till he clicked to what she was preparing and who was going to get it. Maybe that *is* why all the ruction." Then he shrugs, and begins making tea.

"Well?"

"Well, what does it matter? He's still going to perform if he has to visit a strange doctor."

"Not if he knows what scares him. If you know why you're scared, your fear diminishes."

"O yeah? And that's the crunch, Kerewin. Why is he scared of needles?"

"He might have a genuine phobia. That can be dealt with. There might be some other reason. We could try and find out and help."

Joe grimaces.

"I take it you haven't tried yet, asking him questions about his past."

"Nope." A quick riff.

"You get nowhere fast. I think he tries to give you answers, but he doesn't want to remember anything. I don't think he can remember much anyway, and it all seems to have been bad. If you keep on questioning him, he'll weep or get sick or, as he did with Hana one time, have a go at you." He shakes his head. "Maybe it was the only way he could think of then to stop her asking questions but it upset her . . . Himi too. Anyway, if you persist, he'll have nightmares the next time he sleeps, regardless of how much I dope him."

"O," says Kerewin, staring at the sleeping child. "In that case, there goes my next line of investigation." She starts picking a tune, watching her fingers now. "Because of that luverly reaction to my bastard French this morning—you did notice?"

He nods, his eyes cold.

"I was also going to casually sing the odd song, like this," a simple melody, "Sur Le Pont D'Avignon, and see if he reacted at all. I was also going to polish up my school-learnt French and *very* casually drop the odd sentence into ordinary conversation. Just to see what happens." She stops playing abruptly. "Or did you or Hana speak French to him?"

"We did not. I don't know French. Hana couldn't speak French." His voice is clipped. For the first time, his anger is showing through.

She laughs quietly.

"E Joe, my friend, do you think I hate the poor silly little bastard?"

He doesn't mean to, but it bursts out,

"I don't know, but you weren't much bloody help a while ago, and he needed you then. He kept asking . . . o to hell with it."

"Kept asking why I didn't come and play surgical assistant? Because I wouldn't have been any help at all, not even holding him, or offering words of comfort from a distance. I would have been too busy being as sick as he was in the boat, only continually so."

All the taunt and humour has gone from her voice. "I have an achilles heel, Joe, strange in a fighter. I can't stand watching anything get hurt, helpfully or no. I even kill fish as soon as they're caught . . . I couldn't have done anything to help you or Sim, even if I had grogged up large on that revolting port and brandy concoction. I'm sorry it's upset you, and I'll say I'm sorry, and say why, to Simon soon as he wakes. But no way was I going to have any part of your operation."

The guitar begins to sing again in counterpoint to her words.

"Back to what I began to say . . . I wouldn't put Sim on any kind of verbal rack. If he pukes merrily at one mangled phrase, do you think I'd attempt kackhanded questioning like 'Quelle appellez-vous in the dark old days ma petite chou'?" Somehow the first bars of the Marseillais have sneaked into her playing. "I like ould Ireland, and I'll take care not to hurt him with words . . . it'll all be done with extreme and subtle care. The fish is in the freezer next door," an arpeggio of harmonics, "I took some photos of it more or less entire," a series of brisk minor chords, "though I don't suppose he wants to be reminded of it, eh," zing as she brings one high note skating down a dozen frets, "e hoa?"

He is smiling broadly now.

"I dunno, Kerewin, I dunno . . . we couldn't have cared less if it had been anyone else, but we love you. So I think we better kiss and make up at all opportunities," and because he can feel her drawing away from him, even though she's made no overt move, as soon as he mentioned love, he adds quickly, "metaphorically speaking of course, otherwise we'd be doing bloody nothing else down here."

She laughs and sets the guitar down. "Yeah, well, it must be the sea air or something."

"As for the fish, he'll love the photos. He wanted to know when we'd be going fishing again so he could catch another one . . . he suggested this afternoon."

"Ah youth and resilience . . . if he really wants to go fishing again today, I'll get him out even if I have to swim and tow him."

Joe says drily that maybe today was enough of an introduction to the sea again, without getting *that* close to it, and as it happens, the boy sleeps till dark.

He wakes seemingly relaxed and at ease with himself and the world. His thumb isn't hurting him much, and he is made happy when Kerewin explains apologetically why she stayed at the other end of the beach and didn't offer to help. He gloats over his fish, making three trips out to see it, lying stiff and glistening in the freezer. He eats tea, and stays up quite a while, playing cards with Kerewin and Joe, and winning. By cheerfully concealed cardsharping, they deal him hand after hand of straights and flushes and aces fourhigh, just in case his luck isn't it. He swallows his trichloral with a smile, kisses them both goodnight, and goes happily to bed.

And wakes them both at three in the morning, starting up in the dark and screaming uncontrollably. On and on and on.

. . .

Joe strives, cajoling and pleading in English and Maori and begging interrogatives that are beyond language, to reach the child wherever he is.

She shivers. It is totally unlike the boy not to respond.

> So that's what lies behind those throw away phrases
> Joe uses.
> He has nightmares, you know? And, Spooked would
> you believe?
> This is the shadow to Simon's light.
> The selfcontrol, the unchildlike wit and rationality he
> often shows, the strange abilities he has, are paid for in
> this coin.

The noise is full of abject fear, of someone driven to the point where only terror and anguish exist. Nothing else, not even a memory of anything else, sounds as if it remains.

> Worse than the screaming under the shower, o my
> heart . . . and you were going to poke happily round
> and pry something interesting out of that deep? Inter
> esting . . . aue.

It's too cold to stay sitting up in nakedness. She finds her shirt and jersey, and dresses in them, sits tailorfashion in the middle of her blankets and eiderdowns.

Something Joe has said or done has worked.

Or maybe the spasm of terror doesn't last the way it sounds, forever.

Now she can hear the sea again, a breaker line coming down the beach, the dull boom of the blowhole in the northern reef. The hiss of retreating waves.

"Kerewin?

"Kerewin?" says Joe again. "Are you awake?"

There is, strange and wonderful, a glimmer of laughter in his voice.

"Yes," and her voice sounds deadpan, even to her ears.

He chuckles, then sighs.

"Well . . ." if he was going to add anything, he has decided against it. There's a rustling of blankets. "You like a bed companion for a few minutes?"

"Looks like I get one, will I or nill I," says Kerewin drily. "Switch on a torch, e Joe. I put my smokes down somewhere here, but not even my owl-eyes can spy them. O, plonk whosit down first."

She says, "Greetings, and welcome to the ineffable couch of Holmes, my pipkin. Shall we entertain you with silence and wondrous feats of feet, or shall our fealty be wine and song and nightingales' hearts in jars?"

She can spout highflown nonsense for hours on end if need be, her voice resonant and controlled. She makes no mention of the child's shuddering, or that he's wet himself, nor does she enquire why he started shrieking. It might be midnight at the oasis and ten thousand miles away. She holds him comfortingly and pours Holmes-type paraphrases of the Arabian Nights into his ear, until he listens helplessly to that instead of to the drub of his heart.

Joe listens too, and grins often to himself at the frequent punning and double entendre. Kerewin has a strange vast knowledge of pornography, and a hitherto unrevealed sense of ribaldry. He hopes it's all going over the child's head.

By the time he has got the coals wakened into a fire, and milk heating, she has talked Simon into a state of relaxed, albeit bemused, calm.

"You want some milk too?" He takes Simon from her, wrapping a blanket round the boy as he does.

"Yeah, might as well."

"It'll be a minute . . . we'll duck along to the other bach. I left the dope there, but we'll be back in two ticks."

"Okay . . ."

Hope we can bank on the good old NZ tradition of Don't Interfere. I know there's other people here now, and he must have been heard by everyone in every crib along the beach. If anyone thought we were beating him up, and decided to check. . . .

For the first time, it comes home to her that she is aiding and abetting the concealment of a criminal offence.

Whee, outlawry and small wars made to order, mysteries and pandemonium . . . what the hell did I do before the Gillayleys arrived on the scene?

And she wonders how it would be if they left.

. . .

TIDE IN

Joe is an uncannily good darts player.

A gentle heft, and chk! the dart is as firm in the number, the double, the bull, as though it had grown from there. He rarely misses.

He brought the dartboard back from Hamdon, with more groceries and a renewal of their grog supply.

"Ah darts!" Kerewin said gleefully, rubbing her hands and anticipating victory.

Joe had smiled.

He won every game.

"No bloody wonder I've never seen you play at the pub," she grumbles. "You've probably been banned . . . how do you do it? Hypnotise the feathers or magnetise the points?"

"Years of practice. Years and years of practice."

He told her more that night.

They've established a routine now. Tea and a drink or two, get the child settled in bed, and then play chess and swap yarns and confidences until the fire goes out.

> Simon's asleep in the top bunk.
> (He's been listless all day, though goodhumoured enough. "It always knocks some of the stuffing out of him, eh," Joe says in an aside to Kerewin. "It takes a couple of good nights for him to get over it. And me."
> She says, Yeah, she could see about the stuffing part. Must be taken mainly from the head, she thought, straightfaced. "You notice those luverly purple hollows under his eyes? Whoever does the unstuffing has a nice aesthetic sense. Purple shadows and seagreen eyes . . . rather decadent, but an arresting combination.")
> The kettle's singing a thin metallic song on the range; the sea is heard clearly now, washing laplap husssh by the fence; Kerewin is smoking her pipe, having won the chess as usual; the lamp is dying as the pressure falls off, and the kerosene burns out; and Joe says into the easy night,

"About my one skill, darts . . . I had a *funny* childhood."
"Oh?"
"Funny horrible."
She takes the pipe out of her mouth, and squints into the bowl. "I had a good childhood, I suppose."
"You were lucky." He stares into the bright ashes. "I wonder, I've wondered. . . ."
Kerewin is scraping the dottle from the bowl, attentive, but not urging him to continue. Joe goes on:
"I've often thought that maybe what happens to you as a child determines everything about you. What you are and what you do, and somehow, even the things that happen to you."
"To a certain extent I think it does."
"I mean, my mother left her home area and married away from her people. So did I. I was given to my grandmother when I was three, and I get to foster Himi when he's about that. Hana died early, I was only married to her for five years, and my pa died when I was four, eh. I was an only child, and it wasn't planned that way, and he is too, although I didn't intend him to be. It all links."
"Like he's repeating your childhood?"

"In some ways it looks like that . . . or maybe I'm repeating my mother's life. I don't know."

She packs tobacco into the pipe, thumbing wayward strands neatly down.

"When my mother gave me to my Nana, she was expecting to have plenty more children. But my father died a year later . . . and I always used to think it was my fault, I'd gone away and left him alone, you know how kids are eh?" He sighs.

"I never knew him . . . I never saw him buried even. There was some kind of very bad feeling between his mother my Nana, and him, and it wasn't only over me. She used to say things like, 'I hated his guts from the day he was born, he was born bad.' And, 'I'm not having you turn out wrong like him, that's why I've got you.' She never went to the tangihanga. I used to go round feeling like some kind of leper for having a father so bad, so rotten, that his own mother wouldn't go to his burying. I can't remember much about him, but he always seemed good, and kind."

She asks guardedly, "He always treated you well, then?"

"I think I know what you're getting at." He laughs. "Maybe I can blame my grandfather for that in me, eh. He was highly respected and that, an elder too, but of the church, not of the people. He avoided the marae . . . I think he was ashamed, secretly ashamed, of my Nana and her Maoriness. But oowee, was that old lady strong-willed! What she wanted, she got, me or anything else . . . but the old man, I think he took it out on me for being like her, for being dark, and speaking Maori first, all sorts of things . . . he always seemed fair about it, at least, he always gave me a reason, but he was hard on me. And my Nana wasn't one for letting kids take it easy. I don't think she ever wanted me for myself, just to show my father who was boss. Maybe to teach him a lesson for marrying a lady she didn't like or something."

He laughs again.

"Sounds a nutty family set-up eh? It was, in more ways than one. My mother spent about six years in the bin after my father died. She was away from her family, and his people didn't like her, it must have been hard . . . they used to let them out for weekends for good behaviour or something . . . I never found out why. Anyway she used to come and have this big scene with my Nana, and then go weepy over me. Wail and kiss and carry on, but not because she wanted to comfort or make me feel better. She wanted me to make *her* feel better . . . that's what it felt like, eh. O boy, she'd say, e tama, ka aha ra koe? Ka aha ra koe? And I'd cry and carry on, and she'd cry more . . . and the old people would be sneering away in the background . . . *bad* scene. And it was worse when I got older and was going to school, because she'd be just as likely to swoop on me in the street, and there'd be all the kids around that I knew, giggling and nudging each other . . . shit, it was embarrassing. She got sent down to some South Island hutch eventually, when I was seven or so. I came down with something like polio pretty soon after."

"Holy oath, really?" she says in extreme surprise.

"Ae, ko te pono tena."

The lamp has finally failed.

The fire needs more coal.

She feeds it, lump after lump, waiting for the next revelation.

> Heaven and hell, you never knew what people had in their past.

The room lightens. The fire crackles.

Simon stirs in his sleep, swallows hard, turns to his other side.

"E tama, ka aha ra koe?" he says, softly but sarcastically. It seems the sarcasm is directed at himself. "I should know better you'd think, eh?"

"I don't know. I don't know what I would do in your position." She puffs a smokering that sails in the updraught to the ceiling. Then she says,

"You would have come down with polio before the vaccine was out, and before they could treat it properly. How come you aren't mouldering away in an iron lung somewhere? Or does 'something like polio' mean it wasn't?"

"It means the medics weren't quite sure. You see, Nana was a great one for traditional medicine and avoiding Pakeha doctors. Or Maori doctors trained Pakeha fashion, come to that. As far as she was concerned, the old ways and the old treatments were best, even for new diseases, so that's what I got. By the time the fever was all over, the doctors my grandfather had sneaked into the house weren't sure which germ I'd had, except that there I was, flat on my back in bed with legs that might have been rolls of dough for all the use they were in walking . . . sweet Lord! you should

have heard the language my Nana used when she walked in on a
dirty Pakeha doctor actually daring to tamper with one of her
poultices . . . yeehair! I learned about a dozen new words for filth
and pustular excrescences in two minutes flat. She was good at
languages, the old lady, both languages . . . I wasn't shifted into any
hospital. I wouldn't be, save over her dead body, and I suspect she
would have taken a lot of killing, eh. I stayed in my bed and did all
my schoolwork from there, and when that got boring, I was given
potatoes to peel, wool to card, flax to plait—I can plait and weave
as well as any woman, believe you me. Later it was whittling
wood . . . then back to the books. Except, she gave me a dartboard.
I don't know why she brought me that . . . anyway, I used to tie
string onto the darts so I could bring them back out of the board.
When you've played for a couple of years like that, flat on your
back with darts that fly in a lopsided fashion, playing standing up
with ordinary darts is a cinch."

"Two *years* in bed?"

"Well, it was actually closer to four before the old lady got me
walking again. I think she did that by sheer willpower . . . I want
you to walk, and by God you're going to walk, polio or no polio.
Walk! And here I am, walking."

"Unholy oath," awe in her voice this time, "nobody would ever
pick you'd been crook."

"I've got funny skinny legs as a memento, he iwi kaupeka nei?
But at least I'm not a cripple like so many of the poor buggers who
got the plague when I did."

"Right on, your Nana . . . except maybe for the darts part."

"Ae. . . ."

He has slid into a private reverie, and doesn't appear to have
heard her.

She gets up quietly and fetches herself another pouch of tobacco
from the bach next door. She collects a couple of glasses and the
new bottle of whisky, and walks briskly back. Frost glitters in her
torchlight, on the beach gravel path, on the dead grasses beside the
stream. The stars are bright and close, and the moon shines a cold
silver quarter. Back inside, she proposes a toast.

"Here's to the skeletons we all keep in cupboards."

Joe says unsmiling, "Here's to the ones we let out. . . ."

But the whisky unleashes another flow of words. He tells of his grandmother's death in a car accident when he was sixteen, and how he left her home immediately after she'd been buried. He tells of his mother remarrying, "Another loony, but he seemed a good bloke," and shifting to the far North. He says he hasn't seen her since his own marriage, "She regards me as part of the evil past, better forgotten eh. Besides, she didn't like Hana. . . ." He talks briefly about his grandfather, increasingly bitter as he talks. "I've never been back to see him since I left Whakatu, and that was after Nana died. I got the money to put me through my training there, working on the chain. The old bastard can go to hell in a hand-basket as far as I'm concerned. He might be there already. He'll be pushing eighty if he's still alive."

He talks of his two years of religious dedication. "I even started training as a seminarian. It lasted till I met Hana at an interchurch hui. She was Ratana, and I was Catholic, but we were very diplomatic about religion. We agreed to each go our own way, and let the kids decide for themselves . . . kids, aue."

He is silent for quite a time then, sipping his whisky as though it burns his tongue.

He says, finally, that he dropped out of teachers' college before he got his diploma—"Hana wanted me to get through, but I wanted to get her a house, and I couldn't as a student,"—and he dropped religious observance when his wife died. "I tasted both vocations enough to know they weren't for me." He laughs bitterly. "I'm a typical hori after all, made to work on the chain, or be a factory hand, not try for high places."

"High places in whose world? And high is as you decide it . . . I've known roadies who knew theirs was a high place in the scheme of things, and I've met a cabinet minister who realised he was bottom of the dung heap."

She doesn't explain where she knew any of them. She tells very little about herself, while seeming to say a lot. After several more whiskies, she steers the conversation adroitly back to Joe's family, specifically the Tainuis.

"I know you're close to them, e hoa, but I've never quite worked out who they are."

"Wherahiko is my mother's brother." His voice is becoming slurred. "I like him and Marama helluva lot. Not so keen on their sons though, specially that poisonous bastard Luce. Dunno how

Marama could've spawned him eh. He might be adopted or some-thing, I never heard. I never asked. But he doesn't take after either of the old people, and he's not like his brothers either. No," He rubs his forehead, "no, he's not adopted, he's just a shit. He was born bad. I keep on thinking things, you know."

> I'll bet you do. Like how is Sim going to turn out. Any-thing like Luce?
> Ahh man, don't worry . . . he's a different kettle of fish altogether. . . .

Joe is saying,

"Ben's eldest, he's okay. But he's got problems. The farm needs all his time and more money than any of them have got, and he's worried by the old man's heart flutter. Marama's had a stroke too, but she got over it . . . Piri works for Ben now, used to be his own man though. He thinks he runs my life as well as his own, but he's a neat fella to have round most of the time . . . except when he's been drinking. He drinks a bit much these days, and I'm saying it eh? But he doesn't want the separation, and he realises he shouldn't have taken Timote . . . it was mainly to pip Lynn anyhow . . . Marama looks after the kid most of the time. Simon too, a lot more before than now."

She says cautiously, "Simon doesn't seem to like Piri."

Joe laughs and hiccoughs in the middle of it. "Sheesh . . . ah, I don't really know why that is. I know one reason, and that's funny, it truly is. Piri had a fight with me one night because I gave Himi a whacking round there, and Himi got wild as hell when Piri hit me with a bottle. He didn't forgive him that for a long time. Poor Piri couldn't understand it . . . as for now," he shrugs, "maybe Piri knows something about him he doesn't want Piri to know or something . . . they all know about him, they been in on the act for the last two years . . ." he stands up wearily. "O, I'm getting old and tired . . . or is it the whisky?"

"Whisky, and Sim waking you last night eh? You off to bed?"

"Yeah."

"I'll stay up a while and watch the fire die."

. . .

She stays up rearranging the picture she had built in her mind of what Joe is, until it is daylight. When the whisky's finished, and the coal-scuttle is empty of everything including dust, she creeps away to bed.

Very disturbing.

You just get someone neatly arranged in a slot that appears to fit them, and they wriggle on their pins and spoil it all.

Like Simon the sane and smiling of spirit becoming the screamer.

And Joe, holy mother of us all, you thought him to be a self-pitying childbashing ogre, with yeah, a few good points. . . .

What would it feel like, to want to be priest, to want to be teacher, to want to be husband and father of a family, and be thwarted in them all? How would it feel to have that macabre kind of childhood, blighted by insanity, beset with illness? And those veiled hints he dropped of violence done to him . . . no wonder he's sparse on knowledge of how to deal with children.

She can imagine what it must be like to come home to a cold house, still filled with memories of dead wife and dead child, after a day of hard hated monotonous work.

She can imagine what it must feel like to be faced again and again with the knowledge that he's failing in bringing up a chance-given child, an odd, difficult and distressing child, like he feels he's failed with everything else in his bitter past.

And he still tries, and he still cares.

Mind you, says the snark, you have only his word for his history.

To hell, she thinks, you'd have to be a dramatic genius to put on that pain and Joe is a bad actor at the best of times . . . she'd prefer he hadn't started talking, but it's too late now. Thank God for whisky and the sea . . . the sea sweeps in and out of the tide of coming sleep.

> What is your breakfast?
> Whisky, says Kerewin sleepily.
> And your dinner?
> Whisky.
> And for tea?
> Drambuie she says, licking her lips.

And your constant companion? (Whisky, doubtless.)
The shush of my heart in my left ear.
The sea hath all my right. . . .

. . .

TIDE OUT

"You going out in your bare feet?"

The boy nods.

"Well don't expect any sympathy when you come back with a cold," says Joe grimly.

She looks up from the morning paper.

"Don't worry. Kids don't have the same sort of nerves as we do. I think they grow more feeling as they grow older."

Simon blows a raspberry at her.

"Nerves are one thing and cold germs quite another."

Kerewin shrugs. She looks at Sim and shrugs again. He shrugs happily back at her and vanishes out the door.

"And do you know something else?" growls Joe.

"King lists for the Egyptian dynasties, how to construct an oc-topus lure, when. . . ."

"No, damn it. People with your kind of kidneys and constitu-tions shouldn't be allowed."

He wraps another blanket round himself, honks, sips more lemon drink, and goes on angrily incubating his cold.

She giggles gracelessly.

"How could I know you'd develop a cold last night? Anyway, I'll buy you another bottle of whisky to dilute that lemon ick as soon as I finish the paper. Promise."

She goes on reading, whistling to herself, not quite under her breath.

He sighs. No sign of a hangover after drinking the better part of a quart of whisky.

Healthy, thriving, glowing indeed, in this damnable cold. And

Haimona, rushing barefoot out into what's practically snow. When the good Lord made me a Maori and sent me to the cold island, why didn't he ensure I was fat? A neat happy stereotype? Or at least, germ-resistant?

He shivers and coughs hoarsely.

Speaking of the good Lord, keep an eye on my giddy child please, I can't. I'm going back to bed.

Aloud. "I'm going t'bed."

"Okay."

She turns a page, keeps on whistling.

What do I have to do to get sympathy from her. Die?

He goes disconsolately back to the old bach.

. . .

Simon walks along the high tide line. The sand is soft, sand rather than gravel. He hasn't been along this beach before. For that matter, he hasn't been beachwalking by himself before. The other days, Joe, or Kerewin, or both of them, have come too. There's nothing to worry about, walking by the sea, says Kerewin. "One of these times I'll tell you about ponaturi and krakens and other toothy and interesting greebles, but in the meantime, wander in happy ignorance. You may find a seal or two, sunbathing. That's all."

Rather than seals, he's looking for green stones.

Kerewin said she had picked up a pendant along this beach. "An old one? Hei, that's interesting." Joe had been enthusiastic. "Have you got it here? Can I see it?"

She had closed up. "It's at home," she had said cautiously. Joe had sighed. "That's one thing I've always wanted. Nana had an earring, but she left it to my grandfather. That was the only piece the family owned, eh." Kerewin had pursed her lips, as though wondering whether to say anything more. Finally, she had said, "There's a lot in my family's hands. The great grand fatherly progenitor was Ngati Poutini, and so was one of my grandfathers. They didn't exactly eat off pounamu plates, but they left quite a bit to us all. You'll have to come and look, help yourself to something when we get back, eh?" But that hadn't been what she had been going to say at all. Funny, thought Simon, and forgot it.

At the moment, he's got to decide which way to look. By the cliffs, or in the sea? He scans the beach.

Something flaps on the sand by the sea's edge.

. . .

Kerewin finishes the paper and makes herself a coffee. Then she drives to Hamdon, and buys more whisky. She stops at the tavern for a quick drink. It's just eleven, but there's a scattering of fishermen and farming folk having the alcoholic equivalent of smoko. She notices that the signs that used to be everywhere, warning minors and those on prohibition orders not to come in, have gone. The barman says goodbye civilly though she only has a single beer.

Must go for a decent session there, before we leave, she thinks, driving in a leisurely fashion back to Moerangi.

. . .

He can't see what it is.

It looks quite large.

He decides to go that way, looking for green stones on the way. He finds several, but none with the water look of Kerewin's rings. Maybe polished? thinks Simon, and edges closer to the shore.

The thing flaps again.

. . .

She makes a tumbler full of whisky toddy and takes it to Joe. She kneels by the bunk and blows a stream of whisky fumes at the huddle under the blankets.

"A kill or cure machine has arrived and is waiting for you."

"Gur?"

"Whisssky."

"O . . . thag you."

"Sweet hell man, drink it quick. It sounds like the germs are winning." Snigger.

"O?" says Joe, with considerable restraint.

. . .

What do I do? What do I do?

Get them.

It's a long way back.

The bird struggles again, the ruined wing beating sluggishly, the wounded body scuffling in the sand.

Its head tilts further to one side. The beak opens and darkish froth drips out.

A stone. I could throw it hard.

He readies one of the green pebbles in his hand.

I might miss, I might just hurt it.

He drops it.

Clare, do something, hugging himself in misery.

The beak opens and shuts soundlessly.

If I wait, it might die quickly.

The bird flops forward, wing drawn up convulsively, scrabbles again in the sand.

It is trying to get away from him.

. . .

She puts a leg of mutton on to roast, and prepares the vegetables ready in pots.

She helps herself to a whisky, clears away the morning dishes, and sweeps out the bach.

Positively domesticated we are, this morning.

Glancing at the clock,

this afternoon.

This afternoon? Where's the urchin?

She goes to the old bach.

"Hey Joe, wake up a minute."

He is woozy with cold and a septuple whisky, and he doesn't know which way Simon went.

"Doan worrym, he'll comg bag."

"Oath, it's an entire new dialect."

She grins. "I think I'll go look for him anyway. The sandhoppers might have nibbled away his toes, and he's hirpling back on his anklebones."

. . .

If I go . . .

I can't leave it.

I can't watch it die like this.

He drops to his knees beside the bird, closes his eyes, the stone tight in his hand, and hits until he can hear nothing, feel nothing moving any more.

Smell of the sea and the smell of blood.

The bird is reddened. The one wing curves, moves in the air towards the earth. It comes to rest at an awkward upbent angle.

Simon puts his head on his drawnup knees. There is a singing in his head, and a bitter constriction in his throat. He tries to swallow and his gorge rises. He dry-retches repeatedly.

I can't cry.

• • •

Kerewin hunkers down so she can see all the footprints in the sand backlit as it were. There it is, the barefoot trail, heading south. Would you believe everyone else is shod?

He's not on the first beach round from the kaika. The footprint trail begins again after the rocks that mark the beginning of the south reef, and still heads purposefully south.

She follows, swinging the harpoonstick alongside.

Two youths on the clifftop wave to her. One carries a rifle. She waves back.

> That's one of the nice things about being back in me old
> home. The natives aren't suspicious here.

One of them, both of them, may know her by sight, though they would have been children the last time she was here.

She rounds the corner of the beach called King and Queen. Two rock towers give it the name.

And there it is, one Gillayley gremlin, in a desolate-looking hunch on the sand.

> What's the betting its feet have dropped off from
> frostbite?

She lays a large whisky to a lemon drink against it, grinning as she does.

• • •

After a time, he begins to shiver, with cold and shock.

> This place is getting too much.

He opens his eyes and looks at the mutilated dead thing at his feet.

It is quiet and still.

He digs a hole, scraping in the sand with his fingers so the thin bird blood is rubbed off.

He uses the stone to lever and roll the body into the hole. It was the kind of bird Kerewin called mollymawk, and Joe, toroa. Its brown eyes are still open. He drops sand on it, avoiding the eyes as much as he can. He searches for fine sand, then gravel, heaping it over until there is no sign at all except the mound on the beach.

Then he sits back on his heels, keeping his mind dark, and sings to it.

It is a thin reedy sound at first, nasal and highpitched. It is the only sound he can make voluntarily, because even his laughter and screaming are not under his full control, and it is as secret as his name.

The singing rises and builds atonically.

To Kerewin, walking catfooted on the silent sand, it has the strange heady purity of a counter-tenor.

She squats down three yards behind him and waits, not moving a muscle. Not even breathing loudly.

God, if only I had my guitar with me. . . .

A brilliant green-armoured blowfly zzzes onto the mound and picks its way across the wet sand.

The singing stops.

The only sound is the pulse of the sea.

She hasn't moved but somehow he is suddenly aware she is there. His head snaps forward, and he cowers against the sand, his bowels loosening in his terror.

She doesn't move.

Nor does she speak.

She sits, rocksteady. Only her fingers grasping the harpoonstick have tightened until the pressure hurts.

Slowly, fighting against the horror, he drags himself upright again. His body is jerking spasmodically.

I do anything, talk, sing, touch him, anything. I'll push him into convulsions. Wait it out, o soul. God, I'm sorry for you, child.

His mouth drawn down in a rictus of fear, he waits. For lightning, blows, the darkness.

Nothing happens.

The sea rolls in, the sea rolls out.

A gull keens over the island.

Kerewin sits unmoving, watching him.

The green fly gives up its search and buzzes away.

Nothing happens.

The wind blows a little: he feels it shift his hair.

His feet are numb with cold.

I've hurt my thumb.

I've shit myself. Joe'll be mad.

He lets his breath out in one great shuddering sigh.

Nothing happens.

Nothing happens to him at all.

He shivers again, but this time from fiery exultation.

He kneels up, holding himself tightly, but the wild shivering
goes on.

Mother of us all, just when I thought it might be over.

The child's face is the colour of tallow, and all the colour has
gone out of his eyes, except for the black of pupil.

Nothing! She heard me singing! But nothing!

What the hell can I do? Knock him out?

Any time, I can sing!

She swings quickly to her feet, and in the same moment, Simon
stands shakily. He staggers to her and clings as though he is drowning. Kerewin slides her hand gently down his neck, as though in a
caress. Her fingers rest a second, press *there* and he'll go out like a
light, but just before she applies pressure, she looks into his eyes.

The greenblue irises are enlarging by the second, and they are
shining, afire with joy.

She moves her hand smoothly away, laying it on his shoulder.

"Child, you're full of surprises. . . ."

She kneels so their eye-level is the same, still holding his
shoulder.

"That sounded very good . . . you okay now?"

He's still shaking but nothing in his face shows he is suffering any longer.

Icansing!Icansing!Icansing! it sifts him like a wind, a tumult in him like the rush of music . . . smiling and crying at the same time isn't the way to show it to her, but it's all he can do for the moment.

She waits. She says very little, and whatever she says sounds like the sea. But her words come more clearly as the joyous chaos in him settles.

" . . . and there you were. Marvellous. . . ."

A little later she asks, "What happened?"

He looks at the nearby mound.

Bird, he says, hands beating as wings, then makes the cut-throat gesture.

"Dead when you found it?"

No he says, his eyes sombre suddenly.

"You had to put it out of its misery?" Her voice is so gentle it doesn't sound like Kerewin at all.

"Aue," she says to his Yes, "I've had to do that a few times. With animals . . . it is always bad at the time."

The shadow stays on him a few seconds longer, but then excitement sweeps through again. You hear me? touching her face, his ear and mouth, making the circuit twice.

"Of course I heard you singing," now it sounds exactly like Kerewin. "What do you think I was doing? Contemplating the scenery or some damn thing? And yeah, you're a wonderful brat . . . if we don't get home soon though, lunch'll be cooked to a cinder and Joe will be lurching round, spreading the dreaded lurgi everywhere."

Speaking of lurching: just standing the child is so unsteady, he drags on her hand for support. His feet are a dull purple colour.

> Gonna have to be a carry job, Holmes . . . cold and panic
> and relief and whatever else this little executioner has
> been inflicting on himself, have about got him down.

She stands, saying, "Simon Pi Ta Gillayley, and translate that how you like—I can think of fifteen meanings for ta, and quite a few for pi but only one of each that fit—if you've given yourself frostbite, and I have to drink a glass of lemon juice in consequence," picking him up without a visible trace of queasiness, "I'm gonna get drunk tonight just to wash the taste outa my mouth. And a drunk Holmes is a mean kind of spider."

He leans cosily close. Ah, it's all good . . . he doesn't give two knobs, as Piri says, for drunk spiders or Kerewin making puns on his second name. He's got this sweet high feeling everything is going to work out fine from now on, and it's as heady as gorse wine.

He wrinkles his nose. High's the word, he sings in himself, and giggles in a kind of whimper, all the way back home.

6

Ka Tata Te Po

It's been a smooth week: this is the first flaw in it.

For his cold had cleared up in a record two days;

("and two bottles of whisky," says Kerewin, pointedly.)

the weather has held fine and windless;

("Maori summer," he says. "In the middle of winter?" "When better to get a bit of brown in?")

and the fishing has been superb.

Simon's made the acquaintance of barracouta, ling, trumpeter, and rig, and red cod, kelp cod, and rock cod.

He gets taught to use a scrubbing brush without getting his bandaged thumb in the way.

He cleans fillet after fillet after fillet that Kerewin slices away from rigid fish. Sometimes the world seems all silver scales and gelatinous eyeballs and bloodcoloured seawater. And the squabbling squawling greed of gulls.

But Kerewin boasts, "Another record year for the Holmes and Gillayley Smoked Fish Corporation!" The racks in the smokehouse are filled with slabs of ling and couta and cod, already pickled and dried. "A hundredweight in there if there's an ounce—keep us going a while back in Whangaroa, e Joe?"

Ulp, thinks Joe. It's been fish for breakfast, dinner and tea, and it looks like it's going to be fish for snacks, chowders and sandwiches for months ahead. He sighs. You could get tired of fish.

But you don't get tired of this place, he reflects, while standing outside the old bach wondering how to approach Kerewin.

He relishes the days at sea, whether fishing or simply lazing in the weak winter sunshine. He walks the beaches a lot: the reefs aren't alien places any more. The black rocks have their secrets, but he feels welcome there now. And best of all, he loves the quiet evenings when the wind has dropped and the homing birds call high above his head, mysterious and lonely. Ah, peace, peace . . . it is wellnamed, this place of healing beauty where you can, in perfect safety, sleep by day. . . .

Only, at the moment, Kerewin is playing something brutal and discordant.

Aue. If she feels like that sound . . . even Himi wouldn't like *that*.

And his child is now passionately, wholeheartedly, openly in love with music.

("He's worse than the transistors," says Kerewin. "He's been warbling along the beach like a demented canary . . . y'know a way to shut him up?" "No way! It's great." He's still not sure on all the details as to why his son has suddenly discovered he can sing—"Well, port a beul, wordless mouth music," Kerewin the cyclopaedic—but he is as delighted and enthusiastic as the child with the ability. It's the only vocal advance Simon has ever made, and besides, as Joe tells her repeatedly, "Sweet Lord, it's *tuneful*. He really can *sing*.")

Simon's had sound nights all this week, and there's been no trouble of any kind during the days. Ah, we never had it so good, thinks Joe. For the child is sweet-tempered, he's happy, he's helpful, he's entertaining (and he's healing up beautifully, from the belt-cuts on his body to his hook-bitten thumb).

He starts.

"Eh, I must've been dreaming, tama. You want your shirt and suit?"

The boy flips an affirmative, and pulls faces.

"At that?"

Yes.

"I think it's pretty horrible too," he whispers. "But you get your gear, and I'll go and talk," holding up crossed fingers.

("Where's your old jeans?" he'd asked a few days back. Kerewin said blithely that she'd chucked them out. "They fitted where they touched, and that was hardly anywhere. Can't you get him some clothes that fit? I'm tired of seeing the brat go round in what looks like the tailend of the ragbag." "Thanks. Can I help it if he doesn't grow like I'd planned?" But she said since it was her aesthetic sense that was offended, she'd shout the boy new clothes. In an Omaru store she says to Simon, "Open slather, boy. Choose your own gear." She likes his choice of jeans, of a denim suit, but tries to dissuade him when he opts for a florid lime and tangerine silk shirt. "I mean, those bright flowers are okay Himi, but don't you think those blue whirlpool things are a bit much?" "I'll shout you that," says Joe, and to Kerewin's groan, "I think I'll have one myself too." "Ah hell, you'll get mistaken for an Islander, and goodness knows what they'll think of *him*." "I can imagine," says Joe ruefully, looking down on his son. The child's hair reaches half-way down his back now, and with the flowery silk, and his earring, and Kerewin's turquoise pendant he's taken to wearing—"E, they'll think you're some kind of leftover mini-hippy," and both adults laugh. He pushes Simon's fringe out of his eyes. "You look beautiful really, tama. Tika.")

He listens to the savage tune Kerewin is throttling her guitar into producing, and thinks, I'll talk, but will she listen?

It's not blues, it's not rock, it's not folk or imitation electronic, and sure as hell, it's not any Maori music he's heard before. He says, at the inner door,

"E hoa?"

Notes rear and slash at him.

"What *are* you playing?"

"Shark music," says Kerewin sweetly. "Dirges and laments, coronachs and requiems, all for my fellow sharks."

He shudders.

She feels like that?

O God.

He had said to Simon when the two of them came back, "What's the matter? Have you upset her?"

The boy shook his head. I caught two fish, he said, showing off again.

"I heard. Too many times already. That wouldn't make her wild, though."

Kerewin had stalked off to the old bach looking as sour as curdled milk, and she hadn't said a word before she went.

Simon sighed, and wrote BROTHER.

"Hers? Here?"

He took his father to the door, and pointed out where, exactly.

"And so?"

They talked, said the boy, flapping his fingers open and close.

"And that made her mad?"

Simon frowned. It hadn't seemed as though the woman was upset.

She and the stranger had looked at each other for a minute without saying anything. Then the man had said,

"Is, umm, yours?"

"No. A friend's."

"You staying here?"

"For another week or so."

"You're well?"

"Yes." Long pause. "Everyone?"

"Dot and Celia are dead. Mag's married. Two kids. Everyone else is okay."

"Mmmm," said Kerewin.

The man sighed.
"I don't suppose you're coming . . . ?"

"I'm not."

He sighed again.
"Okay then."

"Okay . . . Sim, get a move on home." She had turned on her heel walking back fast to the baches.

He stayed, flashed the man a smile, watched him till he went out of sight. He had been a peculiar looking person, a foot taller than Kerewin, with black eyes and reddishbrown hair, as thick and as curling as Kerewin's.

He had given the boy a sad smile back.

Funny, thought Simon, and ran to catch the woman up.

Who? he asked.

"A brother of mine," and she began kicking the sand, sending it flying in sprays and showers.

Simon stopped dead in his tracks.

"Didn't you know I was part of a family?"

No he didn't. Questions are sprouting from him like fungi from a stump.

"Well, I am. I have a mother and a half a dozen siblings and about a thousand other relations most of whom I only meet when I'm doing something wicked in front of them and they say, I'll tell your mother, Kerewin Holmes. I'm your great-aunt Tilda on your father's side." She booted more sand, viciously. "Now get along home before those fish go off."

He told the gist of this to his father, and Joe said, "Well, I dunno . . . I better go and see if I can smooth things over. Have a wash, put your new duds on, and I'll see if I can't talk our grim lady into having an afternoon out somewhere."

He asks her now,

"What's wrong? What can I do?"

"I'm just playing bad music and—"

"Himi said your brother was here."

"Bloody little telltale." The tone is light.

"I asked him why you'd gone away looking mad. More or less."

"That's the reason, more or less."

"So I thought I better come along and see if you'd like to come with us to that Hamdon tavern, where I'll offer you all the drunk you can drink and all the comfort you want."

> Very subtle, Ngakau. Now she'll probably jump all over
> the top of you.

But she leans against the bunk post, and lets the guitar rest belly-down on her knees.

"You know what, my friend Gillayley? A family can be the bane of one's existence. A family can also be most of the meaning of one's existence. I don't know whether my family is bane or meaning, but they have surely gone away and left a large hole in my heart."

She is very close to weeping and he has never known Kerewin to cry.

"I dunno," she adds. "Maybe they took the heart and left the hole. . . ."

One thing about having Himi for your child: you learn to read what people meant but didn't say.

"I am Kerewin the stony and I never cry. I want to like
or even love you, but I don't trust anyone now."

He waits the space of three breaths before saying, casually, kindly, "And I thought my tribe were the devout cannibals. At least they used to check first whether the dinner still had a use for the heart or not."

He would dearly love to hold her in his arms, as though she were Simon needing comforting. He would dearly love to kiss her, and use the endearments he hasn't said since Hana died. But that would upset her, not help her, and with all his heart he wants to help.

Kerewin makes a sound that could have been a gulp of laughter or a half-swallowed sob.

"Those bastards, and I mean my tribe, never worried about such small tripes or trifles. . . ."

He laughs. He makes sure it doesn't sound like obliging laughter. But he thinks, Aue! Trust her to wriggle away under cover of words. And if she could turn the situation into colour, she'd over-whelm me with rust and verdigris or some such rainbow. . . .

"Aiiieeee. . . ." She lets her breath out noisily, sniffs once, and stands. "It's a good idea, man . . . but what about half-pint? I don't know whether they'll let him in up there."

"You know Sim . . . if we wanted his heart in aspic, to fill a gap so to speak, he'd hand it to us on a plate."

"E you bastard! You're pinching my style!"

"No, no," he says blandly. "It's merely contagion . . . Himi'll stay quite happily by himself in the car, if that's the way it's got to be. We can ferry drinks out to him, and let him get merrily plonked on coke or something."

"After some of his recent performances, it'll take more than coke to set Sim on his ear."

"Or something, I said," grinning.

"Yeah, well . . . heigh ho for revelry and loud indecent cheer." She fits the guitar back in its case and bangs the lid down. "You fel-las getting fancied up?"

"Course . . . we'll startle the natives eh?"

"*You* may. I shall be as conservative as a Tamaki pig."

He thinks, when she gets into the car ten minutes later, that it depends on what your idea of conservatism is—sure, she's wearing a sober denim suit, and a prussianblue highnecked jersey, but it's conservative to wear six large rings? Her left hand is studded by four silverset cabochons of greenstone, and there's a star sapphire with three dolphins circling it deiseal in gold on her right hand. The massive gold signet she always wears is on her right middle finger, and he privately thinks that's enough by itself.

He just says, "You expecting a fight, eh?"

"Tcha, Gillayley. I'm a pacifist, remember?"

"I remember," he says wrily, "very well."

. . .

There's no-one but the barman in the bar.

"Gidday," he says smiling. "Nice weather we're having eh?"

"Best winter I can remember for a while," says Joe. "Can I have a jug and two sevens, and you want anything else, Kere?"

"Not at the moment."

"Two beers coming up." The barman draws the jug. "Nice to have someone in the bar this time of day. It'd make a man cry, the quiet of it normally."

"No afternoon regulars?"

"Not for half an hour or so yet."

Simon slides in round the door, and stands just inside.

"I thought," Joe begins, but the barman grins. "Yours?" he asks, thumb to Kerewin.

"Mine," says Joe. "I'll throw him out eh?"

"Nah, no way. Wanna raspberry drink, ummm?" The barman hisses to them, "Is it a boy or a girl?"

Kerewin guffaws.

"He's a boy," and Joe waits resignedly for a crack about the length of the child's hair.

"Nice kiddie," says the barman. "Got one of me own about his size. What's your name?" he asks Simon.

The boy edges closer, his eyes flicking around their faces.

"Bit shy eh?"

The barman's beaming fondly. He obviously dotes on children.

"I wouldn't call him shy," says Joe. "He can't talk though."

"O hell," the man is blushing as though he should have known about it, "jeez, I really put my foot in it, didn't I?"

"I'm sorry," he says loudly, then drops his voice to whisperlevel. "Is he ahhh backward? He don't look it."

"A little too forward if anything," says Joe. "Come on Haimona, don't skulk."

"Looks like you're allowed in after all," Kerewin turns to the barman for confirmation.

"Yeahyeah, sure, nobody minds. Lotsa them bring their kids in on the weekend. Gives the place a real nice feel if you know what I mean."

"Civilised drinking?"

He agrees heartily. "No fights or swearing or nothing. Even the rough blokes mind their manners ... what'd you call him, mate?"

"Haimona. Maori for Simon."

"Well, glad to meet you Hymornah ehh Simon ... my name's Dave, by the way."

"Kerewin;" says Kerewin, and Joe says, "I'm Joe."

"Great," says Dave. "Now, what'll you have, Simon? What does he drink?" to Joe.

"He'll tell you," he says, and lifts his child onto a bar stool. Simon writes PIA on his pad.

"No way," says Joe firmly, and the barman cranes in for a look. "You write good and neat," he says to Simon, "izzat Maori?" The boy nods and prints BEER beside it.

Dave laughs. "Hey neat!" He taps the jug. "But I can't give you any, sorry, Simon ... the cops wouldn't like it. I'll look the other way if your Dad gives you a sip of his, though." He winks at them all.

"He won't get any of mine ... though it's good to meet a barman like yourself who doesn't treat children as though they're some kind of exotic germ."

"Aw well, this is a bit different from the cities eh?" his quick look at them conveys, With gear like that, you're not country people. "Nobody minds a kiddie being in the bar provided someone's looking after it. Better that than leave them at home uncared for, or stuck out by themselves in a car, isn't it?"

"O yes," say Kerewin and Joe in unison, and when Joe pours the beer out, he avoids Simon's eyes.

"We'll get you a coke or something, okay?" and the boy writes O YES. "Ah smartass," and pushes the beerjug out of his reach.

"Have one with us, Dave?" asks Kerewin.

"I wouldn't say no," pouring himself a seven ounce from their jug, "that's very kind of you, I'll shout the next one, cheers."

Swallow, swallow, swallow.

"Ah look, we've forgotten Simon . . . did he decide on a drink, Joe?"

"Make it a coke, eh."

"On the house," says Dave, and winks again. "Wouldn't get it like that in the cities, now would you?"

"Not even in the best pubs," Kerewin says solemnly, while Joe thinks of Whangaroa, Population 4000 give or take a dog or two, and gives the man his widest whitest smile.

. . .

The regulars trickle in. They say Gidday to Dave, grin to the boy, nod to her and Joe, and settle down at their accustomed tables.

Motley bunch, she thinks. Fisherman. Farmhands. The odd truckie. And barflies . . . like that one there.

A big man, face purple, belly protruding, legs thick with oedema, delivering words in a permanent alcoholic slur.

> Sad. One in every bar. Widowed or unmarried, gone
> beyond taking care. I should be warned maybe.

But the jug gets less: the glass is full again. Down and drown it goes. Our third to date, and he's grinning happily as he gets us another.

Sim's still with the toothrot, but cannily lining his vulnerable gut with potato chips. Neat kid, taking a single crisp at a time and eating it as though it's a communion bread. Sip of softdrink. Then licking the salt off his fingers. Grinning to me, and then back he swings to his da, corroborating all he says with showoff gestures.

Me, still morose, although the beer is beginning to help me deny it.

Dave serving a new one, bang the angostura, swish a glass ... pink gins coming up. The recipient has a high and tenor laugh and a mid-baritone belch, and he swishes too.

Motley the locals may be, they're a helluva lot more tolerant than some other small country pubs I've known. There he goes, bending down to his friend, eyelashes fluttering before he sits. Right on, fella. ...

Did I say tolerant? Next door to them is a fat fellow with a carpenter's folded rule stuck in his rear pocket. Sour and sneering, getting up obviously and pushing rudely past them to the bar. He bears tattoos on his arm muscles like they're emblems of the brave, and he's got a paunch like a sponge pregnancy, overhanging the double ledge of his hips, overlapping his belt in a full flabby fall. Yech. And you can quit trying to sneer on me, mate.

She looks away, hearing Dave, "Wait your hurry now, wait your hurry, I'll get to you in a minute."

Joe's in conversation with a trio, all taking fish and prices and weather flat tack. And they've got Sim deep in the chat with them. Ho hum ... what was that about comfort? Ah hell, the drink'll bring it, and they seem happy enough.

Talk seethes round her, coming in peculiar snatches.

"He's gone queer and he always was a queer bastard. Now he's absolutely queer, and even his housekeeper's left him ..."

". . . and her with muscles like a chicken's instep, not to mention tits like nothing at all, eh. So I. . . ."

"Hey George! Glad to see you're still in the land of the living you old . . ." mumble mumble mumble.

"Who's the crutches?"

"Him? He just came outa hospital falling outa—"

"Hur hur! Ter hur hur hur!"

That's a laugh? Debate, debate, relate, relate, all around the bar. . . .

Dave comes past and fidgets with a sloppy cloth, wiping up the spill.

"Enjoying yourself, Kerewin?"

"In a quiet way, Dave."

"Your mates are cards, eh?"

"They're good company."

"Jeez, I can imagine! They've got themselves quite an audience."

"Mmmm."

He passes on to his next customer, whistling,

> They have, too. Barstools ranged round them in a semi-
> circle, the man and his boy in the middle. Joe grinning like
> a hyena, and Simon showing off. Handsome Joe, brilliant
> sunburst shirt and maroon suit, strong hands bracing the
> child against the pitch of his knees, protective and gentle.
> Really so . . . and the brat leans against them, sure of his
> perch, happy child pretty as a picture. And who'd believe,
> under the flowery silk and fresh blue denim, the fine skin
> is keloid scars and seams from welt laid on welt? Them?

mentally thumbing the grinning chattering crowd,

> They probably think this is the normal routine. . . .

She sweeps up the rest of Simon's chips and eats them sourly.

> I think I'll go home soon. I can drink by myself in as
> good company as here.

"See y'gain." "Hooray." "Chalk it up will ya, Dave?" "Rightio
then." "O David," the willowy man, back again with his two pink
gins. He smiles briefly at her, and goes on arranging his change in
graduating rows on the bar-top.

She stands up, brushing beads of beer and chip-crumbs off her
trousers.

> Have a mimi, grab a couple of half g's, and walk back.
> Or shall I take the car, and leave them loot for a taxi?

"Excuse me," trying to force a way through the crush round
the bar.

"Hey Kerewin, you ready to go?" calls Joe.

"In a minute," she doesn't look round.

When she gets back, Joe is standing, Simon in his arms, saying
goodbyes to his circle. There's a general chorus of "Aw" and "The
night's just begun, mate," and "What's the hurry?"

Except for our fat carpenter friend, she notes.

Lips raised in a sneer, he is glad the strangers are going. As she goes to the bar to ask Dave for the half g's, he says quite loudly, "About bloody time, too. Stinkin' leslies and Mahries and that bloody little freak."

She swings round to him, and he goes on sneering, eyes and lips now, not words. His shoulders jut under her scrutiny.

"Got an uncivil tongue, fella," she places her hands together, rocking slightly, back and forwards on the balls of her feet.

"Yurr."

"Inarticulate with it?"

"Shut yer bloody fancy words," he spits a flake of tobacco off his tongue, and says to the barman, "Fill me glass."

"In a minute," says Dave coldly, suddenly in front of Kerewin. He whispers, "Don't mind him, he's got a bit of a grudge against the world."

"So have I," she says loudly, but seemingly equably, "So have I."

It's grown abruptly quiet, all ears tuned to her.

"Uh, can I get you a drink?" says Dave.

She doesn't say anything, staring the fat man down. He stares back, his eyes blinking. A fly comes buzzing past in the silence.

She doesn't appear to move with haste but her left hand has captured the fly, killed it, and flicked it at her adversary in a split second.

"Ah Kerewin," from Joe, and the silence becomes more intense.

To the onlookers, that jade-laden hand has become frightening. Any comedy about the rings has died.

Dave says haltingly, "Ah some drink?"

She turns to him, smiling. "Yeah. Say a couple of half g's?"

"Right!" The relief makes his voice ring out.

Joe moves in by her, leading Simon now. "I'll get it, e hoa . . . everything okay?"

"O yeah . . ." her smile gone.

"He-ell," says someone behind her. "What is she? Some kind of prizefighter?"

"Dunno, but it looks like it . . . I wouldn't like to get in the way of a punch that fast, woman or no woman," and someone else adds, "With that set of knuckledusters, hell no . . ." and everything else is drowned in a rising tide of talk, as the regulars regroup round the bar.

There's a gap left either side of the carpenter.

He stands, staring in at his glass where the dead fly lies.

He hasn't moved since it arrived.

. . .

"You okay now?"

"Yeah."

She stands with folded arms, watching the waves crest and break, crest and break.

"I'm sorry. I didn't mean for us to ignore you and that. It just happened."

"S'okay. I was in a bitch of a mood anyway. I wouldn't have been any kind of good company."

"You sure you're all right now?"

"Mmm."

He shivers. "You aren't cold?"

"Na . . . I'll be in in a few minutes. I just want to look at the sea awhile."

"Right. I'll go back and see Himi doesn't steal all the grog."

"Unlikely."

"O, he's helped himself to a glass already."

"Struth, that brat's got an unhealthy eagerness to enter into lushdom. He looked like he had some back at the pub too."

"No, that was just high spirits . . . the unbottled kind eh?"

There is pleading in his voice, Laugh with me?

"Pretty good." She makes an effort and smiles at him. "I'm really all right, fella. This bad temper'll wear itself out soon. It's just, o I don't know. I keep on thinking about the things we used to do here, build fires, share dreams, play wild and weird games, all together . . . and it all came to nothing, meant nothing," she ends bleakly.

He hugs her shoulders. "E Kerewin, e Kerewin." He takes his arm away. "We could do some of those things too. . . ."

"Yes."

He sighs.

"I'll get some tea ready . . . we'll see you soon?"

"Very soon."

. . .

The waves march in.

Three herring gulls lift with each breaker, settle back on the sand again as the sea streams out. An old blackback carks and skrees, fossicking along the tideline. The shags sit by their hollow mud nests on Maukiekie. Nothing else is moving. Sometimes, the waves grow hushed, but the sea is always there, touching, caressing, eating the earth. . . .

She can hear Joe singing in the bach behind her. Then the rise and fall of his voice talking, with pauses for the child's answers.

At the horizon, the sky has turned smoked and red: the sea out there looks as though hot blood diffuses the water.

A cloud of midges comes weaving and dancing through the evening air, and she is suddenly precipitated back to the day she had gone floundering in Taiaroa estuary, and fallen asleep, and woken to find midges round her face.

The day she came home to find a mute frightened child in her window.

It seems like years ago.

> Years . . . and it's not much more than a couple of months since he came into my ken. I know him well, and yet I know so very little about him. He's been horribly scared by something in his past. He may understand some French. He's maybe scared of needles; he was definitely scared when he realised I was listening to him sing . . . a frightening secret, a thing he had kept hidden. I wonder what else he keeps hidden from me. Even from Joe. Maybe more from Joe than me. . . .
>
> I know he has his own kind of courage, wry humour, an abnormal compassion, a great capacity for love, and yet. . . .

The colour has faded out of the sky. It is grey, becoming darker as the world turns herself round a little more. The clouds are long and black and ragged, like the wings of stormbattered dragons. Or of hokioi . . . huge birds. . . .

> The bird he killed . . . was it beyond help? Might he have a dark streak in him, as Joe seems to think? And that is why the violence? Flicking matches, throwing things . . . ah, I don't know. I don't know much about him at all.

For that matter, how much do I know about Joe? Only what he's said, and what he's done. And what he's done is a confused mixture of the congenial and the unpleasant. Gentle with his son, and brutal. Drunken boor and sober wit. Too much of the past riding on his shoulders, I think. With too much of an emotional stake in the boy to ever see him clearly, dispassionately . . . maybe. I don't know.

It is becoming night. Pale stars show through the gaps in the clouds.

> Betelgeuse, Achenar. Orion. Aquila. Centre the Cross and you have a steady compass.
> But there's no compass for my disoriented soul, only ever-beckoning ghostlights.
> In the one sure direction, to the one sure end.

She shivers. She is beginning to feel very cold.

> But wait here a little longer, think about it a bit more.
> You're involved with two strangers, different and difficult people. You're different and difficult yourself, but strangely enough, you all get on well together. To the extent that there can be a real fight, and forgiveness and renewed friendship after.
> To what end, my soul?
> Remember how horrifyingly painful it was when you and the family broke apart? So much so, that a brief meeting with one member is enough to put you in despair. The pain is back.
> Be wary. Keep it a cool friendship. Look out for the child by all means—it's the least you can do as a human being—but don't let them get too close.

And as if he were waiting for that cue, Simon takes her hand.

It takes all her self-control not to pull violently away. To wait until the sudden pound of her heart slows to normal, to wait without yelling abuse, until she can say, almost evenly,

"I didn't hear you come up. You been here long?"

A finger pressing once. His eyes glint as he looks at her.

"I've been watching the sea and thinking about things."

He has drawn her hand against his chest. She can feel the steady clock of his heart. He hasn't made any other move, but she feels as though he's saying something.

> Very careful, Holmes . . . that's an aura-watcher, re-member? It's visible to him, the electric perimeter of yourself, the waxing and waning moon of your soul. All the skeins and flickers of your energy, he can see . . . but how the hell

trying vainly to douse the anger she's feeling

> do I project calm ease of spirit when all I feel is misery?

"Get inside eh. I'll be in soon."

The single silent pressure again.

"Hey, inside when you're told," voice sharpened, making no ef-fort to contain her anger now. His heart is beating hard against the back of her hand, and she feels him start to shake. It comes with unpleasant certainty that he is scared of her . . . me? Kerewin the goody, the answering service, the white knight of the ready fist? He is, and how . . . but despite his fear, he still holds her hand against his chest.

> Ah hell, what am I doing?

She sighs hard.

"Hai, fella, let go my hand eh? I'm really coming in soon, but I need to be alone a little longer. Okay?"

He lets go, reluctantly. He leaves her, reluctantly. He goes slow-footed back to the bach, so she can hear each unhappy step.

She calls after the child,

"E Sim, don't worry . . . tomorrow's another day, and it'll all work out. You'll see."

. . .

Alone in the dark, drug-induced sleep near, he thinks

> But it's not going to work out, and there's nothing I can do about it.

It overwhelms him, a sudden flood of despair.

> There's nothing I can do.

The little brown man from the floor smiles sadly at him. He seems to be at the edge of the bunk.

> Can you do anything?
> No, he can't. He's not really here,

but the ghost is singing

> *E tama, i whanake*
> *i te ata o pipiri*

He is falling asleep and the words are muddled with grief

> *Piki nau ake, e tama*

It sounds thinly in his ears as the roaring night comes nearer still

> *ki tou tini i te rangi*

. . .

The lullaby is the ghost's goodbye. He doesn't see the man in the floor again.

. . .

Three days to go, and already they're souveniring.
She grins to herself wrily.

> At least they'll have substantial mementoes. All I've got is a load of smoked fish, and the fog wiped off my memories.

The boy has scoured the beach, gathering shells and seasmoothed glass; tidewashed bones and old seagull feathers; poppable pieces of bladderwrack and dead dried crabs. And stones . . . the kind with holes in them, bored by pholad or piddock, or ground out by other stones. Wounded stones, losers in the tidal wars, soon to become sand except for the urchin's intervening hand.

She had asked, What are you going to do with them?

Not take them home, says Joe, you've got about a hundredweight.

Just some, the boy points, a few.

Don't throw the rest out then. They're Maori sinkers.

Joe: O yeah?

"That's what we say . . . we got a pile of them in the black bach. We figure when the rest of the world runs out of lead, the Holmes tribe will still be able to go fishing."

Blowing a raspberry, "That's going to be my contribution to future family comfort here. Simon's stone collection."

The boy, ordering his finds in piles and patterns, looks over his shoulder. His face reads, O yeah?

> Well, I might get them, and I might not. I certainly won't get Joe's souvenir.
> Talk about a man in love with a stone. . . .

He'd come back from the south reef, whistling. The whistle was strained, and when he stopped it, his lips kept twitching as though he was smothering smiles.

"What's up with you?"

"O, nothing. . . ."

But he didn't want to keep it a secret, just dress the stage.

"Look!" kneeling before them, and holding out his hand.

Slender, coloured like the deep sea, a rich translucent green. . . .

Already, he's planning how to suspend it round his neck. My own greenstone, my own pendant, he says all the time. Given me by the sea, on one of your beaches . . . ah Kerewin, the place loves me!

> So I won't tell him about the graves up on the cliff, and how that probably got washed out with its former owner . . . sour him off if he knew the smell of bones went with it eh? He can be happy with his hei matau . . . because the old ones might have given it to him. They gave mine to me. . . .

. . .

She told them, when the celebrating died down.

"That's the fourth piece I know that's been picked up round by the south reef. One of my brothers found two adzes—they're in the Otago museum now. And I found Tahoro Ruku."

"Whale Diving? Is it a mere? A family mere?"

She grinned. Very polite way to say, Obviously you wouldn't keep a named heirloom if it didn't belong in your family. . . .

"No, it's a weird kind of pendant. I don't know whose family it belongs in. I made enquiries round all of my relations, and most Ngai Tahu hapu. Memory of it is lost. Or maybe," thoughtfully, "they've changed the name of it. You see, when I picked it up—I was just going onto the reef for pupu and a wave uncovered it at my feet—when I picked it up, there seemed to be voices all around me saying 'Te tahoro ruku! Te tahoro ruku!' It was bright sunlight, I wasn't drunk, and there were people further out on the reef who didn't look round or anything, so the voices must have been in my head. But they were loud. They echoed. . . ."

She shivered.

"I picked it up, and the voices went on and on, and I got scared. I said, maybe inside myself, 'E nga iwi! Mo wai tenei?' and there was silence. Only after a little while, one voice returned, an infi-nitely old voice whispering, 'Tahoro ruku, tahoro ruku,'—you know what?"

"No." He whispered it.

"I didn't ask anything more. I just picked it up and ran back to the baches. I didn't show it to anyone for weeks, and then,"

I know I shouldn't look shamefaced, but I always do,

"I didn't exactly say where I got it. That came out later."

"I think I would have left it. . . ."

She sighed.

"I don't know what I should have done . . . I argued with myself, for long enough. The sea wouldn't have given it to me if it hadn't been meant for me. The ghosts of the old people, or whatever the voices were, didn't say it *wasn't* for me. I asked who it was for, they didn't say. I didn't do anything wrong and nothing bad came of it, so it must have been all right. I just had some strange dreams for a while."

Joe nodded gravely.

"They were about Maukiekie out there. Sometimes I saw a hole in the ground. Sometimes I entered it, and in the heart of the island there was a marae. Tukutuku panels and poupou carved into the living rock . . . there was never anyone to welcome me, but there was always breathing. Slow huge breaths . . . it was several dreams before I realised it was breathing, and not an underearth wind. I thought, It's the island breathing, or Papa herself. I don't know."

He just sucked his breath in, Ssseee.

"The dreams were trying to tell me something but I couldn't un-derstand them. I still don't. In the last one, the breathing stopped, and the marae suddenly lightened like something lifted the covering rock off, and a great voice, not human, cried, 'Keria! Keria!' Bloody strange way to end a dream, eh?"

She laughed. "I woke my brother up yelling, 'Dig what?' and he thought I was nuts."

"It was the call of peace, the ancient one. . . ."

"I know. I learned that later. But I still don't know what the dreams meant . . . I've got Tahoro Ruku safely, and it's dear to my heart. Even though I often feel I'm merely its guardian, and some-one else is meant to have it. . . ."

"You don't wear it?"

"No. For one thing, it's too big. For another, I haven't got a suit-able cord. Anyway, you can see it back at Taiaroa, and tell us what you think."

He looks at the pendant in his hand. "I'm glad this didn't have voices with it . . . you ever dig on the island?"

"Yeah. I got a yard of guano and a chipped shovel. Maukiekie is as solid as a bloody rock."

. . .

The dreamhold island.
Shags slide off its top with reptilian grace.
Bullkelp weaves and snakes by the base.

　　Rimu rimu tere tere e. . . .

Why should I feel sad?

My memories are refurbished. They've got their souvenirs. It's been a good holiday. I've enjoyed most of it. They seem to have en-joyed most of it.

So why should I feel sad?

She doesn't know.

She stares at Maukiekie a long time before going back inside the baches.

. . .

The wind rises to gale force, the day before they leave. Seas drive hard up the beach, and out on the reef the blowhole booms above the roar of the waves.

"Winter's back with a vengeance," says Kerewin, and calmly goes on packing.

She has turned the old bach inhumanly tidy. The sand they've trodden in, is swept away and the floor polished. All the familiar dead flies are dusted off the sills. Even the spiderwebs that hung in jointed cables round the lamphooks, and grew in furry webs in the corners, spangled with sucked-dry corpses—even the webs are gone. The bunks are made for the final time, but all the clothes they had hung from convenient projections—top of ladders, bunk ends, or slung over chairs—are sorted and folded into three piles. "Yours, and yours," she says, and goes down the beach, dodging waves, to clean and lockup there. She scrubs down the dinghy, o keep safe till I come back, and stacks the oars, and anchor, and all the fishing gear. Bars the boatshed door, and puts shutters over the windows. The black bach is eyeless again, blinkered against its enemy.

"It's going to be a high wild tide," she tells them when she returns, "but that wind'll drop before too much longer. Then all we have to worry about is rain. Or maybe snow."

"Great." Joe keeps on staring at the fury before him. The great waves roll in, crests streaming away before the wind like long white hair. Near shore, the sea is latticed with a scum of yellowish froth. There is a constant grinding thunder as shoals of rocks rumble up and down in the violent boil of water. At last he says,

"Aue tama, we better get our stuff packed too."

The boy spends an hour going through his hoard. He selects all the seacrystalled glass, two perfect lampshells, one black and one red, and three of the holed stones; a paua shell Joe had garnered from the reef, and the big crab claw Kerewin jokingly calls his roach holder.

("Lookat it, chela of Ozius truncatus, defunct, perfect for gripping the teeniest roach. . . ."

"Struth Kere, he's got more than a taste for booze as it is. Don't encourage him to start on anything else.")

He piles all the rest of his collection into a kete and staggers to the door with it.

"Where are you putting that?"

On the beach, point point.

"What about all those stones Kerewin wanted?"

Simon lifts his eyebrows.

"You're growing to be a bit of meanie, fella. Leave some where she can find them. She might have been serious about keeping them for her family."

OK signs the boy and lurches outside.

He stands behind the fence and throws of each piece to the hungry waves, telling them thank you and goodbye. The bag is still heavy with holey stones when he has finished. He takes it round to the back of the old bach, where there's an alleyway between the building and its landward fence. Some craypots and a rusted tank are stored there, but it doesn't seem used for anything else. All she had done was look into it without commenting, when she was showing them round. He squats beside the tank and forms words with the stones. He croons to himself, They won't know, They won't know, making the letters good and big. But he hasn't enough stones, and the last two letters of the third word have to be left off. He looks at his message for quite a time, wondering whether it would be better, safer, to kick the phrase into disarray. It looks vaguely threatening as it is. He shrugs. It's too late. Whatever is going to happen, will happen, and there is nothing at all he can do about it now.

He leaves the message as it is.

. . .

The rain has ceased. The sky this morning is so pale a blue it appears white at first glance. The wind is gone. The air is very still: the sea roar is magnified, and every birdcall piercingly clear.

A clean refreshed land, she thinks, walking along the tideline for the last time.

> Maybe there are such things as second chances, even if dreams go unanswered. . . .

(Back by the car, Joe says, "I don't want to go either, but you've got school, and I've got work, and we don't have any choice eh?" Sighing, "If only she would. . . ." He smiles unhappily to his child, his words an echo in his head, if only she would, if only. Simon smiles bleakly back. "Would you like it if I asked her to marry me?" and the child's smile lightens and his eyes go bright kingfisher green. "Ah, you would too," the man laughs, and his heart is easy all of a sudden.

Should I ask her when she comes back to us? No, not yet, not yet. . . .)

He contents himself by saying as they leave,

"We been good? We can come back?" grinning broadly, his eyes dancing.

> He's glad to get away from the place? Ah hell, who
> cares?

"Oh yeah," says Kerewin coldly. "There's always next time."

III

The Lightning Struck Tower

7

Mirrortalk

*H*ELLO, AGAIN.
         *I planned to try and unravel the tangle of dream and substance
that is me, my family, Moerangi . . . but I am overwhelmed by futility.
What use is it to know? What use is it, when I am gutted by the sense of
my own uselessness?*

*Through poverty, godhunger, the family debacle, I kept a sense of worth.
I could limn and paint like no-one else in this human-wounded land: I was
worth the while of living. Now my skill is dead. I should be.*

But I can't.

*Let the razor sleek into my flesh. The numb night of overdose send me
stillness.*

So I exist, a husk that wishes decay into sweet earth.

Writing nonsense in a journal no-one ever sees.

"Ah to hell, Holmes, you take yourself far too seriously." Locking the book away in its chest.

> I can hear it whining in the dark to itself, Despair, despair,
> there's no-one here. I should climb in with it, and we
> could whimper in company. Each unaware of the other.

. . .

She had dropped the Gillayleys at Pacific Street, refusing their
offer of dinner.

She had sold the car at the nearest sales yard, and walked home.

> This Tasman sea is grey and wild, and there is no island with dream marae at its core . . . There was a film of dust over everything in the Tower.

The suneater burred on in the late afternoon sun, but its beat is irregular, the crystal mounting hazy.

> Stasis. A hell in itself. No change. All this waiting for me, to no avail.
> Maybe I should load up Aihe and sail off somewhere? Dunno.
> Go back to Moerangi? Dunno. Sleep for a week? Burn my brain with booze? Anything? Dunno. . . .
> You're wounded, soul, too hurt to heal. Maybe so. I dunno. . . .

. . .

He says, stamping up the stairs,

"It was good to go away, but it's better to get back home eh?"

"Yes."

"We were round at Tainuis an hour ago, and Christ, what a re-union! You should've been with us . . . everyone carrying on, Ben, the old people, Piri's up north but he sent a telegram saying hello, even *Luce* . . . you'd think we'd been gone years rather than weeks."

"You're appreciated."

He squeezes her shoulder. "E, so are you. . . ."

He spreads his arms wide at the livingroom circle, "Hai, it's good to get back here too."

"Sim at Tainuis' still?"

"Yeah, being spoilt. Everyone thinks he's looking great. And he was showing off his singing about two seconds after we got in the door. Regular party there now."

> Why aren't you at it? Why bother me here?

The whisky she's been supping since putting her nightmare book away hasn't made her feel more joyful.

He says, out of the blue,

"What do you want most of all?"

"All my life or now or what?" frowning into the fire.

"Say, for the future."

"Nothing much. What I want couldn't happen."

"Just pretend it could."

"It'll be pretending all right . . . I'd like to have a family re-union, reconciliation. Talk, drink, laugh, sing . . . what you fellas were doing, with no recriminations on either side. And most of all, I'd like to paint again as I could before. I don't care if it came hard, if I could make just one painting we could all see a piece of soul in. . . ."

She sounds cool and controlled as though uninvolved with her wishes.

"And that's all? All you want?"

"Yes. Why, what do you want?"

He is silent. He says at last,

"I don't know. It's clear, and unclear . . . I would mainly like for Himi and me to be happy. It was so good there this evening, with Wherahiko and everyone . . . that's what I really want. A good big family group, to help me, for Himi to grow up straight in. With you."

It comes out baldly.

"Hey, Joe. . . ." Her first word is drawled, warningly slow.

"You don't have to say it. I know you don't feel that way. I know you're wary of us all. Maybe that's wise, too. You don't get hurt that way."

She doesn't say anything.

"But it's a dream we've got, Himi and I, that you'll decide to throw your lot back in with humanity again. Specifically, us . . . we can wait a long time. We're masters of patience, both of us, and trained to disappointments." He grins quickly at her, inviting a flip-pant retort.

She gets to her feet. She says in a strained voice,

"I want you to come and look at something."

"Right." He stands gracefully.

. . .

*Thin etched arch of storm
and eggshell blue sky before it;*

far away, goldened by a retreating sun,
grey streak and wash of rainclouds
over the brawling Tasman sea.

> *Lone gull, sentinel, king gull, watch gull,*
> *nightblack wings, head white as a snow wave*
> *and cold barbarian eye:*
> *gull the solidity, all else mist and wraithness*
> *sea spume spun to light.*

A moon shining a broken road
oversea;
A lone woman naked to her waist
waits at the edge of moonlight;
a shadow person watching for meaning
somewhere.

She doesn't say a word, holding up the boards and canvases from behind her desk one at a time.

A group of lights
that look living
crystalled in a circle;
a tree in the middle
waiting.

> *Sunlight metalling horizon to silver;*
> *long stretch of ruffled grey.*
> *A matt white line of breakers.*
> *Behind the steel, clouds reach darkly up*
> *tops shaded by cold still light.*

Abstract, but it is as real a winter sea, winter sun, he has ever seen.

She shuffles through them quickly, paintings full of strange lights and torn lands and odd people who scowl or stare or smile distantly at him.

He practically snatches the last one out of her hand.

Kerewin on a board.

Wildly curly hair, darkly brown, but the normal high-lights have turned to streaks of gold and red and grey, wheat-colour by her temples; bushy hair so alive, he startles himself looking for eyes or fingers among it.

Broad pale face, fleshy cheeks; the V of flesh of her forehead heavily shadowed so it becomes a brand.

Narrowed cynical intense eyes, neither blue nor grey. Lively stone eyes, hating life. Thin twisted upper lip, fat lower lip, chin wedged out, ever-ready to confront the worst.

A grim face, stupid, but redeemed by the harrowing eyes.

Look up from it, and there's the same person staring back. A piece of soul enshrined in paint.

He drinks the painting in.

"These are the only things in my life that are real to me now. Not people. Joe. Not relationships. Not families. Paintings. That re-mind me I could."

She is sliding them back behind the desk, screamers and myster-ies and the weeping loving pieces of her sea and land. She holds out her hand for the self-portrait.

"But something. Something has died. Isn't there now. I can't paint." There are tears in her voice, but none in her eyes. "I am dead inside."

He still holds the painting.

"May I have it?"

There are tears in his eyes.

"Have? Not buy?" The harsh burst of laughter sneers, hits at him.

"Whatever price you ask, I will pay."

She is suddenly very weary. It hasn't meant anything to him.

"Ah, keep it. I see better work in the mirror daily. . . ."

"It is, it is real."

Admiration she is used to. Giving paintings away she is used to. This awe she is inured against. She doesn't reply.

He says softly.

"Whatever you ask of me, I will do. Whatever you want from me, I will give."

"Even absence?"

He draws his breath in sharply.

"If you wish it. . . ."

She hits the desk with the side of her hand and the crack echoes round the library.

"Forget it. Have the painting with my blessing. You're welcome to the gibbering thing, a poor gift to a good friend. But stay a good friend. Don't come any closer to me, just close enough to be always welcome."

He places it down reverently. He leans over and takes her shoulders.

She stiffens, pulling away.

"You don't want to hongi with me?"

Her taut shoulders relax.

> I salute the breath of life in thee, the same life that is
> breathed by me, warm flesh to warm flesh, oily press of
> nose to nose, the hardness of foreheads meeting.
> I salute that which gives us life.

He sighs loudly, then says, strongly, gaily,

"It's a great gift. A time when it's right to hongi, ne?"

She has pulled away again, leaning on the other side of the desk.

"I suppose so."

She shivers. Something is crawling up her spine with claws on all its thousand feet.

"Let's get back to the fire and have another drink, eh? Leave that thing here for the moment. I'll frame it and bring it round for you sometime soon, okay?"

"Okay."

He props the painting against the desk and says, as though he only just thought of it, "Are you afraid of kissing? You know, of men?"

"I don't like kissing."

"I suppose it's a matter of taste." Thoughtfully, as though she'd asked him for his opinion on osculation, instead of giving that flat conclusive answer. "I like kissing . . . Himi likes kissing . . . in fact, he thinks he can cajole and explain and talk his way out of all kinds of trouble with his kisses. Like they're part of language, eh. If he's in a good mood, everyone gets a helping."

"I've noticed."

"I wondered, did anyone ever," shrug, "you know, hurt you so you don't like kissing? Love?"

"Nope."

She picks up the lantern and the shadows spin round the booklined walls.

He doesn't move.

"I thought maybe someone had been bad to you in the past, and that was why you don't like people touching or holding you."

"Ah damn it to hell," she bangs the lamp down on the desk and the flame jumps wildly.

"I said no. I haven't been raped or jilted or abused in any fashion. There's nothing in my background to explain the way I am." She steadies her voice, taking the impatience out of it. "I'm the odd one out, the peculiarity in my family, because they're all normal and demonstrative physically. But ever since I can remember, I've dis-liked close contact . . . charged contact, emotional contact, as well as any overtly sexual contact. I veer away from it, because it always feels like the other person is draining something out of me. I know that's irrational, but that's the way I feel."

She touches the lamp and the flaring flame stills.

"I spent a considerable amount of time when I was, o, adoles-cent, wondering why I was different, whether there were other people like me. Why, when everyone else was fascinated by their developing sexual nature, I couldn't give a damn. I've never been attracted to men. Or women. Or anything else. It's difficult to ex-plain, and nobody has ever believed it when I have tried to explain, but while I have an apparently normal female body, I don't have any sexual urge or appetite. I think I am a neuter."

He picks up the painting again, considering it.

"Maybe you have so much energy tied up in this, you have none left for sex." He doesn't sound doubting, or horrified. "Sublimated is the jargon, eh." He looks at her. "I'm not being funny, but that's a Maori thing in a way . . . I used to carve a lot, and one of the old prohibitions was, while engaged in a carving, you did not lie with a woman or spend your seed, as the euphemism goes. It wasn't that sex was bad, but because all the energy was tied up in a tapu thing, was needed for it."

"Maybe so," says Kerewin heavily. "I don't know."

"Are you a virgin then?"

"Yes."

He puts the painting down and grins impishly at her.

"Well, take it from one who is very experienced, sex is hell of an enjoyable but not the be-all and end-all of things. I had it best in my life with Hana my wife, and it grew better all the time we were with each other. Because we learned to know each other with more than our bodies, sharing more than our physical excitement . . . like that, it's wonderful, it truly is. Otherwise, like now, I feel it as a need, something I want more or less to relieve myself of, but it's not over-powering. You need never be scared my cock's going to rule my head. Or my heart, eh."

He is comforting her.

He is being brotherly, friendly, almost fatherly, she thinks he thinks, denying her difference is ruinously odd.

And she loves him for a moment for his concern.

She picks up the lamp and the shadows gyrate again. "E Joe, e hoa, ka pai."

She adds, "When I was ten years younger, I read all I could to find out the why and wherefore of it. From the Kama Sutra and Kraft-Ebbing to a pile of know-yer-own body books. I decided I was one more variety in varied humanity. It doesn't worry me now, but it does seem to worry others."

"Not me now. You've explained. You're Kerewin, and I love you, as Haimona does, but we'll keep it, as they say, platonic. All right, e hoa?"

"All right," she's smiling for the first time that day. "So let's have that drink. . . ."

"Right on. But I'd better go home soon and get Sim off to bed."

Time, he thinks, as she leads the way downstairs, time and care and tenderness. It'll get through to her. I can wait. I wasn't joking when I said we were masters of patience. I can wait for a year, years if need be, because she is well worth waiting for. O dear Lord, in spite of her arrogance and coldness, she is well worth waiting for.

As he walks down the spiral he thinks it will be far less than years of waiting.

. . .

She dreamed that night she was sitting in front of a table, its edges defined by shadows. There were cards on the table, but they had nothing on them. She picked them up and called, her voice weak and querulous, "Where is the message? Where is the message?"

And at once brightly coloured pictures appeared. Trump cards, Tarot trumps. But they weren't stable. The colours ebbed and flowed and the pictures changed as she looked at them.

The pair chained to the column in the card called The Devil shifted and stretched and became The Lovers. The Fool stepped lightly forever towards the abyss, but the little dog snapping at his heels ran on to bay at the Moon. The benign placid face of the Empress became hollow-eyed, bone-cheeked, and Death rode scything through the people at his horse's feet.

The more she looked, the more the archetypes danced and altered, until they ran together in a rainbow fluidity that turned white. Except one card glowed.

The scene was there for a split second, but in that second she was drawn into the card. The sky split and thunderbolts rained down, and she started falling, wailing in final despair from the lightning struck tower.

And woke, pressed hard against the sheepskin she sleeps upon, heart beating hurtfully fast.

> A falling dream, and the Tower of Babel? Astral travel,
> and the House of God?

She didn't, then, think at all of her Tower.

. . .

She spent most of the day making a frame for the self-portrait. The wood is rewarewa, blond and fine-grained and sanded to satin finish. The frame is an inch wide: the painting life-sized, head and shoulders. Her face glowers back at her, caged with wood.

"Same to you, whatever you're thinking. *I'm* thinking you're just dartboard-sized, so watch it." She grins to herself, scowls back at the portrait.

She waits until after seven, after their tea she figures, before taking a taxi to Pacific Street.

She tucks the painting under one arm and strolls up the path. Say hello, drop the painting, and beat a hasty retreat, she decides.

But she can hear Joe yelling before she's close enough to the door to knock.

Oath, what's up now?

She can't hear the words. She kicks the door so he'll hear, and there's sudden silence after. Rapid heavy footfalls as the man comes striding down the hallway. He jerks the door open and peers out belligerently.

"O it's you," his frown vanishes, "come on in. It's cold eh."

"Very . . . what's the trouble?"

"What?"

"I heard you yelling. I assume it wasn't at the budgie?"

"No it wasn't. Simon threw a plate at me."

"He what?"

"Threw a plate . . . you come and see if you can't talk some sense into him. He's in a real shitty mood."

She leaves the painting by the door.

"Okay . . . that's the picture, by the way," and walks into the kitchen.

The boy is behind the table, pressed against the wall.

"Right," hands on her hips, "why're you chucking the crockery round?"

He snarls.

She pulls a face back, and turns to Joe.

"All I did was suggest his hair needs cutting, and he flings the plate. He very nearly hit me too. Up to then, we'd been having tea, all quiet and amicable. I haven't touched him, just shouted. He zapped round there," pointing to the table end, "as soon as the plate left his hand."

"I'd shout too. More likely I'd throw my plate back, and make sure it hit."

"It's good dinner ware. I can't afford to be hurling it about."

Simon goes on glaring at them both, still tight against the wall.

She faces him again.

"You don't like your hair being cut, I take it?"

"He doesn't. He hates it. There's always a fight over it, but I've got to do it . . . well, you can imagine the scene at the barber's can't you?"

"Yeah. What don't you like though, Sim? It being cut short?"

"But I don't cut it short," says Joe plaintively. "Just trim it, so it doesn't tangle so much. I'm damned if I know why he fights it. I know he gets rubbished by other kids . . . I've heard them."

The boy remains where he is, sullen and unmoving.

Scared as well as defiant, she thinks. Wonder what it feels like to be small and afraid, knowing either of us can do what we like with him? And I wonder how many times he has retreated there, before being hauled out and beaten?

"Mmm," she says to Joe, and walks closer to Simon, standing in front of him, looking him over for a minute and more. He stares up at her. The budgie chitters.

Joe moves to the sink, and opens a cupboard. She hears the susurration of a brush across the floor, then the clink of china pieces being swept up.

The boy's defiant scowl stays in place most of the time, but he can't bear it towards the end. Kerewin just stares, her gaze revealing nothing. He lowers his eyes, and starts to snivel.

"He normally get a hiding for breaking plates?"

Pause in the sweeping.

"Yes," says Joe.

She hears him put the brush down.

"But . . . last time it was breakfast he threw, and I got wild. I was already late for work and him having a tantrum was the last straw."

"O yes. I came round here that night, I remember. Before going pubbing. There was porridge and plate all over the floor. That was the time," she says reflectively, "yeah, that was the time he arrived at Taiaroa with his face punched. Or was it slapped?"

"Slapped." A low voice, but the sound has the flat echo of the action.

Simon is still crying.

"And with a few sundry kicks, I recall."

"Yes."

She hears the broom picked up, the sweeping resumed. He says,

"It was a bit of a fight. He said he wasn't going to school, and like I said, I was late. So when he persisted, I slapped him a couple of times, and slapped him more when he swore at me. Then he hefted the plate at me, and it hit. It hurt too. So I kicked him."

The budgie twitters.

Clatter as the broken bits of plate are dropped in the rubbish tin.

The boy sniffs, tears dripping off his chin.

"Well, to me he got a gross overdose of punishment that time. This time he goes scotfree, eh?"

The boy stares up at her, his mouth opening in surprise.

"I wasn't going to hit him," and the boy's stare switches to him. "I said I wouldn't, without you agreeing, and I meant that."

"I've said."

"Yes."

"Goodoh." She kneels on the floor beside the table, close to the boy. "Now you, what's so terrible about a haircut?"

Scotfree? That means get off? Nothing happens?

He starts to grin.

She has seen him smile through tears a few times now, and it always gets to her. It probably shows how emotionally wobbly he is, but it looks like old hearts and flowers getting on top of his woes, come what hell may.

Joe notes the smile too.

Hell, he's going to be murder to handle from now on. Though I have a suspicion, if he starts behaving badly with our stony lady here, he'll get the biggest comeuppance he's ever had.

"Nothing's terrible about a haircut?" asks Kerewin, and the smiling stops. He raises one hand, eyes narrowing with concentration, and then his fingers curl together and his eyes close. He drops the hand, defeated.

"The sound of scissors cutting through your hair?" she suggests. "Metal by your head? Somebody touching your head? What happens to your hair afterward?"

Simon shakes his head to them all, eyes still closed.

She sits back on her haunches.

"How about a cuppa?" Joe asks quietly.

"Good idea, man . . . would you bring us your scissors over?" and Simon's eyes open immediately. "S'okay sunchild. I'm not going to start cutting against your will."

She leans over and takes a handful of his hair, and he flinches. "Look at it. Look at the ends."

The hair is thick, dead straight, wheatgold with a silver sheen.

"See how that's split? And the tangle it's gotten into there? Guarantee you'd find it hard to brush through there."

"You mean I'd find it hard to brush," says Joe. "I wash and brush him still . . . that's the point, e tama. When you look after your hair, you can wear it how you like, and decide when you want it cut. But not now, right?"

The boy pouts.

"Yik," Kerewin's voice is full of distaste. "I like that about as much as your thumb-sucking routine." She stands, groaning until her stretched ankle and thigh tendons recover. "Oath, I'm unfit . . . e thanks, Joe," as he sets a cup of tea by her. He lays the scissors unobtrusively beside the saucer.

"Simon, you going to stay stuck on the wall like a fly, or do you want a tea too?"

T says the boy, two fingers making one, and he sits beside Kerewin at the table. He spies the scissors a second later. He looks quickly at her, and reaches for them.

She doesn't try to stop him.

> You fling them at me though chief, and I'll knock you
> off your seat,

but she doesn't let the thought show on her face.

To her surprise, the child takes hold of one of the long strands that are always falling in front of his eyes and gingerly cuts it through. He winces, as though it hurt him, and stops, eyes closed tightly again, scissors in one hand, hank of hair in the other.

> Well I never: cliche number two, whatever next?

Nothing, it seems.

The boy stays in the same position. Joe comes with two cups of tea, glances at his son, glances at Kerewin, sits down and begins supping from his cup.

The gas heater hisses. The kitchen is warm, but the air is thick; smells of burnt fat, and underlying stink of coal gas. Yet, with people in it, the kitchen is a friendly and comfortable room, she decides, and remembers her first impression of it. Spartan it may be, but at the moment, the very bareness emphasises the companionship between her and the man, and the boy.

The budgie chirrups again, and cracks its seeds. Her swallow sounds loud in her ears. At last, Simon shifts.

He puts down the cut hair and the scissors, and opens his eyes, sighing.

"Your tea, tama?" and pushes a saucerless cup to him. The boy ignores it, holding his hand out to Joe, palm up.

It's a gesture she hasn't seen before, apparently one of apology, because Joe lays his hand on top of his son's, and says,

"That's okay. Don't throw things any more, eh?"

Simon nods. He looks very tired all of a sudden.

But when the tea has been drunk, and Joe asks, "Will you mind if I cut your hair now?" he doesn't make any demur. He hunches his shoulders and sits rigidly still, until Kerewin offers to hold him.

Why should he be so palpably afraid?

He relaxes, once on her knees. Joe keeps up a cheerful running commentary as he cuts six inches or so off, trimming it to shoulder length. He collects the hair as he goes, piling it on the table.

"You haven't got a plait yet for that pendant of yours, Tahoro Ruku?"

"No."

"Would you like one? It could be for any pendant."

"You mean, made of Sim's hair?"

"Why not?" He grins. "Same colour as flax . . . be all right with you, Himi?"

The boy says Yes with a fingerfall: he is still tense.

"Why not indeed?"

"Okay Kere, I'll make you one . . . hold still, tama, just this end bit of your fringe now."

Joe is deft, and when he asks, "How's it look?" she can say "Ber-loody neat," and mean it. "You ever a professional?"

"No. I had a friend who was though, and he showed me a few tricks of the trade." He holds a mirror up for the child. "Like it, Haimona?"

The boy scans his reflection, grimacing, but the grimace turns to a reluctant and shamefaced grin.

"Lotta fuss over nothing," says Joe, and he ruffles the neatness into disarray fondly.

. . .

The fire in the livingroom circle is out. After the warmth and company of the Gillayleys, the Tower seems as cold and ascetical as a tombstone. Me silent dank grave. And mere months ago, they were the ones who lived in a chilly institutional hutch . . . what's happened? she asks herself, grieving. Even my home is turning against me. . . .

. . .

"Mind you," Joe had said to Kerewin, "that's the first time he's ever sat still long enough for me to do a decent job. Piri tried to hold him once, and got bitten for his trouble. The other times after Hana died," he sighed, "sheesh, all those other times . . . there's only been me here eh, which means I've had to give him a belting so he'll do as he's told . . . you ever try shearing sheep? Unwilling sheep?"

"I've worked as rousie, never shearer, but I've seen them carry on."

"Well, he's a handful like that, only worse. So thank you very much from both of us for making this time easy and good. Maybe he'll be okay from now on?"

"Maybe. Let's hope so."

She left soon after.

. . .

The night is still young, but she can't be bothered relighting the fire.

Shall I drink this depression off? Nah, I'll try sleeping it
out, first.

She doesn't bother with a lamp, plodding up the spiral in the gloomy dark.

She does light the great candle that stands by her bed.

Three foot high, inches wide, intended to provide the easterlight in a church. It is rooted in a massive pottery base she made three years ago: the base is decorated with spirals that wind and flow together, like eddies of smoke, eddies of water.

Spirals make more sense than crosses, joys more than sorrows. . . .

She sits down on the bed edge, watching the flickering candle flame.

A writhing fire, dancing on this candle . . . twisting to an inward wind, then spiring up orange and smoking . . .

There are moths in the room. Willowisp silver of their wings, out in the shadow bounds, a shimmering irregular beat, sought seen caught out of the corner of the eye. . . .

I wonder if Sim sees auras like that? A twist of wayward light, or thick clouding smoke. Lights, he said, but . . .
I wonder if he's dreaming now? Joe says he does, hence the trichloral and put him to bed soon after we finished trimming his hair . . . though it wouldn't have needed dope to make him sleep. He was exhausted . . . and what is there about cutting hair that should bring home his nightmares to him?
And damn it, soul . . . Joe and his care and love of the brat—and then the casual admission that the only way he can control Sim is to whack him into submission. What about korero, Joe? What about our tribe's famous talk-it-out with all concerned? It worked tonight. Give the urchin reasons, and time to think things out, and he responds, even more than you'd expect. You can bring him round with a little talk, a bit of humour and sympathy, round to wherever you want.
E man, you can't be so short on understanding, even given your past, that the *only* way you can handle Simon P is to knock him about. And if he's such a burden, you've said yourself that the Tainuis would take him tomorrow. So, given that you love him, why not take that extra time and trouble with him? Instead of yelling like tonight . . . and I wonder what would've happened if I hadn't come along just then?

To hell, Holmes, what's the point of thinking about this?
You know damn well you'll never say it to Gillayley.

The candle flame has steadied now, and the moths are darting
closer.

If I'm going to sit here, I might as well drink and forget
about bloody Gillayleys. . . .

Down to the cellar, using a torch to explore the labels of the
bottles.

Frontignac, pinotage, port and muscatel;
hock, riesling, sauterne, and liebfraumilch;
mead, burgundy, chianti, and dandelion wine;
Cider? Perry? Arrack? Beer? Stout? Ale?
Holy mother, I didn't realise I had so much grog stored
away. . . .

More labels in the steady beam; rum, tequila, Scotch, bourbon,
cognac, and liqueurs of all degrees . . . claret and sherry, madeira and
sack, and ah hah! what better? Gloom-defeating champagne. . . .

There's half a case of it left. And I thought that bottle I took
from upstairs to Moerangi was the last of it . . . dear spirits, remind
me to visit more often . . . take two, and hope they'll do.

Upstairs rapidly to the livingroom, where the smell of dead ashes
hangs heavily everywhere.

"Ah choices, choices . . ." standing in front of her minor grog
hoard.

"Lessee, what's a fitting cup from which to drink the health of
God in bloodless wine?" She runs her fingers over the wine goblet
collection.

A thin shell of pottery, lopsided, coloured brown and
yellow, speckled like a thrush breast; wooden goblets
with carved stems; the three pure bubbles of crystal,
brittle upon the thinnest possible stalks; matt pewter;
engraved silver; a clear hemisphere of aquamarine,
flawed and scintillating with light on that one side; the
thick, chunky cut glass that Charles, long ago prince of
doomed distant Stuarts, was supposed to have owned;
translucent bowls of porcelain brought back from

Japan; two handsized lacquer bowls; a jade cup that held as much wine as an eggshell on a tall pedestal of fretted ivory . . . no two quite the same. All rare, all strange . . . especially the odd little pottery bowl that Simon used on his drinking spree. . . .

She holds it in her hand a moment, reverently.

Two and a half thousand years old, dug from a gravesite in Greece, my precious . . . what brews were drunk in thee?

But she chooses one of the crystal bubbles, and picks up a bottle-opener, a mirror, and wanders back to her bedroom.

And here I go,
knocking round the bottle,
holding my heart open and
hoping my mind
keeps closed. . . .

Tuneless bellowing, Holmes. . . .

She watches the candle light spurt up, from the wind of the opening door.

Do not dance, do not get excited, flame; it is only me come in. . . .

She opens a bottle of champagne, and sets the mirror by the candle. She can see her face in it, a candlelit ovoid, with gouges for eyes, shadowmouthed.

"Hi me. I shall converse with thee. There is nobody near so fluent, so full of shining wit. You know the right things to say, to titillate me, to appall. I shall assure thee, give me praise, comfort . . . no end of good it'll do, talking to a mirrored me."

Her voice raps into silence.

She shudders.

I think I'm going off my head.
They say if you can think it, you can't be it.

The candle rears up and smoke clouds the mirror.

For no reason, she hears Joe talking in the bach at Moerangi: "It was a good idea. I could see out the window that way, and who came in the door."

> O yes. Mirror of course. From his flat-on-the-back phase of childhood. And he also said—how did those two bits go?

"I used to get afraid that I'd look up into the mirror and see nothing there."

And,

"I had this nightmare eh. One day, I'd look into the mirror and somebody else would be looking back out of my face."

Nasty.

She leans carefully over, and swivels the mirror round so she can't see in it.

It was a nice idea, to practise the old discipline of mirror and candle again, to use image and living light as pointers to the self beyond self.

> But not in this state, gentle soul. It's a bad stage when you get talking to mirrors, and right at the moment, I think you're unstable enough to see other people looking outa your eyes.

She rests back against the headboard of the bed, and begins drinking steadily.

The cold white eye of the moon looks in.
A bottle down, and a bottle to go. . . .

> *Over the lip of wax*
> *a river spills,*
> *flame reddens flickers*
> *flares, stills,*
> *and the river congeals. . . .*

The black wick slopes over, leaning out of the flame.

The world is night, quiet night.

She wets the rim of the bubbleglass, and strokes round and round slowly. The crystal begins to sing.

"Getta guitar?"

She squints at the wine.

In the uneasy light, she can just see her reflection.

"Was it thee or me who spake?"

Silence.

"Musta been me."

She sets the goblet down by the backwards mirror with great care, and fumbles her way downstairs.

"Stuhupid barstard, shoulda brought the light."

The toadstools by the seventh step glow palely green. She reaches into the niche and pinches one off, and splutters into a chuckle.

"Brought it!" triumphantly. But the phosphorescence fades even as she speaks. "Ah sheeit," throwing it down on the stone, "hope I *squash* you."

Darkness, darkness, all around.

The distant crying of the sea . . . or is it my heart in me? Thou nede not be afrayed of any bugges by night . . . it must be the living-room circle by now . . . this step? What if I've stepped out of my retreat and this downward spiral goes on and on in the black for-ever? Steep deep, deep where light suffocates and people become tiny creeping shades unseen ever except by horrible. . . .

"Thank heaven," in a loud voice, stepping out into the livingroom. The great window lets in enough moonlight for her to see by.

Wonder when me new one's coming?

She lights a lamp quickly, and another, and another, and their flames all seem to run together in a blurring winery flicker.

"I can see. Short of. I mean, sort of. Sort. Of. Thank you." She bows to herself, to the lamps, to the moon.

Take it easy, Holmes, take it slow.

"Bugger the guitar, I need tucker, I need food."

Hunting through the cupboards, remembering with a vague despair that she'd eaten the remaining tinned food yesterday and earlier today, and had meant to get more when she went into Whangaroa, but. . . .

"Ah typical," she sneers in derision at herself. "Floating on a lake of grog, and sitting on a mountain of tobacco and assorted weedery, and watch ya got to eat?"

A jar of lumpfish caviar.

She sighs.

"Better than nothing."

She blows out two of the lamps, and takes the other up the spiral with her. On the floor below the toadstool niche there is a small shining smear. Her eyes fill with tears.

"I'm sorry. I shouldn't have done that. Too impatient y'see ... do you see? Don't be berloody dense, woman, how could a toadstool see? Well, the Toad mighta retracted and shat an eye eh?" She starts to giggle. It becomes a dirty lowdown chuckle, blatting out, a gutty bleat she can't stop.

Easy! says herself, cold and furious. Quit it!

She sobers momentarily, bends down swiftly and kisses the slimy patch on the stair.

"Really sorry," she says, and continues upwards, marvelling at the ease with which she'd bent. Never do it sober, sweet, you'll bust your spine. . . .

She stops in the doorway.

"Only half a bottle left? Hell, it'll have to do. . . ."

She puts the lamp by the great candle and slumps onto the bed. The lamp goes out. Face flushdown in the rubicund dark. . . . e hine! Haere mai ki te kai!!

O yeah ... sitting up stupidly, and fishing for the small jar. Sticks her tongue in and sucks a mouthful out. Squelching the tiny oily globules ... dunno whether it's the salt soy taste or the burstingunderteeth scrunch ... delicious anyway.

> You have just eaten enough lumpfish to stock an ocean ... so what? Whattabout me cod roe patties? Millions and millions of codfry, never going to make it ... and for that matter, think of eating a fish of any kind, anything ... all its potential gone ... mind you, snark, you could eat people like me with impunity: we're kind to mother earth, and don't seek to stock her with replicas of self ... we're neither horned nor slatted, a twilight of the genders, as Fletcher rewrote of Agathon ... so come all anthropophagi and feast in innocence, least so far as me potential reproductive processes are concerned ... neat of Joe to be so understanding, or at least show a mask of comprehension, that's more than most

have done . . . damn hell, I've let a Gillayley back in my
brain . . . distant or near, they close in. . . .

She leans on her elbow to stow away the empty caviar jar, and
her elbow collapses under her. She falls forward, on top of the
candle. The flame spurts up and scores through her hair.

She jerks back, rubbing frantically.

There's a charred track through the front curls, and a vile stench
of burnt hair.

"Ahh heeellll," she says wearily. "Ah to hell."

The candle has gone out.

. . .

Woken once by a thin tinny whistling, like breath from a bron-
chial baby.

Then a small moan, and scuffling somewhere under the window.

Stiffen and tense, bent with the ears towards where the sound
last came from.

It doesn't occur again.

The silence is ominous, nervewracking.

. . .

Woken twice by having to get up and urinate.

She sways on the toilet, feeling sick and thickheaded. Her eyes
are sore, and sticky with mucus. Her head is throbbing.

"You getting old. Old, old old. Bladder worn out and self in
misery, just from a few drinks."

There is an odd pressure on her bladder these days.

"Beer belly," she says critically, looking at herself in the mirror.
"Fatgutted pig that you are."

All those innards pressing upon one another, she thinks, angry
at her self-despoliation. No bloody wonder you can't hold your
water anymore.

She goes back to bed, and tosses restlessly for a long time, waiting on sleep.

. . .

When she wakes again, it is late morning, the sun streaming in
through the sea-coloured window.

The air is stale, and soured by the smell of burnt hair.

Running her hand over her head and discovering the burned patch anew,

Sweet hell, what a morning.

She half-expects Simon to come around, even though it is the first day of the new term. But he doesn't turn up.

"Just as well," growling to herself, standing in front of the mirror again. "I am fed up with Gillayleys to here," knifing her hand across her throat, scissors perilously close to the skin.

We did wake in a bad mood, didn't we? says the snark. Just because we got carelessly drunk and burned ourselves, we start taking swipes at our near and dear friends.

"Near and dear friends be damned . . . what the hell are they doing to me? Sucking me dry, it feels like. Emotional vampires, slurping all the juice from my home, that's what." Even with the new lightheaded feeling a haircut gives her, she still feels resentful and ill-at-ease.

Better go back to being your natural self, dear Holmes. The loner on the fringes. Phase Joe and his brat out . . . but I think I'd miss them. Think? You know you would! But don't think . . . play it as it comes. And enjoy this peaceful solitude—it makes a bloody neat change. And speaking of neat . . . this place is becoming a hovel.

She starts a cleaning binge. Niches in the Tower that have been undisturbed since the place was built are rudely dusted. The bonsais get trimmed, the toadstools ruthlessly pruned, and the insect population gets the kind of hurryalong it's never had before. And she discovers mice everywhere.

There are tiny furrows from their teethwork even on the great candle she notices, while cleaning up the splatters of spilt wax.

"Strangle-traps," with heavy emphasis on the strangle. "That's what it's gonna have to be."

What was that line of Nash? In "The Mind of Professor Primrose"? O yeah, "He set a trap for the baby, and dandled the mice." Got his priorities right, that fella. . . .

Normally, she dislikes killing mice. There is something about their beady-eyed furtivity, their wholesale preying on humans, that appeals to her outlaw instincts. But at the moment, they're in her way, and they're doomed.

She fantasises some baby traps though, while baiting the traps for the mice. Glittery things, she decides, that make zing and beep noises to lure the wee souls in. Construct them of shiny fireproof plastic: mould 'em to look like bubbles. And Baby comes to play . . . once yer victim is inside, an automatic dispenser dispenses a whiff of extremely potent anaesthetic, the clear walls turn opaque, and the cell swiftly incinerates its contents. Just turn upside down afterwards, and let the clean ashes sift away. . . .

> You're a morbid abhuman bastard, Holmes . . . where were you when they built Treblinka and Dachau?

It isn't a mood she enjoys. She clenches her shoulder and back muscles, loosens them, tightens them, trying to physically get rid of a grim humour. It works, until she does a round of the strangle-traps in the afternoon and discovers she has caught a fine crop of mice, every size from decrepit patriarch to tender pinknosed fine-furred baby. She flings thirty corpses out to the gulls, and the cold-eyed birds squawl and battle for the stiff little bodies. Some are gulped whole, others torn apart, before she can get away from the view, and she has a new gruesome set of images to fight.

The Tower is clean and sweetsmelling and dustfree by late afternoon. The seawind has blown through it, every window opened wide as could be.

"Foul fug of smoke *every*where . . . strange I never noticed it before now."

She spent some time cleaning her smoking gear.

> If I could see this yech,

a disgusting slime, dark dung of tobacco she's excavated from her pipes and nargheel.

> every time I smoked, I do believe it would put me off for life . . .
> On the other hand, I don't see it.

cheerfully lighting a pipe before going down to make tea.

She is laying the fire when the radiophone buzzes.

Hundred to one it's Gillayley senior. It can buzz its head off.

But the clamour is unrelenting, going on and on, so she snatches up the mike and thumbs home the speak button as though she'd like to push it through the set.

"Ah hah," says the operator brightly. "Don't tell me, I know. I just got you out of the shower."

"You did not."

"O? Is everything all right?"

"Yes. Did you just ring up to say hello?"

"No. I've got your friends on the line," all the good humour has fled the operator's voice. "One moment please,"

switch, click, switch.

"Tena koe e hoa!" bellows Joe. "C'mon down to the Duke, Kerewin! We got all kinds of celebration going on!"

Up you.

"No thanks," she says coldly.

"Huh?"

"I said, No thanks."

"Uh Kerewin, you not feeling well?"

"I'm feeling fine."

He's scratching his head. "I've upset you some way? Himi's upset you?"

"Hell, you're self-centred, bloody self-centred. What makes you think the only thing in the world that could upset me would be you or your son?"

"What's wrong?" bewilderment in his voice. "Whatever's wrong?"

"Nothing. I just don't feel like going out and grogging up tonight."

He must be in the phone booth at the Duke. She hears a door pulled shut, and the babble and clamour in the background dim.

"E Kere, that's okay," he says gently. "I'm sorry if it sounded like

I expected you to drop everything and come out with me. I didn't mean it that way. You see, Piri and his missus are back together, that's why he went north eh. And Ben's just sold a stud heifer for a few hundred more than he expected, and everyone's happy. We're having a bit of a do, and I thought you might be happy to come and join it. Piri's been asking where you are. So's Pi and Polly and the old lady, you know? And I've been wanting you here."

Well want on, man.

"Yeah, but I'm busy."

"Okay, e hoa," and sighs his breath huhhh out. "Ahh, will you be busy tomorrow? Because I've got a sort of present for you if you want it. . . ."

Talk about baits . . . or is it just because I've set too many traps today?

"All right, I bite. What kind of present?"

He laughs.

"I'll give you a clue. He aha koa iti, he pounamu." His voice has grown stronger and more relaxed with each word. "You know last night?"

"What about it?"

"I didn't say anything about the painting, unwrap it or even give a thank you . . . but it's the best self-portrait I've ever seen, Rembrandt included."

"Ha bloody ha."

"No truly, I love it. I hung it up in the sittingroom today eh, right above the fireplace. The frame's perfect. I think I'll do the room up to match it eh?"

His high throbbing giggle.

"Yeah," she drawls.

"I mean that too . . ." she can hear him ripping open a packet of cigarettes, the click and hiss of his lighter. "Well, I was thinking what I could get you. Nothing nearly as good as your gift, but something special. . . ."

"That plait you said you'll be making from Sim's hair will do fine."

"O, I made that already. I stayed up a while last night doing it. I was thinking all kinds of things while I did eh."

"I'll bet," she says drily.

> Hell, imagine. While I was drinking my way through a
> sludge of selfpity, there was the earnest Gillayley wear-
> ing his fingers down to the bone, up all night regardless
> of early morning work, to make me a necklet from his
> son's moonshimmer hair. I'll bet the bugger's lying.

"Anyway, what I was thinking doesn't matter . . . I bought you
this present today, and I was going to give it to you tonight."
Pause.

The harsh eager gasp as he sucks in more smoke, and the long
soft breath out.

> He aha koa iti, he pounamu . . . it doesn't mean that it is
> a gift of greenstone, but that it carries the emotional
> content of jade. The value, the indications of affection
> and respect, the mana of pounamu.

"All right, you've hooked me . . . I'll put away me sour mood, and
crawl along to the Duke."

"E ka pai, ka pai," his delight makes his voice rise to a tenor
pitch. "Look, I'll borrow Piri's truck and come right over, eh?"

"Nah, she's right. I'll ring a taxi. I haven't had much to eat today,
and I better get some food aboard before drinking."

He asks with sudden consternation,

"You haven't had one of those stomach attacks, have you? Like
at Moerangi?"

"Hell no. It's just been a shit of a day . . . I went mad and cut my
hair, cleaned everything out, slaughtered mice . . . a sort of dreary
combination of the murderous and the domestic, you know?"

Joe, giggling, says he doesn't. "But I'm glad you're all right . . . hei,
what does your hair look like? Ah not to worry. I'll see it soon . . . must
be shearing time eh?" Snicker. "I'll chop mine too, and get in on the
act. O by the way, Haimona's with the old people. We were on our
way to you with this koha, and he nearly had us off the bike, shrieking and pointing and carrying on at some kids. Took about ten years
off my life and three inches of rubber off the tyres as we screech to
a halt. And the kids all start yelling and dancing bad as Himi, and it's
Piri's mob, all of them. So we went into the farm quick and you'd
never believe it but Himi and them are all over the top of one another
like they're old mates from way back. And I told you how they used
to fight, eh?"

"Yeah."

"Piri and Lynn are all over the top of each other too, ur, I mean they're hugging us as much as we're hugging them."

"That did sound very much like double entendre."

"Weellll," and she knows he is grinning. "They were kind of close when we barged in . . . anyway, that's where Himi still is. The old people are babysitting while we depraved adults go out and booze."

"Lucky Marama. Lucky Wherahiko," intense sympathy in her voice to pervert her words. . . .

. . .

16 ounces of beer and two whiskies in ten minutes. A bit much too fast for comfort. Particularly after last night's performance. A momentary giddy swirl.

Polly is saying something.

"I said, you done your hair nice."

"Sorry, I was far away . . . you like it? I just hacked, but hair like mine grows quickly over catastrophes."

"Huh, you're lucky. You want to have hair like *mine*." Polly tosses her head and shuffles cards faster.

> My cut hair lying in a woolly pile on the floor . . .
> wondering whether it might be better, more respectful,
> to bury it—but then, worms, mould, decay . . . so, as
> always I burn it, and watch, as always, dismayed to see
> it shrivel to a sticky mass that charred and disintegrated.
> A little more of me gone forever. . . .

"Yeah, I'm lucky," she says to Polly.

Joe comes back with another tray of drinks. He whispers in her ear, "Happy you came?"

She nods. "Ah, I'm glad . . . I'll give it you in private?" laying his hand on her shoulder. Again she nods.

"What're you fellas whispering about?" Piri bawls it out. He is very drunk and very happy, one arm draped about his wife, hugging her tight to him every minute as though he's afraid she'll forget him.

Lynn is smaller than he is, a fine-boned woman with black feathery hair. She reminds Kerewin of a bird in more ways than one, high-voiced, sharp-nosed, full of quick nervous movement. A sparrow of a woman, but without a sparrow's gamin cheerfulness.

"Secrets eh?" says Piri.

"No. I was merely saying this place is filling up." Joe leaves his hand on her shoulder as he sits. The warmth of it soaks through her jacket, through her shirt, warming her skin. "Filling up fast," he says, and takes the hand away, raising his glass to her.

The early evening drinkers are pouring in: the din increases. She can no longer hear what the others are saying, yet through the general uproar some small sounds are abnormally clear. The plic! of a poolball snicking another. The flat knock the shotglass makes when she puts it down. Polly going "Fsss!" under her breath as she plunks down an invincible card. Pi's soft swear. The old lady looks over his shoulder and says, "Heh!", and draws hard on her pipe. It's gone out since the last puff and Kerewin can hear the sucking sound as though it's being played through loudspeakers.

"Umm . . . my turn to get drinks eh." Standing, the floor seems to withdraw a little under her feet. "What are you all having?"

"Just some jugs and a few whiskies," says Pi. "We can share them round eh?"

"Right you are," steadying herself unobtrusively. "Would you help us with the glasses, Joe?"

"Gladly."

At the counter, while waiting for the jugs and glasses to be filled:

> "and what does the bloody borough do? Put 'em through the stonecrusher!"
>
> "Struth mate, at a dollar a sugarsack?"
>
> "And then they plant them in the bloody tarseal!"

"What's all that about?" thumbing towards the group that's doing the talking.

Joe shrugs. The barman shakes his head, eyes on the squirting stream of beer.

"Stones, I think," he says. "They've found a market for those white ones you can pick up by the ton off Bright Street beach."

"Ah they'll be selling the air we breathe next," snarls Kerewin. "First gold, then coal, then all the bush they could axe, and all the fish they could can. And now the very beach. . . ."

"Ah you never know where it'll end," the barman agrees cheerfully. "That'll be four dollars and 91 cents." He whisks the fiver into
the till. "I like your hair like that," dropping the change into her hand.

"My donation to this year's woolclip," she says sourly.

"I like it anyway," Joe smiles, helping load the drinktray.

She has clipped her hair very short: the thick mushroom cloud
that had bloomed has been tamed to a neat tightcurled cap. Not a
sign of singed hair anywhere.

"Ta, mate." She swaps grins with him.

Joe thinks, Hope to hell she didn't hear what else those buggers
said, or that'll really screw things up.

> "S'all right for some to talk," one of the group had said
> after Kerewin's remarks. "She's got more money than
> she knows what to do with they reckon, but how many
> of us can say that?" And another added, "Yeah. Lucky
> bastard Gillayley, looks like he's in on it now."

That had hurt. Thinks Joe, I don't want any part of her money.
I just want her. He had made his compliment in a loud voice, covering whatever else the group said.

The hell with what they think . . . but why can't they keep their
big mouths shut?

. . .

We're a quiet school, she thinks. A little island of peace in all
this racket.

Piri and Lynn are staring tipsily into each other's eyes.

Pi and Polly are intent on their game, cardplayers' eyes flickering
like lizard tongues. The old lady drinks and smokes and stares,
chuckling to herself over jokes only she knows about.

She and Joe drink in companionable silence. Shreds of conversation drift by her. The poolplayers give the game up in disgust,
". . . bloody cue's flawed, not to mention the table," and troop down
to the other end of the bar where the dartboard is. An old old man
to her left is saying, ". . . and the nurse said, Hold my hand then, ever
so nicely."

He's dotted with age freckles, bald but with a thin layer of side
hair combed up and across in a vain attempt to hide the baldness;
he sits stiffly upright like a poker's rammed up him. ". . . and after

my operation on the other side, she said, My, Mr Kissenger, for a man old enough to be my grandfather you certainly know some," she turns her ears away.

A group of men, all dressed in jeans and grey pullovers, discuss fish and boats. One yells, "Hey John! Go get your guitar and we'll have a bit of a song eh?"

"Do, John," she murmurs to herself, and starts as Joe taps her arm.

"You're miles away."

"I was just thinking . . . something the matter?"

"No, Pi's got some sandwiches for us."

"The old lady makes them and keeps them in her bag every time we come here now," says Pi.

"We got caught by the greasy hamburgers they make down the road a couple of times, and as for the pies *here*. . . ."

"Help yourself," urges the old lady.

"Is it okay? There's enough?"

"Man, she got tons in the bag there. She always makes enough for the whole damn family in case they turn up," Polly growls. She lost the last game.

The old lady passes over a gory-looking sandwich.

"Have some proper kai," she says firmly, "not like that filthy pie and stuff."

"Looks interesting," opening it, and wishing she hadn't.

A lot of little baby cockles with their siphons erect like tiny penises, arranged on a bed of lettuce leaf and soaked with tomato sauce.

Keck . . . and I had a greasy hamburger and filthy stuff half an hour ago,

but she takes a mouthful grimly, and is surprised to feel spurts of saliva.

"You know what?" she says after a moment. "I'm really hungry."

Joe grunts, tearing into another sandwich.

Solid chewing all round for the next five minutes.

"Oowe," says Joe, standing suddenly. "Scuse, time for mimi." He clutches at the table, wavering. "Wow, that beer and whisky . . . won't be a minute you fellas."

He pushes away through the crowd.

Pi says,

"Simon okay now?"

She thinks he is asking Piri, but Piri is leaning towards her.

Pi looks at her steadily.

"Joe treated him all right on this holiday of yours?"

So everybody knew but me . . . and nobody said or did a damn thing.

"There was no trouble," she says, cool and hard as a rock.

Lynn winces, her eyes filling with tears.

"You know Kere, the number of times we have, Piri has, fixed up poor Himi . . . he used to come round with terrible weals on him, didn't he Piri? Terrible cuts, and we couldn't say anything to Ma, because she'd get too upset. And we couldn't do anything, because you feel sorry for Joe being alone and all . . . but that poor kid! God, sometimes he could hardly walk . . . I'd never treat one of mine that way, though I suppose it's different him not really being Joe's and all, but sometimes I got so wild, didn't I Piri? Sometimes I could have scratched that bastard's eyes out," she ends viciously.

Piri blinks. He's been nodding pacifically along with all Lynn's been saying, eyes half-closed, face slack.

"Simmer down, Lynnie . . . Kerewin, I thought you might do something as soon as you found out about it, and Joe says you have eh? He didn't say what though."

Meaning, Tell us.

She is silent.

Piri pours the last of the beer out, first in her glass, then in Lynn's; Pi shakes his head and covers his glass, while Polly drains hers and holds it out; some in Polly's, some in Missus' genteel 5 ounce, and winds up giving a half-hearted scowl at the drop left in the bottom.

"Aue . . . well, my shout anyway." He holds the tray limply, leaning his head back. He says quietly.

"Me and Joe had a big fight about a year ago, over the way he treats his kid. I went in punching, but he's bigger than me so in the end I picked up a bottle, and smashed it on him. It skidded all down his shoulder and ribs . . . I was lucky I didn't gut him, the way the glass broke eh?"

He sighs heavily, head still back. "Pa woodened me . . . *and* said he was going to call the cops. Never did though . . . don' think it's a good thing to bring fuzz into family affairs, do you?" his eyes flick open suddenly, the drink drowsiness gone.

"I don't. Provided the family can cope."

"We tried," says Piri very softly. "We did try. Joe's had his troubles though, and you can't kick a man who's down all the time, nei?"

"I'm not civilised like that." She speaks as softly as Piri, aware of the rapt attention, everyone straining to hear. "I said to Joe if he thrashes Sim the way he has in the past, I'll kick him silly." She drains her glass. "I like Joe helluva lot, and I like Himi too, but aside from the damage this business has done to the child, it's warping a good man."

"Exactly," says Piri, no slur at all.

She puts the glass down, and smiles round at them all. "It wasn't an idle threat. I could take on any or all of you right now, and have a neat time, stomping you to mush."

> Great, Holmes! An old lady, a tiny woman, a wee man,
> and a good fat fellow, placid as the day is long . . . kick
> 'em all to death eh? O mighty work, hero stuff that!

The old lady looks at her keenly, and spits to one side. Pi raises his eyebrows, and Polly grins like a dog. She'd obviously like Kerewin to have a go . . . Lynn just swallows.

"Judo or something?" The glaze is coming back into Piri's eyes.

"Or something. But good."

"Joe's found out?"

"By experience, yep."

"Whooo," Piri shakes his head blurrily. "Kinoath . . ." he starts collecting glasses, avoiding her eyes again.

She laughs. "Hey it wasn't much of fight, you fellas . . . we just decided that if Himi ever needs a hiding again, Joe will wait till I agree to it. I'm not muscling into Joe's business or anything . . . it's just we figured that the bashings happened because Joe was by himself, under pressure, and he lashed out on the spur of the moment eh? Sooo," she shrugs, comfortable in her power, "now he's not alone any more, he's got a promise to stand by and reason to keep his temper, and that should prevent Himi from getting damaged again."

Lynn closes her mouth. She looks at Kerewin, her brown eyes gone from birdbright to look strangely like a spaniel's, watery, inane, devoted.

"Well, I'm *glad* you stopped it because it wasn't nice . . . when you said though, about Joe not being alone now and that, did you mean you and Joe're getting married soon?"

Unholy, what the hell has Joe been saying?

She goes from boast to being coldly angry in a second. She says, "Emphatically not."

Silence again.

"Play up," Pi in a low voice to Polly.

"Hold your horse, fuckwit." She picks up her cards deliberately, ears cocked for the next bit.

"O, I thought . . ." Lynn is pleating the edge of her cardigan nervously, seemingly not aware of doing it. "You know, I thought . . . well, you know and all." Piri sighs behind her. "You know," she says again, "I just thought."

Her anger dies as abruptly as it roused.

> Poor little twerp. Sounds like putting her foot in it is a
> regular occupation . . . and she was only trying to be
> polite to what must seem to her to be the ultimate in
> butch strangers, strange butchers.

She grins at her wordplay, grins kindly to Lynn. "My fault, I put it the wrong way. But whatever it looks like, we're just good friends . . ."

Lynn smiles back timidly.

"I'm not the marrying kind, you see," and she feels, rather than sees, Polly's glance rake her over. The big woman grunts to herself in satisfaction.

"Got you this time, Pi," she says, and almost simpers at Kerewin.

Kerewin smiles politely, cups her chin in her hands, and leans on the table, gazing with deep interest at the patterns the beer rings have made there.

> Twixt devil and deep blue sea . . . hurry back, e hoa.

She hears Pi, "You playing these cards or aren't you?"

"Give us time," says Polly. Mumble, mumble, mumble.

She feels a stealthy touch on her foot.

> Ah sheeit, that's all I need . . . overtures from the ambi-
> sextrous . . . she's not a bad sort, I suppose. Just trying.

Without making it look pointed, she stands and stretches.

"We are of the sea, we have tides like the sea," she begins in a chant. "Tears of saltwater, tidal bodies, and seastreamed hair."

"E, that's nice," says Polly. "Whatsit mean?" grinning.

"Something I thought of . . . it means, I gotta go."

"And when you gotta go, you gotta go," says Pi. Fatuous laughter all round, herself included. The old lady joins in, husky aged cough of a laugh, "Huk! Huk! Huk! Ahh, you young people. . . ."

Polly stands too. "Need a mimi myself," hitching her shoulders back.

"It can wait," says Pi calmly, sitting back in his chair. "You haven't played these cards yet, and I don't think Kerewin needs company."

And Kerewin, looking frantically for polite but offputting phrases for Polly, feels a surge of affection for the man. Pub gossip rubbished him for living with a militant and overt bisexual.

> Fatguts they call you, good only at the cardtable, good only for the beer. But man, your discernment and kind-ness puts them all to shame.

It was Pi who first greeted her here, she remembers. Pi who first brought up the question of Simon. She grins widely at him.

"Like you say, e hoa. I don't need the company."

Making it sound a joke to everyone but Pi and Polly. Polly scowls and flounces back down in her seat. Pi looks at her under one lifted eyebrow, and deals out more cards.

. . .

The toilet was empty.

> Thank goodness for that. Much longer and I'd be piss-ing all over the floor. Odd how you can forget about your bladder . . . better than last night, anyhow.

She feels oddly lightheaded after pissing.

> Lightened bladder sure, but lightened head? Less the two are connected in some impure fashion . . . Fill your head with all kinds of spirits, whisky to ghosts, and piss it out again . . . dear soul, imagine if you could pass all memories, but selectively . . . keep the sweet things, the

> first flows of joy at colour and shape and sound (chime
> of tuis, lichen at Moerangi, rich cadmium yellow on
> black and red rock; the ratpad ticker of the clock that
> beat time time time to my guitar; rainbows and storm
> clouds and dragons of the sunset, and mists set in mo-
> tion by the breathing of the sea . . .) and lose everything
> else, festering quarrels and old moneyhurt and the awe-
> some neglect of God. . . . The old horrors I can't forget.

Standing shakily, speaking out loud, "I think I'll drink wine from
now on."

She splashes water on her face, washes her hands.

> Checking in the mirror to see if I'm still there . . . I'm
> there all right, little piggy eyes in a large piggy face,
> swivelling down all your lazygutted blubberarsed
> length . . . what good in you? I don't know. . . .

"I don't want to die, but I don't know why I live. So what's my
reason for living?" she asks the mirror image. "Estranged from my
family, bereft of my art, hollow of soul, I am a rock in the desert.
Pointing nowhere, doing nothing, of no benefit to anything or anyone. Flaking, parched, cracked . . . so why am I?"

The person in the mirror stared emptily back.

"I do have a wish for dying," she said slowly. "A deepheld wish
for dying."

The old lady came through the door. She stood looking a moment, lined face inscrutable next to Kerewin's in the mirror. Then
she hitched up her skirt and began waddling to the toilet.

"They're starting to sing out there. Someone brought in a guitar.
Does you good to sing eh?"

"Too right!" Her face is going scarlet.

> And that's what you get for wringing your weevily lit-
> tle soul for the last casting of self-pity, you disease.

In the bar, there's a crowd gathered round the person playing,
and the way is clear to their tables.

"Pack up your troubles," everyone is roaring beerily," and
SMILE! SMILE! SMILE!"

> Sweet hell, here we go, World War Two all over
> again,

but her fingers are already snapping to the crisp rhythm.

"Greetings, stranger," says Joe as she sits down. "You're just back in time to say hooray to Polly and Pi."

"We're off home to the menagerie," says Pi. Polly grunts. "Have a shout on us."

"Well thanks, but I'm just changing to wine and you've got to buy a bottle at a time here. Tell you what, may I shout you instead?"

"No," says Pi, and Polly says "Yes," and Kerewin is unsure who she is saying that to. Joe stands.

"Look, I'll get the drinks, okay? Specials, topshelf, or whatever, okay?"

He must have had a couple of extra rounds while she's been in the loo. His eyes are unfocused and he's swaying as he stands.

"I'll get my wine though," taking out her wallet.

"No. This is my shout," holding up his hand as though to ward her money off.

"Okay. . . ."

She offers her cigarillo case round. Piri doesn't smoke, it seems, and Lynn says Thanks, but not one of those if you don't mind, and Pi says Ka pai, and Polly takes two and doesn't say anything.

She flicks a flame up from the lighter. There is barely enough gas in it to make a light, but she woos the little blue flame, nuzzling it carefully lest it perish with the effort.

The old lady says, "Can I have a smoke too?"

"O surely," handing the case across. "I didn't see you come back."

"O, I been here," the old lady grins. "Listening. E pai ana."

A smokering flows over the table between them, expanding.

Plonk! into the middle of the curling vapour. A bottle of young port, '76 says the label. Gawd, just put to bed in its bottle. . . .

"Izzit your wine?"

> Urrk never . . . but look at his smile, my soul, floating
> through the thickened air as white and mysterious as
> the cheshire cat's . . . you wanna dim it?

"Ae Joe, it'll do nicely."

She peels away the lead foil, and uncorks the bottle with her knife. Joe's saying, "I got you fellas a whisky apiece," handing them out, "trebles, eh?"

Pi Kopunui groans, Piri shudders, Lynn says O dear, Polly cackles, and Missus just tosses hers straight down, and begins sedately on the beer.

They toast each other, wishing health and long life, Kia ora, Kia ora. . . .

"Look," she says suddenly. "Look, they match exactly," holding her little finger up with the glass of port by it, so all can see the hump of garnet next to the wine. She is bemused by the coincidence. They offer disinterested agreement.

"Ultimate eh, matching your grog to your jewellery. Remind me to get some neat brown bracelets with cream stripes eh?" Pi belches and giggles. "Kelk. Sorry, that beer is getting to me."

"No wonder, you been inviting it in since this morning . . . why do you have so many rings?" Polly's head is cocked on one side and her eyes are partly crossed.

Flicker of sober amusement . . . how many do you see, lady?

"O I like the colour and feel of semi-precious stones . . . so I load 'em on, eh. . . ."

> Each ring feeds my fingers with its particular virtue. A garnet gives courage, a turquoise soothes. Greenstone ennobles. Opal enlivens. Coral is shy, but full of ancient memory. And aquamarine quickens thought, lively as a dolphin in the open sea.
>
> And some stones I avoid like the plague . . . diamonds are obnoxious and leave, somehow, a sick taste in the mouth. Emeralds are cold as death, idol eyes, and rubies are too luxuriantly, unctuously velvet. . . .

"Uhh?"

"Sweet Lord, you're dreamy tonight. I said, Pi and co are away . . . and Lynn's taking Piri home." In a whisper, "He's flaked."

The little woman has Piri propped against her, one limp arm still round her neck. Piri sleepwalks and doesn't say goodbye. Lynn says awkwardly,

"Nice meeting you, Kerewin. Please come round and visit. I hope

you and Joe get on in spite of, you know, Simon and all that . . ." she
smiles entreatingly. "It was *nice* meeting you and having that talk,"
lurching away under Piri's weight, her own drink-riddled feet finding it hard to keep the floor in its proper place.

O God no, Himi's in the way.

It is like a punch in his stomach.

Kerewin is half-rising, bowing a little to the others. "Nice meeting you all again," she is saying, lips curling in a smile, "Pi, Polly,
Missus. . . ."

"Good to see you again too," says Pi. "Get a move on, woman,"
belligerently to Polly who is clattering round, gathering cards and
cans of beer. She heads for the door, and her bag catches on the
corner of a table and she trips. "Hoops!" grabbing a man conveniently close, staggering closer against him, "All right, honey?" and
the man chuckles, his arms moving up her. Pi, upset, roars, "Quit
arsing around there and get cracking," and a dozen heads turn their
way. Polly yells back, "What? Farts?" and slopes off through the
door. Pi shakes his head sorrowfully to Kerewin, and follows.

The old lady, chkchkking them both, turns and says, "She is a
good woman," and Kerewin thinks Polly isn't bad, but she's not
necessarily good. But Missus turns back and calls loudly after Pi, "I
think she's Maori for all that white skin. She'll make Joe a good
wife, nei?" nodding her head firmly, headscarf aflap, and she exits.

"Jesus holy, I'm gonna have to kill that idea fast . . . first Lynn,
now her eh?" Kerewin grins broadly to Joe.

> Aiiee, I should have guessed . . . who would want to
> take him on? But I was sure she liked him. Cared for my
> child. My only son.
> ("Did she like you?"
> NO.)
> But if that's what it is, why didn't she say so the other
> night?
> Instead of all that business about not being ordinary,
> and not liking sex?

He says, ignoring her smile, his voice shaking,

"We'll go and drink by the bar eh? Have a song or two before
we go?"

Singing is the last thing I want to do.
Aue, cry and cry and cry . . . why didn't I see it before?
And what am I going to do now? What now, God?

He stares into his empty beerglass. The broken latticework of foam there begins to blur. "Okay man," she is saying. "Singing might stop the swirl in my head, eh?" Picks up the two thirds full bottle of port and forces her way through the crowd to the bar. She bores past anyone blocking her, not hearing protests. She stiffarms a space for Joe to come beside her.

The guitarist is playing, "It's A Long Way To Tipperary," thunka thunka thunk, and the people round are bellowing out the words. She joins in, her strong voice roughening as she tries to outshout everyone.

Farewell Picadilly! and a germane part of her drink-unsteady mind begins a strange battle paean,

> Ho! the godly scarlet crump of newborn bomb craters
> resounds above the gleeful whistling bullets whee! and
> the gurgling of cheery throttlings going on and on. . . .

Goodbye Leicester Square!

> . . . a tuneful chrrkchrrkkk of thumb-blocked throats serv-
> ing as a discreet melodic line below the sshpluck! of impact
> and the Ur! of pained surprise . . . ahh, rustling crumpling
> figures, blending folding fugueing (hands spreadfingered
> clutching Why?? delicate belly entrails flopping softly o
> he he he!) a resonant yet subtle percussion . . .

It's a long long way to Picadilly

> . . . o splurge life! Encorporate cheerful death! Enjoin
> dismemberment! O! blissful! ahh! happy war!

but my heart's right there!

> But then General Joy had never been considered quite
> sane, quite healthy, even by his nearest and dearest on
> skin. . . .

"Sheeit," she hears herself say to Joe, "Why do they want to go on singing those sorta songs all the time? War songs?" her voice booming out.

The oompa-oompa march strains fade away.

There's a big blond man standing next to her, and a greasy little fellow with buck teeth and hair styled like it was still the rocking fifties, beside him.

Blondie turns and sneers at her,

"What's wrong with war songs, tit? What do you ignorant young grab-arses know that's better? Yahhh," turning to his companion, "they get round with bloody Mahries and behave worse than they do."

She feels Joe tense beside her.

The alcohol fog leaves: she notes and hates the nasal accent, the RSL stickpin in the blazer lapel. She says icily,

"Pig ignorant *old* Australian *bastards* should get back where they belong. To their dead-hearted, deadbeat offal-catering country. Not parasitise here, littering up Godzone."

The guitar group is gone quiet, collectively grinning. The guitar-ist plays little riffs, as though thinking about a song.

"What'd you say?"

"You heard, poof."

"I won't take that from. . . ."

"You'll have to," there's no slur in Joe's voice now either, "be-cause between us, we'll have your guts for garters."

"And goodness knows what we'll do with your balls," says Kerewin.

Mild guffaws from the group. No one makes a move to help or hinder, though several are edging away from the bar. A ring of space miraculously occurs.

The Aussie stands, going tunk! tunk! tunk! on the bartop with a 20 cent piece, a nasty little tocsin of imminent violence.

"Stow it, c'mon stow it," says the fifties-greasy. "They'll do you. Turn it off yer fuckin idiot."

The other man stands uncertainly now, looking at Joe's very broad shoulders, at Kerewin's long tensed hands. He can see curi-ous calluses all down the edges of the palms. His eyebrows stand out silver against the growing flush of his face.

"Arr," inarticulate with indecision.

Kerewin giggles.

His meaty lips twitch.

"Arr yourself. Push off. Get lost." Joe turns deliberately round to the bar. "Fill 'em again Bill. Nother bottle for Kere too, eh."

The Aussie mutters something foul under his breath and rounds on his companion.

"Let's move. Outa this fucking dump."

He stalks away, his heavy paunch taut before him, fists ladling air at either side. The fifties-greasy grins apologetically, downs his beer, and scuttles off after.

"Ahh, fresh air," calls Kerewin loudly.

"Easy, e hoa. Be gentle now. They're gone."

"I," she says sweetly, "am as full of fight as seaweed, and hardened as the unshelled snail . . . lend us that guitar, would you mind?"

"Nah, sure, glad of a break," says the guitarist, bringing the strap over his head, and passing the instrument to her. "Here you go."

She checks the tuning swiftly, harmonics lingering in the air until she cuts them short with the flat of her hand.

On the open strings she picks a quick tune, says to Joe laughing, "I call this Simon's Mead Reel, though you don't know about that," chords A minor, while he shakes his head in bewilderment, and then she sings,

> *E wine,*
> *puts a fog upon the mind,*
> *drowns down those hard old memories*
> *to a thin blear line,*
> *e wine. . . .*

Fingers dancing over the strings, changing the tune an octave lower:

> *E wine,*
> *through the cloud I see*
> *him walk away from me,*
> *but I'm gone beyond the caring time,*

zing, and up again,

> *E wine,*
> *e wine . . .*

a reeling tune, lightfooted, lightheaded, only just catching its balance
as it slips and dances:

E wine,
just a shade that's left behind
caressing this hard bottle as I please,
drinking my shadow blind,
E wine . . . e wine . . . e wine . . .

voice trailing away, the quick picked tune going lighter and lighter
and lighter it's gone. . . .

Clapping and hoots and "E bloody neat!" 's.

She grins round at them, belly of the guitar close to her, strong
hands spreadfingered over the strings.

> What did she mean, Simon's mead reel? Mead's a drink,
> reel's a dance, but what does Haimona have to do with
> them?

"Come on, give us another! More!" they start to drone, "More!"

"You really want another?" her grin sharp, and into the chorus
of Yes, Geddonwithit, she strums a series of major chords. The
crowd quietens fast, and she says, eyes glinting and very blue,

"This is a song for a friend of mine, same one I mentioned before
as a matter of fact. You might know him,"

a note jangles, seemingly mispicked, but it comes again and again,
until all ears are hearing it more than the surrounding chord.

"He's the son of Joe Gillayley here," twang, "a little kid, but very
sharpwitted," a higher note has started to ring against the first jan-
gle, "Heh, mimin' Simon caint talk, but hell he, got hands aint he?"
zang/ping, zaang/piing, they duel back and forth, and the steady
throb of the chords goes on underneath.

"Other words, he uses his hands to talk with, this small friend
of mine, and this song'll let you do that too, if you want. But not at
me, okay?"

Rustle and murmur all round: here and there heads swivel to look
surreptitiously at Joe, and see how he's taking this introduction.

His heart is beating painfully hard, the thud going against the
rhythm of the guitar, faster and louder in his ears.

Ah God, sweet Jesus, look at her . . . leanwristed, lean-
ankled, but strong thickhipped body, ripe for bearing
children no matter what she says . . . Lord, I could have
more children by her . . . narrow waist I could put my
hands around. Swaybacked she says, a draught mare,
she says, paunched before I'm forty, beerbellied and
wellbellied, she says, laughing her head off . . . laughing
at me now, and having a go at Sim, that's not fair, he'd
be hurt, but why? Why God? I love her, and she won't
let me close. Either of us close. Any of us close. . . .

The song has been going on but his ears have been deaf to it.
The chorus has been caught up by the people round him, and is
boisterously chanted complete with the gesture.

O spirals are spirals and sweetly curled,
but two straight fingers can vee the world,

"Vee ther world!" bawls a voice in his ear, and the man, full of
tipsy good humour, punches him lightly on the shoulder. It's all he
can do, heart quaking, fists clenched, to smile tightly at him.

What does she mean by doing this? She knows he isn't
allowed to do that. She's poking shit at me, and saying how little she cares for him? But it doesn't make
sense. . . .

His heart is weeping in him.
Another verse from Kerewin, unheard because the chorus has
taken the tipsy man's fancy and he hums it out loud, ready to
pounce as soon as it comes up again. Whang! as the chorus chord
is struck hard and away the crowd goes, rowdy and laughing and
upping each other as merrily as anarchists through it.
He is sick to his stomach through all the stamping and applause.
The silence, and her voice, come strangely to him.
"Well okay . . . this last one,"
boooo in sustained herd disapproval,
"yeah, definitely last, this is cutting into my drinking time,"
clapple clapple hurr hurr hurr,
"this last one is a bit different. Quiet, eh."

A simple chord sequence, D A7 G. . . .
"Tenei mo Haimona, e hoa," and he stares wildly at her.

This is for Simon? But what about the others?

When I was young and tree was full,
of sweetly singing birds,
then full of heart was I with song,
o'erpowering great for words,

the key changes, slides into a dischord,

Not so now. . . .

Her voice is unstrained, no longer outshouting the crowd, pleasant alto, easy on the ears,

When me and the tree were older both,
and birds had left their young,
words for my song I began to find,
and to the tune give tongue,

again the wandering eddy of discordancy,

With a vow. . . .

Aiee, it's a gentle song, he thinks with thankful wonder. His
heartbeat is calming down. Maybe it's just that I've taken it all up
wrongly, maybe it's all right. . . .

That all the good would sunlike shine,
and beckon me ahead,
but in grey age for my past I pine,
with years my vow is dead,

the small bitter melody again,

Forgotten now. . . .

That's the way it happens, he thinks, we start out bright and something clouds us . . . if it's for Himi, maybe she's saying this won't happen to him, this is her warning for him, her lesson. . . .

The chord sequence changes, Dm Am E, is hit harder,

Lightning blasted the tree,
the birds are fled;
Death hovers here for me,
Yet not all hope is dead . . .

a ragged arpeggio, and then slowly the notes wind back to the original tune. Silence all round the bar, spread to the tables beyond.

His heart has eased to its normal beat, past the strain and pound of desire and bewilderment and hurt. He waits for the chance to sing with her.

O when I was young and tree was full,

he joins in, his bass mellowing the song further, and Kerewin smiles to him,

of sweetly singing birds,
then full of heart was I with song,
o'erpowering great for words. . . .

The last chord dies into silence.

"C'mon, another!"

Again the beat of clapping, and the droning choir of "More!" but Kerewin shakes her head. "That's happy hour over for tonight, kiddies," slipping off the guitarist's stool and passing the guitar back to its owner. She joins Joe at the bar.

He slips an arm round her, whispers smiling, "Those were all your songs?" taking the arm away before she can resent it.

"O yeah. Sort of."

Little caches of verse, the hidden hoarded hopes of yesterday, things to sing and savour, saviour verses s'hope.

She takes a deep mouthful of the wine he had poured out ready for her.

Hear it, hum it, hymn it . . . stuhupid Kerewin.

To her left she can hear Joe bragging,
"Yeah, all songs she wrote for my son eh."

I did not.
"He's a little bastard," wipes mouth on back of hard brown hand, "but a gutsy little bastard. Wouldn't be mine if he wasn't," he boasts, "wouldn't have kept him, eh?"
The man beside him grins. "Yeah? Sounds a good kid. . . ."

From that you can tell? But he is good. Joe's golden boy the sunchild . . . I wonder if *that's* what bothers the man? He said right at the beginning it didn't, but he's changed his tune on a lot of things since . . . maybe it hurts, everytime someone sees you two together, notes that blondness, and looks you over speculating, "Cuckold? Or so Pakeha a wife your blood can't show . . . ?"

She drinks more wine, orders large whiskies in a row for Joe.
"Her?" she hears him say, back to her, "her? NO way, all she's in love with are her bloody paintings."
She could be a thousand miles away.

Who knocks
on the rotten boards of my heart?
Let me in/let me in,
It's me—Kerewin. . . .

Too true.
"Scuse me, Joe," to his unhearing ears, and walks to the toilet, each step purposely in line, effortfully straight and steady.
"Deafer and deafer and drunker and drunker," she croons, and the pub recedes entirely away.
A silence like the most intense music. . . .
. . . the stench of the airfreshener is vilely plastic. She is begin-ning to feel sick. But outside the toilet she is suddenly caught up in

the people swarm. All the tight inner communing with self is given over to the sweep of herd emotion. She stretches her arms, sickness forgotten,

Ae, a wide embrace! A long and broad joying!

At the bar, Joe swipes out with his elbow, catching someone in the back.

"Watch what you're doing!"

"Outa way!" he yells, ignoring the protest, "my lady troubadour is back!"

"Ah to hell!" calling back as loudly, grinning wildly.

The original guitarist is thumping out the coke-song, and all the pub is rocking with the tune.

"And snow white purple doves!" bawls Joe.

"You got that a bit wrong old son," she punches him lightly on the shoulder, still grinning. His shoulder muscles are soft and relaxed. His smile is similarly loose.

"Nice song," he says, slurring it, "very niessh shong."

"Yeah."

It's gone eight o'clock and the after-tea drinkers are swarming everywhere.

Kerewin chattering to herself,

"So ergo, the ego ain't. It's a pervert symptom, a warp of Self. This little warp of human life we weave ... what really is the cockroach individual? A baggage of unthinking urges. A ragbag thing of no account? A freak, a mystery? And does the warring self survive body dissolution? Heaven help us! the ancients' essay and ours to pierce the veil are mere baby meddling, needling into a gloom beyond attempt."

She coughs on a mouthful of wine.

Joe nods.

The man on the right nods. "Go on," he says.

"Come and play darts," urges Joe, which is a suitable comment on the whole, he thinks.

"I can beat you in this state. Let's stay friends."

"Aw, I'd never live it down if you win. Play friendly."

She ponders, the clatter of the crowd growing and growing in her head.

> The rainbow end. The phoenix helix. The joyful Noth-
> ing. The living abyss . . . what does he mean, he'd never
> live it down?

"Aw bullshit. Crap. Shit. Dung. Excreeetia. Processed anything. Come on," dragging herself off the barstool, "I'll give you a game anyway. An I mean, give."

Joe stands up. And promptly sits down on the floor.

"Upsadaisy," says the man on the left, bending down to help.

"Man, that's rude. That's crazy. Upsadaisy s'though I'se Simon's size." Joe is blinking furiously.

"Well downsadaisy then," says the bloke huffily, and lets go his arm.

Joe, on his feet again, pats the man.

"S'okay e hoa. Don, know what'm doin eh. Full right up to here," pointing. He blinks again, tears trickling from his dark eyes. "Hon-ess beer but ah damn deceeful whishky." He sounds as though any moment he's going to break into a full-fledged howl.

"Pissed as farts the both of them," says the rightbarside.

She thinks, Simon.

A start, a wrench, of sickness, deep in her gut. The bright wine flowing in her blood until the blood curdles . . . ah treachery!

"Joe?" the word treacling out. "Ring a taxi, e mate?"

He looks at her blearily, head bobbing up and down.

"S'okay, sokay."

She clenches her glass for self-control.

> Solidity of glass, metal that evaporates under your
> squeezing fist, until the only solidity is your painfully
> ground teeth. That alone is reality. And do this under a
> smile, with guarded face, lest someone see and sneer.

She moves, without haste, over the miles to the toilet again. Brushes past the woman coming out, throws open the toilet door, and throws up down the toilet, violently. Pulls the door hastily closed.

Beer and whisky and wine and little baby cockles . . . she kneels, head on her arms, waiting for the retching to stop.

O mother of us all, that's the first time in my life I've
ever been sick through drinking . . . this is the gift he
would give me?

Her breath condenses on the silver bar of her rings.

Te koha . . . aha koa iti, he pounamu . . . he's probably
forgotten about it, if it existed. I'd better too.

He is standing under the phone, the public phone on the wall. His
head is down, eyes closed, arms folded, slumped against the wall.
"E Joe?" breathing into his ear.
"AieeE!"
"Sorry fella, but you looked like you'd gone to sleep eh?"
"Orrr," he massages his face, his eyes, his neck.
"You all right?"
"Drunker'n hell." Squints at her. "You okay?"
"Worse for wear too. . . ."
He stretches, groaning.
"Got us a taxi ordered . . . said it was for you, but I'll go to Tai-
nuis' eh. Pick up tama. It's on the way."
"Beaudy. I'll shout you home."
His eyes fix on her.
All pupil, black, blank, but with an ice-glitter sheening them.
"Yeah." Eyelids hooding the blackness. "You do that. Shout us
outa the way home."
They wait in awkward silence for the taxi to arrive. They sit in
silence all the way to the Tower. The driver whistles tunelessly
under his breath the whole way.

So much for merrymaking, Holmes . . . you should've
stayed home happily strangling the meece. . . .

She gets out by her bridge. "Goodnight, Joe." And because that
sounds baldly rude, she adds, "Thanks." He smiles, a dark bitter
smiles that makes the deep lines on his face seem more like scars
than ever.
"For nothing, eh?" He leans out. "Open it sometime. You can
have it as a memento of those two idiots who used to bother you
and waste all your valuable time." He puts the small packet in her
hand. She stares at him. His eyelids droop.

"G'night," he says, and leans away from her, into the covering dark.

Her hand tightening into a fist, she goes to the driver's window.

"That should be enough to cover the trip both ways," passing him a note. "Gee thanks," he says guilelessly.

She slams the back door of the taxi. The driver says something like Toodleloo in the background, and puts the car into reverse. It goes, headlights cutting a slice in the night. The lights vanish. The sound dies.

She leans against the Tower door,

"Well, *that* seems to be *that*."

A far-off cloud in the deep of space. The drunken circling stars.

"Aue, Mere-mere quite contrary," she trys to laugh.

Or is it Kere-kere quite contrary?

She closes the door with a thump! as though that would keep the phantoms of the night outside.

8

Nightfall

```
TRY
KEEP
A LITT
    ill lon
        guron
            your feee
```

he slumps.

. . .

    The world goes away some more.
    The night comes closer still.

. . .

    Blinks in weary vagueness.
    Try.
    Keep eyes. Them open. See the dark come.
    Can't.
    Nothing.
    Badbadbad.
    Fucking *useless* Clare.
    Among the chaff and evil reedy voices round that hummock in unconsciousness he can hear the one he hates. Singing. It's too near the threshold but go back up. . . .

Hey! shh Sant' Claro
dulce and gentle

a throbbing double kick, and the plateau tilts. Deeper, it welcomes.
The voices are rejoicing.

"Ah no."

He hears himself say it. For one second the bonds at his throat
loosen. And he is bitterly sick.

Another kick. A raking almost harmless kick, but it tears across
the skin of his chest. Across Kerewin's bruise island. Something
breaks.

He feels the air stir, Joe slip after the kick.

Crush. And the dead weight doubles his pain.

The world tilts more, and helpless he begins to slide, downwards, underground, into the box. Turning pinioned. Sound. A
scream.

Suffocating.

Deep dark.

. . .

It is almost night.

. . .

That morning he watched the sun come up, head on his arms,
his arms on the window sill. That morning Joe was in a bitchy
mood, saying, "Don't go round to the Tower."

That morning, Mr Drew leant across his desk, frowning, and
handed him the envelope. "You'd better take that home to your father, Simon."

. . .

He didn't go back to school after the lunch break.

He went round to Binny Daniels, hoping for money, however he
can get it.

From the gateway he could see the old man was dead.

The flies were humming a strong lively song. They were impatient when he came through them, skidding onto him, face and eyes
and hair, as though they thought he was more of the feast.

Binny Daniels had slipped and fallen. He'd done that often enough.

This time, he'd fallen on top of his half g of sherry. It broke apart under him, bits tinkling down the path. But a long freak shard had daggered in, into the old man's groin. He had bled a lot. Great clots and puddles of blood have spilled on the concrete. The flies seethe merrily over them, jostling and shoving and wanting room for more.

Binny Daniels had tried to hold his artery's pulse to a stop. But his fingers are narrow and fleshless and they ache with arthritis, and the remaining strength ebbs out so fast. He still clutched at the hole through, the glass blade's tip sticking obscenely out. Diamond bright in the afternoon sun.

. . .

He'd been sick, and the odd fly had buzzed eagerly up and landed on the halfdigested pulp, and he'd been sick again.

He went round to the Tower anyway.

Kerewin said,

"You better not come here any more. Your father won't be dead keen on it."

She'd asked, "Where's my knife? The special one?"

She didn't believe he hadn't got it. Wise Kerewin. He'd taken it before the holiday.

The knife is Kerewin's talisman, her athelme. Made from German steel, superbly tempered. The bone handle is riveted with three steel pins, and near the pommel is a brass-lined hole. A thong of rawhide can be twisted through the hole and looped over the knife handle. The thong is attached to the sheath. The knife can't fall out.

"I know I haven't lost it," Kerewin said.

There is no guard on the knife. A dimly golden crosspiece separated the curve of bone from the curving blade.

He can see each detail clearly. In the flaring lights, it is all he can see.

The sheath is made of leather, oiled to a deep russet red. A rim of shagreen capped the sheath above the rivet that completed the stitching. A second thong, which could be tied round the thigh, hung in a plait from a steel-lined hole at the end of the sheath. A long time ago, Kerewin had engraved runes on the leather, filling the gouges with white enamel, and they are still there.

When he first picked up knife and sheath, he had traced the runes and she had said,

"They're letters, but not our kind. They're called runes, cen, os, and hagall. My initials. They also have other meanings. It is a strange and providential chance that what they stand for and my initials, are the same thing."

There are more runes carved into the bone handle. An inscription, said Kerewin.

"Indeed, a dedication," she had added thoughtfully.

These runes are worn down to unreadable fineness.

It is mysterious, but he must remember it all. He is in the mystery, and needs to remember.

It is a small heavy knife, comfortable to hold, and excellently balanced.

It is good for throwing—she had sent it thunking into the wood under the window to show him how.

It is good for gutting, skinning, slicing, chopping, ripping, and killing.

A knife with an edge keen enough for whittling, rugged enough to hack through bone. Kerewin asked, "So where is it?"

She got very angry when he continued to deny he had it.

"I know where all my gear is, at all times. I know what's gone missing from here, and a lot has, boyo. From paperclips to cowries and a helluva stack of smokes somewhere between. I don't give a damn about them but I want my knife back. Get it, and I forget about all the other stuff, okay?"

What knife?

It is a peculiar feeling, sick to the stomach, with the dead Binny Daniels floating in and out of view, flies humming over him in a black racing cloud, a peculiar feeling trying to be angry. To pretend to be angry. It is necessary to be angry. He threw a punch at her, a neat punch sent overhand into the triangle between the wings of her ribs.

He had forgotten how fast she could move.

It was a hard hit to get back, in the centre of his chest. He buckled to the floor and Binny Daniels went flying into a thousand separate pieces, each loaded with a cargo of wildly buzzing flies.

When he got to his feet, she was standing just as she had finished the blow, eyes wide, one hand still balled in a fist.

He staggered over, a hand on the numbness, the other fisted, and went to hit her again. She slid easily to one side yelling "Simon!" High and echoy and shocked. "Simon!"

He tried twice more, and each time she ducked.

So he'd turned fast as possible and before she guessed what he was going to do, kicked in the belly of her amber guitar, lying there by the window.

The room became deathly still.

Huge pale blisters rose and spread under the varnish. The wood was smashed but the strings hung free, still humming in the air.

Binny Daniels and the flies zoom back together.

Kerewin said, "Get out."

Her voice trembled.

Her hands trembled.

He can see them still. Trembling to get hold of any part of him that can feel a hurt, and wreak vengeance on him.

She puts them behind her back.

"Get out."

He stayed as long as he could, but the shaking that envelopes her is frightening.

Besides, Binny Daniels and his retinue of flies has practically come into the Tower now. He left.

. . .

There was a group of men in Binny Daniel's garden, talking in low guarded voices.

They've put a blanket over the twisted old body.

"Jesus," says one, "get that kid away from here."

The flies are everywhere, in high hungry clouds.

. . .

It was nearly dark.

There was nobody in the street.

Just the long line of shop windows, their glass faces bright with the metalling of the dying sun.

He started on the left side, doing one at a time, and he had nearly finished them all, up the street and back down the other side, when the hand closed on his shoulder, and the other hand wrenched the brick from his fists.

It was Constable Morrison.

He said,

"You've done it, Gillayley. This time you've really done it. Christ, what a mess."

Holding both his bleeding hands together in one hand. Saying under his breath, looking down, eyes in the shadow of his helmet rim, "Christ, what a mess."

It didn't sound like he meant all the smashed windows, or the glass all over the street.

. . .

The constables stayed talking to Joe for a long time.

Joe held the top of his arm, tightly. After a while, he couldn't think of anything else except the bite of the fingers, and he lost the thread of the conversation.

The police said,

"He's too young to prosecute, Joe, but it's about time something got done."

The police said,

"There's already a complaint laid with Welfare that he's not receiving proper care and attention. That he's not under proper control."

"Who's laid that? Kerewin Holmes?"

Constable Morrison coughed. "They can't say who lays complaints and nor can we. But it wasn't your lady, Joe."

The police said,

"You'll probably get sued by the shop owners, or their insurance people. He's smashed in nearly all the fronts along Whitau Street. About thirty all told. Plate glass."

Constable Morrison said,

"You better take him to, Lachlan isn't it? Yeah, well get him along there tonight. Constable Murray taped his hands up at the station as best she could, but they're badly cut."

The constable reached down and touched him on the face, a tap, gentle. "Why'd you do it?"

Joe shook him. "Answer."

Constable Morrison took away his hand. "Well, we'll find out one way or the other, you know. Joe, go easy on him. There's more to this than meets the eye."

The talk went on.

In the end, the constables went back to the car.

The top of his arm ached intensely when Joe released him.

Joe said,

"Get inside."

. . .

He stamps back and forth, three steps one way, three steps the other.

"I thought you had gone to Kerewin's. I hoped you had, even though you were told not to. Where did you go?"

Forward.

"Being sullen won't get you anywhere. Answer me." Back.

"Answer me." Forward.

"All right, I'll have to ring Kerewin. A promise is a promise." Back.

"You know what that means." Forward.

"What did you do it for?" Back.

"Answer me." Forward.

"Answer me." Back.

"ANSWER ME!" Forward, away to the door, raging.

"Get your shirt off," as he goes.

The door slammed.

He took off his shirt. And his T-shirt underneath. And he took the glass splinter from his back jeans pocket. It came from the first window smashed: it is triangular, three inches long, and searingly sharp. Good as a knife. He has cut himself on it once already. He tucks it into the loose folds of bandage over his left palm, and keeps the hand stiff.

It is cold in the kitchen, even though the heater is hissing away.

There's a fly buzzing over by Bill's cage.

His hands feel as if they're burning. There is a welt already on the top of his arm, from the grip of Joe's fingers.

The door opens.

Joe beckons him out while he says into the phone, "You tell *him* that, e hoa, not me."

. . .

The phone was awkward to hold. He couldn't keep a proper grip on it. It kept sliding down so the listening end moved away from his ear. It is startlingly black against the white bandages.

Kerewin says,

"Are you listening, bloody Gillayley? Do you know what I think of you?"

Her voice is strange. It rasps; it grates; it abrades. She can't touch him physically so she is beating him with her voice. What she says drums through his head, resounding in waves as though his head were hollow, and the words bound back from one side to smash against the other.

She has finished having anything to do with him.

She hates him.

She loathes every particle of his being.

Did he know what that guitar meant to her?

Did he know what her knife meant to her?

Did he know what he had wrecked?

She hopes his father knocks him sillier than he is now.

She has every sympathy for his father.

She didn't realise what a vicious little reptile he had to endure.

He choked.

Joe took the phone out of his hands almost gently.

He smiled a tight leanlipped smile.

"I think he got the message, e hoa."

The sickness in the pit of his stomach increases. He hasn't stopped feeling sick since he opened Binny's gate. The cold increases, except round his hands. They're glowing.

"No," Joe says, "I won't overdo it. And thanks very much for the offer. I've got a bit put away, but it won't cover this lot. Thank you very much for the offer but . . . get in there, you."

Joe kicked the door shut behind him.

The echo took a long time to die away.

His head is starting to buzz, to hum, as though somehow the flies have finally found a way in.

. . .

When Joe comes back into the kitchen, he is carrying his belt by the leather end. The buckle glints as it swings just above the floor.

His stomach convulses, knotting with fear.

He swallows violently to keep the vomit down.

Joe is surrounded by pulses and flares of dull red light.

He says in a low anguished voice,

"You have ruined me."

He says,

"You have just ruined everything, you shit."

He doesn't say anything more, except when he has turned the chair against the table.

Joe says, "Get over."

He does. He lays his arms in front of him, left hand stiff, and his head on his arms.

He sets his teeth, and waits.

. . .

The world is full of dazzlement, jewel beams, fires of crystal splendour.

I am on fire.

He is aching, he is breaking apart with pain.

The agony is everywhere, hands, body, legs, head.

He is shaking so badly he cannot stand.

The hard wood keeps griding past him.

He keeps trying to stand.

Joe's voice is thin and distant.

"When did you get this?"
"When did Bill Drew give you this?"
"How long have you kept this?"

He is pulled up and held into the door frame.

The wood gnaws his body.

He pushes forward with all his strength against the hand that pins him down.

He is thudded back into all the teeth of the wood.

"When did you do this?"
"When did this happen?"

Sliding the sliver out of the wrapping, his hand trembling uselessly. He fists forward. It seems a foolish feeble blow.

But I need to stop the wood coming through.

Joe screams.

The first punch hit his head.

His head slammed back into the door frame.

The punches keep coming.

Again.

Again.

And again.

The lights and fires are going out.

He weeps for them.

The blood pours from everywhere.

He can feel it spilling from his mouth, his ears, his eyes, and his nose.

The drone of flies gets louder.

The world goes away.

The night has come.

9

Candles in the Wind

IF ONLY was the tapu phrase.

> If only I had
> If only I hadn't

The trench my worried thoughts have worn towers on either side. I can see a bar of sky . . . there is no more room for anything but pacing, wearing down, round and round in my worry trench.

For now it's life on the straight and narrow, the harrowed way. No more casual nights, drunken by candlelight or flare of crowd. No more communion with mirrored self or the uncaring stars.

Communing means uncovering: drinking means thinking.

If I think it becomes if only, and if only is the tapu phrase.

What else can I do?

. . .

She hid all her opal rings. The seaglint disturbs her. Like they're eyes on her fingers.

. . .

Strangely, the worst thing of all—worse than the shambles she had come in on, worse than the disfigurement and non-recognition— was that they had shaved off his hair.

She remembers the shock in his eyes when he saw her cut hair.

If only I had
Shut up.
Taipa.

. . .

The second week, she started packing.

The third week, on a Wednesday morning, she turned from contemplating the bare library walls, and stopped, shocked.

The man is standing in the doorway, watching her.

His face is more dead grey than living brown.

He says softly,

"Piri told me about this. If you want me to, I can maybe help. If
you don't want me to, shake your head and I will go away."

His eyes are fixed on her face, but they don't entreat.

They are lustreless and unsouled.

Except one thing flickers. A last spark of spirit, waiting without
hope. Waiting in the knowledge that she will react with disgust
and horror. Waiting for the final reason to die.

But he has come back this once, to make sure: to offer one last
time whatever of him she will take.

She makes it very short, the waiting time. She folds her hands
over her stomach, containing the dull ache.

"Ngakaukawa, kei te ora taku ngakau. E noho mai."

And he covers his face and weeps.

. . .

Later, his eyelids spongy and fat from crying, he says,

"I have been wanting to weep for a long time, but I couldn't."

"I wept, but only a little. It didn't seem that weeping was going
to do any good."

He sighs.

"It doesn't change anything. It just makes me feel a bit more
alive. I don't know whether that's good. While you're alive, you're
hurting."

"It's the possibility that when you're dead you might still go on
hurting that bothers me," she says grimly.

"Yes." He stares at the broken guitar hanging on the wall.
"Aue, yes."

. . .

The only time she had wept was when she went back to Pacific Street to clean up. Sick stomach or nothing, you can't expect him to come home to this. . . .

Congealed spatters. Against the door. On the floor. Joe's blood, from the glass dagger sent so neatly into his stomach.

("Funny," said Morrison. "Two in one day. D'you know that old fart Daniels?"

"I heard already."

"Yeah, well, he got it from a splinter too . . . broken off a half g of that rotgut he primed himself on. The glass went in a bit lower though."

The constable is weary and ill-looking. He shuts his notebook and puts it back in his tunic pocket. "Christ, if only I'd known," he'd said, shaking his head, and then caught the look in her eyes. "It can't be helped, Miz Holmes," he'd offered. "We none of us have got that kind of foresight. It can't be helped.")

Blood from the child, from his ruined body and head.

> Pretend it's fish blood. Weak cool fish blood. Different lymph, different platelets, non-mammalian. Won't corrode or stain the hands, right?

She managed to clean it all up before she was sick.

Leaning back against the sink thinking, Holy mother, this is a day and a night to forget. Looking round, checking all is normal, no relics of violence left. (Belt picked up and coiled away in a policeman's drawer, glass dagger in safe police hands.)

And on the end chair, out of the way where he'd left them in those careful clumsy folds, Simon's shirt and T-shirt.

The tears stung her eyes. Shaking her head, Stop it, stop it, crying won't help them any, and weeping more and more.

She sobbed uncontrollably for minutes, her voice climbing higher and higher, and at its peak, the violent stabbing pain cut in again, leaving her with breath enough only to gasp.

Beneath her hands, pressed in deep against the agony, she felt the hard alien lump in her belly for the first time.

. . .

She is carefully disinterring the bonsai grove.

"You need a hand with that?"

"No thanks."

"I've finished wrapping all the pounamu . . . God, you've got some beautiful work there."

She glances at him. "You want any bits, help yourself."

He shakes his head.

He asks, scuffing his shoetip against the stone step, "You ever, you know, take a look at it?"

She dusts her hands free of sandy earth fastidiously, and opens the neck of her shirt. "The present? Yes."

It hangs there as he had imagined it: the pale shining braid he'd made, the semicircle of dark green against the pallor of her skin.

She buttons her shirt again without commenting.

He blinks away his ready tears.

"Emmersen's brother spent most of, of Monday engraving that . . . I asked him to get it ready for me by evening no matter what, and he did."

She has turned back to the unearthing of her small trees.

"Mmmm," as though she didn't hear him properly and didn't care to know. "Did you say Marama liked plants?"

"Yes," says Joe sadly.

"I'll give these to her then. They might amuse her."

. . .

The hei matau is hook-shaped, and the inner curve is lined with silver. In tiny italics the jeweller has engraved, Arohanui na H & H.

. . .

Later that day she asks,

"E hoa, would you accept this?"

He stares at the translucent ring poised between her fingers.

"I understand the old people used to fasten the leg of an especially favoured calling-bird with it, but they used them as jewellery too . . . I thought it might um, complement the long and straight of your pendant."

He takes it wordlessly.

Centuries ago, people had laboured with great skill on this piece of unflawed jade. Piercing it to make the side decorations, working the stone-tipped drill with precision and painstaking care. Piercing it again, and smoothing the inside circle to an oily fineness. The kaumatua would have rubbed the finished ring against belly and nose to make that shine, for many months. A long time in the making, a long time worn.

"It hasn't got a name," she is saying. "It's a family piece though, and it is guaranteed pre-pakeha."

She touches it one last time.

"It was one of the bits I got when the family gave me the boot." She doesn't say it was the only piece she got of the family inheritance. All the rest of her collection she has bought.

. . .

She had sneered at the hook when she first unwrapped it. Trite contemporary junk, she thought. Look at that diamond hard shine. She stashed it away with the rest of her pieces, still wrapped in the brown paper Joe had given it to her in. She hadn't noticed the engraving or the braid wrapped in a separate piece of tissue.

The second week she took it out, and looked it over with dry-eyed care. Much love from Hohepa and Haimona, aue . . . the braid is finely-done, five-ply and rounded. Joe has had the jeweller seal the ends with clips of silver, fitted permanently into the hole in the hei matau. The braid is just long enough to go over her head. . . .

She slips it on, and the green jewel lies by the cross and the medal and the pendant she always wears.

> A hook to his jaw and a hook in his thumb and a kind
> of a hook in my heart, by God. . . .

. . .

Each morning, when Joe goes in to Whangaroa to report according to the terms of his bail, Kerewin goes up to the library circle.

It is stripped entirely bare now, except for the forlorn shelves round the walls. The books are packed in cases, and stowed in the cellar. The swords are greased thickly and laid away on a cellar shelf. The chest of jade and the drawers of shells are locked and sealed into three tin trunks. (Joe had played with the shells like he was a child again. "Anana! I never knew fish made such shapes in all the world!" picking up one spiked and trimmed like a pagoda, while holding another as meticulously curved and sharp as a carpenter's bit. "And look at these colours!" Lime green snail shell and flamingo pink conch and a cowrie as gold as the setting sun. "Where'd you get these, e hoa?" as he wraps them up carefully. "O, bought them. A lot in Japan, a lot here. They were supposed to be delight and inspiration. They turned out to be the same sort of detritus as everything else. Junk and mathoms and useless geegaws the lot of them, shells, rings, goblets, books and swords . . . and my pounamu . . . it was beautiful to have them at first, but all the magic has worn off. Little by little it has all gone away.")

There are three things in the library that were never there before: a packing-case; a cushion; and a lump of clay, swathed in wet cloth. And every morning, she kneels down, toes crossed behind her and chin tucked in, as though she were meditating.

But her fingers begin sliding over the clay, moulding. For the first time in a year, she knows exactly what she wants to make and how to make it.

Beads of clay flattened, beads of clay raised. Day by day, the three faces grow. The blunt blind features become definite, refined, awake.

Back of head to back of head to back of head: a tricephalos.

It's easy to model her own face, and that is finished first.

Joe is there each day: she can pick the detail she requires and grow the clay face next morning to match it.

But remembering the child's face pains her. She has to strip away the vision of how it looked the last two times she saw it. The bloody swollen mask on the floor, broken nose and broken jaw. And the horrible indentation in the side of his skull where he had been smashed against the door frame. Or neatened, whitened, bandaged with care, but looking lifeless. O, his eyes had opened several times, but the seacolour had gone and he didn't see her. He didn't see anyone or anything. His eyes look dead.

> (Elizabeth Lachlan said, "We don't know how much damage there is. All we've done is remove the clot and repair the bone. He may not be able to see. It's almost certain he won't be able to hear, and it's likely he has suffered irreversible harm as far as his mental processes are concerned."

You mean mind, lady?

She had stood impassive, saying nothing.

The doctor had shrugged. "But we don't know. We won't know until we've had him over in one of the major hospitals for a head scan. And we won't know fully even then until he's recovered enough for us to as-certain in other ways the sum total of his injuries. If he recovers," she had said finally, "if he ever recovers.")

She concentrates on the way the child was at Moerangi, at the Hamdon pub, out in the boat. By the bonfires, when he sang for them. Peaceful in the firelit bach.

Gradually, his unbroken face is moulded by her hands, small and angular and smiling again.

You were a strange child, Simon gargoyle, an unknown quantity in so many ways. I wonder what you would have turned out like, had you been left to grow up whole?

Smoothing the narrow double point of the cleft chin.

Twisted, with a streak of meanness and sadism in you, as Joe was so plainly afraid? A musician, full of zany fire? The dancer, the sweet singer, the listener to the silence of God on deserted beaches—ae, you had music in you. Ordinary sinner, extraordinary sinner, or some new kind of saint? All too late now. . . .

The clay lips smile as well as the real ones did.

At the end of the fourth week, she has finished it. She lets it dry slowly, so it doesn't crack. She has in mind a wild way to fire it.

. . .

Joe saw it once.

His curiosity bettered his sense of privacy, and he turned back the cloth on the draped hump.

The clay faces are still dark and damp.

Simon smiles at him.

Kerewin is gazing off into infinity.

And he has a look of wondering attentiveness, as though some great good news is about to be broken to him.

He circles the triple head again and again, staring at each lifesize face. The hair of their heads is entwined at the top in a series of spirals. Simon's hair curves back from his neck to link Kerewin and Joe to him. Kerewin wears the greenstone hook, he, his Moerangi pendant.

Round and round, and with each circumambulation, the faces become more alive.

> Aue! She saw us as a whole, as a set. And soon we'll be parted forever. (Not forever, not forever, not forever.)

He covers it with trembling hands.

The next time he was in the library, when they came up the spiral to start knocking the Tower down, the tricephalos had gone.

. . .

His case was stood down: he was remanded on the same terms as when he'd been charged for the next two weeks.

He said in the afternoon, "The lawyer says it's because they're waiting to see what happens. With him."

It's the first time the child has been referred to, even obliquely.

"In case it's murder," he adds shakily.

She grimaced.

"Elizabeth doesn't think it will, will come to that. She went on the plane with him on Friday. She said they didn't learn anything new from the scan. She said it's just a matter of waiting." He shuddered. "E hoa, I don't mind what they do to me, but I hate this waiting."

"So do I," she said sombrely, and she wasn't referring only to the coming trial, or the child's coma. Each day, the pain and pressure in her gut has grown more intense until now it nags like toothache. She dreads the moment when the knife will strike again.

. . .

Everything has been packed away now. The livingroom circle is the only room in use, and it is spartanly furnished. Two stretchers for sleeping on (Piri brought them one morning: he said very little, but they joined in hongi for the first time); some cooking gear; one sheepskin mat in front of the fire; Kerewin's black guitar on the wall.

They spend the afternoons breaking down the upper circles; the neat stone blocks dislodged one by one to hurtle down into the dandelion-studded lawn.

The dandelions are surviving, but only just. They seem to be making a special effort to breed past this menace. The afternoons are full of their ballooning seeds, silver and prodigal in the sun.

They have become expert wreckers. It had been hard at first, blistered hands and stretched aching muscles. But you grew accustomed to the heavy swing of the sledge hammer, built it into a rhythm. You grew wise to the ways of stone and nailed wood, and learned to turn their solidity against them. Lever with a crowbar, tap in a wedge here, a judicious smack with the hammer, and down falls more of the Tower.

She saved very little of the upper levels: the great sister curve from the library, and the seashaded windows from the bedroom, and the golden niche where the boy had stood centuries ago; the plumbing and the solar waterheaters; the handrail of the stairway, taking particular care of the dolphin heads with their benign engraven smiles.

All the rest of the wood and furnishings she sent splintering and crashing downwards in a frenzy of destruction.

Joe protested once.

"It's a waste of good wood, Kere. You might want to build again." She had smiled meanly at him. "I don't think so. Besides, I am short of wood. I need quite a lot of wood. This'll help," smashing the hammer through the smooth floorboards.

He was afraid to ask her what she wanted the wood for.

. . .

They are short evenings.

They spend an hour after tea, sometimes talking about the day, sometimes drinking quietly; sometimes sitting in silence until the fire dies.

She plays her guitar infrequently, and the music is always dispirited and sad. It has the kind of loneliness behind it that haunts old graves. Forgotten, dead, gone . . . she knows a lot of that kind of music.

And when the talk has run out, or the drink has turned sour, or the companionable sitting has grown tense, they say Goodnight and go to their separate beds.

Each night it is the same. They spend a long time listening to each other trying to go to sleep. It is always Joe who sleeps first. He whimpers as he dreams, a small scared animal sound, strange in a grown man.

> And what sound do I make when the memories come crowding in too close? I don't know, and I care even less.

She lies stiffly still, night after night, her mind focused in fear on the thing that has invaded her. The wild spreading cells that grow and grow. It is always near dawn before sleep comes.

. . .

The suneater is still going, perched on the sill of the great living-room window now. Late in the last week, she stops it. Quite simply. She crushes it in her fist.

Looking at the small pile of bits, Nearly two years running and now you're dead. I wonder if someone will make another like you?

She feels no remorse. All her feelings are dulled these days, as though life is already going, slowly leaking out and ebbing away.

> Maybe it will make my dying that much easier . . . when I come to die, there will be little left to die.

I'm already a ghost with set wings, stalking tombstone territory.

. . .

Three days to the firestorm.

Three days to go.

Joe says that morning,

"I'll stay in 'Roa for a couple of days, if that's all right with you?"

"Of course it is."

"Okay then . . . I need to sign the papers for the house, and get everything sorted out. Before."

"Of course," but she says it more gently this time.

He pushes the hair away from his face. "You'll be all right, e Kere? I mean, I'll come out each night if you want some company."

"I'll be fine . . . take good care of yourself, and I'll see you Friday."

"Ae. E noho ra," as he swung away down the steps.

"Haere ra."

She listens to his footsteps clatter away.

"Everything sorted out," means the bare house cleared; the budgie given away to the Tainuis; the lawyer seen again and the house
disposed of. Preparations for what may be a long stay behind ston-
ier walls than these.

She sighs, and starts on the final work on the Tower.

She finishes nailing the last sheets of iron on the temporary roof
to the livingroom circle, and has clipped up a PVC guttering before
the afternoon begins. She no longer marks passing time by meals,
but by the position of the sun. She doesn't feel like eating these
days, though over the past week her appetite for drink has returned. So she is playing a melancholy thoughtful tune, her mind
cloistered in a wine haze, when the radiophone buzzes.

It takes several seconds for her to realise what the sound is.
More than a month gone by since it rang. And last time . . . taipa.

"Ah, hello?"

"Hello," says the operator, in subdued tones. "I've got a call for
you from Doctor Lachlan waiting."

Lachlan? Lachlan? Sheeit, that's Simon's doctor, Simon's?

Her heart has started to beat crazily fast.

"Put her through."

"Right away."

The voice is distant. She turns the volume control full up, concentrating against the haziness of the wine. "Hello, Elizabeth? What'd
you say?"

"I said, is Joseph there?"

"No, he's in town."

"But I've tried his number and he. . . ."

"You'd better leave him a message here if you can. I don't know
exactly where he is at the moment, and he's had his phone cut
off . . . he got some nut calls the week he came out of hospital.
Nasty ones."

"Oh . . ." the voice fades and fuzzes.

"Oath, this is a bad line . . . I can't hear you, Elizabeth."

"I said, in that case would you mind telling him that Simon is
conscious but not recognising me, and not responding to very much
at all."

"O God."

The tinny voice grows stronger.

"He isn't reacting to sounds, and it appears he has difficulty in focusing on anything. We're not sure how much he can see, but he can move his limbs. And he did more or less co-operate when the neurologist carried out a simple test. He can understand some things I think."

The operator has obviously been fiddling with the connection. The line is now clear, free of all hums and buzzes.

"No idea how much?"

"No, though I personally think he's aware of where he is, for instance, and what's happened to him."

"Others don't think so?"

"Well, they don't know Simon's reactions as well as I do, and you know how difficult it can be, trying to understand him."

I never found it that hard . . .

Saying aloud,

"He doesn't recognise you at all?"

"He doesn't, but that kind of amnesia is normal after the sort of head injury that's involved here. And as I said, we don't know how much he can see or hear."

"Do you reckon it'd do some good if Joe caught the late flight and came?"

"No," says Elizabeth decisively, "and dissuade him if he has any idea of visiting. Aside from the fact that the police are sure to object, I think the child is terrified by the possibility of this happening. We're doing our—"

"He's terrified of hospitals, that'd be—"

"In this instance, we are all sure that the source of Simon's very evident fear is a recurrence of what has already happened far too often." Cold, authoritative, brooking no disagreement, and implying that Kerewin is somehow guilty for being involved.

So I am, she thinks dully, and I'm probably wrong for thinking Sim would want Joe to help him now. Would I want someone after they had done such damage to me? Even if I loved them? No way. . . .

The conversation ends in small talk, goodbyes.

She thumbs the operator recall button. He says anxiously, "Is everything all right? I was very upset when I heard what had happened."

"Not half as upset as I was," says Kerewin drily. She sends Joe a long telegram in Maori, and then settles down to drinking in earnest.

The boy entombed by deafness? Possibly blind? Mentally deficient?

Aue. . . .

> He would be better off dead. Better by far that he had never woken again.

. . .

The rain begins to fall that night, the first heavy rain for nearly six weeks. She weeps with it, stirred to tears for the first time since the night of horror.

> Maudlin Holmes, o tearbesotted soul . . . think on the bright side. He may be all right. (What? Frozen deep in his terror, waiting for the next nightmare to happen?) Besides, we use only a, what is it? tenth of our brain? So, if he's lost a bit, it's not to say that he is subnormal, ineducable. (The tenth of the brain theory is estimation and unprovable . . . and who's going to bother to educate the urchin now?)

It's a question she has steadfastly been avoiding since she first heard from Piri that Joe had been charged with assault on the child, and doing grievous bodily harm. She knows with intuitive certainty that the one thing the court will do is order a change of custody. That Joe will lose his child for good, for ill, but definitely forever.

. . .

She works in the cold drizzle, helped by whisky, piling wood in a high teepee. Dribbling fuel oil over it, and ladling out kerosene. It takes all day to build the fire. It has to be done carefully, for in the centre, in a small chamber all of its own, she has set the tricephalos.

> Like unto the phoenix laying its egg, I have laid me down the last work and monument I'll ever make. May this pyre burn it to terracotta. A very hardshelled triumph . . . and who knows what will rise if it hatch?

She pours the rest of the whisky on the completed fire-nest.

She is tired nearly to death.

Her weakness is frightening now. She stands by the cunningly piled wood, wondering that it has taken her ten hours to do what would have been accomplished in two a month ago.

> If I'm going to burn out this quickly, it might not be worth taking off. It might be better to stay here, and just lock the door towards the end . . . but it's too late now. I've done my wrecking . . . besides, someone would have come here eventually and discovered one hell of a mess. I will go away to a quiet desert place and make a skeleton of me in peace and solitude.

What a pity, she thinks, as she drops the bottle at the woodpile's edge, that we humans don't have aesthetically pleasing skeletons. None of the elegance and beauty of your humble mollusc. Just a knobbily serrated jumble, headbone connected to de breastbone etcetera etcetera. On the other hand, maybe just as well . . . something might decide to start collecting *us*. . . .

She goes inside, seeking more whisky to warm the still-living body she owns.

The moon's up, and inching round the world.

. . .

It's outside the window when Joe gets back.

He comes straight across the room and kneels down beside her. "You feeling bad?"

"Quite. Goood. Act-u-ally," looking at him through bleary eyes.

He looks harassed and tired, and the sick greyness is back in his face, and yet for seconds he grins at her, merry and charming as ever he was.

"O ho. Fair enough. In a few minutes, I'll join you. I'll just have a shower and get changed. Trim my hair so I look less of a hard case and outlaw." His grin vanishes, and he is tired and old-looking again. "There's some news," he says gently. "Bad news."

"Sim?" her heart jars suddenly.

"No, no . . . Marama's had another stroke. They've taken her to Christchurch but they don't think she's going to last the night." He sighs. "Just as I was shutting the house, Piri came round and raved at me, and said I was to blame for it. Maybe I am . . . o dear Christ, I'll miss the old lady if she goes. . . ."

"Aue," she says thickly. "So'll I."

One up, one down, and one to go. . . .

He's shaking his head. "I dunno, things happen all of a heap, don't they?"

"Yeash."

"I got your telegram . . . thanks from my heart for it . . . I've been talking to Elizabeth—she came back this morning, and she thinks Himi'll make it now. Morrison says the two charges are the only ones they're preferring, and he thinks I'll get a year. I get the feeling he'd like it to be a century."

Kerewin laughs harshly.

"You wanna hear some of the things Morrison said to me, e hoa. He do not like you, my friend Joe, he do not like you at all."

"I can imagine." He stands. "Anyway . . . can we talk a lot tonight? Because I don't think we'll get the chance for quite a while."

She lets her head fall back so she's staring up at him. Both of him.

"I think that's a good night idea." She shakes her head and both Joes slide into one.

"I mean, a good idea for the night."

"Good," he says drily.

He puts down his briefcase. "There's some stuff in there that's yours . . . and a bottle or two I got in hope of talk. O, and I've left some of our gear," he hesitates, "my gear," in a low voice, "down in the hallway. If it's okay by you, I'd like to store it here."

"Shurrely." She pushes herself up off the hearthrug and stands unsteadily.

"S'matter of fact, I'll put it away for you if there's nothin you don want now?"

"No, I've got all I need in a handcase." He looks across at her quizzically. "You sure you'll be all right?"

She punches out at him, very slowly. A feather punch, but even so, body memory nearly has him lurching to one side to avoid it.

"It's a dire excuse to get still more whisky from me cellar, my sweet covey." She sucks in her breath. "Wow, I drunk a little too much today," eyes closed, head loose, swaying slightly on the balls of her feet. When she opens her eyes however, she looks quite sober. "You want a different drink to help heal the woes of the world?"

"Nope. Whisky's what I brought."

"Goodoh. Have yer last Towershower for the duration, and I'll shuffle down and put away your gear, and shuffle back, and between sober sips, examine whatever it is in there." Momentarily befuddled again, "What *is* in there? I never left anything at your place. . . ."

"Things Himi stole."

. . .

A string of moneycowries she'd used long ago as worrybeads.

A silver religious medal on a too-fine silver chain.

The talisman knife, Seafire.

Seven Cuban cigars, still in their cedar-veneer wrappings.

About 200 paper clips.

A small piece of machinery she had stolen for herself from the first factory she worked in: it had a fascinating and now totally useless action. Press the top button and a thin spiked disk the size of a five cent slid out, spun round, whirred to a halt, and retreated back into the housing. You could do it again and again, the disk never got tired. It never varied either.

An agate from the heap of polished stones she used to keep on her desk.

The miniature travelling chess-set.

A tiny bottle of the patchouli-scented oil she uses to perfume her hairbrushes.

Three felt pens and an oblong block of Chinese ink.

A heavy silver thumbring with a bezel of turquoise.

And a wad of the visiting cards she had used in Japan (engraved with three dolphins going deiseal round the Southern Cross, her name in Japanese and English, and the proud boast, Artist, which she had been then.)

Some of it she had known to be missing.

Except for the knife Seafire she didn't miss any of it.

O my strange little filcher, the magpie child, what in the name of hell did you want with all this? Not that it mat-

ters now, but I have a suspicion that, despite Joe's ef-
forts, you never had any sense of property, just that of
need, and you thought everyone else was really the
same way too. . . .

She swept all the junk back into the brown paper bag, keeping
aside her knife. She put the bag in an envelope, and sealed it, stamped
it, and addressed it to the child, care of the public hospital. She
didn't send a letter with it. She went down the stairs in a skittering
hurry, while Joe was in the makeshift shower, and left the envelope
out in the letterbox for the postman to collect next morning.

. . .

The gear Joe spoke of is three suitcases and a forlorn carton of
books and jugs and old shoes. A small pair of sandals on top. Two
guitars, one cased, lean against the suitcases. That's all.

She piles it on top of one of the large packing cases of books,
stowed round the border of the cellar.

It's a large cool vaulted room, the cellar: before, she could wander round and admire all the wine and liquor, the basic preserved
food she had stored away. Now it is full of cases and trunks and
furniture, and there is little room to move.

They travelled lightly, the Gillayleys, not loaded down
with trivia. But then, in the end we all travel very lightly
indeed. Nothing to carry more substantial than memories . . . and maybe that's the heaviest baggage of all. . . .
Philosophising while partially embalmed with whisky
never does produce much more than a whining little
tribe of cliches. . . .

She picks up the lamp and plods sadly up to the livingroom.

Time, time, it's all running out and it could have been a
season of rare vintage, this coming summer. Now it has
sunk to this vinegary lees,

up a step, another step, up yet again,

my cask hollowlight, the rich wine about done. Ah
come on, me chortling ghoul . . . we'll hold a premature

lyke-wake, and make merry for the bitterhearted
man . . . God, his mother named him true, Ngakaukawa
to the very marrow I'll bet he is . . . he's looking a bit
grey tonight, I'd better check he hasn't split a stitch or
a gut . . . shall we reveal about our gut, ghoulie? Piti (one
step) piti (two step) potara (three) a . . . the top . . . nah,
we go away because we have a simple ulcer, and because we are tired/depressed/rundown as all afore-
said. Because we want to build up strength again . . .
mother of us all, the lies we tell to salve hearts. So be
it, I go on my mythical painting safari for recuperation,
and yeah Joe, we'll meet again next spring if you're
sprung by then. . . .

She lays out the last of her smokes, cheroots and bidis and
Kreetax, pipe tobacco and the last quarter-ounce of Coast gold
grass. She ranges the two bottles of whisky and the squat little
flask of Drambuie by the selection.

Should do us . . . and *do* is the right word. . . .

She washes her face and head in cold water, and sits back down
by the fire, feeling cool and high and relaxed.

She lies on her side, head propped on hand: the hardness in her
gut is felt less that way. Water from her wet curls drips steadily
down her supporting arm: the soles of her kaibab clad feet, turned
to the fire, are already hotter than is comfortable. She moves
one leg at a time slowly out of range, back again into the fiery
shadow, out. . . .

He thinks,

She has this curious heavy grace, like something out of
its element making do in a thinner medium. Like she
should be living in water. If only I could lie down beside her and tenderly, by firelight. . . .

"Joe, do us a favour please?"

"Whatever you want."

"Pass us the guitar down . . . I seem to have grown roots here."

As he lifts the instrument down, she hears him grunt with
pain.

He brings the guitar back and lays it by her: his face is rigid.

"Fretting you?" she brushes the air by her belly in a gesture the child could have made.

"Sometimes it twinges."

He pours himself a strong whisky and swallows it like medicine; pours another, and groaning, settles his length by the other side of the fire.

"Kia ora," lifting the glass briefly to her.

"Kia ora." She rearranges herself, back supported by the side of the fireplace, guitar cradled in one arm, bottle conveniently close. She sips whisky slowly. No more throwing down drams, she thinks. It's time for quiet considered drinking.

He says,

"If I could start from the beginning—not my beginning, but from the time we became just me and him, when Hana and Timote died— you know what I'd do? I'd stop work. Stay home most of the time. I was thinking yesterday, what a waste it all was . . . I'd worked hard, pakeha fashion, for nearly six solid years, making money to make a home. And the one thing I never made was a home . . . now it's sold, finished, and all I'm left with is a few thousand dollars. Maybe nothing else at all. Do you think they'll let me keep him?"

The question comes jolting out, bare as a bone, sharp as a razor.

"No," She says it very softly. Then more firmly, "No, they won't. Joe, dear heart, if there's one thing certain, it's that they'll remove him from your custody tomorrow. I hate to say this, but if he was your natural son, they'd be reluctant to make him a ward of the state or whatever, even now. If he was properly adopted, it'd be the same as if you'd sired him. But you said things were never finalised. . . ."

He's nodding, the silver tears sliding down his cheeks.

"So in view of the evidence of all the past, um, past abuse on his body, they'll be making very sure you don't get another chance to dole out more of the same."

She takes another sip of whisky.

"Look at it through their eyes: you no longer have a wife, and you've hurt him badly, in the past as well as this time. As far as they're concerned, he's not looked after properly, he plays truant, and he's a vandal . . . they'll think people who don't know him will make a better job of bringing him up. They think."

Her voice is as level and uninflected as though she's discussing shell nomenclature or how to make mead.

"The pity of it all is that they're wrong . . . I've been fascinated by you two these past few months. You've got, you had genuine love between you. You've given him a solid base of love to grow from, for all the hardship you've put him through. You've been mother and father and home to him. And probably tomorrow they'll read you a smug little homily, castigating you for ill-treatment and neglect. And they'll congratulate themselves quite publicly for rescuing the poor urchin from this callous ogre, this nightmare of a parent . . . you got your lawyer clued up on all the background? The real background, the one that counts? Being both parents to him, helping him over his bad dreams, picking him up from all round the countryside, going along to school to find out what the matter is *this* time . . . it all shows you cared deeply. In a negative way, so does the fact that you beat him. At least, you worried enough about what you considered was his wrongdoing to try and correct it."

Joe says dully, "I told him a bit."

"Tell him all of it, if there's still time . . . and if he's good, it may just swing things far enough for the court to appreciate the pressures on you both."

She's been using her voice deliberately, pitching timbre and tone to comfort him. Not giving false hope, or weeping with him. Not praising him or denigrating him or the boy. Trying to inject a little objectivity, a little distance, to make the matter a little less hurtful.

"Jesus, I feel so bad about it all." The tears are rolling down unheeded. "I feel so bad."

"I feel as bad. As guilty. As criminal."

"But you didn't do anything. . . ."

The tapu on 'if only' is hereby lifted, soul. . . .

"No? Two things, Joe. Sim came here and kicked in my guitar as you know, but I provoked that. I kept interrogating him, no other word for it, as to where he'd put my damn bloody knife. When I think back—and I've been avoiding doing that—but now it comes to mind that he was very upset over something and I never bothered to find out what it was. Just harped on about the knife."

"School," says Joe, staring into his shot glass. "He was in deep trouble there. He had a note on him from Bill Drew saying they were thinking about expelling him."

"It was something, certainly . . . anyway, when he finally broke under my barrage of questions, he went to hit me. He did, actually, and it was so unexpected it hurt for a moment. Did I remember what you said, that he'll eventually fight when he wants you to understand? Did I, hell. I punched him so hard he was down on the floor a minute catching his breath again. It was only after that, he kicked my guitar. You finished it, but I started it . . . if I had shown more understanding, he wouldn't have tried to start a fight with me. He wouldn't have gone away and vented his anger on the windows. He wouldn't have been picked up by the cops. He would have been home with you . . . point two, I started the next stage too. I flayed him with words, and I've got a vicious tongue . . . you know what particularly sticks in my craw?"

He shakes his head numbly.

"I said, I hope your father knocks you sillier than you are now, you stupid little bastard. I said many such pleasantries, all intended to hurt . . . damn it Joe, I'm just as culpable as you are. More so, in that I could have stopped it happening and I jumped in to inflame the whole thing. If I'd said, No, don't hit him, or No, wait till I get round there and we'll talk it out. If I'd said . . . to hell, I didn't, and there's nothing I can do about it now."

She gulps down the remainder of her drink, and refills the glass.

"I did plenty, e hoa, and I'm not likely to forget any of it. Not least, that when I hung the mike up after talking to you, I knew Simon was in for one hell of a hiding, and I was glad."

She holds the bottle out to him. "The bad part for me is that you're paying and I'm not. You'll have a definite penance, and I'll have only the miasma of memory to endure. Which is plenty in one way, and nothing in another. Drink up."

Her voice is still cool and detached.

> She is making it easy on me, trying to share the
> blame . . . but it makes sense. She did have the chance
> to stop me thrashing him.

And he recalls the wordless choking of pain the child had made, holding the phone in his ineffectual grip while Kerewin hit him with words.

Aue, that must have hurt him to hear things like
that. . . .

He doesn't feel as leprous with guilt, as isolated and criminal any
more. He wipes away his tears with the heel of his palm, and takes
the whisky bottle. Clink clink, and another golden measure poured.
He selects himself a smoke, one of the clove-impregnated Indone-
sian ones, and lights it on an ember. It crackles and sparks as he
inhales.

"Ah, e hoa, you didn't do much bad . . . I did so much more."

"The intent is sin as much as the action, and believe you me, if I
could have hurt Sim without killing him that afternoon, I would
have hurt him . . . hell, I was wild." Her fingers are plucking the guitar strings lute fashion. "So stupidly wild . . . I could buy a thousand
guitars like that . . . it was just that it was special. The second guitar
I ever owned—I literally played the first to death—and given to me
by my mother. I used it as comforter and cocelebrant and resonance
chamber for my thoughts for over twenty years. . . ."

She settles the black guitar body close to her, and begins to
play.

It's a slow haunting tune; melancholy, yet it embraces the listener, drawing one onward rather than down.

He remembers it in the months to come, playing it so often in his
mind that when he next picks up a guitar, his fingers settle into the
melody without him meaning them to.

"Pavane for a dead infanta, by Ravel," she says at the music's
end. She plays it again and again that night, seeming to have forgotten all the rest of her repertoire.

. . .

As Joe drinks more, he becomes garrulous. Several times he goes
over the way he beat up the child, seeking to find a pattern in it, a
meaning for what happened. Each time it comes up, he exclaims in
wonder,

"You know, that's the first time he's ever hit me? First time, and
what a hit," shaking his head, halfpuzzled and halfproud, that Simon
had had the forethought to conceal the splinter, and the initiative
to use it.

A hit indeed. A little deeper, and the glass shard would have sliced through another artery and bled him dry before Kerewin's arrival.

"It wasn't that hard but God! did it hurt . . . I never thought he would go for me like that, not using a knife or anything. He's never even hit me before . . . he fights sometimes, beforehand, you've got to struggle with him but he never tried to hurt me. He always gives up, he always does what he's told. So I never looked for it to happen . . . e Kere, when he started moving his hands I thought he was going to say something about Bill Drew's note and then wham. Oath, it went in so easy, he didn't have to push. Just like a knife into hot butter, whizz and there it was, deep in my gut and me bleeding like a stuck pig. I was so mad he'd thumped me back, ah Jesus I just hit him as hard as I could till he went out. Then I went down too."

"You know what?" he asks yet again, on the last recital, and she shakes her head tiredly. She has become more and more sober as the night has worn on. "I think I was trying to beat him dead," says Joe. "I think I was trying to kill him then."

. . .

He says something in passing that Kerewin wishes he had never revealed. A few words, but they make for horror.

He says, "I don't think I'm the only one that's hurt him. He had some bloody funny marks on him when he arrived."

. . .

He falls asleep before dawn.

She watches the moon draw away to the west, and the southern cross take a header down the south horizon. Orion pales to a distant ice glitter, and one by one, his stars go out.

The sky flushes brilliant crimson.

Red sky in the morning. Warning. O I know it's only weather words, but . . .

watching the blood sky swell and grow, dyeing the rainclouds ominously, making the far edge of the sea blistered and scarlet.

Dawn, and in the east, another star dies.

. . .

It made the national news on Friday evening.

"And in Taiwhenuawera today, a man was sentenced to three months' imprisonment for what prosecuting counsel called a savage and brutal attack on a defenceless handicapped child. However, the magistrate, Mr P. S. Seward, commented that the child involved could hardly be called defenceless since he had stabbed his foster father, Joseph Gillayley, in the stomach during the assault. Gillayley, a 33 year old labourer, spent two weeks in hospital recovering from the wound. His seven year old foster son has been removed from his custody which, as Mr Seward remarked drily, will be a move beneficial to both parties.

The government intends to introduce new legislation during the coming session which will . . ."

snap.

And that's the end of the news.

She stood up and flexed her shoulder muscles.

Time to hit the road, Holmes. Time to get gone.

She wondered if she would still be alive three months from now.

. . .

She folded the stretchers and left them outside under a canvas for Piri.

She packed away the sleeping bags, and cleared out all the remaining food.

Have a feast, gulls. . . .

She stowed her backpack into a large suitcase, added a few clothes, all her remaining smokes, the last of the bottle of Drambuie, Simon's rosary and three books.

One is the Book of the Soul, the one she normally keeps under lock and key.

One is the Concise Oxford Dictionary.

The last is peculiarly her own.

It is entitled, in hand-lettered copper uncials, "Book of God-head", and the title page reads,

"BOG: for spiritual small-players to lose themselves in."

It contains an eclectic range of religious writing.

The Diamond Sutra and The Wisdom of the Idiots.

The Tao te Ching, and Julian of Norwich's Revelations of Divine Love.

The Bardo Thedol, and extracts from Buber's Hasidism.

The first, second, and fourth wings of the I Ching, and Hahlevi's Tree of Life.

Selections from the Upanishads and the works of the sixteenth century Beguine, Hadewych.

Teilhard de Chardin's Hymn of the Universe, and Reps's Zen Flesh, Zen Bones.

The Book of Job, and Ecclesiastes, and the Song of Solomon.

"The New Testament of Jesus Christ, and Masnawi by the Sufi, Jalal-uddin al Rumi.

It has illustrations. Da Vinci's Vitruvian Man. Blake's Ghost of a Flea. A drawing of Pallas Athene she'd made after a dream. Thirty mandalas, from the Grand Terminus to one she'd created three years ago, a steady indrawing of spirals and psirals and stars.

It was a book she had designed to cater for all the drifts and vagaries of her mind. To provide her with information, rough maps and sketches of a way to God.

She has a feeling her need for the numinous will increase dramatically from now on.

. . .

Left bereft, go sift the wide expanse of wind . . . take issue with any straw that blows across your path and conjure hopes from sticks that lie in the sand. Soul, your hopes are my hopes and my hopes are insane. So the meaning and signpost for the journey is Hope Obscure.
And the sign is a ghost, still whining and bound in a cart.

. . .

There's a fine mist falling and the world is close about her. The truncated mass of the Tower looms behind. The sea is hushed.

The suitcase, and the Ibanez in its travelling case, are sitting by the locked Tower door.

She waits patiently under an umbrella for the night to become complete.

She has made a torch of rags and tow soaked in kerosene, wrapped round a billet of wood. It waits at her feet.

> If I was an honest uncompromising soul, if I wasn't riddled by this disease called hope, I'd climb into the middle of my pyre and light a phoenixfire from there. . . .

The dandelions look luminous in the evening. Many of the aureoles are wide open, as though the sun still shone.

> On the other hand, my cardinal virtue is hope. Forlorn hope, hope in extremity. Not Christian hope, but an innate rebellion against the inevitable dooms of suffering, death, and despair. A senseless hope. . . .

The great pile of wood waits darkly.

Pale moths are flitting all around, hordes of them like insect ghosts, flicking in and out of her vision. Time. . . .

She lights the torch. It smokes blackly, then bursts into flame.

She flings it and it travels like a comet into the waiting wood.

The pile explodes, fire jetting, soaring, enfolding wood with eager flowers of flame. They rush and roar up in a tall soaring column.

> If I hadn't my hope, I might have lasted ten seconds there . . . the air is all gone from round it . . . splendid dragon . . . the glory of the salamander. . . .

It burns down to a bed of embers ten feet across. Even then the dying fire is enough to light the side of the struck-down Tower. O dandelions, you must have known what was coming. . . .

The moths are back after the firestorm: they fleet and tumble round her head and hands as she shifts the embers into a pile with a shovel. When it's complete, she digs the shovel into the ground, leaving it there. One more thing to do. . . .

She takes a silk handkerchief from her pocket, and with her bare hands, scoops up soil, enough to fill the hollow of her palm. She secretes handkerchief and earth back in her pocket.

> Wherever I go, however I go, I carry this earth for memory. And should I die in a strange land, there is a little more than just my flesh to make a friend and sanc-tuary of alien ground.

Kerewin picked up her cases, and walked away into the night.

IV

Feldapart Sinews,
Breaken Bones

10

The Kaumatua and the Broken Man

I

"HERE?" says the bus driver incredulously. "Here?"

"Here," says Joe.

"But it's in the middle of bloody nowhere!"

"That doesn't matter. I can walk to where I'm going."

The bus pulled away in a rising whine of gears. The late afternoon sun glinted on the back window until it turned a corner. The noise faded.

It began to rain, a thick drizzle that clung to his clothes without really wetting them. He shifted off the road and started walking through the scrub towards the sea. It wasn't hard going: there was little gorse and less blackberry, mainly acre upon acre of manuka, stands of bracken, the occasional coprosma, no tall trees. But the scrub was high enough to prevent him seeing where he was going.

The bus driver had said,

"Well, you might meet old Jack in there. He comes out to the turnoff sometimes to collect his sack of flour and tea and tobacco. They call him the last of the cannibals, but I don't think he really is," and he'd laughed.

The sentence joggled in his mind.

"I don't think he's really the *last* of the cannibals," or "I don't think he's really a cannibal, but you never know. . . ."

He could never imagine his great-grandfather, who had taken part in several feasts of people, as a cannibal. He remembered the old man only as a picture of a silver-haired fiercely dignified chief. He'd always imagined cannibals to be little wizened people, with pointy teeth.

"We're meat, same as anything else," his grandmother had said.

He shivered.

The manukas were blackened with blight and there was a pervading stink of swampwater throughout the bush. Even the concrete rooms and corridoring with their discreet bars and locks seemed more pleasant now.

He shoved his way onward, his pack catching and smashing branches, and all at once stopped.

He was on the edge of a bluff: below him, a scoured stone beach, with driftwood in tangled piles along the tideline. It was thirty shadowed feet to the bottom.

. . .

The kaumatua:

> I have watched the river and the sea for a lifetime. I have seen rivers rob soil from the roots of trees until the giants came foundering down. I have watched shores slip and perish, the channels silt and change; what was beach become a swamp and a headland tumble into the sea. An island has eroded in silent pain since my boyhood, and reefs have become islands.
>
> Yet the old people used to say, People pass away, but not the land. It remains forever.
>
> Maybe that is so. The land changes. The land continues. The sea changes. The sea remains.
>
> Since I came here, I have left this land only twice. I walked the streets of towns the first time, and was ignored. The second time, people laughed behind their hands at my stilted speech, and stared at my face. "Keerist, what an antique," said one.
>
> So I quickly learnt the results of my desertion. I am tied irrevocably to this land.

And so. For this past life, I have kept watch, from dawn till star-pierced night. For this past life, I have waited, from the sun's dying until the bright midday. Watching over, watching for awakening: waiting for the sign. There is not long left for me to watch or wait, and still the stranger does not come. The digger has not delved. The broken man has not been found and healed.

Yet those were the ones you instructed me to watch and wait for.

Was it all illusion? Were your eyes blinded in the moments before your death? Have I cast aside the pleasures of life to endure only this pointless watch?

. . .

He stood sweating, looking down at the beach for a long time. A shag flew past in the twilight, and gulls wheeled and keened above his head. It could be Moerangi, four hundred miles south; it could be Moerangi, and nothing has happened, and along the beach in a firelit bach, they wait for him. . . .

He shook his head, and stumbled back.

As though in a dream, he began to run. Somewhere near, he could hear a river that he hadn't heard before. You learned not to hear too much in prison. The manukas slashed at him as he blundered through, ears full of the river. The packstraps ate into his shoulders. You grew flabby and soft in prison, playing at working, ignoring the talk, enduring the time.

He stopped, breathing heavily, and shrugged the pack off. He listened carefully. The bush is filled with the sound of the river but he can't tell which way it is. Something moves and grunts nearby, and he turns sharply, his fists clenched.

The grunts stop. His heart settles again.

It grows very dark as he stands there. At last, he sighs and sits down beside the pack. He doesn't feel like eating, wanting only deep, dreamless sleep. He fumbles through the pack, sorting out the bivsac, and sets it up. The pencil torch is blindingly useless. It is better to work in the dark, even though he bangs into stones and bushes. He grows more and more tired.

Prop the pack against a stunted manuka: turn the boots upside down beside it: wriggle into sleeping bag, and again into the bivsac, and wait for sleep.

The ground is surprisingly springy except for a branch buried under his shoulders. And an evil little breeze drives straight into his face. It is bitingly cold, and the drizzle slides in with it. He puts his head inside his sleeping bag, and moisture from his breath builds up and wets the area by his face. His feet are numb.

He cannot recall falling asleep, but the wetness and the cold wake him. There's a thin whining of insects. In the chill gloom, all else is silent. Slatebodied midges begin crawling in every gap, hordes of them, slow but thorough biters, driving him to get up.

In the grey half-light, he discovers he has gone to sleep in a bog. A small bog, crawling with every kind of biting life. Midges and daylight mosquitos of all varieties. They whine joyfully.

He stands, incomparably miserable, the soles of his socks wet and growing wetter, letting the creatures bite their fill.

Ngakau, wake up. Look, the sky is lightening. Make a tea. Dry out your gear. Pull yourself together, man.

Two kinds of manuka, he thinks, consciously observing as he spreads the bivsac and sleepingbag. One with white flowers and fat leaf lobes, and that one has smaller diamond leaves and pinkish flowers. Wonder which one she made the sedative from? Or was it both? He notices sundews, some vivid red, some tall with a dozen green sticky heads per stem. Kerewin would love 'em, eh, she had a mind for the macabre. Probably spend hours watching until some poor bastard of a fly got snared. Fern curls, bracken, pollen-like dust round the rims of puddles. Cracked white rocks edging out of the soil. An odd bleak place, but better than the concrete desert.

As he lit the spirit-cooker, a seagull flew overhead and made a raucous noise. He was reminded of the boy imitating the mollymawk, and the minding made him smile. You learnt to remember the sweet things and squash down the bad ones. It works until sleep comes.

The sun is out: the bivsac is drying, and the wet patches at the mouth of the sleepingbag have dried. His sad fey mood begins to pass.

Midges in the tea ... he scoops them out, frowning ... what was that childhood horror? Ah yes, Kohua-ora, meaning "Cooked alive in an earthoven." Refers, the book has said, to an ancient event near Papatoetoe. He had stumbled across the reference in one of the useful books his grandmother gave him, and it brought him nightmares for months.

You have plenty of time to think when you're sick and helpless, when you're cooped up and made to feel useless.

Had it been deliberate, the slow cooking of a hated rival? Or someone laid in the hole, who though thought dead, was still alive and showed it? She told him what a noble fighter the old Maori was, and the school texts repeated it whenever they mentioned the Maori at all . . . God, what lies we get taught. Exemplify the honourable incidents, and conceal the children who got the chop, the women and old men stampeded over cliffs, the bloody endless feuding . . . yet the gallantry according to the code was there, the wit in the face of inevitable death . . . besides, he grins to himself, as a race, we *like* fighting. We're not too far from the old people, Kerewin and me . . . but Kohuaora? Thinking about old horrors somehow lessens the impact of the new ones.

As he flicks away the last waterlogged midge, the sun shines more brightly, and his heart lightens with the morning.

. . .

The kaumatua:

plaited a kete.

He put in it: cold potatoes; fresh cress; old corn; and the last piece of fried bread. He filled the battered thermos with strong sugared milkless tea.

"That is all there is, for now."

There was half an ounce of tobacco left in his tin. He put it, and a dozen wax matches and a strip of coarse sandpaper, into the kete too.

"This person, they may smoke."

There is a person, digger or stranger or broken man.

Last night, a huhu beetle tapped on the window.

He sat wrapped in the blanket from his bed, candle glimmering on the floor beside him, and watched it knock and walk over the pane for an hour.

He did not let it in.

Then he dreamed, although he did not think he fell asleep. And his grandmother, whom he had last seen as oiled ochred bones, spoke to him.

"I wasn't feebleminded, I did not speak of illusions before I died," she said acidly. "It was the way things had to be done. The waiting was as much for your good as for that which you watch over. It is finished now."

The candle had sunk and died. The huhu had gone. He had sat, shivering, waiting for the dawn.

Even though I have had a long life; even though I have been taught and prepared for this time, I am not ready for it.

Are all people so wary of their death?

. . .

He took off his pack, lay down, and looked over the face of the bluff.

A greyblue clay-like material, slippery-looking; no handhold visible, no purchase for feet.

"Ah, screw it." He sat up, leaning against the pack.

It had begun to drizzle again an hour ago. He had tramped two miles looking for the river, and hadn't found it. Wet branches smacked into him viciously, his shoulders still ached from the pack-straps, and he was beginning to feel sick and faint.

He had last eaten yesterday afternoon, when the bus had stopped at a tearooms. Cardboardy sandwiches with limp tomato insides. This morning's tea had used all his water, and the freeze-dried food he carried needed water for cooking it.

He had turned for the beach, and the bluff still confronted him.

On the beach I'd have water. And there might be some decent food, there *will* be . . . pipi, karengo, kina, something . . . but I'm not a bloody bird.

He gestured over the bluff with his thumb, and then snarled at himself . . . you're going round the twist, Ngakau. . . .

There was a quart flask of rum in the pack, and three of Kerewin's cigars left in their case. Might stimulate some useful thinking. *Some* thinking, eh. And dear Lord, it'd make me feel warmer.

Despite his parka, he was cold, even while he had been walking. Now the cold had pierced bonedeep.

He pours the cap full of rum and swallows. Fills it again, and tosses that down too. The stinging warmth sweeps down his gullet, and his skin contracts and tingles; his stomach opens wide. He fills the cap again, and balances it carefully: it holds three nips, and it is a long time since he had a drink.

"That is better," and his voice sounds cheerful and confident.

Days in pubs . . . long long days and nights, days soaking, and blind nights . . . and those three mixed-up sweet times of song and talk and happy heavy drinking . . . though Kerewin pake could never forget herself and come home, it was so good.

He can feel his face flushing, beginning to sweat. He throws back the hood of his parka and lets the drizzle fall on his hair. Clipped hair, prison cut.

He drinks the capful slowly.

. . .

The kaumatua:

"Now," he says, sitting down beside the little mound of earth, "where do I go?"

The top of the mound is smoothed flat, and he has traced where the river flows, where the inland track is, where the five beaches are, and their headlands.

So many years. . . .

He shuts his eyes, and drops the twig of karamu he holds in his left hand. In the dark at the back of his mind, he hears his grand-mother whisper. He lifts his right hand and lets the other twig fall. It leaves his hand slowly, not like a stick dropping at all.

It falls without a sound.

Then, his eyes tightly closed, he says haltingly, fearfully under his breath, the old words.

He sighs when they are finished. I must do this, for my strength is waning, but the cold, aiee, the cold is almost too much.

He opens his eyes.

The dart he had first dropped lies on the third beach. It is twisted as though something had snapped at it in midair.

The other, the seeker from his right hand, has inched its way to meet it, and now lies quiescent, touching the first.

He can see its thin trail quite clearly on the smoothed earth.

But it is as the first time: the twigs have moved and he never saw what moved them.

And as before, he feels the dry harsh laughter of his grandmother rustle through his mind.

. . .

"It's a bloody long way to jump."

The smoke from his cigar curls back and stings his eyes.

Those legs, thin-calved, weak-thewed, with brittle ankles. So
painstakingly, painfully massaged back into usefulness. The old cold
hands pressed back and forth; the rank smell of acetic acid and oil;
the pinching and kneading of wasted muscles, "E boy, *move* your
foot," pummelled to walking again.

> So, I'm a shattered heap down there. The tide will roll
> in and sweep me away. Stronger logs are disposed be-
> neath the sea.

He got up unsteadily, and began to shuffle back and forth, a foot
from the edge.

The space was small. No more than two yards free of scrub,
but the shuffling became a dance, a dance of abandon, of pain, of
illusion. Stagger of despairing hope forward; a step of beaten-by-
circumstance back. It's become the sin dance of forlornness, the
one dance of death.

But this lone dance is wrong, he thinks hazily. Even in hell, there
should be lines, ranks of sinewed legs beating down beside mine.
Ka mate, ka mate. . . .

He fell down against the pack.

> Why am I sitting down?
> When all I need to do
> to get to the bottom
> is jump?

A three-note saw, a whining vicious singing: Jump Nga Kau.

He pounded on his head. His fist made a dull sound but didn't
hurt. Beat your brains out, Ngakau, beat your sense back in. Because you do know what you're doing . . . o yes. All those nights in
the dark alone, and his face came before you as you split his lips,
and bruised and cut and broke his face. Cracked his skull, and that
was just the beginning. Now they're gone, gone, gone beyond,

"O I need you!" he screams, "I need you both!"

Fists clenched against the sides of his head as though he would press more sound free, as though to make his screams lightning edged to split this coming dark.

If I make it, it will be a sign.

Rocks await.

He tosses the pack to them.

It falls, tumbling briefly, thwacking against the bank below.

> Thud. Imagine that's you. And the snap is your barrelchest giving way at the stays, the heartcask battered and broke.

He throws down the empty flask, and a spin of last drops zags out golden.

> A measure as an offering. Lucky gods. You get five full drops as a libation.

"The last measure is me," saying it loudly, but not in a scream, "I have rum for blood, and blood in plenty. Measure me!"

He spreads his arms to the lowering sky and runs over the edge.

For a moment he seems to hang there, space below his feet, and then he plummets with sickening speed.

The first hardness is his breath, thudded out of him leaving him groaning with no air to groan on.

The second is his arm snapping like a stick beneath him.

And the third is himself swearing, You stupid shit, you could've killed yourself, and for fucking nothing.

He says it again and again, like a litany, while the blackness retreats and his breath comes back in shuddering sobs.

He struggles to sit up, holding his arm so the bone doesn't move. He leans his head against his shaking knees: his whole body shakes, with shock and hurt and crying.

> E atua ma, wairua ma, if there are gods, if there are spirits, o, people of this place, I am made known by my stupidity. Aid me.

. . .

His own bone sticking out of the flesh, a weak china blue colour, like a pig bone in a butcher's shop freshly laid from the meat.

God god god make the pain go away. . . .

He presses it back into his arm and blood pours out. He retches.

I've got to keep it in but o god what with?

He gains two pieces of wood in a staggering search, neither of them wholly straight nor smooth. He binds them on his arm with his handkerchiefs. He is weak and clumsyhanded, and it takes a long hurtful time. He derides himself when he moans,
"You can hand it out but you can't take it,"
but he is sick again before he finishes the binding, and cannot talk then, even to spur himself on.
He watches his hand darken and engorge, but he hasn't any more strength to loosen the sticks.

Look at my veins. Gnarled and thick like I'm already an old man. Jesus, I'm cold.

He pulls himself slowly to his feet. He can't feel the stones he walks on. Painfully, he gathers dryish chips from beneath the damp piles of driftwood. He collects several large knots of wood. Each time he bends over, he feels sick, as though he must fall.
He piles the kindling in a heap; holding the matchbox in his mouth, lights it.
He huddles over the little flame, sheltering it with his body. It smoulders a long minute before flaring. Gradually, gingerly, he adds the bigger pieces, building them round the flames in a cone shape . . .

"Lang doon the cluny isles," sings Kerewin, balancing another chunk.
"What does that mean?"
"How the berloody hell should I know?"
She twists a piece of wood to one side. "Hey look! See how perfectly that reciprocates that shadow?"
"It's drizzling again."
"You couldn't shift anything more, or the whole lot would topple, visually."
"And we're cold to boot."
"O to hell with the weather," snaps Kerewin. "You're not dying of it. *Look!*"

"Himi's shivering. And my teeth are chattering."

"Ah ruin it then." She squats by the pile and strikes the match.

The flames creep along the twists of grass, flare and soar into cracks between logs. Very soon the fire is roaring: Kerewin builds more towers and wigwams about it, containing and directing the flames.

The drizzle has no effect. Simon crouches close as he can to the artistic inferno, and he kneels behind him, arms outspread, catching the warmth and keeping his son from the draught.

She loved to sit and talk by those masterpiece fires of hers, to keep watch until they sank to quiet ashes. He could name them all; the pipi and potato fire they taught Simon to cook on; the fire when all the flames had been tinged with violet; the rata fire by the Tower; and the fire on top of Moerangi hill, the witch fire, when streaks and spires of green and blue ran riot through the heart of the flames. And this one, the spider fire, when the katipo crawled out and Kerewin let it crawl into the palm of her hand.

"Seen many?"

He looks cursorily into her hand.

"Jesus! Drop it!"

"Why? It won't hurt me. Or you either." The little katipo strolls unhurriedly across her palm. "I'm not squashing it. It's not bothered. It's not going to sink its fangs into me. And it wouldn't do me much harm if it did. Although it might skedaddle *you*," she says warningly to Simon, who comes finger forward, closer. "Take a good look at it, Sim. Aside from the seasnake, and you'll usually find that only in the heathen north, this is New Zealand's sole poisoner."

Little Death, examining unfamiliar ground.

Kerewin put her hand on the ground, and after a while, the spider vanished into the marram grass.

Or did it?

His arm is bloated and aching, as if all his nightmares were spiderpoison dreams, and nothing else.

"But I'm not mad yet." He murmurs it. "I'm sitting by a smoking fire on some godforsaken beach with a compound fracture of my forearm. I'm sane and nearly sober and about had it."

He lies down wearily by the fire's edge.

"Ten minutes," he says, more lowly still.

. . .

> I am a waste, a wilderness of alien gorse and stone that scores all who enter. O, Kerewin can stalk through in her grim and withering way, because she is self-contained, wrapped in iron, and I cannot reach her except on the terms she admits. Very few, very hard. . . .
>
> And Haimona . . . ah dear God, my Haimona . . . Haimona storms through any wilderness though it tears him bloody. I am afraid of his ardour. I am afraid of him. So they track my waste, and the waste yields nothing blessed yet. And no-one else attempts this desert. . . .
>
> O, I am hamstrung by foreign images . . . all the luminous childhood pictures are sunk beneath the gorse, the stones . . . I cannot warm or heal the woman. I cannot warm or heal the child. . . .
>
> Any of them. . . .

Coming home that Thursday, with no idea, no hint of what was to come. What already was. Ae, she'd been sick. But it was the 'flu. Everybody gets the 'flu in winter. And Timote was colicky, but that was probably a virus. Everybody gets a virus in winter. And then the terrible bare unbelief. I had no shield for that mood of death. I could not believe so much of me could be cut out so swiftly, leaving only a gaping depth of anguish.

And there was nothing, no-one to take their place.

I could not cry for days. My chest was tight, my jaw muscles clenched so hard they ached all the time, even when I drank myself into a stupor. It might have been better if I had gone with her, home for the burying but . . . aie, everything I looked at, thought of, touched or tasted or smelt carried a burden of memories. Reminded me that they were gone. For ever. And only Haimona left behind. . . .

The best part of me was lost then. What remains is a deep ulcer that will not heal, a waste.

I have nothing to give Kerewin that she will have. I have nothing to give Himi, not even the shelter of my arms and heart. I know I exacerbated his reckless wounding of himself, but now I am not allowed to give him even shelter. . . .

I am just a waste . . . and the worst thing I bear is the knowledge that others have borne far worse distress and not buckled like this under it. They have been ennobled by their suffering, have discovered meaning and requital in loss . . . O Hana Mere, why did you eat the food they offered you? Why did you not return to me?

Aue, the roots of the tree are long and descend into darkness. The shore is wavebeaten, and there is nothing beyond but the unceasing immeasurable sea.

. . .

The kaumatua:

> He is not a big man, not tall, but he is very heavy. To lever him off his side and wrap the blanket round him, has tested my strength to the limit. I have spread his coat over him, and built the fire a little closer, and rested. His arm is badly broken, and badly set. Shortly, I will undo the cloths and wash away the blood, and reset the bone. I shall try to rouse him then, and feed him whatever he will eat. Afterwards, there will be time to consider what to do.

He breathed out deeply, and cautiously inhaled. The pains that felt like bubbles exploding in his chest did not return.

He took out his pipe and filled it carefully, picking up the shreds of tobacco that fell into his palm, and returning them to the tin. He smiled to himself as he did it.

"Ah, the habit of frugality is hard to lose," he said softly.

He reached across the still form in front of him, and removed a stick from the fire, and lit his pipe.

"Still, it is nothing to be ashamed of, this being careful of what one has. Just a little ridiculous when one is going to die."

As he smoked, he studied the face before him.

> I am glad you're Maori. It would be very hard to explain things if you were a European.

The tendrils of smoke spread over the unconscious man, hang in swathes about himself. The cold at his back is intense, but the rain has stopped, and there is no wind.

. . .

The voice is high and husky.

"This is food, a piece of bread. Open your mouth and chew it."

He chews obediently, puzzled by the taste. It is slightly fatty, more like a scone than bread.

It's fried bread, but I'm not . . . where am I?

He opens his eyes cautiously.

The face above him smiles.

Joe shuts his eyes quickly.

That can't be Kahutea feeding me fried bread. He's a photograph somewhere north and he's been dead for fifty years.

He shook his head side to side quickly. I'm hallucinating.

"He aha tou mate?"

"Who is there?" asks Joe, and his voice sounds loud and harsh to himself. "Who is that?"

There is a long silence.

Sweet Lord, prays Joe beneath his breath, if that is food I should not have eaten, I ate it in ignorance. I don't want to stay dead.

The voice says,

"I was Tiaki Mira. But it is a long time since anyone called me that. I think of myself as the keeper."

Joe lifts his hand, passes it over his body. He is solid, he feels like himself, and his forearm still aches. His fingers rest on it briefly: it has been rebound, and the fierce pain has dulled.

He exhales and it sounds like a sob.

"Where is this place?"

"On maps, it is the Three Mile beach."

"There are many Three Mile beaches," says Joe doubtfully, his eyes still shut.

But the weird feeling is going. The discomfort of the stones he is lying on is too normal, the hurt in his arm too continuous.

"Tiaki Mira, thank you for the bread. Have you anything I can drink?"

"Ae," says the high voice. There was a scraping sound. "This is tea, with sugar in it."

It is strong and acrid, and some of it dribbles out of his mouth and down his neck, but the rest flows into him like fresh blood.

He hears Tiaki Mira shift, hears him clear his throat. He draws in his breath, presses down hard with his good arm and levers himself up. He sits, eyes still shut until the throbbing in his head recedes.

"That is good," says the other man. There is a hesitancy to his phrasing, a pause between words as though he must think about what he is saying before saying it.

Joe looks at him.

The old man smiles, and pushes the kete across to him.

"Eat," he says, and lights his pipe.

As Joe eats, hesitantly at first, and then with a relish approaching greed, he glances again and again at the man.

The same stern time-sharpened face,

> only here the features are sharpened by pain as well:
> the old man's cheekbones press eagerly out, making the
> brown skin there a yellowish waxy colour;
> the eyes are similar, deepset and always seeming to look
> down on you from above. Only these eyes smile. The
> hawklike stare of Kahutea is missing.

But the really astonishing thing, he thinks, is the two parallel blue lines across this kaumatua's face. A truly archaic moko, te moko-a-Tamatea.

He had thought the people who had worn that tattoo dead for centuries.

The eyes do not flinch under his scrutiny, nor does the expression of benevolence alter. The old man waits.

"Ahh, good," sighs Joe at last. "That was good. Thank you for the food, and for, for," he touches his arm.

Despite the pain—for he can now feel an ache in his thigh and bruises coming out on his shoulders, as well as the nagging throb from the broken arm—and despite the shuddering that shakes him occasionally, he feels well. As though, he dare not think it clearly, as though an expiation has been made. As though the benumbing burden he has been carrying for years is about to be removed.

The kaumatua smiles again. He knocks the dottle from his pipe, and repacks the kete.

Then he picks it up, and unfolds his tall thin body to its height.

"My home is an hour's walk from here," he says carefully, "I can help you if you need the help to walk."

Joe grimaces. He gestures to his pack.

"If you can help me on with that, I'll be OK," stopping as the old man shows puzzlement, "I think I'll be well enough to walk an hour or two."

Just the food, he thinks in wonder, the food and the drink and the time I slept for. He stands up: he does not feel faint or sick any more. He slides his right arm through the pack strap with extreme care, settles the pack on his shoulders uncomfortably. Too bad, he tells himself, but you can endure a few bruises. You've given enough. Before they leave, he kills the fire, pushing sand over the embers, separating the burning logs. When he is satisfied it is dead, that smoke now rising is the smoke of extinction, he turns away from the kaumatua, and glances up at the bluff.

"Ka maharatia tenei i ahau e ora ana," he says, very quick and soft. "E pai ana."

"Ka pai," says the old man behind him, "he tika tonu ano tena."

Joe stares at him. He couldn't have heard. . . .

The seasound quickens in his ears.

The kaumatua smiles sadly back, and begins walking north.

. . .

It is smoky inside, and very quiet.

"What is that?"

"An antiseptic." The old man grunts. "A bush antiseptic. . . ."

He had steeped and kneaded broad green leaves in a basin of water. The juice that he bathes Joe's arm with is mildly astringent.

"You were limping," he says, some time later.

Joe stretches his right leg cautiously: his jeans are stuck to the outer side of his thigh.

"I've cut the skin there, that's all," he says, pointing. "Nothing's broken."

The kaumatua tore another piece off his shirt.

"Can you bathe yourself there?"

Joe reaches awkwardly, careful not to move his forearm.

"Yes."

The kaumatua purses his lips, and rips off three more strips. He rolls them neatly, and then stands.

"I will be back in a short while."

He draws his greatcoat tightly round him, and walks noiselessly outside.

"E, what a weird old bird,"

but he says it quietly lest the elder hear. He thinks, That's the first time I've ever met anyone who literally gave you the shirt off their back.

He balls the worn scrap in his hand. I can always buy him another . . . you're getting as bad as Kerewin, Ngakau. . . .

He washes the crust of blood away; the stones have bitten into his flesh as well as scraping long grazes on his hip and thigh. More scars, he thinks morosely. All self-inflicted more or less. I don't think I've ever had an honest accident or an honourable wound. . . .

The washing reopens the cuts. He rearranges the piece of shirt into a wad, and holds it against his thigh, staunching the flow with difficulty.

> Kerewin said at Moerangi, "Suffering is undignified."
> Suffering ennobles, I said, but I smiled to show her that
> I thought that was really bullshit. What was noble
> about enduring a hook in your thumb? And she said,
> "Sometimes, the dross is burnt off your character," and
> moodily added, "but the scars that result from burning
> can be a worse exchange."

"Come on, says Joe to Joe, "you're *here*. God knows where, but *here*. They're, they're anywhere."

He blinks furiously, and scans the room for something to look at.

Opposite him is the range. The cover over the firebox is cracked, and smoke leaks out in pungent clouds. There is a piece of twine strung above the range: a pair of grey socks hang from it. On the mantelpiece above is an ornate black clock. The clock is stopped.

"Figures," says Joe.

There are books on the mantelpiece, but he can't read the titles from here. That used to be a thing Kerewin did, read the book titles in any room she came into. "You want to know about anybody? See what books they read, and how they've been read. . . ." By the door, thinks Joe firmly, by the door, on the same side of the room as the range, is a sink and bench. There are rust stains in the sink where the tap drips. One tap—for hot water, boil it. Hence the two battered iron kettles steaming gently on the stove.

At the far end of the whare there's a wooden bed. Beside it, a tin trunk. Then there's a single window, with spiderwebs growing out from the corners. And lastly, the table he sits beside. One chair, and one stool.

"Ascetical. Or bloody poor."

There are two incongruities.

Above the table, leaning out from the wall as though to remind you they're there, are three black-framed photographs. One is a faded sepia picture of a mother and child: both are Maori, the woman with long hair, the child practically hairless with narrow eyes and a sulky downturned mouth. The middle photograph is Michael Joseph Savage, amicable smile, bookish air, mildly looking the world over through wire-rimmed spectacles. The official portrait put-out.

The last is a colour photograph, much more recent. A young blond-haired man, long blond hair, ahh Jesus Ngakau, don't look at that one, but he does. The young man is gaunt and ill-looking, with deep hollows under his oblique eyes. His smile is somehow wildly merry, as though he has fallen into a terrifying joke. Pointed chin and high cheekbones . . . man, you're getting sick again, seeing him in *every*one. He looks hurriedly away, to the other strange thing in the room.

It's a worn hexagonal pincushion made of black velvet. It hangs on the wall above the head of the bed, and is studded with needles and long antique hat pins.

"Odd religion this man must have," and he grins to himself.

The kaumatua, standing hitherto silent in the doorway, says,

"My grandmother always wore a hat when she went to town. Bare feet, but wellclad head. She spent most of her money on hats. A small vanity, and a permissible one."

He adds after a minute of silence,

"This room has been left unchanged since her death, with two exceptions. That I hung on the wall," stabbing a finger at the cadaverous young man, "and this," poking at his barechested body, "sleeps on her bed instead of the floor. She died outside," he says.

He lays the materials he has gathered on the table. The rough bandages have been soaked in a secretion that is powerfully redo-lent of turpentine. There are lengths of flax fibres, freshly scraped and rubbed into raw string, and two flat footlong shafts of wood. And clear gum in a mussel shell.

From one of the cupboards under the bench, the kaumatua brings a saucepan. He adds a little hot water to the gum in the musselshell, until it slides easily into the pot: he heats the mix on the range. When the gum has melted and blended with the water, he cools it.

"You could call this bush-lotion. Or Maori ointment. It heals well, whatever the name given to it."

Joe has been watching him with growing resentment. After the sudden shock the old man's silent appearance and words had caused, he found his feelings of awe and thanksgiving had some-how been displaced by a strong antagonism with undertones of contempt. He says abruptly,

"I know its healing properties. It's miro gum. The antiseptic was probably tutu. I asked you what it was because I couldn't see what leaves you had in the bowl. The bandages smell like you've ex-pressed oil from miro fruit onto them. The only thing I don't bloody know is where you'd find a miro tree round here."

"Ka pai," says the old man. "In my garden as a matter of fact. I planted it there forty years ago. It's quite a big tree now. Good for people who fall over bluffs, as well as the pigeons."

He sounds mildly amused.

He brings the melted mirogum over.

"I suppose you know it stings too, o man of wisdom?" He smiles slowly, his lips thinning and edging away from his teeth. It isn't re-ally a smile.

"Yes," says Joe shortly.

The kaumatua is very skilful, both in applying the lotion to the deep wound in his arm, and in rebinding the arm later, so his wrist is immobilised. But the gum burns like fire, and for all the elder's skill, the shattered bone is moved more than once.

"Stand up," says the kaumatua, when he has done bandaging.

"My jeans'll fall down," says Joe, and realises with horror that he has whined like a petulant child.

The kaumatua doubles up with laughter. "Hei!" he gasps huskily, between spasms of laughter, "maybe this is a new kind of man after all! E hei!" He collapses onto the stool, cackling to himself, brushing tears away from his eyes.

"Hei?" asks Joe warily, unsmiling.

The other wipes his eyes again.

"O not 'hei'," he says at last. "Just a noise." He grins wickedly. "I'll look the other way, man, until your modesty is recovered, in case I see a sight not meant for mortal eyes."

Joe bends his head. "I'm sorry," he says in a low shaky voice. "My thigh won't stop bleeding. That's why I'm holding it. That's why I didn't want to stand. That's why," he stops, feeling his eyes overflow. God I'm either going to faint or bawl out loud like a baby.

The kaumatua stands quickly, his humour gone as fast as it came. He moves Joe's hand aside, washing over the cuts with his lotion. It stings hard but the bleeding diminishes.

"Now stand carefully, please. I shall do up your jeans for you. Good. Place your arm across your chest. That is right, good. Lift your other arm. Hei, now you can lower it. Good man. That is firm? Ah, see if you can move the broken arm? No? Very good. Now lean against me. Walk a little more, a little more, just two steps more . . . e very good."

The soft high voice is receding into darkness. The bands holding his right arm to his chest feel uncomfortably tight, but the arm is secure. He can feel the old man taking his boots off him, can hear him saying, "E, that is good, now lean back. That is the pillow there. Gently now."

The bed is hard but the blankets are soft and warm. A little while of darkness later, he hears the kaumatua say,

"Open your mouth. This is medicine." A soft distant chuckle. "Not a concoction of manuka bark or anything so interesting, e kare, but a modern medicine that brings sleep."

The taste is sweetly familiar.

"Kerewin," he murmurs, "e Kere, I smell like your painting and now I taste like him," and he smiles as he sleeps.

. . .

He is swimming down a foul mud-coloured river.

Not really swimming: the water gets so shallow that he can pull himself along, hands walking on the river bottom.

He knows he must not get his hair wet by the foulness. But already the long strands at the back of his neck are contaminated, and he is horrified corruption has touched him. He paddles and hand-walks along, head reared high out of the water.

Immediately in front of him, is a very low bridge. He has no choice but to lower his head into the stinking stream. Retching, he slides down, water creeps into his mouth, and to his surprise it is sweet. . . .

Ahead, weeping willows, foreigners, trail into the water. The stream narrows until he has to stand up, for he can no longer float. The water trickles over his feet, sparkling and ice-clear now.

He looks down at Hana, who lies on her back smiling up at him, her face relaxed and full of joy. The stream flows from her vagina in a steady pure rivulet.

"E honey, I thought you were asleep. . . ."

"Joe, why would I sleep? It's time to feed Timote, ne?" She shakes her head from side to side, and amidst her thick long hair he sees his little son moving his toes back and forward with his fingers as though to find out how far they'll go. He smiles gravely at Joe, but goes on playing, absorbed in these mobile toes.

He lies down beside Hana, stroking her forehead softly. The grass beneath his hips is warm and dry and prickly, but the sensation is not uncomfortable.

"E Hana," he says, beginning to breathe more quickly, "e taku hine."

Hana reaches for his hands and brings them to her lips. She kisses them. She says,

"Well Joe my love, you'd better feed first then." Her breasts before him are still swollen with milk. The milk is sweeter than the riverwater. Timote crawls out of the soft deeps of Hana's hair, and falls asleep near Hana's other breast. A hand strokes his hair, a small pale crooked hand. "Ssss," says Haimona. "Ae," says Hana to him, her face sleepy now but still calm, "you suck by Timote, my Himi, my heart child, my honey." But as the boy begins to drink, Hana's face changes. Her skin goes grey and begins to run with sweat.

"Aue, the moths, the moths!" she cries out, and her voice is harsh with terror.

To his horror, he discovers he is sucking the fat furred end of an enormous moth. Hana and Timote begin to dissolve, to break up into whirling clouds of fire-eyed moths. Haimona cries out, wretched and forlorn, and he echoes the cry.

"Aue, Hana, Hana!" he calls in anguish, grasping at her fading body. His hand is full of sliminess and a fine hairy powder. The moths begin to swirl round him, their bodies slapping against his bare flesh with a pattering sound that becomes louder and louder as the moths swarm out of the ground in their millions.

He gasps, spitting out moth-dust,

"Hana! O God, Hana! Help me!"

"Hana!" His heart is pounding in his breast, and it feels like a thumb is blocking his throat.

"Hana is dead," says a calm voice.

Joe raises himself on his left elbow, shaking.

"I was dreaming," falling back against the pillow, "a nightmare."

The kaumatua is sitting by the range. The door to the fire-cavity is open, and he is partly lit by firelight, a dark straight figure wrapped in his greatcoat.

He says again.

"Hana is dead."

"I know."

"When the dead are dead, you cannot bring them back. Not by memory, or desire, or love."

"I know," says Joe, more softly.

The kaumatua sighs.

"But you are still calling to her. I have been listening to your dream. It is eery listening to a man talk to ghosts in his sleep."

"I did not ask to dream of her," anger in his voice, "I did not mean to. It just happened."

"The interesting thing," says the kaumatua, as though he had not heard Joe's last words, "is that she has now become a moth."

He shakes his head gently.

"And you must know what that means, o man of wisdom, hmmm?"

"No I bloody don't. I don't want to find out either." Even as he speaks, he feels unpardonably rude.

"But you do," says the kaumatua. "You slept well, but now you are afraid to return to sleep. It is better that we talk. Or that I talk," he amends, and smiles his thin no-smile to Joe lying in the shadows at the end of the room. His teeth glint.

The last of the cannibals . . . Joe is silent. He is afraid to go back to sleep, but not because of the busdriver's careless phrase. The dream would continue, would worsen unbearably. He had wondered, when the nightmares began two years ago, whether he had infected Simon with his bad dreams. Or whether Simon had infected him.

Now, he grits his teeth until his jaw aches. The old man knows too much, if he can listen in to dreams. . . .

"Maybe you know about moths, eh?"

Rain batters the old roof. A burst of wind makes the metal groan, as though it is tired of standing alone against the weather. The kaumatua clears his throat. There is the sudden flare of a match, then a sucking noise as he draws on his pipe.

"When it came time to bury my grandmother, I was instructed to eat part of the corpse, and let the rest of her decay. I was to clean and oil and ochre the bones, and hide them away. Then, she said, she would rest in peace and not bother me."

He spits into the firebox.

"Well, I got the piece prepared and cooked, but I couldn't eat it. I carried out the rest of her commands, but it hasn't seemed sufficient. She buzzes in the back of my head like a bluebottle sometimes."

The iron stirs, moaning again, and the rain beats steadily down.

"E well," says the kaumatua. "All that used to give me bad dreams. Now I just wonder what she would have tasted like."

He puts sticks on the fire, and leans back in his chair again.

"After all, she told me how to make her rest. It's my fault that she lingers, waiting, nei?"

He takes the pipe out of his mouth, and blows the ashes from the top of the bowl.

"In a lot of ways, I am stronger than she is, now. So, if she has any thought of revenge for my neglect of her instructions, there could be an interesting scene."

Sweet Christ, he's as barmy as a coot.

"No, I'm not mad," says the old man gently, and Joe jerks, because he hadn't spoken it.

"I was trying to show how the dead return as voices and dreams quite often. Sometimes, there are very good reasons for their persistence in our world. Sometimes, we have failed them."

Joe lies very quietly, biting his lips.

> Look after our child, she had said. And I have hurt him.
> And I have lost him.

"You see that my grandmother is still here because I failed her in a small way. But it was necessary she stayed, because otherwise I would have failed her in a big way. I would have left."

Joe asks in a small voice, "How long have you been here?"

"All my life, since I was a small boy. Waiting for you."

The kaumatua sighs.

"It must seem very strange to you, a young man from the world outside, that someone has been waiting for you from before the time when you were born. But wait until tomorrow has gone. Then you will know whether I was mad or sane."

"You helped me," says Joe, and sees the old man nod, as if that is the proper answer.

"Now about moths," says the old man briskly. "When one dies, one must journey. The journey is well-known. You must know it. One goes north to Te Rerenga-wairua, down the grey root of Akakitererenga, onto the rock platform and into the sea. Into the seahole that leads into Te Reinga."

"It is all myths and legends," says Joe, "and I never liked any of it."

"Tsk," says the kaumatua, "and your wife still returns to you as a moth?"

"Sometimes she turns into moths. Sometimes she decays in my arms. Sometimes she eats one of my sons and then starts on me, beginning at my privates. That is all business for a psychiatrist maybe, but not any exemplar of Maori truths."

The kaumatua drew on his pipe.

"I think it is," he says at last. "I have more experience in these matters than you. Listen! There are three versions of what happens to you after death. If you go to Te Reinga, it is held that you live as you did here. Eventually, you die again. And then the rot sets in. If you get past the spirit-eaters, Tuapiko and Tuwhaitiri, if you get past them, there is underworld after underworld, each less pleasant than the last. In the end one of all you get a choice. The choice is to become nothing, or to return to earth as a moth. When the moth dies, that's you gone forever—just putting off the evil day, hei?" Cackle.

He simmers down. "But that is allegory, I think. It means you journey on and on, becoming less human and more . . . something else. Your wife has just about reached the end of that road, I think."

He leans forward a little.

"The second way is to journey along the sea path. You surface once to say goodbye to Ohau, the last of this land you'll ever see, and then go ever westwards till you reach Te Honoiwairua in Irihia. There, there is a judgement, and you're thrust into heaven or hell."

He spits at the fire again, thoughtfully.

"I think that idea is cribbed. It doesn't sound quite Maori. The third version however, I like, therefore," chuckle, "it is more sophisticated. Some of us believe that the soul has a choice of which journey to make, to stay with Papa, or to join Rangi. Graveminders used to put a toetoe stalk, a tiri, into the ground at the end of the grave so it pointed to the sky. Then the soul could leave the body, and hang in the sun awhile, like a cicada crawled from its larval husk. It would choose which way it wanted to develop, the earthly, or the heavenly, and if it chose Rangi, away into the firmament it would go. Maybe as far as the tenth heaven where Rehua of the long hair smiles hospitably; Rehua the giver, eldest child of Rangi and Papa, Rehua the star of kindness with the lightning flashing from his armpits, Rehua who disperses sadness from strong and weak alike. Today I shall call, 'Ki a koe, Rehua! Rehua, ki a koe!"

His voice rings out, stronger than Joe has heard it yet. It is the voice of a triumphant young man.

There is a long time of silence. The fire dies down. The rain pours down, now hard and wind-driven, now in steady and soothing rhythm.

"Aue," mourns the old man at last, and his voice is cracked and thin and high again, "that is how I would like things to be, but do you know? I am more scared than a child would be. I have no faith in the old ways and no hope in the new."

"Are you dying?"

"I am nearly dead."

It was said matter-of-factly.

"Sometime today, it will end for me. Don't shiver like that."

He bent over, and picked up more wood, coaxed the fire to burn brightly. Then he said, "It is nearly dawn. I have some things to tell you, but you must be strong when you hear them. They are not frightening, but they are grave matters. Matters of importance to you, and all people. So go to sleep again. You will not dream."

Joe says hoarsely.

"I think I am in a nightmare. I think I've been in a nightmare for months. Or maybe forever."

"Rupahu! You are a sick man, a broken man, but now it is time for you to heal, to be whole. To flourish and bear fruit. Go to sleep."

The old man wraps himself firmly in his overcoat again, sits down in the chair, and motionless, stares into the fire.

> I am not sleepy. In this fug of smoke and turpentine, who could sleep? I suppose I should feel guilty lying on his bed. I suppose I should give it back and let him have some rest, especially if he thinks he's going to die soon. But he can't die on me now.
> For all his arrogance and rambling, I think the old bloke just cleared up a nightmare for me. I can see where the thing got its root. And I can see what Hana meant when she said. . . .

The kaumatua smiles to himself as the sound of breathing becomes louder, becomes a steady, even snore. O man, he thinks, you are still very young, and while your life has broken you, you can still heal yourself. With a little help, with a little help. And you, cackling away there in the back of my mind—o yes! I heard you start when I told him those things you made me do so long ago, for it was your idea of a joke, nei?—very soon I will be in the back of my mind with you, and the thought does not increase my respect . . . indeed, my hands are knotting with rage, old woman. Watch out! There is not long to go now!

He thinks with wonder and easy tears, I still have the certainty of meeting her.

And the dry voice says from the dark,
I told you. You have never lost that.

. . .

II

The whare shuddered.

A draught of wind forced smoke back down the chimney, and ash spun out of the grate.

"Ata! Do you like ashes with your soup?"

The old man's voice is sprightly, and his eyes gleam with mischief.

"Not really," says Joe, and sips another mouthful of tea. He winces. It is nearly black, and as bitter as anything he has tasted. "But if they're in there, they're in there."

He thinks,

Strange . . . I feel gay and, o, I don't know . . . unburdened?

He considers that, sipping more of the hellbrew gingerly.

Yes, unburdened. As though something's climbed off my shoulders. Yet nothing's different. I still remember everything.
God, I can even feel my arm as bad as yesterday.

He stares into his cup.

Very strange. The talk this early morning? My dreams?
Nah, it must be the change in the weather. . . .

The sky outside is intensely blue. Patches of whitish cloud spear across it, moving eastwards. The wind blows strongly.

"E ka pai," the old man says. "There's not that many. Maybe enough to make a new flavour."

He stirs the soup busily. "You look much better today."

"I feel much better," says Joe, grinning. "I'm not usually a bastard, I'm sorry for my bad temper."

The kaumatua grins back. It's an impish grin, much like Himi's when he's done something not bad, but not good either.

"And I do not usually bait guests," he answers gently, and the grin fades. "It was necessary to spark a little anger in you, to begin the healing. So much better if the anger began on me. That may sound vague and mystical, but you were the broken man who had to come."

"You didn't bait me!"

"I did. I was taught early in my life how to manipulate people, by someone who was far too wise. You can antagonise people, by posture and tone of voice, without them being aware this is being done. Of course, you can do the opposite thing too, and be concilia' tory. Or make people go to sleep."

Joe looks at him sideways.

"And there is no mystery to it," says the kaumatua sadly. "It is horrifyingly easy to make people perform as you wish, if they think they are in control all the time."

"Like me, early this morning?"

"And yesterday afternoon. It is easier, naturally, when someone is bound by pain or pleasure, mental or physical."

He takes another two cups from the cupboard under the sink, and ladles soup into them. He sets them down by a plate of fried bread.

"Eat well," he says.

The soup is greenish. The taste is peppery, yet reminiscent of chicken.

"What's in this?"

"Eels mainly. The odd bird. Greens."

"O," He blows cautiously into his cup. It is awkward, having only one hand to eat with.

"What kinds of birds? Greens?"

The old man dips a piece of bread into the soup. "As I remember, it started with a duck, and six potatoes. Then one night I added two silverbelly eels. After that, more water, a pigeon, cresses, puwha, more potato, o the soup grew." Shaking his head, laughing silently.

"What's funny? It sounds a good way to build a soup."

"I had always imagined one's death day to be a solemn ritual af' fair, not a matter of discussing the contents of a soup!"

"I could think of worse ways to spend it . . . do you really think you're going to die?"

"I know," says the kaumatua. "As soon as we have finished, I will tell you the story, and show you what must be shown, and hear your answer. And then," he shrugs, "haere. Mou tai ata, moku tai ahiahi."

. . .

He lights his pipe and settles back against his chair.

"Na, I have not asked you before, but what is your name, and who are your people?"

"I am Joseph Ngakaukawa Gillayley, and I am Ngati Kahungunu."

"Ah, ah, good . . . I won't ask you what you are doing on this land. . . ."

"I will tell you because you should know," says Joe quickly. "I was just wandering. I came out of jail last week, and I had, I had nowhere to go. I sold my house before I was imprisoned, my son has been taken away from me, and my friend has vanished. I mean, she's somewhere, but she isn't at her home any more. I had nowhere to go."

The old man's face has been impassive: he doesn't look surprised or disturbed to hear that Joe is newly free of jail, but as soon as he mentions friend, the impassivity vanishes.

"This friend . . . is she a gardener, perhaps?"

Joe grins.

"No, she's a painter . . . though she does take good care of her dandelions!"

The other frowns.

"She doesn't have anything to do with digging or cultivation then?"

"Nope," and suddenly he hears Kerewin telling the dream that came with Tahoro Ruku,

"Keria! Keria!" she says again, "bloody strange way to end a dream eh?"

"She had a dream of being told to dig. Dig something, she didn't know what," he says slowly.

The old man leans forward a little, stabbing the air with his pipe.

"Ah!" he says, his eyes very bright, "pardon this discourtesy, this curiosity . . . but is there someone close to you who might be called a stranger?"

And how the hell would he know this?

Joe shivers. "Yes," hesitantly, "my son. I went to jail for beating him up." He darts a look at the old man. "I hurt him badly and they, the court, you know the welfare people, have taken him off me. I'm not even allowed to see him . . . but you could call him a stranger."

Understatement of the year, Ngakau.

"I mean, I know him, I've known him for four years, but he wasn't mine to begin with, and his background is a mystery. No-one knows his name or where he came from. He was too little to let us know when we found him, and besides, he can't talk." Or do anything much now, he thinks, his heart aching.

It is long seconds before he dares take another look at the old man. He is smiling with delight it seems, but tears are squeezing past his shut eyes. For Himi? thinks Joe in astonishment, but then the man says,

"Well, Joseph of sorrows, man from the east coast, when you are old you cry easy. You are young, your tears will keep. You may even find that you needn't weep, for this strange friend and your lost hurt son. If I'm given time, I'll find out for you, but now I must talk, for a long time, uninterruptedly."

Joe nods to him, Yes, I understand.

Tiaki Mira is greyfaced, and the lines about his mouth and eyes are eaten in sharp and dark against the pallid skin. Pained and dying.

But he is chuckling to himself, saying, "E kui, how could I have guessed such a riddle as that? Stranger and digger and broken man all in one. All in one . . . how could I know? I was just looking for one of them. . . ."

He sighs, and looks at Joe.

"It began with my grandmother. O, it had been in existence a long time before that, but it needed someone with my grandmother's foresight and intelligence, and sense of what was proper, and I say it, fanaticism, for it to continue. Otherwise it would have become, even in her time, just one more piece of lost knowledge. Another legend. One more of the old people's dreaming lies. But my grand-mother heard, and searched, and found, and stayed as a guardian. She got herself a husband, and bred of him two children. None of them, husband or children, were as strong as she was. They all died before her, and because she had these strange skills, she knew they would die, and she didn't tell any of them. When my mother died, my father sent word to my grandmother, and she came to get me.

"I was ten years old, a smart child. I'd been brought up to speak English. I even thought in English. I still can . . . they spoke Maori on the farm sometimes, but they were no longer Maori. They were husks, aping the European manners and customs. Maori on the out-side, with none of the heart left. One cannot blame them. Maori were expected to become Europeans in those days. It was thought that the Maori could not survive, so the faster they become Euro-peans the better for everyone, nei?"

The old eyes are as blank of sympathy as a hawk's, watching fiercely for any sign of agreement.

Joe stares unwaveringly back.

The kaumatua lowers his glare.

"My grandmother was not like that. The only European thing about her was her hat . . . ahh, the hats she used to wear! Great wheels covered with fruit, with birds, with all manner of wax fak-ery. Stuck with steel pins like daggers . . . ahh, her hats . . ." shaking his head, "but aside from those hats, she was one of the old people. She didn't wear shoes, and her feet had soles as hard as leather. She was tall, taller than I am, and heavy with muscle and fat. A big woman, a very big woman . . . she had a disease in her private parts, and her smell was offensive. Her hair was rusty black, and her teeth were huge, like a horse's. She stood in the doorway, and called to me, 'Mokopuna! Tamaiti!' and I was terrified, and squashed myself in by my father lest she seize me, and maybe devour me. I was a smart child, but I imagined too much . . . she knelt in the door, and tears streamed down her face. 'Come to me!' she called, 'o little child, come to me! I have such a need for you!' And she called and wept until I was no longer afraid, because how could someone who needed you so much harm you?

"I went into her arms, and she hugged me tightly, and then she stood up, and with her great hard hand, smacked me round the ears. 'Next time, come at the first call,' she said, and I was dazed and confused. Such a mixture . . . I learned, over the next twenty years, that she could be as tender as any person born, and as hard as stone. She was herself, and a very strange woman indeed. I was lonely, too much by myself as a child, and more lonely and even more by myself as a young man. She perceived this, and judged the exact time I could no longer endure the vigil and the learning she imposed on me. Then she gave me a handful of money, a literal handful of gold sovereigns, and her hand was large, remember.

"And she said, 'Go away, learn some limits of yourself. Learn to enjoy all that towns and people can offer you. Get married if you must. But when I send for you, come back!' By then I had learned to obey her least word without hesitation. She was a terrifying old woman, and she had more knowledge than any one person should have.

"I went, and I found I was a stranger wherever I went. Women were afraid of me. I was too serious for the men to find me a good companion. I drank and learned to dislike drinking. I took to smoking, and enjoyed that. I went to bed with whores and easy women, and found my imagination and the blurred pictures I had retained from childhood were more vivid that what occurred. I read a lot. I listened a lot. Then I came back to my grandmother, and returned to her seventeen gold sovereigns. I didn't say much about what I had done, and she didn't ask at all.

"Since then I have left this place one time only. That was two years ago, when I became ill with phlegm in my chest . . . it wasn't the illness that drove me away, but fear that I would die before the people I was waiting for arrived, digger and stranger and broken man. I made a deal with a lawyer in Durville, that is the town nearest here . . . a strange deal he called it, but an acceptable one. I made a will, which is unsigned as yet, with no beneficiary, yet. I left with the lawyer a complicated design which I said I would draw over the name of the beneficiary and my own name on my copy of the will, so he would know I had completed it with a sound mind, without being under duress. I told him if he never received the will, if I died too soon, he must hold the land in trust, and find a suitable person . . . but I didn't think that would happen, even then. The lawyer directed me to a doctor, and the doctor healed the lung disease, and then, days later, I returned home.

"My grandmother died nearly forty years ago, and she died hard. She whispered to me, before she choked, that I *must* wait until the stranger came home, or until the digger began the planting, or until the broken man was found and healed. Then they could bear my charge. They could keep the watch. They could decide the next step on the way . . . she instructed me to dispose of her as I told you. She said if I deserted this place, the land would curse me beyond my death. 'Keep watch!' she cried to me, 'Keep watch as I have taught you! While you watch, it will be safe, and when your watch is done, if you have kept faith with me, it will be safe . . .' she pleaded in the end, when her mind snapped, pleaded with me, which she had not done since that long-ago day she collected me from the farm.

"I have remained, and kept watch here. Many times, I have cursed bitterly, because I am doomed to live alone and lonely, and to what end? To keep guard over something that modern people deem superstitious nonsense. Something modern people decry as an illusion. And yet, forty years after the death of my grandmother, I am visited by the person who bears in his heart two of the people my grandmother foretold. And he is the broken man . . . is it not strange?"

The soft high voice has been hypnotic. The old-fashioned phrases slide easily into Joe's ears. He has been staring, eyes fixed on the fierce sharpened face. He hasn't been aware of thinking anything while the voice told the tale.

Told what? he asks himself, told me nothing. A tale of a lonely old man, warped and defeated by a domineering old woman . . . but he says,

"Yes, very strange," quietly.

The old man chuckles. It has a breathless sound to it, as though there is not enough air left in his lungs to support mirth.

"And you think I have gone off my head with the pressure of loneliness and the years, eh? Or maybe you think I was like that to begin with? heh!"

Joe looks at the table, blushing. He studies his soup cup; the mouthful left in the bottom has a scum on top, with golden globules of fat studded over its surface. He doesn't say anything. The old man wheezes again.

"Small wonder!" he adds, "I think I would too, if I were you. But let me tell you some more . . . o Joseph, would you have some tobacco with you? See," taking out his battered tin, and holding it out open, "mine is nearly finished. Like me." Cackle, cackle.

No-one can laugh at their madness if they're mad, can they? Joe stands clumsily.

"I've got some smokes in my pack, I'll get them."

He fetches the two cigars and places them on the kaumatua's lap.

"Anana!" he says with surprise and delight. "These were the kind I smoked first of all . . . what a kind gift."

He's peeling the wrapping off one with shaky fingers.

"My friend Kerewin left those for me. She left them with my relations in the town I came from, with a letter. Well, it isn't really a letter. . . ."

The old man nods.

"Tell me soon, if there is time . . . but first I must finish what I have to tell you."

He lights the cigar carefully, and breathes out smoke with a deep sigh of satisfaction.

"It is odd how the mouth and nose remember, nei? Well, let me see how to reassure you . . . I think the heart of the matter is that I was waiting for you, the broken man. Or one of the other two people, right?"

To Joe's nod, he answers,

"I have been here for fifty years, no, nearly sixty years, and very few people have come during that time. There was a sawmill here at one time, but they quickly cut down all the trees, and it ceased to operate before my grandmother died. After her death, there have come pig and deer shooters. Once, three men, looking for gold. Some survey people. I watched what they did, and where they went. I followed them secretly. And never did any of them fit the descriptions. They were all whole people, rough strong ordinary men. There was one man who was very different, and for a while. . . ."

For a minute, the old man muses, his eyes clouded. Then he shakes his head, and his eyes become bright and aware again.

"When I came back from the town, after preparing this will of mine, I didn't come back alone. There was a man with me, who wanted to die in peace. He had been in hospital, in the bed next to mine, and he had said this, and I invited him to come here to die. That is his picture," gesturing to the photograph of the young white man, "and his name was Timon. He was a singer, he said. He had no family. His wife was dead, and his child gone too, he said, and soon they would all meet again. He seemed very happy at that thought. Though it may have been the drugs. He injected himself with them many times a day, and he was always resigned and placid afterwards. One day, a week after he arrived, I found him dead outside the door, the needle still in his arm. He looked so peaceful that I wept. I stopped the bus the following day, and told the driver, and later that afternoon, the police arrived and took him away."

A puff of smoke.

The old man says,

"He was a beautiful man, or he had been beautiful. He had a marvellous voice, that even in his pain could ring and soar. He didn't say very much about himself, only that he had been a singer, and that he lived with a lady old enough to be his mother. Those were his words. 'She's old enough to be my mother, and mother of god, she's lovely. I mean, she was. She wasn't lovely when she died.' He cried sometimes for her and his child. He cried at other times because he said they were all far from home. And sometimes, he cried for me. 'A wait I could sing of,' he said, 'the wait of a hero indeed . . . may it finish soon, sir, very soon.' He never called me anything but Sir, although I had given him my name and circumstances."

He shrugs.

"The day before he died, he sang a song for me. I don't know what the language was, but the melody has haunted me since. That day he gave me the photograph. He had had it taken before he went into hospital, he said, because he thought he was going to die there, and he wanted to send it to someone, a woman I think, as a memento of him. But he said he wanted to give me all there was to give, and that was all there was, his song and his picture. I wish I could remember enough of his song to give it to you. It is a shame I cannot keep his song going."

He drew a last inhalation of smoke and coughed as he breathed out.

"I have spent too much time on Timon the singer . . . but he was the only different man of those few who came here. Besides, he died. . . . Two nights ago, a green gecko lay on my bed. That night a huhu stayed on the window until I slept. My grandmother has been talking a lot to me. I cast twigs to see what I should do and where I should go. One broke. The other found it at a place I had designated the Three Mile beach. I knew you had come at last. Not before time!" and he laughs again.

I wish he wouldn't, thinks Joe. It's too harsh. It sounds as though he's going to go at any moment. He looks as though he might too.

He says, to cover his dismay,

"You are a keeper, you say. And I am the person who was fore-told, to keep watch after you. What do I look after?"

"I will show it to you very soon . . . but you must know what it is before I show you. Otherwise it will seem to be shadows in the water. . . ."

He stands, bending up slowly from the waist, standing piece by piece as it were, chest, shoulders, neck, head. He looks at Joe for a long time, and he doesn't say anything.

"Maybe I can't put it in the proper words," he says finally.

He bows his head.

"I was told about it, taught about it, for a long time before I met it. I was prepared, and aue! there isn't time to prepare you. I think it best to say it bluntly. I guard a stone that was brought on one of the great canoes. I guard the canoe itself. I guard the little god that came with the canoe. The god broods over the mauriora, for that is what the stone is home to, but the mauri is distinct and great be-yond the little god . . . the canoe rots under them both . . . aie, he is a little god, no-one worships him any longer. But he hasn't died yet. He has his hunger and his memories and his care to keep him tenu-ously alive. If you decide to go, he will be all there is left as a watcher, as a guardian."

The old voice limps and stutters. The kaumatua does not look up. There is a shudder running constantly through him now.

> Sweet Jesus Christ alive! You'd better humour him Ngakau, but he's mad! Watching for sixty years over a canoe. A mauriora! a little god! Doesn't he know the museums are full of them.

But like an unseen current, there's a darker thought—

> Maybe a priestly canoe? A live god? A live mauriora?

He says, with real bewilderment,

"What can I say? What do I do? I've seen them in museums,

Tiaki. Pierced stones and old wooden sticks where the gods were supposed to live. Where the vital part of a thing was supposed to rest. But aren't they temporary? And can't they look after themselves?"

The old man mumbles,

"Not this one . . . it is the heart of this country. The heart of this land."

He straightens his shoulders, his dark eyes burning. In a stronger voice,

"By accident or design, when the old people arrived here, they induced, or maybe it arrived of itself, the spirit of the islands, part of the spirit of the earth herself, it rested in the godholder they had brought. O it isn't able to go now. It is both safe, it is vulnerable." He stops, aware suddenly that the phrases are mixed up, that he is speaking garble.

"O Joseph, my time is coming faster than I thought it would . . . there will be no time for ceremonies, you will have to take the land without prayers, but you will have my blessing . . . listen carefully. I was taught that it was the old people's belief that this country, and our people, are different and special. That something very great had allied itself with some of us, had given itself to us. But we changed. We ceased to nurture the land. We fought among ourselves. We were overcome by those white people in their hordes. We were broken and diminished. We forgot what we could have been, that Aotearoa was the shining land. Maybe it will be again . . . be that as it will, that thing which allied itself to us is still here. I take care of it, because it sleeps now. It retired into itself when the world changed, when the people changed. It can be taken and destroyed while it sleeps, I was told . . . and then this land would become empty of all the shiningness, all the peace, all the glory. Forever. The canoe . . . it has power, because of where it came from, and who built it, but it is just a canoe. One of the great voyaging ships of our people . . . but a ship, by itself, is not that important. And there are many little gods in the world yet, some mean, others impotently benign, some restless, others sleeping . . . but I am afraid for the mauri! Aue! How can I make you understand? How? How? How?"

He beats his fist against his thigh, drawing in his breath with a great sucking sound. He holds it, his bony chest swelling beneath the wings of his coat. Then, exhausted, he lets it stream out, and stands still, grey and anguished and weary.

"Three days ago, I would have laughed you to scorn, now I believe you," says Joe simply. "You came up the beach, prepared to meet someone and help someone. You've helped me. You've told of all the years you waited, keeping guard. You've told me why. You are a sane man, and a wise man. I believe you. I don't understand it all, but I believe you."

He stands up, cradling his arm.

"Show me where it is, and I will look after it until it tells me otherwise."

He rests the broken arm against his belt, and holds out his other hand to the kaumatua.

"Show me," he says again.

. . .

It is a long slow march, paced for a funeral, a march of death.

The kaumatua shuffles, bonefingered hand grasping Joe's forearm. He moves blindly; his feet catch on sticks and stumble on stones. He mutters to himself continuously. He is failing horribly fast, the upright man of yesterday become this scarecrow of bones mere hours later.

> I have seen dead people, but I have never seen someone die.
> What do you do? Hold their hand and let them get on with it?
> Pray? Tangi? Listen?

The old man trips again, and nearly falls. Joe steadies him with his body.

"Corner. Left."

The words are forced out. Thick veins in the old man's forehead pulse alarmingly.

The beaten earth track forks. Joe helps him down the left-hand path. They come to rocks, worn and broken, but still towering above them. An ancient gorge where the river ran aeons ago, and carved this place for part of its bed. A silent place: ochre and slate-grey stones. No birds. No insects. The only plants are weeds, stringy and grey and subdued.

The old man pulls on Joe's arm. He points with a trembling hand.

"Cave. In ground." He tightens his lips and closes his eyes, con-centrating. "I don't. Want. To be put there. In the *town*. . . ."

> Burial cave . . . and his grandmother will lie up there. Somewhere. There's a rock like a saddle about fifty yards away, in a direct line with where he's pointing. I'll take a look later. Maybe.

Joe shivers.

"E pou, don't worry. I won't put you there. You want to be bur-ied in the town, I will take you there . . . but what marae? Who are your people?"

"No. People. They're dead. The town. . . ."

"You want to go to the cemetery in the town?"

A whisper of sound, Ae.

"So be it."

The kaumatua edges forward again. "Tauranga atua . . ." he says softly. Under his breath, again and again, "Tauranga atua, tauranga atua," as though those words give strength and enable him to walk.

> Tauranga . . . a resting place for canoes, an anchorage.
> For a god canoe, what anchorage?
> I remember a wet afternoon, when I was a child, and I read a magazine. It had the pictures and story of how they found an old canoe of the Egyptians . . . the sun ship of Cheops, that was it, a burial ship for a pharaoh to ride in. And I thought then—to think of it now!— how much more exciting it would be to find a ship of ours . . . not a dusty narrow craft in the desert sand, a river-craft if it sailed at all, but one of the fartravelled saltsea ships, that knifed across great Kiwa centuries ago . . . guided by stars, powered by the winds and by the muscles of stronghearted women and men. . . .
> But Cheops' canoe travelled the way of the dead, and

that's a journey and a half . . . confined it was, confined between stone blocks.

Where will I find this ship? In stone? In water as he suggested?

Or only in the clouded remnants of an old man's mind?

The kaumatua's grasp on his arm tightens again.

"Here," he says in a choked whisper, "here."

The earth track goes on a way yet, turning a corner to head towards the sea. The sea is loud here, as though the diminishing rock walls, by some freak of acoustics, channel the sound in. There doesn't appear to be anything different about this part of the gorge. Joe looks sadly round.

Mad and stricken after all. . . .

"See. It?"

The rasping urgency of the tired voice makes him stare at the bare surrounding rocks as hard as he can. Tears blur his vision.

I can't say even Yes for him. I can't tell him a lie.

The wind blows a little more strongly, and the white streamers of cloud shift away from the face of the sun.

Over by the cliff, something glints.

"Is it water?" asks Joe sharply.

The old man sags.

"Haere . . ." pushing himself away from Joe, go, you go, I cannot go.

As gently as possible, Joe helps him lie down at the side of the track. He takes off his parka and wraps it into a pad, a pillow for the kaumatua's head. The old man's eyes are closed.

"I'll come right back."

Don't die yet, he thinks fiercely. He clambers over the rocks towards the glint, his heart pounding.

A weathered stratum of rock makes an overhang. It is almost a cave. But it hasn't a floor. A great natural well, like a sinkhole, a cenote, has been formed in the rock.

The water is pale green and milky, as though it contains lime dust in suspension. It is opaque at first glance. But in a very short time—trick of the light, or his eyes adjusting—he can see shadows in the pool. He can't tell how deep the water is, or how large the things that show as shadows are. They cover the bottom of the pool, with patches and gaps between them. Long angular shadows mainly, with two round ones at the far side.

> It can't be one of the great ships ... the pool's only, what? twenty feet in diameter . . . but there's *something* down there . . . rock debris? Old logs? Dunno . . . where does the water come from? Underground spring maybe ... there doesn't seem to be any outflow or overflow. ...

He puts his hand in the water cautiously, meaning to see whether the water is coloured or contains stoneflour, and snatches it out again before his fingers go in past the knuckles.

Jesus Holy!

It's like ten thousand tiny bubbles bursting on his skin, a mild electric current, an aliveness.

He notices that the water is not still at the far end of the pool. Fine tendrils, filaments of clearness, rise and meld with the pale green, like an ice-cube melting in whisky and spinning lucid threads into the surrounding colour.

He edges back from the side of the pool. Peace, peace, I'm just looking . . . maybe I should introduce myself?

Feeling foolish, squatting on his haunches by the overhang, he tells the water his name and his tribe, that Tiaki Mira has named him as his replacement.

> Stupid fool, Ngakau ... what do words mean to, whatever it is? If it's anything. ...

He says "E noho ra" before he goes, though.

The old man is sitting, back against a rock, when he returns.

"Not dead yet!" He calls cheerfully, triumphantly. "I am staggering on the edge of corruption, but I'm not dead yet!"

Fresh strength has been infused into him, from the rest or by Joe finding what he was sent to find. His eyes are bright and see the present again, and he no longer mumbles unintelligibly to the ghosts that surround him.

He produces Kerewin's last cigar from the pocket of his great-coat, and lights it, passing it then to Joe.

> E hoa, if only you could see where your smokes
> went ... where are you now? And the last time I shared
> a smoke, it was with Haimona. ...
> O boy, what are they doing to you? Though maybe you
> can't know. ...

They smoke in silence, sharing the cigar puff and puff about.

"Pity we didn't bring the tea," says the kaumatua suddenly. "It's a good place for a picnic nei?"

Joe looks at him sideways. "A bit too quiet for my liking."

"O, it's not like this all the time ... plenty of noise in a thunder-storm! It booms and echoes all up the gorge like giant men yell-ing ... and when there's an earthquake! Ahh, I've been here when the earth was creaking and groaning as if she were giving birth ... and sometimes, on long summer evenings when the flies are humming, sometimes ..." the bantering note is gone, and his voice is low and dreamy, "the old people come back. I've seen them standing round the mouth of that shelter up there, watching and talking softly. With their long oiled hair, and their fine strong bodies, and proud free-eyed faces ... sometimes they talk, and sometimes they walk, filing away down a track that isn't there anymore, silent under the sun ... maybe they don't come back, maybe I've gone into their time, because they've looked to where I sit and shaded their eyes, squinting, as though they could see something but not enough. And once, a woman threw a piece of cooked kumara at me and I ducked, and laughed ... and once I looked at my dog, and he'd gone misty. Insubstantial, until I put my hand on him, and he whined and licked my hand, and when I looked back, the old ones had gone ... mysteries, o Joseph. All the land is filled with mysteries, and this place fairly sings with them."

"I don't think I'd like to meet any of the old folk."

> I don't think I could look them straight in the eye. I'd
> feel like a thing of no account, less than a slave.

"You may, and you may not."

The old man shrugs, and begins talking about other days and

happenings, when he was younger and spent much of his time
hunting pig and deer through the scrub.

"Fishing and hunting and looking after my garden," he finishes,
"that's how my life has been spent. It has been a very easy life, I
suppose. No wars or great doings. Just watching things grow,
and catching things for food. No family worries after the old
woman died. No money problems, always enough to eat, enough to
smoke, a roof over my head. A man can find satisfaction with
enough."

"Yes," says Joe.

His thigh has started to ache after all the walking and scrambling
over the rocks, and his arm is throbbing hard.

> I'd like to stretch out in the sun and go to sleep while
> he talks, but I can't do that.

He says with an effort,

"Your dogs, e pou? Where did you get them?"

"O, the old lady had a bitch, that somehow got herself in
pup . . . a dog from a hunter's pack maybe? They bred among themselves, never too many, all good strong dogs, not a mean or bad
cur among them. The last one, he died about two years ago, and I
didn't have the heart to start again. Just as well, ne? It's not
good for a dog to outlive his master . . . they were company as well
as hunting companions. That last one, Tika he was called, must
have been the only dog in the country who was brought up and
lived on fish, eh. I haven't hunted pig or deer for many years now,
but I can still fish . . . o, he used to get a bit of bird now and then,
but mainly fish. . . ." He sits in the sun, his hands folded in his lap,
remembering the dogs, retelling their exploits as they come into his
mind.

> It's maybe his last talk, Ngakau. Make it happy for him.

So he chuckles amiably at the funny stories, and clucks his
tongue at the bad ones, and mourns with the old man over the
deaths of long-dead dogs. The ache in his arm and leg grows, but
he doesn't let it show on his face.

At last the kaumatua reaches out his hand to him. "Help me up,
o Joseph."

When standing, he cries out in a loud voice, something that is gutteral and archaic and incomprehensible to Joe. The chant rings in the gorge, an echo dying seconds after the last word has been called out.

"A farewell," says the old man, turning to him, answering his question before it is asked. "I don't think the mauriora or the little god recognise we who watch over them as individuals. My grand-mother thought of us as an attendant stream of awareness, and said they knew when we left. Now, they'll know I'm leaving."

Joe, rubbing his thigh awkwardly with his left hand,

"I told them when I said hello. Sort of."

"What did you see to say hello to?" asks the old man, grinning. Joe flushes.

"What looked like long shadows in the water," his words echo-ing the kaumatua's earlier words.

The old man says gently,

"It's all in pieces, you know . . . and not all of it is there. The old people managed to get the stern and the prows and a few of the hull sections to that safety . . . I know they used pieces of the hull to carry the little god and the mauri to the tarn."

"They're the round shadows?"

He smiles with satisfaction. "Ah, you're a discerning one after all . . . it took me days to see them properly. Yes, I think they may be unwrapped now, but when my grandmother brought them to the surface they were covered with the remains of cloaks. Red feather cloaks, too."

"She swam in *that?*"

The old man smiles more widely still.

"You touched, eh? It's a surprise isn't it! No, she called them to the top, and the little god came with the mauri on his back, and they stayed there for minutes while she sang, and then sank back to safety. Believe it, or disbelieve it, that was how the matter was. I tried once, using the words she taught me, but the water started boiling, and that hadn't happened when she sang, so I was afraid and stopped. My grandmother was a very strong-minded woman, remember, and she had knowledge she maybe never should have had."

Joe shivers, partly from the growing pain, partly from the magic.

"Where did she get hold of it?" he asks, not really wanting to know.

The old man waves a hand in the air. "From her girlhood, she was curious about this place . . . her grandfather doted on her, and told her many things from the past. What he told her of the burial of this canoe, and what it contained, fascinated her mind. She sought out the people who had knowledge, and one way or another, obtained all she needed to know. She had the right to this piece of land, through her mother's sister, who never was married. She had to wait years until she got it though, and when she got it, she made sure, pakeha fashion, that it would never pass out of her hands except to someone she was confident would look after what it bore. Me. Now you."

He looks up to the strange well in the gorge-side.

"Remember, it was a time of flux and chaos when she sought her knowledge. No-one can be blamed for giving her information that she maybe should never have known. And she can be praised for having that staunch courage and intelligence to preserve something she believed, as I believe, to be of unusual value. Incalculable value. How do you weigh the value of this country's soul?"

Joe shakes his head. He doesn't want to think of what could be lying there in the cool green and stinging water.

He does say, tentatively, as they're walking slowly away, "If it is, the heart of Aotearoa . . . why isn't this whole place . . . flowering? Something as strong as that, would make the very stones flower, ne? And there is nothing at all . . . no birds . . . flies, you say, but . . . flies?"

The kaumatua waits until the halting sentences are finished.

"It despaired of us, remember. It is asleep . . . maybe its very sleep keeps the living things away, except for flies, who come to the sleeping and the dead alike. Aue! the one thing I regret about dying is that, secretly, in the marrow of my heart, I have always wanted to see what happens when it wakes up." He sighs. "Maybe we have gone too far down other paths for the old alliance to be reformed, and this will remain a land where the spirit has withdrawn. Where the spirit is still with the land, but no longer active. No longer loving the land." He laughs harshly. "I can't imagine it loving the mess the Pakeha have made, can you?"

Joe thought of the forests burned and cut down; the gouges and scars that dams and roadworks and development schemes had made; the peculiar barren paddocks where alien animals, one kind of crop, grazed imported grasses; the erosion, the overfertilisation, the pollution. . . .

"No, it wouldn't like this at all. We might have started some of the havoc, but we would never have carried it so far. I don't think." He adds thoughtfully, after a pause of seconds, "I can't see that," nodding back towards the hidden well, "ever waking now. The whole order of the world would have to change, all of humanity, and I can't see that happening, e pou, not ever."

"Eternity is a long time," says the kaumatua comfortably. "Every-thing changes, even that which supposes itself to be unalterable. All we can do is look after the precious matters which are our heritage, and wait, and hope."

The lively glint is back in his eyes.

"Well, at least *you* can do that . . . this one is going to take things easy from now on!" He rubs his belly. "Though I might wait long enough for tea, Joseph. Yes, I think I'll take you through my garden, and we'll gather food for tea. We'll eat a last good meal together, and you can tell me all about your dead family that was, and your live one which you have lost, and I'll be as polite as you were while I was boring you with tales of my dogs, hei?"

Joe grins shamefacedly.

"I wasn't that bored . . . I hope it's not our last meal. Maybe you won't be called away so fast now they," gesturing with his hand to the pale shining sky, "know how inept and unlearned I am."

"Ah, you'll do, you'll do," says the old man cryptically, and they walk on, limp on, in silence.

. . .

In the garden, under that bright sky, the kaumatua clutched at his chest, and fell heavily to the ground. Ahh, he gasps, trying to regain his breath, but with each exhalation there is less left. His body jerks spasmodically. Then slowly, he curls up, withering round his anguish like a burning leaf.

Joe started to run towards the whare, turned and came back. No phone no nothing no doctor what good would a doctor be? He knelt by the man.

His face is suffused and his eyes are screwed tightly shut. One hand scrabbles on the ground.

It is a deliberate motion, Joe realises after a moment. Writing . . . aie, the will. . . .

"Where is it? The will you want? Where?" he asks urgently, bending over and loosing his voice like an arrow into the old man's ear.

Somehow the thin shaking limbs are drawn together, driven by an inordinate effort of will. He is nearly to his knees.

Joe unstraps his right hand from his belt, and clenching his teeth against the tearing ache, picks him up, cradles him, arm beneath back, head lolling, arm under the long legs. For the strength in my shoulders, praise, going one halt step after the other; for the strength in my shoulders, praise, arm feeling like it is breaking anew; for the strength in my shoulders, praise, a slow torturous ripping apart of bone and muscle fibre; for the strength in my shoulders, praise, staggering, skinning round the doorframe, grating against it, using it as a prop to hold himself up a little longer. He stumbles across the room and lays the old man on his bed.

The sweat rolls into his eyes, stinging them blind.

A whistling croaking voice, pausing after each word, an inhuman voice, says,

"In. The Bible. Pen. On clock."

He wheels round and lurches over, fingers fumbling, words ticking like an inexorable clock, "Bible pen bible pen bible pen."

He shakes the bible and a piece of folded typescript falls out, snatches the pen off the clock knocking over a key a candle butt, and races back to the bed.

"Ahh!" he calls wildly, "somethingtowriteon!" picking up the fallen bible and bringing it back. He is dizzy and sick, both with his own pain and the knowledge that the old man, however strenuous and gallant his effort, is too nearly dead to succeed in writing his name, drawing his secret design.

Like a puppet lifted by its strings, the old man rises up. His hand outstretched, he receives the pen. His eyes stare fixedly ahead, looking at the end of his bed.

"Where?" pen poised.

Joe stares at him, cold with horror.

For it is as though the old man has already vacated his body and he—or something else—is directing it from the outside.

"Here," he whispers, through numb lips. Blinking against the tears and sweat of pain, he guides the stiff hand. "My name," he whispers, "here."

In beautiful copperplate, the letters form: mechanically, each letter separate then joined by an eerily serene curve: Joseph Kakaukawa Gillayley, Kati Kahukunu. . . .

"It is done. Where?"

The voice is not the kaumatua's, the eyes still stare blankly ahead.

"Here." Joe is shaking and trembling, his voice chilled to an almost noiseless whimper, fear growing in him like crystals of ice.

The signature flows swiftly, appearing on the paper as if tipped from a strange container. T. M. Mira, a flourish, two dots. The pen falls.

As though someone struck him, the old man winces and jerks. For a second he is present again. Joe seizes the pen and returns it to the cold grasp, ice deep in his heart now as he touches the fingers to close them round the barrel.

As though the fingers have eyes, they take the pen back to Joe's name, and quickly draw a complicated maze of spirals and spreading lines. Too quickly. No calligraphist could have drawn the moko so perfectly in the short time the fingers execute it. With the same horrid fluidity, a second pattern is drawn over the kaumatua's signature.

"Yours . . . Joseph. My. Blessing."

Joe eases the paper away, avoiding another touch of the living dead hand. The pen falls. As though a string has been cut, the thin body flops bonelessly on the bed, the eyes closing.

"Aue," Joe says softly, "it is ended. It is done."

But the old body convulses once, twice, and the bowel contents spurt out. The stench of excrement is overpowering. The old man moans, his fingers twitching helplessly by his sides.

"Not like this," a husky thread of protest, "not like this . . . aue . . . aue, the shame, the shame. . . ."

Joe takes hold of the hands, enfolding them.

He says, weeping,

"E pou, tipuna, we all die like this, do not worry, I will be a son to you, be content to let a son perform this office for you, there is no shame, no shame," his words strangle in his sobbing.

"Aue, te whakama," says the kaumatua wearily.

"No shame, no shame,"
but he is talking to empty ears.

. . .

"Today I shall cry, Ki a koe, Rehua! Rehua, ki a koe!"
"Aue, te whakama. . . ."

. . .

He washes the body.
He clothes it in a pair of his jeans and his shirt.
The jeans are short, and the thin ankles stick out ridiculously.
The shirt could be wrapped round the body twice.
There are no shoes he can put on the body's feet, no shoes any-
where in the whare.

. . .

He walks out and waits by the side of the road.
A passing motorist stops, and when she hears someone has died,
she is shocked and sympathetic. She takes him right to the police
station in Durville. Joe doesn't speak. He feels as hollow and dry as
a cicada husk.

. . .

He watches as they casually pick up the brittle old body and
tuck it up on the stretcher, blanket across the face.

The roots of the tree
snake down the cliff.
There is nothing beyond them
but the endless sea.

. . .

"Lucky for you he found you, mate." The police sergeant is
roughly jovial.
"Yes."
"I suppose it was lucky for him too, in a way eh?"
"Yes."
"Going into town to get that arm of yours seen to?"

"Yes."

"I can give you a ride back in the patrol car if you like."

"Yes."

Shocked, poor bastard, thinks the sergeant, and leads the way to the car.

. . .

His arm is set under anaesthetic, and the other cuts stitched. They had burst open when he carried the dying man back to his home.

The surgeon says later,

"Well, you've been lucky. Not many splinters, and not much torn muscle. You'll probably have difficulty using your arm initially, the tendon's damaged quite extensively, and it'll be a while before you're carrying weights again. But with rest and physiotherapy you'll come right."

He smiles. Joe says dully,

"I'll be discharging myself tomorrow."

The smile vanishes. "No way, man. You'll be here a couple of weeks before I'll. . . ."

"Tomorrow," says Joe. "There are some things I *must* do."

. . .

Thin darned socks, and old old clothes. The greatcoat. A superb weka feather cloak.

Odds and ends of fishing tackle, and the battered tobacco tin. Two pipes. The hexagonal pin cushion. The photographs off the wall. The books. The clock and all the things off the mantelpiece. A pouwhenua. Toilet gear.

He puts them all in a sugarsack, setting aside the cloak and the pouwhenua.

As he is putting in the photographs, something says, "Keep Timon," and he can't tell whether it's a voice in his head or outside of him. He takes the photograph of the young man out again, numbly, and lays it on the bed.

He cleans out the whare thoroughly, clumsy and restricted with one arm only to use.

He burns the mattress outside.

While it smoulders, he looks at the hut.

The iron of the roof is piled in layers, a kind of metal thatching. Rusted and raineaten, flaking away piece by piece, it'll decay entirely soon.

The wood of the studs and rafters is borer-eaten. A little while, and it will all subside into dust.

> I won't burn it. It can die at its own rate.

. . .

He searches for nearly an hour before he finds a toetoe bush. He takes one short strong golden-stemmed spear.

. . .

Back in Durville he applies for, and is granted permission to bury the body.

"79 years old, hale and sound except for one heart vessel," says the coroner drily. "Is this kind of tattoo common? In his time, I mean?"

"No. I think, I think he wore it as a reminder of a dead people."

"Hmmm . . . are you a relation?"

"No, I was a guest in his house when he died. He has no family."

"And you feel this obligation to um," checking the certificate, "Tiakinga Meto Mira, because of that?"

"It's the least I can do for him."

The coroner raises his eyebrows. "Hmmm," he says again.

. . .

He takes the cloak and pouwhenua, and his greenstone chisel, pierced now and strung on a plaited cord, to the undertaker's. He helps them clothe the body with the cloak. He places the greenstone round the withered neck, and the wooden spearclub between the cold hands.

> This is nearly all the rite and ceremony I can make for
> you, Tiaki. I am nearly dead inside as well.

. . .

In the afternoon, he visits the solicitor whose name is on the titlehead of the will.

The solicitor looks at him a long time, taking in the broken arm, the strained face, the dark furrows under the eyes.

He says,

"Where are you living?"

"Nowhere. I have a mind to go back and live in his house. For a while."

The solicitor offers a cigarette case, "Smoke?"

"Not now, thank you."

The man lights up, and looks at the will, and a sheet of paper he has taken from a wall safe. He compares the designs on each like a detective comparing fingerprints. The cigarette ash grows longer and longer. At last, he puts the papers down.

"Tell me, if you will, how the old man came to die?" He stubs the butt out. "And how you came to be with him?"

"Why?"

He is sick, and tired to the limit of his endurance. And there is still tomorrow to be got through.

The solicitor looks at him again for a time.

"I knew Tiaki Mira for an afternoon, and visited him twice in hospital. I don't make hasty judgements . . . I don't know whether you'd agree that you can make a friend in a few short hours. I felt I had. He was one of the most noble and dignified people I have ever met, yet he was warm-hearted . . . it was only because I felt him to be a friend that I agreed to act as his trustee."

"For no other reason would I tell you, unless it was going to frustrate his will."

He leans his head against his left hand. In a flat voice, he relates most of what happened, even including some of his own past.

"I read about that," says the solicitor, but doesn't make any other comment.

At the end, he picks up the will.

"There will be no trouble with this. The title will pass to you, after probate has been filed. You will then own 796 acres of pakihi and private sea beaches. The land itself is nearly worthless unless you care to develop it. If you spent a million dollars and half a century, for instance, you might make a farm out of it. But that is all its potential, overt value. . . ."

The words hang in the air.

He adds softly,

"Tiaki only said there was something of extraordinary value on the property that needed watching. I assume you know, and you are the new watcher?"

"If I can be," says Joe wearily, "if I can be."

. . .

He stays in a hotel overnight.

There is a short report in the paper of the old man's death. "Local Identity Dead" it says, and not very much more.

The body is buried in the morning.

It is raining, a fine misty drizzle, when the hearse arrives at the cemetery. He is surprised to see another car standing there.

The solicitor waits beside it. He doesn't say anything, just takes off his hat and follows the coffin that the undertaker's people carry. Joe, feeling out of place in his jacket and jeans, follows him. He carries the sugarsack with the old man's belongings in it, and the toetoe stalk in his right hand.

When the short service is finished, before the sexton fills in the hole, he lowers the sugarsack onto the coffin. The undertaker watches with astonishment, the solicitor, calmly. Joe kneels, and plants the tiri at the foot of the grave. It sways gently a minute, and stills.

The drizzle continues. The silver drops slide down the golden stalk.

That is all, Tiaki.

Sleep in peace, or find your way home.

. . .

The solicitor says,

"Stay with me and my wife tonight, please."

"Thank you," says Joe, smiling brittlely. "Do you often put up crims?"

"No. Only people I like and respect."

The dry hollow in Joe fills alarmingly fast with tears.

. . .

He talks a lot that night.

About the kaumatua. About Simon. About Kerewin. About the dream world, and the world of the dead. About legends and myths, and nine canoes, tatau pounamu, the possible new world, the impossible new world.

The solicitor and his wife seem stolid educated middleclass people, but they know what he talks about. They agree and sympathise and draw him out, until he is talked out. He goes to bed weary, but rested. He sleeps soundly and dreamlessly.

The solicitor says to his wife as they undress for bed,

"He is one hell of a man, but you'd never pick it just by looking at him. Like the old man, very like the old man . . . isn't it odd how it's worked out? Him arriving just before Tiaki died? And the old man meeting him in his need?"

His wife is a woman of much thought but few words.

"Ordained," she answers.

. . .

"Keep in touch," they say after breakfast.

"I will. Kia ora korua!" he says, and is gone.

. . .

Two things more to do, and then he can rest as long as he likes.

He buys what he needs, food and clothing, and a set of wood chisels. New bedding and a guitar.

Then he goes to the police-station.

"Gidday, you're looking a bit better," says the sergeant. "Everything okay now?"

"Yes thanks, more or less . . . but I'm wondering if you could help with something. The old man, you know Tiaki Mira?"

The sergeant nods.

"Well, he told me about this man," handing over the photograph,

"staying with him, and dying with him, but he said he never knew who he was."

The sergeant looks at it, pursing his lips.

"Can't say I do either . . . was he a criminal? Do you want us to check through the files or something?"

"I don't know . . . I thought maybe there was someone who should have the photo. Tiaki said he injected himself with drugs, and I thought, if he was a heroin addict or something, you might know him . . ." voice trailing away.

"Can I have a look?" says a constable, coming to their side. "O him," he says, after a cursory glance, "that's that hippy fella . . . before your time Dave, you wouldn't have known about him."

He says to Joe,

"He was called Timon Padraic MacDonnagh, I remember that, I'm Irish background myself. Spoke well, but a right layabout. He did cause quite a stir when he first came here, as there was a bit of a drug-scandal going on, and he was a registered heroin addict. Harmless enough though, just did himself in. Arrived from Auckland in ahh, late 1976. His wife and kid were killed in a car accident there . . . he had to report to us on a regular basis because he was more or less an illegal immigrant as well as the other business. I think the Ministry let him stay on for compassionate reasons, eh. He died at Mira's place about six months after he arrived anyway. I was one of the lot who brought the body out. Thin as a bloody rake he was . . . I felt sort of sorry for the bloke, you know, not having any reason to live, and killing himself by degrees."

"Yeah, I can understand," says Joe. "And his wife and child were both dead, eh?"

"Yeah. Auckland, as I said. I've got a good memory for things like that, though I say. . . ."

". . . though you say it yourself," says the sergeant grinning. Joe grins too.

Then he sighs,

"Well, that's one more mystery wrapped up . . . it's a pity I can't tell Tiaki. I was curious myself, too."

"Understandably," says the sergeant. "That old man had a lot of secrets you could be curious about . . . know what they call him here? The last of the cannibals. They reckoned he ate his grandmother in the old days. All I've heard of is that the old lady just disappeared and. . . ."

Joe grins again.

"Well, he was nice enough to me, and that's all I worried about. And he had plenty of chances to make me kai if he wanted."

The police laugh.

Forgive me, Tiaki. But if we keep talking this way, they
might get curious about some of your other secrets. Kill
it with a foolish joke. . . .

. . .

Outside the station, he looks at the photograph again. It had
been a slim chance, going on no more than the young man's colouring, and the pointed chin, and something about the eyes, an impossible chance . . . Ahh, forget it, Ngakau. What does it matter now?

. . .

He hired a truck to carry his gear to the track turnoff, but he
carted the gear in on his back. It took three trips. The new mattress
was worst. It kept slipping away from his one-handed grasp. By the
time all the stuff was packed away, he was exhausted.

He sat on the doorstep, propped against the frame, and watched
the stars come out, one by one by three by a hundred. The air was
still.

I'll stay here, he thought, until things make sense again. Until I'm
healed anyway. Until I know more about the pool, the mauri. Until
the title's mine, and I've set up some proper boundary markers.
Until, God help me! I know what to do.

The cry that came out of him was not intended to happen. It
burst out, while his mind listened amazed. And then he was caught
up in the streaming sound. It was full of grief, a lamentation without words.

When it stopped, there was silence.

Then the treefrogs begin their chirruping again: a cricket zitzits
close by: down by the river, a morepork calls.

Life goes on, Ngakau.
The weeping doesn't last forever.
Nor does the waiting.
You'll heal, man, back together again.

In the deep south, a shooting star blazes brightly, and is extin-
guished by the night.

III

The earthquake hit on Saturday morning, just before dawn.

He wakes a second before the first shock strikes, the air full of cavernous rumbling, and slides off the bed before the shaking starts.

It grows in intensity, becoming violent.

"Be still, o God be still," while the earth groans,

> Jesus the ground's gonna open right under here in a dirty great crack what are my rahui doing that noise is murder the mauri'll die

"stopit stopit STOPIT!!"

bellowing furiously, and over the earth moaning and the skriek of iron grating all round him, surprises himself by laughing loudly.

> Jesus, Ngakau! *This*'ll take heed of *you!?*

The tumult suddenly ceases. His heart pounds on in the preter-natural quiet.

> If this keeps going I'm not going to make it to any Christmas party . . .

Face on the hard dirt floor, waiting uneasily.

> If this is an allover one, she won't either. If she's still alive. . . .

The earth shudders again.

The window behind him splits with a ringing crack!—

Stillness.

Ready for it, sphincters clenched in all directions. Nothing happens.

> You might as well get back to bed, man. Damn cold here.

For all that, sweat is trickling down his face.

He stands up, his feet meeting the ground unsteadily, still ex-pecting it to jolt.

> Might as well stay up . . . it's getting light anyway.
> But Haimona honey, where are you? Kerewin, Kerewin, where are you?

He rakes away the soft ash and lays wads of fuchsia bark on the still-glowing coals. It smokes immediately. Twigs, larger pieces of driftwood, hunks of heartwood to top it off. . . .

> It's not that I haven't been thinking of you both . . . but it's been rearranging it. Not falsifying, but trying to see the whole thing as an outsider would.

His thought is as calm as his face. He fills the kettle, and dresses in front of the range.

> But I've done as much as I can with the past.
> I know my child was a gift, and that I loved him too hard, hated him too much. That I was ashamed of him. I wanted him as ordinarily complex and normally simple as one of Piri's rowdies. I resented his difference, and therefore, I tried to make him as tame and malleable as possible, so I could show myself, "You've made him what he is, even if you didn't breed him."
> And I loved and hated him for the way he remained himself, and still loved me despite it all.
> Now, the gift has been taken back, and I have only myself to blame. As I have only the memory left, of his love and his pain, his joy and badness and sadness, of four years, almost, of growing. That is that.

Another tremor.

He glances at the roof, the cracked window. The whare is creaking and shivering all round, but shows no signs of falling down yet.

> Soon as it's light, I'd better go and check what's happened up the gorge.

The kettle has started to sing.

He lays out a cup, and the ready made skim milk, and puts half a handful of tealeaves in the pot. There's a bread left and butter still in the safe. While eating:

> Kerewin . . . I was trying to make her fit my idea of what a friend, a partner was. I could see only the one way . . . whatever she thought she was, bend her to the idea that lovers are, marriage is, the only sanity. Don't

accept merely what she can offer, make her give and
take more . . . now I can see other possibilities, other
ways, and there is still a hope. . . .

The birds are starting to make a noise, but it isn't the gradual
growing chorus that normally wakes him. They're calling, Alarum!
Alarum!

All shook up with nests in the roots of trees he thinks, and giggles. But he loses the gaiety quickly.

The hope is still a hope while Kerewin lives, but if she has died, as
her note gloomily foretold, he has decided to stay here. Hermit and
recluse number three, the unsung guardian of a madwoman's dream.

Aie, Ngakau, little did the old lady know what she was
bringing you up for! But I can pray and play and carve
again . . . I've got the garden to take care of—if this
hasn't shaken it to bits—and my food to catch. Strange
old cold trails to follow.

He has begun a correspondence with several North Island elders
and two libraries, trying to find out, without giving too much information away, what one of the founding canoes could be buried here.
Whether there was any ancient lore concerning a pact with such a
nebulous entity as the mauri of Aotearoa and any tribe of the old
people. He goes into town each fortnight, staying overnight with
the solicitor and his wife. He buys food, checks his mail and writes
replies, says Hello to the pub at the edge of the town, and leaves it
quickly after a single beer each time. Somehow, it has got round
who he is and what he's done, and the incident is still fresh in people's minds. It is a relief to return to eyeless tongueless bush.

He sips his tea thoughtfully.

Next week is Christmas week, and he has still some final ar-
rangements to make for a sneaky happening he has set going. If
Kerewin doesn't turn up, he will look all kinds of fool, but if she
does . . . that might be a new beginning.

If the lady lives . . . look in the tea leaves, Ngakau, some
people say they tell you things. She used to play with
oracles . . . and the kaumatua had some tame demons or
something. Old karakia he mentioned to make stones
float, and find halfdead people cluttering up his beaches.

My beaches, now. Well, I don't have second sights or insights or even the uncanny sense Himi had ... music-hutches and lights around people:

shaking his head,

e tama, you were a strange one.

He stands abruptly. The day is growing bright.

Time to go round and check the damage.

He fills the thermos and takes an extra packet of cigarettes, and the last of the bread filled with cheese. It will take most of the day to go round his rahui.

I'll leave the gorge to last. If one of these neat little wriggles go off while I'm there ... aue! a nice career as a hermit ended by a few ton of stone.

There's still enough hope for that to have no appeal at all.

. . .

The land shows little damage. Some of the seaward bluffs have crumbled further, and there are several deep rifts by the river, too narrow for anyone to slip down them. All the rahui except one are standing.

When he carved them, he had thought of a person and put all that he felt about them into the work. He had erected them in places that reflected an aspect of each person. The kaumatua stood nearest the gorge. Wherahiko and Marama were close to one another, on the northern track. Luce was planted in the swamp, and other Tainuis bordered the road. Hana and Timote and Simon stand close to the whare, on the southern boundary. And at the western sea border, planted by herself in a place he loved to sit and watch the sea from, Kerewin had stood.

That rahui is angled drunkenly, nearly on the ground.

His heart pounds: "Aieee," flinging down the kete, and racing to prop it up.

You superstitious nga bush, that'll teach you to go thinking a person into a piece of wood, it doesn't mean anything, it doesn't mean anything,

gibbering and praying it didn't.

And all the while, the odd phrases of Kerewin's note pass through his mind:

> E Joe Ngakau, I'm in the lost country. And would you believe the crab has me in thrall? A deft pincer caused that alarm at Moerangi, remember the pale and gasping state? Medics chorus dividedly, but a friend in my soul whispers Death sweet Death, and that will probably be the way of it. But if I exist this coming Christ Mass, rejoin me at the Tower eh? O the groaning table of cheer ... speaking of tables, does commensalism appeal to you as an upright vertebrate? Common quarters wherein we circulate like corpuscles in one blood stream, joining (I won't say like clots) for food and drink and discussion and whatever else we feel like ... a way to keep unjoy at bay, like those last few weeks before they haled your corpus away. With no obligation on your part, I could provide a suitable shell. If, if ... I drivel. If you turn up for Christmas, maybe I do too. Then we see, right? In the mean mean time, thus think and drink tobacco. Piri says he'll pass on this to you. I'm stoned the noo. Kia koa koe.

No address, no date, no signature, the small box of cigars as an envelope, and nothing heard from her since.

A tumbled rahui means nothing, it was a random chance, an accident of the earthquake ... Sweet Lord, he thinks, why couldn't it have been Luce in the bog where the ground is naturally shaky? Going flat on his face in the slime, I couldn't give a damn for him, the two-faced stirrer, going to the police behind everyone's back. ...

He stamps the earth down hard round the re-erected pole.

The free-flowing spirals face the sea once more. He lays his hand on it a moment, and then sets off for the gorge.

. . .

The great overhang has gone.

There is a pale gash on the freshly exposed rock above the pool.

And the pool, the living green pool, is buried under a thousand tons of rubble.

He stands on the track, stunned.

> This is not real. It is nightmare country. It can't have happened.

He stumbles up the rock-strewn slope.

"No it isn't, no, not all dead, no please, please no please no," begging like a child in the end.

His arms outstretched, standing on the edge of ruin, *Why?*

And one part of his mind says sagely, It was all an old man's dreams and fancies, and there were explanations for what you saw and felt that have nothing to do with mysteries, and another part says Listen, and the sage bit goes on, It's just some rocks that have fallen in a rainwater well, and the other says Listen, and the wise bit over-rides it saying, You are a young man yet with plenty of things to do, you're whole and healed and flourishing, and you're released from any promise you gave; you've a future now, not an immurement in dank swamp country, and the other side says LISTEN!

"Just crickets and treefrogs," he says dully. "Just beetles and mothwings thrumming."

Here?

He's been here at night and in the day and there have been flies. Some flies. A few flies.

A morepork calls close by, and its mate answers from further up the gorge.

The early evening air is alive with noise.

His breath held until it's painful, he searches round the buried pool.

It's a hump in the dusk, a round, a disk, a thing the size he could hold in his two spread palms. Settled on a broken-backed rock, balanced on the crack as though it had grown there. It looks very black or very green, and from the piercing, the hole in the centre, light like a glow-worm, aboriginal light.

. . .

"You're cheerful, mate."

"Yep. Nice day and all eh?"

"Too right . . . pack go in the back?"

"You mind if I keep it in the cab? It can stay on my lap?"

The driver shrugs.

"Suit yourself, mate. There's room down by your feet. Shove her there."

"Right." Whistling merrily, propping his feet on the pack.

He had been afraid to touch it, but the drawing power of it was immense.

He had walked to it, sat by it, hands over it, hands on it.

It felt like stone, it was stone, finegrained cold stone . . . no tingling or warmth, nothing out of the ordinary, Ngakau.

The light is just phosphorescence, eh? but when he lifts the thing, he nearly falls.

He's tensed his muscles and pulled, and it's light light light, no weight at all.

And there's an ecstasy as he carries it, a live buoying stream of joy that makes him want to shout and sing and dance.

He can see streamers and fields of brightness round everything he looks at: the very weeds and stones at his feet coruscate with brilliant fire.

That's what Haimona meant by light? Aie!

Past the cave where the old woman's bones are entombed forever—he ran to look there, and the stone in his hands grew too heavy to carry. He took the hint and turned back onto the track.

Past the kaumatua's ruined garden, the miro tree uprooted, the careful lines of corn and other vegetables fallen in disarray.

Not to worry, man, this is someone else's place now. Not mine.

For sure as the light that lives steadily in the stone, he's going home.

"Where you going, mate?"

"Anywhere south," says Joe, his grin wide, "I'm taking the south road home."

11

The Boy By His Own

I

The night gives up its hold reluctantly, but slowly, very slowly, the world comes back.

Because he kept attempting to remove the useful tubes they inserted, they restrained his hands.

He was still after that, for over a week.

Lying in the dark, lying without moving, listening helplessly to the voices.

It doesn't seem that the night is giving ground.

No familiar touch, no handholding, no-one he knows.

There is never anybody he knows.

So he lies withdrawn again, his tied hands clenched to the deep of nails in despair.

But little by little, the night is lifting.

Instead of the shifting shattered brightness, he begins to see outlines. The light is shot through with forms. They crack and vanish and unexpectedly reappear; they splinter like a broken mirror when he blinks, but now, for seconds at a time, he can see the chair. The cabinet at the side. His feet. They look, somehow, cut off from his legs. He can see people again, briefly, as people, instead of dark cores in the centre of lightning oscillations.

He watches, his hope never quite dead, for them to enter.

In time, says his heart.

Wait, says his heart.

They'll come, says his heart.

They don't.

He weeps in the dead silence and he can't hear himself cry. It is only by the wet of tears that he knows it is real crying.

Yet the night is ebbing away.

The hated voice grows weaker, cannot sing as freely. The old fears seem impotent in the face of what has happened.

He shrinks from the impersonally gentle hands that feed and clean him, but he glimpses the faces now, and they smile.

He doesn't smile back.

One morning, he discovers his hands are free again. For minutes, he doesn't dare move them. But nothing happens. No-one comes in.

The hands feel strange; they've been restrained for so long they're apart from him, as though they belong to someone else.

He brings them in front of his face. He stares at them as long as he can without blinking.

There is a network of pink scars over them he hasn't seen before. Cuts? Glass? Windows? Binny . . . wait. With a new keen instinct for self-preservation, he stops thinking about the windows right then. He just stares at the scars, fresh and shiny and jagged.

There is a plastic bangle round his left arm.

He brings it close to his eyes, squinting to keep it in focus. There are letters of some kind or another. He doesn't know what they are.

I never had a bangle?

He spends the morning watching his hands, opening and closing his fingers, touching them together. Absorbed in rediscovery.

But he keeps them by his sides when someone finally comes in with food. He accepts the food passively, but instead of closing his eyes after seeing who the person is, he watches her as dedicatedly as he has been watching his hands. He discovers the longer he watches the steadier his vision becomes. The nurse smiles at him all the time, and speaks often. He can't hear what she says, and he can't tell what she is talking about from the way her lips move. They don't shape themselves in the shape of words. He is frowning with concentration at the end of lunch, and he still hasn't understood a word.

It's all silence.

During that afternoon, he sends his hands on forays round his body. By drawing up his legs, he learns that the two cut-off lines at his ankles are bandages, covering what feel like holes. Once he has felt his legs and feet with his hands, he can feel them again.

Which is very odd.

He realises he hasn't been conscious of his body for a long time. The half-moon marks in the palms of his hands where his nails had bitten in haven't hurt him at all until now.

The fingers explore on.

The label on the chain round his neck is gone.

His face feels strange, with lumps in the bone of his jaw.

His scalp is half-covered by padded bandaging. He can feel stiff bristles of very short hair. His fingers stay on the remains of his hair for minutes.

I dreamed of that. . . .

They move on, following the contours of the pads at the side of his head.

He can feel three things now; the itching of his scalp; the long scar lines under the pads; the band that holds them in place. It runs round his head. It covers his ears.

That's why I can't hear?

He snaps his fingers very close to his right ear. Nothing. Not a click, not the ghost of a click. Nor by his left ear . . . hold on, something like a very distant thud? It doesn't sound like the sharp click! he normally hears, but he can hear something. Or is it feel something?

By evening, he has wakened—it is as if he just climbed back into it again—all his body. Some of it is uncomfortable: his ankles ache, and there is a pain like a headache bothering him, and he's learned that if he breathes in deeply, both sides of his chest get something like cramp.

Joe kicked . . . stop it there.

Mostly however, it is very reassuring, a feeling like coming home. He no longer feels fuzzy, just puzzled and worried.

Where are they?

He has been here a long time. He knows, because all the cuts Joe dealt him have healed.

Weeks? Months? Years? If it was years you would have grown, Clare.

But do you grow when you're asleep?

. . .

Are they being kept out?

He tries to go back over the obscure days, but there is not enough in them to make sense. He cannot remember, he cannot remember . . . so he returns to the morning again, when he got up early and watched the sun rise. Find them in that day, bring them back . . . going through the day slowly (blanking quick that out that didn't happen not now) to Kerewin in the Tower . . . she turns away, shaking, so go on, on to the night-time, through the night-time, happening by happening.

He won't let it overwhelm him. He couldn't stop it before, the day happened again and again, inexorably, but now, but now. . . .

He reaches the doorframe again, and the hard hand pressing his hurt against it, and then his own slow drifting blow.

He can't see where it lands. He can only hear the man's high scream. It hits him near the waist . . . can you kill somebody hitting them with glass in the waist? Are they crippled?

His head hits the doorpost again.

Can you break ears?

. . .

He is whimpering uncontrollably when the nurse arrives, and shaking uncontrollably by the time the pediatrician gangles in. He can see enough to know they are exchanging mysterious words, and though he begs with one clasped hand, they don't know the sign and they can't read his eyes. The needle slides into his vein, and he can't do anything about the night closing over again.

. . .

But it's the last fling of horror, the final clawing grasp of the night.

. . .

Piri, who has come over the hill to see Marama:
(she is recovering valiantly, though worried sick she says by what has happened, and how are Ben and Luce behaving? Not fighting, tell them please no . . . and, o dear, look after Pa, take care of him for me, don't let him get upset and excited, and

"Course, Ma. Fine, Ma. No trouble, Ma. For goodness sake

stop worrying Ma, and get some rest, eh? What'll all these fellas," pointing in a swathe at the other three elderly ladies, all lacking visitors, so snoring with their mouths and ears wide open, "think of us?"

Marama retorts, What does it matter *what* they think? The whole world and her brother knows . . .) takes time before he goes back, to try yet again to see Simon.

The other times the doctors and staff have smiled blandly, and said he's as well as could be expected, off the seriously ill list, and progressing normally.

Which says fat bugger all, thinks Piri. We're still family, he tells himself stoutly. If I could be sure that shitarse would stay away, I'd ask for Himi. He's too good a kid to waste, however damaged he is . . . but if Joe comes back, ahh it'd never work. That mutt would always stick a finger in. Or his fist.

"Uhh hello," he says to the head nurse, avoiding her eyes, "would it be possible I see . . ." and before he gets any further the nurse gushes.

"O good, Mr Tainui isn't it? Would you come this way please? Doctor won't be a moment, and I know he'll be glad to see you."

Doctor?

What about Himi?

The nurse turns and beckons from further down the corridor. by the door at the end.

"Would you come in here now, Mr Tainui?" she says, her smile all teeth.

. . .

He expects distortion, disfigurement: maybe an inert and help-less log of a child.

What he gets is one astounded Simon.

O yeah: his hair is gone to a fine gold fuzz, and there's a set of godawful purple-red scars welting the side of his head, and those neat dark circles he'll produce on the slightest provocation ring his eyes, and make them look inhumanly large, and he's whiter than the sheet he's sitting on, and it looks like

(squeezing his eyes narrow and checking fast)

he's lost three more teeth—mouth hung open, eyes fixed on him.

Am I unwelcome? Or don't he know me now? his heart shrinks inside him.

One eye isn't tracking properly either, but damnall Haimona! do something! Don't just stay static like that,

and the child shrieks, flinging his arms wide open, and the bloke sitting by the bedside gets an ear full of fist.

One thing about having four kids: you know when you're wanted, needed hard.

. . .

After a while the hoha dies down. The doctor rubs his ear ruefully. Simon burrows in against Piri as though he'd like to get inside him, arms and legs wrapped round all he can reach. Piri murmurs to him, questions he isn't supposed to answer, endearments for his heart, "E taku hei piripiri, what you been doin? What they done to you, eh? Gentleheart, we miss you, you been feeling bad alone? Lonely, e tawhiri? Never mind, ease up now, Piri's here, Piri's here."

It takes a long time even for Piri's practised hands and voice to get him calm again, he is so hungry for the affection, the cuddling, Piri thinks.

> Well, I suppose all these fellas are kind enough, but they wouldn't have time to hold him and that . . . holy hell! What a room! Bare except for two sticks of furniture, no colour, no nothing for him . . . and why's he all by himself?
>
> Just as bloody well I called by.

The doctor's been silent all this while, just fingering the ear Simon clouted every now and then, and watching them with a detached sort of grin on his face.

"Come on e Himi, sit round now boy."

and stops, realising at last that the boy isn't responding to his voice, but to the movement of his hands.

"If you yell loudly, he'll pick up some of it," says the doctor softly. "He's got residual hearing in one ear."

"Ah Christ," says Piri. "Ah Christ, this isn't fair."

He doesn't yell: he catches Simon's eye and then asks him fingerfashion, You can't hear me? and the boy says No.

"Christ," says Piri again.

He takes a felt-tip out and writes on the back of his tobacco pack, I AM V. SORRY ABOUT THAT, LOVE, YOU WANT ANYTHING? and the boy snatches the pencil and box as though he's been starved of them.

Once he's got hold of them however, it takes him a minute to get them settled to write on, and longer to print the words. The printing is awkward and cramped and slow.

Piri says in a cold voice,

"When I get hold of my cousin, I'm gonna beat his head in and see how *he* likes it."

The other man doesn't comment, watching the child narrowly.

He says in his soft accented drawl,

"A week ago, he couldn't really write. Or read . . . two months ago, I would have said he'd never communicate in any way again. He's getting better very quickly, you know."

Piri, bitterly:

"Not long ago he could read and write better than my ten year old, and now look at him."

"Given enough time, and the right kind of care, he'll read and write as well as ever he did, I think."

"Yeah?" says Piri, with a world of doubt behind the sound. He looks down at the note Simon is holding for him.

JOE OK AND WHERE AND K PIRI HOW LONG I HERE CAN I COME HOME

"Don't worry if it's a bit scrambled," says the doctor. "He's getting there, but it takes him time."

The boy keeps his eyes fixed on Piri's face in a disconcerting unlevel stare.

Piri looks over it, over to the doctor.

"I can make it out, but it's not how he used to do it. And bloody hell, would you believe the first thing he asks is how that prick is?"

And while the doctor blinks over that, Piri writes swiftly,

JOE'S FINE. HE'S IN JAIL. I DON'T KNOW WHERE KERE-WIN IS. YOU BEEN IN HOSPITAL FOR TEN WEEKS, HIMI, AND YOU HAVE TO STAY IN A WHILE YET.

The boy reads it, and reads it, and reads it again, as though the words don't make sense, while Piri begs him in his heart not to ask any more questions.

These bastards haven't told him anything, and no way
am I going to be the one who breaks his heart. How can
I say he hasn't got a home any more? That Kerewin's
knocked down her Tower and apparently gone for
good? Or that my triple-dyed shit of a cousin isn't his
father any more?"

He avoids Simon's eyes then, too. He writes, GET BETTER
QUICK. I WILL COME BACK NEXT WEEK, ignores the fact
that the child is obviously loaded with more questions and implor-
ing him with his eyes to stay, and gives him a fast final hug.

It can be Lynn's turn next time, thinks Piri, this is killing me, watching the doctor handle Simon, reluctant and upset, back into bed.

He doesn't wave back when Piri waves him goodbye.

. . .

He keeps the tobacco packet for days.

He takes it a question and answer at a time, working them out
in his mind.

Joe okay?

Yeah, writes Piri, Joe's fine.

That's good. I didn't hurt him then. He's fine.

That's not why he can't come.

Where's Joe?

In jail, Piri's reply . . . but why's Joe in jail? Was it the windows?
Did he get the blame because I was in here? I hope not, he'll be
wilder than hell. But why else?

That is why he can't come though. . . . Jail, he means jail, ah yes,
penitentiary. Aside from the penitential part, says Kerewin, floating
out the door and going down the Tower stairs . . . where would she
be but at the tower? Piri knows, he's been there.

But where's Kerewin?

I don't know where Kerewin is, writes Piri. Which means she
must have gone away.

Why has she gone away? Because Joe's in jail, and I'm here?

And I've been in here how long?

Ten weeks. Ten weeks! That's a hell of a long time.

And I can't come home because Joe's in jail, and Kerewin's gone
away because he's in jail and I'm here.

It starts to tie itself in knots, the question and answer way. But the crux of it is,

You'll have to stay here a while yet, Himi.

How long's a while yet?

For days he asks it, writing on the pad they gave him (it isn't paper, but a square of plastic with a transparent sheet on top. You can write on it with your nail if there's nothing else, and when you lift the transparency, the words vanish.)

WHEN AM I GOING HOME? SP to all and sundry.

"You're writing very well today, Simon," and the male nurse hurries away.

WHEN DO I GO HOME? SP

"When you're better, dear, I expect." The wardsmaid smiles, and goes out, shutting the door on him.

WHEN DO I GO HOME? SP

"As soon as you're walking properly, we'll be thinking about that . . . excuse me, Nurse Campbell, would we have . . ." the pediatrician called Fayden lowers his voice and he can't hear any more.

WHEN DO I GO HOME? SP

"I don't know, Himi, only the doctors can say that," Lynn shakes her head and smiles and cries at the same time. "Your hair's growing nice . . . you like those grapes eh?"

Chatter chatter chatter and say *nothing*. It's her third visit, and her last one, because they're taking Marama home this weekend.

> ("Don't tell him we won't be seeing him again . . . Jesus!"
> he says explosively, "I'd rather see him with Joe again
> than stuck in a home. He'll *rot* there."
> "I still don't see why they won't let us have him. . . ."
> "Because we haven't got much money and we're Maori
> and we're not *really* relations and we got four kids already
> and another one on the way . . . ahh Lynnie, don't cry, I
> didn't mean it like that," Piri trying his consoling best.)

WHEN DO I GO HOME? SP

"Come off it, young man. This is getting past a joke."

Ploy number two: if they won't answer you, don't answer them properly until they do.

So, seven times the audiologist has asked, "Do you hear that?"

and each time he has handed back the pad with the same question on it, a bland expression on his face.

The man is red in the face, and saying things under his breath.

Simon watches the muttering with interest. As well as getting to hear quite a lot with the help of the amplifiers he wears, he's got fairly good at lipreading.

"You're well on the way to becoming a first class bloody nuisance," says the head nurse of the children's ward the next day.

He's been showing an interested group of ambulant children how far you can piss if you really set your mind to it i.e. right down the stairwell. He doesn't look apologetic.

He writes, WHEN DO I GO HOME? SP (Plot three: be a nark.)

"As soon as I can arrange it if you keep on behaving like this!" she snaps, and is instantly aware that that was the wrong thing to say. There is a demoniac glint in the crooked green eyes.

Now there's nothing else for it, she thinks, or God knows what he'll be up to next.

"I think you'd better come into my office a minute, Simon. I have something very important to tell you." She holds out her hand.

He ignores it, but follows her, heart beating hard.

It had dawned on him days ago that They didn't have any intention of sending him home. And the suspicion has been steadily growing ever since Piri and Lynn stopped coming, that They don't want him to have anything more to do with the people he knows. Both things would have broken him before, but today's child is way harder than the gullible soft-hearted Clare of four months back, he thinks.

They stare at one another.

The woman:

It should be Fayden doing this, he can handle you . . . why do I always feel uneasy? Your appearance? Thin so your bones show, eyes vividly alive now despite the bruised-looking sockets, hair regrown to a spiky aureole concealing all the damage except for that crooked face . . . you don't look child-like, more a shrunken bitter adult . . . or is it the way you move, that lurch, a drunken sort of scuttle when you want to get out of our way? Or the way you refuse to accept us? You're a cool arrogant bandit of a child; you don't owe us obedience and you show it hourly, by the minute if you can . . . and Fayden jokes about it, eggs you on . . . can't he see you need a good stable place to grow up in, a place of kind authority, a normal background at last? Can't he understand as we do, that "home" means, "When am I better?"—not really going back to that, that ghoul. . . .

Simon keeps his mind blank. He just stares at her.

She takes a deep breath.

I know we're right, and Fayden's wrong.

She checks that the door is shut, and switches on the Don't Disturb sign. She pitches her voice more loudly than normal.

She explains, using simple terms, why Joe was sent to jail, what custody is, why he has been removed from Joe's custody.

"He was never really your father, you know, it was never properly finished, you see?"

She explains what a handicap is, what multi-handicapped means, what normal means.

"So you'll need very special care and teaching so you can, when you're grown up, fit in with all the other people. You see that, don't you?"

No response.

He stands unmoving, one hand steadying himself against the wall. His face is absolutely still.

She explains why, in short, they'll be sending him away soon, to a very nice home and school where there will be kind and understanding people who will love him for himself, take good care of him, and teach him all,

"Simon, you can hear me?"

His eyes are fixed on her face.

He hasn't shown any reaction whatsoever. Except, queerly, his eyes have become darker.

Pupil enlargement of course . . . but where's the green gone to?

"Simon?" standing up, "Simon? Are you all right? Simon?"

Her voice is coming from the far dark distance, and sounds like a cry for help.

. . .

They can't do this to me.
And he knew they could.

• • •

He had endured it all. Whatever they did to him, and however long it was going to take, he could endure it. Provided, at the end, he went home.

And home is Joe, Joe of the hard hands but sweet love. Joe who can comfort, Joe who takes care. The strong man, the man who cries with him. And home has become Kerewin, Kerewin the distant who is so close. The woman who is wise, who doesn't tell him lies. The strong woman, the woman of the sea and the fire.

And if he can't go home, he might as well not be. They might as well not be, because they only make sense together. He knew that in the beginning with an elation beyond anything he had ever felt. He has worked at keeping them together whatever the cost. He doesn't know the words for what they are. Not family, not whanau . . . maybe there aren't words for us yet? (E nga iwi o nga iwi, whispers Joe; o my serendipitous elf, serendipitous self, whispers Kerewin, we are the waves of future chance) he shakes the voices out of his head. But we have to be together. If we are not, we are nothing. We are broken. We are nothing.

It is almost worse than the night.

Because now he can see nothing ahead, nothing at all.

• • •

He stopped communicating.

The pad would gather dust if it wasn't a hospital.

The male nurse said,

"He does exactly what you tell him to do as though he hadn't heard you, unless you tell him to answer. Then he doesn't hear you."

It was a wall he had built in one night, with consummate care, and there was only one entry point.

They didn't know it.

They tried cajolery. He could come and go as he pleased. He stayed in the single room he'd been put back into, stayed rocking on the bed.

They gave him something that'd been kept aside for months,

Kerewin's parcel of the things he'd looted. They watched when they gave it, hoping for a chink to show in the wall.

He sorted through the stuff mechanically, not hesitating over any of it.

Moneycowries in his pocket, paperclips on the table. The gadget in his pocket, the cigars on the table. The agate and the scented oil in his pocket, the felt-tips on the table. The chess-set jammed in his pocket, the ink-block on the table. The visiting cards slipped in beside, except for one, on the table.

He strung the turquoise ring on the small medallion's chain and hung it round his neck.

"Hey, do you like jewellery? (Remember his earring?)
I know, we'll get your earring, okay? (Get his earring.)"

He looks at his hands. He doesn't watch people's faces anymore. He knows what his eyes can give away.

"Hold on a minute . . . there we are? My, you look grand!
We'll get a mirror and then you can see how good it looks, eh?"

He avoids looking in the mirror. His earring could be a thousand miles away, instead of in the lobe of his ear again. So could everyone round him.

("Well, we tried," said the head nurse. "What next?")

They tried a form of simply bullying—anything to crack the facade. Like the physiotherapist saying, "Walk. Stop. Walk. Stop," about twenty times in a row. The child obeyed like a zombie soldier, and the only result was his footwork deteriorated to lurching.

The wall is seemingly a complete barrier. The male nurse was reduced, one afternoon, to shaking the wooden child. He stopped himself hurriedly.

There was nothing in Simon's downcast eyes, not even fear.

. . .

But there is a way in, and Fayden found it.

He's the pediatrician, recently graduated, an ebullient young foreigner not especially liked by the rest of the staff. He's inclined to wear peacock shirts under his uniform whites, and he whistles and sings and talks too much to the patients. For all his inexperience, he's apt to disagree with his colleagues in all departments over the way they handle the people they serve. "Man, they're peeople," he drawls, a dozen times a day, and "Peeeple Fayden" he's become.

At the last staff meeting on Simon, he says.

"Man, he loves that Gillayley, it's obvious what we do."

"Aw . . . come on. He's been scared into pathetic submission by him and—"

"Not from what I've heard. Those Tainui people said—"

"They're biased. Haven't you read the welfare reports? And our social worker's comments? We've agreed as a group that placement in a Hohepa home will provide the most advantageous start for—"

"I dissent."

"Your opinion is noted."

Nothing else for it now, he thinks. The afternoon before the boy leaves, he moves in.

"Hullo, you."

The room is too quiet. The child hasn't seen him. He's doing what he mainly does these days: legs drawn up and crossed at the ankles, arms wrapped round his knees, chin sunk on them, he rocks back and forth. His eyes are closed.

"Stop it eh, Simon."

The rocking into oblivion goes on.

He looks at the bedside table, and yeah, the kid's taken out his aids again. The ultimate go away. Each time before, they've waited until he puts them back, taking it as an encouraging sign he wants the world to include him sometimes.

But this time we gonna intrude. It's worth a try, man.

He sneaks over and lays a hand on the unsuspecting child's shoulders.

The boy jerks once, then holds himself rigidly still.

Fayden sits down on the chair, and holds out the three things he has in his hand.

The aids and Kerewin's card.

For a minute, nothing happens.

Then, slowly, the child takes the aids, and adjusts them in his ears.

He thinks I'm gonna bite him? Cautious and shaky and slower than a crippled snail. . . .

"You know I'm Doctor Fayden, right? Well, my real name is Sinclair, Sinclair Fayden,"

Sinclare? Clare? My name?

"so forget the doctor bit for a while, and think of me as a helpful fellow called Sinclair. Okay? I think I can be helpful . . . with your help. And this,"
tapping the little ivory card with a casual forefinger.

It's the magic word all right, the golden key, the open sesame.

The boy's unwinding from his unholy huddle. Propped by his elbows, head back, he stares up at the man as though it's the first time he's seen one.

It's strange how discomforting the askew green stare can be, but Sinclair grins it away.

"It's going to take some time to explain all this. It's about you, and your dad, and this lady, Kerewin Holmes, uh huh?"

Pause: wait for it: we get a Yes.

Sinclair mentally rubs his hands.

This ain't gonna be a disaster area after all.

"There's other people in it too, and there's places . . . what's up?"
But he's only turning over to pick up his pad.

By the ineffable name, I think he's finally gonna risk it, break that record and actually SMILE for the first time . . . not quite a smile, more like a twitch . . . nuts, nobody here to corroborate

(he's smiling franctically back).

QUESTIONS? scarred thumb jammed back to himself like it's a cocked trigger.

"You wanna ask me questions, boy? You ask all the questions you like, and I will answer them truthfully as I can. Cross my heart and hope to die," giving him the cross on the heart and chop across the throat, that the kids seem to take more seriously than the words themselves.

"You askin now?"

The boy shakes his finger, wriggling up to sit closer, still watching him intently.

Fuck, it's like someone threw a switch. He's a different child altogether.

> None of the brittle defiance, and none of this horrid apathetic docility we've been getting lately either. Alive again, naturalleee,

all the while he says aloud,

"Okay, anything you want to know more about, stop me and we'll talk. Now, I think I'm right when I say you want to go home, and home means your dad?"

He retreats before the avid hunger in the child's eyes.

"It means this lady Kerewin Holmes, too?"

It does, it does. He's shaking with Yes's, fingers and head.

Sinclair says blandly.

"I see. Well, y'know they're all convinced here that you've been scared and hurt too often to want to go back to your dad . . . what do you call him?"

JOE

"Makes sense. How do you . . . hey, d'you know what I was just gonna ask you? How do you say Joe's second name?" high giggling, and the boy, we didn't know about this, joins in with a strange throaty chuckle.

I CANT WRITE IT ASK PIRI

"Yeah, I'll do that . . . anyway, the other doctors and nurses think they're doin you a *big* favour sending you away. They haven't asked you about it, but they *know* they know best. So off you go to a Hohepa home," watching the child frown. "I found out that means Joseph . . . ironic, isn't it? Won't let you go to Joseph, but they'll send you . . . ahh, never mind," squeezing the thin shoulder gently. "You goin away tomorrow, you know that?"

He adds hastily,

"Hey, it'll be good, I hear they're *good* places, and everyone'll be sweet to you there . . . and if things work out the way I want them to, and you want them to, it'll be a holiday. You think of it as a holiday," damn, I've unleashed tears too early, he won't listen now,

"hey child, it won't be forever, I promise, I promise it, honey,"

rash bugger Sinclair, now how you gonna make that stick?

"Look," urgently, "I been talking to a lot of people, your teachers, the old lady Marama Tainui when she was here,"

ahh, goody, consternation.

A finger swivels in the air making a—was that a question mark? Gulps and sighs when I don't respond, and he takes up the pad—hell, he don't *like* writing things.

"I'm dumb, Simon, I'm thick, you be patient with me. You tell me your own, thanks," as the pad's shoved across nearly into him.

MARAMA SICK HERE?
"Hoowee, I let that out, and I shouldn't have done,"

liar man, you hoped he might get interested in some-thing other than his own trouble. The Tainuis said he was compassionate; rather, that Piri said he was a sucker for anyone else's woes.

Glancing down quickly,

but I'd better not keep you quiverin there too long.

"She was here, she's better now, but she was very sick. Sick as you were," brushing his hand lightly over the boy's ragged gold hair. "You know what a stroke is?"

Very puzzled look. Holy ghost, it's easy to talk with him . . . where'd Lachlan get this shit about him being a difficult kid to talk to *all* the time?

"Let's say it means a part of her broke inside. It happens some-times to old people . . . she's really all right now, you needn't worry for her. She was here for two months though, and when I found you were related, I went and talked some. She loves you, right?"

He gets the real McCoy this time, a full-fledged Simon smile. He grins back. Maan, just as well they're still your milk teeth. . . .

"You know what, chicken? You got a lovely smile, you want to indulge yourself more often," but it fades quickly.

> Well, I suppose he ain't got much to be happy about right now.

"Well, this Marama," becoming businesslike, "she had a lot to say about you and Joe. She knew you got hidings, but she said, 'I thought he just got a smack. Like all kids get a smack eh? Otherwise he would have showed it, nei?' You don't give too much away, you know that?"

The look he gets back is deadpan.

"She was very upset when she learned how you were hurt, but more upset that they've separated you. She kept saying, 'But Joe loves his boy, this was just an accident.' It don't look that way to other people though. Not to the police or the doctors . . . but they only get to hear the bad parts. I've been hearing all about the good parts. There were a lot of good parts, right?"

The fingers fan out and close and spread again and again and again.

Sinclair giggles.

"I get the message . . . millions. Simon, shift over would you, honey? This old chair's hard as a navvy's arse and it's cutting right through me. Thanks. That's another thing, can I borrow one of your cigars while I smoke it?" giving him the clown face he knows turns kids on, rolling eyes and looselip smile and eyebrows wagging Hey? hey?

The boy laughs and pats him on the shoulder. He kneels up and passes him a cigar from the discard pile.

"Ahh, that's good . . . settle down by me now," peeling the cigar and lighting it. He puffs it awhile in silence, then gives it to Simon saying, "Your head teacher told me you've got this bad habit of smoking, but as your personal physician I say you can smoke this once and it won't stunt your growth or nothing."

He curls his long limbs up on the bed, arm out for the child to pillow his head on.

> Right on, Sinclair man, you doin this your way and it's working, but you can guarantee those stiff-face cheeses won't understand one bit of it if they come in at the wrong time. They'll foul it up and *how* they can foul it up. A bit of time—give me that and I'll have him started the right way.

Between sharing the cigar, he tells the boy who he has talked to, and what they said, and how he built up a picture of the situation gradually. "I don't do nothing in a hurry, child," chuckling, "nor something either." It's a much different picture to the one the Social Welfare and other medical people hold.

"I think you'll do better all ways back home with your own folk. There'll be enough of them looking out for you now everything's come bang into the open. I don't think nobody'll let it happen again. And to make that sure, I aim to find out whether this Kerewin'll take responsibility for you, while Joe gets access."

The two solicitors had been dubious about that. "Possible," they'd said, "but very unlikely unless the bloke has had a complete change of heart and lifestyle."

Sinclair smiles to the boy,

"From what I hear, the access part shouldn't be a problem far as you and Kerewin are concerned, right?"

Agreement.

The child is relaxed and interested. Even when he starts coughing on the smoke, he attempts to keep his eyes on Sinclair's face.

"Easy now, I'd better finish that off . . . well, you got all that part? Right, here's where I need your help. It'll have to be surreptitious, sneaky you know? You won't have to let *any* of them know Sinclair put you up to this, you keep a still tongue in your head?" broad smile taking the edge off that.

Course, mouths Simon, and the man blinks.

"What you *say?*" tipping the boy's face gently round towards him. "You say course?"

"Wow," says Sinclair, "you put a mite more air behind that word, any word, and one of these days you gonna surprise yourself and talk right out loud," though he's swallowing now like he's going to be sick at any moment. Cigar? "Speaking of air, boy, you think some fresh stuff be a good idea?"

The NO is so emphatic it surprises him.

K SMOKES THIS.

"And you've missed the smell, huh?" Sinclair shakes his head. "I'm looking forward to meeting this lady. How'd you call her? Unique? Speaking of meeting her," taking a cagy sideways look through the blue screen of smoke, "you know where she is?"

Obviously no. And he's fighting tears again, while he writes
TOWER? MORANGI? and losing by the time he's finished.

"Ah c'mon Simon honey, don't break your heart . . . Morangi?
Nobody's suggested *there*. Where is it, north or south? I'll try
and find her, I really will because I been looking allover already,
truly now,"
watching tears trickle down into the gutter of the child's smile.

"Fuck me, why can't they *see* you're missing your home so
much?"

> Calm down man, everything works for the best . . . made
> an impression on Greeneyes here though. That smile is
> rueful and knowing and about two hundred years old.
> Who's the child?

He leans over and kisses the boy quickly and tenderly, and then
sits up.

"Look Simon P Gillayley, I'll work on things from my end, but
you'll have to be doin something too."

> You'll get hung, man, this ever comes out . . . inciting
> rebellion and riot in minors, shithot!

"It's like this. If you settle down and get happy in this place
they're sending you tomorrow, that's fine, it makes everyone happy,
they were right, you see?"

He says Yes like an ancient, still crying noiselessly.

"But if you show you aren't happy—and I don't know *how* you
goin to do that, everyone will start to see they've made a mistake,
okay?"

Standing, looking down at him stranded on the bed.

"So don't hold everything in, honey. Don't behave like you've
been doin here, all quiet and good and do as you're bid. If you stay
biddable, they goin to ignore you, right? They'll think you're happy,
right?"

The odd eyes hood. The boy gathers himself up, and curls round
his pad as he writes. He holds the note out to Sinclair, sitting still,
one shoulder hunched higher than the other, head angled against it,
staring at the man.

His eyes might be washed by tears but they're hard and bright,
the pupils retracted to points, emphasising the glittering sea-colour.

I WAS NOT GOING TO BE GOOD. I WAS GOING
AWAY.

Sinclair laughs, his black eyes full of fire.

"Great souls suffer in silence, and us great minds think alike?
Simon child, they don't know what they've taken on!"

Right, thinks Simon, right.

II

"The one that smells like a two-bit whore? The one with the
hippy jewellery? Brother, you've got to be kidding!"

Brother Kennan leaned back in his chair.

This isn't a good idea at all, he thought tiredly. Who else can we
ask though?

He said in a mild voice,

"I don't know about the whore part, but yes, he's the child who
wears the earring and the necklace. He does use scent, but it has
some meaning for him we haven't been able to find out. It is not
because he is particularly effeminate."

The other man snorts. He still looks affronted.

What had Brother Antony said? "Pat O'Donaghue," the brother
has a rich Irish brogue, and the congenial syllables fairly melted
from his mouth, "he's oh, a shortback&sides man I suppose. But a
good man, now, a good man. A sergeant in the North Africa and
Italian campaigns, rugby player once, now a referee. A father of
seven, all good children and most of 'em married, but always room
in his heart, God bless him, for a foster child or two. Pillar of the
local church," says Brother Antony, "Holy Name society, parish
council, Legion of Mary, and good for a tithe of whatever he
earns."

Not the sort of person I would pick myself for this child, thinks
Brother Keenan, but who else, who else?

The other man is saying,

"Beats me how you let him get round like that. I mean, you could
take it off him."

"What? Scent, or jewellery?"

"All of it! Struth, he looks a proper little queer, untidy hair and
scruffy jeans and all that muck on him."

Brother Keenan presses his fingertips together, and looks at them fixedly.

"I mean, there's all the kids in uniform and looking smart and healthy, and there's *him* . . . and you expect. . . ."

"We don't expect anything of course, Mr O'Donaghue. Brother Antony thought," emphasis, "thought you might be able to help."

He lets the chair rock forward.

"You see, it's not a case of letting him go round, or taking his things away from him, or making him wear what the other boys wear. It's a case of giving him enough love and security for him to realise that he doesn't have to behave outrageously for people to notice him. We don't think we can give him that. That's why we are looking for a suitable foster home."

The other man nods.

"You know a lot of our children are disturbed. You've looked after some of them yourself," another nod, "so you can appreciate that disturbed behaviour takes all kinds of forms. This child insists on carrying as much of his past around with him as he can lay hold of, at all times. In a self-destructive fashion, he invites our criticism, our disapproval. It reassures him that we notice him, even if only in a punitive way."

He leans the chair back again.

"When he came to us from the Masterton Hohepa home, we knew he would be a difficult child to look after, and to place."

He reaches into a drawer, and takes out a file.

"He was sent to Masterton from Christchurch hospital in October. He ran away the second day after he arrived. He didn't get very far on that occasion—he has difficulty in walking distances— but one week afterwards, he was picked up twenty miles out of town. He'd apparently hitched a ride. During the next three weeks, he set fire to a garden shed, provoked several fights with other members of the Hohepa household, destroyed quite an amount of their play equipment, and absconded a total of seven times. On the last occasion, he was picked up on the Picton ferry, and nobody knows how he got that far, or how he got on it. He's an uncommonly resourceful child—in what he thinks are his interests. But the Hohepa people, understandably, can't appreciate that kind of resourcefulness. They have the rest of their people to consider, so they gave up. The Social Welfare sent him to us."

"Sounds a charming sort of a boy."

Brother Keenan looks at him. "Curiously, he is. Or can be, on occasion. However, he is totally uncontrollable."

"An uncontrollable seven year old? Aw, come on Brother!"

"This is a seven year old who is very different to any other seven year old I have ever encountered. And I have been involved with children in church organisations for nearly thirty years. I have seen a great many seven year olds."

"But there must be dozens of ways you could put a bit of pressure on him, to make him toe the line. For his own good, he needs to have a bit of. . . ."

"May I tell you what has happened since he's arrived here? So you will be completely in the picture, and can make a wise decision?"

"Oh sure, Brother. Fire ahead."

"He's been here a month, yes, arrived November the fifth. He was wearing the shirt and jeans and jacket and gear you've seen him in. As always, we removed those and gave him one of our uniforms. He didn't protest at first. But the following day, he simply took off all the new clothes, and refused to wear them. We explained, we cajoled, we even threatened—to no avail. We thought, he needs a little time to settle in, and after that he'll accept the uniform quite happily when he sees he is differently dressed from everyone else. He is quite happy to be differently dressed from everyone else, however. He still refuses to wear any clothes other than the ones he arrived in. When they're being washed, he wears nothing. And if they look a little scruffy," peering at the man opposite him, "it's because they're apparently the clothes he was admitted to hospital in, or was given there, and he's been wearing them ever since. We attempted to trim his hair. He tried and nearly succeeded, in stabbing Brother Antony with the scissors, and when held, screamed himself rapidly into hysteria. We haven't tried to cut his hair again."

"Aw, but good heavens, what's a bit of an uproar when—"

Brother Keenan interrupts,

"You haven't seen or heard him scream." He adds drily, "It's quite a performance."

He scans the file pages. "Now, what's next? O yes. November 11th: disappeared. Brought back by the police from Christchurch railway station. November 12th: disappeared. Picked up by the local policeman at Otira from the Coast railcar. November 25th: disappeared. Returned from Whangaroa railway station, once again by the police. We were reduced to threatening him with corporal punishment the second time. The third time, he was strapped. He laughed. It upset Brother Antony, rather."

"A bit harder, and he wouldn't have laughed."

Brother Keenan presses his fingers together again. Sacred Heart of Jesus, teach me compassion for all Thy people. He says after a moment,

"It is very difficult to have to hit a child at all. To hit a child who is literally covered in scars from previous whippings is distasteful in the extreme. That kind of punishment doesn't seem to bother him, however. As far as we know, no punishment bothers him. There isn't very much you can threaten or entice a child with, who is impervious to peer group pressure, who simply refuses to write lines, who regards being detained in a solitary bedroom as pleas- ant relaxation, and who thinks any of the special treats we have to offer, very boring. Therefore, their curtailment is quite, quite immaterial."

"Mmmm, yeah. . . ."

"We could, I suppose, if we merely wanted to make him con- form to our standards, be brutal to him. Take away all his small treasures, insist he does as he's told, and order things in such a man- ner that he's obliged to. Starve him, or beat him, or something dis- gusting like that," says Brother Keenan wearily. "But we are here to help him. He simply doesn't want to be helped by us. He ignores the psychologist. I understand he actually goes to sleep during school classes. He will not participate in any game or recreation. He has cold-shouldered all attempts by boys and staff to make friends with him. He has no interest in church activities. He has no interest in anything whatsoever, except returning to his home."

"I don't want to seem rude, Brother, but if he's as uncooperative as all that, why not let him?"

"For one thing, he is now a ward of the State. For another, there is no home for him to return to. His former foster parent has van- ished, and has sold the house where he and the child used to live. I have told him this, several times. He does not believe me, and like everything else, you can not make him do anything, even be- lieve the truth."

"Why not show him it?"

"Pardon?"

"Let him go all the way home to . . . where is it? Whangaroa? and find out for himself. That'd probably bring him back to his senses."

Brother Keenan, saying it quite gently, admonishes, "It would probably drive him out of them entirely."

The big man opposite coughs.

"Oh. Well. Ah, I see it's a bit more complicated than I thought."

"Yes," says Brother Keenan, and thinks that maybe this time hasn't been wasted after all.

"Well, d'you want me to take him home, and show him a bit of real family life?"

"Brother Antony says you have an enviable record in dealing with children from this home, and a particular understanding when it comes to disturbed children." He thinks, I still have my doubts, but who else is there, Lord?

"Yeah, well," Pat O'Donaghue is saying, "there was Felix, and Julian, Mata, I suppose you could call them all a bit round the twist. Bedwetters, destructive, rowdy, liars, that sort of thing. But they're all great kids now. Me and Ann can handle that sort of thing. We're used to kids, disturbed ones and all, and we love them."

"Well, Mr O'Donaghue, this child is certainly in dire need of genuine love and care. You know I am a newcomer to this parish and this home. I think in this instance, I will rely on Brother Antony's judgement, and ask you formally whether you are willing to look after the boy for a trial period, with a view to placing him with you permanently as a foster-son."

"Yeah Brother, that'll be great . . . there's always room for someone who needs it at us O'Donaghues, and this kid, like you say, sounds like he needs it. We'll take good care and I'll bet in a few months, you won't recognise him, he'll be so much changed for the better."

"I hope so," says Brother Keenan.

> Indeed, I pray so . . . dear Father, I commend the child
> especially to Your care,

pressing the button on his desk,

it is time he was looked after as he deserves.

"O, Brother Michael, would you find Simon Gillayley and ask him to come to my office? On second thoughts, would you bring him yourself?"

"Of course, Brother."

They wait for quite a long time.

III

One step, two step, three step, four, walking down the sandy track, transistor turned up full bore and pressed against his ear.

Keep on goin Clare, you nearly home.

It has been a long two days, and a very long walk, and he is so tired he can't see or walk straight any more.

But I'm nearly there. So what if no-one came for me, I have come home by myself. Shrugging off the pain again, no-one came.

He had a vague feeling you got ill-treated in some fashion in jail. He's thought that Joe might've gone to Moerangi afterward, to get over it. That Kerewin might've gone with him, and they'd had to stay for a while. Which is why they never came.

It had been a considerable shock to find other people in his home at Pacific Street. Warily wise now, he had checked the station platform before getting off the train. No police standing ready. This time.

He had slipped off the train and gone home the back way, by the wharves. It was early evening, fine and mild, which was just as well. His shirt was cotton, and the denim jacket Sinclair had given him wasn't all that warm.

There was nobody in the street except some children, stranger children, playing outside his gate. He walked up the path, his tiredness dropping from him with each step.

Shall I go straight in? Or knock and wait?

Knock and wait would be the better surprise . . . e, imagine his face!

The door opened.

"Yeah? Waddya want?"

The woman stood looking down at him angrily. "You been playin with my kids?" he's backing off the frontdoor step, eyes staring, his heart almost stopped, "You tell 'em their father's coming home any minute now and they'd better get inside and quick about it."

He's back down the path, faltering.

He said, he said. . . .

The brother's soft voice, and his worried eyes, and his tightened lips above the choke of his collar.

What do I do? What do I do now?

The night was growing darker, colder. He watched the house from the other side of the road, and the man who went in the door wasn't Joe.

What the hell can I do now? Where is he, why'd he leave me behind?

And suddenly he had enough anger to walk away, not knowing where to go, but needing to leave the house with its children and baleful woman and sad-looking man behind.

He *said* he'd gone away, he *said* . . . but he can't have, he wouldn't go and not take me, he wouldn't,

and it comes as sudden and fiery as lightning,

Of course! He's gone to live with Kerewin!

Hugging himself and weak with the relief of it all,

Jesus you stupid Clare, I knew it was lies all the time . . . why didn't you think before? You could've been home now, instead of stuck in the dark. I can't get there tonight.

His legs are shaking, and his head has begun to hurt again. He makes it as far as the park, just past the wharves. It is quiet and peopleless, only a weka scrabbling near the garden-shed. He used the shed as a hideout once before: the brass padlock on the door looks impressive, but nobody seems to realise the side window is always open, and big enough for him to get in by.

He climbs through the windows with difficulty, the hinges grating, and the weka squawks and scuttles into the night.

His last conscious thought, curled up on papersacks watching two moons loom glowing outside the window, was, Talk about me saying where I'm going, you gonna hear about *this*, e pa, for bloody weeks. . . .

. . .

He wakes very early, stiff and aching and as thirsty as he's ever been in his life. Looking blearily round the shed for something to ease him . . . nothing much here . . . there's a dufflebag hanging on the wall, and he climbs the bench to get it. And when he reaches it, sweating and unsteady, wonder of wonders it holds two oranges, a parka, and a small transistor radio.

Hey loot galore Gillayley! Slinging it over his shoulder, and clambering back down.

It takes him three goes to get out the window, but there's no one around outside.

He walks away as quickly as he can.

There's a mist about, sea fetch, breath of the sea, says Kerewin. It makes him feel safe, all the houses cloudy, the sky-height hidden, the lamp-posts obscure, a car going past with dim yellow headlights, as he goes walking through the town. He sees two people but neither take any notice of him.

It's still early morning when he arrives at the side road going past the Tainui farm.

Shall I visit? No way, I'll never make the Tower.

Another mile, plod, plod, and he reaches the turnoff. He knows it's a mile from Tainuis to the track, and three miles to the Tower to go.

The sun has wheeled round to be halfway up the sky and the covering mist has gone.

It's growing hot, he feels slack and faint, and his tongue is so dry he can't spit even.

Take a break, Claro. A fast break. A breakfast,

mentally groaning at that, but delighted by his wit. Words mean a lot more, these days. He wilts to the grass on the side of the track, spreading out the parka with shaking hands and lying down on it. He holds the oranges up in front of him to peel them. Any juice that dribbled could then be drunk. That was the theory. But it went down his neck and into unlickable regions like his eyes.

Damn and damn again.

The oranges are sweet and still juicy, even when he's finished mutilating them. And they're sticky. His fingers cling together when they're dry.

There isn't any water until just before the Tower, where the river comes out. So he scoots out onto the track, and rubs his hands with dust. The stickiness is absorbed. Indeed, if you rub your hands hard, it sort of peels off, dust and dried juice, in long spindrils. Interesting in a quiet sort of way.

He's so interested that he doesn't hear the car pull up behind him until a door slams.

He's jolted to his feet and running the other way into the bush before he has realised what he is doing. To get away before they catch him is now instinctive.

Someone's yelling, "Hey Simon! Stop!"

No way, crashing on through the broom and manuka until his feet betray him and he comes down hard. Not again, not again, not so close, pushing himself up. His heart is hammering, sight and sound drowned by its beating.

They're going to get me again

but as his vision and hearing clear, he realises there are no sounds of pursuit.

He can hear voices calling down the track, but no other noise.

He crouches down, listening as intently as he can.

The voices stop, the car doors slam: the engine starts. The car drives off.

Trust nobody. They'll be waiting again, Clare, someone will be hiding and waiting. . . .

The car noise dies away.

No other sound.

Just the flies, an occasional bird, his heart beat.

Carefully, he creeps forward, pausing after each step, waiting for sounds.

There are none.

He steps forward more confidently.
Still nothing.
Cautiously onto the track.
No-one.
Hugging himself with pure joy, Fooled you!

I'll get home now!

He is singing with delight.
They haven't touched the parka or the dufflebag. It's all there, just as he left it.

Talk about dumb, they can't even catch my gear,

packing the parka back in the bag, but keeping the transistor out. Music to march home by, one step two step, winding the volume up and walking steadily along the righthand rut to the Tower.
He's sagging before he's gone another mile.

It never used to be this long, I know it didn't.

One foot in front of the other, stumbling forward, counting the steps in his head. The music still pours into his ear, but he can't keep any kind of pace with it.

I will say hellos. I will give them all my love. And then
I am going to bed for a week.

The thought of bed and sleeping makes him tireder than ever. One step, two step, take it a step at a time.

This bend to go, and the next bend to go, and then there's the bridge, and over the bridge, there's the Tower.

Over the bridge, there's a ruin.
The music blares on.
He shakes his head, squinching his eyes shut and squinting when they're open.

It's my eyes again, it can't be like that.

Half the Tower seems to have fallen down.
He drives himself onward at a lurching run, over the bridge, over the dandelion studded lawn. The grass is long and snatches at his feet.

Up to the Tower door. Shut Tower door. Locked Tower door.

Standing there in the warm mid-December sunshine, both hands fastened on the great iron ring of the door handle, hands fastened as though they had melted there, transistor dropped and still shouting from the tall green grass.

A long time later, his hands drop numbly to his sides.

His bruised heart still beats, but he no longer cares.

Where? Where? Where have they gone? turning blindly away from the door and staggering as he goes, anywhere, nowhere, I don't care where, where have they gone?

The black burn scar reels past, black grass? no longer thinking just seeing, then his heel catches against something and he goes down backwards into the middle of ashes and cinders and small charred pieces of wood.

The world has burned and he is in the midst of desolation.

Lying in the ashes staring up at the wheeling sky. The black world round . . . why bother to sit up?

Because it looks like Kerewin by his feet.

Kerewin's head in the blackness at his feet. That is too terrible to endure looking at. He crouches, his eyes hidden,

> but touch it, touch it, even if she has been burned here,
> touch her. Let her know you came back.

And the head is cold and hard as stone beneath his searching fingers.

Gone beyond thinking, drawn forward by his hands, he kneels in front of the thing. There are shadows and voices coming towards him, from all sides over the lawn.

It is Kerewin, it is Joe, turning round the third face, aiee it is me, and even though he is moaning aloud, somewhere in the cloudy anguish a thready voice says, Together, all together, a message left for you, and he clasps it to his chest as hard as he can, and will never let it go.

Not even when the hands come down on his shoulders, and take him again.

12

The Woman at the
Wellspring of Death

S he travelled for weeks in an aimless way, all round the South
Island.

Uprooted again. Truly Kerewin te kaihau . . . but I seek
always for homes. I find, then I lose. And I'm not a trav-
eller at heart, just a casual gypsy wandering out from
my base and back. No more, because no base . . . and
nowhere to go, no-one to trust. No marae for beginning
or ending. No family to help and salve and save. No-one
no-one no-one at all.

She arrived in the town, smaller than a city, larger than a country stop, and sat at the bus-station, wondering what to do.

Stranded again, me soul. Dreary bloody place this looks
too.

She stood at last and gathered her guitar and suitcase in one
hand, the harpoonstick in the other, and walked to the heart of the
town. At the first hotel she came across, she entered and signed for
a room. Sitting on the immaculate bed, she stared at her oppressive
comforts and wished for a hand, to hold or be held by.

O for a voiceless pantomime . . . a celebrated fuckoff to
all this.
Wonder whether he's up and about? Or playing the
discreet vegetable still?

She took off her jacket and unbelted the knife from round her waist.

> I can't play pirates in the bar . . . Seafire, Troublemaker would be your better name . . . but I can hardly blame you for my shortcomings . . . and if I do, you may yet have the pleasure of slicing my sweet and tender blue veins. When the going gets too tough.

She polished the hook round her neck against her nose and shirt lapel for minutes (pale hair, dark hair, talking fingers, lovebent fingers) and then slid down to the bar and drank whisky until tea, and then drank whisky until the bar closed, and still as sober and clear-headed as when she started off, gloomed her way back to her room to contemplate emptiness again.

The whisky had one effect: she slept easily.

But only for a time. In the very early morning she woke, sweating and itching unbearably. Not only in the usual places, wrists and neck and hands, but also in hitherto pacific regions, centre of her back and the middle of each shoulder blade. She writhed and blamed it on the whisky, but secretly knew better. An old enemy had returned. One which was impossible to fight. Damn thee, itch of my own sick soul.

It was most persistent and unbearable on her hands. The joints and creases of each finger developed small spot-like sacs. Scratch them until they were torn, and your own skin and blood lined your nails, and the eczematous torture persisted. Then the soft bases of her wrists. Then the entire hand.

An old foe, this, thought beaten years ago. The antagonist of childhood, known in all its degrading forms of ambush and sabotage. She waged the old hopeless campaign. Cold water, and anything that hurt the itching areas into temporary passivity. Salt, or alcohol. Even ash.

She bought antihistamines as soon as a chemist opened, and spent the day feeling doped and sluggish, and especially, at war with herself.

And the knife-paining slid sharply into her stomach before the day died, and this time, it stayed.

After the first minutes, she found she could endure it, but felt if she moved suddenly it really would turn into a knife and cut the coils of her intestines to shreds.

Aiee, instant harakiri, sickly jokes, sweating, crying without sound, staying immobile all the long tense night,

But even in the anguish, the busy noisy part of her mind still analyses.

You have given up your home. Because the burden of uselessness became too much. Because the loneliness of being a stranger to everyone grows. Because knowledge of your selfishness has grown to be unendurable. Mentally, I am almost drowned. I'm not made for fighting this kind of battle. Spiritually, I still hope ... idiot Holmes, you are not charitable, you do not have the gracemeet of faith, faith in anything. Why hope? Because, because, I can do nothing else ... and you call yourself bright? Hah!

When the pain did knife in, despite her rigid stillness, she bit her lips bloody to stop from screaming.

God not here I can't.

It seared.

For dislocated minutes.

Suddenly ceased.

Shortly after, weak with relief that the knife had been withdrawn, she slept. The itch was in abeyance. As she sank wearily through a sea that seemed to have neither touch nor bottom, she collected the tears that slid down her cheeks and grinned in their salt embrace.

. . .

"Why do you want sleeping tablets?"

"Because I want to sleep eh."

The doctor smiles, a little superciliously.

"We can gather that, but what is preventing you from sleeping?"

"Nervous eczema," she flicks a scarred wrist briefly towards him, "annnd," she hesitates, but ahh what the hell, "stomach pain."

"Indigestion? Or, umm, heartburn?"

"Oath, no. I could clear those up fast. This feels like, well, like a knife might if you were being stabbed."

He seems surprised.

"Does it occur often?"

"It's happened twice before, but this time was too bad. I couldn't take it."

He notes something on a pad.

"Nothing unusual to eat or drink beforehand?"

"Nope."

"Are you, umm, entirely regular in your toilet habits? Any recent alteration in them, or discharge?"

"I never looked. I shit the same as I always have."

The doctor sniffs.

"Where does this pain occur precisely?"

She pointed.

"Would you lift your clothes a little?"

Denim jacket, sharkskin jerkin bedecked with fringes, silk shirt, mushroom white Holmes type skin. . . .

He palpated the area with his fingers. They are soft and cold and dry.

He frowns.

"You haven't had a blow to the stomach recently?"

"Nope."

"You have noticed the swelling and hardness there?"

"Yep."

He asks, full of non-professional curiosity, "Well, why didn't you ask me about it first? It's the real reason for your visit, isn't it?"

"It isn't. I came because I needed something to help me sleep. Whisky gets to be too hard on the liver. That, that swelling is a matter about which I am entirely incurious."

"When it causes you substantial distress? Come, come. I think we'd better have some tests done right away."

"I think we won't," says Kerewin coldly. "I said I wasn't interested."

The doctor puts his pen down, and polishes his glasses slowly.

"I think," he says, searching for gentleness, "that this may be rather more serious than you imagine. I think it would be better if we found out what the swelling was, and why it is causing you pain."

He has found a certain professional gentleness, speaking to her as though she were an excited idiot child.

She takes the same tone for her answer.

"I think I have a generously large imagination. I think I have covered all possibilities ranging from tumorous growth to invasion by
alien fungi. And as I said, it doesn't interest me further. I wish for
something to assist me to sleep. If you will also prescribe a strong
painkiller, I'll even manifest gratefulness. If you won't do either, I'll
stick to my whisky."

He says bluntly,

"It may be cancer. There is definitely an unusual growth there,
not an intestinal blockage. The sooner it is examined and removed,
the better your chance of survival."

"I am not interested. Ah, do you have difficulty understanding
English? I've said that three times."

He looks like he's going to froth at the mouth. "Do you know,"
speaking quickly and intensely, "have you any idea of what someone dying of cancer goes through? The agony they suffer? Do you
know—"

"You are getting beyond yourself, little medicine man," her voice
is controlled and gentle. "How do you know I want to live? What
say this is a nice neat no-questions-asked-after way of committing
suicide?"

His jaw hangs open.

There is a curious inevitability about the whole scene, as though
it were destined to be played out like this from the moment she arrived in town. It was remote, like watching someone else in a play.
It didn't feel real.

"Don't talk to me anymore," she says quietly. "Just write me a
prescription. After all, that's what most of you jokers do, most of
the time. Oblige me, continue the practice. In your code put, for
pain, and for sleeping when needed. And I'll say ta and go away
forever, okay?"

He had spoken more, passionately.

Kerewin had sat and looked at him with the same sort of expression she kept for viewing new varieties of spiders. He had finished
abruptly, flushing under her stare.

"It is your life," he had said.

And she made him an answer that surprised her as much as it
did the helpless medic.

"It was," she said.

But somewhere long ago it left me.

The promised joys were arid nothings.

The destiny was never proclaimed, and never fulfilled.

. . .

She was walking in the park. Park? Several dozen trees, all exotics, and neatly trimmed lawns. A forlorn pondshell, empty of water and children, filled with dead leaves.

The leaves were everywhere, in deep piles, brown and wilted. When she scuffled through them, they rustled sullenly as if the movement annoyed them.

Snarling leaves, eh Holmes? and threw back her head and surprised herself again, with laughter.

There was a bolete under a nearby beech. She squatted down and examined it carefully. The slightly viscid top was hole-free. Ah, no maggots have chanced upon this feast . . . she plucked it carefully, and held it in her cracked and weeping hands. The cap spread a royal nine inches. She felt in her pocket for a collecting bag, and fitted the bolete carefully in.

"I'll cook it in butter with herbs even," she whispered to herself, and as she stood, the two phials of pills clinked a merry requiem in her pocket.

. . .

FIRSTLY

"Is it possible to diagnose a condition without hospitalisation or intrusive tests?"

A brisk woman, as young or as old as Kerewin:

"In your case, not surely. I've made a tentative diagnosis, but without a biopsy or other explorative operation, I can not tell you definitely. The pain you describe, the weight loss and waning appetite, the site and form of the probable tumour, are all pointers, but there could be explanations other than carcinoma."

"Could similar symptoms be initiated by stress and mental discontent?"

The woman shrugs.

"I don't know. The way the human organism reacts to stress and anxiety is extremely variable."

"If I have stomach cancer, how long will it be before I die, given that I won't accept any form of treatment?"

"That is impossible to answer without knowledge of how far the disease has progressed. Even then, it is uncertain. You might live for a year and longer, or succumb within the month. It depends on many factors, not least your desire to live."

Kerewin smiles. The dark violet shadows under her eyes give a strange highlight to that smile.

"What is your objection to hospitalisation and treatment?" The doctor is curious but dispassionate.

"Primarily, that I forgo control over myself and my destiny. Secondly, medicine is in a queer state of ignorance. It knows a lot, enough to be aware that it is ignorant, but practitioners are loath to admit that ignorance to patients. And there is no holistic treatment. Doctor does not confer with religious who does not confer with dietician who does not confer with psychologist. And from what I can learn about cancer treatment, the attempted cure is often worse than the disease. . . ."

"What you are saying basically is that you have no trust in doctors or current medicine."

"Right on."

Her cigar smoke makes a silent barrier between them.

The specialist says coolly,

"Well, all I can do in that case is refer you to my colleague with a recommendation that he gives you what you have asked for."

"Thank you. That is more than I hoped for."

. . .

SECONDLY

"All right, I give you this and you go away, but there's one thing," he holds up his hands, "doesn't it strike you as selfish? I mean, who cleans up the mess afterwards?"

Kerewin is silent a moment.

He goes on, almost eagerly,

"You must have relations who have some good feelings for you, even if they're presently estranged as you say."

"I don't give a damn for my relations. They feel, I assure you, the same way about me. As to cleaning up the mess—I've left a written explanation with my lawyer as to why I chose not to receive med-ical care. My legal and financial affairs are in perfect order. Granted, removing a mouldering corpse isn't pleasant, but there is every chance I won't be found until I'm a nice clean skeleton."

"What about dying by yourself?"

"What about it? Everyone does. The company you keep at death is, of all things, most dependent on chance. I am outside my faith with no need of its ministrations. And I function best by myself."

He sighs.

"Okay, blunt words don't affect you and you make your points coherently. Would you consider this? How about living with my wife and me instead of going away to god knows where? She is trained as a nurse, and we're both sympathetic to your point of view. We'd leave you alone until you wanted our help. I mean, you never really know how you're going to feel dying until it happens . . . you might want a hand to hold after all."

"Thanks but no thanks. It's very kind of you to offer but," she hesitates before saying it,

"I vant to be alone."

He grins, "Okay. And you never signed this," holding out the slip for her to sign, "as far as the fuzz are concerned. It's just for my own files." He asks wistfully, "I don't suppose you'd be able to keep any kind of record as to how they help?"

"I'll do me everlivin' best . . . don't expect it to be too coherent, that's all. I'll leave any notes in an envelope for you."

He grimaces.

"Yes . . . if you change your mind, please let us know."

"Rightio," standing up, feeling nearly lighthearted now, "and as they say, hooray."

All that talk and time for this, a brown glass jar full of gelatinous capsules.

Extract of mushroom, potent hallucinogen, a painkiller of un-known strength.

Sweet weed, sweet wine, sweet taker-out of self, I have you all,
she sang to herself.

And now, begin.

. . .

THIRDLY

She left a lot of her gear in a commercial holdingplace, with
sealed instructions to be opened a year from now if she didn't come
back for them.

Into the aluminium-framed silk pack she gathers the basics for a
tilt against oncoming death.

The three books. Simon's rosary. The Ibanez in its travelling
case, with a spare set of silver strings. The hallucinogen. The
month's supply of smoke. A quart of whisky for a kickoff.

Painkillers of the orthodox kind, antihistamine, Vitamin E and
C and Laetrile in 1000 mg tablets.

A spare pair of jeans, another silk shirt, change of socks, under-
pants, leather gloves. Anorak. Very light very warm waterproof
down sleeping bag.

A billy and two messtins. Firelighters and small compact set of
cooking instruments.

A packet of coffee and a container of salt and some cooking oil.

The heaviest item is a drawing board with extendable legs. The
pocket at the back of it contains paper and brushes and felt-tips,
and two blocks of ink.

If and when I find a place to die in, I'll stock it.

Meantime, I roam again. Hai, Te Kaihau.

The pain is always present now.

. . .

FOURTHLY

An odd little set of thesaurisms kept running versewise through
her head:

> geegaw
> knicknack
> kicksure
> bric-a-brac

That's all the whole thing matters eh, as this snowflake world splinters and glistens. Gimcrack trumpery in gold and azure and scarlet and a glory silver . . . becasually nerthing is. . . .

. . .

Stink of last night's drink thick in her nostrils. Raw throated, and febrile clots of words still hanging everywhere . . . how did it go?

> *Little febrile clots of words*
> *that choir in earfuls*
> *humping off the page*

I declaimed to the sea awash in rainbows. . . .

The earth is wet, rained on, and the coffin smell trails out from roots and leaves.

"This," says Kerewin in a soft slurred voice, "s'll never do. Kidneys aching from the perversity of hard drinking and lying anywhere along the sandhills. And while for a sweet night me mushroom potion supplies peace, the unreeling mind ain't worth it."

She stood herself up and groaned.

It is a lonely stretch of beach. No eyes for miles. No people.

"I'm grateful, herr Gott, grateful."

She shrugged the twisted sleeping bag off her. It seemed a waste of time and effort to recall her wandering thought, and wash herself, and see about something to eat and drink, and excrete the last day's food.

She sat crosslegged awhile, hating the hard pressing growth in her suppliant stomach. In a little time, the day became a day. She washed in a rivulet, gasping at the chill of the water. Her breasts hang; her belly has developed new folds, and a horrid offcentre prominence. The trickle of water lipped it, as though reluctant to come closer. The fat cover she had sneered at, that lapped her body in protective covering, had vanished. The muscles of her arms were grotesquely exposed, while thighs and buttocks had thinned beyond recognition. As she contemplated the ruin of her body, she experienced an odd urging of protectiveness, a desire to renew it. There is only one of thee, and now nearly none. . . .

Sombrely, she drank a cup of coffee. The sullen smoke of her cooking fire trailed off to one side. Clasping the cup, still filled with this new feeling of pity for her body, she scans her hands.

For some time, they had been infected. When journeying through a town she hid them in gloves. Since it was the tail-end of winter, no-one commented.

Swollen, empurpled, leaking pus from every crack.

> In this disease
> part spiritual
> my hands are betrayed
> gross, flaccid
> decayed to illuse
> and all the silent
> tender strength
> they hold is
> in abeyance
> out of their reach.

She has a sudden desire to play her guitar. But two days ago, she had sent it to her family's home. No letter. Just the Ibanez.

Now the need to take the dark and pale between her arms, pear-wood surface and ebony underbody. The black neck fretted with silver. Recollection of the palace of shadows.

O God, even my guitar wore mourning.

. . .

FIFTHLY

I went away. Now, I am come.

The gorse is still yellow on the hill. The rich musty smell still drifts downwind. She had found new strength after deciding to come here. South into the high barren hills, the anchored remote land, the intense country of shades and storms and snows and sun . . . crystals and desert. The McKenzie country where the wind-swept hut belonging to her family still stood. Unused since the long-ago summer when three of them had searched for gold, the door was loose on its hinges, and the glass in the one window was cracked and coated with spiderwebs. The floor was rammed earth: she kicked the refuse on it outside. The fireplace under the massive chimney that formed the far wall, was marred by broken bottles and a dead mouse. She kicked them out too.

There were two bunks in the hut. The sacking on the top one had rotted: she tore it off and burned it as soon as the fireplace was cleared and laid.

On the shelf under the window, she set out her books and paper and art gear. She placed the drawing board on its legs at an angle that let it serve as easel and desk without further adjustment.

She hung the pack with her clothes on it at the end of the bunk.

By this time, her gift of new strength was fading. In a long effortful day, she hitched into the nearest town, and bought a new guitar, two crates of whisky, and three cartons of foodstuffs, salami and milkpowder and dried bananas and everything else the store had, that she could keep without a refrigerator. She travelled back as far as she could in a taxi, but it took six trips to transport it all to the hut.

As she looked at it piled on the floor, her hands trembling, her legs weak, the pain in her gut overwhelming, she fainted for the first time in her life. The last piece of visual consciousness showed the corner of a crate before she hit it.

. . .

A little thread of bright crawling awareness.

Then a slow weary return to light.

It had taken the night to arrange the hut. When she dragged herself to the bunk, a fire gleamed on the hearth, the cupboards were full, and there was water in the tank outside.

She slept the next day and night through. Woke still tired, full of tension ache, with a thick bruise on the side of her face to warn against going beyond her strength again. She washed, dressed, ate her mixtures slowly, drank little, and crawled to the doorway. There she soaked up the sun when it was fine, and watched the rain with detachment when it rained. So she had grown into a habit of days.

Joy of the worm is upon thee.

Most afternoons she would walk, not for pleasure but because she deemed it necessary. Past the boulder-riven stream. Past the triangular tussock that marked the halfway point. Past the gorsewoman, huddled and weeping with the wind's stroke. Limping, bent, weary to death, back home.

At evening, she lit the fire, and made the only cooked meal of her day. She would paint, or write as the mood took her, all the pain down. Notes for a mushroom dealer. And then, until the fire died, would strum the guitar, or pluck untunes, or simply hold it in weeping hands.

I am decaying piece by piece.

The skin of her face has gone taut and masklike. Lizardskin eyelids and scales that disguise the lines that meant laughter. And once, high and uncaring under the benefice of the mushrooms, she caught herself laughing at the way a bead of pus leaked from the bend in her wrist down her sloping forearm onto the guitar's strings. It shocked her momentarily, the whole stupid end. But then she had giggled again, not in despair or dismay, but because that was the only way it was, and always had been, except for the lucid luminous days when the paintings grew like music under her brushes, and it was apt and fitting to go this way, to end the stupidity, decaying piece by piece.

The nights were full of the musk of gorse.

. . .

SIXTHLY

It is calm outside tonight, no wind, frost, bright stars. I have lit the fire.

There is a constant rustling . . . moths, fluttering, flattening, giddying at the window. For now, we are uninhabited by Mothon, goblin spirit of drunkenness and bestiality.

A sober night, straitly joyful is looked forward to. For some deep mystery has decreed the momentary relaxation of battle. The canker is there, but not omnipresent. I no longer feel drained by its growth. Drawing breath for the next round? Maybe. And yet . . .

despite this truce, I am bothered. For all the calm stillness, a despair pulls at me from beyond the doorway. An alien despair.

It seems unfair that on this rare eve of peace, something other than my own revolting condition should interpose itself.

Try the guitar . . . I could get to love this badly varnished parody. For it gives me back music, music to match the images in my mind, to draw them out and make a realm of exultant leaping joy.

Something calls in the dark beyond and I must fret strings until I can answer it.

Let the door creak open. For this moment, I need the cold sweep of air over my skin.

There are trees, like dim stagmen on that shadowed hill, caught and frozen by the over-riding moon. The ground is uneasy under the frost. I feel it mourning. So back to the fire.

It's dying slowly. Whole areas of ash and then sudden blazing flare, one high arm of flame aloft, unfurled. A sap reservoir, amber and sizzling, that lasts for minutes of sparking fire.

A moth has come in.

Furry, and horned like a foreign owl.

> *E, silvergrey fleeting-feelered*
> *moth messenger of night,*
> *who cries out there?*

It leaves my finger and flies heavily away. It is a gravid female, plump banded body ripe with eggs, O lay my loverly, lay. . . .

I keep hearing someone walking.

The feet have a rustly echo echo that sounds about my dreaming . . . the moth brushes past and the tickle persists, itching my nose . . . there is no-one here, just feathered air. . . .

But who is it?

I can feel that despair out there, closer now, crouched and solitary. Let me in, it whimpers.

I am minded of that night in Whangaroa, at the pub with Joe, when that voice beat against my heartboards. I am minded of the child in his silent darkness.

But I can no longer share even my thoughts with them. I am too near my death.

And why must I be bothered by the ills of the world at this late time?

Ah berloody hell, pass me the whisky bottle, self, and down drown the whole berloody sickness.

Shitworld, I leave thee in thy chamber.

Without even prayers.

. . .

SEVENTHLY

For most of the third week, she lay unmoving in bed.

Reduced to unsteady crawling, she shitted outside, but only just.

Part blind, and the world growing dimmer daily, she no longer painted.

The dead fire stayed cold. She no longer ate.

She didn't endure pain any more either, but swallowed whisky and hallucinogen water that stood in the billy by her bunk.

"Every pig to its trough," huskily one daynight, before lapsing back into slurred horrifying confusions of dreams.

Something screamed.

> Simon stands, with strange crooked eyes. His lips are corroded with small slots of ulcers. A worm writhes out of his mouth. Hi! he gurgles, I'm clear. He dissolves into sanies.

Something screamed.

> Rich red ash on the ledge of the fire. There are bones under it. They begin to inch forward, wriggling like maggots. She prods them back, but there is a suffocating weight on her chest and she falls under it. She recognises the weight as a head, Joe's head, his black hair curling dreamily round the sawn bloody edge of his neck.

Something screams.

> Her family stand with bird spears, laughing and chattering, and poke at her in the pit. Fat bubbles break around her ears, cracking with rich shit voices that sneer You? You? You? She calls to her mother, her brothers, Help

me out! her sister, Give me a hand! but the bone tips of
the spears pierce as they push her under.

Something screams.

The seagull cry, the world wound.

> *God!*
> *It's not the gullcry that perturbs me*
> *but all the waves*
> *falling on the sand. . . .*

And in the quiet, the dream sea resounds like a wind, crying
round the hills.

. . .

EIGHTHLY

I feel obscurely wet.

It is very very cold.

That little toadstool over there, the one with the pale grey cap?
Look at the perfection of its gills . . . see? Delicate, shadowed,
full of subtle silent life . . . it tastes watery. In fact, it doesn't taste
damnall.

There are little pearls all over this grass!

More toadstools over there.

Come on, c'mon, no need to cram. They grow in circles, you can
get plenty if you crawl right limberly.

Somehow I can't get warm. I feel cold to my very bones.

But I haven't got bones now. They're fired, dissolved, earth to
earth again.

"But if I had bones mister, I did say *if*, what would they show in
the cold? The skeletal leftover . . . and she was rough flesh, blunt
and gentle and silver-refined. Above all, she was incredibly incur-
ably sense-able. To all modes, declensions, conduits and canticles
of feeling—she would never, could never, stop being conscious.
And thinking of herself. Her gift and her burden. Not bones."

"What do you love?"

"Seriously, my only lonely love, what do I love?"

(Dreamily smothering the drops of frozen pearls over her body.)

"Hey you! You really want to know?"

"Yes."

"What do I love?" musing on it.

"Very little. The earth. The stars. The sea. Cool classical guitar. Throbbing flamenco. Any colour under the sun or hidden deep in the breast of my mother Earth. Ah Papa my love, what joys do you yet conceal? And storms . . . and the thunderous breaking surf. And the farout silent waves . . . and o, dolphins and whales! The singing people, my sisters in the sea . . . and anything that displays gentle courage, steadfast love. The still brilliance of garnet, all wine, water of life and bread of heaven and grave shimmering moon. . . ."

"Yes. . . . can you stand?"

"Sure, anything. Whoops! Those pearl things are berloody slippery y'know."

Chanting,

"Rain jetting, whirl of gut, cut and shielding skin, let me in, let me in, o it's me, Kerewin. . . ."

Steady on her feet, bare arms spread, stopped in surprise,

"but not me alone. He's the bright sun in the eastern sky, and he's the moon's bridegroom at night, and me, I'm the link and life between them. We're chance we three, we're the beginning free."

She sighs.

"It don't make sense but it's the only sense, and o lady of the southern land, dear dear to me are my loves."

"Yes. That is good."

Of a sudden, crystal distilled clarity. A small dark person, all etched sharp. She blinks and it splinters.

"I can't see you any mind more." She murmurs it sleepily.

"You will."

"I have just discovered," says Kerewin. And fell.

Life is lonely.
Foe we all are,
one apart from the other.

. . .

There is a time, when passing through a light, that you walk in
your own shadow.

. . .

LASTLY

All fall down. But gone on up. A funny feeling. Light as a bal-
loon, light as a cloud. She raises herself easily on an elbow, floating
upright, and looks toward the fireplace, and there, poking through
the ashes, is a thin wiry person of indeterminate age.

Of indeterminate sex. Of indeterminate race.

Browned and lined, and swathed in layers of old blanket weathered and sundyed. Silver hair. Silver eyebrows. A massive burnscar
for half a face, with mouth and eyebrows wreaked and twisted by
pink keloid tissue.

Watery eyes. Snaggle teeth.

It says, coming over and bending in by the bunk,

"You can understand now?"

The whispery hoarse voice has no accent: a flat papery enuncia-
tion of words.

"Kkkik," says Kerewin, meaning Yes.

Her mouth and throat are webbed with mucus, strings of it,
thick and partly dried.

She swallows, but it isn't much better.

The odd head vanishes.

"It doesn't contain your, hur, additives."

She takes the proffered cup with a shaking hand. It takes seconds to steady her hand, more to bring the cup to her mouth. She
drinks deeply. A sour brew. Red currant juice? Here? After she
drains the cup she holds it out.

"Thank you."

Questions are swivelling round her like small green bats. She is
half-inclined to swat some of them.

"That's okay." It takes the cup carefully. "I'll be going now."

"Who are you though? I owe you sanity, if not life, I think."

"O, you'll live long enough," it answers. "And your mind would have straightened, you're lovestrong enough. I just cleaned up a bit." The snaggletooth grin. "My name wouldn't mean anything, now or later. You're an artist by the look of things. I saw your sketches. And your writings. So paint me down, write me down. That'll mean something."

It pulls the blanket wrappers closer, and glides towards the door.

"There isn't any debt of gratitude. I didn't really do anything."

It chuckles, a croupy bubbling wet-level version of its speaking voice.

"See you round," and vanishes into the misty outside.

She drifts back to lie down in the sleeping bag again.

Her body is a fined down version of itself, but itself alone.

The thing that had blocked her gut and sucked her vitality is gone.

A growing fire of joy flares through her as she sinks into sleep.

II

It's a dismaying face, encompassed in a pocket mirror. Thin and rigid under layers of peeling skin. Panning the mirror down, migod whatta sight. Wizened dirty skin.

The great muscles gather and stretch under my foul hide, feeling a way out. Slack belly . . . folds of flab, but better than deadly mounds . . . and breasts dangling, not in the natural aging curve though. All the fat flesh has melted and left bare gland in a flap of skin.

"A bit close to the skeletal for comfort, my soul."

And,

"Hell, this place stinks." Sniffing again. "Correction. I stink. Like an old fart or stale stale."

Away with the mirror and the horrid scrutiny, and arrange a spring clean. Even though it's getting on for summer.

. . .

Bless the dear little soul. As well as cleaning up the shit, it's filled the tank. And stop calling it 'it': yer got yer one great invention, remember Holmes? The neuter personal pronoun; ve/ver/vis, I am not his, vis/ve/ver, nor am I for her, ver/vis/ve, a pronoun for me, (slopping another tin of water out ready).

She boils the water and scrubs herself down while the stones heat,

> mess tin of hot to billy of cold, nice lukewarm blend to which we added schloop, a dash of disinfectant and generous amounts of soap.

By the time she's clean, the stones are ready, not hangi-hot but hot enough. She piles armloads of manuka on them, and then pours a bucket of water over the pile at a time, while she stands on the springy bed.

The steam is hot and aromatic.

> An illusion, dear heart, but it feels like all my individual pores are unplugging and gulping it in. And what they're sweating out is nobody's business,

rubbing herself down with a cloth and sweating on gleefully.

> Can you get drunk on manuka steam? O pungent o resinous o beautiful plant, none of your tender buds which died today died in vain. . . .

stepping away from the steampit, relaxed to the point where she feels boneless.

Flopping down on her springcleaned bed and bag in naked ease, looking round the doubly springcleaned hut through half-closed eyes.

The clothes hang drying by the fire, the fire is loaded with wood: they'll dry while I snooze . . . Jesus holy, I musta been far far gone, I've never got into such slack filthiness in all my years . . . beating my denims down on the rocks and all kinds of debris floating free with the suds. Part drying them on the bushes . . . they'll be steeped in the scent of gorse and me in manuka, and I look kinda twiggy, mistaken for ambulant scrub when seen wandering by. . . .

She wakes with a start, peering into the red eyes of the coals . . . who said that?

> Haere mai!
> Nau mai!
> Haere mai!

an earthdeep bass, a sonorous rolling call that reverberates still in my gut. Getting up cautiously, her skin feeling pleasantly tight and new, sniffing the plant-sweet air.

> No-one's here? No-one living could have that voice anyway. . . .

She shakes her head, and stretches her thin body until the useless muscles crack and the misaligned vertebrae pop into place. A sudden tide of wellbeing floods through her, a fierce joy at being alive.

And she is hungry enough to eat anything on legs or off 'em . . . there's a pound of oatmeal in the cupboard, some honey; two bottles of whisky; a covered jug—the creature must have left that—it *lives* somewhere near?—the sour red juice is from currants; skim milk and potato flakes, and that's all? That's all, unless you count the dried moth or two and a curled bunch of a spider. . . .

She makes a billy full of porridge, and devours it and its syrup of milk and honey, and surprises herself by making and eating a second, a third.

Satiated; stretched now, in front of the rebuilt fire. Full of new wiry strength and gentle energy, and determined not to wreck it . . . she drinks a whisky in civilised measure, and in between sips, practises scales on the guitar.

> Nice to see those hands looking so neat . . . guitar's a hard funky sound, but you'll do, friend instrument, you'll do. . . .

"You're lucky Holmes, my harmonious soul. Not everyone gets second chances."

She thinks, while her fingers slip into picking tunes,

> I can paint again, and I will.
> I will make overtures to the family soon, because now I can.
> Whether they accept or reject me, is up to them.
> Rebuild at Taiaroa? We have might and money and

we may. . . .
And then?

She steps lightly round the quagmires and sinking sands of what comes next to the tune she picked in a long-ago pub, Simon's mead reel.

And what about them?
If Joe picked up the note, he might come home for Christmas.
He might like the commensal idea. I think I rambled a bit in that note, but he'll understand . . . God, I hope he hasn't been warped too badly by jail, and the jail of memories. . . . And the goblin brat, oddbod spiderchild indeed, the catalytic urchin who touched this off?
Cataleptic then, bald as an egg on the palm of God, with shookup brain and terrible blank eyes where once the sly underhand mischief flickered; where once the strange self-awareness showed; where once the love-light shone. All gone. Unseeing, the sunchild. Too deep in the dark to know anymore. If he hasn't come back to himself, he's dead to me. Dead to us.

But as the overture to La Gaza Ladra swoops and soars and dips,

I'll enquire. I'll see if I can be of use. . . .

She thinks, by the firelight,

Art and family by blood; home and family by love . . . regaining any one was worth this fiery journey to the heart of the sun.

. . .

It was that hour before dawn when souls are least attached to bodies. When kehua roam. When, particularly if the tide is going out, old people slip easily away from deathbeds. The eery hour when dreams are real.
She sat outside the door, and thought the dream over.

The land is unknown. Bare and deserted, no trees, no obvious rocks, just low brown rolling hills.

"Haere mai!"
Welcome!
But also, Come here. . . .
She had been aware enough to ask, Kei whea?
"Haere mai,"
now a deep insistent pulse.

A light came up, and the scene began to turn, as though
a camera was panning slowly round 180 degrees.
Bare waiting hills, and the aged night sky . . . but down
in the gullies, she can see bush starting to grow and
straggle up the bare slopes. The landscape keeps turning, and the next sign of life is a wrecked rusting building, squat on a tableland.
She walks to it, "Haere mai!" chanted by many voices
now, filling the land like the thunderous pulse of a
mighty sea.
She touched the threshold, and the building sprang
straight and rebuilt, and other buildings flowed out of
it in a bewildering colonisation. They fit onto the land
as sweet and natural as though they'd grown there.
The karanga grows wilder, stronger.
The light bursts into bright blue daylight, and the people mill round, strangely clad people, with golden eyes,
brown skin, all welcoming her.
They touch and caress with excited yet gentle hands
and she feels herself dissolving piece by piece with each
touch. She diminishes to bones, and the bones sink into
the earth which cries "Haere mai!" and the movement
ceases.
The land is clothed in beauty and the people sing.

Very peculiar, my soul. I have never dreamed like that before.
The welcome chant lingered in her ears.
A cool wing of wind brushed her face.

Where is the land I am invited to?

She reached into her pocket and took out a smoke for the first
time in a month, and lit up.

> The only wrecked buildings I have any connection with
> are my Tower . . . and the old Maori hall at Moerangi.

The smoke spreads out and away.

. . .

She packs all her gear next morning, except for the guitar and a bottle of whisky. And Simon's rosary draped round the bottle and lying shining on her note: "My name is Kerewin Holmes. My home is The Tower, Private Bag, Taiaroa. Communicate that my joy may be full, okay? Kia koa koe. . . ."

Then she walks out, closing the groaning door behind her for the last time.

The pack is light: books and board, bits of food and the remaining bottle of whisky, a few clothes. The only other thing she carries is the harpoon stick.

> Kerewin te kaihau indeed . . . if I don't find a town soon,
> that'll be all I eat for a while, too,

grinning to herself.

Under this sun, with this new buoyant body, she feels nothing will go wrong.

Three miles up the road, she's picked up by a sheep-truck driver, and he lets her down at the next small town, just in time to satisfy the appetite the walking grew.

She replenishes her wallet, has a couple of beers in the local pub, some quiet conversation about the weather, and then sets off again.

She's not in a hurry, or worried about getting there, but the transport is strangely available for her. Another lift from a truckie in time to catch a Railways bus in time to catch the train.

She's walking into the kaika by nightfall.

Whistling to some words that have come into her mind, and wishing for a guitar to make it a processional, stick swung alongside instead, matching her easy stride,

> *O, never silent by the sea*
> *always something talking*
> *water on rocks*

> *water on sand*
> *wind and birds*
> *your heartbeat and*
> *others' words*
> *whatever knocks*
> *keep right on walking*
> *Listening is for free. . . .*

There is no-one at the baches. She breaks into the old one, and settles in.

. . .

The sea rolls on.
A sheep coughs asthmatically behind the hill.
A beetle burrs past.
She stands on the old marae site.
The halldoor hangs crookedly open.
"Tena koe . . . whakautua mai tenei patai aku. He aha koe i karanga ai ki a au?"
It is very still.
Kerewin waits, hands on her hips, head cocked to one side, listening.

> What do I expect? I come and say hello, I've come back,
> did you call me, and wait for . . . lightning? Burning
> bushes?

It is very dark behind the door.
"He aha te mahi e mea nei koe kia mahia?"
Sea distant on the beach; birds in the night; her breath coming and going. Nothing else.

> I ask what it wants me to do, and there's silence.

Nothing else.
She sighs.

> Typical, Holmes . . . expectations always greater than
> reality.
> So be it. I'll come again tomorrow when it's light.

As she turns away, a great warmth flows into her. Up from the earth under her feet into the pit of her belly, coursing up like benevolent fire through her breast to the crown of her head.

She feels her hair literally start to move.

Shaking with laughter, shaking with tears, shook to the core by joy.

III

Sitting in front of a Moerangi fire, the last for some time.
Cat purring on my lap. I'm contemplating leavetaking.

She unlocks the small wooden chest that holds her Book of the Soul.

Pretentious bugger, Holmes, taking yourself that seriously. . . .

She weighs the book in her hand. A thousand pages of Oxford India paper, bound with limp black leather covers, the title blocked in silver.

You could expose me to hell, you could give all my secrets away, little miseries and whining self-pities cloistered together . . . but you've been my last resort, a soul-hold beyond even the bottle.

She opens it at the last page she filled in, a third of the way through. Sees, in her thin Italic hand, the lines,

So I exist, a husk that wishes decay into sweet earth. Writing nonsense in a journal no-one ever sees.

Bloody hell, we've come a way since then. Where to start?

She writes:

It's been a rare year, o paper soul, not least because this is the third time I've talked to you. It is now nearly the great Christ Mass, the start of another year, the start of another life. Great changes—where to begin to record them?

With me, natch.

I'm weaker and whiter and wambling, but growing fatter and stronger as the days go. A feeling of burgeoning . . . it's the only simple word that encapsules the flight and the flower.

I'm working hard, I'm painting easily, fluently, profoundly. I smile often. I have direction in my life again, four directions—make that five—no, six. I am weaving webs, and building dreams and every so often this this wonder seizes me unawares. Which is a far distance on from the moribund bag of bones of a month ago.

You know what? I lost three and a half stone . . . imagine the glowering heavyweight, twelve stone plus in its bare feet and britches, reduced to that extremity!

But I'm putting fat back on with devotion, eating as though my life depended on it. I'm nine and a half stone, rising ten . . . I still do interesting things like fold up under weights I would have hefted easily not that many months ago (for instance, tried carrying four sheets of iron, sevenfooters, 26 gauge, pitched over and damn near cut my head off). But we work full days, and we sleep, how we sleep! peaceful and pleasant dreams of nights.

History, facts, practicalities: I started rebuilding the Maori hall because it seemed, in my spiral fashion, the straight-forward thing to do. It didn't take long for curious locals to drift round to find out who I was and why I was playing with their relic. I was recognised, saluted, and they shrugged when they found it was my time and money being given free, and left me to it . . . only on the Saturday, a few came by to help prop up bits of four by two and a handle up the tin. And by late Sunday, we've got the roof done and the outside straight and sober looking. A real working party (we weren't that straight and sober Sunday night).

I was left to me own devices for the week—it was only a matter of relining walls and putting down new floor boards. Light carpentry, and it all fitted together so easy and slick, it might have been building itself.

And on Friday, they came with the new door, and the windows we'd decided to order. They came with a keg, and blankets, and mattresses, and guitars, and two blank-eyed sheep that were promptly converted to mutton. They came with gallons of glorious rainbows, a tin of paint from everyone's shed. They came with a surplus of song and willing hands.

And on Sunday I'm greasy with picking mutton-bones, and more than slightly riddled with good brown beer, and I'm singing with the rest inside the tight sweet hall that's got a heart of people once more.

The prayers and the hallowing will be done this coming Sunday, and, glory of glories, the old gateposts from the old marae, each with their own name, will be re-erected.

We have not just a hall, but a marae again. The fire's been relit, and I sink gracefully back into oblivion having lit it.

"It's so easy," they kept on saying. "It's the right time to do it, eh?"

Timing is all, my friends.

"What'd you get out of it though?"

A party, I say grinning. Laughs.

But I also got two strange and unlooked-for bonuses.

When the first half sheep was outside cooling, a cat wraith came round.

Dear ghost, I was thin but this was parchment skin on starved bones. It gnawed at the scraps of fat on the ground, at tiny bits of leftover offal. Nobody kicked, but nobody stroked it; nobody owned and nobody wanted it . . . with an excess of kindness brought on by the beer, I shared my lunch with it, and now find the first of my responsibilities hath come home to roost. Maybe in that way, its thinness was advantageous. It slid into the bach without me noticing, and then fed itself into my heart.

It is a very young cat, not much more than a kitten indeed. From the pale-brown colour and wedgehead, I'd say it was a Siamese's bastard. It has the dark brown mask, but no other markings. Its tail is another leg, a feeler, a toucher, a finger.

It needs such a subtle tail. It has no eyes.

I thought it was the starvation, eh. But the sockets are empty and sealed. I don't think it ever had eyes. The mask has no relief.

I named it. One must name cats, people, whoever whatever comes close, even though they carry their real names hidden inside them. I named this one, Li.

The hexagram name, The Fire, Brilliant Beauty.

For it is not a remote cat, as one would think blindness would make it. It winds about me, begging for touch. It sits on my shoulders, throbbing with the small rough sound of content. It can perch there, admirably balanced, while I walk.

It is a civilised cat, and a keen and curious cat. It gets to know where it is very quickly; who is there, what is there. It is an armed and raking cat, with wicked scythe claws, always retracted when I touch but otherwise ready for anything (as a luckless gull, disputing Li's food this morning, discovered). It devours food—but it has a stronger need for affection. (It hates other cats . . . it's a female, and since I suspect bastard Siamese are as randy *as the true breed, that'll probably soon change . . . but for the moment, other cats are greeted with an edgy growl, and the dull dun fur stands up in ridges and flakes.) Fiery cat. Strange cat. Neat cat.*

I have never owned an animal before. I am glad of her.

My second bonus was a man, and his trade.

He was beery-eyed, a droop-bellied fellow who wobbled over to where I was sitting, and flopped down. Nearly went through the clean new floorboards of the hall we've yet to name.

He said, "Hiccup. Sheesh. How're yer goin' mate?"

I tried a basso profundo. More than one word and it tickled the throat to a desperate squeak. So he discovered I wasn't male under the denim and leather and silk.

"Censored. Never thought a woman could use a hammer like that . . . don't tell me yer rar carpenter by trade?"

"Nope. I paint pictures for a living and hunt snarks for a hobby," said glibly while already teetering to my feet away.

"Gawn . . . I'm a deepsea diver," blink blink, "yer really a painter though?"

"Yeah," receding.

"I'm really a diver."

"O really? In that case, I've got work for you mate," thinking, if he's a deepsea diver, I'm a pickled prawn.

He was.

He hunted all round the baches. He hunted me down. The next day indeed. He was sheepish and hungover and he asked lamely,

"On the offchance yer know, did yer really have work? Or yer joking?"

I had been joking, but suddenly wasn't.

He had the slenderest of hopes that I was a generous eccentric who wanted yet another go at the "General Grant". I destroyed that, but offered him a little sugarlolly consolation prize. He snapped it up with astonishing haste.

"It's the challenge I love," he said, diver Finnegan of the deep. He explained morosely that there wasn't any work these days, no-one getting wrecked, no oil-rigs to bolt down, just pissy surface work he made do with, waiting without hope for real dives.

"This'll be a challenge all right. It's in deep and dirty water. There's a reef and rocks and currents all round. It's probably in pieces, but I want as much as possible brought up and how much will it cost?"

Am I becoming responsible about my whims? I thought about that for all of a minute while he scribbled away in the back of a dirty little notebook, scratched his head, hummed, and finally said,

"About $450 a day. Dunno how long it'll take either. Have to be two of us, good surface joker, and then there's the boat etcetera etcetera."

He didn't exactly end it like that, but I accepted his quote and put a limit of two weeks on the operation. See? Responsibility creeping into me from all angles . . . he went off happy to Whangaroa, laden with something else that had nothing to do with the stranger cruiser—a set of plans, and an offer for Piri Tainui to become my building and salvage-operation supervisor. (About ten minutes after the offer was communicated to Piri, I got a telegram back. Damn thing said simply "AE" one hundred times, and I swear it was still smoking when I took it out of the envelope.)

I had spent many nights happily drawing and redrawing those plans. I decided on a shell-shape, a regular spiral of rooms expanding around the decapitated Tower . . . privacy, apartness, but all connected and all part of the whole. When finished, it will be studio and hall and church and guest-house, whatever I choose, but above all else, HOME. Home in a larger sense than I've used the term before.

Because.

Because when I rang the fuzz in 'Roa to get permission to go ahead salvaging, I was enthusiastically greeted and enthusiastically permitted. Actually Morrison said, "You don't need permission from us. We couldn't spend thousands of the taxpayers' money finding out the identity of a couple of corpses, but if you're that curious, we. . . ."

"The corpses don't interest me a damn," and that was when I heard about all kinds of escapades and peregrinations, and had this o so hesitant and gingerly feeler extended to me. I said I'd think about it. Morrison, bless those dewy eyes and that fluffy copper mustache, reduced himself to plead. "Look, there's sure to be a next time, he's made it back once already, can we let you know so I don't have to, to—look, can I ring you?"

Sure, I said, and gave him the number of my headquarters, the Hamdon pub.

Holy Mother! Did I say I would think about it?

It made me want to dance. It made me want to weep. It made rebuilding so bloody pointed and poignant and REAL. Commensalism—right on. But this had a dawn air to it, the day yet to come. And what we could do with the day. . . .

Learn to label with new names, for a small start.

Yesterday, the cat Li went exploring. It wauled from the alley round by the tankstand, back of the bach. I didn't hurry to find out why. It wasn't a distressed yowl, just a come-hither call. I strolled round to her, smoking my pipe.

"Watcha got, Li? Too big a spider?"

And I nearly choked. I nearly swallowed my whole bloody pipe. The cat was most perturbed, coiling into my arms asking in a guttural croak why all the smoke? A screen, Li . . . Jesus in hell, who left those stones there like that?

You see, my dear alter ego, I collected memories here in the mayday holidays. Joe collected a pounamu chisel and large lungfuls of fresh air. And the urchin went in mainly for stones, Maori sinkers, the whole beach's worth.

And did he arrange them in six inch capitals, CLARE WAS HE?

It occurred to me while I watched the stone words blur, that I'd never asked him what he called himself. Just, what do they call you?

Well, I shall enquire of him discreetly and call him whatever he likes, though I would find it peculiar to fit my tongue round son. I think I will leave that to Gillayley-senior.

Plots and plans flowering all over the show—I've found out where he is, back of beyond, being mysterious, carving he says, heading homewards and I'll see him at Christmas. He has a present for me, he says. He giggled when he said it. Two can play that game: I shall have a present for him, strange and legal (by that time). Ho ho ho!

We're nearing the end now, soul of the book. We're coming to the new beginning. This afternoon, Finnegan rang. He said the police were all over what he'd rescued like flies on a dead sheep (his simile, not mine) and they'll be ringing yer and bloody good he'd made it just in time eh mate?

Yes, I said, and thanks, I said, and didn't offer any bonus which wasn't quite fair, because it's apparently damnably dirty and cold down there, a gloom of current-stirred soup . . . but Finnegan didn't care. He'd triumphed over the sea again, lorded it over the deeps. "You shoulda been there," he crowed, "you shoulda seen her break top . . . hull dripping crawlies and things and barnacles from here to my arse. Like she's been down centuries not a few years. She's whole, nearly whole, though mind yet there's nothin' yer can have that'll be worth much. . . ."

I should have been warned by that "yer can have. . . ."

Piri was next.

"You heard from the inspector yet? You heard from Morrison?" and I

could hear him hopping up and down with some kind of joy. It giggles through his voice. It makes him sing the words gaily down the line. "O I won't say nothing yet Kere, they got to let you know officialeee. . . ."

I should have been warned by the officialeee.

But no.

I'm sitting sipping beer, stroking Li, wondering what price for each crawlie on the hull, when Dave says,

"Phone again, Kerewin me love . . . take it in the office eh, you'll be able to hear yourself think in there."

"Miz Holmes?"

"Myself."

"Detective Inspector Gil Price here, Miz Holmes . . . your salvage expert will have let you know that he was successful in recovering the hull of the launch that sank on. . . ."

Oath!

He drones on in formal statement-sheet phraseology, and I hang there in suspense, smoothing Li beneath my hand.

"There are several urrr," first human comment, "relics you will find interesting. They have enabled us to close our file on the ah Gillayley child. The most interesting item, or should I say items rather, we found behind the bulkheads however."

Very stagy pause.

"You found?" I oblige.

"Heroin," says the detective inspector smugly. You can hear him smack his lips fatly. "Nearly twenty pounds of pure heroin. Worth about three million dollars on the street."

More lipsmacking. Such bonuses don't often come the way of smalltown fuzz.

I am taking some time to catch my breath, because some happenings are starting to go click click click quite nastily into place . . . put together needles and drugsmuggling and nightmares and threats and o there's worlds to go into yet, hells to explore. . . .

"Wow," I say at last, coherent and apt and precise as always.

"I'm afraid you won't be able to claim this," he heheheh's discreetly and I he-he-he back with distinct undertones of hysteria, "but we hope to be able to assist with your expenses for, just a minute constable, well, I suppose this can wait . . . Miz Holmes, if you've got a minute more, Constable Morrison and friend are waiting to talk to you."

And then it was three again, the trinity regained in a microcosmic way. Well, numero deus impare gaudet.

She flexes her fingers. She's been writing for over an hour. The cat yawns and stretches on her lap.

"A few more minutes, Li, so settle down. I want to do this properly."

Not an arbitrary end, like when I crushed the suneater to death. Something of tender ritual, an exorcism of all the past despair. A meet to make a fit beginning.

She picks up the pen again, thinks a minute.

So we'll make that seven new directions for my life—Deity might as well delight in yet another odd number . . . imagine this a skewed compass rose, with a tempered steel needle flexing before a magnetic wind; rose and needle myself, and the wind? the wind, my dear sour other self, is that of chance and change. Direction one, is recovery; two, a renewed talent; three, rebuilding; and four, tying up loose ends, making the net whole. Direction five is endeavouring not to dodge responsibilities, for me, or a wandering cat, or whomever. Six is related: I know I can move, can lead, can direct. Therefore, I will. No more sequestration, no more Holmes against the world. And seven is the pivot, the point of balance for the needle of my true soul—I have faced Death. I have been caught in the wild weed tangles of Her hair, seen the gleam of her jade eyes. I will go when it is time—no choice!—but now I want life.

It's been a rare year, o paper soul, and against all the preceding bitterness and bile, this one shining scrawl . . . maybe I should fold you away to pull you out again in a decade, see whether the flowering, that now seems promised, came; see whether it was untimely frostbit, or died without fruit, because you chart the real deeps of me. No: I hold you a pelorus, a flexing mirror, strange quarters for the wind of God.

I follow the Chinese: on the funeral pyre of our dead selves, I place a paper replica of what is real. Ghost, follow the other ghosts—haere, haere, haere ki te po! Go easy to the Great Lady of the Night, and if we ever meet in the dimension where dreams are real, I shall embrace you and we shall laugh, at last.

She caps the pen, closes the book softly. Packs it gently away in the wooden chest. Leans over and places it in the heart of the fire, and closes the range door upon it. The blind cat leaps from her lap, and dances highpawed on lean back legs.

"Yeah, cat Li, it's time to go."

Time to hit the high road.

Time to go home.

Epilogue

Moonwater Picking

Ice crystal haloes round the stars, the crash of waves down on the beach, sweet-scented air breathed in with the wine on my breath. breath.

It doesn't really matter, any of it . . . and on the instant, it *does* matter, and I hesitate to upset the moonshadow of a stone.

Sudden flare and splash of light. The crack of fireworks brazen-ing through the night. It's still dark, but the day is drawing near.

Shaking her head over the din,

> As well we're an outaway place . . . someone's playing that accordion again, and there goes a guitar. They're never all going to go to sleep at the same time. Someone always wakes up. Wakes everyone else up.

The reedy song winds plaintively above the throb of the guitars.

> It's music and singing and talk talk talk . . . I come out into the dying night air and a bunch of rockets charge moonwards. Shrieks and whoops and hollering as another snail-hunting party seeks its quarry in the dew-wet grass. "Getit! Yeehai! EEEEK!" . . . maybe an espe-cially speedy fella? The ones I saw inside were looking distinctly puzzled by all the free greenery. Teach Luce to ask for a real French salad. . . . We play on, apes and larrikins all.

Walking down the sinew of track stretched white and tight through the muscle of the hill. Seaward, to that finger of land where the mauri waits, and spins its magic in deep silence.

. . .

He wanders through the brandnew rooms, through knots of happy people, chattering people, singing-tired and weeping-drunk people. Couples of all kinds.

Two wrinkled old bodies, Kerewin's greatgreat aunts, cossetted together, full of mothmirth and dry seedy shadows of laughter. Knocking each other's ribs with sharp elbows, plucking at one another with bony fingers, flickering from flame of dirty memory to flame of dirty joke. "So I sol' mesel' soul an' arse'ol, an' never did regret it," husk husk croak croak tee hee hee.

He inclines his head to them.

Two people, pulsing by themselves in a darkish corner.

He steps over them.

Two more, his own relations, Wherahiko and Marama, arms about each other, keeping themselves warm. Pile of grandchildren sprawled round asleep, young arms at angles and curve of sleeping cheek . . . but no bright head here. Search on . . . his eyes do, while he stands.

Wherahiko: We don't want to be left out, to sit ignored in the corner, but we might as well
be. All the things we've got to tell, years
of love and life and hate. We'd be a good
drink for them, a fullbodied mature wine,
and look at them! Overcome by fizzy pop,
lollywater brew . . .

sweeping his eyes round, fierce as a hawk, over the grandchildren pile.

Winking to Joe.

Marama: When they want to listen, they'll listen. We
can't wake them up just to tell them our stories. They're busy making their own. And in
the meantime, my love, we've got each other,

sliding her plump arm closer, tighter.

Winking to Joe.

A wave of flat and heavy music drowns the homemade plunk and whine and chorus. Stereo blaring, ingots of sound beating the ears, people stirring fukthisracket, louder louder LOUDER and someone bawls out and somebody else switches it off. Ahhh, snore, snore, except for Timote, whimpering out of sleep.

Marama picks him up.

"Over there," she croons to Joe, "over there," cuddling the sleepy child quiet.

Here's the other one, his smile riddled by sleep, nearly out on his feet.

Pick him up, kiss him, give him goodnight.

The rangy black man, spruce in midnight velvet, steps to his side. He watches with a possessive love and pride.

"Want to wish him sweet dreams?"

"Surely, man."

Sharing a look that is communion, black eyes to brown eyes, O we've all had a hand in this venture.

Stepping over more feet and busy bodies.

Sunflowers and seashells and logarithmic spirals (said Kerewin); sweep of galaxies and the singing curve of the universe (said Kerewin);
the oscillating wave thrumming in the nothingness of every atom's heart (said Kerewin);
did you think I could build a square house?

So the round shell house holds them all in its spiralling embrace. Noise and riot, peace and quiet, all is music in this sphere.

It's sweet to walk through it, looking for a calm place to put him to bed.

Yesterday afternoon, back I came, crowded round with strangers who had taken my invitation for hers, and were too eager to recognise a mistake. My battleready Kerewin went down under the peaceflags. There's herself, content in the long wordless embrace given by her mother. Herself pushed and pummelled and hugged as though she were a child by all her tall brothers (he sniggers, watching as they duck and swerve away from her return punches, all of them aware of how lethal a woman she is). Herself, propped against her fat and comfortable moon-eyed sister, arms round each other's necks all good cheers and covered tears and matey friendship.

Her grin to him is sharp and fanged.

"Gillayley, I'll get you for this."

"O yeah?" he replies. "Like how? I done you this one good turn and," turning, hearing the slipping step, "My God," his heart stopping.

"Ahh Jesus, no!" as the child comes creeping up beside, his face alight.

Stooping, weeping, cupping both hands about the small face, framing it, fingers spread back in a protective flange for the thin bone cradle of his skull, "Ahh, Jesus yes!"

Now I'm the wordless one, what can I say?

Hupe nose and eyes dripping as though this is a tangi, not a return. So gather him up, gather him in, arms tight full, and spin round and round and round in a giddy dance of ecstasy, aching with love to give, smothered by love in return.

No sign of reproach.

The unlevel gaze is bright, brimming, but every time I look, the loveshine's there.

But ahh Ngakau. . . .

In the early night, when it's still orderly, less of an orgy, Kerewin plays. The child listens on the fringes, but soon comes to her knee, leaning there, head down. His hair has regrown in fine straggling flakes and shades his crooked face: silvery moon hair pressed against the dark body of the guitar as he strains to hear the high notes sing. Kerewin, used to it already, plays on unmoved.

"What have I done," whispering it, crushing down his crying, "What have I done? I've taken away his music. . . ."

"O, not all of it," says Kerewin the stony.

There's memory in all the eyes round him, furtive glances that rake him, all saying, The quick light is dimmed, the dancer's grace is gone. Damn you.

He endures all the hate. We can endure anything. We are toughened, different, an annealed steel, triple-forged. But if I were alone. . . .

Piri says,

"Give him here."

"No."

"Give."

The Tainuis are still wild. Liz punched Joe in the stomach first chance she got, and Piri looked the other way. When she kept it up though, past the first wild swing, he said, "Lay off, miss. Smack her down, man."

"No," said Joe, "I understand why." Bending down to the furious little girl, breathing hurt and hard, "Liz, I am very sorry for it, but it's past. It's all over now." And he hopes the Tainuis will see, will learn, will agree.

Passing the boy carefully into Piri's arms, It's past, but we live with it forever. As Kerewin said, he's mainly calm and good as bread. But, she added, you should've seen the performance at the copshop when I arrived ... wheeee! Shaking her head at them both, spitting casually on her dandelions, Pah! Gillayleys, I dunno. ... So she had offered them both that unlikely gift, her name. As umbrella, as shelter, not as a binding. No sentiment about it, says Kerewin, just good legal sense.

The cold-forged lady, aue!

"Ah sheeit ..." coming through a wall, over the buzzzz and jingle of music and talk; only she has that penetrating drawling way with swearwords, "I thought it was a beerloody funny coffee bean."

"Lookit its little legs. ..."

"Nothing else left after going through the grinder ... you like your coffee?"

Choke.

Luce glides up to them, elegantly dressed in katipo colours. Cool hand on Piri's shoulder, cool eyes on Simon Clare, cool smile turned to see itself in Joe's eyes.

"Happy, Hohepa?"

"Yes, Luce." Get lost.

"With everything, cos? Every tiny thing?"

"No, Luce." Bugger off.

He stirs the silvergold hair with one cool finger. Not deep enough to touch the skull, enough to make his cool cool point.

The gentleness goes from his tired son's eyes, and something iron and quick takes its place. The fingers veer up into Luce's face, effoff. Right on, tama.

"Manners need mending too," lidded mean gaze turned back to Joe.

"Piss off, Luce," says Piri, handing the child back. Right on, Piri.

(But all the while, the old man while, instinct fought against my clavicle and told me sin, hop in, the livin' water's warm. No way. Not that way ever again.)

"As the lady said, a hen is an egg's deeplaid plot to get itself more company."

There she goes out the door, weaving round and singing to her-self, guitar slung over her shoulder, not seeing us in the gloom.

Follow follow, we're the led, e tama?

and he nods to me, without a word being said.

Out under the cold dimming stars, drawn on by her moon-shadow.

(Yesterday afternoon, I turned aside this way. "Excuse, I need a mimi please," the pack growing so heavy I was sure I would drop. But I have grown strong. I got out of sight, and the mauri, set down, sunk itself into the hard ground. Or maybe the earth turned willing water beneath its touch. It vanished completely. But we all came back to it, after the hoha died down, and each of us can feel where it is resting. A sort of pricket and tremble in our gut.)

And there she stands, over the place, throwing away sparks of words. All to a sly fast-picked tune, the mead reel, his dance, bring-ing out last, steps to her.

O the spun shiny surface,
mica and stars,
I span: stand stunned
reeling over night and mind,
so far, no sand
or chance strange feeling
blunts my eyes blind. . . .

"You took a helluva long time coming. . . ."

Reaching out with one hand to join us, "Ka ao, ka ao, ka awatea. . . ."

It is dawn, indeed it is dawn, and bright broad daylight braiding our home."

TE MUTUNG—RANEI TE TAKE

Translation of
Maori Words and Phrases

Page

14 **Aue** = exclamation of dismay, or despair

15 **Te Kaihau** = lit. windeater. Can mean either wanderer or loafer
Tena koe = hello, greeting to one person

17 **Raupo** = a variety of weed
Ngaio = a coastal tree

19 **Pounamu** = New Zealand jade, also called "greenstone"

29 **Manuka** = useful shrub, also called "tea tree"

36 **Kia ora koe** = good health to you (singular)

41 **Mere** = a short flat weapon of stone (often greenstone) for hand to hand fighting. Other terms on this page (hei matau, patu pounamu, kuru, marakihau etc are translated in text)

44 **Hinatore** = glow with an unsteady light, phosphorescent things in general

58 **Pake** = Simon pake means stubborn Simon

65 **E tama** = son, kid, boy

70 **E noho ki raro. Hupeke tou waewae** = Sit down. Hold your foot
E whakama ana au ki a koe = I'm ashamed of you

70 Kei whea te rini = Where's the ring?
    Kaua e tahae ano = Don't steal again

71 E korero Maori ana koe? = Do you speak Maori?
    He iti iti noa iho taku mohio = O, I understand a bit

72 Ka pai = good, great, thanks mate etc.

74 E hoa = friend, mate etc

75 Nga Bush = bush people, primitives
    Makutu, nei = hoodoo, eh?

76 Maoritanga = Maori culture, Maoriness
    Ka whakapai au ki a koe mo tau atawhai = Thanks very
    much for your kindness
    Ka pai, e hoa = That's okay, mate

85 Na tou hoa = from your friend

96 Kia ora korua = Good luck you two

101 E moe koe = Goodnight

108 Hongi = greeting or salutation by two people pressing noses
    with each other

110 Pakeha = stranger, now used for a New Zealander of European
    descent. Used here as an adjective, hence the lower case.

112 Kaika = Ngai Tahu dialect for home, or village
    Te Ao Hou = the new world, the shining world

122 Whakapapa = genealogies, family trees
    Rangatira = chiefly or noble person/people

127 Kina = sea-egg or sea urchin, delicious!
    Pikopiko = fern, young fronds of which are edible
    Puha/Puwha = edible weed
    Kai moana = seafood

130 Karengo = edible seaweed

138 Haere mai! Nau mai! Haere mai! = a formal chant of welcome
    Tena koutou katoa = greeting to more than two people
    Kei te pehea koe? = How're you?

139 He puku mate, nei? = Crook stomach, eh?
Ae = yes

145 E pai ana = also means, Thank you

148 Muri iho = Later

151 E noho ra = Goodbye, said to the person(s) staying
Haere ra = Goodbye, said to the person(s) going

152 Pipi = edible shellfish

153 Kete = basket, generally made of plaited or woven flax

157 E hine = woman or girl

174 Tika = right, appropriate, correct

191 Kahikatea = white pine, a beautiful native tree fond of swamps

196 Koromiko = useful tree if you've got a crook stomach or diarrhoea

199 Tihe mauriora = lit. sneeze of life, fig. I salute the breath of life in you, said at the beginning of formal speeches; with hongi; or at times like this.

204 Taniwha = a mythical (?) water terror/monster

208 Tamaiti = child
Taku aroha ki a koe = I love you

209 Aroha = love
Utu = revenge

214 Ka nui taku mate = I'm really sick

216 Anana = exclamation of surprise

218 Mimi = piss

223 Kawau pateketeke, K. paka, K. tuawhenua, K. tui = all kinds of shag

225 Haere mai = as well as a greeting, this phrase means Come here

230 Pupu = edible green snail, also called a catseye

242 Taipo = demon, night goblin (a word of dubious origin)

245 Arohanui = much love

248 Paua = succulent marine univalve

260–61 Terakihi, hapuku = delicious fishes

278 Tangihanga = funeral, and the ceremonies connected with it
Marae = a place for gathering, to learn, to mourn, teach, welcome and rejoice

279 Ae, ko te pono tena = Yes, that's the exact truth
E tama, ka aha ra koe? = O child, what will become of you?

280 Iwi kaupeka, nei = would you believe, "Funny skinny legs"?
Lit. legs like sticks

281 Hui = gathering
Hori = lit. George. Used by Maori among themselves in a jocular fashion but is an insult when used by an unfriendly Pakeha

285 Ponaturi = rather nasty mythical beings who sleep on land but live undersea

291 Pi Ta = in this case it translates as shitty nestling

293 Ka Tata Te Po = Night is Near

306 Hokioi = unknown (and maybe legendary) kind of bird

309 The song the ghost sings is an old lullaby and translates roughly as "O child, winterborn, ascend/rise up and join your forbears in the heavens"

311 Hapu = next tribal division down from "iwi"
E nga iwi! Mo wai tenei? = O people! Who is this for?
Tukutuku/poupou = forms of wall decoration

312 Rimu, rimu, tere tere e = lines from a popular song, "Seaweed, seaweed, drifting, drifting . . ."

334 Korero = talk, argument

339 **Haere mai ki te kai!** = Come and get it! lit. come here for the food!

345 **He aha koa iti, he pounamu** = although it's little, it's jade
Koha = gift

363 **Tenei mo Haimona** = This is for Simon

369 **Mere-mere** = Venus the evening star

380 **Tapu** = can mean forbidden in a secular sense

381 **Taipa** = Keep quiet
Ngakaukawa, kei te ora taku ngakau. E noho mai = Bitter heart, you heal my heart. Stay here

384 **Kaumatua** = an elder/elders

413 **Huhu** = NZ's largest beetle, in some areas symbolic of Death

422 **He aha tou mate?** = What's wrong with you?/Where is your sickness?

424 **Ka maharatia tenei i ahau e ora ana** = I shall remember it as long as I live
He tika tonu ano tena = That is natural, that's the right thing (to do)

427 **Tutu** = a useful shrub, to be used with extreme care

429 **E taku hine** = o my girl, o my woman

433 **Papa** = the name of Earth herself; **Rangi** = the Sky-father
Ki a koe, Rehua! = To you, Rehua!

434 **Rupahu** = nonsense

437 **Haere, mou tai ata, moku tai ahiahi** = Go, the morning tide for you, the evening tide for me (an old saying)

438 **E kui** = a term of address and respect to an aged woman

439 **Mokopuna** = grandchild

444 Mauri/Mauriora = Life principle, thymos of humans; talisman or material symbol of that secret and mysterious principle protecting the mana (power/vitality) of people, birds, land, forests, whatever . . .

446 Tangi = weep, mourn

447 Tauranga atua = resting place for a god
Kiwa = god, also very old name for Pacific

448 Haere = Go

451 E pou = affectionate term of respect for an old person

456 Moko = facial tattoo pattern, sometimes used as a signature in the old days
Tipuna = grandfather/mother

458 Pouwhenua = a long spear-club
Whare = house

460 Pakihi = a term for a swampy acidic barren type of land

463 Kai = food

467 Aotearoa = the shining bright land, an old name for New Zealand

468 Karakia = prayers, sacred chants
Rahui = boundary markers, essentially tapu

469 Kia koa koe = wishing you joy

477 Hoha = fuss, nuisance
E taku hei piripiri, E tawhiri = endearments for children

483 Whanau = extended family group—a general term for "family" now
E nga iwi o nga iwi = this is a pun. It means, O the bones of the people (where 'bones' stands for ancestors or relations), or, O the people of the bones (i.e. the beginning people, the people who make another people)

498 Weka = hensized bird with inordinate curiosity. Tastes good, too.

524 **Kehua** = ghosts

525 **Kei whea?** = Where?
Karanga = call of invitation, welcome, mourning, onto a marae

527 **Whakautua mai tenei patai aku** = Answer this question of mine
He aha kow i karanga ai ki a au? What did you call me for? Did you call me?
He aha te mahi e mea nei koe kia mahia? = What do you want me to do?

545 **Ka ao, ka ao, ka awatea** = it is dawn, it is dawn, it is daylight
Te mutunga—ranei te take = the end—or the beginning

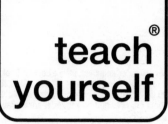

Buddhism
clive erricker

For over 60 years, more than
50 million people have learnt over
750 subjects the **teach yourself**
way, with impressive results.

be where you want to be
with **teach yourself**

For UK order enquiries: please contact Bookpoint Ltd, 130 Milton Park, Abingdon, Oxon, OX14 4SB. Telephone: +44 (0) 1235 827720. Fax: +44 (0) 1235 400454. Lines are open 09.00–17.00, Monday to Saturday, with a 24-hour message answering service. Details about our titles and how to order are available at www.teachyourself.co.uk

For USA order enquiries: please contact McGraw-Hill Customer Services, PO Box 545, Blacklick, OH 43004-0545, USA. Telephone: 1-800-722-4726. Fax: 1-614-755-5645.

For Canada order enquiries: please contact McGraw-Hill Ryerson Ltd, 300 Water St, Whitby, Ontario, L1N 9B6, Canada. Telephone: 905 430 5000. Fax: 905 430 5020.

Long renowned as the authoritative source for self-guided learning – with more than 50 million copies sold worldwide – the **teach yourself** series includes over 500 titles in the fields of languages, crafts, hobbies, business, computing and education.

British Library Cataloguing in Publication Data: a catalogue record for this title is available from the British Library.

Library of Congress Catalog Card Number: on file.

First published in UK 1995 by Hodder Education, 338 Euston Road, London, NW1 3BH.

First published in US 1995 by The McGraw-Hill Companies, Inc.

This edition published 2003.

The **teach yourself** name is a registered trade mark of Hodder Headline.

Copyright © 1995, 2001, 2003 Clive Erricker

Typeset by Transet Limited, Coventry, England.
Printed in Great Britain for Hodder Education, a division of Hodder Headline, 338 Euston Road, London, NW1 3BH, by Cox & Wyman Ltd, Reading, Berkshire.

The publisher has used its best endeavours to ensure that the URLs for external websites referred to in this book are correct and active at the time of going to press. However, the publisher and the author have no responsibility for the websites and can make no guarantee that a site will remain live or that the content will remain relevant, decent or appropriate.

Hodder Headline's policy is to use papers that are natural, renewable and recyclable products and made from wood grown in sustainable forests. The logging and manufacturing processes are expected to conform to the environmental regulations of the country of origin.

Impression number   10 9 8
Year   2010 2009 2008 2007